THE
UNREAL
AND THE
REAL

STORY COLLECTIONS
The Wind's Twelve Quarters
Orsinian Tales
The Compass Rose
Buffalo Gals
Searoad
A Fisherman of the Inland Sea
Four Ways to Forgiveness
Unlocking the Air
The Birthday of the World
Changing Planes
The Unreal and the Real:
    Selected Stories, Volume One:
    Where on Earth
The Unreal and the Real:
    Selected Stories, Volume Two:
    Outer Space, Inner Lands
The Found and the Lost

TRANSLATIONS
Lao Tzu: Tao Te Ching
The Twins, the Dreams/Las
    Gemelas, El Sueño
    (with Diana Bellessi)
Kalpa Imperial

Selected Poems of Gabriela Mistral

CRITICISM
Dancing at the Edge of the World
The Language of the Night
The Wave in the Mind
Cheek by Jowl
Steering the Craft
Words Are My Matter

THE UNREAL

AND THE

REAL

— THE —

SELECTED SHORT STORIES

— OF —

URSULA K. Le GUIN

SAGA PRESS

LONDON SYDNEY **NEW YORK** TORONTO NEW DELHI

SAGA PRESS

AN IMPRINT OF SIMON & SCHUSTER, INC.

1230 AVENUE OF THE AMERICAS, NEW YORK, NEW YORK 10020

The Unreal and the Real: Selected Stories of Ursula K. Le Guin Volume I: Where On Earth copyright © 2012 by Ursula K. Le Guin | *The Unreal and the Real: Selected Stories of Ursula K. Le Guin Volume II: Outer Space, Inner Lands* copyright © 2012 by Ursula K. Le Guin | Originally published in two editions in 2012 by Small Beer Press | Published by arrangement with Small Beer Press | "The Jar of Water" copyright © 2014 by Ursula K. Le Guin | Pages 717–721 function as an extension of the copyright page. | Cover photograph of Mt. Hood copyright © 2016 by Don Smith/ Getty Images | Author photograph by Arwen Curry from The Worlds of Ursula K. Le Guin | All rights reserved, including the right to reproduce this book or portions thereof in any form whatsoever. For information address Saga Press Subsidiary Rights Department, 1230 Avenue of the Americas, New York, NY 10020 | SAGA PRESS and colophon are trademarks of Simon & Schuster, Inc. | For information about special discounts for bulk purchases, please contact Simon & Schuster Special Sales at 1-866-506-1949 or business@simonandschuster.com. | The Simon & Schuster Speakers Bureau can bring authors to your live event. For more information or to book an event, contact the Simon & Schuster Speakers Bureau at 1-866-248-3049 or visit our website at www.simonspeakers.com. | Also available in a Saga Press hardcover edition | The text for this book was set in Adobe Garamond Pro. | Manufactured in the United States of America | First Saga Press edition October 2016 | First Saga Press paperback edition November 2017 | 10 9 8 7 6 5 4 3 | The Library of Congress has cataloged the hardcover edition as follows: ISBN 978-1-4814-7596-9 (hc) | ISBN 978-1-4814-7597-6 (pbk) | ISBN 978-1-4814-7598-3 (eBook)

THE
UNREAL
AND THE
REAL

CONTENTS

PART II: OUTER SPACE, INNER LANDS

PART I:

WHERE ON EARTH

INTRODUCTION

Choosing and Dividing

I BEGGED PEOPLE—EDITORS, FRIENDS, THIRD COUSINS ONCE removed—to help me select stories for this collection, but nobody would. So all the credit for good choices and all the blame for bad ones is mine. If something you rightfully expected to find here isn't here, I'm sorry. I had to leave out a lot of stories, because I've written a lot of them.

The first way I found to reduce the mob to a manageable size was: limit it to short stories. No novellas—even though the novella is my favorite story-form, a lovely length, in which you can do just about what a novel does without using all those words. But each novella would crowd out three, four, five short stories. So they all had to be shut out, tearfully.

There were still way too many stories, so I had to make arbitrary restrictions. I mostly avoided stories closely tied to novels, set on Gethen or on Anarres, etc.—and stories forming an integral part of story-suites, where the pieces are linked by characters, setting, and chronology, forming an almost-novelistic whole. But "May's Lion" is closely tied to *Always Coming Home*, and three of the stories from *Orsinian Tales* form a loose, many-decade sort of suite. . . . Oh well. Consistency is a virtue until it gets annoying.

So there I was with enough stories, still, to make a book about the size of the *Shorter Oxford Dictionary.* I therefore developed extremely scientific and methodical criteria for my choices.

The first criterion was: Do I like the story?

The answer was almost invariably Yes, so it wasn't much of a criterion. I refined it to: Do I really like the story a lot? That worked better. It resulted in a very large pile of stories I liked a lot.

I then exercised the next criterion: How well would this story work with all the others? which was very difficult to put into operation, but did eliminate some. And by then a further principle of selection had appeared as a question: Should I put a story in this collection because I think it has been overshadowed, has received less attention than it maybe deserved?

That's a tricky call. Luck, fashion, literary awards, and other uncontrollable factors play a part in when and whether a story gets noticed. The only near certainty is that the more often it's reprinted, the more often it will be reprinted. Familiarity sells. "Nine Lives" was republished more often than any of my other stories for years, until "The Ones Who Walk Away from Omelas" (after a slowish start despite winning the Hugo Award) took a handy lead and is still galloping happily along like Seabiscuit.

I did decide to include some stories partly because I wanted to bring them back into the light. Most of them, but not all, are in this first volume.

And here we arrive at the next choice I had to make, once I had chosen all the stories I wanted in the collection. They were to go in two volumes. How should I divide them?

At first I thought I should simply put them in chronological order as written. I tried it, and didn't like the effect. I ended up sorting them into the two parts I call "Where on Earth" and "Outer Space, Inner Lands."

I think the two titles are sufficiently descriptive and need no further explanation. Some people will identify the first volume as "mundane" and the second as "science fiction," but they will be wrong. All the science-fiction stories are in the second volume, but not all the stories in the second volume are science fiction by any definition. I'll talk more about all that in the introduction to the second volume. Let's now find out where on earth we're going.

THE STORIES IN THIS VOLUME

WHEN I WAS A SOPHOMORE IN COLLEGE, I CAME UPON OR DIS-covered or invented a country in central Europe called Orsinia. Orsinia gave me an entry to fiction. It gave me the ground, the room I needed. I had been writing realistic stories (bourgeois-U.S.A.-1948) because realism was what a serious writer was supposed to write under the rule of modernism, which had decreed that non-realistic fiction, if not mere kiddilit, was trash.

I was a very serious young writer. I never had anything against realistic novels, and loved many of them. I am not theory-minded, and did not yet try to question or argue with this arbitrary impoverishment of literature. But I was soon aware that the ground it offered my particular talent was small and stony. I had to find my own way elsewhere.

Orsinia was the way, lying between actuality, which was supposed to be the sole subject of fiction, and the limitless realms of the imagination. I found the country, drew the map, wrote stories about it, wrote two novels about it, one of which was published later as *Malafrena*, and revisited it happily now and then for many years. The first four stories in this volume are Orsinian tales, and the first of them, "Brothers and Sisters," was the first story I wrote that I knew was good, was right, was as close as I could come. I was in my mid-twenties by then.

Since the story "Unlocking the Air," written in 1990, I have had no word from Orsinia. I miss hearing from my people there.

I don't think "The Diary of the Rose" takes place in Orsinia, it seems more like South America to me, but the protagonist has an Orsinian name.

By the early Sixties, when I finally began getting stories published, I was quite certain that reality is often best represented slantwise, backwards, or as if it were an imaginary country, and also that I could write about anywhere and anything I liked, with a hope though no expectation that somebody, somewhere, would publish it.

I could even write realism, if I wanted to.

The stories "Texts," "Sleepwalkers," and "Hand, Cup, Shell," all from the collection *Searoad*, take place in present-day Oregon, in a semi-disguised beach-town I call Klatsand. The protagonist of "The Direction of the Road" still lives beside Highway 18, near McMinnville, in Oregon. "Buffalo Gals" is set in the high desert of Eastern Oregon. "Ether, OR" moves between the dry East side and the green West side of the state in a peaceful, improbable, taken-for-granted way that I think is something I learned from living in Oregon for fifty years.

"The White Donkey" seems to be in a dreamed India, and "Gwilan's Harp" somewhere along the borders of a fantasy-Wales. Spatial location of stories like "The Water is Wide" or "The Lost Children" is irrelevant, other than that they are in America—reflections of a moment in American time. "May's Lion" is set in the Napa Valley of California, where I spent the timeless summers of my childhood, and "Half Past Four" is mostly in Berkeley, where I grew up.

"Half Past Four" is pure realism, but in a somewhat unusual form. In a one-day writing workshop in San Jose, the poetry teacher and I traded classes after lunch: he got my fiction-writers and made them write poems, and I got his poets, to whom I was supposed to teach story-writing. They put up a huge fuss—poets always do. No, no, I am a Poet and cannot possibly tell stories! I said yes you can. I'll give you the names of four people and tell you their relative status; and you'll put them together in a specific place, and look at them for a while, and see that their relationship gives you the beginning of a story. (I made this all up on the spot.) The four character names I gave them were:

Stephen, an older man in a position of relative power or authority; Ann, young, without authority; Ella, older, without much authority; and Todd, young or very young, without any authority.

One brave poet went home and did the assignment; she sent me her story, and it was good. I went home and did the assignment eight times, using those same four names (plus a few extras, such as Marie and Bill). I sent it to *The New Yorker*. They were game and published the piece. The feedback I got showed that many readers tried hard to make the eight Stephens into one Stephen, the eight Ellas into one Ella. It can't be done. The eight brief stories in "Half Past Four" are about thirty-two different people, thirty-two different characters, plus Marie and Bill sometimes. All eight stories have to do with power, identity, and relationship; certain themes and images recur in them and interweave; and they all take place at about four-thirty in the afternoon. I'm still pleased with my assignment.

—Ursula K. Le Guin. August 2012.

BROTHERS

AND

SISTERS

THE INJURED QUARRIER LAY ON A HIGH HOSPITAL BED. HE HAD
not recovered consciousness. His silence was grand and oppressive; his
body under the sheet that dropped in stiff folds, his face were as indifferent
as stone. The mother, as if challenged by that silence and indifference,
spoke loudly: "What did you do it for? Do you want to die before I do?
Look at him, look at him, my beauty, my hawk, my river, my son!" Her
sorrow boasted of itself. She rose to the occasion like a lark to the morning. His silence and her outcry meant the same thing: the unendurable
made welcome. The younger son stood listening. They bore him down
with their grief as large as life. Unconscious, heedless, broken like a
piece of chalk, that body, his brother, bore him down with the weight of
the flesh, and he wanted to run away, to save himself.

The man who had been saved stood beside him, a little stooped fellow, middle-aged, limestone dust white in his knuckles. He too was
borne down. "He saved my life," he said to Stefan, gaping, wanting an
explanation. His voice was the flat toneless voice of the deaf.

"He would," Stefan said. "That's what he'd do."

He left the hospital to get his lunch. Everybody asked him about
his brother. "He'll live," Stefan said. He went to the White Lion for

lunch, drank too much. "Crippled? Him? Kostant? So he got a couple of tons of rock in the face, it won't hurt him, he's made of the stuff. He wasn't born, he was quarried out." They laughed at him as usual. "Quarried out," he said. "Like all the rest of you." He left the White Lion, went down Ardure Street four blocks straight out of town, and kept on straight, walking northeast, parallel with the railroad tracks a quarter mile away. The May sun was small and greyish overhead. Underfoot there were dust and small weeds. The karst, the limestone plain, jigged tinily about him with heatwaves like the transparent vibrating wings of flies. Remote and small, rigid beyond that vibrant greyish haze, the mountains stood. He had known the mountains from far off all his life, and twice had seen them close, when he took the Brailava train, once going, once coming back. He knew they were clothed in trees, fir trees with roots clutching the banks of running streams and with branches dark in the mist that closed and parted in the mountain gullies in the light of dawn as the train clanked by, its smoke dropping down the green slopes like a dropping veil. In the mountains the streams ran noisy in the sunlight; there were waterfalls. Here on the karst the rivers ran underground, silent in dark veins of stone. You could ride a horse all day from Sfaroy Kampe and still not reach the mountains, still be in the limestone dust; but late on the second day you would come under the shade of trees, by running streams. Stefan Fabbre sat down by the side of the straight unreal road he had been walking on, and put his head in his arms. Alone, a mile from town, a quarter mile from the tracks, sixty miles from the mountains, he sat and cried for his brother. The plain of dust and stone quivered and grimaced about him in the heat like the face of a man in pain.

He got back an hour late from lunch to the office of the Chorin Company where he worked as an accountant. His boss came to his desk: "Fabbre, you needn't stay this afternoon."

"Why not?"

"Well, if you want to go to the hospital . . ."

"What can I do there? I can't sew him back up, can I?"

"As you like," the boss said, turning away.

"Not me that got a ton of rocks in the face, is it?" Nobody answered him.

When Kostant Fabbre was hurt in the rockslide in the quarry he was twenty-six years old; his brother was twenty-three; their sister Rosana was thirteen. She was beginning to grow tall and sullen, to weigh upon the earth. Instead of running, now, she walked, ungainly and somewhat hunched, as if at each step she crossed, unwilling, a threshold. She talked loudly, and laughed aloud. She struck back at whatever touched her, a voice, a wind, a word she did not understand, the evening star. She had not learned indifference, she knew only defiance. Usually she and Stefan quarrelled, touching each other where each was raw, unfinished. This night when he got home the mother had not come back from the hospital, and Rosana was silent in the silent house. She had been thinking all afternoon about pain, about pain and death; defiance had failed her.

"Don't look so down," Stefan told her as she served out beans for supper. "He'll be all right."

"Do you think . . . Somebody was saying he might be, you know. . . ."

"Crippled? No, he'll be all right."

"Why do you think he, you know, ran to push that fellow out of the way?"

"No why to it, Ros. He just did it."

He was touched that she asked these questions of him, and surprised at the certainty of his answers. He had not thought that he had any answers.

"It's queer," she said.

"What is?"

"I don't know. Kostant . . ."

"Knocked the keystone out of your arch, didn't it? Wham! One rock falls, they all go." She did not understand him; she did not recognise the place where she had come today, a place where she was like other people, sharing with them the singular catastrophe of being alive. Stefan was not the one to guide her. "Here we all are," he went on, "lying around each of us under our private pile of rocks. At least they got Kostant out from under his and filled him up with morphine. . . . D'you remember once when you were little you said 'I'm going to marry Kostant when I grow up.'"

Rosana nodded. "Sure. And he got real mad."

"Because mother laughed."

"It was you and dad that laughed."

Neither of them was eating. The room was close and dark around the kerosene lamp.

"What was it like when dad died?"

"You were there," Stefan said.

"I was nine. But I can't remember it. Except it was hot like now, and there were a lot of big moths knocking their heads on the glass. Was that the night he died?"

"I guess so."

"What was it like?" She was trying to explore the new land.

"I don't know. He just died. It isn't like anything else."

The father had died of pneumonia at forty-six, after thirty years in the quarries. Stefan did not remember his death much more clearly than Rosana did. He had not been the keystone of the arch.

"Have we got any fruit to eat?"

The girl did not answer. She was gazing at the air above the place at the table where the elder brother usually sat. Her forehead and dark eyebrows were like his, were his: likeness between kin is identity, the brother and sister were, by so much or so little, the curve of brow and temple, the same person; so that, for a moment, Kostant sat across the table mutely contemplating his own absence.

"Is there any?"

"I think there's some apples in the pantry," she answered, coming back to herself, but so quietly that in her brother's eyes she seemed briefly a

woman, a quiet woman speaking out of her thoughts; and he said with
tenderness to that woman, "Come on, let's go over to the hospital. They
must be through messing with him by now."

The deaf man had come back to the hospital. His daughter was with
him. Stefan knew she clerked at the butcher's shop. The deaf man, not
allowed into the ward, kept Stefan half an hour in the hot, pine-floored
waiting room that smelled of disinfectant and resin. He talked, walking
about, sitting down, jumping up, arguing in the loud even monotone
of his deafness. "I'm not going back to the pit. No sir. What if I'd said
last night I'm not going into the pit tomorrow? Then how'd it be now,
see? I wouldn't be here now, nor you wouldn't, nor he wouldn't, him in
there, your brother. We'd all be home. Home safe and sound, see? I'm
not going back to the pit. No, by God. I'm going out to the farm, that's
where I'm going. I grew up there, see, out west in the foothills there, my
brother's there. I'm going back and work the farm with him. I'm not going
back to the pit again."

The daughter sat on the wooden bench, erect and still. Her face
was narrow, her black hair was pulled back in a knot. "Aren't you hot?"
Stefan asked her, and she answered gravely, "No, I'm all right." Her voice
was clear. She was used to speaking to her deaf father. When Stefan said
nothing more she looked down again and sat with her hands in her lap.
The father was still talking. Stefan rubbed his hands through his sweaty
hair and tried to interrupt. "Good, sounds like a good plan, Sachik.
Why waste the rest of your life in the pits." The deaf man talked right on.

"He doesn't hear you."

"Can't you take him home?"

"I couldn't make him leave here even for dinner. He won't stop talking."

Her voice was much lower saying this, perhaps from embarrassment,
and the sound of it caught at Stefan. He rubbed his sweaty hair again
and stared at her, thinking for some reason of smoke, waterfalls, the
mountains.

"You go on home." He heard in his own voice the qualities of hers, softness and clarity. "I'll get him over to the Lion for an hour."

"Then you won't see your brother."

"He won't run away. Go on home."

At the White Lion both men drank heavily. Sachik talked on about the farm in the foothills, Stefan talked about the mountains and his year at college in the city. Neither heard the other. Drunk, Stefan walked Sachik home to one of the rows of party-walled houses that the Chorin Company had put up in '95 when they opened the new quarry. The houses were on the west edge of town, and behind them the karst stretched in the light of the half-moon away on and on, pocked, pitted, level, answering the moonlight with its own pallor taken at third-hand from the sun. The moon, second-hand, worn at the edges, was hung up in the sky like something a housewife leaves out to remind her it needs mending. "Tell your daughter everything is all right," Stefan said, swaying at the door. "Everything is all right," Sachik repeated with enthusiasm, "aa-all right."

Stefan went home drunk, and so the day of the accident blurred in his memory into the rest of the days of the year, and the fragments that stayed with him, his brother's closed eyes, the dark girl looking at him, the moon looking at nothing, did not recur to his mind together as parts of a whole, but separately with long intervals between.

ON THE KARST THERE ARE NO SPRINGS; THE WATER THEY DRINK in Sfaroy Kampe comes from deep wells and is pure, without taste. Ekata Sachik tasted the strange spring-water of the farm still on her lips as she scrubbed an iron skillet at the sink. She scrubbed with a stiff brush, using more energy than was needed, absorbed in the work deep below the level of conscious pleasure. Food had been burned in the skillet, the water she poured in fled brown from the bristles of the brush, glittering in the lamplight. They none of them knew how to cook here at the farm. Sooner or later she would take over the cooking and they could eat properly. She liked housework, she liked to clean, to bend hot-faced to the oven of a woodburning range, to call people in to supper; lively, complex work, not a bore like clerking at the butcher's shop, making change, saying "Good day" and "Good day" all day. She had left town with her family because she was sick of that. The farm family had taken the four of them in without comment, as a natural disaster, more mouths to feed, but also more hands to work. It was a big, poor farm. Ekata's mother, who was ailing, crept about behind the bustling aunt and cousin; the men, Ekata's uncle, father, and brother, tromped in and out in dusty boots; there were long discussions about buying another pig. "It's better here than in the town, there's nothing in the town," Ekata's widowed cousin said; Ekata did not answer her. She had no answer. "I think Martin will be going back," she said finally, "he never thought to be a farmer." And in fact her brother, who was sixteen, went back to Sfaroy Kampe in August to work in the quarries.

He took a room in a boarding house. His window looked down on the Fabbres' back yard, a fenced square of dust and weeds with a sadlooking fir tree at one corner. The landlady, a quarrier's widow, was dark, straight-backed, calm, like Martin's sister Ekata. With her the boy felt manly and easy. When she was out, her daughter and the other boarders, four single men in their twenties, took over; they laughed and slapped one another on the back; the railway clerk from Brailava would take out his guitar and play music-hall songs, rolling his eyes like raisins set in lard. The daughter, thirty and unmarried, would laugh and move about a great deal, her shirtwaist would come out of her belt in back and she would not tuck it in. Why did they make so much fuss? Why did they laugh, punch one another's shoulders, play the guitar and sing? They would begin to make fun of Martin. He would shrug and reply gruffly. Once he replied in the language used in the quarry pits. The guitar player took him aside and spoke to him seriously about how one must behave in front of ladies. Martin listened with his red face bowed. He was a big, broad-shouldered boy. He thought he might pick up this clerk from Brailava and break his neck. He did not do it. He had no right to. The clerk and the others were men; there was something they understood which he did not understand, the reason why they made a fuss, rolled their eyes, played and sang. Until he understood that, they were justified in telling him how to speak to ladies. He went up to his room and leaned out the window to smoke a cigarette. The smoke hung in the motionless evening air which enclosed the fir tree, the roofs, the world in a large dome of hard, dark-blue crystal. Rosana Fabbre came out into the fenced yard next door, dumped out a pan of dishwater with a short, fine swing of her arms, then stood still to look up at the sky, foreshortened, a dark head over a white blouse, caught in the blue crystal. Nothing moved for sixty miles in all directions except the last drops of water in the dishpan, which one by one fell to the ground, and the smoke of Martin's cigarette curling and dropping away from his fingers. Slowly he drew in his hand so that her eye would not be caught by the tiny curl of smoke. She sighed, whacked the dishpan on the jamb of the door to shake out the last drops, which had already run out, turned, went in; the door slammed. The blue air rejoined without a flaw where she had stood. Martin murmured to that flawless air the word he had been advised not to say in front of ladies, and in a moment, as if in answer, the evening star shone out northwestwards high and clear.

Kostant Fabbre was home, and alone all day now that he was able to get across a room on crutches. How he spent these vast silent days no one considered, probably least of all himself. An active man, the strongest and most intelligent worker in the quarries, a crew foreman since he was twenty-three, he had had no practice at all at idleness, or solitude. He had always used his time to the full in work. Now time must use him. He watched it at work upon him without dismay or impatience, carefully, like an apprentice watching a master. He employed all his strength to learn his new trade, that of weakness. The silence in which he passed the days clung to him now as the limestone dust had used to cling to his skin.

The mother worked in the dry-goods shop till six; Stefan got off work at five. There was an hour in the evening when the brothers were together alone. Stefan had used to spend this hour out in the back yard under the fir tree, stupid, sighing, watching swallows dart after invisible insects in the interminably darkening air, or else he had gone to the White Lion. Now he came home promptly, bringing Kostant the *Brailava Messenger.* They both read it, exchanging sheets. Stefan planned to speak, but did not. The dust lay on his lips. Nothing happened. Over and over the same hour passed. The older brother sat still, his handsome, quiet face bowed over the newspaper. He read slowly; Stefan had to wait to exchange sheets; he could see Kostant's eyes move from word to word. Then Rosana would come in yelling good-bye to schoolmates in the street, the mother would come in, doors would bang, voices ring from room to room, the kitchen would smoke and clatter, plates clash, the hour was gone.

One evening Kostant, having barely begun to read, laid the newspaper down. There was a long pause which contained no events and which Stefan, reading, pretended not to notice.

"Stefan, my pipe's there by you."

"Oh, sure," Stefan mumbled, took him his pipe. Kostant filled and lit it, drew on it a few times, set it down. His right hand lay on the arm of the chair, hard and relaxed, holding in it a knot of desolation too heavy to lift. Stefan hid behind his paper and the silence went on.

I'll read out this about the union coalition to him, Stefan thought, but he did not. His eyes insisted on finding another article, reading it. Why can't I talk to him?

"Ros is growing up," Kostant said.

"She's getting on," Stefan mumbled.

"She'll take some looking after. I've been thinking. This is no town for a girl growing up. Wild lads and hard men."

"You'll find them anywhere."

"Will you; no doubt," Kostant said, accepting Stefan's statement without question. Kostant had never been off the karst, never been out of Sfaroy Kampe. He knew nothing at all but limestone, Ardure Street and Chorin Street and Gulhelm Street, the mountains far off and the enormous sky.

"See," he said, picking up his pipe again, "she's a bit wilful, I think."

"Lads will think twice before they mess with Fabbre's sister," Stefan said. "Anyhow, she'll listen to you."

"And you."

"Me? What should she listen to me for?"

"For the same reasons," Kostant said, but Stefan had found his voice now—"What should she respect me for? She's got good enough sense. You and I didn't listen to anything dad said, did we? Same thing."

"You're not like him. If that's what you meant. You've had an education."

"An education, I'm a real professor, sure. Christ! One year at the Normal School!"

"Why did you fail there, Stefan?"

The question was not asked lightly; it came from the heart of Kostant's silence, from his austere, pondering ignorance. Unnerved at finding himself, like Rosana, included so deeply in the thoughts of this reserved and superb brother, Stefan said the first thing that came to mind—"I was afraid I'd fail. So I didn't work."

And there it was, plain as a glass of water, the truth, which he had never admitted to himself.

Kostant nodded, thinking over this idea of failure, which was surely not one familiar to him; then he said in his resonant, gentle voice, "You're wasting your time here in Kampe."

"I am? What about yourself?"

"I'm wasting nothing. I never won any scholarship." Kostant smiled, and the humor of his smile angered Stefan.

"No, you never tried, you went straight to the pit at fifteen. Listen, did you ever wonder, did you ever stop a minute to ask what am I doing here, why did I go into the quarries, what do I work there for, am I going to work there six days a week every week of the year every year of my life? For pay, sure, there's other ways to make a living. What's it *for*? Why does anybody stay here, in this Godforsaken town on this Godforsaken piece of rock where nothing grows? Why don't they get up and go somewhere? Talk about wasting your time! What in God's name is it all for— is this all there is to it?"

"I have thought that."

"I haven't thought anything else for years."

"Why not go, then?"

"Because I'm afraid to. It'd be like Brailava, like the college. But you—"

"I've got my work here. It's mine, I can do it. Anywhere you go, you can still ask what it's all for."

"I know." Stefan got up, a slight man moving and talking restlessly, half finishing his gestures and words. "I know. You take yourself with yourself. But that means one thing for me and something else again for you. You're wasting yourself here, Kostant. It's the same as this business, this hero business, smashing yourself up for that Sachik, a fool who can't even see a rockslide coming at him—"

"He couldn't *hear* it," Kostant put in, but Stefan could not stop now. "That's not the point; the point is, let that kind of man look after himself, what's he to you, what's his life to you? Why did you go in after him when you saw the slide coming? For the same reason as you went into the pit, for the same reason as you keep working in the pit. For no reason. Because it just came up. It just happened. You let things happen to you, you take what's handed you, when you could take it all in your hands and do what you wanted with it!"

It was not what he had meant to say, not what he had wanted to say. He had wanted Kostant to talk. But words fell out of his own mouth and bounced around him like hailstones. Kostant sat quiet, his strong hand closed not to open; finally he answered: "You're making something of me I'm not." That was not humility. There was none in him. His patience was that of pride. He understood Stefan's yearning but could not share it, for he lacked nothing; he was intact. He would go forward in the same, splendid, vulnerable integrity of body and mind towards whatever came to meet him on his road, like a king in exile on a land of stone, bearing all his kingdom—cities, trees, people, mountains, fields and flights of birds in spring—in his closed hand, a seed for the sowing; and, because there was no one of his language to speak to, silent.

"But listen, you said you've thought the same thing, what's it all for, is this all there is to life—If you've thought that, you must have looked for the answer!"

After a long pause Kostant said, "I nearly found it. Last May."

Stefan stopped fidgeting, looked out the front window in silence. He was frightened. "That—that's not an answer," he mumbled.

"Seems like there ought to be a better one," Kostant agreed.

"You get morbid sitting here. . . . What you need's a woman," Stefan said, fidgeting, slurring his words, staring out at the early-autumn evening rising from stone pavements unobscured by tree branches or smoke, even, clear, and empty. Behind him, his brother laughed. "It's the truth," Stefan said bitterly, not turning.

"Could be. How about yourself?"

"They're sitting out on the steps there at widow Katalny's. She must be night nursing at the hospital again. Hear the guitar? That's the fellow from Brailava, works at the railway office, goes after anything in skirts. Even goes after Nona Katalny. Sachik's kid lives there now. Works in the New Pit, somebody said. Maybe in your crew."

"What kid?"

"Sachik's."

"Thought he'd left town."

"He did, went to some farm in the west hills. This is his kid, must have stayed behind to work."

"Where's the girl?"

"Went with her father as far as I know."

The pause this time lengthened out, stretched around them like a pool in which their last words floated, desultory, vague, fading. The room was full of dusk. Kostant stretched and sighed. Stefan felt peace come into him, as intangible and real as the coming of the darkness. They had talked, and got nowhere; it was not a last step; the next step would come in its time. But for a moment he was at peace with his brother, and with himself.

"Evenings getting shorter," Kostant said softly.

"I've seen her once or twice. Saturdays. Comes in with a farm wagon."

"Where's the farm at?"

"West, in the hills, was all old Sachik said."

"Might ride out there, if I could," Kostant said. He struck a match for his pipe. The flare of the match in the clear dusk of the room was also a peaceful thing; when Stefan looked back at the window the evening seemed darker. The guitar had stopped and they were laughing out on the steps next door.

"If I see her Saturday I'll ask her to come by."

Kostant said nothing. Stefan wanted no answer. It was the first time in his life that his brother had asked his help.

The mother came in, tall, loud-voiced, tired. Floors cracked and cried under her step, the kitchen clashed and steamed, everything was noisy in her presence except her two sons, Stefan who eluded her, Kostant who was her master.

Stefan got off work Saturdays at noon. He sauntered down Ardure Street looking out for the farm wagon and roan horse. They were not in town, and he went to the White Lion, relieved and bored. Another Saturday came and a third. It was October, the afternoons were shorter. Martin Sachik was walking down Gulhelm Street ahead of him; he caught up and said, "Evening, Sachik." The boy looked at him with blank grey eyes; his face, hands, and clothes were grey with stone-dust and he walked as slowly and steadily as a man of fifty.

"Which crew are you in?"

"Five." He spoke distinctly, like his sister.

"That's my brother's."

"I know." They went on pace for pace. "They said he might be back in the pit next month."

Stefan shook his head.

"Your family still out there on that farm?" he asked.

Martin nodded, as they stopped in front of the Katalny house. He revived, now that he was home and very near dinner. He was flattered by Stefan Fabbre's speaking to him, but not shy of him. Stefan was clever, but he was spoken of as a moody, unsteady fellow, half a man where his brother was a man and a half. "Near Verre," Martin said. "A hell of a place. I couldn't take it."

"Can your sister?"

"Figures she has to stay with Ma. She ought to come back. It's a hell of a place."

"This isn't heaven," Stefan said.

"Work your head off there and never get any money for it, they're all loony on those farms. Right where Dad belongs." Martin felt virile, speaking disrespectfully of his father. Stefan Fabbre looked at him, not with respect, and said, "Maybe. Evening to you, Sachik." Martin went into the house defeated. When was he going to become a man, not subject to other men's reproof? Why did it matter if Stefan Fabbre looked at him and turned away? The next day he met Rosana Fabbre on the street. She was with a girl friend, he with a fellow quarrier; they had all been in school together last year. "How you doing, Ros?" Martin said loudly, nudging his friend. The girls walked by haughty as cranes. "There's a hot one," Martin said. "Her? She's just a kid," the friend said. "You'd be surprised," Martin told him with a thick laugh, then looked up and saw Stefan Fabbre crossing the street. For a moment he realised that he was surrounded, there was no escape.

Stefan was on the way to the White Lion, but passing the town hotel and livery stable he saw the roan horse in the yard. He went in, and sat in the brown parlour of the hotel in the smell of harness grease and dried spiders. He sat there two hours. She came in, erect, a black kerchief on her hair, so long awaited and so fully herself that he watched her go by with simple pleasure, and only woke as she started up the stairs. "Miss Sachik," he said.

She stopped, startled, on the stairs.

"Wanted to ask you a favor." Stefan's voice was thick after the strange timeless waiting. "You're staying here over tonight?"

"Yes."

"Kostant was asking about you. Wanted to ask about your father. He's still stuck indoors, can't walk much."

"Father's fine."

"Well, I wondered if—"

"I could look in. I was going to see Martin. It's next door, isn't it?"

"Oh, fine. That's—I'll wait."

Ekata ran up to her room, washed her dusty face and hands, and put on, to decorate her grey dress, a lace collar that she had brought to wear to church tomorrow. Then she took it off again. She retied the black kerchief over her black hair, went down, and walked with Stefan six blocks through the pale October sunlight to his house. When she saw Kostant Fabbre she was staggered. She had never seen him close to except in the hospital where he had been effaced by casts, bandages, heat, pain, her father's chatter. She saw him now.

They fell to talking quite easily. She would have felt wholly at ease with him if it had not been for his extraordinary beauty, which distracted her. His voice and what he said was grave, plain, and reassuring. It was the other way round with the younger brother, who was nothing at all to look at, but with whom she felt ill at ease, at a loss. Kostant was quiet and quieting; Stefan blew in gusts like autumn wind, bitter and fitful; you didn't know where you were with him.

"How is it for you out there?" Kostant was asking, and she replied, "All right. A bit dreary."

"Farming's the hardest work, they say."

"I don't mind the hard, it's the muck I mind."

"Is there a village near?"

"Well, it's halfway between Verre and Lotima. But there's neighbors, everybody within twenty miles knows each other."

"We're still your neighbors, by that reckoning," Stefan put in. His voice slurred off in midsentence. He felt irrelevant to these two. Kostant sat relaxed, his lame leg stretched out, his hands clasped round the other knee; Ekata faced him, upright, her hands lying easy in her lap. They did not look alike but might have been brother and sister. Stefan got up with a mumbled excuse and went out back. The north wind blew. Sparrows hopped in the sour dirt under the fir tree and the scurf of weedy grass. Shirts, underclothes, a pair of sheets snapped, relaxed, jounced on the clothesline between two iron posts. The air smelt of ozone. Stefan vaulted the fence, cut across the Katalny yard to the street, and walked westward. After a couple of blocks the street petered out. A track led on to a quarry, abandoned twenty years ago when they struck water; there was twenty feet of water in it now. Boys swam there, summers. Stefan had swum there, in terror, for he had never learned to swim well and there was no foothold, it was all deep and bitter cold. A boy had drowned there years ago, last year a man had drowned himself, a quarrier going blind from stone-splinters in his eyes. It was still called the West Pit. Stefan's father had worked in it as a boy. Stefan sat down by the lip of it and watched the wind, caught down in the four walls, eddy in tremors over the water that reflected nothing.

"I have to go meet Martin," Ekata said. As she stood up Kostant put a hand out to his crutches, then gave it up: "Takes me too long to get afoot," he said.

"How much can you get about on those?"

"From here to there," he said, pointing to the kitchen. "Leg's all right. It's the back's slow."

"You'll be off them—?"

"Doctor says by Easter. I'll run out and throw 'em in the West Pit. . . ." They both smiled. She felt tenderness for him, and a pride in knowing him.

"Will you be coming in to Kampe, I wonder, when bad weather comes?"

"I don't know how the roads will be."

"If you do, come by," he said. "If you like."

"I will."

They noticed then that Stefan was gone.

"I don't know where he went to," Kostant said. "He comes and he goes, Stefan does. Your brother, Martin, they tell me he's a good lad in our crew."

"He's young," Ekata said.

"It's hard at first. I went in at fifteen. But then when you've got your strength, you know the work, and it goes easy. Good wishes to your family, then." She shook his big, hard, warm hand, and let herself out. On the doorstep she met Stefan face to face. He turned red. It shocked her to see a man blush. He spoke, as usual leaping straight into the subject— "You were the year behind me in school, weren't you?"

"Yes."

"You went around with Rosa Bayenin. She won the scholarship I did, the next year."

"She's teaching school now, in the Valone."

"She did more with it than I would have done.—I was thinking, see, it's queer how you grow up in a place like this, you know everybody, then you meet one and find out you don't know them."

She did not know what to answer. He said good-bye and went into the house; she went on, retying her kerchief against the rising wind.

Rosana and the mother came into the house a minute after Stefan. "Who was that on the doorstep you were talking to?" the mother said sharply. "That wasn't Nona Katalny, I'll be bound."

"You're right," Stefan said.

"All right, but you watch out for that one, you're just the kind she'd like to get her claws into, and wouldn't that be fine, you could walk her puppydog whilst she entertains her ma's gentlemen boarders." She and Rosana both began to laugh their loud, dark laughter. "Who was it you were talking to, then?"

"What's it to you?" he shouted back. Their laughter enraged him; it was like a pelting with hard clattering rocks, too thick to dodge.

"What is it to me who's standing on my own doorstep, you want to know, I'll let you know what it is to me—" Words leapt to meet her anger as they did to all her passions. "You so high and mighty all the time with all your going off to college, but you came sneaking back quick enough to this house, didn't you, and I'll let you know I want to know who comes into this house—" Rosana was shouting, "I know who it was, it was Martin Sachik's sister!" Kostant loomed up suddenly beside the three of them, stooped and tall on his crutches: "Cut it out," he said, and they fell silent.

Nothing was said, then or later, to the mother or between the two brothers, about Ekata Sachik's having been in the house.

Martin took his sister to dine at the Bell, the café where officials of the Chorin Company and visitors from out of town went to dine. He was proud of himself for having thought of treating her, proud of the white table-clothes and the forks and soupspoons, terrified of the waiter. He in his outgrown Sunday coat and his sister in her grey dress, how admirably they were behaving, how adult they were. Ekata looked at the menu so calmly, and her face did not change expression in the slightest as she murmured to him, "But there's two kinds of soup."

"Yes," he said, with sophistication.

"Do you choose which kind?"

"I guess so."

"You must, you'd bloat up before you ever got to the meat—" They snickered. Ekata's shoulders shook; she hid her face in her napkin; the napkin was enormous—"Martin, look, they've given me a bedsheet—" They both sat snorting, shaking, in torment, while the waiter, with another bedsheet on his shoulder, inexorably approached.

Dinner was ordered inaudibly, eaten with etiquette, elbows pressed close to the sides. The dessert was a chestnut-flour pudding, and Ekata, her elbows relaxing a little with enjoyment, said, "Rosa Bayenin said when she wrote the town she's in is right next to a whole forest of chestnut trees, everybody goes and picks them up in autumn, the trees grow thick as night, she said, right down to the river bank." Town after six weeks on the farm, the talk with Kostant and Stefan, dining at the restaurant had excited her. "This is awfully good," she said, but she could not say what she saw, which was sunlight striking golden down a river between endless dark-foliaged trees, a wind running upriver among shadows and the scent of leaves, of water, and of chestnut-flour pudding, a world of forests, of rivers, of strangers, the sunlight shining on the world.

"Saw you talking with Stefan Fabbre," Martin said.

"I was at their house."

"What for?"

"They asked me."

"What for?"

"Just to find out how we're getting on."

"They never asked me."

"You're not on the farm, stupid. You're in his crew, aren't you? You could look in sometime, you know. He's a grand man, you'd like him."

Martin grunted. He resented Ekata's visit to the Fabbres without knowing why. It seemed somehow to complicate things. Rosana had probably been there. He did not want his sister knowing about Rosana. Knowing what about Rosana? He gave it up, scowling.

"The younger brother, Stefan, he works at the Chorin office, doesn't he?"

"Keeps books or something. He was supposed to be a genius and go to college, but they kicked him out."

"I know." She finished her pudding, lovingly. "Everybody knows that," she said.

"I don't like him," Martin said.

"Why not?"

"Just don't." He was relieved, having dumped his ill humor onto Stefan. "You want coffee?"

"Oh, no."

"Come on. I do." Masterful, he ordered coffee for both. Ekata admired him, and enjoyed the coffee. "What luck, to have a brother," she said. The next morning, Sunday, Martin met her at the hotel and they went to church; singing the Lutheran hymns each heard the other's strong clear voice and each was pleased and wanted to laugh. Stefan Fabbre was at the service. "Does he usually come?" Ekata asked Martin as they left the church.

"No," Martin said, though he had no idea, having not been to church himself since May. He felt dull and fierce after the long sermon. "He's following you around."

She said nothing.

"He waited for you at the hotel, you said. Takes you out to see his brother, he says. Talks to you on the street. Shows up in church." Self-defense furnished him these items one after another, and the speaking of them convinced him.

"Martin," Ekata said, "if there's one kind of man I hate it's a meddler."

"If you weren't my sister—"

"If I wasn't your sister I'd be spared your stupidness. Will you go ask the man to put the horse in?" So they parted with mild rancor between them, soon lost in distance and the days.

In late November when Ekata drove in again to Sfaroy Kampe she went to the Fabbre house. She wanted to go, and had told Kostant she would, yet she had to force herself; and when she found that Kostant and Rosana were home, but Stefan was not, she felt much easier. Martin had troubled her with his stupid meddling. It was Kostant she wanted to see, anyhow.

But Kostant wanted to talk about Stefan.

"He's always out roaming, or at the Lion. Restless. Wastes his time. He said to me, one day we talked, he's afraid to leave Kampe. I've thought about what he meant. What is it he's afraid of?"

"Well, he hasn't any friends but here."

"Few enough here. He acts the clerk among the quarrymen, and the quarryman among the clerks. I've seen him, here, when my mates come in. Why don't he be what he is?"

"Maybe he isn't sure what he is."

"He won't learn it from mooning around and drinking at the Lion," said Kostant, hard and sure in his own intactness. "And rubbing up quarrels. He's had three fights this month. Lost 'em all, poor devil," and he laughed. She never expected the innocence of laughter on his grave face. And he was kind; his concern for Stefan was deep, his laughter without a sneer, the laughter of a good nature. Like Stefan, she wondered at him, at his beauty and his strength, but she did not think of him as wasted. The Lord keeps the house and knows his servants. If he had sent this innocent and splendid man to live obscure on the plain of stone, it was part of his housekeeping, of the strange economy of the stone and the rose, the rivers that run and do not run dry, the tiger, the ocean, the maggot, and the not eternal stars.

Rosana, by the hearth, listened to them talk. She sat silent, heavy and her shoulders stooped, though of late she had been learning again to hold herself erect as she had when she was a child, a year ago. They say one gets used to being a millionaire; so after a year or two a human being begins to get used to being a woman. Rosana was learning to wear the rich and heavy garment of her inheritance. Just now she was listening, something she had rarely done. She had never heard adults talk as these two were talking. She had never heard a conversation. At the end of twenty minutes she slipped quietly out. She had learned enough, too much, she needed time to absorb and practice. She began practicing at once. She went down the street erect, not slow and not fast, her face composed, like Ekata Sachik.

"Daydreaming, Ros?" jeered Martin Sachik from the Katalny yard.

She smiled at him and said, "Hello, Martin." He stood staring.

"Where you going?" he asked with caution.

"Nowhere; I'm just walking. Your sister's at our house."

"She is?" Martin sounded unusually stupid and belligerent, but she stuck to her practicing: "Yes," she said politely. "She came to see my brother."

"Which brother?"

"Kostant, why would she have come to see Stefan?" she said, forgetting her new self a moment and grinning widely.

"How come you're barging around all by yourself?"

"Why not?" she said, stung by "barging" and so reverting to an extreme mildness of tone.

"I'll go with you."

"Why not?"

They walked down Gulhelm Street till it became a track between weeds.

"Want to go on to the West Pit?"

"Why not?" Rosana liked the phrase; it sounded experienced.

They walked on the thin stony dirt between miles of dead grass too short to bow to the northwest wind. Enormous masses of cloud travelled backward over their heads so that they seemed to be walking very fast, the grey plain sliding along with them. "Clouds make you dizzy," Martin said, "like looking up a flagpole." They walked with faces upturned, seeing nothing but the motion of the wind. Rosana realised that though their feet were on the earth they themselves stuck up into the sky, it was the sky they were walking through, just as birds flew through it. She looked over at Martin walking through the sky.

They came to the abandoned quarry and stood looking down at the water, dulled by flurries of trapped wind.

"Want to go swimming?"

"Why not?"

"There's the mule trail. Looks funny, don't it, going right down into the water."

"It's cold here."

"Come on down the trail. There's no wind inside the walls hardly. That's where Penik jumped off from, they grappled him up from right under here."

Rosana stood on the lip of the pit. The grey wind blew by her. "Do you think he meant to? I mean, he was blind, maybe he fell in—"

"He could see some. They were going to send him to Brailava and operate on him. Come on." She followed him to the beginning of the path down. It looked very steep from above. She had become timorous the last year. She followed him slowly down the effaced, boulder-smashed track into the quarry. "Here, hold on," he said, pausing at a rough drop; he took her hand and brought her down after him. They separated at once and he led on to where the water cut across the path, which plunged on down to the hidden floor of the quarry. The water was lead-dark, uneasy, its surface broken into thousands of tiny pleatings, circles, counter-circles by the faint trapped wind jarring it ceaselessly against the walls. "Shall I go on?" Martin whispered, loud in the silence.

"Why not?"

He walked on. She cried, "Stop!" He had walked into the water up to his knees; he turned, lost his balance, careened back onto the path with a plunge that showered her with water and sent clapping echoes round the walls of rock. "You're crazy, what did you do that for?" Martin sat down, took off his big shoes to dump water out of them, and laughed, a soundless laugh mixed with shivering. "What did you do that for?"

"Felt like it," he said. He caught at her arm, pulled her down kneeling by him, and kissed her. The kiss went on. She began to struggle, and pulled away from him. He hardly knew it. He lay there on the rocks at the water's edge laughing; he was as strong as the earth and could not lift his hand. . . . He sat up, mouth open, eyes unfocussed. After a while he put on his wet, heavy shoes and started up the path. She stood at the top, a windblown stroke of darkness against the huge moving sky. "Come on!" she shouted, and wind thinned her voice to a knife's edge. "Come on, you can't catch me!" As he neared the top of the path, she ran. He ran, weighed down by his wet shoes and trousers. A hundred yards from the quarry he caught her and tried to capture both her arms. Her wild face was next to his for a moment. She twisted free, ran off again, and he followed her into town, trotting since he could not run any more. Where Gulhelm Street began she stopped and waited for him. They walked down the pavement side by side. "You look like a drowned cat," she jeered in a panting whisper. "Who's talking," he answered the same way, "look at the mud on your skirt." In front of the boarding house they stopped and looked at each other, and he laughed. "Good night, Ros!" he said. She wanted to bite him. "Good night!" she said, and walked the few yards to her own front door, not slow and not fast, feeling his gaze on her back like a hand on her flesh.

Not finding her brother at the boarding house, Ekata had gone back to the hotel to wait for him; they were to dine at the Bell again. She told the desk clerk to send her brother up when he came. In a few minutes there was a knock; she opened the door. It was Stefan Fabbre. He was the color of oatmeal and looked dingy, like an unmade bed.

"I wanted to ask you . . ." His voice slurred off. "Have some dinner," he muttered, looking past her at the room.

"My brother's coming for me. That's him now." But it was the hotel manager coming up the stairs. "Sorry, miss," he said loudly. "There's a parlour downstairs." Ekata stared at him blankly. "Now look, miss, you said to send up your brother, and the clerk he don't know your brother by sight, but I do. That's my business. There's a nice parlour downstairs for entertaining. All right? You want to come to a respectable hotel, I want to keep it respectable for you, see?"

Stefan pushed past him and blundered down the stairs. "He's drunk, miss," said the manager.

"Go away," Ekata said, and shut the door on him. She sat down on the bed with clenched hands, but she could not sit still. She jumped up, took up her coat and kerchief, and without putting them on ran downstairs and out, hurling the key onto the desk behind which the manager stood staring. Ardure Street was dark between pools of lamplight, and the winter wind blew down it. She walked the two blocks west, came back down the other side of the street the length of it, eight blocks; she passed the White Lion, but the winter door was up and she could not see in. It was cold, the wind ran through the streets like a river running. She went to Gulhelm Street and met Martin coming out of the boarding house. They went to the Bell for supper. Both were thoughtful and uneasy. They spoke little and gently, grateful for companionship.

Alone in church next morning, when she had made sure that Stefan was not there, she lowered her eyes in relief. The stone walls of the church and the stark words of the service stood strong around her. She rested like a ship in haven. Then as the pastor gave his text, "I will lift up mine eyes unto the hills, whence cometh my help," she shivered, and once again looked all about the church, moving her head and eyes slowly, surreptitiously, seeking him. She heard nothing of the sermon. But when the service was over she did not want to leave the church. She went out among the last of the congregation. The pastor detained her, asking about her mother. She saw Stefan waiting at the foot of the steps.

She went to him.

"Wanted to apologise for last night," he brought out all in one piece.

"It's all right."

He was bareheaded and the wind blew his light, dusty-looking hair across his eyes; he winced and tried to smooth it back. "I was drunk," he said.

"I know."

They set off together.

"I was worried about you," Ekata said.

"What for? I wasn't that drunk."

"I don't know."

They crossed the street in silence.

"Kostant likes talking with you. Told me so." His tone was unpleasant. Ekata said drily, "I like talking with him."

"Everybody does. It's a great favor he does them."

She did not reply.

"I mean that."

She knew what he meant, but still did not say anything. They were near the hotel. He stopped. "I won't finish ruining your reputation."

"You don't have to grin about it."

"I'm not. I mean I won't go on to the hotel with you, in case it embarrassed you."

"I have nothing to be embarrassed about."

"I do, and I am. I am sorry, Ekata."

"I didn't mean you had to apologise again." Her voice turned husky so that he thought again of mist, dusk, the forests.

"I won't." He laughed. "Are you leaving right away?"

"I have to. It gets dark so early now."

They both hesitated.

"You could do me a favor," she said.

"I'd do that."

"If you'd see to having my horse put in, last time I had to stop after a mile and tighten everything. If you did that I could be getting ready."

When she came out of the hotel the wagon was out front and he was in the seat. "I'll drive you a mile or two, all right?" She nodded, he gave her a hand up; they drove down Ardure Street westward to the plain.

"That damned hotel manager," Ekata said. "Grinning and scraping this morning . . ."

Stefan laughed, but said nothing. He was cautious, absorbed; the cold wind blew, the old roan clopped along; he explained presently, "I've never driven before."

"I've never driven any horse but this one. He's never any trouble."

The wind whistled in miles of dead grass, tugged at her black kerchief, whipped Stefan's hair across his eyes.

"Look at it," he said softly. "A couple of inches of dirt, and under it rock. Drive all day, any direction, and you'll find rock, with a couple of inches of dirt on it. You know how many trees there are in Kampe? Fifty-four. I counted 'em. And not another, not one, all the way to the mountains." His voice as he talked as if to himself was dry and musical. "When I went to Brailava on the train I looked out for the first new tree. The fifty-fifth tree. It was a big oak by a farmhouse in the hills. Then all of a sudden there were trees everywhere, in all the valleys in the hills. You could never count 'em. But I'd like to try."

"You're sick of it here."

"I don't know. Sick of something. I feel like I was an ant, something smaller, so small you can hardly see it, crawling along on this huge floor. Getting nowhere because where is there to get. Look at us now, crawling across the floor, there's the ceiling. . . . Looks like snow, there in the north."

"Not before dark, I hope."

"What's it like on the farm?"

She considered some while before answering, and then said softly, "Closed in."

"Your father happy with it?"

"He never did feel easy in Kampe, I think."

"There's people made out of dirt, earth," he said in his voice that slurred away so easily into unheard monologue, "and then there's some made out of stone. The fellows who get on in Kampe are made out of stone." "Like my brother," he did not say, and she heard it.

"Why don't you leave?"

"That's what Kostant said. It sounds so easy. But see, if he left, he'd be taking himself with him. I'd be taking myself. . . . Does it matter where you go? All you have is what you are. Or what you meet."

He checked the horse. "I'd better hop off, we must have come a couple of miles. Look, there's the ant-heap." From the high wagon seat looking back they saw a darkness on the pale plain, a pinpoint spire, a glitter where the winter sun struck windows or roof-slates; and far behind the town, distinct under high, heavy, dark-grey clouds, the mountains.

He handed the traces to her. "Thanks for the lift," he said, and swung down from the seat.

"Thanks for the company, Stefan."

He raised his hand; she drove on. It seemed a cruel thing to do, to leave him on foot there on the plain. When she looked back she saw him far behind already, walking away from her between the narrowing wheel-ruts under the enormous sky.

Before she reached the farm that evening there was a dry flurry of snow, the first of an early winter. From the kitchen window all that month she looked up at hills blurred with rain. In December from her bedroom, on days of sun after snow, she saw eastward across the plain a glittering pallor: the mountains. There were no more trips to Sfaroy Kampe. When they needed market goods her uncle drove to Verre or Lotima, bleak villages foundering like cardboard in the rain. It was too easy to stray off the wheel-ruts crossing the karst in snow or heavy rain, he said, "and then where are ye?"

"Where are ye in the first place?" Ekata answered in Stefan's soft dry voice. The uncle paid no heed.

Martin rode out on a livery-stable horse for Christmas day. After a few hours he got sullen and stuck to Ekata. "What's that thing Aunt's got hanging round her neck?"

"A nail through an onion. To keep off rheumatism."

"Christ Almighty!"

Ekata laughed.

"The whole place stinks of onion and flannel, can't you air it out?"

"No. Cold days they even close the chimney flues. Rather have the smoke than the cold."

"You ought to come back to town with me, Ekata."

"Ma's not well."

"You can't help that."

"No. But I'd feel mean to leave her without good reason. First things first." Ekata had lost weight; her cheekbones stood out and her eyes looked darker. "How's it going with you?" she asked presently.

"All right. We've been laid off a good bit, the snow."

"You've been growing up," Ekata said.

"I know."

He sat on the stiff farm-parlour sofa with a man's weight, a man's quietness.

"You walking out with anybody?"

"No." They both laughed. "Listen, I saw Fabbre, and he said to wish you joy of the season. He's better. Gets outside now, with a cane."

Their cousin came through the room. She wore a man's old boots stuffed with straw for warmth getting about in the ice and mud of the farmyard. Martin looked after her with disgust. "I had a talk with him.

Couple of weeks ago. I hope he's back in the pits by Easter like they say. He's my foreman, you know." Looking at him, Ekata saw who it was he was in love with.

"I'm glad you like him."

"There isn't a man in Kampe comes up to his shoulder. You liked him, didn't you?"

"Of course I did."

"See, when he asked about you, I thought—"

"You thought wrong," Ekata said. "Will you quit meddling, Martin?"

"I didn't say anything," he defended himself feebly; his sister could still overawe him. He also recalled that Rosana Fabbre had laughed at him when he had said something to her about Kostant and Ekata. She had been hanging out sheets in the back yard on a whipping-bright winter morning a few days ago, he had hung over the back fence talking to her. "Oh Lord, are you crazy?" she had jeered, while the damp sheets on the line billowed at her face and the wind tangled her hair. "Those two? Not on your life!" He had tried to argue; she would not listen. "He's not going to marry anybody from here. There's going to be some woman from far off, from Krasnoy maybe, a manager's wife, a queen, a beauty, with servants and all. And one day she'll be coming down Ardure Street with her nose in the air and she'll see Kostant coming with his nose in the air, and crack! that's it."

"That's what?" said he, fascinated by her fortune-teller's conviction.

"I don't know!" she said, and hoisted up another sheet. "Maybe they'll run off together. Maybe something else. All I know is Kostant knows what's coming to him, and he's going to wait for it."

"All right, if you know so much, what's coming your way?"

She opened her mouth wide in a big grin, her dark eyes under long dark brows flashed at him. "Men," she said like a cat hissing, and the sheets and shirts snapped and billowed around her, white in the flashing sunlight.

January passed, covering the surly plain with snow, February with
a grey sky moving slowly over the plain from north to south day after
day: a hard winter and a long one. Kostant Fabbre got a lift sometimes
on a cart to the Chorin quarries north of town, and would stand watching the work, the teams of men and lines of wagons, the shunting box-
cars, the white of snow and the dull white of new-cut limestone. Men
would come up to the tall man leaning on his cane to ask him how he
did, when he was coming back to work. "A few weeks yet," he would
say. The company was keeping him laid off till April as their insurers
requested. He felt fit, he could walk back to town without using his cane,
it fretted him bitterly to be idle. He would go back, to the White Lion,
and sit there in the smoky dark and warmth till the quarrymen came in,
off work at four because of snow and darkness, big heavy men making
the place steam with the heat of their bodies and buzz with the mutter
of their voices. At five Stefan would come in, slight, with white shirt
and light shoes, a queer figure among the quarriers. He usually came
to Kostant's table, but they were not on good terms. Each was waiting
and impatient.

"Evening," Martin Sachik said passing the table, a tired burly lad, smiling.
"Evening, Stefan."

"I'm Fabbre and Mr. to you, laddie," Stefan said in his soft voice that
yet stood out against the comfortable hive-mutter. Martin, already past,
chose to pay no attention.

"Why are you down on that one?"

"Because I don't choose to be on first names with every man's brat
that goes down in the pits. Nor every man either. D'you take me for the
town idiot?"

"You act like it, times," Kostant said, draining his beermug.

"I've had enough of your advice."

"I've had enough of your conceit. Go to the Bell if the company here
don't suit you."

Stefan got up, slapped money on the table, and went out.

It was the first of March; the north half of the sky over the streets was heavy, without light; its edge was silvery blue, and from it south to the horizon the air was blue and empty except for a fingernail moon over the western hills and, near it, the evening star. Stefan went silent through the streets, a silent wind at his back. Indoors, the walls of the house enclosed his rage; it became a square, dark, musty thing full of the angles of tables and chairs, and flared up yellow with the kerosene lamp. The chimney of the lamp slithered out of his hand like a live animal, smashed itself shrilly against the corner of the table. He was on all fours picking up bits of glass when his brother came in.

"What did you follow me for?"

"I came to my own house."

"Do I have to go back to the Lion then?"

"Go where you damned well like." Kostant sat down and picked up yesterday's newspaper. Stefan, kneeling, broken glass on the palm of his hand, spoke: "Listen. I know why you want me patting young Sachik on the head. For one thing he thinks you're God Almighty, and that's agreeable. For another thing he's got a sister. And you want 'em all eating out of your hand, don't you? Like they all do? Well by God here's one that won't, and you might find your game spoiled, too." He got up and went to the kitchen, to the trash basket that stood by the week's heap of dirty clothes, and dropped the glass of the broken lamp into the basket. He stood looking at his hand: a sliver of glass bristled from the inner joint of his second finger. He had clenched his hand on the glass as he spoke to Kostant. He pulled out the sliver and put the bleeding finger to his mouth. Kostant came in. "What game, Stefan?" he said.

"You know what I mean."

"Say what you mean."

"I mean her. Ekata. What do you want her for anyhow? You don't need her. You don't need anything. You're the big tin god."

"You shut your mouth."

"Don't give me orders! By God I can give orders too. You just stay away from her. I'll get her and you won't, I'll get her under your nose, under your eyes—" Kostant's big hands took hold of his shoulders and shook him till his head snapped back and forth on his neck. He broke free and drove his fist straight at Kostant's face, but as he did so he felt a jolt as when a train-car is coupled to the train. He fell down backwards across the heap of dirty clothes. His head hit the floor with a dead sound like a dropped melon.

Kostant stood with his back against the stove. He looked at his right-hand knuckles, then at Stefan's face, which was dead white and curiously serene. Kostant took a pillowcase from the pile of clothes, wet it at the sink, and knelt down by Stefan. It was hard for him to kneel, the right leg was still stiff. He mopped away the thin dark line of blood that had run from Stefan's mouth. Stefan's face twitched, he sighed and blinked, and looked up at Kostant, gazing with vague, sliding recognition, like a young infant.

"That's better," Kostant said. His own face was white.

Stefan propped himself up on one arm. "I fell down," he said in a faint, surprised voice. Then he looked at Kostant again and his face began to change and tighten.

"Stefan—"

Stefan got up on all fours, then onto his feet; Kostant tried to take his arm, but he stumbled to the door, struggled with the catch, and plunged out. At the door, Kostant watched him vault the fence, cut across the Katalny yard, and run down Gulhelm Street with long, jolting strides. For several minutes the elder brother stood in the doorway, his face rigid and sorrowful. Then he turned, went to the front door and out, and made off down Gulhelm Street as fast as he could. The black cloud-front had covered all the sky but a thin band of blue-green to the south; the moon and stars were gone. Kostant followed the track over the plain to the West Pit. No one was ahead of him. He reached the lip of the quarry and saw the water quiet, dim, reflecting snow that had yet to fall. He called out once, "Stefan!" His lungs were raw and his throat dry from the effort he had made to run. There was no answer. It was not his brother's name that need be called there at the lip of the ruined quarry. It was the wrong name, and the wrong time. Kostant turned and started back towards Gulhelm Street, walking slowly and a little lame.

"I've got to ride to Kolle," Stefan said. The livery-stable keeper stared at his blood-smeared chin.

"It's dark. There's ice on the roads."

"You must have a sharp-shod horse. I'll pay double."

"Well . . ."

Stefan rode out of the stable yard, and turned right down Ardure Street towards Verre instead of left towards Kolle. The keeper shouted after him. Stefan kicked the horse, which fell into a trot and then, where the pavement ceased, into a heavy run. The band of blue-green light in the southwest veered and slid away, Stefan thought he was falling sideways, he clung to the pommel but did not pull the reins. When the horse ran itself out and slowed to a walk it was full night, earth and sky all dark. The horse snorted, the saddle creaked, the wind hissed in frozen grass. Stefan dismounted and searched the ground as best he could. The horse had kept to the wagon road and stood not four feet from the ruts. They went on, horse and man; mounted, the man could not see the ruts; he let the horse follow the track across the plain, himself following no road.

After a long time in the rocking dark something touched his face once, lightly.

He felt his cheek. The right side of his jaw was swollen and stiff, and his right hand holding the reins was locked by the cold, so that when he tried to change his grip he did not know if his fingers moved or not. He had no gloves, though he wore the winter coat he had never taken off when he came into the house, when the lamp broke, a long time ago. He

got the reins in his left hand and put the right inside his coat to warm
it. The horse jogged on patiently, head low. Again something touched
Stefan's face very lightly, brushing his cheek, his hot sore lip. He could
not see the flakes. They were soft and did not feel cold. He waited for
the gentle, random touch of the snow. He changed hands on the reins
again, and put the left hand under the horse's coarse, damp mane, on
the warm hide. They both took comfort in the touch. Trying to see
ahead, Stefan knew where sky and horizon met, or thought he did, but
the plain was gone. The ceiling of sky was gone. The horse walked on
darkness, under darkness, through darkness.

Once the word "lost" lit itself like a match in the darkness, and Stefan
tried to stop the horse so he could get off and search for the wheel-ruts,
but the horse kept walking on. Stefan let his numb hand holding the
reins rest on the pommel, let himself be borne.

The horse's head came up, its gait changed for a few steps. Stefan
clutched at the wet mane, raised his own head dizzily, blinked at a spiderweb of light tangled in his eyes. Through the splintery blur of ice on
his lashes the light grew square and yellowish: a window. What house
stood out alone here on the endless plain? Dim blocks of pallor rose up
on both sides of him—storefronts, a street. He had come to Verre. The
horse stopped and sighed so that the girths creaked loudly. Stefan did
not remember leaving Sfaroy Kampe. He sat astride a sweating horse
in a dark street somewhere. One window was alight in a second storey.
Snow fell in sparse clumps, as if hurled down in handfuls. There was
little on the ground, it melted as it touched, a spring snow. He rode to
the house with the lighted window and called aloud, "Where's the road
to Lotima?"

The door opened, snow flickered whirling in the shaft of light. "Are
ye the doctor?"

"No. How do I get on to Lotima?"

"Next turn right. If ye meet the doctor tell him hurry on!"

The horse left the village unwillingly, lame on one leg and then the other. Stefan kept his head raised looking for the dawn, which surely must be near. He rode north now, the snow blowing in his face, blinding him even to the darkness. The road climbed, went down, climbed again. The horse stopped, and when Stefan did nothing, turned left, made a couple of stumbling steps, stopped again shuddering and neighed. Stefan dismounted, falling to hands and knees because his legs were too stiff at first to hold him. There was a cattle-guard of poles laid across a side-road. He let the horse stand and felt his way up the side-road to a sudden house lifting a dark wall and snowy roof above him. He found the door, knocked, waited, knocked; a window rattled, a woman said frightened to death over his head, "Who's that?"

"Is this the Sachik farm?"

"No! Who's that?"

"Have I passed the Sachiks'?"

"Are ye the doctor?"

"Yes."

"It's the next but one on the left side. Want a lantern, doctor?"

She came downstairs and gave him a lantern and matches; she held a candle, which dazzled his eyes so that he never saw her face.

He went at the horse's head now, the lantern in his left hand and the reins in his right, held close to the bridle. The horse's docile, patient, stumbling walk, the liquid darkness of its eye in the gleam of the lantern, grieved Stefan sorely. They walked ahead very slowly and he looked for the dawn.

A farmhouse flickered to his left when he was almost past it; snow, windplastered on its north wall, caught the light of the lantern. He led the horse back. The hinges of the gate squealed. Dark outbuildings crowded round. He knocked, waited, knocked. A light moved inside the house, the door opened, again a candle held at eye-level dazzled him.

"Who is that?"

"That's you, Ekata," he said.

"Who is that? Stefan?"

"I must have missed the other farm, the one in between."

"Come in—"

"The horse. Is that the stable?"

"There, to the left—"

He was all right while he found a stall for the horse, robbed the Sachiks' roan of some hay and water, found a sack and rubbed the horse down a bit; he did all that very well, he thought, but when he got back to the house his knees went weak and he could scarcely see the room or Ekata who took his hand to bring him in. She had on a coat over something white, a nightgown. "Oh lad," she said, "you rode from Kampe tonight?"

"Poor old horse," he said, and smiled. His voice said the words some while after he thought he had said them. He sat down on the sofa.

"Wait there," she said. It seemed she left the room for a while, then she was putting a cup of something in his hands. He drank; it was hot; the sting of brandy woke him long enough to watch her stir up the buried coals and put wood on the fire. "I wanted to talk to you, see," he said, and then he fell asleep.

She took off his shoes, put his legs up on the sofa, got a blanket and put it over him, tended the reluctant fire. He never stirred. She turned out the lamp and slipped back upstairs in the dark. Her bed was by the window of her attic room, and she could see or feel that it was now snowing soft and thick in the dark outside.

She roused to a knock and sat up seeing the even light of snow on walls and ceiling. Her uncle peered in. He was wearing yellowish-white woollen underwear and his hair stuck up like fine wire around his bald spot. The whites of his eyes were the same color as his underwear. "Who's that downstairs?"

Ekata explained to Stefan, somewhat later in the morning, that he was on his way to Lotima on business for the Chorin Company, that he had started from Kampe at noon and been held up by a stone in his horse's shoe and then by the snow.

"Why?" he said, evidently confused, his face looking rather childish with fatigue and sleep.

"I had to tell them something."

He scratched his head. "What time did I get here?"

"About two in the morning."

He remembered how he had looked for the dawn, hours away.

"What did you come for?" Ekata said. She was clearing the breakfast table; her face was stern, though she spoke softly.

"I had a fight," Stefan said. "With Kostant."

She stopped, holding two plates, and looked at him.

"You don't think I hurt him?" He laughed. He was lightheaded, tired out, serene. "He knocked me cold. You don't think I could have beat him?"

"I don't know," Ekata said with distress.

"I always lose fights," Stefan said. "And run away."

The deaf man came through, dressed to go outside in heavy boots, an old coat made of blanketing; it was still snowing. "Ye'll not get on to Lotima today, Mr. Stefan," he said in his loud even voice, with satisfaction. "Tomas says the nag's lame on four legs." This had been discussed at breakfast, but the deaf man had not heard. He had not asked how Kostant was getting on, and when he did so later in the day it was with the same satisfied malice: "And your brother, he's down in the pits again, no doubt?" He did not try to hear the answer.

Stefan spent most of the day by the fire sleeping. Only Ekata's cousin was curious about him. She said to Ekata as they were cooking supper, "They say his brother is a handsome man."

"Kostant? The handsomest man I ever saw." Ekata smiled, chopping onions.

"I don't know as I'd call this one handsome," the cousin said tentatively.

The onions were making Ekata cry; she laughed, blew her nose, shook her head. "Oh no," she said.

After supper Stefan met Ekata as she came into the kitchen from dumping out peelings and swill for the pigs. She wore her father's coat, clogs on her shoes, her black kerchief. The freezing wind swept in with her till she wrestled the door shut. "It's clearing," she said, "the wind's from the south."

"Ekata, do you know what I came here for—"

"Do you know yourself?" she said, looking up at him as she set the bucket down.

"Yes, I do."

"Then I do, I suppose."

"There isn't anywhere," he said in rage as the uncle's clumping boots approached the kitchen.

"There's my room," she said impatiently. But the walls were thin, and the cousin slept in the next attic and her parents across the stairwell; she frowned angrily and said, "No. Wait till the morning."

In the morning, early, the cousin went off alone down the road. She was back in half an hour, her straw-stuffed boots smacking in the thawing snow and mud. The neighbor's wife at the next house but one had said, "He said he was the doctor, I asked who it was was sick with you. I gave him the lantern, it was so dark I didn't see his face, I thought it was the doctor, he said so." The cousin was munching the words sweetly, deciding whether to accost Stefan with them, or Ekata, or both before witnesses, when around a bend and down the snow-clotted, sun-bright grade of the road two horses came at a long trot: the livery-stable horse and the farm's old roan. Stefan and Ekata rode; they were both laughing. "Where ye going?" the cousin shouted, trembling. "Running away," the young man called back, and they went past her, splashing the puddles into diamond-slivers in the sunlight of March, and were gone.

A WEEK
IN THE
COUNTRY

ON A SUNNY MORNING OF 1962 IN CLEVELAND, OHIO, IT WAS
raining in Krasnoy and the streets between grey walls were full of men.
"It's raining down my neck in here," Kasimir complained, but his friend
in the adjoining stall of the streetcorner W.C. did not hear him because
he was also talking: "Historical necessity is a solecism, what is history
except what had to happen? But you can't extend that. What happens
next? God knows!" Kasimir followed him out, still buttoning his trousers,
and looked at the small boy looking at the nine-foot-long black coffin leaning against the W.C. "What's in it?" the boy asked. "My great-aunt's body,"
Kasimir explained. He picked up the coffin, hurried on with Stefan
Fabbre through the rain. "A farce, determinism's a farce. Anything to
avoid awe. Show me a seed," Stefan Fabbre said stopping and pointing
at Kasimir, "yes, I can tell you what it is, it's an apple seed. But can I tell
you that an apple tree will grow from it? No! Because there's no freedom,
we think there's a law. But there is no law. There's growth and death,
delight and terror, an abyss, the rest we invent. We're going to miss the
train." They jostled on up Tiypontiy Street, the rain fell harder. Stefan
Fabbre strode swinging his briefcase, his mouth firmly closed, his white
face shining wet. "Why didn't you take up the piccolo? Give me that

awhile," he said as Kasimir tangled with an office-worker running for a bus. "Science bearing the burden of Art," Kasimir said, "heavy, isn't it?" as his friend hoisted the case and lugged it on, frowning and by the time they reached West Station gasping. On the platform in rain and steam they ran as others ran, heard whistles shriek and urgent Sanskrit blare from loudspeakers, and lurched exhausted into the first car. The compartments were all empty. It was the other train that was pulling out, jammed, a suburban train. Theirs sat still for ten minutes. "Nobody on this train but us?" Stefan Fabbre asked, morose, standing at the window. Then with one high peep the walls slid away. Raindrops shook and merged on the pane, tracks interwove on a viaduct, the two young men stared into bedroom windows and at brick walls painted with enormous letters. Abruptly nothing was left in the rain-dark evening sliding backwards to the east but a line of hills, black against a colorless clearing sky.

"The country," Stefan Fabbre said.

He got out a biochemical journal from amongst socks and undershirts in his briefcase, put on dark-rimmed glasses, read. Kasimir pushed back wet hair that had fallen all over his forehead, read the sign on the windowsill that said DO NOT LEAN OUT, stared at the shaking walls and the rain shuddering on the window, dozed. He dreamed that walls were falling down around him. He woke scared as they pulled out of Okats. His friend sat looking out the window, white-faced and black-haired, confirming the isolation and disaster of Kasimir's dream. "Can't see anything," he said. "Night. Country's the only place where they have night left." He stared through the reflection of his own face into the night that filled his eyes with blessed darkness.

"So here we are on a train going to Aisnar," Kasimir said, "but we don't know that it's going to Aisnar. It might go to Peking."

"It might derail and we'll all be killed. And if we do come to Aisnar? What's Aisnar? Mere hearsay."—"That's morbid," Kasimir said, glimpsing again the walls collapsing.—"No, exhilarating," his friend answered.

"Takes a lot of work to hold the world together, when you look at it that way. But it's worthwhile. Building up cities, holding up the roofs by an act of fidelity. Not faith. Fidelity." He gazed out the window through his reflected eyes. Kasimir shared a bar of mud-like chocolate with him. They came to Aisnar.

Rain fell in the gold-paved, ill-lit streets while the autobus to Vermare and Prevne waited for its passengers in South Square under dripping sycamores. The case rode in the back seat. A chicken with a string round its neck scratched the aisle for grain, a bushy-haired woman held the other end of the string, a drunk farm-worker talked loudly to the driver as the bus groaned out of Aisnar southward into the country night, the same night, the blessed darkness.

"So I says to him, I says, you don't know what'll happen tomorrow—"

"Listen," said Kasimir, "if the universe is infinite, does that mean that everything that could possibly happen, is happening, somewhere, at some time?"

"Saturday, he says, Saturday."

"I don't know. It would. But we don't know what's possible. Thank God. If we did, I'd shoot myself, eh?"

"Come back Saturday, he says, and I says, Saturday be damned, I says."

In Vermare rain fell on the ruins of the Tower Keep, and the drunk got off leaving silence behind him. Stefan Fabbre looked glum, said he had a sore throat, and fell into a quick, weary sleep. His head jiggled to the ruts and bumps of the foothill road as the bus ran westward clearing a tunnel through solid black with its headlights. A tree, a great oak, bent down suddenly to shelter it. The doors opened admitting clean air, flashlights, boots and caps. Brushing back his fair hair Kasimir said softly, "Always happens. Only six miles from the border here." They felt in their breast-pockets, handed over. "Fabbre Stefan, domicile 136 Tome Street, Krasnoy, student, MR 64100282A. Augeskar Kasimir, domicile 4 Sorden Street, Krasnoy, student, MR 80104944A. Where are you

going?"—"Prevne."—"Both of you? Business?"—"Vacation. A week in
the country."—"What's that?"—"A bass-viol case."—"What's in it?"—"A
bass viol." It was stood up, opened, closed again, lugged out, laid on the
ground, opened again, and the huge viol stood fragile and magnificent
among flashlights over the mud, boots, belt-buckles, caps. "Keep it off
the ground!" Kasimir said in a sharp voice, and Stefan pushed in front
of him. They fingered it, shook it. "Here, Kasi, does this unscrew?—No,
there's no way to take it apart." The fat one slapped the great shining
curve of wood saying something about his wife so that Stefan laughed,
but the viol tilted in another's hands, a tuning-peg squawked, and
on the patter of rain and mutter of the bus-engine idling, a booming
twang uncurled, broken off short like the viol-string. Stefan took hold
of Kasimir's arm. After the bus had started again they sat side by side
in the warm stinking darkness. Kasimir said, "Sorry, Stefan. Thanks."

"Can you fix it?"

"Yes, just the peg snapped. I can fix it."

"Damn sore throat." Stefan rubbed his head and left his hands over
his eyes. "Taking cold. Damn rain."

"We're near Prevne now."

In Prevne very fine rain drifted down one street between two street-
lamps. Behind the roofs something loomed—treetops, hills? No one met
them since Kasimir had forgotten to write which night they were coming.
Returning from the one public telephone, he joined Stefan and the bass-viol
case at a table of the Post-Telephone Bar. "Father has the car out on a call.
We can walk or wait here. Sorry." His long fair face was discouraged;
contrite. "It's a couple of miles." They set off. They walked in silence
up a dirt road in rain and darkness between fields. The air smelt of wet
earth. Kasimir began to whistle but the rain wet his lips, he stopped. It
was so dark that they walked slowly, not able to see where each step took
them, whether the road was rough or plain. It was so still that they heard
the multitudinous whisper of the rain on fields to left and right. They

were climbing. The hill loomed ahead of them, solider darkness. Stefan stopped to turn up his wet coatcollar and because he was dizzy. As he went forward again in the chill whispering country silence he heard a soft clear sound, a girl laughing behind the hill. Lights sprang up at the hillcrest, sparkling, waving. "What's that?" he said stopping unnerved in the broken dark. A child shouted, "There they are!" The lights above them danced and descended, they were encircled by lanterns, flashlights, voices calling, faces and arms lit by flashes and vanishing again into night; clearly once more, right at his side, the sweet laugh rang out. "Father didn't come back and you didn't come, so we all came to meet you."—"Did you bring your friend, where is he?"—"Hello, Kasi!" Kasimir's fair head bent to another in the gleam of a lantern. "Where's your fiddle, didn't you bring it?"—"It's been raining like this all week."—"Left it with Mr. Praspayets at the Post-Telephone."—"Let's go on and get it, it's lovely walking."—"I'm Bendika, are you Stefan?" She laughed as they sought each other's hands to shake in darkness; she turned her lantern round and was dark-haired, as tall as her brother, the only one of them he saw clearly before they all went back down the road talking, laughing, flashing lightbeams over the road and roadside weeds or up into the rain-thick air. He saw them all for a moment in the bar as Kasimir got his bull-fiddle: two boys, a man, tall Bendika, the young blonde one who had kissed Kasimir, another still younger, all of them he saw all at once and then they were off up the road again and he must wonder which of the three girls, or was it four, had laughed before they met. The chill rain picked at his hot face. Beside him, beaming a flashlight so they could see the road, the man said, "I'm Joachim Bret."—"Enzymes," Stefan replied hoarsely.—"Yes, what's your field?"—"Molecular genetics."—"No! too good! you work with Metor, then? Catch me up, will you? Do you see the American journals?" They talked helices for half a mile, Bret voluble, Stefan laconic as he was still dizzy and still listened for the laugh; but all of them laughed, he could not be sure. They all fell silent a moment, only the two boys ran far ahead, calling. "There's the house," tall Bendika said beside him; pointing to a yellow gleam. "Still with us, Stefan?" Kasimir called from somewhere in the dark. He growled yes, resenting the silly good cheer, the running and calling and laughing, the enthusiastic jerky Bret, the yellow windows that to all of them were home but to him not. Inside the house they shed wet coats, spread, multiplied, regathered around a table in a high dark room shot through with noise and lamplight, for coffee and coffeecake borne in by Kasimir's mother. She walked hurried and tranquil under a grey and dark-brown coronet of braids. Bass-viol-shaped, mother of seven, she merged Stefan with all the other young people whom she distinguished one from another only by name. They were named Valeria, Bendika, Antony, Bruna, Kasimir, Joachim, Paul. They joked and chattered, the little dark girl screamed with laughter, Kasimir's fair hair fell over his eyes, the two boys of eleven squabbled, the gaunt smiling man sat with a guitar and presently played, his face beaked like a crow's over the instrument. His right hand plucking the strings was slightly crippled or deformed. They sang, all but Stefan who did not know the songs, had a sore throat, would not sing, sat rancorous amid the singers. Dr. Augeskar came in. He shook Kasimir's hand, welcoming and effacing him, a tall king with a slender and unlikely heir. "Where's your friend? Sorry I couldn't meet you, had an emergency up the road. Appendectomy on the dining table. Like carving the Christmas goose. Get to bed, Antony. Bendika, get me a glass. Joachim? You, Fabbre?" He poured out red wine and sat down with them at the great round table. They sang again. Augeskar suggested the songs, his voice led the others; he filled the room. The fair daughter flirted with him, the little dark one screeched with laughter, Bendika teased Kasimir, Bret sang a love-song in Swedish; it was only eleven o'clock. Dr. Augeskar had grey eyes, clear under blond brows. Stefan met their stare. "You've got a cold?"—"Yes."—"Then go to bed. Diana! where does Fabbre sleep?" Kasimir jumped up contrite, led Stefan upstairs and through corridors and rooms all smelling of hay and rain. "When's breakfast?"—"Oh, anytime," for Kasimir never knew the time of any event. "Good night, Stefan." But it was a bad night, miserable, and all through it Bret's crippled hand snapped off one great coiling string after another with a booming twang while he explained, "This is how you go after them the latest," grinning. In the morning Stefan could not get up. Sunlit walls leaned inward over the bed and the sky came stretching in the windows, a huge blue balloon. He lay there. He hid his pin-stiff aching black hair under his hands and moaned. The tall golden-grey man came in and said to him with perfect certainty, "My boy, you're sick." It was balm. Sick, he was sick, the walls and sky were all right. "A very respectable fever you're running," said the doctor and Stefan smiled, near tears, feeling himself respectable, lapped in the broad indifferent tenderness of the big man who was kingly, certain, uncaring as sunlight in the sky. But in the forests and caves and small crowded rooms of his fever no sunlight came, and after a time no water.

The house stood quiet in the September sunlight and dark.

That night Mrs. Augeskar, yarn, needle, sock poised one moment in her hands, lifted her braid-crowned head, listening as she had listened years ago to her first son, Kasimir, crying out in sleep in his crib upstairs. "Poor child," she whispered. And Bruna raised her fair head listening too, for the first time, hearing the solitary cry from the forests where she had never been. The house stood still around them. On the second day the boys played outdoors till rain fell and night fell. Kasimir stood in the kitchen sawing on his bull-fiddle, his face by the shining neck of the instrument quiet and closed, keeping right on when others came in to perch on stools and lean against the sink and talk, for after all there were seven young people there on vacation, they could not stay silent. But under their voices the deep, weak, singing voice of Kasimir's fiddle went on wordless, like a cry from the depths of the forest; so that Bruna suddenly past patience and dependence, solitary, not the third daughter and fourth child and one of the young people, slipped away and went upstairs to see what it was like, this grave sickness, this mortality.

It was not like anything. The young man slept. His face was white, his hair black on white linen: clear as printed words, but in a foreign language.

She came down and told her mother she had looked in, he was sleeping quietly; true enough, but not the truth. What she had confirmed up there was that she was now ready to learn the way through the forest; she had come of age, and was now capable of dying.

He was her guide, the young man who had come in out of the rain with a case of pneumonia. On the afternoon of the fifth day she went up to his room again. He was lying there getting well, weak and content, thinking about a morning ten years ago when he had walked out with his father and grandfather past the quarries, an April morning on a dry plain awash with sunlight and blue flowers. After they had passed the Chorin Company quarries they suddenly began to talk politics, and he understood that they had come out of town onto the empty plain in order to say things aloud, in order to let him hear what his father said: "There'll always be enough ants to fill up all the ant-hills—worker ants, army ants." And the grandfather, the dry, bitter, fitful man, in his seventies angrier and gentler than his son, vulnerable as his thirteen-year-old grandson: "Get out, Kosta, why don't you get out?" That was only a taunt. None of them would run away, or get away. A man, he walked with men across a barren plain blue with flowers in brief April; they shared with him their anger, their barren helpless obduracy and the brief blue fire of their anger. Talking aloud under the open sky, they gave him the key to the house of manhood, the prison where they lived and he would live. But they had known other houses. He had not. Once his grandfather, Stefan Fabbre, put his hand on young Stefan's shoulder while he spoke. "What would we do with freedom if we had it, Kosta? What has the West done with it? Eaten it. Put it in its belly. A great wondrous belly, that's the West. With a wise head on top of it, a man's head, with

a man's mind and eyes—but the rest all belly. He can't walk any more.
He sits at table eating, eating, thinking up machines to bring him more
food, more food. Throwing food to the black and yellow rats under
the table so they won't gnaw down the walls around him. There he sits,
and here we are, with nothing in our bellies but air, air and cancer, air
and rage. We can still walk. So we're yoked. Yoked to the foreign plow.
When we smell food we bray and kick. —Are we men, though, Kosta? I
doubt it." All the time his hand lay on the boy's shoulder, tender, almost
deferent, because the boy had never seen his inheritance at all but had
been born in jail, where nothing is any good, no anger, understanding,
or pride, nothing is any good except obduracy, except fidelity. Those
remain, said the weight of the old man's hand on his shoulder. So when
a blonde girl came into his room where he lay weak and content, he
looked at her from that sunwashed barren April plain with trust and
welcome, it being irrelevant to this moment that his grandfather had
died in a deportation train and his father had been shot along with
forty-two other men on the plain outside town in the reprisals of 1956.
"How do you feel?" she said, and he said, "Fine."

"Can I bring you anything?"

He shook his head, the same black-and-white head she had seen clear
and unintelligible as Greek words on a white page, but now his eyes were
open and he spoke her language. It was the same voice that had called
faintly from the black woods of fever, the neighborhood of death, a few
nights ago, which now said, "I can't remember your name." He was very
nice, he was a nice fellow, this Stefan Fabbre, embarrassed by lying there
sick, glad to see her. "I'm Bruna, I come next after Kasi. Would you like
some books? Are you getting bored yet?"—"Bored? No. You don't know
how good it is to lie here doing nothing, I've never done that. Your
parents are so kind, and this big house, and the fields outside there—I
lie here thinking, Jesus, is this me? In all this peace, in all this space, in
a room to myself doing nothing?" She laughed, by which he knew her:

the one who had laughed in rain and darkness before lights broke over the hill. Her fair hair was parted in the middle and waved on each side down nearly to the light, thick eyebrows; her eyes were an indeterminate color, unclear, grey-brown or grey. He heard it now indoors in daylight, the tender and exultant laugh. "Oh you beauty, you fine proud filly-foal never broken to harness, you scared and restive, gentle girl laughing. . . ."

Wanting to keep her he asked, "Have you always lived here?" and she said, "Yes, summers," glancing at him from her indeterminate, shining eyes in the shadow of fair hair. "Where did you grow up?"

"In Sfaroy Kampe, up north."

"Your family's still there?"

"My sister lives there." She still asked about families. She must be very innocent, more elusive and intact even than Kasimir, who placed his reality beyond the touch of any hands or asking of identity. Still to keep her with him, he said, "I lie here thinking. I've thought more already today than in the last three years."

"What do you think of?"

"Of the Hungarian nobleman, do you know that story? The one that was taken prisoner by the Turks, and sold as a slave. It was in the sixteenth century. Well, a Turk bought him, and yoked him to a plow, like an ox, and he plowed the fields, driven with a whip. His family finally managed to buy him back. And he went home, and got his sword, and went back to the battlefields. And there he took prisoner the Turk that had bought him, owned him. Took the Turk back to his manor. Took the chains off him, had him brought outside. And the poor Turk looked around for the impaling stake, you know, or the pitch they'd rub on him and set fire to, or the dogs, or at least the whip. But there was nothing. Only the Hungarian, the man he'd bought and sold. And the Hungarian said, 'Go on back home. . . .'"

"Did he go?"

"No, he stayed and turned Christian. But that's not why I think of it."

"Why do you?"

"I'd like to be a nobleman," Stefan Fabbre said, grinning. He was a tough, hard fellow, lying there nearly defeated but not defeated. He grinned, his eyes had a black flicker to them; at twenty-five he had no innocence, no confidence, no hope at all of profit. The lack of that was the black flicker, the coldness in his eyes. Yet he lay there taking what came, a small man but hard, possessing weight, a man of substance. The girl looked at his strong, blunt hands on the blanket and then up at the sunlit windows, thinking of his being a nobleman, thinking of the one fact she knew of him from Kasimir, who seldom mentioned facts: that he shared a tenement room in Krasnoy with five other students, three beds were all they could fit into it. The room, with three high windows, curtains pulled back, hummed with the silence of September afternoon in the country. A boy's voice rang out from fields far away. "Not much chance of it these days," she said in a dull soft voice, looking down, meaning nothing, for once wholly cast down, tired, without tenderness or exultation. He would get well, would go back a week late to the city, to the three bedsteads and five roommates, shoes on the floor and rust and hairs in the washbasin, classrooms, laboratories, after that employment as an inspector of sanitation on State farms in the north and northeast, a two-room flat in State housing on the outskirts of a town near the State foundries, a black-haired wife who taught the third grade from State-approved textbooks, one child, two legal abortions, and the hydrogen bomb. Oh was there no way out, no way? "Are you very clever?"

"I'm very good at my work."

"It's science, isn't it?"

"Biology. Research."

Then the laboratories would persist; the flat became perhaps a four-room flat in the Krasnoy suburbs; two children, no abortions, two-week vacations in summer in the mountains, then the hydrogen bomb. Or no hydrogen bomb. It made no difference.

"What do you do research on?"

"Certain molecules. The molecular structure of life."

That was strange, the structure of life. Of course he was talking down to her; things are not briefly described, her father had said, when one is talking of life. So he was good at finding out the molecular structure of life, this fellow whose wordless cry she had heard faintly from congested lungs, from the dark neighborhood and approaches of his death; he had called out and "Poor child," her mother had whispered, but it was she who had answered, had followed him. And now he brought her back to life.

"Ah," she said, still not lifting her head, "I don't understand all that. I'm stupid."

"Why did they name you Bruna, when you're blonde?"

She looked up startled, laughed. "I was bald till I was ten months old." She looked at him, seeing him again, and the future be damned, since all possible futures ever envisaged are—rusty sinks, two-week vacations and bombs or collective fraternity or harps and houris—endlessly, sordidly dreary, all delight being in the present and its past, all truth too, and all fidelity in the word, the flesh, the present moment: for the future, however you look at it, contains only one sure thing and that is death. But the moment is unpredictable. There is simply no telling what will happen. Kasimir came in with a bunch of red and blue flowers and said, "Mother wants to know if you'd like milk-toast for supper."

"Oatbread, oatbread," Bruna sang arranging the cornflowers and poppies in Stefan's water-glass. They ate oats three times a day here, some poultry, turnips, potatoes; the little brother Antony raised lettuce, the mother cooked, the daughters swept the big house; there was no wheat-flour, no beef, no milk, no housemaid, not any more, not since before Bruna was born. They camped here in their big old country house, they lived like gypsies, said the mother: a professor's daughter born in the middle class, nurtured and married in the middle class, giving up order, plenty, and leisure without complaint but not giving up the least scruple of the discriminations she had been privileged to learn. So Kasimir for all his gentleness could still hold himself untouched. So Bruna still thought of herself as coming next after Kasimir, and asked about one's family. So Stefan knew himself here in a fortress, in a family, at home. He and Kasimir and Bruna were laughing aloud together when the father came in. "Out," Dr. Augeskar said, standing heroic and absolute in the doorway, the sun-king or a solar myth; his son and daughter, laughing and signalling child-like to Stefan behind his back, went out. "Enough is enough," Augeskar said, ausculting, and Stefan lay guilty, smiling, child-like.

The seventh day, when Stefan and Kasimir should have taken bus and train back to Krasnoy where the University was now open, was hot. Warm darkness followed, windows open, the whole house open to choruses of frogs by the river, choruses of crickets in the furrows, a southwest wind bearing odors of the forest over dry autumn hills. Between the curtains billowing and going slack burned six stars, so bright in the dry dark sky that they might set fire to the curtains. Bruna sat on the floor by Stefan's bed, Kasimir lay like a huge wheatstalk across the foot of it, Bendika, whose husband was in Krasnoy, nursed her five-month-old firstborn in a chair by the empty fireplace. Joachim Bret sat on the windowsill, his shirtsleeves rolled up so that the bluish figures OA46992 were visible on his lean arm, playing his guitar to accompany an English lute-song:

> *Yet be just and constant still,*
> *Love may beget a wonder,*
> *Not unlike a summer's frost or*
> *winter's fatal thunder:*
> *He that holds his sweetheart dear*
> *until his day of dying*
> *Lives of all that ever lived*
> *most worthy the envying.*

Then, since he liked to sing praise and blame of love in all the languages he knew and did not know, he began to strum out "Plaisir d'Amour," but came to grief on the shift of key, while the baby was sat up to belch loudly causing merriment. The baby was flung aloft by Kasimir while Bendika protested softly, "He's full, Kasi, he'll spill."—"I am your uncle. I am Uncle Kasimir, my pockets are full of peppermints and papal indulgences. Look at me, whelp! You don't dare vomit on your uncle. You don't dare. Go vomit on your aunt." The baby stared unwinking at Bruna and waved its hands; its fat, silky belly showed between shirt and diaper. The girl returned its gaze as silently, as steadily. "Who are you?" said the baby. "Who are you?" said the maiden, without words, in wonder, while Stefan watched and faint chords in A sobbed joyously on Bret's guitar between the lighted room and the dark dry night of autumn. The tall young mother carried the baby off to bed, Kasimir turned off the light. Now the autumn night was in the room, and their voices spoke among the choruses of crickets and frogs on the fields, by the streams. "It was clever of you to get sick, Stefan," said Kasimir, lying again across the foot of the bed, long arms white in the dusk. "Stay sick, and we can stay here all winter."

"All year. For years. Did you get your fiddle fixed?"

"Oh yes. Been practicing the Schubert. Pa, pa, poum *pah.*"

"When's the concert?"

"Sometime in October. Plenty of time. Poum, poum—swim, swim, little trout. Ah!" The long white arms sawed vaguely a viol of dusk. "Why did you choose the bass viol, Kasimir?" asked Bret's voice among frogs and crickets, across marshbottoms and furrows, from the windowsill. "Because he's shy," said Bruna's voice like a country wind. "Because he's an enemy of the feasible," said Stefan's dark dry voice. Silence. "Because I showed extraordinary promise as a student of the cello," said Kasimir's voice, "and so I was forced to consider, did I want to perform the Dvorak Concerto to cheering audiences and win a People's Artist

award, or did I not? I chose to be a low buzz in the background. Poum,
pa poum. And when I die, I want you to put my corpse in the fiddle
case, and ship it rapid express deep-freeze to Pablo Casals with a label
saying 'Corpse of Great Central European Cellist.'" The hot wind blew
through the dark. Kasimir was done, Bruna and Stefan were ready to
pass on, but Joachim Bret was not able to. He spoke of a man who
had been helping people get across the border; here in the southwest
rumors of him were thick now; a young man, Bret said, who had been
jailed, had escaped, got to England, and come back; set up an escape
route, got over a hundred people out in ten months, and only now had
been spotted and was being hunted by the secret police. "Quixotic?
Traitorous? Heroic?" Bret asked. "He's hiding in the attic now," Kasimir
said, and Stefan added, "Sick of milk-toast." They evaded and would
not judge; betrayal and fidelity were immediate to them, could not be
weighed any more than a pound of flesh, their own flesh. Only Bret,
who had been born outside prison, was EXCITED, insistent. Prevne was
crawling with agents, he went, even if you went to buy a newspaper your
identification was checked. "Easier to have it tattooed on, like you," said
Kasimir. "Move your foot, Stefan."—"Move your fat rump, then."—
"Oh, mine are German numbers, out of date. A few more wars and I'll
run out of skin."—"Shed it, then, like a snake."—"No, they go right
down to the bone."—"Shed your bones, then," Stefan said, "be a jelly-
fish. Be an amoeba. When they pin me down, I bud off. Two little spine-
less Stefans where they thought they had one MR 64100282A. Four of
them, eight, sixteen thirty-two sixty-four a hundred and twenty-eight. I
would entirely cover the surface of the globe were it not for my natural
enemies." The bed shook, Bruna laughed in darkness. "Play the English
song again, Joachim," she said.

Yet be just and constant still,
Love may beget a wonder . . .

"Stefan," she said in the afternoon light of the fourteenth day as she sat, and he lay with his head on her lap, on a green bank above the river-marshes south of the house. He opened his eyes: "Must we go?"

"No."

He closed his eyes again, saying, "Bruna." He sat up and sat beside her, staring at her. "Bruna, oh God! I wish you weren't a virgin." She laughed and watched him, wary, curious, defenseless. "If only—here, now—I've got to go away day after tomorrow!"—"But not right under the kitchen windows," she said tenderly. The house stood thirty yards from them. He collapsed by her burying his head in the angle of her arm, against her side, his lips on the very soft skin of her forearm. She stroked his hair and the nape of his neck.

"Can we get married? Do you want to get married?"

"Yes, I want to marry you, Stefan."

He lay still awhile longer, then sat up again, slowly this time, and looked across the reeds and choked, sunlit river to the hills and the mountains behind them.

"I'll have my degree next year."

"I'll have my teaching certificate in a year and a half."

They were silent awhile.

"I could quit school and work. We'll have to apply for a place . . ." The walls of the one rented room facing a courtyard strung with sooty washing rose up around them, indestructible. "All right," he said. "Only I hate to waste this." He looked from the sunlit water up to the mountains. The warm wind of evening blew past them. "All right. But Bruna, do you understand . . ." that all this is new to me, that I have never waked before at dawn in a high-windowed room and lain hearing the perfect silence, never walked out over fields in a bright October morning, never sat down at table with fair, laughing brothers and sisters, never spoken in early evening by a river with a girl who loved me, that I have known that order, peace, and tenderness must exist but never hoped even to witness them, let alone possess them? And day after tomorrow I must go back. No, she did not understand. She was only the country silence and the blessed dark, the bright stream, the wind, the hills, the cool house; all that was hers and her; she could not understand. But she took him in, the stranger in the rainy night, who would destroy her. She sat beside him and said softly, "I think it's worth it, Stefan, it's worthwhile."

"It is. We'll borrow. We'll beg, we'll steal, we'll filch. I'll be a great scientist, you know. I'll create life in a test-tube. After a squalid early career Fabbre rose to sudden prominence. We'll go to meetings in Vienna. In Paris. The hell with life in a test-tube! I'll do better than that, I'll get you pregnant within five minutes, oh you beauty, laugh, do you? I'll show you, you filly, you little trout, oh you darling—" There under the windows of the house and under the mountains still in sunlight, while the boys shouted playing tennis up beside the house, she lay soft, fair, heavy in his arms under his weight, absolutely pure, flesh and spirit one pure will: to let him come in, let him come in.

Not now, not here. His will was mixed, and obdurate. He rolled away and lay face up in the grass, a black flicker in his eyes looking at the sky. She sat with her hand on his hand. Peace had never left her. When he sat up she looked at him as she had looked at Bendika's baby, steadily, with pondering recognition. She had no praise for him, no reservation, no judgment. Here he is; this is he.

"It'll be meager, Bruna. Meager and unprofitable."

"I expect so," she said, watching him.

He stood up and brushed grass off his trousers. "I love Bruna!" he shouted, lifting his hand; and from the sunlit slopes across the river-marshes where dusk was rising came a vague short sound, not her name, not his voice. "You see?" he said standing over her, smiling. "Echoes, even. Get up, the sun's going, do you want me to get pneumonia again?" She reached out her hand, he took it and pulled her up to him. "I'll be very loyal, Bruna," he said. He was a small man and when they stood together she did not look up to him but straight at him at eye level. "That's what I have to give," he said, "that's all I have to give. You may get sick of it, you know." Her eyes, grey-brown or grey, unclear, watched him steadily. In silence he raised his hand to touch for a moment, with reserve and tenderness, her fair parted hair. They went back up to the house, past the tennis court where Kasimir on one side of the net and the two boys on the other swung, missed, leapt and shouted. Under the oaks Bret sat practicing a guitar-tune. "What language is that one?" Bruna asked, standing light in the shadow, utterly happy. Bret cocked his head to answer, his misshapen right hand lying across the strings. "Greek; I got it from a book; it means, 'O young lovers who pass beneath my window, can't you see it's raining?'" She laughed aloud, standing by Stefan who had turned to watch the three run and poise on the tennis court in rising shadow, the ball soar up from moment to moment into the level gold light.

He walked into Prevne next day to buy their tickets with Kasimir, who wanted to see the weekly market there; Kasimir took joy in markets, fairs, auctions, the noise of people getting and selling, the barrows of white and purple turnips, racks of old shoes, mounds of print cotton, stacks of bluecoated cheese, the smell of onions, fresh lavender, sweat, dust. The road that had been long the night they came was brief in the warm morning. "Still looking for that get-em-out-alive fellow, Bret says," said Kasimir. Tall, frail, calm, he moseyed along beside his friend, his bare head bright in the sunlight. "Bruna and I want to get married," Stefan said.

"You do?"

"Yes."

Kasimir hesitated a moment in his longlegged amble, went on, hands in his pockets. Slowly on his face appeared a smile. "Do you really?"

"Yes."

Kasimir stopped, took his right hand out of his pocket, shook Stefan's.

"Good work," he said, "well done." He was blushing a little. "Now that's something real," he said, going on, hands in his pockets; Stefan glanced at his long, quiet young face. "That's absolute," Kasimir said, "that's real." After a while he said, "That beats Schubert."

"Main problem is finding a place to live, of course, but if I can borrow something to get started on, Metor still wants me for that project— we'd like to do it straight off—if it's all right with your parents, of course." Kasimir listened fascinated to these chances and circumstances confirming the central fact, just as he watched fascinated the buyers and sellers, shoes and turnips, racks and carts of a market-fair that confirmed men's need of food and of communion. "It'll work out," he said. "You'll find a place."—"I expect so," said Stefan never doubting it. He picked up a rock, tossed it up and caught it, hurled it white through sunlight far into the furrows to their left. "If you knew how happy I am, Kasimir—" His friend answered, "I have some notion. Here, shake hands again." They stopped again to shake hands. "Move in with us, eh, Kasi?"—"All right, get me a truckle-bed." They were coming into town. A khaki-colored truck crawled down Prevne's main street between flyblown shops, old houses painted with garlands long faded; over the roofs rose high yellow hills. Under lindens the market square was dusty and sun-dappled: a few racks, a few stands and carts, a noseless man selling sugarcandy, three dogs cringingly, unwearyingly following a white bitch, old women in black shawls, old men in black vests, the lanky keeper of the Post-Telephone Bar leaning in his doorway and spitting, two fat men dickering in a mumble over a pack of cigarettes. "Used to be more to it," Kasimir said. "When I was a kid here. Lots of cheese from Portacheyka, vegetables, mounds of 'em. Everybody turned out for it." They wandered between the stalls, content, aware of brotherhood. Stefan wanted to buy Bruna something, anything, a scarf; there were buttonless mud-colored overalls, cracked shoes. "Buy her a cabbage," Kasimir said, and Stefan bought a large red cabbage. They went

into the Post-Telephone Bar to buy their tickets to Aisnar. "Two on the
S.W. to Aisnar, Mr. Praspayets."—"Back to work, eh?"—"Right." Three
men came up to the counter, two on Kasimir's side one on Stefan's.
They handed over. "Fabbre Stefan, domicile 136 Tome Street, Krasnoy,
student, MR 64100282A. Augeskar Kasimir, domicile 4 Sorden Street,
Krasnoy, student, MR 80104944A. Business in Aisnar?"—"Catching the
train to Krasnoy." The men returned to a table. "In here all day, past
ten days," the innkeeper said in a thready mumble, "kills my business.
I need another hundred kroner, Mr. Kasimir; trying to short-change
me?" Two of the men, one thickset, the other slim and wearing an army
gunbelt under his jacket, were by them again. The smiling innkeeper
went blank like a television set clicked off. He watched the agents go
through the young men's pockets and feel up and down their bodies;
when they had gone back to the table he handed Kasimir his change,
silent. They went out in silence. Kasimir stopped and stood looking at
the golden lindens, the golden light dappling dust where three dogs still
trotted abased and eager after the white bitch, a fat housewife laughed
with an old cackling man, two boys dodged yelling among the carts, a
donkey hung his grey head and twitched one ear. "Oh well," Stefan said.
Kasimir said nothing. "I've budded off," Stefan said, "come on, Kasi."
They set off slowly. "Right," Kasimir said straightening up a little. "It's
not relevant, you know," said Stefan. "Is the innkeeper really named
Praspayets?"—"Evander Praspayets. Has a brother runs the winery here,
Belisarius Praspayets." Stefan grinned, Kasimir smiled a little vaguely.
They were at the edge of the market-place about to cross the street.
"Damn, I forgot my cabbage in the bar," Stefan said, turning, and saw
some men running across the market-place between the carts and stalls.
There was a loud clapping noise. Kasimir grabbed at Stefan's shoulder
for some reason, but missed, and stood there with his arms spread out,
making a coughing, retching sound in his throat. His arms jerked wider
and he fell down, backwards, and lay at Stefan's feet, his eyes open, his

mouth open and full of blood. Stefan stood there. He looked around. He dropped on his knees by Kasimir who did not look at him. Then he was pulled up and held by the arm; there were men around him and one of them was waving something, a paper, saying loudly, "This is him, the traitor, this is what happens to traitors. These are his forged papers. This is him." Stefan wanted to get to Kasimir, but was held back; he saw men's backs, a dog, a woman's red staring face in the background under golden trees. He thought they were helping him to stand, for his knees had given under him, but as they forced him to turn and walk he tried to pull free, crying out, "Kasimir!"

He was lying on his face on a bed, which was not the bed in the high-windowed room in the Augeskar house. He knew it was not but kept thinking it was, hearing the boys calling down on the tennis court. Then understanding that it was his room in Krasnoy and his roommates were asleep he lay still for a long time, despite a fierce headache. Finally he sat up and looked around at the pine-plank walls, the grating in the door, the stone floor with cigarette butts and dried urine on it. The guard who brought his breakfast was the thickset agent from the Post-Telephone Bar, and did not speak. There were pine splinters in the quicks of his nails on both his hands; he spent a long time getting them out.

On the third day a different guard came, a fat dark-jowled fellow reeking of sweat and onions like the market under the lindens. "What town am I in?"—"Prevne." The guard locked the door, offered a ciga-rette through the grating, held a lighted match through. "Is my friend dead? Why did they shoot him?"—"Man they wanted got away," said the guard. "Need anything in there? You'll be out tomorrow."—"Did they kill him?" The guard grunted yes and went off. After a while a half-full pack of cigarettes and a box of matches dropped in through the grating near Stefan's feet where he sat on the cot. He was released next day, seeing no one but the dark-jowled guard who led him to the door of the village lock-up. He stood on the main street of Prevne half a block

down from the market-place. Sunset was over, it was cold, the sky clear
and dark above the lindens, the roofs, the hills.

His ticket to Aisnar was still in his pocket. He walked slowly and
carefully to the market-place and across it under dark trees to the Post-
Telephone Bar. No bus was waiting. He had no idea when they ran. He
went in and sat down, hunched over, shaking with cold, at one of the
three tables. Presently the owner came out from a back room.

"When's the next bus?" He could not think of the man's name, Praspets,
Prayespets, something like that. "Aisnar, eight-twenty in the morning,"
the man said.—"To Portacheyka?" Stefan asked after a pause.—"Local
to Portacheyka at ten."—"Tonight?"—"Ten tonight."—"Can you
change this for a . . . ticket to Portacheyka?" He held out his ticket for
Aisnar. The man took it and after a moment said, "Wait, I'll see." He
went off again to the back. Stefan got change ready for a cup of coffee,
and sat hunched over. It was seven-ten by the white-faced alarm clock
on the bar. At seven-thirty when three big townsmen came in for a beer
he moved as far back as he could, by the pool table, and sat there facing
the wall, only glancing round quickly now and then to check the time
on the alarm clock. He was still shaking, and so cold that after a while
he put his head down on his arms and shut his eyes. Bruna said, "Stefan."

She had sat down at the table with him. Her hair looked pale as
cotton round her face. His head still hunched forward, his arms on the
table, he looked at her and then looked down.

"Mr. Praspayets telephoned us. Where were you going?"

He did not answer.

"Did they tell you to get out of town?"

He shook his head.

"They just let you go? Come on. I brought your coat, here, you must
be cold. Come on home." She rose, and at this he sat up; he took his coat
from her and said, "No. I can't."

"Why not?"

"Dangerous for you. Can't face it, anyway."

"Can't face us? Come on. I want to get out of here. We're driving back to Krasnoy tomorrow, we were waiting for you. Come on, Stefan." He got up and followed her out. It was night now. They set off across the street and up the country road, Bruna holding a flashlight beamed before them. She took his arm; they walked in silence. Around them were dark fields, stars.

"Do you know what they did with . . ."

"They took him off in the truck, we were told."

"I don't—When everybody in the town knew who he was—" He felt her shrug. They kept walking. The road was long again as when he and Kasimir had walked it the first time without light. They came to the hill where the lights had appeared, the laughter and calling all round them in the rain. "Come faster, Stefan," the girl beside him said timidly, "you're cold." He had to stop soon, and breaking away from her went blind to the roadside seeking anything, a fencepost or tree, anything to lean against till he could stop crying; but there was nothing. He stood there in the darkness and she stood near him. At last he turned and they went on together. Rocks and weeds showed white in the ragged circle of light from her flashlight. As they crossed the hillcrest she said with the same timidity and stubbornness, "I told mother we want to marry. When we heard they had you in jail here I told her. Not father, yet. This was—this was what he couldn't stand, he can't take it. But mother's all right, and so I told her. I'd like to be married quite soon, if you would, Stefan." He walked beside her, silent. "Right," he said finally. "No good letting go, is there." The lights of the house below them were yellow through the trees; above them stars and a few thin clouds drifted through the sky. "No good at all."

UNLOCKING
THE
AIR

THIS IS A FAIRY TALE. PEOPLE STAND IN THE LIGHTLY FALLING snow. Something is shining, trembling, making a silvery sound. Eyes are shining. Voices sing. People laugh and weep, clasp one another's hands, embrace. Something shines and trembles. They live happily ever after. The snow falls on the roofs and blows across the parks, the squares, the river.

THIS IS HISTORY. ONCE UPON A TIME A GOOD KING LIVED IN HIS palace in a kingdom far away. But an evil enchantment fell upon that land. The wheat withered in the ear, the leaves dropped from the trees of the forest, and no thing thrived.

THIS IS A STONE. IT'S A PAVING STONE OF A SQUARE THAT SLANTS downhill in front of an old, reddish, almost windowless fortress called the Roukh Palace. The square was paved nearly three hundred years ago, so a lot of feet have walked on this stone, bare feet and shod, children's little pads, horses' iron shoes, soldiers' boots; and wheels have gone over and over it, cart wheels, carriage wheels, car tires, tank treads. Dogs' paws every now and then. There's been dogshit on it, there's been blood, both soon washed away by water sloshed from buckets or run from hoses or dropped from the clouds. You can't get blood from a stone, they say, nor can you give it to a stone; it takes no stain. Some of the pavement, down near that street that leads out of Roukh Square through the old Jewish quarter to the river, got dug up once or twice and piled into a barricade, and some of the stones even found themselves flying through the air, but not for long. They were soon put back in their place, or replaced by others. It made no difference to them. The man hit by the flying stone dropped down like a stone beside the stone that killed him. The man shot through the brain fell down and his blood ran out on this stone, or another one maybe, it makes no difference to them. The soldiers washed his blood away with water sloshed from buckets, the buckets their horses drank from. The rain fell after a while. The snow fell. Bells rang the hours, the Christmases, the New Years. A tank stopped with its treads on this stone. You'd think that that would leave a mark, a huge heavy thing like a tank, but the stone shows nothing. Only all the feet bare and shod over the centuries have worn a quality into it, not a smoothness exactly but a kind of softness like leather or like skin. Unstained, unmarked, indifferent, it does have that quality of having been worn for a long time by life. So it is a stone of power, and who sets foot on it may be transformed.

THIS IS A STORY. SHE LET HERSELF IN WITH HER KEY AND CALLED, "Mama? It's me, Fana," and her mother in the kitchen of the apartment called, "I'm in here," and they met and hugged in the doorway of the kitchen.

"Come on, come on!"

"Come where?"

"It's Thursday, Mama!"

"Oh," said Bruna Fabbre, retreating towards the stove, making vague protective gestures at the saucepans, the dishcloths, the spoons.

"You said."

"But it's nearly four already—"

"We can be back by six-thirty."

"I have all the papers to read for the advancement tests."

"You have to come, Mama. You do. You'll see!"

A heart of stone might resist the shining eyes, the coaxing, the bossiness. "Come on!" she said again, and the mother came.

But grumbling. "This is for you," she said on the stairs.

On the bus she said it again. "This is for you. Not me."

"What makes you think that?"

Bruna did not reply for a while, looking out the bus window at the grey city lurching by, the dead November sky behind the roofs.

"Well, you see," she said, "before Kasi, my brother Kasimir, before he was killed, that was the time that would have been for me. But I was too young. Too stupid. And then they killed Kasi."

"By mistake."

"It wasn't a mistake. They were hunting for a man who'd been getting people out across the border, and they'd missed him. So it was to . . ."

"To have something to report to the Central Office."

Bruna nodded. "He was about the age you are now," she said. The bus stopped, people climbed on, crowding the aisle. "Since then, twenty-seven years, always since then it's been too late. For me. First too stupid, then too late. This time is for you. I missed mine."

"You'll see," Stefana said. "There's enough time to go round."

THIS IS HISTORY. SOLDIERS STAND IN A ROW BEFORE THE REDDISH, almost windowless palace; their muskets are at the ready. Young men walk across the stones towards them, singing,

Beyond this darkness is the light,
O Liberty, of thine eternal day!
The soldiers fire their guns. The young men live happily ever after.

THIS IS BIOLOGY.

"Where the hell is everybody?"

"It's Thursday," Stefan Fabbre said, adding, "Damn!" as the figures on the computer screen jumped and flickered. He was wearing his topcoat over sweater and scarf, since the biology laboratory was heated only by a spaceheater which shorted out the computer circuit if they were on at the same time. "There are programs that could do this in two seconds," he said, jabbing morosely at the keyboard.

Avelin came up and glanced at the screen. "What is it?"

"The RNA comparison count. I could do it faster on my fingers."

Avelin, a bald, spruce, pale, dark-eyed man of forty, roamed the laboratory, looked restlessly through a folder of reports. "Can't run a university with this going on," he said. "I'd have thought you'd be down there."

Fabbre entered a new set of figures and said, "Why?"

"You're an idealist."

"Am I?" Fabbre leaned back, stretched, rolled his head to get the cricks out. "I try hard not to be," he said.

"Realists are born, not made." The younger man sat down on a lab stool and stared at the scarred, stained counter. "It's coming apart," he said.

"You think so? Seriously?"

Avelin nodded. "You heard that report from Prague."

Fabbre nodded.

"Last week . . . This week . . . Next year—Yes. An earthquake. The stones come apart—it falls apart—there was a building, now there's not. History is made. So I don't understand why you're here, not there."

"Seriously, you don't understand that?"

Avelin smiled and said, "Seriously."

"All right." Fabbre stood up and began walking up and down the long room as he spoke. He was a slight, grey-haired man with youthfully intense, controlled movements. "Science or political activity, either/or: choose. Right? Choice is responsibility, right? So I chose my responsibility responsibly. I chose science and abjured all action but the acts of science. The acts of a responsible science. Out there they can change the rules; in here they can't change the rules; when they try to I resist. This is my resistance." He slapped the laboratory bench as he turned round. "I'm lecturing. I walk up and down like this when I lecture. So. Background of the choice. I'm from the northeast. '56, in the northeast, do you remember? My grandfather, my father—reprisals. So, in '60, I come here, to the university. '62, my best friend, my wife's brother. We were walking through a village market, talking, then he stopped, he stopped talking, they had shot him. A kind of mistake. Right? He was a musician. A realist. I felt that I owed it to him, that I owed it to them, you see, to live carefully, with responsibility, to do the best I could do. The best I could do was this," and he gestured around the laboratory. "I'm good at it. So I go on trying to be a realist. As far as possible under the circumstances, which have less and less to do with reality. But they are only circumstances. The circumstances in which I do my work as carefully as I can."

Avelin sat on the lab stool, his head bowed. When Fabbre was done, he nodded. After a while he said, "But I have to ask you if it's realistic to separate the circumstances, as you put it, from the work."

"About as realistic as separating the body from the mind," Fabbre said. He stretched again and reseated himself at the computer. "I want to get this series in," he said, and his hands went to the keyboard and his gaze to the notes he was copying. After five or six minutes he started the printer and spoke without turning. "You're serious, Givan, you think it's coming apart as a whole?"

"Yes. I think the experiment is over."

The printer scraped and screeched, and they raised their voices to be heard over it.

"Here, you mean."

"Here and everywhere. They know it, down at Roukh Square. Go down there. You'll see. There could be such jubilation only at the death of a tyrant or the failure of a great hope."

"Or both."

"Or both," Avelin agreed.

The paper jammed in the printer, and Fabbre opened the machine to free it. His hands were shaking. Avelin, spruce and cool, hands behind his back, strolled over, looked, reached in, disengaged the corner that was jamming the feed.

"Soon," he said, "we'll have an IBM. A Mactoshin. Our hearts' desire."

"Macintosh," Fabbre said.

"Everything can be done in two seconds."

Fabbre restarted the printer and looked around. "Listen, the principles—"

Avelin's eyes shone strangely, as if full of tears; he shook his head. "So much depends on the circumstances," he said.

THIS IS A KEY. IT LOCKS AND UNLOCKS A DOOR, THE DOOR TO Apartment 2–1 of the building at 43 Pradinestrade in the Old North Quarter of the city of Krasnoy. The apartment is enviable, having a kitchen with saucepans, dishcloths, spoons, and all that is necessary, and two bedrooms, one of which is now used as a sitting room with chairs, books, papers, and all that is necessary, as well as a view from the window between other buildings of a short section of the Molsen River. The river at this moment is lead-colored and the trees above it are bare and black. The apartment is unlighted and empty. When they

left, Bruna Fabbre locked the door and dropped the key, which is on a
steel ring along with the key to her desk at the Lyceum and the key to
her sister Bendika's apartment in the Trasfiuve, into her small imitation
leather handbag, which is getting shabby at the corners, and snapped
the handbag shut. Bruna's daughter Stefana has a copy of the key in
her jeans pocket, tied on a bit of braided cord along with the key to the
closet in her room in Dormitory G of the University of Krasnoy, where
she is a graduate student in the department of Orsinian and Slavic
Literature working for a degree in the field of Early Romantic Poetry.
She never locks the closet. The two women walk down Pradinestrade
three blocks and wait a few minutes at the corner for the number 18 bus,
which runs on Bulvard Settentre from North Krasnoy to the center of
the city.

Pressed in the crowded interior of the handbag and the tight warmth
of the jeans pocket, the key and its copy are inert, silent, forgotten. All a
key can do is lock and unlock its door; that's all the function it has, all
the meaning; it has a responsibility but no rights. It can lock or unlock.
It can be found or thrown away.

THIS IS HISTORY. ONCE UPON A TIME IN 1830, IN 1848, IN 1866,
in 1918, in 1947, in 1956, stones flew. Stones flew through the air like
pigeons, and hearts, too, hearts had wings. Those were the years when
the stones flew, the hearts took wing, the young voices sang. The soldiers raised their muskets to the ready, the soldiers aimed their rifles,
the soldiers poised their machine guns. They were young, the soldiers.
They fired. The stones lay down, the pigeons fell. There's a kind of red
stone called pigeon's blood, a ruby. The red stones of Roukh Square
were never rubies; slosh a bucket of water over them or let the rain fall
and they're grey again, lead grey, common stones. Only now and then
in certain years they have flown, and turned to rubies.

THIS IS A BUS. NOTHING TO DO WITH FAIRY TALES AND NOT romantic; certainly realistic; though in a way, in principle, in fact, it is highly idealistic. A city bus crowded with people in a city street in Central Europe on a November afternoon, and it's stalled. What else? Oh, dear. Oh, damn. But no, it hasn't stalled; the engine, for a wonder, hasn't broken down; it's just that it can't go any farther. Why not? Because there's a bus stopped in front of it, and another one stopped in front of that one at the cross street, and it looks like everything's stopped. Nobody on this bus has yet heard the word "gridlock," the name of an exotic disease of the mysterious West. There aren't enough private cars in Krasnoy to bring about a gridlock even if they knew what it was. There are cars, and a lot of wheezing idealistic busses, but all there is enough of to stop the flow of traffic in Krasnoy is people. It is a kind of equation, proved by experiments conducted over many years, perhaps not in a wholly scientific or objective spirit but nonetheless presenting a well-documented result confirmed by repetition: there are not enough people in this city to stop a tank. Even in much larger cities it has been authoritatively demonstrated as recently as last spring that there are not enough people to stop a tank. But there are enough people in this city to stop a bus, and they are doing so. Not by throwing themselves in front of it, waving banners, or singing songs about Liberty's eternal day, but merely by being in the street getting in the way of the bus, on the supposition that the bus driver has not been trained in either homicide or suicide; and on the same supposition— upon which all cities stand or fall—they are also getting in the way of all the other busses and all the cars and in one another's way, too, so that nobody is going much of anywhere, in a physical sense.

"We're going to have to walk from here," Stefana said, and her mother clutched her imitation leather handbag. "Oh, but we can't, Fana. Look at that crowd! What are they—Are they—?"

"It's Thursday, ma'am," said a large, red-faced, smiling man just behind them in the aisle. Everybody was getting off the bus, pushing and talking. "Yesterday I got four blocks closer than this," a woman said crossly, and the red-faced man said, "Ah, but this is Thursday."

"Fifteen thousand last time," said somebody, and somebody else said, "Fifty, fifty thousand today!"

"We can never get anywhere near the Square, I don't think we should try," Bruna told her daughter as they squeezed into the crowd outside the bus door.

"You stay with me, don't let go, and don't worry," said the student of Early Romantic Poetry, a tall, resolute young woman, and she took her mother's hand in a firm grasp. "It doesn't really matter where we get, but it would be fun if you could see the Square. Let's try. Let's go round behind the post office."

Everybody was trying to go the same direction. Stefana and Bruna got across one street by dodging and stopping and pushing gently; then turning against the flow they trotted down a nearly empty alley, cut across the cobbled court back of the Central Post Office, and rejoined an even thicker crowd moving slowly down a wide street and out from between the buildings. "There, there's the palace, see!" said Stefana, who could see it, being taller. "This is as far as we'll get except by osmosis." They practised osmosis, which necessitated letting go of each other's hands, and made Bruna unhappy. "This is far enough, this is fine here," she kept saying. "I can see everything. There's the roof of the palace. Nothing's going to happen, is it? I mean, will anybody speak?" It was not what she meant, but she did not want to shame her daughter with her fear, her daughter who had not been alive when the stones turned to rubies. And she spoke quietly because although there were so many people pressed and pressing into Roukh Square, they were not noisy. They talked to one another in ordinary, quiet voices. Only now and then somebody down nearer the palace shouted out a name, and then many, many other voices would repeat it with a roll and crash like a wave breaking. Then they would be quiet again, murmuring vastly, like the sea between big waves.

The street lights had come on. Roukh Square was sparsely lighted by tall, old, cast-iron standards with double globes that shed a soft light high in the air. Through that serene light, which seemed to darken the sky, came drifting small, dry flecks of snow.

The flecks melted to droplets on Stefana's dark, short hair and on the scarf Bruna had tied over her fair, short hair to keep her ears warm.

When Stefana stopped at last, Bruna stood up as tall as she could, and because they were standing on the highest edge of the Square, in front of the old Dispensary, by craning she could see the great crowd, the faces like snowflakes, countless. She saw the evening darkening, the snow falling, and no way out, and no way home. She was lost in the forest. The palace, whose few lighted windows shone dully above the crowd, was silent. No one came out, no one went in. It was the seat of government; it held the power. It was the powerhouse, the powder magazine, the bomb. Power had been compressed, jammed into those old reddish walls, packed and forced into them over years, over centuries, till if it exploded it would burst with horrible violence, hurling pointed shards of stone. And out here in the twilight in the open there was nothing but soft faces with shining eyes, soft little breasts and stomachs and thighs protected only by bits of cloth.

She looked down at her feet on the pavement. They were cold. She would have worn her boots if she had thought it was going to snow, if Fana hadn't hurried her so. She felt cold, lost, lonely to the point of tears. She set her jaw and set her lips and stood firm on her cold feet on the cold stone.

There was a sound, sparse, sparkling, faint, like the snow crystals. The crowd had gone quite silent, swept by low laughing murmurs, and through the silence ran that small, discontinuous, silvery sound.

"What is that?" asked Bruna, beginning to smile. "Why are they doing that?"

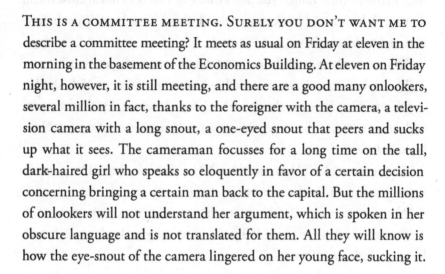

THIS IS A COMMITTEE MEETING. SURELY YOU DON'T WANT ME TO describe a committee meeting? It meets as usual on Friday at eleven in the morning in the basement of the Economics Building. At eleven on Friday night, however, it is still meeting, and there are a good many onlookers, several million in fact, thanks to the foreigner with the camera, a television camera with a long snout, a one-eyed snout that peers and sucks up what it sees. The cameraman focusses for a long time on the tall, dark-haired girl who speaks so eloquently in favor of a certain decision concerning bringing a certain man back to the capital. But the millions of onlookers will not understand her argument, which is spoken in her obscure language and is not translated for them. All they will know is how the eye-snout of the camera lingered on her young face, sucking it.

THIS IS A LOVE STORY. TWO HOURS LATER THE CAMERAMAN WAS long gone but the committee was still meeting.

"No, listen," she said, "seriously, this is the moment when the betrayal is always made. Free elections, yes, but if we don't look past that now, when will we? And who'll do it? Are we a country or a client state changing patrons?"

"You have to go one step at a time, consolidating—"

"When the dam breaks? You have to shoot the rapids! All at once!"

"It's a matter of choosing direction—"

"Exactly, direction. Not being carried senselessly by events."

"But all the events are sweeping in one direction."

"They always do. Back! You'll see!"

"Sweeping to what, to dependence on the West instead of the East, like Fana said?"

"Dependence is inevitable—realignment, but not occupation—"

"The hell it won't be occupation! Occupation by money, materialism, their markets, their values, you don't think we can hold out against them, do you? What's social justice to a color TV set? That battle's lost before it's fought. Where do we stand?"

"Where we always stood. In an absolutely untenable position."

"He's right. Seriously, we are exactly where we always were. Nobody else is. We are. They have caught up with us, for a moment, for this moment, and so we can act. The untenable position is the center of power. Now. We can act *now*."

"To prevent color-TV-zation? How? The dam's broken! The goodies come flooding in. And we drown in them."

"Not if we establish the direction, the true direction, right now—"

"But will Rege listen to us? Why are we turning back when we should be going forward? If we—"

"We have to establish—"

"No! We have to act! Freedom can be established only in the moment of freedom—"

They were all shouting at once in their hoarse, worn-out voices. They had all been talking and listening and drinking bad coffee and living for days, for weeks, on love. Yes, on love; these are lovers' quarrels. It is for love that he pleads, it is for love that she rages. It was always for love. That's why the camera snout came poking and sucking into this dirty basement room where the lovers meet. It craves love, the sight of love; for if you can't have the real thing you can watch it on TV, and soon you don't know the real thing from the images on the little screen where everything, as he said, can be done in two seconds. But the lovers know the difference.

THIS IS A FAIRY TALE, AND YOU KNOW THAT IN THE FAIRY TALE, after it says that they lived happily ever after, there is no after. The evil enchantment was broken; the good servant received half the kingdom as his reward; the king ruled long and well. Remember the moment when the betrayal is made, and ask no questions. Do not ask if the poisoned fields grew white again with grain. Do not ask if the leaves of the forests grew green that spring. Do not ask what the maiden received as her reward. Remember the tale of Koshchey the Deathless, whose life was in a needle, and the needle was in an egg, and the egg was in a swan, and the swan was in an eagle, and the eagle was in a wolf, and the wolf was in the palace whose walls were built of the stones of power. Enchantment within enchantment! We are a long way yet from the egg that holds the needle that must be broken so that Koshchey the Deathless can die. And so the tale ends. Thousands and thousands and thousands of people stood on the slanting pavement before the palace. Snow sparkled in the air, and the people sang. You know the song, that old song with words like "land," "love," "free," in the language you have known the longest. Its words make stone part from stone, its words prevent tanks, its words transform the world, when it is sung at the right time by the right people, after enough people have died for singing it.

A thousand doors opened in the walls of the palace. The soldiers laid down their arms and sang. The evil enchantment was broken. The good king returned to his kingdom, and the people danced for joy on the stones of the city streets.

AND WE DO NOT ASK WHAT HAPPENED AFTER. BUT WE CAN TELL the story over, we can tell the story till we get it right.

"My daughter's on the Committee of the Student Action Council," said Stefan Fabbre to his neighbor Florens Aske as they stood in a line outside the bakery on Pradinestrade. His tone of voice was complicated.

"I know. Erreskar saw her on the television," Aske said.

"She says they've decided that bringing Rege here is the only way to provide an immediate, credible transition. They think the army will accept him."

They shuffled forward a step.

Aske, an old man with a hard brown face and narrow eyes, stuck his lips out, thinking it over.

"You were in the Rege Government," Fabbre said.

Aske nodded. "Minister of Education for a week," he said, and gave a bark like a sea lion, *owp!*—a cough or a laugh.

"Do you think he can pull it off?"

Aske pulled his grubby muffler closer round his neck and said, "Well, Rege is not stupid. But he's old. What about that scientist, that physicist fellow?"

"Rochoy. She says their idea is that Rege's brought in first, for the transition, for the symbolism, the link to '56, right? And if he survives, Rochoy would be the one they'd run in an election."

"The dream of the election . . ."

They shuffled forward again. They were now in front of the bakery window, only eight or ten people away from the door.

"Why do they put up the old men?" asked the old man. "These boys and girls, these young people. What the devil do they want us for again?"

"I don't know," Fabbre said. "I keep thinking they know what they're doing. She had me down there, you know, made me come to one of their meetings. She came to the lab—Come on, leave that, follow me! I did. No questions. She's in charge. All of them, twenty-two, twenty-three, they're in charge. In power. Seeking structure, order, but very definite: violence is defeat, to them, violence is the loss of options. They're absolutely certain and completely ignorant. Like spring—like the lambs in spring. They have never done anything and they know exactly what to do."

"Stefan," said his wife, Bruna, who had been standing at his elbow for several sentences, "you're lecturing. Hello, dear. Hello, Florens, I just saw Margarita at the market, we were queueing for cabbages. I'm on my way downtown, Stefan. I'll be back, I don't know, sometime after seven, maybe."

"Again?" he said, and Aske said, "Downtown?"

"It's Thursday," Bruna said, and bringing up the keys from her handbag, the two apartment keys and the desk key, she shook them in the air before the men's faces, making a silvery jingle; and she smiled.

"I'll come," said Stefan Fabbre.

"Owp! owp!" went Aske. "Oh, hell, I'll come too. Does man live by bread alone?"

"Will Margarita worry where you are?" Bruna asked as they left the bakery line and set off towards the bus stop.

"That's the problem with the women, you see," said the old man, "they worry that she'll worry. Yes. She will. And you worry about your daughter, eh, your Fana."

"Yes," Stefan said, "I do."

"No," Bruna said, "I don't. I fear her, I fear for her, I honor her. She gave me the keys." She clutched her imitation leather handbag tight between her arm and side as they walked.

THIS IS THE TRUTH. THEY STOOD ON THE STONES IN THE lightly falling snow and listened to the silvery, trembling sound of thousands of keys being shaken, unlocking the air, once upon a time.

IMAGINARY COUNTRIES

"WE CAN'T DRIVE TO THE RIVER ON SUNDAY," THE BARON SAID, "because we're leaving on Friday." The two little ones gazed at him across the breakfast table. Zida said, "Marmalade, please," but Paul, a year older, found in a remote, disused part of his memory a darker dining-room from the windows of which one saw rain falling. "Back to the city?" he asked. His father nodded. And at the nod the sunlit hill outside these windows changed entirely, facing north now instead of south. That day red and yellow ran through the woods like fire, grapes swelled fat on the heavy vines, and the clear, fierce, fenced fields of August stretched themselves out, patient and unboundaried, into the haze of September. Next day Paul knew the moment he woke that it was autumn, and Wednesday. "This is Wednesday," he told Zida, "tomorrow's Thursday, and then Friday when we leave."

"I'm not going to," she replied with indifference, and went off to the Little Woods to work on her unicorn trap. It was made of an egg-crate and many little bits of cloth, with various kinds of bait. She had been making it ever since they found the tracks, and Paul doubted if she would catch even a squirrel in it. He, aware of time and season, ran full speed to the High Cliff to finish the tunnel there before they had to go back to the city.

Inside the house the baroness's voice dipped like a swallow down the attic stairs. "O Rosa! Where is the blue trunk then?" And Rosa not answering, she followed her voice, pursuing it and Rosa and the lost trunk down stairs and ever farther hallways to a joyful reunion at the cellar door. Then from his study the baron heard Tomas and the trunk come grunting upward step by step, while Rosa and the baroness began to empty the children's closets, carrying off little loads of shirts and dresses like delicate, methodical thieves. "What are you doing?" Zida asked sternly, having come back for a coat-hanger in which the unicorn might entangle his hoof. "Packing," said the maid. "Not my things," Zida ordered, and departed. Rosa continued rifling her closet. In his study the baron read on undisturbed except by a sense of regret which rose perhaps from the sound of his wife's sweet, distant voice, perhaps from the quality of the sunlight falling across his desk from the uncurtained window.

In another room his older son Stanislas put a microscope, a tennis racket, and a box full of rocks with their labels coming unstuck into his suitcase, then gave it up. A notebook in his pocket, he went down the cool red halls and stairs, out the door into the vast and sudden sunlight of the yard. Josef, reading under the Four Elms, said, "Where are you off to? It's hot." There was no time for stopping and talking. "Back soon," Stanislas replied politely and went on, up the road in dust and sunlight, past the High Cliff where his half-brother Paul was digging. He stopped to survey the engineering. Roads metalled with white clay zigzagged over the cliff-face. The Citroen and the Rolls were parked near a bridge spanning an erosion-gully. A tunnel had been pierced and was in process of enlargement. "Good tunnel," Stanislas said. Radiant and filthy, the engineer replied, "It'll be ready to drive through this evening, you want to come to the ceremony?" Stanislas nodded, and went on. His road led up a long, high hillslope, but he soon turned from it and, leaping the ditch, entered his kingdom and the kingdom of the trees.

Within a few steps all dust and bright light were gone. Leaves overhead and underfoot; an air like green water through which birds swam and the dark trunks rose lifting their burdens, their crowns, towards the other element, the sky. Stanislas went first to the Oak and stretched his arms out, straining to reach a quarter of the way around the trunk. His chest and cheek were pressed against the harsh, scored bark; the smell of it and its shelf-fungi and moss was in his nostrils and the darkness of it in his eyes. It was a bigger thing than he could ever hold. It was very old, and alive, and did not know that he was there. Smiling, he went on quietly, a notebook full of maps in his pocket, among the trees towards yet-uncharted regions of his land.

Josef Brone, who had spent the summer assisting his professor with documentation of the history of the Ten Provinces in the Early Middle Ages, sat uneasily reading in the shade of elms. Country wind blew across the pages, across his lips. He looked up from the Latin chronicle of a battle lost nine hundred years ago to the roofs of the house called Asgard. Square as a box, with a sediment of porches, sheds, and stables, and square to the compass, the house stood in its flat yard; after a while in all directions the fields rose up slowly, turning into hills, and behind them were higher hills, and behind them sky. It was like a white box in a blue and yellow bowl, and Josef, fresh from college and intent upon the Jesuit seminary he would enter in the fall, ready to read documents and make abstracts and copy references, had been embarrassed to find that the baron's family called the place after the home of the northern gods. But this no longer troubled him. So much had happened here that he had not expected, and so little seemed to have been finished. The history was years from completion. In three months he had never found out where Stanislas went, alone, up the road. They were leaving on Friday. Now or never. He got up and followed the boy. The road passed a ten-foot bank, halfway up which clung the little boy Paul, digging in the dirt with his fingers, making a noise in his throat: *rrrm, rrrrm.* A couple

of toy cars lay at the foot of the bank. Josef followed the road on up
the hill and presently began expecting to reach the top, from which he
would see where Stanislas had gone. A farm came into sight and went
out of sight, the road climbed, a lark went up singing as if very near the
sun; but there was no top. The only way to go downhill on this road was
to turn around. He did so. As he neared the woods above Asgard a boy
leapt out onto the road, quick as a hawk's shadow. Josef called his name,
and they met in the white glare of dust. "Where have you been?" asked
Josef, sweating.—"In the Great Woods," Stanislas answered, "that grove
there." Behind him the trees gathered thick and dark. "Is it cool in
there?" Josef asked wistfully. "What do you do in there?"—"Oh, I map
trails. Just for the fun of it. It's bigger than it looks." Stanislas hesitated,
then added, "You haven't been in it? You might like to see the Oak."
Josef followed him over the ditch and through the close green air to
the Oak. It was the biggest tree he had ever seen; he had not seen very
many. "I suppose it's very old," he said, looking up puzzled at the reach
of branches, galaxy after galaxy of green leaves without end. "Oh, a century or two or three or six," said the boy, "see if you can reach around it!"
Josef spread out his arms and strained, trying vainly to keep his cheek
off the rough bark. "It takes four men to reach around it," Stanislas
said. "I call it Yggdrasil. You know. Only of course Yggdrasil was an
ash, not an oak. Want to see Loki's Grove?" The road and the hot white
sunlight were gone entirely. The young man followed his guide farther
into the maze and game of names which was also a real forest: trees, still
air, earth. Under tall grey alders above a dry streambed they discussed
the tale of the death of Baldur, and Stanislas pointed out to Josef the
dark clots, high in the boughs of lesser oaks, of mistletoe. They left the
woods and went down the road towards Asgard. Josef walked along
stiffly in the dark suit he had bought for his last year at the University,
in his pocket a book in a dead language. Sweat ran down his face, he
felt very happy. Though he had no maps and was rather late arriving,

at least he had walked once through the forest. They passed Paul still burrowing, ignoring the clang of the iron triangle down at the house, which signalled meals, fires, lost children, and other noteworthy events. "Come on, lunch!" Stanislas ordered. Paul slid down the bank and they proceeded, seven, fourteen and twenty-one, sedately to the house.

That afternoon Josef helped the professor pack books, two trunks full of books, a small library of medieval history. Josef liked to read books, not pack them. The professor had asked him, not Tomas, "Lend me a hand with the books, will you?" It was not the kind of work he had expected to do here. He sorted and lifted and stowed away load after load of resentment in insatiable iron trunks, while the professor worked with energy and interest, swaddling incunabula like babies, handling each volume with affection and despatch. Kneeling with keys he said, "Thanks, Josef! That's that," and lowering the brass catchbars locked away their summer's work, done with, that's that. Josef had done so much here that he had not expected to do, and now nothing was left to do. Disconsolate, he wandered back to the shade of the elms; but the professor's wife, with whom he had not expected to fall in love, was sitting there. "I stole your chair," she said amiably, "sit on the grass." It was more dirt than grass, but they called it grass, and he obeyed. "Rosa and I are worn out," she said, "and I can't bear to think of tomorrow. It's the worst, the next-to-last day—linens and silver and turning dishes upside down and putting out mousetraps and there's always a doll lost and found after everybody's searched for hours under a pile of laundry—and then sweeping the house and locking it all up. And I hate every bit of it, I hate to close this house." Her voice was light and plaintive as a bird's calling in the woods, careless whether anybody heard its plaintiveness, careless of its plaintiveness. "I hope you've liked it here," she said.

"Very much, baroness."

"I hope so. I know Severin has worked you very hard. And we're so disorganised. We and the children and the visitors, we always seem to scatter

so, and only meet in passing. . . . I hope it hasn't been distracting." It
was true; all summer in tides and cycles the house had been full or half
full of visitors, friends of the children, friends of the baroness, friends,
colleagues and neighbors of the baron, duck-hunters who slept in the
disused stable since the spare bedrooms were full of Polish medieval his-
torians, ladies with broods of children the smallest of whom fell inevitably
into the pond about this time of the afternoon. No wonder it was so still,
so autumnal now: the rooms vacant, the pond smooth, the hills empty
of dispersing laughter.

"I have enjoyed knowing the children," Josef said, "particularly Stanislas."
Then he went red as a beet, for Stanislas alone was not her child. She
smiled and said with timidity, "Stanislas is very nice. And fourteen—
fourteen is such a fearful age, when you find out so fast what you're
capable of being, but also what a toll the world expects. . . . He handles
it very gracefully. Paul and Zida now, when they get that age they'll
lump through it and be tiresome. But Stanislas learned loss so young. . . .
When will you enter the seminary?" she asked, moving from the boy to
him in one reach of thought. "Next month," he answered looking down,
and she asked, "Then you're quite certain it's the life you want to lead?"
After a pause and still not looking at her face, though the white of her
dress and the green and gold of leaves above her filled his eyes, he said,
"Why do you ask, baroness?"

"Because the idea of celibacy terrifies me," she replied, and he wanted
to stretch out on the ground flecked with elm leaves like thin oval coins
of gold, and die.

"Sterility," she said, "you see, sterility is what I fear, I dread. It is my enemy.
I know we have other enemies, but I hate it most, because it makes life
less than death. And its allies are horrible: hunger, sickness, deformation,
and perversion, and ambition, and the wish to be secure. What on earth
are the children doing down there?" Paul had asked Stanislas at lunch
if they could play Ragnarok once more. Stanislas had consented, and

so was now a Frost Giant storming with roars the ramparts of Asgard represented by a drainage ditch behind the pond. Odin hurled lightning from the walls, and Thor—"Stanislas!" called the mother rising slender and in white from her chair beside the young man, "don't let Zida use the hammer, please."

"I'm Thor, I'm Thor, I got to have a hammer!" Zida screamed. Stanislas intervened briefly, then made ready to storm the ramparts again, with Zida now at his side, on all fours. "She's Fenris the Wolf now," he called up to the mother, his voice ringing through the hot afternoon with the faintest edge of laughter. Grim and stern, one eye shut, Paul gripped his staff and faced the advancing armies of Hel and the Frozen Lands.

"I'm going to find some lemonade for everybody," the baroness said, and left Josef to sink at last face down on the earth, surrendering to the awful sweetness and anguish she had awakened in him, and would it ever sleep again? while down by the pond Odin strove with the icy army on the sunlit battlements of heaven.

Next day only the walls of the house were left standing. Inside it was only a litter of boxes and open drawers and hurrying people carrying things. Tomas and Zida escaped, he, being slow-witted amid turmoil and the only year-round occupant of Asgard, to clean up the yard out of harm's way, and she to the Little Woods all afternoon. At five Paul shrilled from his window, "The car! The car! It's coming!" An enormous black taxi built in 1923 groaned into the yard, feeling its way, its blind, protruding headlamps flashing in the western sun. Boxes, valises, the blue trunk and the two iron trunks were loaded into it by Tomas, Stanislas, Josef, and the taxi-driver from the village, under the agile and efficient supervision of Baron Severin Egideskar, holder of the Follen Chair of Medieval Studies at the University of Krasnoy. "And you'll get us back together with all this at the station tomorrow at eight—right?" The taxi-driver, who had done so each September for seven years, nodded. The taxi laden with the material impediments of seven people lumbered away,

changing gears down the road in the weary, sunny stillness of late afternoon, in which the house stood intact once more room after empty room.

The baron now also escaped. Lighting a pipe he strolled slowly but
softly, like one escaping, past the pond and past Tomas's chickencoops,
along a fence overgrown with ripe wild grasses bowing their heavy, sunlit heads, down to the grove of weeping birch called the Little Woods.
"Zida?" he said, pausing in the faint, hot shade shaken by the ceaseless
trilling of crickets in the fields around the grove. No answer. In a cloud
of blue pipe-smoke he paused again beside an egg-crate decorated with
many little bits of figured cloth and colored paper. On the mossy, much-
trodden ground in front of it lay a wooden coat hanger. In one of the
compartments of the crate was an eggshell painted gold, in another a bit
of quartz, in another a breadcrust. Nearby, a small girl lay sound asleep
with her shoes off, her rump higher than her head. The baron sat down
on the moss near her, relit his pipe, and contemplated the egg-crate.
Presently he tickled the soles of the child's feet. She snorted. When she
began to wake, he took her onto his lap.

"What is that?"

"A trap for catching a unicorn." She brushed hair and leafmold off her
face and arranged herself more comfortably on him.

"Caught any?"

"No."

"Seen any?"

"Paul and I found some tracks."

"Split-hoofed ones, eh?"

She nodded. Delicately through twilight in the baron's imagination
walked their neighbor's young white pig, silver between birch trunks.

"Only young girls can catch them, they say," he murmured, and then
they sat still for a long time.

"Time for dinner," he said. "All the tablecloths and knives and forks
are packed. How shall we eat?"

"With our fingers!" She leapt up, sprang away. "Shoes," he ordered, and laboriously she fitted her small, cool, dirty feet into leather sandals, and then, shouting "Come on, papa!" was off. Quick and yet reluctant, seeming not to follow and yet never far behind her, he came on between the long vague shadows of the birch trees, along the fence, past the chicken-coops and the shining pond, into captivity.

They all sat on the ground under the Four Elms. There was cold ham, pickles, cold fried eggplant with salt, hard bread and hard red wine. Elm leaves like thin coins stuck to the bread. The pure, void, windy sky of after-sunset reflected in the pond and in the wine. Stanislas and Paul had a wrestling match and dirt flew over the remains of the ham; the baroness and Rosa, lamenting, dusted the ham. The boys went off to run cars through the tunnel in High Cliff, and discuss what ruin the winter rains might cause. For it would rain. All the nine months they were gone from Asgard rain would beat on the roads and hills, and the tunnel would collapse. Stanislas lifted his head a moment thinking of the Oak in winter when he had never seen it, the roots of the tree that upheld the world drinking dark rain underground. Zida rode clear round the house twice on the shoulders of the unicorn, screaming loudly for pure joy, for eating outside on the ground with fingers, for the first star seen (only from the corner of the eye) over the high fields faint in twilight. Screaming louder with rage she was taken to bed by Rosa, and instantly fell asleep. One by one the stars came out, meeting the eye straight on. One by one the young people went to bed. Tomas with the last half-bottle sang long and hoarsely in the Dorian mode in his room above the stable. Only the baron and his wife remained out in the autumn darkness under leaves and stars.

"I don't want to leave," she murmured.

"Nor I."

"Let's send the books and clothes on back to town, and stay here without them. . . ."

"Forever," he said; but they could not. In the observance of season lies order, which was their realm. They sat on for a while longer, close side by side as lovers of twenty; then rising he said, "Come along, it's late, Freya." They went through darkness to the house, and entered.

In coats and hats, everyone ate bread and drank hot milk and coffee out on the porch in the brilliant early morning. "The car! It's coming!" Paul shouted, dropping his bread in the dirt. Grinding and changing gears, headlamps sightlessly flashing, the taxi came, it was there. Zida stared at it, the enemy within the walls, and began to cry. Faithful to the last to the lost cause of summer, she was carried into the taxi head first, screaming, "I won't go! I don't want to go!" Grinding and changing gears the taxi started. Stanislas's head stuck out of the right front window, the baroness's head out of the left rear, and Zida's red, desolate, and furious face was pressed against the oval back window, so that those three saw Tomas waving good-bye under the white walls of Asgard in the sunlight in the bowl of hills. Paul had no access to a window; but he was already thinking of the train. He saw, at the end of the smoke and the shining tracks, the light of candles in a high dark dining-room, the stare of a rockinghorse in an attic corner, leaves wet with rain overhead on the way to school, and a grey street shortened by a cold, foggy dusk through which shone, remote and festive, the first streetlight of December.

But all this happened a long time ago, nearly forty years ago; I do not know if it happens now, even in imaginary countries.

THE DIARY

OF THE

ROSE

30 AUGUST

DR. NADES RECOMMENDS THAT I KEEP A DIARY OF MY WORK.
She says that if you keep it carefully, when you reread it you can remind
yourself of observations you made, notice errors and learn from them,
and observe progress in or deviations from positive thinking, and so
keep correcting the course of your work by a feedback process.

I promise to write in this notebook every night, and reread it at the
end of each week.

I wish I had done it while I was an assistant, but it is even more important now that I have patients of my own.

As of yesterday I have six patients, a full load for a scopist, but four of
them are the autistic children I have been working with all year for Dr.
Nades's study for the Nat'l Psych. Bureau (my notes on them are in the
cli psy files). The other two are new admissions:

Ana Jest, 46, bakery packager, md., no children, diag. depression,
referral from city police (suicide attempt).

Flores Sorde, 36, engineer, unmd., no diag., referral from TRTU
(Psychopathic behavior—Violent).

Dr. Nades says it is important that I write things down each night just as they occurred to me at work: it is the spontaneity that is most informative in self-examination (just as in autopsychoscopy). She says it is better to write it, not dictate onto tape, and keep it quite private, so that I won't be self-conscious. It is hard. I never wrote anything that was private before. I keep feeling as if I was really writing it for Dr. Nades! Perhaps if the diary is useful I can show her some of it, later, and get her advice.

My guess is that Ana Jest is in menopausal depression and hormone therapy will be sufficient. There! Now let's see how bad a prognostician I am.

Will work with both patients under scope tomorrow. It is exciting to have my own patients, I am impatient to begin. Though, of course, teamwork was very educational.

31 AUGUST

HALF-HOUR SCOPE SESSION WITH ANA J. AT 8:00. ANALYZED SCOPE material, 11:00–17:00. N.B.: Adjust right-brain pickup next session! Weak visual Concrete. Very little aural, weak sensory, erratic body image. Will get lab analyses tomorrow of hormone balance.

It is amazing how banal most people's minds are. Of course the poor woman is in severe depression. Input in the Con dimension was foggy and incoherent, and the Uncon dimension was deeply open, but obscure. But the things that came out of the obscurity were so trivial! A pair of old shoes, and the word "geography"! And the shoes were dim, a mere schema of a pair-of-shoes, maybe a man's maybe a woman's, maybe dark blue maybe brown. Although definitely a visual type, she does not see anything clearly. Not many people do. It is depressing. When I was a student in first year I used to think how wonderful other people's minds would be, how wonderful it was going to be to share in all the different worlds, the different colors of their passions and ideas. How naive I was!

I realised this first in Dr. Ramia's class when we studied a tape from a very famous successful person, and I noticed that the subject had never looked at a tree, never touched one, did not know any difference between an oak and a poplar, or even between a daisy and a rose. They were all just "trees" or "flowers" to him, apprehended schematically. It was the same with people's faces, though he had tricks for telling them apart: mostly he saw the name, like a label, not the face. That was an Abstract mind, of course, but it can be even worse with the Concretes, whose perceptions come in a kind of undifferentiated sludge—bean soup with a pair of shoes in it.

But aren't I "going native"? I've been studying a depressive's thoughts all day and have got depressed. Look, I wrote up there, "It is depressing." I see the value of this diary already. I know I am over-impressionable.

Of course, that is why I am a good psychoscopist. But it is dangerous.

No session with F. Sorde today, since sedation had not worn off. TRTU referrals are often so drugged that they cannot be scoped for days.

REM scoping session with Ana J. at 4:00 tomorrow. Better go to bed!

1 SEPTEMBER

DR. NADES SAYS THE KIND OF THING I WROTE YESTERDAY IS pretty much what she had in mind, and invited me to show her this diary again whenever I am in doubt. Spontaneous thoughts—not the technical data, which are recorded in the files anyhow. Cross nothing out. Candor all-important.

Ana's dream was interesting but pathetic. The wolf who turned into a pancake! Such a disgusting, dim, hairy pancake, too. Her visuality is clearer in dream, but the feeling tone remains low (but remember: *you* contribute the affect—don't read it in). Started her on hormone therapy today.

F. Sorde awake, but too confused to take to scope room for session. Frightened. Refused to eat. Complained of pain in side. I thought he was unclear what kind of hospital this is, and told him there was nothing wrong with him physically. He said, "How the hell do you know?" which was fair enough, since he was in a straitjacket, due to the V notation on his chart. I examined and found bruising and contusion, and ordered X-ray, which showed two ribs cracked. Explained to patient that he had been in a condition where forcible restraint had been necessary to prevent self-injury. He said, "Every time one of them asked a question the other one kicked me." He repeated this several times, with anger and confusion. Paranoid delusional system? If it does not weaken as the drugs wear off, I will proceed on that assumption. He responds fairly well to me, asked my name when I went to see him with the X-ray plate, and agreed to eat. I was forced to apologise to him, not a good beginning with a paranoid. The rib damage should have been marked on his chart by the referring agency or by the medic who admitted him. This kind of carelessness is distressing.

But there's good news too. Rina (Autism Study subject 4) saw a first-person sentence today. Saw it: in heavy, black, primer print, all at once in the high Con foreground: *I want to sleep in the big room.* (She sleeps alone because of the feces problem.) The sentence stayed clear for over 5 seconds. She was reading it in her mind just as I was reading it on the holoscreen. There was weak subverbalisation, but not subvocalisation, nothing on the audio. She has not yet spoken, even to herself, in the first person. I told Tio about it at once and he asked her after the session, "Rina, where do you want to sleep?"—"Rina sleep in the big room." No pronoun, no cona-tive. But one of these days she will say *I want*—aloud. And on that build a personality, maybe, at last: on that foundation. I want, therefore I am.

There is so much fear. Why is there so much fear?

4 SEPTEMBER

WENT TO TOWN FOR MY TWO-DAY HOLIDAY. STAYED WITH B. IN her new flat on the north bank. Three rooms to herself!!! But I don't really like those old buildings, there are rats and roaches, and it feels so old and strange, as if somehow the famine years were still there, waiting. Was glad to get back to my little room here, all to myself but with others close by on the same floor, friends and colleagues. Anyway I missed writing in this book. I form habits very fast. Compulsive tendency.

Ana much improved: dressed, hair combed, was knitting. But session was dull. Asked her to think about pancakes, and there it came filling up the whole Uncon dimension, the hairy, dreary, flat wolf-pancake, while in the Con she was obediently trying to visualize a nice cheese blintz. Not too badly: colors and outlines already stronger. I am still willing to count on simple hormone treatment. Of course they will suggest ECT, and a co-analysis of the scope material would be perfectly possible, we'd start with the wolf-pancake, etc. But is there any real point to it? She has been a bakery packager for 24 years and her physical health is poor. She cannot change her life situation. At least with good hormone balance she may be able to endure it.

F. Sorde: rested but still suspicious. Extreme fear reaction when I said it was time for his first session. To allay this I sat down and talked about the nature and operation of the psychoscope. He listened intently and finally said, "Are you going to use only the psychoscope?"

I said Yes.

He said, "Not electroshock?"

I said No.

He said, "Will you promise me that?"

I explained that I am a psychoscopist and never operate the electro-convulsive therapy equipment, that is an entirely different department. I said my work with him at present would be diagnostic, not therapeutic.

He listened carefully. He is an educated person and understands distinctions such as "diagnostic" and "therapeutic." It is interesting that he asked me to *promise*. That does not fit a paranoid pattern, you don't ask for promises from those you can't trust. He came with me docilely, but when we entered the scope room he stopped and turned white at sight of the apparatus. I made Dr. Aven's little joke about the dentist's chair, which she always used with nervous patients. F.S. said, "So long as it's not an electric chair!"

I believe that with intelligent subjects it is much better not to make mysteries and so impose a false authority and a feeling of helplessness on the subject (see T. R. Olma, *Psychoscopy Technique*). So I showed him the chair and electrode crown and explained its operation. He has a layman's hearsay knowledge of the psychoscope, and his questions also reflected his engineering education. He sat down in the chair when I asked him. While I fitted the crown and clasps he was sweating profusely from fear, and this evidently embarrassed him, the smell. If he knew how Rina smells after she's been doing shit paintings. He shut his eyes and gripped the chair arms so that his hands went white to the wrist. The screens were almost white too. After a while I said in a joking tone, "It doesn't really hurt, does it?"

"I don't know."

"Well, does it?"

"You mean it's on?"

"It's been on for ninety seconds."

He opened his eyes then and looked around, as well as he could for the head clamps. He asked, "Where's the screen?"

I explained that a subject never watches the screen live, because the objectification can be severely disturbing, and he said, "Like feedback from a microphone?" That is exactly the simile Dr. Aven used to use. F.S. is certainly an intelligent person. N.B.: Intelligent paranoids are dangerous!

He asked, "What do you see?" and I said, "Do be quiet, I don't want to see what you're saying, I want to see what you're thinking," and he said, "But that's none of your business, you know," quite gently, like a joke. Meanwhile the fear-white had gone into dark, intense, volitional convolutions, and then, a few seconds after he stopped speaking, a rose appeared on the whole Con dimension: a full-blown pink rose, beautifully sensed and visualised, clear and steady, whole.

He said presently, "What am I thinking about, Dr. Sobel?" and I said, "Bears in the Zoo." I wonder now why I said that. Self-defense? Against what? He gave a laugh and the Uncon went crystal-dark, relief, and the rose darkened and wavered. I said, "I was joking. Can you bring the rose back?" That brought back the fear-white. I said, "Listen, it's really very bad for us to talk like this during a first session, you have to learn a great deal before you can co-analyse, and I have a great deal to learn about you, so no more jokes, please? Just relax physically, and think about anything you please."

There was flurry and subverbalisation on the Con dimension, and the Uncon faded into grey, suppression. The rose came back weakly a few times. He was trying to concentrate on it, but couldn't. I saw several quick visuals: myself, my uniform, TRTU uniforms, a grey car, a kitchen, the violent ward (strong aural images—screaming), a desk, the papers on the desk. He stuck to those. They were the plans for a machine. He began going through them. It was a deliberate effort at suppression, and quite effective. Finally I said, "What kind of machine is that?" and he began to answer aloud but stopped and let me get the answer subvocally in the earphone: "Plans for a rotary engine assembly for traction," or something like that, of course the exact words are on the tape. I repeated it aloud and said, "They aren't classified plans, are they?" He said, "No," aloud, and added, "I don't know any secrets." His reaction to a question is intense and complex, each sentence is like a shower of pebbles thrown into a pool, the interlocking rings spread out quick and wide over the Con and into the Uncon, responses rising on all levels. Within a few seconds all that was hidden by a big signboard that appeared in the high Con foreground, deliberately visualised like the rose and the plans, with auditory reinforcement as he read it over and over: KEEP OUT! KEEP OUT! KEEP OUT!

It began to blur and flicker, and somatic signals took over, and soon he said aloud, "I'm tired," and I closed the session (12.5 min.).

After I took off the crown and clamps I brought him a cup of tea from the staff stand in the hall. When I offered it to him he looked startled and then tears came into his eyes. His hands were so cramped from gripping the armrests that he had trouble taking hold of the cup. I told him he must not be so tense and afraid, we are trying to help him not to hurt him.

He looked up at me. Eyes are like the scope screen and yet you can't read them. I wished the crown was still on him, but it seems you never catch the moments you most want on the scope. He said, "Doctor, why am I in this hospital?"

I said, "For diagnosis and therapy."

He said, "Diagnosis and therapy of *what*?"

I said he perhaps could not now recall the episode, but he had behaved strangely. He asked how and when, and I said that it would all come clear to him as therapy took effect. Even if I had known what his psychotic episode was, I would have said the same. It was correct procedure. But I felt in a false position. If the TRTU report was not classified, I would be speaking from knowledge and the facts. Then I could make a better response to what he said next:

"I was waked up at two in the morning, jailed, interrogated, beaten up, and drugged. I suppose I did behave a little oddly during that. Wouldn't you?"

"Sometimes a person under stress misinterprets other people's actions," I said. "Drink up your tea and I'll take you back to the ward. You're running a temperature."

"The ward," he said, with a kind of shrinking movement, and then he said almost desperately, "Can you really not know why I'm here?"

That was strange, as if he has included me in his delusional system, *on "his side."* Check this possibility in Rheingeld. I should think it would involve some transference and there has not been time for that.

Spent pm analysing Jest and Sorde holos. I have never seen any psychoscopic realisation, not even a drug-induced hallucination, so fine and vivid as that rose. The shadows of one petal on another, the velvety damp texture of the petals, the pink color full of sunlight, the yellow central crown—I am sure the scent was there if the apparatus had olfactory pickup—it wasn't like a mentifact but a real thing rooted in the earth, alive and growing, the strong thorny stem beneath it.

Very tired, must go to bed.

Just reread this entry. Am I keeping this diary right? All I have written is what happened and what was said. Is that spontaneous? But it was *important* to me.

5 September

DISCUSSED THE PROBLEM OF CONSCIOUS RESISTANCE WITH DR. Nades at lunch today. Explained that I have worked with unconscious blocks (the children, and depressives such as Ana J.) and have some skill at reading through, but have not before met a conscious block such as F.S.'s KEEP OUT sign, or the device he used today, which was effective for a full 20-minute session: a concentration on his breathing, bodily rhythms, pain in ribs, and visual input from the scope room. She suggested that I use a blindfold for the latter trick, and keep my attention on the Uncon dimension, as he cannot prevent material from appearing there. It is surprising, though, how large the interplay area of his Con and Uncon fields is, and how much one resonates into the other. I believe his concentration on his breathing rhythm allowed him to achieve something like "trance" condition. Though, of course, most so-called "trance" is mere occultist fakirism, a primitive trait without interest for behavioral science.

Ana thought through "a day in my life" for me today. All so grey and dull, poor soul! She never thought even of food with pleasure, though she lives on minimum ration. The single thing that came bright for a moment was a child's face, clear dark eyes, a pink knitted cap, round cheeks. She told me in post-session discussion that she always walks by a school playground on the way to work because "she likes to see the little ones running and yelling." Her husband appears on the screen as a big bulky suit of work clothes and a peevish, threatening mumble. I wonder if she knows that she hasn't seen his face or heard a word he says for years? But no use telling her that. It may be just as well she doesn't.

The knitting she is doing, I noticed today, is a pink cap.

Reading De Cams's *Disaffection: A Study*, on Dr. Nades's recommendation.

6 SEPTEMBER

IN THE MIDDLE OF SESSION (BREATHING AGAIN) I SAID LOUDLY: "Flores!"

Both psy dimensions whited out but the soma realisation hardly changed. After 4 seconds he responded aloud, drowsily. It is not "trance," but autohypnosis.

I said, "Your breathing's monitored by the apparatus. I don't need to know that you're still breathing. It's boring."

He said, "I like to do my own monitoring, Doctor."

I came around and took the blindfold off him and looked at him. He has a pleasant face, the kind of man you often see running machinery, sensitive but patient, like a donkey. That is stupid. I will not cross it out. I am supposed to be spontaneous in this diary. Donkeys do have beautiful faces. They are supposed to be stupid and balky but they look wise and calm, as if they had endured a lot but held no grudges, as if they knew some reason why one should not hold grudges. And the white ring around their eyes makes them look defenseless.

"But the more you breathe," I said, "the less you think. I need your cooperation. I'm trying to find out what it is you're afraid of."

"But I know what I'm afraid of," he said.

"Why won't you tell me?"

"You never asked me."

"That's most unreasonable," I said, which is funny, now I think about it, being indignant with a mental patient because he's unreasonable. "Well, then, now I'm asking you."

He said, "I'm afraid of electroshock. Of having my mind destroyed. Being kept here. Or only being let out when I can't remember anything." He gasped while he was speaking.

I said, "All right, why won't you think about that while I'm watching the screens?"

"Why should I?"

"Why not? You've said it to me, why can't you think about it? I want to see the color of your thoughts!"

"It's none of your business, the color of my thoughts," he said angrily, but I was around to the screen while he spoke, and saw the unguarded activity. Of course it was being taped while we spoke, too, and I have studied it all afternoon. It is fascinating. There are two subverbal levels running aside from the spoken words. All sensory-emotive reactions and distortions are vigorous and complex. He "sees" me, for instance, in at least three different ways, probably more, analysis is impossibly difficult! And the Con-Uncon correspondences are so complicated, and the memory traces and current impressions inter-weave so rapidly, and yet the whole is unified in its complexity. It is like that machine he was studying, very intricate but all one thing in a mathematical harmony. Like the petals of the rose.

When he realised I was observing he shouted out, "Voyeur! Damned voyeur! Let me alone! Get out!" and he broke down and cried. There was a clear fantasy on the screen for several seconds of himself breaking the arm and head clamps and kicking the apparatus to pieces and rushing out of the building, and there, outside, there was a wide hilltop, covered with short dry grass, under the evening sky, and he stood there all alone. While he sat clamped in the chair sobbing.

I broke session and took off the crown, and asked him if he wanted some tea, but he refused to answer. So I freed his arms, and brought him a cup. There was sugar today, a whole box full. I told him that and told him I'd put in two lumps.

After he had drunk some tea he said, with an elaborate ironical tone, because he was ashamed of crying, "You know I like sugar? I suppose your psychoscope told you I liked sugar?"

"Don't be silly," I said, "everybody likes sugar if they can get it."

He said, "No, little doctor, they don't." He asked in the same tone how old I was and if I was married. He was spiteful. He said, "Don't want to marry? Wedded to your work? Helping the mentally unsound back to a constructive life of service to the Nation?"

"I like my work," I said, "because it's difficult, and interesting. Like yours. You like your work, don't you?"

"I did," he said. "Good-bye to all that."

"Why?"

He tapped his head and said, "Zzzzzzt!—All gone. Right?"

"Why are you so convinced you're going to be prescribed electroshock? I haven't even diagnosed you yet."

"Diagnosed me?" he said. "Look, stop the playacting, please. My diagnosis was made. By the learned doctors of the TRTU. Severe case of disaffection. Prognosis: Evil! Therapy: Lock him up with a roomful of screaming thrashing wrecks, and then go through his mind the same way you went through his papers, and then burn it . . . burn it out. Right, Doctor? Why do you have to go through all this posing, diagnosis, cups of tea? Can't you just get on with it? Do you have to paw through everything I am before you burn it?"

"Flores," I said very patiently, "*you're* saying 'Destroy me'—don't you hear yourself? The psychoscope destroys nothing. And I'm not using it to get evidence, either. This isn't a court, you're not on trial. And I'm not a judge. I'm a doctor."

He interrupted—"If you're a doctor, can't you see that I'm not sick?"

"How can I see anything so long as you block me out with your stupid KEEP OUT signs?" I shouted. I did shout. My patience *was* a pose and it just fell to pieces. But I saw that I had reached him, so I went right on. "You look sick, you act sick—two cracked ribs, a temperature, no appetite, crying fits—is that good health? If you're not sick, then prove it to me! Let me see how you are inside, inside all that!"

He looked down into his cup and gave a kind of laugh and shrugged. "I can't win," he said. "Why do I talk to you? You *look* so honest, damn you!"

I walked away. It is shocking how a patient can hurt one. The trouble is, I am used to the children, whose rejection is absolute, like animals that freeze, or cower, or bite, in their terror. But with this man, intelligent and older than I am, first there is communication and trust and then the blow. It hurts more.

It is painful writing all this down. It hurts again. But it is useful. I do understand some things he said much better now. I think I will not show it to Dr. Nades until I have completed diagnosis. If there is any truth to what he said about being arrested on suspicion of disaffection (and he is certainly careless in the way he talks), Dr. Nades might feel that she should take over the case, due to my inexperience. I should regret that. I need the experience.

7 SEPTEMBER

STUPID! THAT'S WHY SHE GAVE YOU DE CAMS'S BOOK. OF COURSE she knows. As Head of the Section she has access to the TRTU dossier on F.S. She gave me this case deliberately.

It is certainly educational.

Today's session: F.S. still angry and sulky. Intentionally fantasized a sex scene. It was memory, but when she was heaving around underneath him he suddenly stuck a caricature of my face on her. It was effective. I doubt a woman could have done it, women's recall of having sex is usually darker and grander and they and the other do not become meat-puppets like that, with switchable heads. After a while he got bored with the performance (for all its vividness there was little somatic participation, not even an erection) and his mind began to wander. For the first time. One of the drawings on the desk came back. He must be a designer, because he changed it, with a pencil. At the same time there was a tune going on the audio, in mental puretone; and in the Uncon lapping over into the interplay area, a large, dark room seen from a child's height, the windowsills very high, evening outside the windows, tree branches darkening, and inside the room a woman's voice, soft, maybe reading aloud, sometimes joining with the tune. Meanwhile the whore on the bed kept coming and going in volitional bursts, falling apart a little more each time, till there was nothing left but one nipple. This much I analysed out this afternoon, the first sequence of over 10 sec. that I have analysed clear and entire.

When I broke session he said, "What did you learn?" in the satirical voice.

I whistled a bit of the tune.

He looked scared.

"It's a lovely tune," I said, "I never heard it before. If it's yours, I won't whistle it anywhere else."

"It's from some quartet," he said, with his "donkey" face back, defenseless and patient. "I like classical music. Didn't you—"

"I saw the girl," I said. "And my face on her. Do you know what I'd like to see?"

He shook his head. Sulky, hangdog.

"Your childhood."

That surprised him. After a while he said, "All right. You can have my childhood. Why not? You're going to get all the rest anyhow. Listen. You tape it all, don't you? Could I see a playback? I want to see what you see."

"Sure," I said. "But it won't mean as much to you as you think it will. It took me eight years to learn to observe. You start with your own tapes. I watched mine for months before I recognised anything much."

I took him to my seat, put on the earphone, and ran him 30 sec. of the last sequence.

He was quite thoughtful and respectful after it. He asked, "What was all that running-up-and-down-scales motion in the, the background I guess you'd call it?"

"Visual scan—your eyes were closed—and subliminal proprioceptive input. The Unconscious dimension and the Body dimension overlap to a great extent all the time. We bring the three dimensions in separately, because they seldom coincide entirely anyway, except in babies. The bright triangular motion at the left of the holo was probably the pain in your ribs."

"I don't see it that way!"

"You don't see it; you weren't consciously feeling it, even, then. But we can't translate a pain in the rib onto a holoscreen, so we give it a visual symbol. The same with all sensations, affects, emotions."

"You watch all that at once?"

"I told you it took eight years. And you do realise that that's only a fragment? Nobody could put a whole psyche onto a four-foot screen. Nobody knows if there are any limits to the psyche. Except the limits of the universe."

He said after a while, "Maybe you aren't a fool, Doctor. Maybe you're just very absorbed in your work. That can be dangerous, you know, to be so absorbed in your work."

"I love my work, and I hope that it is of positive service," I said. I was alert for symptoms of disaffection.

He smiled a little and said, "Prig," in a sad voice.

Ana is coming along. Still some trouble eating. Entered her in George's mutual-therapy group. What she needs, at least one thing she needs, is companionship. After all why should she eat? Who needs her to be alive? What we call psychosis is sometimes simply realism. But human beings can't live on realism alone.

F.S.'s patterns do not fit any of the classical paranoid psychoscopic patterns in Rheingeld.

The De Cams book is hard for me to understand. The terminology of politics is so different from that of psychology. Everything seems backwards. I must be genuinely attentive at P.T. sessions Sunday nights from now on. I have been lazy-minded. Or, no, but as F.S. said, too absorbed in my work—and so inattentive to its context, he meant. Not thinking about what one is working *for*.

10 SEPTEMBER

HAVE BEEN SO TIRED THE LAST TWO NIGHTS I SKIPPED WRITING this journal. All the data are on tape and in my analysis notes, of course.

Have been working really hard on the F.S. analysis. It is very exciting. It is a truly unusual mind. Not brilliant, his intelligence tests are
good average, he is not original or an artist, there are no schizophrenic
insights, I can't say what it is, I feel honored to have shared in the childhood he remembered for me. I can't say what it is. There was pain and fear
of course, his father's death from cancer, months and months of misery
while F.S. was twelve, that was terrible, but it does not come out pain
in the end, he has not forgotten or repressed it but it is all changed, by
his love for his parents and his sister and for music and for the shape
and weight and fit of things and his memory of the lights and weathers
of days long past and his mind always working quietly, reaching out,
reaching out to be whole.

There is no question yet of formal co-analysis, it is far too early, but
he cooperates so intelligently that today I asked him if he was aware
consciously of the Dark Brother figure that accompanied several Con
memories in the Uncon dimension. When I described it as having a matted
shock of hair he looked startled and said, "Dokkay, you mean?"

That word had been on the subverbal audio, though I hadn't connected it with the figure.

He explained that when he was five or six Dokkay had been his name
for a "bear" he often dreamed or daydreamed about. He said, "I rode him.
He was big, I was small. He smashed down walls, and destroyed things,
bad things, you know, bullies, spies, people who scared my mother, prisons,
dark alleys I was afraid to cross, policemen with guns, the pawnbroker.
Just knocked them over. And then he walked over all the rubble on up
to the hilltop. With me riding on his back. It was quiet up there. It was
always evening, just before the stars come out. It's strange to remember
it. Thirty years ago! Later on he turned into a kind of friend, a boy or
man, with hair like a bear. He still smashed things, and I went with him.
It was good fun."

I write this down from memory as it was not taped; session was

interrupted by power outage. It is exasperating that the hospital comes
so low on the list of Government priorities.

Attended the Pos. Thinking session tonight and took notes. Dr. K.
spoke on the dangers and falsehoods of liberalism.

11 SEPTEMBER

F.S. TRIED TO SHOW ME DOKKAY THIS MORNING BUT FAILED. HE
laughed and said aloud, "I can't see him any more. I think at some point
I turned into him."

"Show me when that happened," I said, and he said, "All right," and
began at once to recall an episode from his early adolescence. It had
nothing to do with Dokkay. He saw an arrest. He was told that the man
had been passing out illegal printed matter. Later on he saw one of these
pamphlets, the title was in his visual bank, "Is There Equal Justice?" He
read it, but did not recall the text or managed to censor it from me. The
arrest was terribly vivid. Details like the young man's blue shirt and the
coughing noise he made and the sound of the hitting, the TRTU agents'
uniforms, and the car driving away, a big grey car with blood on the
door. It came back over and over, the car driving away down the street,
driving away down the street. It was a traumatic incident for F.S. and may
explain the exaggerated fear of the violence of national justice justified
by national security which may have led him to behave irrationally when
investigated and so appeared as a tendency to disaffection, falsely I believe.

I will show why I believe this. When the episode was done I said,
"Flores, think about democracy for me, will you?"

He said, "Little doctor, you don't catch old dogs quite that easily."

"I am not catching you. Can you think about democracy or can't you?"

"I think about it a good deal," he said. And he shifted to right-brain
activity, music. It was a chorus of the last part of the Ninth Symphony

by Beethoven, I recognised it from the Arts term in high school. We sang it to some patriotic words. I yelled, "Don't censor!" and he said, "Don't shout, I can hear you." Of course the room was perfectly silent, but the pickup on the audio was tremendous, like thousands of people singing together. He went on aloud, "I'm not censoring. I'm thinking about democracy. That is democracy. Hope, brotherhood, no walls. All the walls unbuilt. You, we, I make the universe! Can't you hear it?" And it was the hilltop again, the short grass and the sense of being up high, and the wind, and the whole sky. The music was the sky.

When it was done and I released him from the crown I said, "Thank you."

I do not see why the doctor cannot thank the patient for a revelation of beauty and meaning. Of course the doctor's authority is important but it need not be domineering. I realise that in politics the authorities must lead and be followed but in psychological medicine it is a little different, a doctor cannot "cure" the patient, the patient "cures" himself with our help, this is not contradictory to Positive Thinking.

14 SEPTEMBER

I AM UPSET AFTER THE LONG CONVERSATION WITH F.S. TODAY and will try to clarify my thinking.

Because the rib injury prevents him from attending work therapy, he is restless. The Violent ward disturbed him deeply so I used my authority to have the V removed from his chart and have him moved into Men's Ward B, three days ago. His bed is next to old Arca's, and when I came to get him for session they were talking, sitting on Arca's bed. F.S. said, "Dr. Sobel, do you know my neighbor, Professor Arca of the Faculty of Arts and Letters of the University?" Of course I know the old man, he has been here for years, far longer than I, but F.S. spoke so courteously and gravely that I said, "Yes, how do you do, Professor Arca?" and shook the old man's hand. He greeted me politely as a stranger—he often does not know people from one day to the next.

As we went to the scope room F.S. said, "Do you know how many electroshock treatments he had?" and when I said no he said, "Sixty. He tells me that every day. With pride." Then he said, "Did you know that he was an internationally famous scholar? He wrote a book, *The Idea of Liberty*, about twentieth-century ideas of freedom in politics and the arts and sciences. I read it when I was in engineering school. It existed then. On bookshelves. It doesn't exist any more. Anywhere. Ask Dr. Arca. He never heard of it."

"There is almost always some memory loss after electroconvulsive therapy," I said, "but the material lost can be relearned, and is often spontaneously regained."

"After sixty sessions?" he said.

F.S. is a tall man, rather stooped, even in the hospital pajamas he is an impressive figure. But I am also tall, and it is not because I am shorter than he that he calls me "little doctor." He did it first when he was angry at me and so now he says it when he is bitter but does not want what he says to hurt me, the me he knows. He said, "Little doctor, quit faking. You know the man's mind was deliberately destroyed."

Now I will try to write down exactly what I said, because it is important.

"I do not approve of the use of electroconvulsive therapy as a general instrument. I would not recommend its use on my patients except perhaps in certain specific cases of senile melancholia. I went into psychoscopy because it is an integrative rather than a destructive instrument."

That is all true, and yet I never said or consciously thought it before.

"What will you recommend for me?" he said.

I explained that once my diagnosis is complete my recommendation will be subject to the approval of the Head and Assistant Head of the Section. I said that so far nothing in his history or personality structure warranted the use of ECT but that after all we had not got very far yet.

"Let's take a long time about it," he said, shuffling along beside me with his shoulders hunched.

"Why? Do you like it?"

"No. Though I like you. But I'd like to delay the inevitable end."

"Why do you insist that it's inevitable, Flores? Can't you see that your thinking on that one point is quite irrational?"

"Rosa," he said, he has never used my first name before. "Rosa, you can't be reasonable about pure evil. There are faces reason cannot see. Of course I'm irrational, faced with the imminent destruction of my memory—my self. But I'm not inaccurate. You know they're not going to let me out of here un . . ." He hesitated a long time and finally said, "unchanged."

"One psychotic episode—"

"I had no psychotic episode. You must know that by now."

"Then why were you sent here?"

"I have some colleagues who prefer to consider themselves rivals, competitors. I gather they informed the TRTU that I was a subversive liberal."

"What was their evidence?"

"Evidence?" We were in the scope room by now. He put his hands over his face for a moment and laughed in a bewildered way. "Evidence? Well, once at a meeting of my section I talked a long time with a visiting foreigner, a fellow in my field, a designer. And I have friends, you know, unproductive people, bohemians. And this summer I showed our section head why a design he'd got approved by the Government wouldn't work. That was stupid. Maybe I'm here for, for imbecility. And I read. I've read Professor Arca's book."

"But none of that matters, you think positively, you love your country, you're not disaffected!"

He said, "I don't know. I love the idea of democracy, the hope, yes, I love that. I couldn't live without that. But the country? You mean the thing on the map, lines, everything inside the lines is good and nothing outside them matters? How can an adult love such a childish idea?"

"But you wouldn't betray the nation to an outside enemy."

He said, "Well, if it was a choice between the nation and humanity, or the nation and a friend, I might. If you call that betrayal. I call it morality."

He *is* a liberal. It is exactly what Dr. Katin was talking about on Sunday.

It is classic psychopathy: the absence of normal affect. He said that quite unemotionally—"I might."

No. That is not true. He said it with difficulty, with pain. It was I who was so shocked that I felt nothing—blank, cold.

How am I to treat this kind of psychosis, a *political* psychosis? I have read over De Cams's book twice and I believe I do understand it now, but still there is this gap between the political and the psychological, so that the book shows me how to think but does not show me how to *act* positively. I see how F.S. should think and feel, and the difference between that and his present state of mind, but I do not know how to educate him so that he can think positively. De Cams says that disaffection is a negative condition which must be filled with positive ideas and emotions, but this does not fit F.S. The gap is not in him. In fact that gap in De Cams between the political and the psychological is exactly where *his* ideas apply. But if they are wrong ideas how can this be?

I want advice badly, but I cannot get it from Dr. Nades. When she gave me the De Cams she said, "You'll find what you need in this." If I tell her that I haven't it is like a confession of helplessness and she will take the case away from me. Indeed I think it is a kind of test case, testing me. But I need this experience, I am learning, and besides, the patient trusts me and talks freely to me. He does so because he knows that I keep what he tells me in perfect confidence. Therefore I cannot show this journal or discuss these problems with anyone until the cure is under way and confidence is no longer essential.

But I cannot see when that could happen. It seems as if confidence will always be essential between us.

I have got to teach him to adjust his behavior to reality, or he will be sent for ECT when the Section reviews cases in November. He has been right about that all along.

9 OCTOBER

I STOPPED WRITING IN THIS NOTEBOOK WHEN THE MATERIAL from F.S. began to seem "dangerous" to him (or to myself). I just reread it all over tonight. I see now that I can never show it to Dr. N. So I am going to go ahead and write what I please in it. Which is what she said to do, but I think she always expected me to show it to her, she thought I would want to, which I did, at first, or that if she asked to see it I'd give it to her. She asked about it yesterday. I said that I had abandoned it, because it just repeated things I had already put into the analysis files. She was plainly disapproving but said nothing. Our dominance-submission relationship has changed these past few weeks. I do not feel so much in need of guidance, and after the Ana Jest discharge, the autism paper, and my successful analysis of the T. R. Vinha tapes she cannot insist upon my dependence. But she may resent my independence. I took the covers off the notebook and am keeping the loose pages in the split in the back cover of my copy of Rheingeld, it would take a very close search to find them there. While I was doing that I felt rather sick at the stomach and got a headache.

Allergy: A person can be exposed to pollen or bitten by fleas a thousand times without reaction. Then he gets a viral infection or a psychic trauma or a bee sting, and next time he meets up with ragweed or a flea he begins to sneeze, cough, itch, weep, etc. It is the same with certain other irritants. One has to be sensitized.

"Why is there so much fear?" I wrote. Well now I know. Why is there no privacy? It is unfair and sordid. I cannot read the "classified" files kept in her office, though I work with the patients and she does not. But I am not to have any "classified" material of my own. Only persons in authority can have secrets. Their secrets are all good, even when they are lies.

Listen. Listen Rosa Sobel. Doctor of Medicine, Deg. Psychotherapy, Deg. Psychoscopy. Have you gone native?

Whose thoughts are you thinking?

You have been working 2 to 5 hours a day for 6 weeks inside one person's mind. A generous, integrated, sane mind. You never worked with anything like that before. You have only worked with the crippled and the terrified. You never met an equal before.

Who is the therapist, you or he?

But if there is nothing wrong with him what am I supposed to cure? How can I help him? How can I save him?

By teaching him to lie?

(UNDATED)

I SPENT THE LAST TWO NIGHTS TILL MIDNIGHT REVIEWING THE diagnostic scopes of Professor Arca, recorded when he was admitted, eleven years ago, before electroconvulsive treatment.

This morning Dr. N inquired why I had been "so far back in the files." (That means that Selena reports to her on what files are used. I know every square centimeter of the scope room but all the same I check it over daily now.) I replied that I was interested in studying the development of ideological disaffection in intellectuals. We agreed that intellectualism tends to foster negative thinking and may lead to psychosis, and those suffering from it should ideally be treated, as Prof. Arca was treated, and released if still competent. It was a very interesting and harmonious discussion.

I lied. I lied. I lied. I lied deliberately, knowingly, well. She lied. She is a liar. She is an intellectual too! She is a lie. And a coward, afraid.

I wanted to watch the Arca tapes to get perspective. To prove to myself that Flores is by no means unique or original. This is true. The differences are fascinating. Dr. Arca's Con dimension was splendid, architectural, but the Uncon material was less well integrated and less interesting. Dr. Arca knew very much more, and the power and beauty of the motions of his thought was far superior to Flores's. Flores is often extremely muddled. That is an element of his vitality. Dr. Arca is an, was an Abstract thinker, as I am, and so I enjoyed his tapes less. I missed the solidity, spatiotemporal realism, and intense sensory clarity of Flores's mind.

In the scope room this morning I told him what I had been doing. His reaction was (as usual) not what I expected. He is fond of the old man and I thought he would be pleased. He said, "You mean they saved the tapes, and destroyed the mind?" I told him that all tapes are kept for use in teaching, and asked him if that didn't cheer him, to know that a record of Arca's thoughts in his prime existed: wasn't it like his book, after all, the lasting part of a mind which sooner or later would have to grow senile and die anyhow? He said, "No! Not so long as the book is banned and the tape is classified! Neither freedom nor privacy even in death? That is the worst of all!"

After session he asked if I would be able or willing to destroy his diagnostic tapes, if he is sent to ECT. I said such things could get misfiled and lost easily enough, but that it seemed a cruel waste. I had learned from him and others might, later, too. He said, "Don't you see that I will not serve the people with security passes? I will not be used, that's the whole point. You have never used me. We have worked together. Served our term together."

Prison has been much in his mind lately. Fantasies, daydreams of jails, labor camps. He dreams of prison as a man in prison dreams of freedom.

Indeed as I see the way narrowing in I would get him sent to prison if I could, but since he is *here* there is no chance. If I reported that he is, in fact, politically dangerous, they will simply put him back in the

Violent ward and give him ECT. There is no judge here to give him a life sentence. Only doctors to give death sentences.

What I can do is stretch out the diagnosis as long as possible, and put in a request for full co-analysis, with a strong prognosis of complete cure. But I have drafted the report three times already and it is very hard to phrase it so that it's clear that I know the disease is ideological (so that they don't just override my diagnosis at once) but still making it sound mild and curable enough that they'd let me handle it with the psychoscope. And then, why, spend up to a year, using expensive equipment, when a cheap and simple instant cure is at hand? No matter what I say, they have that argument. There are two weeks left until Sectional Review. I have got to write the report so that it will be really impossible for them to override it. But what if Flores is right, all this is just playacting, lying about lying, and they have had orders right from the start from TRTU, "wipe this one out"—

(Undated)

Sectional Review today.

If I stay on here I have some power, I can do some good No no no but I don't I don't even in this one thing even in this what can I do now how can I stop

(Undated)

Last night I dreamed I rode on a bear's back up a deep gorge between steep mountainsides, slopes going steep up into a dark sky, it was winter, there was ice on the rocks

(Undated)

Tomorrow morning will tell Nades I am resigning and requesting transfer to Children's Hospital. But she must approve the transfer. If not I am out in the cold. I am in the cold already. Door locked to write this. As soon as it is written will go down to furnace room and burn it all. There is no place any more.

We met in the hall. He was with an orderly.

I took his hand. It was big and bony and very cold. He said, "Is this it, now, Rosa—the electroshock?" in a low voice. I did not want him to lose hope before he walked up the stairs and down the corridor. It is a long way down the corridor. I said, "No. Just some more tests—EEG probably."

"Then I'll see you tomorrow?" he asked, and I said yes.

And he did. I went in this evening. He was awake. I said, "I am Dr. Sobel, Flores. I am Rosa."

He said, "I'm pleased to meet you," mumbling. There is a slight facial paralysis on the left. That will wear off.

I am Rosa. I am the rose. The rose, I am the rose. The rose with no flower, the rose all thorns, the mind he made, the hand he touched, the winter rose.

DIRECTION
OF THE
ROAD

THEY DID NOT USE TO BE SO DEMANDING. THEY NEVER HURRIED us into anything more than a gallop, and that was rare; most of the time it was just a jigjog foot-pace. And when one of them was on his own feet, it was a real pleasure to approach him. There was time to accomplish the entire act with style. There he'd be, working his legs and arms the way they do, usually looking at the road, but often aside at the fields, or straight at me: and I'd approach him steadily but quite slowly, growing larger all the time, synchronizing the rate of approach and the rate of growth perfectly, so that at the very moment that I'd finished enlarging from a tiny speck to my full size—sixty feet in those days—I was abreast of him and hung above him, loomed, towered, overshadowed him. Yet he would show no fear. Not even the children were afraid of me, though often they kept their eyes on me as I passed by and started to diminish.

Sometimes on a hot afternoon one of the adults would stop me right there at our meeting-place, and lie down with his back against mine for an hour or more. I didn't mind in the least. I have an excellent hill, good sun, good wind, good view; why should I mind standing still for an hour or an afternoon? It's only a relative stillness, after all. One need only look at the sun to realize how fast one is going; and then, one grows continually—especially in summer. In any case I was touched by the way they would entrust themselves to me, letting me lean against their little warm backs, and falling sound asleep there between my feet. I liked them. They have seldom lent us Grace as do the birds; but I really preferred them to squirrels.

In those days the horses used to work for them, and that too was enjoyable from my point of view. I particularly liked the canter, and got quite proficient at it. The surging and rhythmical motion accompanied shrinking and growing with a swaying and swooping, almost an illusion of flight. The gallop was less pleasant. It was jerky, pounding: one felt tossed about like a sapling in a gale. And then, the slow approach and growth, the moment of looming-over, and the slow retreat and diminishing, all that was lost during the gallop. One had to hurl oneself into it, cloppety-cloppety-cloppety! and the man usually too busy riding, and the horse too busy running, even to look up. But then, it didn't happen often. A horse is mortal, after all, and like all the loose creatures grows tired easily; so they didn't tire their horses unless there was urgent need. And they seemed not to have so many urgent needs, in those days.

It's been a long time since I had a gallop, and to tell the truth I shouldn't mind having one. There was something invigorating about it, after all.

I remember the first motorcar I saw. Like most of us, I took it for a mortal, some kind of loose creature new to me. I was a bit startled, for after a hundred and thirty-two years I thought I knew all the local fauna. But a new thing is always interesting, in its trivial fashion, so I observed this one with attention. I approached it at a fair speed, about the rate of a canter, but in a new gait, suitable to the ungainly looks of the thing: an uncomfortable, bouncing, rolling, choking, jerking gait. Within two minutes, before I'd grown a foot tall, I knew it was not mortal creature, bound or loose or free. It was a making, like the carts the horses got hitched to. I thought it so very ill-made that I didn't expect it to return, once it gasped over the West Hill, and I heartily hoped it never would, for I disliked that jerking bounce.

But the thing took to a regular schedule, and so, perforce, did I. Daily at four I had to approach it, twitching and stuttering out of the West, and enlarge, loom-over, and diminish. Then at five back I had to come, poppeting along like a young jackrabbit for all my sixty feet, jigging and jouncing out of the East, until at last I got clear out of sight of the wretched little monster and could relax and loosen my limbs to the evening wind. There were always two of them inside the machine: a young male holding the wheel, and behind him an old female wrapped in rugs, glowering. If they ever said anything to each other I never heard it. In those days I overheard a good many conversations on the road, but not from that machine. The top of it was open, but it made so much noise that it overrode all voices, even the voice of the song-sparrow I had with me that year. The noise was almost as vile as the jouncing.

I am of a family of rigid principle and considerable self-respect. The Quercian motto is "Break but bend not," and I have always tried to uphold it. It was not only personal vanity, but family pride, you see, that was offended when I was forced to jounce and bounce in this fashion by a mere making.

The apple trees in the orchard at the foot of the hill did not seem to mind; but then, apples are tame. Their genes have been tampered with for centuries. Besides, they are herd creatures; no orchard tree can really form an opinion of its own.

I kept my own opinion to myself.

But I was very pleased when the motorcar ceased to plague us. All month went by without it, and all month I walked at men and trotted at horses most willingly, and even bobbed for a baby on its mother's arm, trying hard though unsuccessfully to keep in focus.

Next month, however—September it was, for the swallows had left a few days earlier—another of the machines appeared, a new one, suddenly dragging me and the road and our hill, the orchard, the fields, the farm-house roof, all jigging and jouncing and racketing along from East to West; I went faster than a gallop, faster than I had ever gone before. I had scarcely time to loom, before I had to shrink right down again.

And the next day there came a different one.

Yearly then, weekly, daily, they became commoner. They became a major feature of the local Order of Things. The road was dug up and re-metalled, widened, finished off very smooth and nasty, like a slug's trail, with no ruts, pools, rocks, flowers, or shadows on it. There used to be a lot of little loose creatures on the road, grasshoppers, ants, toads, mice, foxes, and so on, most of them too small to move for, since they couldn't really see one. Now the wise creatures took to avoiding the road, and the unwise ones got squashed. I have seen all too many rabbits die in that fashion, right at my feet. I am thankful that I am an oak, and that though I may be wind-broken or uprooted, hewn or sawn, at least I cannot, under any circumstances, be squashed.

With the presence of many motorcars on the road at once, a new level of skill was required of me. As a mere seedling, as soon as I got my head above the weeds, I had learned the basic trick of going two directions at once. I learned it without thinking about it, under the simple pressure of circumstances on the first occasion that I was a walker in the East and a horseman facing him in the West. I had to go two directions at once, and I did so. It's something we trees master without real effort, I suppose. I was nervous, but I succeeded in passing the rider and then shrinking away from him while at the same time I was still jigjogging towards the walker, and indeed passed him (no looming, back in those days!) only when I had got quite out of sight of the rider. I was proud of myself, being very young, that at first time I did it; but it sounds more difficult than it really is. Since those days of course I had done it innumberable times, and thought nothing about it; I could do it in my sleep. But have you ever considered the feat accomplished, the skill involved, when a tree enlarges, simultaneously yet at slightly different rates and in slightly different manners, for each one of forty motorcar drivers facing two opposite directions, while at the same time diminishing for forty more who have got their backs to it, meanwhile remembering to loom over each single one at the right moment: and to do this minute after minute, hour after hour, from daybreak till nightfall or long after?

For my road had become a busy one; it worked all day long under almost continual traffic. It worked, and I worked. I did not jounce and bounce so much any more, but I had to run faster and faster: to grow enormously, to loom in a split second, to shrink to nothing, all in a hurry, without time to enjoy the action, and without rest: over and over and over.

Very few of the drivers bothered to look at me, not even a seeing glance. They seemed, indeed, not to see any more. They merely stared ahead. They seemed to believe that they were "going somewhere." Little mirrors were affixed to the front of their cars, at which they glanced to see where they had been; then they stared ahead again. I had thought that only beetles had this delusion of Progress. Beetles are always rushing about, and never looking up. I had always had a pretty low opinion of beetles. But at least they let me be.

I confess that sometimes, in the blessed nights of darkness with no moon to silver my crown and no stars occluding with my branches, when I could rest, I would think seriously of escaping my obligation to the general Order of Things: of *failing to move*. No, not seriously. Half-seriously. It was mere weariness. If even a silly, three-year-old, female pussy willow at the foot of the hill accepted her responsibility, and jounced and rolled and accelerated and grew and shrank for each motorcar on the road, was I, an oak, to shirk? Noblesse oblige, and I trust I have never dropped an acorn that did not know its duty.

For fifty or sixty years, then, I have upheld the Order of Things, and have done my share in supporting the human creatures' illusion that they are "going somewhere." And I am not unwilling to do so. But a truly terrible thing has occurred, which I wish to protest.

I do not mind going two directions at once; I do not mind growing and shrinking simultaneously; I do not mind moving, even at the disagreeable rate of sixty or seventy miles an hour. I am ready to go on doing all these things until I am felled or bulldozed. They're my job. But I do object, passionately, to being made eternal.

Eternity is none of my business. I am an oak, no more, no less. I have my duty, and I do it; I have my pleasures, and enjoy them, though they are fewer, since the birds are fewer, and the wind's foul. But, long-lived though I may be, impermanence is my right. Mortality is my privilege. And it has been taken from me.

It was taken from me on a rainy evening in March last year.

Fits and bursts of cars, as usual, filled the rapidly moving road in both directions. I was so busy hurtling along, enlarging, looming, diminishing, and the light was failing so fast, that I scarcely noticed what was happening until it happened. One of the drivers of one of the cars evidently felt that his need to "go somewhere" was exceptionally urgent, and so attempted to place his car in front of the car in front of it. This maneuver involves a temporary slanting of the Direction of the Road and a displacement onto the far side, the side which normally runs the other direction (and may I say that I admire the road very highly for its skill in executing such maneuvers, which must be difficult for an unliving creature, a mere making). Another car, however, happened to be quite near the urgent one, and facing it, as it changed sides; and the road could not do anything about it, being already overcrowded. To avoid impact with the facing car, the urgent car totally violated the Direction of the Road, swinging it round to North-South in its own terms, and so forcing me to leap directly at it. I had no choice. I had to move, and move fast—eighty-five miles an hour. I leapt: I loomed enormous, larger than I have ever loomed before. And then I hit the car.

I lost a considerable piece of bark, and, what's more serious, a fair bit of cambium layer; but as I was seventy-two feet tall and about nine feet in girth at the point of impact, no real harm was done. My branches trembled with the shock enough that a last-year's robin's nest was dislodged and fell; and I was so shaken that I groaned. It is the only time in my life that I have ever said anything out loud.

The motorcar screamed horribly. It was smashed by my blow, squashed, in fact. Its hinder parts were not much affected, but the forequarters knotted up and knurled together like an old root, and little bright bits of it flew all about and lay like brittle rain.

The driver had no time to say anything; I killed him instantly.

It is not this that I protest. I had to kill him, I had no choice, and therefore have no regret. What I protest, what I cannot endure, is this: as I leapt at him, he saw me. He looked up at last. He saw me as I have never been seen before, not even by a child, not even in the days when the people looked at things. He saw me whole, and saw nothing else—then, or ever.

He saw me under the aspect of eternity. He confused me with eternity. And because he died in that moment of false vision, because it can never change, I am caught in it, eternally.

This is unendurable. I cannot uphold such an illusion. If the human creatures will not understand Relativity, very well; but they must understand Relatedness.

If it is necessary to the Order of Things, I will kill drivers of cars, though killing is not a duty usually required of oaks. But it is unjust to require me to play the part, not of the killer only, but of death. For I am not death. I am life: I am mortal.

If they wish to see death visibly in the world, that is their business, not mine. I will not act Eternity for them. Let them not turn to the trees for death. If that is what they want to see, let them look into one another's eyes and see it there.

THE
WHITE DONKEY

THERE WERE SNAKES IN THE OLD STONE PLACE, BUT THE GRASS grew so green and rank there that she brought the goats back every day. "The goats are looking fat," Nana said. "Where are you grazing them, Sita?" And when Sita said, "At the old stone place, in the forest," Nana said, "It's a long way to take them," and Uncle Hira said, "Look out for snakes in that place," but they were thinking of the goats, not of her, so she did not ask them, after all, about the white donkey.

She had seen the donkey first when she was putting flowers on the red stone under the pipal tree at the edge of the forest. She liked that stone. It was the Goddess, very old, round, sitting comfortably among the roots of the tree. Everybody who passed by there left the Goddess some flowers or poured a bit of water on her, and every spring her red paint was renewed. Sita was giving the Goddess a rhododendron flower when she looked round, thinking one of the goats was straying off into the forest; but it wasn't a goat. It was a white animal that had caught her eye, whiter than a Brahminee bull. Sita followed it to see what it was. When she saw the neat round rump and the tail like a rope with a tassel, she knew it was a donkey; but such a beautiful donkey! And whose? There were three donkeys in the village, and Chandra Bose owned two, all of them grey, bony, mournful, laborious beasts. This was a tall, sleek, delicate donkey, a wonderful donkey. It could not belong to Chandra Bose, or to anybody in the village, or to anybody in the other village. It wore no halter or harness. It must be wild; it must live in the forest alone.

Sure enough, when she brought the goats along by whistling to clever Kala, and followed where the white donkey had gone into the forest, first there was a path, and then they came to the place where the old stones were, blocks of stone as big as houses all half buried and overgrown with grass and kerala vines; and there the white donkey was standing looking back at her from the darkness under the trees.

She thought then that the donkey was a god, because it had a third eye in the middle of its forehead like Shiva. But when it turned she saw that that was not an eye, but a horn—not curved like a cow's or a goat's horns, a straight spike like a deer's—just the one horn, between the eyes, like Shiva's eye. So it might be a kind of god donkey; and in case it was, she picked a yellow flower off the kerala vine and offered it, stretching out her open palm.

The white donkey stood a while considering her and the goats and the flower; then it came slowly back among the big stones towards her. It had split hooves like the goats, and walked even more neatly than they did. It accepted the flower. Its nose was pinkish-white, and very soft where it snuffled on Sita's palm. She quickly picked another flower, and the donkey accepted it too. But when she wanted to stroke its face around the short, white, twisted horn and the white, nervous ears, it moved away, looking sidelong at her from its long dark eyes.

Sita was a little afraid of it, and thought it might be a little afraid of her, so she sat down on one of the half-buried rocks and pretended to be watching the goats, who were all busy grazing on the best grass they had had for months. Presently the donkey came close again, and standing beside Sita, rested its curly-bearded chin on her lap. The breath from its nostrils moved the thin glass bangles on her wrist. Slowly and very gently she stroked the base of the white, nervous ears, the fine, harsh hair at the base of the horn, the silken muzzle; and the white donkey stood beside her, breathing long, warm breaths.

Every day since then she brought the goats there, walking carefully because of snakes; and the goats were getting fat; and her friend the donkey came out of the forest every day, and accepted her offering, and kept her company.

"One bullock and one hundred rupees cash," said Uncle Hira, "you're crazy if you think we can marry her for less!"

"Moti Lal is a lazy man," Nana said. "Dirty and lazy."

"So he wants a wife to work and clean for him! And he'll take her for only one bullock and one hundred rupees cash!"

"Maybe he'll settle down when he's married," Nana said.

So Sita was betrothed to Moti Lal from the other village, who had watched her driving the goats home at evening. She had seen him watching her across the road, but had never looked at him. She did not want to look at him.

"This is the last day," she said to the white donkey, while the goats cropped the grass among the big, carved, fallen stones, and the forest stood all about them in the singing stillness. "Tomorrow I'll come with Uma's little brother to show him the way here. He'll be the village goatherd now. The day after tomorrow is my wedding day."

The white donkey stood still, its curly, silky beard resting against her hand.

"Nana is giving me her gold bangle," Sita said to the donkey. "I get to wear a red sari, and have henna on my feet and hands."

The donkey stood still, listening.

"There'll be sweet rice to eat at the wedding," Sita said; then she began to cry.

"Good-bye, white donkey," she said. The white donkey looked at her sidelong, and slowly, not looking back, moved away from her and walked into the darkness under the trees.

GWILAN'S HARP

THE HARP HAD COME TO GWILAN FROM HER MOTHER, AND SO
had her mastery of it, people said. "Ah," they said when Gwilan played,
"you can tell, that's Diera's touch," just as their parents had said when
Diera played, "Ah, that's the true Penlin touch!" Gwilan's mother had
had the harp from Penlin, a musician's dying gift to the worthiest of
pupils. From a musician's hands Penlin, too, had received it; never had
it been sold or bartered for, nor any value put upon it that can be said
in numbers. A princely and most incredible instrument it was for a poor
harper to own. The shape of it was perfection, and every part was strong
and fine: the wood as hard and smooth as bronze, the fittings of ivory
and silver. The grand curves of the frame bore silver mountings chased
with long intertwining lines that became waves and the waves became
leaves, and the eyes of gods and stags looked out from among the leaves
that became waves and the waves became lines again. It was the work
of great craftsmen, you could see that at a glance, and the longer you
looked the clearer you saw it. But all this beauty was practical, obedient,
shaped to the service of sound. The sound of Gwilan's harp was water
running and rain and sunlight on the water, waves breaking and the
foam on the brown sands, forests, the leaves and branches of the forest

and the shining eyes of gods and stags among the leaves when the wind blows in the valleys. It was all that and none of that. When Gwilan played, the harp made music; and what is music but a little wrinkling of the air?

Play she did, wherever they wanted her. Her singing voice was true but had no sweetness, so when songs and ballads were wanted she accompanied the singers. Weak voices were borne up by her playing, fine voices gained a glory from it; the loudest, proudest singers might keep still a verse to hear her play alone. She played along with the flute and reed flute and tambour, and the music made for the harp to play alone, and the music that sprang up of itself when her fingers touched the strings. At weddings and festivals it was, "Gwilan will be here to play," and at music-day competitions, "When will Gwilan play?"

She was young; her hands were iron and her touch was silk; she could play all night and the next day too. She travelled from valley to valley, from town to town, stopping here and staying there and moving on again with other musicians on their wanderings. They walked, or a wagon was sent for them, or they got a lift on a farmer's cart. However they went, Gwilan carried her harp in its silk and leather case at her back or in her hands. When she rode she rode with the harp and when she walked she walked with the harp and when she slept, no, she didn't sleep with the harp, but it was there where she could reach out and touch it. She was not jealous of it, and would change instruments with another harper gladly; it was a great pleasure to her when at last they gave her back her own, saying with sober envy, "I never played so fine an instrument." She kept it clean, the mountings polished, and strung it with the harp strings made by old Uliad, which cost as much apiece as a whole set of common harp strings. In the heat of summer she carried it in the shade of her body, in the bitter winter it shared her cloak. In a firelit hall she did not sit with it very near the fire, nor yet too far away, for changes of heat and cold would change the voice of it, and perhaps harm the frame. She did not look after herself with half the care. Indeed she saw no need to. She knew there were other harpers, and would be other harpers; most not as good, some better. But the harp was the best. There had not been and there would not be a better. Delight and service were due and fitting to it. She was not its owner but its player. It was her music, her joy, her life, the noble instrument.

She was young; she travelled from town to town; she played "A Fine Long Life" at weddings, and "The Green Leaves" at festivals. There were funerals, with the burial feast, the singing of elegies, and Gwilan to play the Lament of Orioth, the music that crashes and cries out like the sea and the seabirds, bringing relief and a burst of tears to the grief-dried heart. There were music days, with a rivalry of harpers and a shrilling of fiddlers and a mighty outshouting of tenors. She went from town to town in sun and rain, the harp on her back or in her hands. So she was going one day to the yearly music day at Comin, and the landowner of Torm Vale was giving her a lift, a man who so loved music that he had traded a good cow for a bad horse, since the cow would not take him where he could hear music played. It was he and Gwilan in a rickety cart, and the lean-necked roan stepping out down the steep, sunlit road from Torm.

A bear in the forest by the road, or a bear's ghost, or the shadow of a hawk: the horse shied half across the road. Torm had been discussing music deeply with Gwilan, waving his hands to conduct a choir of voices, and the reins went flipping out of those startled hands. The horse jumped like a cat, and ran. At the sharp curve of the road the cart swung round and smashed against the rocky cutting. A wheel leapt free and rolled, rocking like a top, for a few yards. The roan went plunging and sliding down the road with half the wrecked cart dragging behind, and was gone, and the road lay silent in the sunlight between the forest trees.

Torm had been thrown from the cart, and lay stunned for a minute or two.

Gwilan had clutched the harp to her when the horse shied, but had lost hold of it in the smash. The cart had tipped over and dragged on it. It was in its case of leather and embroidered silk, but when, one-handed, she got the case out from under the wheel and opened it, she did not take out a harp, but a piece of wood, and another piece, and a tangle of strings, and a sliver of ivory, and a twisted shell of silver chased with lines and leaves and eyes, held by a silver nail to a fragment of the frame.

IT WAS SIX MONTHS WITHOUT PLAYING AFTER THAT, SINCE HER arm had broken at the wrist. The wrist healed well enough, but there was no mending the harp; and by then the landowner of Torm had asked her if she would marry him, and she had said yes. Sometimes she wondered why she had said yes, having never thought much of marriage before, but if she looked steadily into her own mind she saw the reason why. She saw Torm on the road in the sunlight kneeling by the broken, harp, his face all blood and dust, and he was weeping. When she looked at that she saw that the time for rambling and roving was over and gone. One day is the day for moving on, and overnight, the next day, there is no more good in moving on, because you have come where you were going to.

Gwilan brought to the marriage a gold piece, which had been the prize last year at Four Valleys music day; she had sewn it to her bodice as a brooch, because where on earth could you spend a gold piece. She also had two silver pieces, five coppers, and a good winter cloak. Torm contributed house and household, fields and forests, four tenant farmers even poorer than himself, twenty hens, five cows, and forty sheep.

They married in the old way, by themselves, over the spring where the stream began, and came back and told the household. Torm had never suggested a wedding, with singing and harp-playing, never a word of all that. He was a man you could trust, Torm was.

What began in pain, in tears, was never free from the fear of pain. The two of them were gentle to each other. Not that they lived together thirty years without some quarrelling. Two rocks sitting side by side would get sick of each other in thirty years, and who knows what they say now and then when nobody is listening. But if people trust each other they can grumble, and a good bit of grumbling takes the fuel from wrath. Their quarrels went up and burnt out like bits of paper, leaving nothing but a feather of ash, a laugh in bed in the dark. Torm's land never gave more than enough, and there was no money saved. But it was a good house, and the sunlight was sweet on those high stony fields. There were two sons, who grew up into cheerful sensible men. One had a taste for roving, and the other was a farmer born; but neither had any gift of music.

Gwilan never spoke of wanting another harp. But about the time her wrist was healed, old Uliad had a travelling musician bring her one on loan; when he had an offer to buy it at its worth, he sent for it back again. At that time Torm would have it that there was money from selling three good heifers to the landowner of Comin High Farm, and the money should buy a harp, which it did. A year or two later an old friend, a flute player still on his travels and rambles, brought her a harp from the South as a present. The three-heifers harp was a common instrument, plain and heavy; the Southern harp was delicately carved and gilt, but cranky to tune and thin of voice. Gwilan could draw sweetness from the one and strength from the other. When she picked up a harp, or spoke to a child, it obeyed her.

She played at all festivities and funerals in the neighborhood, and with the musician's fees she bought good strings; not Uliad's strings, though, for Uliad was in his grave before her second child was born. If there was a music day nearby she went to it with Torm. She would not play in the competitions, not for fear of losing, but because she was not a harper now, and if they did not know it, she did. So they had her judge the competitions, which she did well and mercilessly. Often in the early years musicians would stop by on their travels and stay two or three nights at Torm; with them she would play the Hunts of Orioth, the

Dances of Cail, the difficult and learned music of the North, and learn
from them the new songs. Even in winter evenings there was music
in the house of Torm: she playing the harp—usually the three-heifers
one, sometimes the fretful Southerner—and Torm's good tenor voice,
and the boys singing, first in sweet treble, later on in husky unreliable
baritone; and one of the farm's men was a lively fiddler; and the shepherd Keth, when he was there, played on the pipes, though he never
could tune them to anyone else's note. "It's our own music day tonight,"
Gwilan would say. "Put another log on the fire, Torm, and sing 'The
Green Leaves' with me, and the boys will take the descant."

Her wrist that had been broken grew a little stiff as the years went
on; then the arthritis came into her hands. The work she did in house
and farm was not easy work. But then who, looking at a hand, would
say it was made to do easy work? You can see from the look of it that
it is meant to do difficult things, that it is the noble, willing servant of
the heart and mind. But the best servants get clumsy as the years go
on. Gwilan could still play the harp, but not as well as she had played,
and she did not much like half measures. So the two harps hung on the
wall, though she kept them tuned. About that time the younger son
went wandering off to see what things looked like in the North, and the
elder married and brought his bride to Torm. Old Keth was found dead
up on the mountain in the spring rain, his dog crouched silent by him
and the sheep nearby. And the drouth came, and the good year, and the
poor year, and there was food to eat and to be cooked and clothes to
wear and to be washed, poor year or good year. In the depth of a winter
Torm took ill. He went from a cough to a high fever to quietness, and
died while Gwilan sat beside him.

Thirty years, how can you say how long that is, and yet no longer
than the saying of it: thirty years. How can you say how heavy the
weight of thirty years is, and yet you can hold all of them together in
your hand lighter than a bit of ash, briefer than a laugh in the dark. The

thirty years began in pain; they passed in peace, contentment. But they did not end there. They ended where they began.

Gwilan got up from her chair and went into the hearth room. The rest of the household were asleep. In the light of her candle she saw the two harps hung against the wall, the three-heifers harp and the gilded Southern harp, the dull music and the false music. She thought, "I'll take them down at last and smash them on the hearthstone, crush them till they're only bits of wood and tangles of wire, like my harp." But she did not. She could not play them at all any more, her hands were far too stiff. It is silly to smash an instrument you cannot even play.

"There is no instrument left that I can play," Gwilan thought, and the thought hung in her mind for a while like a long chord, till she knew the notes that made it. "I thought my harp was myself. But it was not. It was destroyed, I was not. I thought Torm's wife was myself, but she was not. He is dead, I am not. I have nothing left at all now but myself. The wind blows from the valley, and there's a voice on the wind, a bit of a tune. Then the wind falls, or changes. The work has to be done, and we did the work. It's their turn now for that, the children. There's nothing left for me to do but sing. I never could sing. But you play the instrument you have." So she stood by the cold hearth and sang the melody of Orioth's Lament. The people of the household wakened in their beds and heard her singing, all but Torm; but he knew that tune already. The untuned strings of the harps hung on the wall wakened and answered softly, voice to voice, like eyes that shine among the leaves when the wind is blowing.

MAY'S LION

JIM REMEMBERS IT AS A BOBCAT, AND HE WAS MAY'S NEPHEW, and ought to know. It probably was a bobcat. I don't think May would have changed her story, though you can't trust a good story-teller not to make the story suit herself, or get the facts to fit the story better. Anyhow she told it to us more than once, because my mother and I would ask for it; and the way I remember it, it was a mountain lion. And the way I remember May telling it is sitting on the edge of the irrigation tank we used to swim in, cement rough as a lava flow and hot in the sun, the long cracks tarred over. She was an old lady then with a long Irish upper lip, kind and wary and balky. She liked to come sit and talk with my mother while I swam; she didn't have all that many people to talk to. She always had chickens, in the chickenhouse very near the back door of the farmhouse, so the whole place smelled pretty strong of chickens, and as long as she could she kept a cow or two down in the old barn by the creek. The first of May's cows I remember was Pearl, a big, handsome Holstein who gave fourteen or twenty-four or forty gallons or quarts of milk at a milking, whichever is right for a prize milker. Pearl was beautiful in my eyes when I was four or five years old; I loved and admired her. I remember how excited I was, how I reached upward to

them, when Pearl or the workhorse Prince, for whom my love amounted
to worship, would put an immense and sensitive muzzle through the
three-strand fence to whisk a cornhusk from my fearful hand; and then
the munching; and the sweet breath and the big nose would be at the
barbed wire again: the offering is acceptable. . . . After Pearl there was
Rosie, a purebred Jersey. May got her either cheap or free because she
was a runt calf, so tiny that May brought her home on her lap in the
back of the car, like a fawn. And Rosie always looked like she had some
deer in her. She was a lovely, clever little cow and even more willful than
old May. She often chose not to come in to be milked. We would hear
May calling and then see her trudging across our lower pasture with the
bucket, going to find Rosie wherever Rosie had decided to be milked
today on the wild hills she had to roam in, a hundred acres of our and
Old Jim's land. Then May had a fox terrier named Pinky, who yipped
and nipped and turned me against fox terriers for life, but he was long
gone when the mountain lion came; and the black cats who lived in the
barn kept discreetly out of the story. As a matter of fact now I think of
it the chickens weren't in it either. It might have been quite different if
they had been. May had quit keeping chickens after old Mrs. Walter
died. It was just her all alone there, and Rosie and the cats down in the
barn, and nobody else within sight or sound of the old farm. We were
in our house up the hill only in the summer, and Jim lived in town,
those years. What time of year it was I don't know, but I imagine the
grass still green or just turning gold. And May was in the house, in the
kitchen, where she lived entirely unless she was asleep or outdoors, when
she heard this noise.

Now you need May herself, sitting skinny on the edge of the irrigation tank, seventy or eighty or ninety years old, nobody knew how old
May was and she had made sure they couldn't find out, opening her
pleated lips and letting out this noise—a huge, awful yowl, starting
soft with a nasal hum and rising slowly into a snarling gargle that sank

away into a sobbing purr. . . . It got better every time she told the story.

"It was some meow," she said.

So she went to the kitchen door, opened it, and looked out. Then she shut the kitchen door and went to the kitchen window to look out, because there was a mountain lion under the fig tree.

Puma, cougar, catamount; *Felis concolor,* the shy, secret, shadowy lion of the New World, four or five feet long plus a yard of black-tipped tail, weighs about what a woman weighs, lives where the deer live from Canada to Chile, but always shyer, always fewer; the color of dry leaves, dry grass.

There were plenty of deer in the Valley in the forties, but no mountain lion had been seen for decades anywhere near where people lived. Maybe way back up in the canyons; but Jim, who hunted, and knew every deer-trail in the hills, had never seen a lion. Nobody had, except May, now, alone in her kitchen.

"I thought maybe it was sick," she told us. "It wasn't acting right. I don't think a lion would walk right into the yard like that if it was feeling well. If I'd still had the chickens it'd be a different story maybe! But it just walked around some, and then it lay down there," and she points between the fig tree and the decrepit garage. "And then after a while it kind of meowed again, and got up and come into the shade right there." The fig tree, planted when the house was built, about the time May was born, makes a great, green, sweet-smelling shade. "It just laid there looking around. It wasn't well," says May.

She had lived with and looked after animals all her life; she had also earned her living for years as a nurse.

"Well, I didn't know exactly what to do for it. So I put out some water for it. It didn't even get up when I come out the door. I put the water down there, not so close to it that we'd scare each other, see, and it kept watching me, but it didn't move. After I went back in it did get up and tried to drink some water. Then it made that kind of meowowow. I do believe it come here because it was looking for help. Or just for company, maybe."

The afternoon went on, May in the kitchen, the lion under the fig tree.

But down in the barnyard by the creek was Rosie the cow. Fortunately the gate was shut, so she could not come wandering up to the house and meet the lion; but she would be needing to be milked, come six or seven o'clock, and that got to worrying May. She also worried how long a sick mountain lion might hang around, keeping her shut in the house. May didn't like being shut in.

"I went out a time or two, and went shoo!"

Eyes shining amidst fine wrinkles, she flaps her thin arms at the lion. "Shoo! Go on home now!"

But the silent wild creature watches her with yellow eyes and does not stir.

"So when I was talking to Miss Macy on the telephone, she said it might have rabies, and I ought to call the sheriff. I was uneasy then. So finally I did that, and they come out, those county police, you know. Two carloads."

Her voice is dry and quiet.

"I guess there was nothing else they knew how to do. So they shot it."

She looks off across the field Old Jim, her brother, used to plow with Prince the horse and irrigate with the water from this tank. Now wild oats and blackberry grow there. In another thirty years it will be a rich man's vineyard, a tax write-off.

"He was seven feet long, all stretched out, before they took him off. And so thin! They all said, 'Well, Aunt May, I guess you were scared there! I guess you were some scared!' But I wasn't. I didn't want him shot. But I didn't know what to do for him. And I did need to get to Rosie."

I HAVE TOLD THIS TRUE STORY WHICH MAY GAVE TO US AS TRULY as I could, and now I want to tell it as fiction, yet without taking it from her: rather to give it back to her, if I can do so. It is a tiny part of the history of the Valley, and I want to make it part of the Valley outside history. Now the field that the poor man plowed and the rich man harvested lies on the edge of a little town, houses and workshops of timber and fieldstone standing among almond, oak, and eucalyptus trees; and now May is an old woman with a name that means the month of May: Rains End. An old woman with a long, wrinkled-pleated upper lip, she is living alone for the summer in her summer place, a meadow a mile or so up in the hills above the little town, Sinshan. She took her cow Rose with her, and since Rose tends to wander she keeps her on a long tether down by the tiny creek, and moves her into fresh grass now and then. The summerhouse is what they call a nine-pole house, a mere frame of poles stuck in the ground—one of them is a live digger-pine sapling—with stick and matting walls, and mat roof and floors. It doesn't rain in the dry season, and the roof is just for shade. But the house and its little front yard where Rains End has her camp stove and clay oven and matting loom are well shaded by a fig tree that was planted there a hundred years or so ago by her grandmother.

Rains End herself has no grandchildren; she never bore a child, and her one or two marriages were brief and very long ago. She has a nephew and two grandnieces, and feels herself an aunt to all children, even when they are afraid of her and rude to her because she has got so ugly with old age, smelling as musty as a chickenhouse. She considers it natural for children to shrink away from somebody partway dead, and knows that when they're a little older and have got used to her they'll ask her for stories. She was for sixty years a member of the Doctors Lodge, and though she doesn't do curing any more people still ask her to help with nursing sick children, and the children come to long for the kind, authoritative touch of her hands when she bathes them to bring a fever down, or changes a dressing, or combs out bed-tangled hair with witch hazel and great patience.

So Rains End was just waking up from an early afternoon nap in the heat of the day, under the matting roof, when she heard a noise, a huge, awful yowl that started soft with a nasal hum and rose slowly into a snarling gargle that sank away into a sobbing purr. . . . And she got up and looked out from the open side of the house of sticks and matting, and saw a mountain lion under the fig tree. She looked at him from her house; he looked at her from his.

And this part of the story is much the same: the old woman; the lion; and, down by the creek, the cow.

It was hot. Crickets sang shrill in the yellow grass on all the hills and canyons, in all the chaparral. Rains End filled a bowl with water from an unglazed jug and came slowly out of the house. Halfway between the house and the lion she set the bowl down on the dirt. She turned and went back to the house.

The lion got up after a while and came and sniffed at the water. He lay down again with a soft, querulous groan, almost like a sick child, and looked at Rains End with the yellow eyes that saw her in a different way than she had ever been seen before.

She sat on the matting in the shade of the open part of her house and did some mending. When she looked up at the lion she sang under her breath, tunelessly; she wanted to remember the Puma Dance Song but could only remember bits of it, so she made a song for the occasion:

> *You are there, lion.*
> *You are there, lion. . . .*

As the afternoon wore on she began to worry about going down to milk Rose. Unmilked, the cow would start tugging at her tether and making a commotion. That was likely to upset the lion. He lay so close to the house now that if she came out that too might upset him, and she did not want to frighten him or to become frightened of him. He had evidently come for some reason, and it behoved her to find out what the reason was. Probably he was sick; his coming so close to a human person was strange, and people who behave strangely are usually sick or in some kind of pain. Sometimes, though, they are spiritually moved to act strangely. The lion might be a messenger, or might have some message of his own for her or her townspeople. She was more used to seeing birds as messengers; the four-footed people go about their own business. But the lion, dweller in the Seventh House, comes from the place dreams come from. Maybe she did not understand. Maybe someone else would understand. She could go over and tell Valiant and her family, whose summerhouse was in Gahheya meadow, farther up the creek; or she could go over to Buck's, on Baldy Knoll. But there were four or five adolescents there, and one of them might come and shoot the lion, to boast that he'd saved old Rains End from getting clawed to bits and eaten.

Mooooo! said Rose, down by the creek, reproachfully.

The sun was still above the southwest ridge, but the branches of pines were across it and the heavy heat was out of it, and shadows were welling up in the low fields of wild oats and blackberry.

Mooooo! said Rose again, louder.

The lion lifted up his square, heavy head, the color of dry wild oats, and gazed down across the pastures. Rains End knew from that weary movement that he was very ill. He had come for company in dying, that was all.

"I'll come back, lion," Rains End sang tunelessly. "Lie still. Be quiet. I'll come back soon." Moving softly and easily, as she would move in a room with a sick child, she got her milking pail and stool, slung the stool on her back with a woven strap so as to leave a hand free, and came out of the house. The lion watched her at first very tense, the yellow eyes firing up for a moment, but then put his head down again with that little grudging, groaning sound. "I'll come back, lion," Rains End said. She went down to the creekside and milked a nervous and indignant cow. Rose could smell lion, and demanded in several ways, all eloquent, just what Rains End intended to *do?* Rains End ignored her questions and sang milking songs to her: "Su bonny, su bonny, be still my grand cow . . ."Once she had to slap her hard on the hip. "Quit that, you old fool! Get over! I am *not* going to untie you and have you walking into trouble! I won't let him come down this way."

She did not say how she planned to stop him.

She retethered Rose where she could stand down in the creek if she liked. When she came back up the rise with the pail of milk in hand, the lion had not moved. The sun was down, the air above the ridges turning clear gold. The yellow eyes watched her, no light in them. She came to pour milk into the lion's bowl. As she did so, he all at once half rose up. Rains End started, and spilled some of the milk she was pouring. "Shoo! Stop that!" she whispered fiercely, waving her skinny arm at the lion. "Lie down now! I'm afraid of you when you get up, can't you see that, stupid? Lie down now, lion. There you are. Here I am. It's all right. You know what you're doing." Talking softly as she went, she returned to her house of stick and matting. There she sat down as before, in the open porch, on the grass mats.

The mountain lion made the grumbling sound, ending with a long sigh, and let his head sink back down on his paws.

Rains End got some cornbread and a tomato from the pantry box while there was still daylight left to see by, and ate slowly and neatly. She did not offer the lion food. He had not touched the milk, and she thought he would eat no more in the House of Earth.

From time to time as the quiet evening darkened and stars gathered thicker overhead she sang to the lion. She sang the five songs of *Going Westward to the Sunrise,* which are sung to human beings dying. She did not know if it was proper and appropriate to sing these songs to a dying mountain lion, but she did not know his songs.

Twice he also sang: once a quavering moan, like a housecat challenging another tom to battle, and once a long, sighing purr.

Before the Scorpion had swung clear of Sinshan Mountain, Rains

End had pulled her heavy shawl around herself in case the fog came in, and had gone sound asleep in the porch of her house.

She woke with the grey light before sunrise. The lion was a motionless shadow, a little farther from the trunk of the fig tree than he had been the night before. As the light grew, she saw that he had stretched himself out full length. She knew he had finished his dying, and sang the fifth song, the last song, in a whisper, for him:

> *The doors of the Four Houses*
> *are open.*
> *Surely they are open.*

Near sunrise she went to milk Rose, and to wash in the creek. When she came back up to the house she went closer to the lion, though not so close as to crowd him, and stood for a long time looking at him stretched out in the long, tawny, delicate light "As thin as I am!" she said to Valiant, when she went up to Gahheya later in the morning to tell the story and to ask help carrying the body of the lion off where the buzzards and coyotes could clean it.

It's still your story, Aunt May; it was your lion. He came to you. He brought his death to you, a gift; but the men with the guns won't take gifts, they think they own death already. And so they took from you the honor he did you, and you felt that loss. I wanted to restore it. But you don't need it. You followed the lion where he went, years ago now.

BUFFALO GALS,
WON'T YOU
COME OUT TONIGHT

I

"You fell out of the sky," the coyote said.

Still curled up tight, lying on her side, her back pressed against the overhanging rock, the child watched the coyote with one eye. Over the other eye she kept her hand cupped, its back on the dirt.

"There was a burned place in the sky, up there alongside the rimrock, and then you fell out of it," the coyote repeated, patiently, as if the news was getting a bit stale. "Are you hurt?"

She was all right. She was in the plane with Mr. Michaels, and the motor was so loud she couldn't understand what he said even when he shouted, and the way the wind rocked the wings was making her feel sick, but it was all right. They were flying to Canyonville. In the plane.

She looked. The coyote was still sitting there. It yawned. It was a big one, in good condition, its coat silvery and thick. The dark tear-line from its long yellow eye was as clearly marked as a tabby cat's.

She sat up, slowly, still holding her right hand pressed to her right eye.

"Did you lose an eye?" the coyote asked, interested.

"I don't know," the child said. She caught her breath and shivered. "I'm cold."

"I'll help you look for it," the coyote said. "Come on! If you move around you won't have to shiver. The sun's up."

Cold lonely brightness lay across the falling land, a hundred miles of sagebrush. The coyote was trotting busily around, nosing under clumps of rabbit-brush and cheatgrass, pawing at a rock. "Aren't you going to look?" it said, suddenly sitting down on its haunches and abandoning the search. "I knew a trick once where I could throw my eyes way up into a tree and see everything from up there, and then whistle, and they'd come back into my head. But that goddam bluejay stole them, and when I whistled nothing came. I had to stick lumps of pine pitch into my head so I could see anything. You could try that. But you've got one eye that's okay, what do you need two for? Are you coming, or are you dying there?"

The child crouched, shivering.

"Well, come if you want to," said the coyote, yawned again, snapped at a flea, stood up, turned, and trotted away among the sparse clumps of rabbit-brush and sage, along the long slope that stretched on down and down into the plain streaked across by long shadows of sagebrush. The slender, grey-yellow animal was hard to keep in sight, vanishing as the child watched.

She struggled to her feet, and without a word, though she kept saying in her mind, "Wait, please wait," she hobbled after the coyote. She could not see it. She kept her hand pressed over the right eyesocket. Seeing with one eye there was no depth; it was like a huge, flat picture. The coyote suddenly sat in the middle of the picture, looking back at her, its mouth open, its eyes narrowed, grinning. Her legs began to steady and her head did not pound so hard, though the deep, black ache was always there. She had nearly caught up to the coyote when it trotted off again. This time she spoke. "Please wait!" she said.

"Okay," said the coyote, but it trotted right on. She followed, walking downhill into the flat picture that at each step was deep.

Each step was different underfoot; each sage bush was different, and all the same. Following the coyote she came out from the shadow of the rimrock cliffs, and the sun at eyelevel dazzled her left eye. Its bright warmth soaked into her muscles and bones at once. The air, that all night had been so hard to breathe, came sweet and easy.

The sage bushes were pulling in their shadows and the sun was hot on the child's back when she followed the coyote along the rim of a gully. After a while the coyote slanted down the undercut slope and the child scrambled after, through scrub willows to the thin creek in its wide sandbed. Both drank.

The coyote crossed the creek, not with a careless charge and splashing like a dog, but singlefoot and quiet like a cat; always it carried its tail low. The child hesitated, knowing that wet shoes make blistered feet, and then waded across in as few steps as possible. Her right arm ached with the effort of holding her hand up over her eye. "I need a bandage," she said to the coyote. It cocked its head and said nothing. It stretched out its forelegs and lay watching the water, resting but alert. The child sat down nearby on the hot sand and tried to move her right hand. It was glued to the skin around her eye by dried blood. At the little tearing-away pain, she whimpered; though it was a small pain it frightened her. The coyote came over close and poked its long snout into her face. Its strong, sharp smell was in her nostrils. It began to lick the awful, aching blindness, cleaning and cleaning with its curled, precise, strong, wet tongue, until the child was able to cry a little with relief, being comforted. Her head was bent close to the grey-yellow ribs, and she saw the hard nipples, the whitish belly-fur. She put her arm around the she-coyote, stroking the harsh coat over back and ribs.

"Okay," the coyote said, "let's go!" And set off without a backward glance. The child scrambled to her feet and followed. "Where are we going?" she said, and the coyote, trotting on down along the creek, answered, "On down along the creek . . ."

THERE MUST HAVE BEEN A WHILE SHE WAS ASLEEP WHILE SHE walked, because she felt like she was waking up, but she was walking along, only in a different place. She didn't know how she knew it was different. They were still following the creek, though the gully was flattened out to nothing much, and there was still sagebrush range as far as the eye could see. The eye—the good one—felt rested. The other one still ached, but not so sharply, and there was no use thinking about it. But where was the coyote?

She stopped. The pit of cold into which the plane had fallen re-opened and she fell. She stood falling, a thin whimper making itself in her throat.

"Over here!"

The child turned. She saw a coyote gnawing at the half-dried-up carcass of a crow, black feathers sticking to the black lips and narrow jaw.

She saw a tawny-skinned woman kneeling by a campfire, sprinkling something into a conical pot. She heard the water boiling in the pot, though it was propped between rocks, off the fire. The woman's hair was yellow and grey, bound back with a string. Her feet were bare. The upturned soles looked as dark and hard as shoe soles, but the arch of the foot was high, and the toes made two neat curving rows. She wore bluejeans and an old white shirt. She looked over at the girl. "Come on, eat crow!" she said. The child slowly came toward the woman and the fire, and squatted down. She had stopped falling and felt very light and empty; and her tongue was like a piece of wood stuck in her mouth.

Coyote was now blowing into the pot or basket or whatever it was. She reached into it with two fingers, and pulled her hand away shaking it and shouting, "Ow! Shit! Why don't I ever have any spoons?" She broke off a dead twig of sagebrush, dipped it into the pot, and licked it. "Oh, boy," she said. "Come on!"

The child moved a little closer, broke off a twig, dipped. Lumpy pinkish mush clung to the twig. She licked. The taste was rich and delicate.

"What is it?" she asked after a long time of dipping and licking.

"Food. Dried salmon mush," Coyote said. "It's cooling down." She stuck two fingers into the mush again, this time getting a good load, which she ate very neatly. The child, when she tried, got mush all over her chin. It was like chopsticks, it took practice. She practiced. They ate turn and turn until nothing was left in the pot but three rocks. The child did not ask why there were rocks in the mush-pot. They licked the rocks clean. Coyote licked out the inside of the pot-basket, rinsed it once in the creek, and put it onto her head. It fit nicely, making a conical hat. She pulled off her bluejeans. "Piss on the fire!" she cried, and did so, standing straddling it. "Ah, steam between the legs!" she said. The child, embarrassed, thought she was supposed to do the same thing, but did not want to, and did not. Bareassed, Coyote danced around the dampened fire, kicking her long thin legs out and singing,

"Buffalo gals, won't you come out tonight,
Come out tonight, come out tonight,
Buffalo gals, won't you come out tonight,
And dance by the light of the moon?"

She pulled her jeans back on. The child was burying the remains of the fire in creek-sand, heaping it over, seriously, wanting to do right. Coyote watched her.

"Is that you?" she said. "A Buffalo Gal? What happened to the rest of you?"

"The rest of me?" The child looked at herself, alarmed.

"All your people."

"Oh. Well, Mom took Bobbie, he's my little brother, away with Uncle Norm. He isn't really my uncle, or anything. So Mr. Michaels was going there anyway so he was going to fly me over to my real father, in Canyonville. Linda, my stepmother, you know, she said it was okay for the summer anyhow if I was there, and then we could see. But the plane."

In the silence the girl's face became dark red, then greyish white. Coyote watched, fascinated. "Oh," the girl said, "Oh—Oh—Mr. Michaels—he must be—Did the—"

"Come on!" said Coyote, and set off walking.

The child cried, "I ought to go back—"

"What for?" said Coyote. She stopped to look round at the child, then went on faster. "Come on, Gal!" She said it as a name; maybe it was the child's name, Myra, as spoken by Coyote. The child, confused and despairing, protested again, but followed her. "Where are we going? Where *are* we?"

"This is my country," Coyote answered, with dignity, making a long, slow gesture all round the vast horizon. "I made it. Every goddam sage bush."

And they went on. Coyote's gait was easy, even a little shambling, but she covered the ground; the child struggled not to drop behind. Shadows were beginning to pull themselves out again from under the rocks and shrubs. Leaving the creek, they went up a long, low, uneven slope that ended away off against the sky in rimrock. Dark trees stood one here, another way over there; what people called a juniper forest, a desert forest, one with a lot more between the trees than trees. Each juniper they passed smelled sharply, cat-pee smell the kids at school called it, but the child liked it; it seemed to go into her mind and wake her up. She picked off a juniper berry and held it in her mouth, but after a while spat it out. The aching was coming back in huge black waves, and she kept stumbling. She found that she was sitting down on the ground. When she tried to get up her legs shook and would not go under her. She felt foolish and frightened, and began to cry.

"We're home!" Coyote called from way on up the hill.

The child looked with her one weeping eye, and saw sagebrush, juniper, cheatgrass, rimrock. She heard a coyote yip far off in the dry twilight.

She saw a little town up under the rimrock, board houses, shacks, all unpainted. She heard Coyote call again, "Come on, pup! Come on, Gal, we're home!" She could not get up, so she tried to go on all fours, the long way up the slope to the houses under the rimrock. Long before she got there, several people came to meet her. They were all children, she thought at first, and then began to understand that most of them were grown people, but all were very short; they were broad-bodied, fat, with fine, delicate hands and feet. Their eyes were bright. Some of the women helped her stand up and walk, coaxing her, "It isn't much farther, you're doing fine." In the late dusk lights shone yellow-bright through doorways and through unchinked cracks between boards. Woodsmoke hung sweet in the quiet air. The short people talked and laughed all the time, softly. "Where's she going to stay?"—"Put her in with Robin, they're all asleep already!"—"Oh, she can stay with us."

The child asked hoarsely, "Where's Coyote?"

"Out hunting," the short people said.

A deeper voice spoke: "Somebody new has come into town?"

"Yes, a new person," one of the short men answered.

Among these people the deep-voiced man bulked impressive; he was broad and tall, with powerful hands, a big head, a short neck. They made way for him respectfully. He moved very quietly, respectful of them also. His eyes when he stared down at the child were amazing. When he blinked, it was like the passing of a hand before a candle-flame.

"It's only an owlet," he said. "What have you let happen to your eye, new person?"

"I was—We were flying—"

"You're too young to fly," the big man said in his deep, soft voice. "Who brought you here?"

"Coyote."

And one of the short people confirmed: "She came here with Coyote, Young Owl."

"Then maybe she should stay in Coyote's house tonight," the big man said.

"It's all bones and lonely in there," said a short woman with fat cheeks and a striped shirt. "She can come with us."

That seemed to decide it. The fat-cheeked woman patted the child's arm and took her past several shacks and shanties to a low, windowless house. The doorway was so low even the child had to duck down to enter. There were a lot of people inside, some already there and some crowding in after the fat-cheeked woman. Several babies were fast asleep in cradle-boxes in corners. There was a good fire, and a good smell, like toasted sesame seeds. The child was given food, and ate a little, but her head swam and the blackness in her right eye kept coming across her left eye so she could not see at all for a while. Nobody asked her name or told her what to call them. She heard the children call the fat-cheeked woman Chipmunk. She got up courage finally to say, "Is there somewhere I can go to sleep, Mrs. Chipmunk?"

"Sure, come on," one of the daughters said, "in here," and took the child into a back room, not completely partitioned off from the crowded front room, but dark and uncrowded. Big shelves with mattresses and blankets lined the walls. "Crawl in!" said Chipmunk's daughter, patting the child's arm in the comforting way they had. The child climbed onto a shelf, under a blanket. She laid down her head. She thought, "I didn't brush my teeth."

II

SHE WOKE; SHE SLEPT AGAIN. IN CHIPMUNK'S SLEEPING ROOM it was always stuffy, warm, and half-dark, day and night. People came in and slept and got up and left, night and day. She dozed and slept, got down to drink from the bucket and dipper in the front room, and went back to sleep and doze.

She was sitting up on the shelf, her feet dangling, not feeling bad any more, but dreamy, weak. She felt in her jeans pockets. In the left front one was a pocket comb and a bubblegum wrapper; in the right front, two dollar bills and a quarter and a dime.

Chipmunk and another woman, a very pretty dark-eyed plump one, came in. "So you woke up for your dance!" Chipmunk greeted her, laughing, and sat down by her with an arm around her.

"Jay's giving you a dance," the dark woman said. "He's going to make you all right. Let's get you all ready!"

There was a spring up under the rimrock, that flattened out into a pool with slimy, reedy shores. A flock of noisy children splashing in it ran off and left the child and the two women to bathe. The water was warm on the surface, cold down on the feet and legs. All naked, the two soft-voiced laughing women, their round bellies and breasts, broad hips and buttocks gleaming warm in the late afternoon light, sluiced the child down, washed and stroked her limbs and hands and hair, cleaned around the cheekbone and eyebrow of her right eye with infinite softness, admired her, sudsed her, rinsed her, splashed her out of the water, dried her off, dried each other off, got dressed, dressed her, braided her hair, braided each other's hair, tied feathers on the braid-ends, admired her and each other again, and brought her back down into the little straggling town and to a kind of playing field or dirt parking lot in among the houses. There were no streets, just paths and dirt, no lawns and gardens, just sagebrush and dirt. Quite a few people were gathering or wandering around the open place, looking dressed up, wearing colorful shirts, print dresses, strings of beads, earrings. "Hey there, Chipmunk, Whitefoot!" they greeted the women.

A man in new jeans, with a bright blue velveteen vest over a clean, faded blue workshirt, came forward to meet them, very handsome, tense, and important. "All right, Gal!" he said in a harsh, loud voice, which startled among all these soft-speaking people. "We're going to get that eye fixed right up tonight! You just sit down here and don't worry about a thing." He took her wrist, gently despite his bossy, brassy manner, and led her to a woven mat that lay on the dirt near the middle of the open place. There, feeling very foolish, she had to sit down, and was told to stay still. She soon got over feeling that everybody was looking at her, since nobody paid her more attention than a checking glance or, from Chipmunk or Whitefoot and their families, a reassuring wink. Every now and then Jay rushed over to her and said something like, "Going to be as good as new!" and went off again to organize people, waving his long blue arms and shouting.

Coming up the hill to the open place, a lean, loose, tawny figure—and the child started to jump up, remembered she was to sit still, and sat still, calling out softly, "Coyote! Coyote!"

Coyote came lounging by. She grinned. She stood looking down at the child. "Don't let that Bluejay fuck you up, Gal," she said, and lounged on.

The child's gaze followed her, yearning.

People were sitting down now over on one side of the open place, making an uneven half-circle that kept getting added to at the ends until there was nearly a circle of people sitting on the dirt around the child, ten or fifteen paces from her. All the people wore the kind of clothes the child was used to, jeans and jeans-jackets, shirts, vests, cotton dresses, but they were all barefoot, and she thought they were more beautiful than the people she knew, each in a different way, as if each one had invented beauty. Yet some of them were also very strange: thin black shining people with whispery voices, a long-legged woman with eyes like jewels. The big man called Young Owl was there, sleepy-looking and dignified, like Judge McCown who owned a sixty-thousand acre ranch; and beside him was a woman the child thought might be his sister, for like him she had a hook nose and big, strong hands; but she was lean and dark, and there was a crazy look in her fierce eyes. Yellow eyes, but round, not long and slanted like Coyote's. There was

Coyote sitting, yawning, scratching her armpit, bored. Now somebody was entering the circle: a man, wearing only a kind of kilt and a cloak painted or beaded with diamond shapes, dancing to the rhythm of the rattle he carried and shook with a buzzing fast beat. His limbs and body were thick yet supple, his movements smooth and pouring. The child kept her gaze on him as he danced past her, around her, past again. The rattle in his hand shook almost too fast to see, in the other hand was something thin and sharp. People were singing around the circle now, a few notes repeated in time to the rattle, soft and tuneless. It was exciting and boring, strange and familiar. The Rattler wove his dancing closer and closer to her, darting at her. The first time she flinched away, frightened by the lunging movement and by his flat, cold face with narrow eyes, but after that she sat still, knowing her part. The dancing went on, the singing went on, till they carried her past boredom into a floating that could go on forever.

Jay had come strutting into the circle, and was standing beside her. He couldn't sing, but he called out, "Hey! Hey! Hey! Hey!" in his big, harsh voice, and everybody answered from all round, and the echo came down from the rimrock on the second beat. Jay was holding up a stick with a ball on it in one hand, and something like a marble in the other. The stick was a pipe: he got smoke into his mouth from it and blew it in four directions and up and down and then over the marble, a puff each time. Then the rattle stopped suddenly, and everything was silent for several breaths. Jay squatted down and looked intently into the child's face, his head cocked to one side. He reached forward, muttering something in time to the rattle and the singing that had started up again louder than before; he touched the child's right eye in the black center of the pain. She flinched and endured. His touch was not gentle. She saw the marble, a dull yellow ball like beeswax, in his hand; then she shut her seeing eye and set her teeth.

"There!" Jay shouted. "Open up. Come on! Let's see!"

Her jaw clenched like a vise, she opened both eyes. The lid of the right one stuck and dragged with such a searing white pain that she nearly threw up as she sat there in the middle of everybody watching.

"Hey, can you see? How's it work? It looks great!" Jay was shaking her arm, railing at her. "How's it feel? Is it working?"

What she saw was confused, hazy, yellowish. She began to discover, as everybody came crowding around peering at her, smiling, stroking and patting her arms and shoulders, that if she shut the hurting eye and looked with the other, everything was clear and flat; if she used them both, things were blurry and yellowish, but deep.

There, right close, was Coyote's long nose and narrow eyes and grin. "What is it, Jay?" she was asking, peering at the new eye. "One of mine you stole that time?"

"It's pine pitch," Jay shouted furiously. "You think I'd use some stupid secondhand coyote eye? I'm a doctor!"

"Ooooh, ooooh, a doctor," Coyote said. "Boy, that is one ugly eye. Why didn't you ask Rabbit for a rabbit-dropping? That eye looks like shit." She put her lean face yet closer, till the child thought she was going to kiss her; instead, the thin, firm tongue once more licked accurate across the pain, cooling, clearing. When the child opened both eyes again the world looked pretty good.

"It works fine," she said.

"Hey!" Jay yelled. "She says it works fine! It works fine, she says so! I told you! What'd I tell you?" He went off waving his arms and yelling. Coyote had disappeared. Everybody was wandering off.

The child stood up, stiff from long sitting. It was nearly dark; only the long west held a great depth of pale radiance. Eastward the plains ran down into night.

Lights were on in some of the shanties. Off at the edge of town somebody was playing a creaky fiddle, a lonesome chirping tune.

A person came beside her and spoke quietly: "Where will you stay?"

"I don't know," the child said. She was feeling extremely hungry. "Can I stay with Coyote?"

"She isn't home much," the soft-voiced woman said. "You were staying with Chipmunk, weren't you? Or there's Rabbit or Jackrabbit, they have families . . ."

"Do you have a family?" the girl asked, looking at the delicate, soft-eyed woman.

"Two fawns," the woman answered, smiling. "But I just came into town for the dance."

"I'd really like to stay with Coyote," the child said after a little pause, timid, but obstinate.

"Okay, that's fine. Her house is over here." Doe walked along beside the child to a ramshackle cabin on the high edge of town. No light shone from inside. A lot of junk was scattered around the front. There was no step up to the half-open door. Over the door a battered pine board, nailed up crooked, said BIDE-A-WEE.

"Hey, Coyote? Visitors," Doe said. Nothing happened.

Doe pushed the door farther open and peered in. "She's out hunting, I guess. I better be getting back to the fawns. You going to be okay? Anybody else here will give you something to eat—you know . . . okay?"

"Yeah. I'm fine. Thank you," the child said.

She watched Doe walk away through the clear twilight, a severely elegant walk, small steps, like a woman in high heels, quick, precise, very light.

Inside Bide-A-Wee it was too dark to see anything and so cluttered that she fell over something at every step. She could not figure out where or how to light a fire. There was something that felt like a bed, but when she lay down on it, it felt more like a dirty-clothes pile, and smelt like one. Things bit her legs, arms, neck, and back. She was terribly hungry. By smell she found her way to what had to be a dead fish hanging from the ceiling in one corner. By feel she broke off a greasy flake and tasted it. It was smoked dried salmon. She ate one succulent piece after another until she was satisfied, and licked her fingers clean. Near the open door starlight shone on water in a pot of some kind; the child smelled it cautiously, tasted it cautiously, and drank just enough to quench her thirst, for it tasted of mud and was warm and stale. Then she went back to the bed of dirty clothes and fleas, and lay down. She could have gone to Chipmunk's house, or other friendly households; she thought of that as she lay forlorn in Coyote's dirty bed. But she did not go. She slapped at fleas until she fell asleep.

Along in the deep night somebody said, "Move over, pup," and was warm beside her.

BREAKFAST, EATEN SITTING IN THE SUN IN THE DOORWAY, WAS dried-salmon-powder mush. Coyote hunted, mornings and evenings, but what they ate was not fresh game but salmon, and dried stuff, and any berries in season. The child did not ask about this. It made sense to her. She was going to ask Coyote why she slept at night and waked in the day like humans, instead of the other way round like coyotes, but when she framed the question in her mind she saw at once that night is when you sleep and day when you're awake; that made sense too. But one question she did ask, one hot day when they were lying around slapping fleas.

"I don't understand why you all look like people," she said.

"We are people."

"I mean, people like me, humans."

"Resemblance is in the eye," Coyote said. "How is that lousy eye, by the way?"

"It's fine. But—like you wear clothes—and live in houses—with fires and stuff—"

"That's what you think . . . If that loudmouth Jay hadn't horned in, I could have done a really good job."

The child was quite used to Coyote's disinclination to stick to any one subject, and to her boasting. Coyote was like a lot of kids she knew, in some respects. Not in others.

"You mean what I'm seeing isn't true? Isn't real—like on TV, or something?"

"No," Coyote said. "Hey, that's a tick on your collar." She reached over, flicked the tick off, picked it up on one finger, bit it, and spat out the bits.

"Yecch!" the child said. "So?"

"So, to me you're basically greyish yellow and run on four legs. To that lot"—she waved disdainfully at the warren of little houses next down the hill—"you hop around twitching your nose all the time. To Hawk, you're an egg, or maybe getting pinfeathers. See? It just depends on how you look at things. There are only two kinds of people."

"Humans and animals?"

"No. The kind of people who say, 'There are two kinds of people' and the kind of people who don't." Coyote cracked up, pounding her thigh and yelling with delight at her joke. The child didn't get it, and waited.

"Okay," Coyote said. "There's the first people, and then the others. That's the two kinds."

"The first people are—?"

"Us, the animals . . . and things. All the old ones. You know. And you pups, kids, fledglings. All first people."

"And the—others?"

"Them," Coyote said. "You know. The others. The new people. The ones who came." Her fine, hard face had gone serious, rather formidable. She glanced directly, as she seldom did, at the child, a brief gold sharpness. "We were here," she said. "We were always here. We are always here. Where we are is here. But it's their country now. They're running it . . . Shit, even I did better!"

The child pondered and offered a word she had used to hear a good deal: "They're illegal immigrants."

"Illegal!" Coyote said, mocking, sneering. "Illegal is a sick bird. What the fuck's illegal mean? You want a code of justice from a coyote? Grow up, kid!"

"I don't want to."

"You don't want to grow up?"

"I'll be the other kind if I do."

"Yeah. So," Coyote said, and shrugged. "That's life." She got up and went around the house, and the child heard her pissing in the back yard.

A lot of things were hard to take about Coyote as a mother. When her boyfriends came to visit, the child learned to go stay with Chipmunk or the Rabbits for the night, because Coyote and her friend wouldn't even wait to get on the bed but would start doing that right on the floor or even out in the yard. A couple of times Coyote came back late from hunting with a friend, and the child had to lie up against the wall in the same bed and hear and feel them doing that right next to her. It was something like fighting and something like dancing, with a beat to it, and she didn't mind too much except that it made it hard to stay asleep.

Once she woke up and one of Coyote's friends was stroking her stomach in a creepy way. She didn't know what to do, but Coyote woke up and realized what he was doing, bit him hard, and kicked him out of bed. He spent the night on the floor, and apologized next morning—"Aw, hell, Ki, I forgot the kid was there, I thought it was you—"

Coyote, unappeased, yelled, "You think I don't got any standards? You think I'd let some coyote rape a kid in my bed?" She kicked him out of the house, and grumbled about him all day. But a while later he spent the night again, and he and Coyote did that three or four times.

Another thing that was embarrassing was the way Coyote peed anywhere, taking her pants down in public. But most people here didn't seem to care. The thing that worried the child most, maybe, was when Coyote did number two anywhere and then turned around and talked to it. That seemed so awful. As if Coyote was—the way she often seemed, but really wasn't—crazy.

The child gathered up all the old dry turds from around the house one day while Coyote was having a nap, and buried them in a sandy place near where she and Bobcat and some of the other people generally went and did and buried their number twos.

Coyote woke up, came lounging out of Bide-A-Wee, rubbing her hands through her thick, fair, greyish hair and yawning, looked all around once with those narrow eyes, and said, "Hey! Where are they?" Then she shouted, "Where are you? Where are you?"

And a faint, muffled chorus came from over in the sandy draw, "Mommy! Mommy! We're here!"

Coyote trotted over, squatted down, raked out every turd, and talked with them for a long time. When she came back she said nothing, but the child, redfaced and heart pounding, said, "I'm sorry I did that."

"It's just easier when they're all around close by," Coyote said, washing her hands (despite the filth of her house, she kept herself quite clean, in her own fashion).

"I kept stepping on them," the child said, trying to justify her deed.

"Poor little shits," said Coyote, practicing dance-steps.

"Coyote," the child said timidly. "Did you ever have any children? I mean real pups?"

"Did I? Did I have children? Litters! That one that tried feeling you up, you know? That was my son. Pick of the litter . . . Listen, Gal. Have daughters. When you have anything, have daughters. At least they clear out."

III

THE CHILD THOUGHT OF HERSELF AS GAL, BUT ALSO SOMETIMES as Myra. So far as she knew, she was the only person in town who had two names. She had to think about that, and about what Coyote had said about the two kinds of people; she had to think about where she belonged. Some persons in town made it clear that as far as they were concerned she didn't and never would belong there. Hawk's furious stare burned through her; the Skunk children made audible remarks about what she smelled like. And though Whitefoot and Chipmunk and their families were kind, it was the generosity of big families, where one more or less simply doesn't count. If one of them, or Cottontail, or Jackrabbit, had come upon her in the desert lying lost and half-blind, would they have stayed with her, like Coyote? That was Coyote's craziness, what they called her craziness. She wasn't afraid. She went between the two kinds of people, she crossed over. Buck and Doe and their beautiful children weren't really afraid, because they lived so constantly in danger. The Rattler wasn't afraid, because he was so dangerous. And yet maybe he was afraid of her, for he never spoke, and never came close to her. None of them treated her the way Coyote did. Even among the children, her only constant playmate was one younger than herself, a preposterous and fearless little boy called Horned Toad Child. They dug and built together, out among the sagebrush, and played at hunting and gathering and keeping house and holding dances, all the great games. A pale, squatty child with fringed eyebrows, he was a self-contained but loyal friend; and he knew a good deal for his age.

"There isn't anybody else like me here," she said, as they sat by the pool in the morning sunlight.

"There isn't anybody much like me anywhere," said Horned Toad Child.

"Well, you know what I mean."

"Yeah . . . There used to be people like you around, I guess."

"What were they called?"

"Oh—people. Like everybody . . ."

"But where do my people live? They have towns. I used to live in one. I don't know where they are, is all. I ought to find out. I don't know where my mother is now, but my daddy's in Canyonville. I was going there when."

"Ask Horse," said Horned Toad Child, sagaciously. He had moved away from the water, which he did not like and never drank, and was plaiting rushes.

"I don't know Horse."

"He hangs around the butte down there a lot of the time. He's waiting till his uncle gets old and he can kick him out and be the big honcho. The old man and the women don't want him around till then. Horses are weird. Anyway, he's the one to ask. He gets around a lot. And his people came here with the new people, that's what they say, anyhow."

Illegal immigrants, the girl thought. She took Horned Toad's advice, and one long day when Coyote was gone on one of her unannounced and unexplained trips, she took a pouchful of dried salmon and salmon-berries and went off alone to the flat-topped butte miles away in the southwest.

There was a beautiful spring at the foot of the butte, and a trail to it with a lot of footprints on it. She waited there under willows by the clear pool, and after a while Horse came running, splendid, with copper-red skin and long, strong legs, deep chest, dark eyes, his black hair whipping his back as he ran. He stopped, not at all winded, and gave a snort as he looked at her. "Who are you?"

Nobody in town asked that—ever. She saw it was true: Horse had come here with her people, people who had to ask each other who they were.

"I live with Coyote," she said, cautiously.

"Oh, sure, I heard about you," Horse said. He knelt to drink from the pool, long deep drafts, his hands plunged in the cool water. When he had drunk he wiped his mouth, sat back on his heels, and announced, "I'm going to be king."

"King of the Horses?"

"Right! Pretty soon now. I could lick the old man already, but I can wait. Let him have his day," said Horse, vainglorious, magnanimous. The child gazed at him, in love already, forever.

"I can comb your hair, if you like," she said.

"Great!" said Horse, and sat still while she stood behind him, tugging her pocket comb through his coarse, black, shining, yard-long hair. It took a long time to get it smooth. She tied it in a massive ponytail with willowbark when she was done. Horse bent over the pool to admire himself. "That's great," he said. "That's really beautiful!"

"Do you ever go . . . where the other people are?" she asked in a low voice.

He did not reply for long enough that she thought he wasn't going to; then he said, "You mean the metal places, the glass places? The holes? I go around them. There are all the walls now. There didn't used to be so many. Grandmother said there didn't used to be any walls. Do you know Grandmother?" he asked naively, looking at her with his great, dark eyes.

"Your grandmother?"

"Well, yes—Grandmother—You know. Who makes the web. Well, anyhow, I know there's some of my people, horses, there. I've seen them across the walls. They act really crazy. You know, we brought the new people here. They couldn't have got here without us, they only have two legs, and they have those metal shells. I can tell you that whole story. The King has to know the stories."

"I like stories a lot."

"It takes three nights to tell it. What do you want to know about them?"

"I was thinking that maybe I ought to go there. Where they are."

"It's dangerous. Really dangerous. You can't go through—they'd catch you."

"I'd just like to know the way."

"I know the way," Horse said, sounding for the first time entirely adult and reliable; she knew he did know the way. "It's a long run for a colt." He looked at her again. "I've got a cousin with different-color eyes," he said, looking from her right to her left eye. "One brown and one blue. But she's an Appaloosa."

"Bluejay made the yellow one," the child explained. "I lost my own one. In the . . . when . . . You don't think I could get to those places?"

"Why do you want to?"

"I sort of feel like I have to."

Horse nodded. He got up. She stood still.

"I could take you, I guess," he said.

"Would you? When?"

"Oh, now, I guess. Once I'm King I won't be able to leave, you know. Have to protect the women. And I sure wouldn't let my people get anywhere near those places!" A shudder ran right down his magnificent body, yet he said, with a toss of his head, "They couldn't catch me, of course, but the others can't run like I do . . ."

"How long would it take us?"

Horse thought awhile. "Well, the nearest place like that is over by the red rocks. If we left now we'd be back here around tomorrow noon. It's just a little hole."

She did not know what he meant by "a hole," but did not ask.

"You want to go?" Horse said, flipping back his ponytail.

"Okay," the girl said, feeling the ground go out from under her.

"Can you run?"

She shook her head. "I walked here, though."

Horse laughed, a large, cheerful laugh. "Come on," he said, and knelt and held his hands backturned like stirrups for her to mount to his shoulders. "What do they call you?" he teased, rising easily, setting right off at a jogtrot. "Gnat? Fly? Flea?"

"Tick, because I stick!" the child cried, gripping the willowbark tie of the black mane, laughing with delight at being suddenly eight feet tall and traveling across the desert without even trying, like the tumbleweed, as fast as the wind.

❧

MOON, A NIGHT PAST FULL, ROSE TO LIGHT THE PLAINS FOR
them. Horse jogged easily on and on. Somewhere deep in the night they
stopped at a Pygmy Owl camp, ate a little, and rested. Most of the owls
were out hunting, but an old lady entertained them at her campfire,
telling them tales about the ghost of a cricket, about the great invisible
people, tales that the child heard interwoven with her own dreams as
she dozed and half-woke and dozed again. Then Horse put her up on
his shoulders and on they went at a tireless slow lope. Moon went down
behind them, and before them the sky paled into rose and gold. The
soft nightwind was gone; the air was sharp, cold, still. On it, in it, there
was a faint, sour smell of burning. The child felt Horse's gait change,
grow tighter, uneasy.

"Hey, Prince!"

A small, slightly scolding voice: the child knew it, and placed it as soon
as she saw the person sitting by a juniper tree, neatly dressed, wearing an
old black cap.

"Hey, Chickadee!" Horse said, coming round and stopping. The child
had observed, back in Coyote's town, that everybody treated Chickadee
with respect. She didn't see why. Chickadee seemed an ordinary person,
busy and talkative like most of the small birds, nothing like so endear-
ing as Quail or so impressive as Hawk or Great Owl.

"You're going on that way?" Chickadee asked Horse.

"The little one wants to see if her people are living there," Horse said,
surprising the child. Was that what she wanted?

Chickadee looked disapproving, as she often did. She whistled a few
notes thoughtfully, another of her habits, and then got up. "I'll come
along."

"That's great," Horse said, thankfully.

"I'll scout," Chickadee said, and off she went, surprisingly fast, ahead
of them, while Horse took up his steady long lope.

The sour smell was stronger in the air.

Chickadee halted, way ahead of them on a slight rise, and stood still. Horse dropped to a walk, and then stopped. "There," he said in a low voice.

The child stared. In the strange light and slight mist before sunrise she could not see clearly, and when she strained and peered she felt as if her left eye were not seeing at all. "What is it?" she whispered.

"One of the holes. Across the wall—see?"

It did seem there was a line, a straight, jerky line drawn across the sagebrush plain, and on the far side of it—nothing? Was it mist? Something moved there—"It's cattle!" she said. Horse stood silent, uneasy. Chickadee was coming back toward them.

"It's a ranch," the child said. "That's a fence. There's a lot of Herefords." The words tasted like iron, like salt in her mouth. The things she named wavered in her sight and faded, leaving nothing—a hole in the world, a burned place like a cigarette burn. "Go closer!" she urged Horse. "I want to see."

And as if he owed her obedience, he went forward, tense but unquestioning.

Chickadee came up to them. "Nobody around," she said in her small, dry voice, "but there's one of those fast turtle things coming."

Horse nodded, but kept going forward.

Gripping his broad shoulders, the child stared into the blank, and as if Chickadee's words had focused her eyes, she saw again: the scattered whitefaces, a few of them looking up with bluish, rolling eyes—the fences—over the rise a chimneyed house-roof and a high barn—and then in the distance something moving fast, too fast, burning across the ground straight at them at terrible speed. "Run!" she yelled to Horse, "run away! Run!" As if released from bonds he wheeled and ran, flat out, in great reaching strides, away from sunrise, the fiery burning chariot, the smell of acid, iron, death. And Chickadee flew before them like a cinder on the air of dawn.

IV

"HORSE?" COYOTE SAID. "THAT PRICK? CATFOOD!"

Coyote had been there when the child got home to Bide-A-Wee, but she clearly hadn't been worrying about where Gal was, and maybe hadn't even noticed she was gone. She was in a vile mood, and took it all wrong when the child tried to tell her where she had been.

"If you're going to do damn fool things, next time do 'em with me, at least I'm an expert," she said, morose, and slouched out the door. The child saw her squatting down, poking an old, white turd with a stick, trying to get it to answer some question she kept asking it. The turd lay obstinately silent. Later in the day the child saw two coyote men, a young one and a mangy-looking older one, loitering around near the spring, looking over at Bide-A-Wee. She decided it would be a good night to spend somewhere else.

The thought of the crowded rooms of Chipmunk's house was not attractive. It was going to be a warm night again tonight, and moonlit. Maybe she would sleep outside. If she could feel sure some people wouldn't come around, like the Rattler . . . She was standing indecisive halfway through town when a dry voice said, "Hey, Gal."

"Hey, Chickadee."

The trim, black-capped woman was standing on her doorstep shaking out a rug. She kept her house neat, trim like herself. Having come back across the desert with her the child now knew, though she still could not have said, why Chickadee was a respected person.

"I thought maybe I'd sleep out tonight," the child said, tentative.

"Unhealthy," said Chickadee. "What are nests for?"

"Mom's kind of busy," the child said.

"Tsk!" went Chickadee, and snapped the rug with disapproving vigor. "What about your little friend? At least they're decent people."

"Horny-toad? His parents are so shy . . ."

"Well. Come in and have something to eat, anyhow," said Chickadee.

The child helped her cook dinner. She knew now why there were rocks in the mush-pot.

"Chickadee," she said, "I still don't understand, can I ask you? Mom said it depends who's seeing it, but still, I mean if I see you wearing clothes and everything like humans, then how come you cook this way, in baskets, you know, and there aren't any—any of the things like they have—there where we were with Horse this morning?"

"I don't know," Chickadee said. Her voice indoors was quite soft and pleasant. "I guess we do things the way they always were done. When your people and my people lived together, you know. And together with everything else here. The rocks, you know. The plants and everything." She looked at the basket of willowbark, fernroot and pitch, at the blackened rocks that were heating in the fire. "You see how it all goes together . . . ?"

"But you have fire—That's different—"

"Ah!" said Chickadee, impatient, "you people! Do you think you invented the sun?"

She took up the wooden tongs, plopped the heated rocks into the water-filled basket with a terrific hiss and steam and loud bubblings. The child sprinkled in the pounded seeds, and stirred.

Chickadee brought out a basket of fine blackberries. They sat on the newly shaken-out rug, and ate. The child's two-finger scoop technique with mush was now highly refined.

"Maybe I didn't cause the world," Chickadee said, "but I'm a better cook than Coyote."

The child nodded, stuffing.

"I don't know why I made Horse go there," she said, after she had stuffed. "I got just as scared as him when I saw it. But now I feel again like I have to go back there. But I want to stay here. With my, with Coyote. I don't understand."

"When we lived together it was all one place," Chickadee said in her slow, soft home-voice. "But now the others, the new people, they live apart. And their places are so heavy. They weigh down on our place, they press on it, draw it, suck it, eat it, eat holes in it, crowd it out . . . Maybe after a while longer there'll only be one place again, their place. And none of us here. I knew Bison, out over the mountains. I knew Antelope right here. I knew Grizzly and Greywolf, up west there. Gone. All gone. And the salmon you eat at Coyote's house, those are the dream salmon, those are the true food; but in the rivers, how many salmon now? The rivers that were red with them in spring? Who dances, now, when the First Salmon offers himself? Who dances by the river? Oh, you should ask Coyote about all this. She knows more than I do! But she forgets . . . She's hopeless, worse than Raven, she has to piss on every post, she's a terrible housekeeper . . ." Chickadee's voice had sharpened. She whistled a note or two, and said no more.

After a while the child asked very softly, "Who is Grandmother?"

"Grandmother," Chickadee said. She looked at the child, and ate several blackberries thoughtfully. She stroked the rug they sat on.

"If I built the fire on the rug, it would burn a hole in it," she said. "Right? So we build the fire on sand, on dirt . . . Things are woven together. So we call the weaver the Grandmother." She whistled four notes, looking up the smokehole. "After all," she added, "maybe all this place, the other places too, maybe they're all only one side of the weaving. I don't know. I can only look with one eye at a time, how can I tell how deep it goes?"

LYING THAT NIGHT ROLLED UP IN A BLANKET IN CHICKADEE'S back yard, the child heard the wind soughing and storming in the cottonwoods down in the draw, and then slept deeply, weary from the long night before. Just at sunrise she woke. The eastern mountains were a cloudy dark red as if the level light shone through them as through a hand held before the fire. In the tobacco patch—the only farming anybody in this town did was to raise a little wild tobacco—Lizard and Beetle were singing some kind of growing song or blessing song, soft and desultory, huh-huh-huh-huh, huh-huh-huh-huh, and as she lay warm-curled on the ground the song made her feel rooted in the ground, cradled on it and in it, so where her fingers ended and the dirt began she did not know, as if she were dead, but she was wholly alive, she was the earth's life. She got up dancing, left the blanket folded neatly on Chickadee's neat and already empty bed, and danced up the hill to Bide-A-Wee. At the half-open door she sang,

> *"Danced with a gal with a hole in her stocking*
> *And her knees kept a knocking and her toes kept*
> *   a rocking,*
> *Danced with a gal with a hole in her stocking,*
> *Danced by the light of the moon!"*

Coyote emerged, tousled and lurching, and eyed her narrowly. "Sheeeoot," she said. She sucked her teeth and then went to splash water all over her head from the gourd by the door. She shook her head and the water-drops flew. "Let's get out of here," she said. "I have had it. I don't know what got into me. If I'm pregnant again, at my age, oh, shit. Let's get out of town. I need a change of air."

In the foggy dark of the house, the child could see at least two coyote men sprawled snoring away on the bed and floor. Coyote walked over to the old white turd and kicked it. "Why didn't you stop me?" she shouted.

"I *told* you," the turd muttered sulkily.

"Dumb shit," Coyote said. "Come on, Gal. Let's go. Where to?" She didn't wait for an answer. "I know. Come on!"

And she set off through town at that lazy-looking rangy walk that was so hard to keep up with. But the child was full of pep, and came dancing, so that Coyote began dancing too, skipping and pirouetting and fooling around all the way down the long slope to the level plains. There she slanted their way off north-eastward. Horse Butte was at their backs, getting smaller in the distance.

Along near noon the child said, "I didn't bring anything to eat."

"Something will turn up," Coyote said, "sure to." And pretty soon she turned aside, going straight to a tiny grey shack hidden by a couple of half-dead junipers and a stand of rabbit-brush. The place smelled terrible. A sign on the door said: FOX. PRIVATE. NO TRESPASSING!—but Coyote pushed it open, and trotted right back out with half a small smoked salmon. "Nobody home but us chickens," she said, grinning sweetly.

"Isn't that stealing?" the child asked, worried.

"Yes," Coyote answered, trotting on.

They ate the fox-scented salmon by a dried-up creek, slept a while, and went on.

Before long the child smelled the sour burning smell, and stopped. It was as if a huge, heavy hand had begun pushing her chest, pushing her away, and yet at the same time as if she had stepped into a strong current that drew her forward, helpless.

"Hey, getting close!" Coyote said, and stopped to piss by a juniper stump.

"Close to what?"

"Their town. See?" She pointed to a pair of sage-spotted hills. Between them was an area of greyish blank.

"I don't want to go there."

"We won't go all the way in. No way! We'll just get a little closer and look. It's fun," Coyote said, putting her head on one side, coaxing. "They do all these weird things in the air."

The child hung back.

Coyote became business-like, responsible. "We're going to be very careful," she announced. "And look out for big dogs, okay? Little dogs I can handle. Make a good lunch. Big dogs, it goes the other way. Right? Let's go, then."

Seemingly as casual and lounging as ever, but with a tense alertness in the carriage of her head and the yellow glance of her eyes, Coyote led off again, not looking back; and the child followed.

All around them the pressures increased. It was as if the air itself was pressing on them, as if time was going too fast, too hard, not flowing but pounding, pounding, pounding, faster and harder till it buzzed like Rattler's rattle. Hurry, you have to hurry! everything said, there isn't time! everything said. Things rushed past screaming and shuddering. Things turned, flashed, roared, stank, vanished. There was a boy—he came into focus all at once, but not on the ground: he was going along a couple of inches above the ground, moving very fast, bending his legs from side to side in a kind of frenzied swaying dance, and was gone. Twenty children sat in rows in the air all singing shrilly and then the walls closed over them. A basket no a pot no a can, a garbage can, full of salmon smelling wonderful no full of stinking deerhides and rotten cabbage stalks, keep out of it, Coyote! Where was she?

"Mom!" the child called. "Mother!"—standing a moment at the end of an ordinary small-town street near the gas station, and the next moment in a terror of blanknesses, invisible walls, terrible smells and pressures and the overwhelming rush of Time straight forward rolling her helpless as a twig in the race above a waterfall. She clung, held on, trying not to fall—"Mother!"

Coyote was over by the big basket of salmon, approaching it, wary, but out in the open, in the full sunlight, in the full current. And a boy and a man borne by the same current were coming down the long, sage-spotted hill behind the gas station, each with a gun, red hats, hunters, it was killing season. "Hell, will you look at that damn coyote in broad daylight big as my wife's ass," the man said, and cocked aimed shot all as Myra screamed and ran against the enormous drowning torrent. Coyote fled past her yelling, "Get out of here!" She turned and was borne away.

Far out of sight of that place, in a little draw among low hills, they sat and breathed air in searing gasps until after a long time it came easy again.

"Mom, that was *stupid*," the child said furiously.

"Sure was," Coyote said. "But did you see all that food!"

"I'm not hungry," the child said sullenly. "Not till we get all the way away from here."

"But they're your folks," Coyote said. "All yours. Your kith and kin and cousins and kind. Bang! Pow! There's Coyote! Bang! There's my wife's ass! Pow! There's anything—BOOOOM! Blow it away, man! BOOOOOOM!"

"I want to go home," the child said.

"Not yet," said Coyote. "I got to take a shit." She did so, then turned to the fresh turd, leaning over it. "It says I have to stay," she reported, smiling.

"It didn't say anything! I was listening!"

"You know how to understand? You hear everything, Miss Big Ears? Hears all—Sees all with her crummy gummy eye—"

"You have pine-pitch eyes too! You told me so!"

"That's a story," Coyote snarled. "You don't even know a story when you hear one! Look, do what you like, it's a free country. I'm hanging around here tonight. I like the action." She sat down and began patting her hands on the dirt in a soft four-four rhythm and singing under her breath, one of the endless tuneless songs that kept time from running too fast, that wove the roots of trees and bushes and ferns and grass in the web that held the stream in the streambed and the rock in the rock's place and the earth together. And the child lay listening.

"I love you," she said.

Coyote went on singing.

Sun went down the last slope of the west and left a pale green clarity over the desert hills.

Coyote had stopped singing. She sniffed. "Hey," she said. "Dinner."

She got up and moseyed along the little draw. "Yeah," she called back softly. "Come on!"

Stiffly, for the fear-crystals had not yet melted out of her joints, the child got up and went to Coyote. Off to one side along the hill was one of the lines, a fence. She didn't look at it. It was okay. They were outside it.

"Look at that!"

A smoked salmon, a whole chinook, lay on a little cedar-bark mat. "An offering! Well, I'll be darned!" Coyote was so impressed she didn't even swear. "I haven't seen one of these for years! I thought they'd forgotten!"

"Offering to who?"

"Me! Who else? Boy, *look* at that!"

The child looked dubiously at the salmon.

"It smells funny."

"How funny?"

"Like burned."

"It's smoked, stupid! Come on."

"I'm not hungry."

"Okay. It's not your salmon anyhow. It's mine. My offering, for me. Hey, you people! You people over there! Coyote thanks you! Keep it up like this and maybe I'll do some good things for you too!"

"Don't, don't yell, Mom! They're not that far away—"

"They're all my people," said Coyote with a great gesture, and then sat down cross-legged, broke off a big piece of salmon, and ate.

Evening Star burned like a deep, bright pool of water in the clear sky. Down over the twin hills was a dim suffusion of light, like a fog. The child looked away from it, back at the star.

"Oh," Coyote said. "Oh, shit."

"What's wrong?"

"That wasn't so smart, eating that," Coyote said, and then held herself and began to shiver, to scream, to choke—her eyes rolled up, her long arms and legs flew out jerking and dancing, foam spurted out between her clenched teeth. Her body arched tremendously backward, and the child, trying to hold her, was thrown violently off by the spasms of her limbs. The child scrambled back and held the body as it spasmed again, twitched, quivered, went still.

By moonrise Coyote was cold. Till then there had been so much warmth under the tawny coat that the child kept thinking maybe she was alive, maybe if she just kept holding her, keeping her warm, she would recover, she would be all right. She held her close, not looking at the black lips drawn back from the teeth, the white balls of the eyes. But when the cold came through the fur as the presence of death, the child let the slight, stiff corpse lie down on the dirt.

She went nearby and dug a hole in the stony sand of the draw, a shallow pit. Coyote's people did not bury their dead, she knew that. But her people did. She carried the small corpse to the pit, laid it down, and covered it with her blue and white bandanna. It was not large enough; the four stiff paws stuck out. The child heaped the body over with sand and rocks and a scurf of sagebrush and tumbleweed held down with more rocks. She also went to where the salmon had lain on the cedar mat, and finding the carcass of a lamb, heaped dirt and rocks over the poisoned thing. Then she stood up and walked away without looking back.

At the top of the hill she stood and looked across the draw toward the misty glow of the lights of the town lying in the pass between the twin hills.

"I hope you all die in pain," she said aloud. She turned away and walked down into the desert.

V

It was Chickadee who met her, on the second evening, north of Horse Butte.

"I didn't cry," the child said.

"None of us do," said Chickadee. "Come with me this way now. Come into Grandmother's house."

It was underground, but very large, dark and large, and the grandmother was there at the center, at her loom. She was making a rug or blanket of the hills and the black rain and the white rain, weaving in the lightning. As they spoke she wove.

"Hello, Chickadee. Hello, New Person."

"Grandmother," Chickadee greeted her.

The child said, "I'm not one of them."

Grandmother's eyes were small and dim. She smiled and wove. The shuttle thrummed through the warp.

"Old Person, then," said Grandmother. "You'd better go back there now, Granddaughter. That's where you live."

"I lived with Coyote. She's dead. They killed her."

"Oh, don't worry about Coyote!" Grandmother said, with a little huff of laughter. "She gets killed all the time."

The child stood still. She saw the endless weaving.

"Then I—Could I go back home—to her house—?"

"I don't think it would work," Grandmother said. "Do you, Chickadee?"

Chickadee shook her head once, silent.

"It would be dark there now, and empty, and fleas . . . You got outside your people's time, into our place; but I think that Coyote was taking you back, see. Her way. If you go back now, you can still live with them. Isn't your father there?"

The child nodded.

"They've been looking for you."

"They have?"

"Oh, yes, ever since you fell out of the sky. The man was dead, but you weren't there—they kept looking."

"Serves him right. Serves them all right," the child said. She put her hands up over her face and began to cry terribly, without tears.

"Go on, little one, Granddaughter," Spider said. "Don't be afraid. You can live well there. I'll be there too, you know. In your dreams, in your ideas, in dark corners in the basement. Don't kill me, or I'll make it rain . . ."

"I'll come around," Chickadee said. "Make gardens for me."

The child held her breath and clenched her hands until her sobs stopped and let her speak.

"Will I ever see Coyote?"

"I don't know," the Grandmother replied.

The child accepted this. She said, after another silence, "Can I keep my eye?"

"Yes. You can keep your eye."

"Thank you, Grandmother," the child said. She turned away then and started up the night slope toward the next day. Ahead of her in the air of the dawn for a long way a little bird flew, black-capped, light-winged.

HORSE CAMP

ALL THE OTHER SENIORS WERE OVER AT THE STREET SIDE OF the parking lot, but Sal stayed with Norah while they waited for the bus drivers. "Maybe you'll be in the creek cabin," Sal said, quiet and serious. "I had it second year. It's the best one. Number Five."

"How do they, when do you, like find out, what cabin?"

"They better remember we're in the same cabin," Ev said, sounding shrill. Norah did not look at her. She and Ev had planned for months and known for weeks that they were to be cabin-mates, but what good was that if they never found their cabin, and also Sal was not looking at Ev, only at Norah. Sal was cool, a tower of ivory. "They show you around, as soon as you get there," she said, her quiet voice speaking directly to Norah's lastnight dream of never finding the room where she had to take a test she was late for and looking among endless thatched barracks in a forest of thin black trees growing very close together like hair under a handlens. Norah had told no one the dream and now remembered and forgot it. "Then you have dinner, and First Campfire," Sal said. "Kimmy's going to be a counselor again. She's really neat. Listen, you tell old Meredy . . ."

Norah drew breath. In all the histories of Horse Camp which she had asked for and heard over and over for three years—the thunderstorm story,

the horsethief story, the wonderful Stevens Mountain stories—in all of them
Meredy the handler had been, Meredy said, Meredy did, Meredy knew.

"Tell him I said hi," Sal said, with a shadowy smile, looking across the
parking lot at the far, insubstantial towers of downtown. Behind them the
doors of the Junior Girls bus gasped open. One after another the engines
of the four busses roared and spewed. Across the asphalt in the hot morning light small figures were lining up and climbing into the Junior Boys
bus. High, rough, faint voices bawled. "OK, hey, have fun," Sal said. She
hugged Norah and then, keeping a hand on her arm, looked down at her
intently for a moment from the tower of ivory. She turned away. Norah
watched her walk lightfoot and buxom across the black gap to the others
of her kind who enclosed her, greeting her, "Sal! Hey, Sal!"

Ev was twitching and nickering, "Come on, Nor, come on, we'll have
to sit way at the back, come on!" Side by side they pressed into the line
below the gaping doorway of the bus.

IN NUMBER FIVE CABIN FOUR IRON COTS, THIN-MATTRESSED,
grey-blanketed, stood strewn with bottles of insect repellent and styling
mousse, T-shirts lettered UCSD and I ♥ Teddy Bears, a flashlight, an
apple, a comb with hair caught in it, a paperback book open face down:
The Black Colt of Pirate Island. Over the shingle roof huge second-
growth redwoods cast deep shade, and a few feet below the porch the
creek ran out into sunlight over brown stones streaming bright green
weed. Behind the cabin Jim Meredith the horse-handler, a short man
of fifty who had ridden as a jockey in his teens, walked along the well-
beaten path, quick and a bit bowlegged. Meredith's lips were pressed
firmly together. His eyes, narrow and darting, glanced from cabin to
cabin, from side to side. Far through the trees high voices cried.

THE COUNSELORS KNOW WHAT IS TO BE KNOWN. RED GINGER, blonde Kimmy, and beautiful black Sue: they know the vices of Pal, and how to keep Trigger from putting her head down and drinking for ten minutes from every creek. They strike the great shoulders smartly, "Aw, get over, you big lunk!" They know how to swim underwater, how to sing in harmony, how to get seconds, and when a shoe is loose. They know where they are. They know where the rest of Horse Camp is. "Home Creek runs into Little River here," Kimmy says, drawing lines in the soft dust with a redwood twig that breaks. "Senior Girls here, Senior Boys across there, Junior Birdmen about here."—"Who needs 'em?" says Sue, yawning. "Come on, who's going to help me walk the mares?"

THEY WERE ALL AROUND THE CAMPFIRE ON QUARTZ MEADOW after the long first day of the First Overnight. The counselors were still singing, but very soft, so soft you almost couldn't hear them, lying in the sleeping bag listening to One Spot stamp and Trigger snort and the shifting at the pickets, standing in the fine, cool alpine grass listening to the soft voices and the sleepers shifting and later one coyote down the mountain singing all alone.

"NOTHING WRONG WITH YOU. GET UP!" SAID MEREDY, AND slapped her hip. Turning her long, delicate head to him with a deprecating gaze, Philly got to her feet. She stood a moment, shuddering the reddish silk of her flank as if to dislodge flies, tested her left foreleg with caution, and then walked on, step by step. Step by step, watching, Norah went with her. Inside her body there was still a deep trembling. As she passed him, the handler just nodded. "You're all right," he meant. She was all right.

❧

FREEDOM, THE FREEDOM TO RUN, FREEDOM IS TO RUN. FREEDOM
is galloping. What else can it be? Only other ways to run, imitations of
galloping across great highlands with the wind. Oh Philly sweet Philly
my love! If Ev and Trigger couldn't keep up she'd slow down and come
round in a while, after a while, over there, across the long, long field of
grass, once she had learned this by heart and knew it forever, the purity,
the pure joy.

"RIGHT LEG, NOR," SAID MEREDY. AND PASSED ON TO CASS AND
Tammy.
     You have to start with the right fore. Everything else is all right. Free-
dom depends on this, that you start with the right fore, that long leg
well balanced on its elegant pastern, that you set down that tiptoe middle-
fingernail so hard and round, and spurn the dirt. Highstepping, trot past
old Meredy, who always hides his smile.

SHOULDER TO SHOULDER, SHE AND EV, IN THE LONG HEAT OF
afternoon, in a trance of light, across the home creek in the dry wild oats
and cow parsley of the Long Pasture. "I was afraid before I came here,"
thinks Norah, incredulous, remembering childhood. She leans her head
against Ev's firm and silken side. The sting of small flies awakens, the
swish of long tails sends to sleep. Down by the creek in a patch of coarse
grass Philly grazes and dozes. Sue comes striding by, winks wordless,
beautiful as a burning coal, lazy and purposeful, bound for the shade of
the willows. Is it worth getting up to go down to get your feet in the
cool water? Next year Sal will be too old for a camper, but can come
back as a counselor, come back here. Norah will come back a second-year
camper, Sal a counselor. They will be here. This is what freedom is, what
goes on, the sun in summer, the wild grass, coming back each year.

COMING BACK FROM THE LONG PACK TRIP TO STEVENS MOUNTAIN weary and dirty, thirsty and in bliss, coming down from the high places, in line, Sue jogging just in front of her and Ev half asleep behind her, some sound or motion caught and turned Norah's head to look across the alpine field. On the far side under dark firs a line of horses, mounted and with packs—"Look!"

Ev snorted, Sue flicked her ears and stopped. Norah halted in line behind her, stretching her neck to see. She saw her sister going first in the distant line, the small head proudly borne. She was walking lightfoot and easy, fresh, just starting up to the high passes of the mountain. On her back a young man sat erect, his fine, fair head turned a little aside, to the forest. One hand was on his thigh, the other on the reins, guiding her. Norah called out and then broke from the line, going to Sal, calling out to her. "No, no, no, no!" she called. Behind her Ev and then Sue called to her, "Nor! Nor!"

Sal did not hear or heed. Going straight ahead, the color of ivory, distant in the clear, dry light, she stepped into the shadow of the trees. The others and their riders followed, jogging one after the other till the last was gone.

Norah had stopped in the middle of the meadow, and stood in grass in sunlight. Flies hummed.

She tossed her head, turned, and trotted back to the line. She went along it from one to the next, teasing, chivying, Kimmy yelling at her to get back in line, till Sue broke out of line to chase her and she ran, and then Ev began to run, whinnying shrill, and then Cass, and Philly, and all the rest, the whole bunch, cantering first and then running flat out, running wild, racing, heading for Horse Camp and the Long Pasture, for Meredy and the long evening standing in the fenced field, in the sweet dry grass, in the fetlock-shallow water of the home creek.

THE
WATER IS WIDE

"YOU HERE?"

"To see you."

After a while he said, "Where's here?" He was lying flat, so could not have much in view but ceiling and the top third of Anna; in any case his eyes looked unfocussed.

"Hospital."

Another pause. He said something like, "Is it me that's here?" The words were slurred. He added clearly enough, "It's not you. You look all right."

"I am. You're here. And I'm here. To see you."

This made him smile. The smile of an adult lying flat on his back resembles the smile of an infant, in that gravity works with it, not against it.

"Can I be told," he said, "or will the knowledge kill me?"

"If knowledge could kill you, you'd have been dead for years."

"Am I sick?"

"Do you feel well?"

He turned his head away, the first bodily movement he had made. "I feel ill." The words were slurred. "Full of drugs, some kind drugs." The head moved again, restless. "Don't like it," he said. He looked straight at her now. "I don't feel well," he said. "Anna, I'm cold. I feel cold." Tears filled the eyes and ran down from them into the greying hair. This happens in cases of human suffering, when the sufferer is lying face up and is middle-aged.

Anna said his name and took his hand. Her hand was somewhat smaller than his, several degrees warmer, and very similar in structure and texture; even the shape of the nails was similar. She held his hand. He held her hand. After some time his hand began to relax.

"Kind drugs," he said. The eyes were shut now.

He spoke once more; he said either "Wait," or "Weight." Anna answered the first, saying, "I will." Then she thought he had spoken of a weight that lay upon him. She could see the weight in the way he breathed, asleep.

"It's the drugs," she said, "he's asked every time if you could stop giving him the drugs. Could you decrease the dose?"

The doctor said, "Chemotherapy," and other words, some of which were the names of drugs, ending in zil and ine.

"He says that he can't sleep, but he can't wake up either. I think he needs to sleep. And to wake up."

The doctor said many other words. He said them in so rapid, distinct, and fluent a manner, and with such assurance, that Anna believed them all for at least three hours.

"Is this a loony bin?" Gideon inquired with perfect clarity.

"Mhm." Anna knitted.

"Thought wards."

"Oh, it's all private rooms here. It's a nice private sort of place. Rest home. Polite. Expensive."

"Senile, incont . . . incontinent. Can't talk. Anna."

"Mhm?"

"Stroke?"

"No, no." She put her knitting down on her knee. "You got overtired."

"Tumor?"

"No. You're sound as a bell. Only a little cracked. You got tired. You acted funny."

"What'd I do?" he asked, his eyes brightening.

"Made an awful fool of yourself."

"Did?"

"Well, you washed all the blackboards. At the Institute. With soap and water."

"That all?"

"You said it was time to start all over. You made the Dean fetch the soap and buckets." They both jolted softly with laughter at the same time. "Never mind the rest. You had them all quite busy, believe me."

THEY ALL UNDERSTOOD NOW THAT HIS MUCH PUBLICISED NEW Year's Day letter to the *Times,* which he had defended with uncharacteristic vehemence, had been a symptom. This was a relief to many people, who had uncomfortably been thinking of the letter as a moral statement. Looking back, everyone at the Institute could now see that Gideon had not been himself for some months. Indeed the change could be traced back three years, to the death of his wife Dorothea of leukemia. He had borne his loss well, of course, but had he not remained somewhat withdrawn—increasingly withdrawn? Only no one had noticed it, because he had been so busy. He had ceased to take vacations at the family cabin up at the lake, and had done a good deal of public speaking in connection with the peace organisation of which he was co-chairman. He had been working much too hard. It was all clear now. Unfortunately it had not become clear until the evening in April when he began a public lecture on the Question of Ethics in Science by gazing at the audience in silence for 35 seconds (approx.: one of the mathematical philosophers present in the audience had begun to time the silence at the point when it became painful, though not yet unendurable), and then, in a slow, soft, rough voice which no one who heard it could forget, announced, "The quantification of Death is now the major problem facing theoretical physicists in the latter half of the Western Hemisphere." He had then closed his mouth and stood gazing at them.

Hansen, who had introduced his talk and sat on the speakers' platform, was a large man and a quick-witted one. He had without much trouble induced Gideon to come backstage with him, to one of the seminar rooms. It was there that Gideon had insisted that they wash all the blackboards perfectly clean. He had not become violent, though his behavior had been what Hansen termed "extraordinarily wilful." Later on, in private, Hansen wondered whether Gideon's behavior had not always been wilful, in that it had always been self-directed, and whether he should not have used, instead, the word "irrational." That would have been the expectable word. But its expectability led him to wonder if Gideon's behavior (as a theoretical physicist) had ever been rational; and, in fact, if his own behavior (as a theoretical physicist, or otherwise) had ever been adequately describable by the term "rational." He said nothing, however, of these speculations, and worked very hard for several weekends at building a rock garden at the side of his house.

Though he offered no violence to others or himself, Gideon had attempted escape. At a certain moment he appeared to understand suddenly that medical aid had been summoned. He acted with decision. He told the Dean, Dr. Hansen, Dr. Mehta, and the student Mr. Chew, all of whom were with him (several other members of the audience or of the Institute were busy keeping busybodies and reporters out), "You finish the blackboards in here, I'll do Room 40," and taking up a bucket and a sponge went rapidly across the hall into a vacant classroom, where

Chew and Hansen, following him at once, prevented him from opening a window. The room was on the ground floor, and his intention
was made clear by his saying, "Let me get out, please, help me get out."
Chew and Hansen were compelled to restrain his arms by force. He
struggled briefly to free himself; failing, he became silent and apparently
thoughtful. Shortly before the medical personnel arrived he suggested
in a low voice to Chew, "If we sat down on the floor here they might not
see us." When the medical personnel entered the room and came close
to him he said loudly, "All right, have it your way," and at once began to
yell wordlessly, or scream. The graduate student Chew, a brilliant young
biophysicist who had not had much experience of human suffering, let
go of his arm and broke into tears. The medical personnel, having had
perhaps excessive experience of human suffering, promptly administered
a quick-acting sedative or tranquilliser by hypodermic. Within 35 seconds
(approx.) the patient fell silent and became tractable, accepting the straitjacket without resistance, and with only a slight expression (facial, not
verbal) of bewilderment, or, possibly, curiosity.

"I HAVE TO GET OUT OF HERE."
    "Oh, Gid, not yet, you need to rest. It's a decent place. They've eased
up on the drugs. I can see the difference."
    "I have to get out, Anna."
    "You're not well yet."
    "I am not a patient. I am impatient. Help me get out. Please."
    "Why, Gid? What for?"
    "They won't let me go where I have to go."
    "Where do you have to go?"
    "Mad."

Dear Lin,

They continue to let me visit Gideon every afternoon from five to six, because I am his only relative, the widower's widowed sister, and I just sort of barge in. I don't think the doctor approves of my visits, I think he thinks I leave the patient disturbed, but he hasn't the authority to keep me out, I guess, until Gideon is committed. I guess he doesn't really have any authority, in a private rest home like this, but he makes me feel guilty. I never did understand when to obey people. He is supposed to be the best man here for nervous breakdowns. He has been disapproving lately and says Gideon is deteriorating, ceasing to respond, but all he gives him to respond to is drugs. What is he supposed to say to them? He hasn't eaten for four days. He responds to me, when nobody else is there, or anyhow he talks, and I respond. He asked me about you kids yesterday. I told him about Kate's divorce. It made him sad. "Everybody is divorcing everybody else," he said. I was sad, too, and I said, "Well, we didn't. You and Dorothea, me and Louis. Death us did part. Which is preferable, I wonder?" He said, "It comes out much the same. Fission, fusion. The human race is one great Nuclear Family." I wondered if the doctor would think that's the way an insane person talks. Maybe he would think that's the way two insane people talk.

Later on Gideon told me what the weight is. It is all the people who are dying. A lot of them are children, little, hollow, empty children. Some of them are old people, very light, hollow, old men and women. They don't weigh much separately, but there are so many of them. The old people lie across his legs. The children are in a great heap on his chest, across his breastbone. It makes it hard for him to breathe.

Today he only asked me to help him get out and go where he has to go. When he speaks of that he cries. I always hated for him to cry when we were children, it made me cry, too, even when I was thirteen or fourteen. He only cried for real griefs. The doctor says that what he has is an acute depression, and it should be cured with chemicals. But Gideon

is not depressed. I think what he has is grief. Why can't he be allowed
to grieve? Would it destroy the rest of us, his grief? It's the people who
don't grieve who are destroying us, it seems to me.

"HERE'S YOUR CLOTHES. YOU'LL HAVE TO GET UP AND GET DRESSED,
Gideon. If you want to come away with me. I didn't get permission. I
just can't get through to that doctor, he wants to cure you. If you want
to go, you'll have to get up and walk."

"Shall I take up my bed?"

"Don't be silly."

"Bible."

"For God's sake don't go religious now. If you do I'll bring you right
back here. Hurry up. Here's your pants."

"Please get off me just for a minute," he said to the dying children and
old men and women.

"Oof, how thin you are. Let me button that. All right. Can you manage?
Hang on. No! hang onto me. You haven't been eating, you're dizzy."

"Dizzy Giddy."

"Do shut up! Try to look ordinary."

"We are ordinary."

They walked out of the room and down the hall arm in arm, an
ordinary middle-aged couple. They walked past the old woman in the
wheelchair nursing her doll, and past the room of the young man who
stared. They walked past the receptionist's desk. Anna smiled and
said in a peculiar voice at the receptionist, "Going out for a walk in
the garden." The receptionist smiled and said, "Lovely weather." They
walked out onto the brick front path of the rest home, and down it,
between lawns, to the iron gate. They walked through the gate and
turned left. Anna's car was parked halfway down the block, under
elm trees.

"Oh, oh, if I have a heart attack it's all your fault. Wait. I'm so shaky I can't get the key in. You all right?"

"Sure. Where are we going?"

"To the lake."

"HE WENT OUT WITH HIS SISTER, DOCTOR. FOR A WALK. ABOUT half an hour ago."

"A walk, my God," the doctor said. "Where to?"

I AM ANNA. I AM GIDEON. I AM GIDEANNA. I AM SISTER'S BROTHER, brother's sister. I am Gideon who am dying, but it is your death I die, not mine. I am Anna who am not mad, but I am your brother, who is mad. Take my hand, brother, from the dark! Reich' mir das Hand, mein Leben, komm' in mein Schloss mit mir. O, but that castle I do not want to enter, brother mine; that is the castle I do not want to enter. It has a dark tower. Who do you think I am, Childe Roland? A Roland to your Oliver? No, look, we know this place, this is the old place, where we were children. Let's dance here, on the lakeshore, by the water. You be the tower, I will be the lake. You will dance in me reflected, I will be full of you, of the wave-broken shimmering stones. Lie lightly on me, tower, brother, see, if you lie lightly we are one. But we have always been one, sisterbrother. We have always danced alone. I am Gideon who dances in your soul, and I am dying. I can't dance any longer. I am borne down, borne down, borne down. I cannot lie, I cannot dance. All the reflections are dissolved. I cannot dance. I cannot breathe. They lie on me, they lie in me. How can the starving be so heavy, Anna?

Gideon, is it our fault? It can't be your fault. You never harmed a living soul.

But I am the fault, you know, the fault in my soul and yours, the fault itself. The line on which the ground moves. So the earthquake comes, and the people die, the little puzzled children, and the young men with guns, and the women pausing shopping bag in hand in the dissolving supermarket, and the old people who crouch down and reach out with wrinkled fingers to the faltering earth. I have betrayed them all. I did not give them enough food to eat.

How could you have? You're not God!

Oh yes I am. We are.

We are?

Yes, we are. Indeed we are. If I weren't God how should I be dying now? God is what dies. God is bereavement. We all die for each other.

If I am God I am the Woman-God, and I shall be reborn. Out of my own body I shall bear my birth.

Surely you will, but only if I die; and I am you. Or do you deny me, at the grave's edge, after fifty years?

No, no, no. I don't deny you, though I've often wanted to. But that's not a grave's edge, my young darkness, my terror, my little brother soul. It's only a lakeshore, see?

There is no other shore.

There must be.

No; all seas have one shore only. How could they have more?

Well, there's only one way to find out.

I'M COLD. IT'S COLD, THE WATER'S COLD.

Look: there they are. So many of them, so many. The children float because they're hollow, swollen up with air. The older people swim, for a while. Look how that old man holds a clod of earth in his hand, the piece of the world he held to when the earthquake came. A little island, not quite big enough. Look how she holds her baby up above the water. I must help her, I must go to her!

If I touch one, they will take hold of me. They will clutch me with the grip of the drowning and drag me down with them. I'm not that good a swimmer. If I touch them, I'll drown.

Look there, I know that face. Isn't that Hansen? He's holding onto a rock, poor soul, a plank would serve him better.

There's Kate. There's Kate's ex-husband. And there's Lin. Lin's a good swimmer, always was, I'm not worried about Lin. But Kate's in trouble. She needs help. Kate! Don't wear yourself out, honey, don't kick so hard. The water's very wide. Save your strength, swim slowly, sweetheart, Kate my child!

There's young Chew. And look there, there's the doctor, in right over his head. And the receptionist. And the old woman with the doll. But there are so many more, so many. If I reach out my hand to one, a hundred will reach for it, a thousand, a thousand million, and pull me down and drown me. I can't save one child, one single child. I can't save myself.

Then let it be so. Take my hand, child! stranger in the darkness, in the deep waters, take my hand. Swim with me, while we can. Let us be drowned together, for it's certain we shall not be saved alone.

It's silent, out here in the deep waters. I can't see the faces any more.

DOROTHEA, THERE'S SOMEONE FOLLOWING US. DON'T LOOK BACK.

I'm not Lot's wife, Louis, I'm Gideon's wife. I can look back, and still not turn to salt. Besides, my blood was never salt enough. It's you who shouldn't look back.

Do you take me for Orpheus? I was a good pianist, but not that good. But I admit, it scares me to look back. I don't really want to.

I just did. There's two of them. A woman and a man.

I was afraid of that.

Do you think it's them?

Who else would follow us?

Yes, it's them, our husband and our wife. Go back! Go back! This is no place for you!

This is the place for everyone, Dorothea.

Yes, but not yet, not yet. O Gideon, go back! He doesn't hear me. I can't speak clearly any more. Louis, you call to them.

Go back! Don't follow us! They can't hear us, Dorothea. Look how they come, as if the sand were water. Don't they know there's no water here?

I don't know what they know, Louis. I have forgotten. Gideon, O Gideon, take my hand!

Anna, take my hand!

Can they hear us? Can they touch us?

I don't know. I have forgotten.

IT'S COLD, I'M COLD. IT'S TOO DEEP, TOO FAR TO GO. I HAVE reached out my hand, and reached out my hand into the darkness, but I couldn't tell what good it did; if I held up some child for a while, or if some shadow hand reached back to me, I don't know. I can't tell the way. Back on the dry land they were right. They told me not to grieve. They told me not to look. They told me to forget. They told me eat my lunch and take my pills that end in zil and ine. And they were right. They told me to be quiet, not to shout, not to cry out aloud. Be quiet now, be good. And they were right. What's the good in shouting? What's the good in shouting Help me, help, I'm drowning! when all the rest of them are drowning too? I heard them crying Help me, help me, please. But now I hear nothing. I hear the sound of the deep waters only. O take my hand, my love, I'm cold, cold, cold.

> *The water is wide, I cannot get over,*
> *And neither have I wings to fly.*

Give me a boat that will carry two,
And both shall row, my love and I.

There is, oh, there is another shore! Look at the light, the light of morning on the rocks, the light on the shores of morning. I am light. The weight's gone. I am light.

But it is the same shore, Gideanna.

Then we have come home. We rowed all night in darkness, in the cold, and we came home: the home where we have never been before, the home we never left. Take my hand, and step ashore with me, my sister life, my brother death. Look: it is the beginning place. Here we begin, here by the flood that parts us.

THE
LOST CHILDREN

HE LIFTED THE SILVER PIPE TO HIS LIPS AND PLAYED. IN HIS patchwork jacket and multistripe pants and two-tone shoes, he walked the city streets piping a tune. What tune? They turned and listened, passersby, businessmen, shoppers, secretaries, smokers, tourists, bag ladies, beggars. As the piper went past they cocked their heads, straining their ears, with an inward look in their eyes. Did they hear the tune? Yes—No—? Some of them followed him a little way, trying to hear what he was playing on his pipe. A bag lady shook her shopping cart in rage and shouted obscenities after him. A Japanese visitor ran to get ahead of him to take his photograph, but lost him in the crowds. A lawyer fell into step beside him, trying to hear the sound of the pipe, which surely was very high and sweet; but he could catch only the faintest sound on the very edge of hearing, and he turned off at Broadway. Three boys ran shoving and yelling past the piper through the crowds, their canvas and plastic shoes gaudier than his jacket. A woman coming out of a clothing store stopped, her back stooped, her lips parted, and gazed after him. Her little daughter tugged at her hand, impatient. "Mama, I want to go home, let's go to the bus stop, mama!" Inside the mother, inside each of the women and the men he passed, a child jumped up crying in a high voice, "I hear it! I hear it! Listen!" But she could not hear, and her daughter paid no attention, did not listen, tugged at her hand, and she followed, obedient. Children shot past running or on skateboards or rollerblades. Men and women strolled or hurried on, turned to their business with a shrug or a comment about street musicians, continued their conversation about municipal bonds, the football game, the price of halibut, the trial, the election, the breakdown. Some of the men, some of the women felt a little flutter of the breath, a kind of gasp or a slight pang at the breastbone, and others felt nothing at all, when the child inside them broke out, broke free, and ran invisibly after the piper, inaudibly crying, "Wait! Wait for me!" as the gaudy, nimble figure passed on through the throngs, threading the traffic at the crossings, always playing his silver pipe. Among the crowds these escaped children passed quick and slight as dust motes or wisps of steam, more and more of them, a cloud, a comet-tail of immaterial children following the piper, skipping, capering, dancing to the tune he played, dancing right out of the city, through the suburbs, across the superhighways, till they came at last to the malls and the fast food strip. Did the piper go on past the malls towards the hidden country or did he slip away from the children among the endless aisles of the vast, windowless buildings? Did the children catch up to him or did they lose him, distracted by the signs and the goods, the toy stores, the candy stores? They dispersed quite suddenly, all the escaped children, wandering off into the shops and theaters and arcades to enter into electronic games, jumping and shooting and destroying one another in puffs of sparks, to enter into videos of isneyland and whizneyland and busineyland, running through towers and castles of smiling machinery and tunnels and orbits of machinery screaming. There the lost children are. When they are hungry they feed on the sweet greasy smoke from the grills where hamburger meat is fried forever, while the loudspeakers forever play the piper's tune.

TEXTS

MESSAGES CAME, JOHANNA THOUGHT, USUALLY YEARS TOO LATE, or years before one could crack their code or had even learned the language they were in. Yet they came increasingly often and were so urgent, so compelling in their demand that she read them, that she do something, as to force her at last to take refuge from them. She rented, for the month of January, a little house with no telephone in a seaside town that had no mail delivery. She had stayed in Klatsand several times in summer; winter, as she had hoped, was even quieter than summer. A whole day would go by without her hearing or speaking a word. She did not buy the paper or turn on the television, and the one morning she thought she ought to find some news on the radio she got a program in Finnish from Astoria. But the messages still came. Words were everywhere.

Literate clothing was no real problem. She remembered the first print dress she had ever seen, years ago, a genuine *print* dress with typography involved in the design—green on white, suitcases and hibiscus and the names *Riviera* and *Capri* and *Paris* occurring rather blobbily from shoulder seam to hem, sometimes right side up, sometimes upside down. Then it had been, as the saleswoman said, very unusual. Now it was hard to find a T-shirt that did not urge political action, or quote lengthily from a dead physicist, or at least mention the town it was for sale in. All this she had coped with, she had even worn.

But too many things were becoming legible.

She had noticed in earlier years that the lines of foam left by waves on the sand after stormy weather lay sometimes in curves that looked like handwriting, cursive lines broken by spaces, as if in words; but it was not until she had been alone for over a fortnight and had walked many times down to Wreck Point and back that she found she could read the writing. It was a mild day, nearly windless, so that she did not have to march briskly but could mosey along between the foam-lines and the water's edge where the sand reflected the sky. Every now and then a quiet winter breaker driving up and up the beach would drive her and a few gulls ahead of it onto the drier sand; then as the wave receded she and the gulls would follow it back. There was not another soul on the long beach. The sand lay as firm and even as a pad of pale brown paper, and on it a recent wave at its high mark had left a complicated series of curves and bits of foam. The ribbons and loops and lengths of white looked so much like handwriting in chalk that she stopped, the way she would stop, half willingly, to read what people scratched in the sand in summer. Usually it was "Jason + Karen" or paired initials in a heart; once, mysteriously and memorably, three initials and the dates 1973–1984, the only such inscription that spoke of a promise not made but broken. Whatever those eleven years had been, the length of a marriage? a child's life? they were gone, and the letters and numbers also were gone when she came back by where they had been, with the tide rising. She had wondered then if the person who wrote them, had written them to be erased. But these foam words lying on the brown sand now had been written by the erasing sea itself. If she could read them they might tell her a wisdom a good deal deeper and bitterer than she could possibly swallow. Do I want to know what the sea writes? she thought, but at the same time she was already reading the foam, which though in vaguely cuneiform blobs rather than letters of any alphabet was perfectly legible as she walked along beside it. "Yes," it read, "esse hes hetu tokye to' ossusess ekyes. Seham hute' u." (When she wrote it down later she used the apostrophe to represent a kind of stop or click like the last sound in "Yep!") As she read it over, backing up some yards to do so, it continued to say the same thing, so she walked up and down it several times and memorized it. Presently, as bubbles burst and the blobs began to shrink, it changed here and there to read, "Yes, e hes etu kye to' ossusess kye. ham te u." She felt that this was not significant change but mere loss, and kept the original text in mind. The water of the foam sank into the sand and the bubbles dried away till the marks and lines lessened into a faint lacework of dots and scraps, half legible. It looked enough like delicate bits of fancywork that she wondered if one could also read lace or crochet.

When she got home she wrote down the foam words so that she would not have to keep repeating them to remember them, and then she looked at the machine-made Quaker lace tablecloth on the little round dining table. It was not hard to read but was, as one might expect, rather dull. She made out the first line inside the border as "pith wot pith wot pith wot" interminably, with a "dub" every thirty stitches where the border pattern interrupted.

But the lace collar she had picked up at a secondhand clothing store in Portland was a different matter entirely. It was handmade, handwritten. The script was small and very even. Like the Spencerian hand she had been taught fifty years ago in the first grade, it was ornate but surprisingly easy to read. "My soul must go," was the border, repeated many times, "my soul must go, my soul must go," and the fragile webs leading inward read, "sister, sister, sister, light the light." And she did not know what she was to do, or how she was to do it.

SLEEPWALKERS

John Felburne

I TOLD THE MAID NOT TO COME TO CLEAN THE CABIN BEFORE four o'clock, when I go running. I explained that I'm a night person and write late and sleep in, mornings. Somehow it came out that I'm writing a play. She said, "A stage play?" I said yes, and she said, "I saw one of those once." What a wonderful line. It was some high school production, it turned out some musical. I told her mine was a rather different kind of play, but she didn't ask about it. And actually there would be no way to explain to that sort of woman what I write about. Her life experience is so incredibly limited. Living out here, cleaning rooms, going home and watching TV—*Jeopardy!* probably. I thought of trying to put her in my characters notebook and got as far as "Ava: the Maid," and then there was nothing to write. It would be like trying to describe a glass of water. She's what people who say "nice" mean when they say, "She's nice." She'd be completely impossible in a play, because she never does or says anything but what everybody else does and says. She talks in clichés. She *is* a cliché. Forty or so, middle-sized, heavy around the hips, pale, not very good complexion, blondish—half the white women in America look like that. Pressed out of a mold, made with a cookie cutter. I run for an hour, hour and a half, while she's cleaning the cabin, and I was thinking, she'd never do anything like running, probably doesn't do any exercise at all. People like that don't take any control over their lives. People like her in a town like this live a mass-produced existence, stereotypes, getting their ideas from the TV. Sleepwalkers. That would make a good title, *Sleepwalkers.* But how could you write meaningfully about a person who's totally predictable? Even the sex would be boring.

There's a woman in the creekside cabin this week. When I jog down to the beach, afternoons, she watches me. I asked Ava about her. She said she's Mrs. McAn, comes every summer for a month. Ava said, "She's very nice," of course. McAn has rather good legs. But old.

Katharine McAn

IF I HAD AN AIR GUN I COULD HIDE ON MY DECK AND POP THAT young man one on the buttock when he comes pumping past in his little purple stretchies. He eyes me.

I saw Virginia Herne in Hambleton's today. Told her the place was turning into a goddamn writers colony, with her collecting all these Pulitzers or whatever they are, and that young man in the shingled cabin sitting at his computer till four in the morning. It's so quiet at the Hideaway that I can hear the thing clicking and peeping all night. "Maybe he's a very diligent accountant," Virginia said. "Not in shiny purple stretch shorts," I said. She said, "Oh, that's John" Somebody, "yes, he's had a play produced, in the East somewhere, he told me." I said, "What's he doing here, sitting at your feet?" and she said, "No, he told me he needed to escape the pressures of culture, so he's spending a summer in the West." Virginia looks very well. She has that dark, sidelong flash in her eye. A dangerous woman, mild as milk. "How's Ava?" she asked. Ava housesat her place up on Breton Head last summer when she and Jaye were traveling, and she takes an interest in her, though she doesn't know the story Ava told me. I said Ava was doing all right.

I think she is, in fact. She still walks carefully, though. Maybe that's what Virginia saw. Ava walks like a tai ji walker, like a woman on a high wire. One foot directly in front of the other, and never any sudden movements.

I had tea ready when she knocked, my first morning here. We sat at the table in the kitchen nook, just like the other summers, and talked. Mostly about Jason. He's in tenth grade now, plays baseball, skateboards, surfboards, crazy to get one of those windsail things and go up to Hood River—"Guess the ocean isn't enough for him," Ava said. Her voice is without color, speaking of him. My guess is that the boy is like his father, physically at least, and that troubles or repels her, though she clings to him loyally, cleaves to him. And there might be a jealousy of him as the survivor: *Why you, and not her?* I don't know what Jason knows or feels about all that. The little I've seen of him when he comes by here, he seems a sweet boy, caught up in these sports boys spend themselves on, I suppose because at least they involve doing something well.

Ava and I always have to re-agree on what work she's to do when I'm here. She claims if she doesn't vacuum twice a week and take out the trash, Mr. Shoto will "get after" her. I doubt he would, but it's her job and her conscience. So she's to do that, and look in every day or so to see if I need anything. Or to have a cup of tea with me. She likes Earl Grey.

Ken Shoto

SHE'S RELIABLE. I TOLD DEB AT BREAKFAST, YOU DON'T KNOW how lucky we are. The Brinnesis have to hire anything they can pick up, high school girls that don't know how to make a bed and won't learn, ethnics that can't talk the language and move on just when you've got them trained. After all, who wants a job cleaning motel rooms? Only somebody who hasn't enough education or self-respect to find something better. Ava wouldn't have kept at it if I treated her the way the Brinnesis treat their maids, either. I knew right away we were in luck with this one. She knows how to clean and she'll work for a dollar over minimum wage. So why shouldn't I treat her like one of us? After four years? If she wants to clean one cabin at seven in the morning and another one at four in the afternoon, that's her business. She works it out with the customers. I don't interfere. I don't push her. "Get off Ava's case, Deb," I told her this morning. "She's reliable, she's honest, and she's permanent— she's got that boy in the high school here. What more do you want? I tell you, she takes half the load off my back!"

"I suppose you think *I* ought to be running after her supervising her," Deb says. God, she can drive me crazy sometimes. What did she say that for? I wasn't blaming her for anything.

"She doesn't need supervising," I said.

"So you think," Deb said.

"Well, what's she done wrong?"

"Done? Oh, nothing. She couldn't do anything wrong!"

I don't know why she has to talk like that. She couldn't be jealous, not of Ava, my God. Ava's all right looking, got all her parts, but hell, she doesn't let you see her that way. Some women just don't. They just don't give the signals. I can't even think about thinking about her that way. Can't Deb see that? So what the hell does she have against Ava? I always thought she liked her OK.

"She's sneaky," is all she'd say. "Creepy."

I told her, "Aw, come on, Deb. She's quiet. Maybe not extra bright. I don't know. She isn't talkative. Some people aren't."

"I'd like to have a woman around who could say more than two words. Stuck in the woods out here."

"Seems like you spend all day in town anyhow," I said, not meaning it to be a criticism. It's just the fact. And why shouldn't she? I didn't take on this place to work my wife to death, or tie her down to it. I manage it and keep it up, and Ava Evans cleans the cabins, and Deb's free to do just what she wants to do. That's how I meant it to be. But it's like it's not enough, or she doesn't believe it, or something. "Well," she said, "if *I* had any responsibility, I wonder if you'd find *me* reliable." It is terrible how she cuts herself down. I wish I knew how to stop her from cutting herself down.

Deb Shoto

IT'S THE DEMON THAT SPEAKS. KEN DOESN'T KNOW HOW IT got into me. How can I tell him? If I tell him, it will kill me from inside.

But it knows that woman, Ava. She looks so mild and quiet, *yes Mrs. Shoto, sure Mrs. Shoto,* pussyfooting it around here with her buckets and mops and brooms and wastebaskets. She's hiding. I know when a woman is hiding. The demon knows it. It found me. It'll find her.

There isn't any use trying to get away. I have thought I ought to tell her that. Once they put the demon inside you, it never goes away. It's instead of being pregnant.

She has that son, so it must have happened to her later, it must have been her husband.

I wouldn't have married Ken if I'd known it was in me. But it only began speaking last year. When I had the cysts and the doctor thought they were cancer. Then I knew they had been put inside me. Then when they weren't cancerous, and Ken was so happy, it began moving inside me where they had been, and then it began saying things to me, and now it says things in my voice. Ken knows it's there, but he doesn't know how it got there. Ken knows so much, he knows how to live, he lives for me, he is my life. But I can't talk to him. I can't say anything before it comes into my mouth just like my own tongue and says things. And what it says hurts Ken. But I don't know what to do. So he leaves, with his heavy walk and his mouth pulled down, and goes to his work. He works all the time, but he's getting fat. He shouldn't eat so much cholesterol. But he says he always has. I don't know what to do.

I need to talk to somebody. It doesn't talk to women, so I can. I wish I could talk to Mrs. McAn. But she's snobbish. College people are snobbish. She talks so quick, and her eyebrows move. Nobody like that would understand. She'd think I was crazy. I'm not crazy. There is a demon in me. I didn't put it there.

I could talk to the girl in the A-frame cabin. But she is so young. And they drive away every day in their pickup truck. And they are college people, too.

There is a woman comes into Hambleton's, a grandmother. Mrs. Inman. She looks kind. I wish I could talk to her.

Linsey Hartz

THE PEOPLE HERE IN HANNAH'S HIDEAWAY ARE SO WEIRD, I can't believe them. The Shotos. Wow. He's really sweet, but he goes around this place all day digging in the little channel he's cut from the creek to run through the grounds, a sort of toy creek, and weeding, and pruning, and raking, and the other afternoon when we came home he was picking up spruce needles off the path, like a housewife would pick threads off a carpet. And there's the little bridges over the little toy creek, and the rocks along the edges of the little paths between the cabins. He rearranges the rocks every day. Getting them lined up even, getting the sizes matched.

Mrs. Shoto watches him out her kitchen window. Or she gets in her car and drives one quarter mile into town and shops for five hours and comes back with a quart of milk. With her tight, sour mouth closed. She hates to smile. Smiling is a big production for her, she works hard at it, probably has to rest for an hour afterwards.

Then there's Mrs. McAn, who comes every summer and knows everybody and goes to bed at nine p.m. and gets up at five a.m. and does Chinese exercises on her porch and meditates on her roof. She gets onto the roof from the roof of her deck. She gets onto the roof of the deck from the window of the cabin.

And then there's Mr. Preppie, who goes to bed at five a.m. and gets up at three p.m. and doesn't mingle with the aborigines. He communicates only with his computer, and his modems, no doubt, and probably he has a fax in there. He runs on the beach every day at four, when the most people are on the beach, so that they can all see his purple spandex and his muscley legs and his hundred-and-forty-dollar running shoes.

And then there's me and George going off every day to secretly map where the Forest Service and the lumber companies are secretly cutting old growth stands illegally in the Coast Range so that we can write an article about it that nobody will publish even secretly.

Three obsessive-compulsives, one egomaniac, and two paranoids.

The only normal person at Hannah's Hideaway is the maid, Ava. She just comes and says "Hi," and "Do you need towels?" and she vacuums while we're out logger-stalking, and generally acts like a regular human being. I asked her if she was from around here. She said she'd lived here several years. Her son's in the high school. "It's a nice town," she said. There's something very clear about her face, something pure and innocent, like water. This is the kind of person we paranoids would be saving the forests for, if we were. Anyhow, thank goodness there are still some people who aren't totally fucked up.

Katharine McAn

I asked Ava if she thought she'd stay on here at the
Hideaway.

She said she guessed so.

"You could get a better job," I said.

"Yeah, I guess so," she said.

"Pleasanter work."

"Mr. Shoto is a really nice man."

"But Mrs. Shoto—"

"She's all right," Ava said earnestly. "She can be hard on him sometimes,
but she never takes it out on me. I think she's a really nice person, but—"

"But?"

She made a slow, dignified gesture with her open hand: I don't know,
who knows, it's not her fault, we're all in the same boat. "I get on OK with
her," she said.

"You get on OK with anybody. You could get a better job, Ava."

"I got no skills, Mrs. McAn. I was brought up to be a wife. Where I
lived in Utah, women are wifes." She pronounced it with the f, wifes. "So
I know how to do this kind of job, cleaning and stuff. Anyhow."

I felt I had been disrespectful of her work. "I guess I just wish you
could get better pay," I said.

"I'm going to ask Mr. Shoto for a raise at Thanksgiving," she said, her
eyes bright. Obviously it was a long-thought-out plan. "He'll give it to
me." Her smile is brief, never lingering on her mouth.

"Do you want Jason to go on to college?"

"If he wants to," she said vaguely. The idea troubled her. She winced
away from it. Any idea of leaving Klatsand, of even Jason's going out
into a larger world, scares her, probably will always scare her.

"There's no danger, Ava," I said very gently. It is painful to me to see her
fear, and I always try to avoid pain. I want her to realize that she is free.

"I know," she said with a quick, deep breath, and again the wincing movement.

"Nobody's after you. They never were. It was a suicide. You showed me the clipping."

"I burned that," she said.

LOCAL MAN SHOOTS, KILLS DAUGHTER, SELF

She had showed the newspaper clipping to me summer before last. I could see it in my mind's eye with extreme clarity.

"It was the most natural thing in the world for you to move away. It wasn't 'suspicious.' You don't have to hide, Ava. There's nothing to hide from."

"I know," she said.

She believes I know what I'm talking about. She accepts what I say, she believes me, as well as she can. And I believe her. All she told me I accepted as the truth. How do I know it's true? Simply on her word, and a newspaper clipping that might have been nothing but the seed of a fantasy? Certainly I have never known any truth in my life like it.

Weeding the vegetable garden behind their house in Indo, Utah, she heard a shot, and came in the back door and through the kitchen to the front room. Her husband was sitting in his armchair. Their twelve-year-old daughter Dawn was lying on the rug in front of the TV set. Ava stood in the doorway and asked a question, she doesn't remember what she asked, "What happened?" or "What's wrong?" Her husband said, "I punished her. She has polluted me." Ava went to her daughter and saw that she was naked and that her head had been beaten in and that she had been shot in the chest. The shotgun was on the coffee table. She picked it up. The stock was slimy. "I guess I was afraid of him," she said to me. "I don't know why I picked it up. Then he said, 'Put that down.' And I backed off towards the front door with it, and he got up. I cocked it, but he came towards me. I shot him. He fell down forwards, practically onto me. I put the gun down on the floor near his head, just inside the door. I went out and went down the road. I knew Jason would be coming home from baseball practice and I wanted to keep him out of the house. I met him on the road, and we went to Mrs.—" She halted herself, as if her neighbor's name must not be spoken—"to a neighbor's house, and they called the police and the ambulance." She recited the story quietly. "They all thought it was a murder and suicide. I didn't say anything."

"Of course not," I murmured, dry of tongue.

"I did shoot him," she said, looking up at me, as if to make certain that I understood. I nodded.

She never told me his name, or their married name. Evans was her middle name, she said.

Immediately after the double funeral, she asked a neighbor to drive her and Jason to the nearest town where there was an Amtrak station. She had taken all the cash her husband had kept buried in the cellar under their stockpile of supplies in case of nuclear war or a Communist takeover. She bought two coach seats on the next train west. It went to Portland. At first sight she knew Portland was "too big," she said. There was a Coast Counties bus waiting at the Greyhound station down the street from the train station. She asked the driver, "Where does this bus go?" and he named off the little coast towns on his loop. "I picked the one that sounded fartherest," she said.

She and ten-year-old Jason arrived in Klatsand as the summer evening was growing dark. The White Gull Motel was full, and Mrs. Brinnesi sent her to Hannah's Hideaway.

"Mrs. Shoto was nice," Ava said. "She didn't say anything about us coming in on foot or anything. It was dark when we got here. I couldn't believe it was a motel. I couldn't see anything but the trees, like a forest. She just said, 'Well, that young man looks worn out,' and she put us in the A-frame, it was the only one empty. She helped me with the rollabed for Jason. She was really nice." She wanted to linger on these details of finding haven. "And next morning I went to the office and asked if they knew anyplace where I could find work, and Mr. Shoto said they needed a full-time maid. It was like they were waiting for me," she said in her earnest way, looking up at me.

Don't question the Providence that offers shelter. Was it also Providence that put the gun in her hand? Or in his?

She and Jason have a little apartment, an add-on to the Hanningers' house on Clark Street. I imagine that she keeps a photograph of her daughter Dawn in her room. A framed five-by-seven school picture, a smiling seventh-grader. Maybe not. I should not imagine anything about Ava Evans. This is not ground for imagination. I should not imagine the child's corpse on the rug between the coffee table and the TV set. I should not have to imagine it. Ava should not have to remember it. Why do I want her to get a better job, nicer work, higher wages—what am I talking about? The pursuit of happiness?

"I have to go clean Mr. Felburne's cabin," she said. "The tea was delicious."

"Now? But you're off at three, aren't you?"

"Oh, he keeps funny hours. He asked me not to come and clean till after four."

"So you have to wait around here an hour? The nerve!" I said. Indignation, the great middle-class luxury. "So he can go *running?* I'd tell him to go jump in the creek!" Would I? If I was the maid?

She thanked me again for the tea. "I really enjoy talking with you," she said. And she went down the neatly raked path that winds between the cabins, among the dark old spruce trees, walking carefully, one foot in front of the other. No sudden movements.

HAND, CUP, SHELL

THE LAST HOUSE ON SEAROAD STOOD IN THE FIELD BEHIND THE dunes. Its windows looked north to Breton Head, south to Wreck Rock, east to the marshes, and from the second story, across the dunes and the breakers, west to China. The house was empty more than it was full, but it was never silent.

The family arrived and dispersed. Having come to be together over the weekend, they fled one another without hesitation, one to the garden, one to the kitchen, one to the bookshelf, two north up the beach, one south to the rocks.

Thriving on salt and sand and storms, the rosebushes behind the house climbed all over the paling fence and shot up long autumn sprays, disheveled and magnificent. Roses may do best if you don't do anything for them at all except keep the sword fern and ivy from strangling them; bronze Peace grows wild as well as any wild rose. But the ivy, now. Loathsome stuff. Poisonous berries. Crawling out from hiding everywhere, stuffed full of horrors: spiders, centipedes, millipedes, billipedes, snakes, rats, broken glass, rusty knives, dog turds, dolls' eyes. I must cut the ivy right back to the fence, Rita thought, pulling up a long stem that led her back into the leafy mass to a parent vine as thick as a garden hose. I must come here oftener, and keep the ivy off the spruce trees. Look at that, it'll have the tree dead in another year. She tugged. The cable of ivy gave no more than a steel hawser would. She went back up the porch steps, calling, "Are there any pruning shears, do you think?"

"Hanging on the wall there, aren't they?" Mag called back from the kitchen. "Anyway, they ought to be." There ought to be flour in the canister, too, but it was empty. Either she had used it up in August and forgotten, or Phil and the boys had made pancakes when they were over last month. So where was the list pad to write *flour* on for when she walked up to Hambleton's? Nowhere to be found. She would have to buy a little pad to write *pad* on. She found a ballpoint pen in the things drawer. It was green and translucent, imprinted with the words HANK'S COAST HARDWARE AND AUTO SUPPLIES. She wrote *flour, bans, o.j., cereal, yog, list pad* on a paper towel, wiping blobs of excess green ink off the pen-point with a corner of the towel. Everything is circular, or anyhow spiral. It was no time at all, certainly not twelve months, since last October in this kitchen, and she was absolutely standing in her tracks. It wasn't *déjà vu* but *déjà vécu*, and all the Octobers before it, and still all the same this was now, and therefore different feet were standing in her tracks. A half size larger than last year, for one thing. Would they go on breaking down and spreading out forever, until she ended up wearing men's size 12 logging boots? Mother's feet hadn't done that. She'd always worn 7N, still wore 7N, always would wear 7N, but then she always wore the same kind of shoes, too, trim inch-heel pumps or penny loafers, never experimenting with Germanic clogs, Japanese athletics, or the latest toe-killer fad. It came of having had to dress a certain way, of course, as the Dean's wife, but also of being Daddy's girl, small-town princess, not experimenting just knowing.

"I'm going on down to Hambleton's, do you want anything?" Mag called out the kitchen door through the back-porch screen to her mother fighting ivy in the garden.

"I don't think so. Are you going to walk?"

"Yes."

They were right: it took a certain effort to say *yes* just flatly, to refrain from qualifying it, softening it: *Yes, I think so; Yes, I guess so; Yes I thought I would.* . . . Unqualified *yes* had a gruff sound to it, full of testosterone. If Rita had said *no* instead of *I don't think so*, it would have sounded rude or distressed, and she probably would have responded in some way to find out what was wrong, why her mother wasn't speaking in the mother tongue. "Going to Hambleton's," she said to Phil, who was kneeling at the bookcase in the dark little hall, and went out. She went down the four wooden steps of the front porch and through the front gate, latched the gate behind her, and turned right on Searoad to walk into town. These familiar movements gave her great pleasure. She walked on the dune side of the road, and between dunes saw the ocean, the breakers that took all speech away. She walked in silence, seeing glimpses between dune grass of the beach where her children had gone.

Gret had gone as far as the beach went. It ended in a tumble of rusty brown basalt under Wreck Point, but she knew the ways up through the rocks to the slopes and ledges of the Point, places where nobody came. Sitting there on the wind-bitten grass looking out over the waves bashing on Wreck Rock and the reef Dad called Rickrack and out to the horizon, you could keep going farther still. At least you ought to be able to, but there wasn't any way to be alone any more. There was a beer can in the grass, a tag of orange plastic ribbon tied to a stake up near the summit, a Coast Guard helicopter yammering and prying over the sea up to Breton Head and back south again. Nobody wanted anybody to be alone, ever. You had to do away with that, unmake it, all the junk, trash, crap, trivia, David, the midterms, Gran, what people thought, other people. You had to go away from them. All the way away. It used to be easy to do that, easy to go and hard to come back, but now it was harder and harder to go: and she never could go all the way. To sit up here and stare at the ocean and be thinking about stupid David, and what's that stake for, and why did Gran look at my fingernails that way, what's wrong with me? Am I going to be this way the rest of my life? Not even seeing the ocean? Seeing stupid beer cans? She stood, raging, backed up, aimed, and kicked the beer can in a low, fast arc off the cliff into the sea unseen below. She turned and scrambled up to the summit, braced her knees in soggy bracken, and wrenched the orange-ribboned stake out of the ground. She hurled it southward and saw it fall into bracken and salal scrub and be swallowed. She stood up, rubbing her hands where the raw wood had scraped the skin. The wind felt cold on her teeth. She had been baring them, an angry ape. The sea lay grey at eye level, taking her immediately now into its horizontality. Nothing cluttered. As she sucked the heel of her thumb and got her front teeth warm, she thought, My soul is ten thousand miles wide and extremely invisibly deep. It is the same size as the sea, it is bigger than the sea, it *holds* the sea, and you cannot, you cannot cram it into beer cans and fingernails and stake it out in lots and own it. It will drown you all and never even notice.

But how old I am, thought the grandmother, to come to the beach and not look at the sea! How horrible! Straight out into the backyard, as if all that mattered was grubbing ivy. As if the sea belonged to the children. To assert her right to the ocean, she carried ivy cuttings to the trash bin beside the house and after cramming them into the bin stood and looked at the dunes, across which it was. It wasn't going to go away, as Amory would have said. But she went on out the garden gate, crossed sandy-rutted Searoad, and in ten more steps saw the Pacific open out between the grass-crowned dunes. There you are, you old grey monster. You aren't going to go away, but I am. Her brown loafers, a bit loose on her bony feet, were already full of sand. Did she want to go on down, onto the beach? It was always so windy. As she hesitated, looking about, she saw a head bobbing along between the crests of dune grass. Mag coming back with the groceries. Slow black bobbing head like the old mule coming up the rise to the sagebrush ranch when? old Bill the mule—Mag the mule, trudging obstinate silent. She went down to the road and stood first on one foot then the other emptying sand out of her shoes, then walked to meet her daughter. "How are things at Hambleton's?"

"Peart," Mag said. "Right peart. When is whatsername coming?"

"By noon, I think she said." Rita sighed. "I got up at five. I think I'm going to go in and have a little lie-down before she comes. I hope she won't stay hours."

"Who is she, again?"

"Oh . . . damn . . ."

"I mean, what's she doing?"

Rita gave up the vain search for the lost name. "She's some sort of assistant research assistant I suppose to whatsisname at the University, you know, doing the book about Amory. I expect somebody suggested to him that maybe it would look odd if he did a whole biography without talking to the widow, but of course it's really only Amory's ideas that interest him, I believe he's very theoretical the way they are now. Probably bored stiff at the idea of actual *people*. So he's sending the young lady into the hencoop."

"So that you don't sue him."

"Oh you don't think so."

"Certainly. Co-optation. And you'll get thanked for your invaluable assistance, in the acknowledgments, just before he thanks his wife and his typist."

"What was that terrible thing you told me about Mrs. Tolstoy?"

"Copied *War and Peace* for him six times by hand. But you know, it would beat copying most books six times by hand."

"Shepard."

"What?"

"Her. The girl. Something Shepard."

"Whose invaluable assistance Professor Whozis gratefully . . . no, she's only a grad student, isn't she. Lucky if she gets mentioned at all. What a safety net they have, don't they? All the women the knots in the net."

But that cut a bit close to the bones of Amory Inman, and his widow did not answer his daughter as she helped her put away the flour, cornflakes, yogurt, cookies, bananas, grapes, lettuce, avocado, tomatoes, and vinegar Mag had bought (she had forgotten to buy a list pad). "Well, I'm off, shout when she comes," Rita said, and made her way past her son-in-law, who was sitting on the hall floor by the bookcase, to the stairs.

The upstairs of the house was simple, rational, and white: the stairs landing and a bathroom down the middle, a bedroom in each corner. Mag and Phil SW, Gran NW, Gret NE, boys SE. The old folks got the sunset, the kids got dawn. Rita was the first to listen and hear the sea in the house. She looked out over the dunes and saw the tide coming in and the wind combing the manes of the white horses. She lay down and looked with pleasure at the narrow, white-painted boards of the ceiling in the sea-light like no other light. She did not want to go to sleep but her eyes were tired and she had not brought a book upstairs. She heard the girl's voice below, the girls' voices, piercing soft, the sound of the sea.

"Where's Gran?"

"Upstairs."

"This woman's come."

Mag brought the dish towel on which she was drying her hands into the front room, a signal flag: I work in the kitchen and have nothing to do with interviews. Gret had left the girl standing out on the front deck. "Won't you come in?"

"Susan Shepard."

"Mag Rilow. That's Greta. Gret, go up and tell Gran, OK?"

"It's so lovely here! What a beautiful place!"

"Maybe you'd like to sit out on the deck to talk? It's so mild. Would you like some coffee? Beer, anything?"

"Oh, yes—coffee—"

"Tea?"

"That would be wonderful."

"Herbal?" Everybody there at the University in the Klamath Time Warp drank herbal tea. Sure enough, chamomile-peppermint would be wonderful. Mag got her sitting in the wicker chair on the deck and came back in past Phil, who was still on the floor in the hall by the bookcase, reading. "Take it into the *light,*" she said, and he said, "Yeah, I will," smiling, and turned a page. Gret, coming down the stairs, said, "She'll be down in a minute."

"Go talk to the girl. She's at the U."

"What in?"

"I don't know. Find out."

Gret snarled and turned away. Edging past her father in the narrow hall, she said, "Why don't you get some *light?*" He smiled, turned a page, and said, "Yeah, I will." She strode out onto the deck and said, "My mother says you're at the U," at the same time as the woman said, "You're at the U, aren't you?"

Gret nodded.

"I'm in Ed. I'm Professor Nabe's research assistant for his book. It's really exciting to be interviewing your grandmother."

"It seems fairly weird to me," Gret said.

"The University?"

"No."

There was a little silence filled by the sound of the sea.

"Are you a freshman?"

"Freshwoman." She edged towards the steps.

"Will you major in Education, do you think?"

"Oh, God, no."

"I suppose having such a distinguished grandfather, people always just expect. Your mother's an educator, too, isn't she?"

"She teaches," Gret said. She had got as far as the steps and now went down them, because they were the shortest way to get away, though she had been coming into the house to go to her room when Sue Student drove up and she got caught.

Gran appeared in the open doorway, looking wary and rather bleary, but using her politically correct smile and voice: "Hello! I'm Rita Inman." While Sue Student was jumping up and being really excited, Gret got back up the steps, past Gran, and into the house.

Daddy was still sitting on the floor in the dark hall by the bookcase, reading. She unplugged the gooseneck lamp from the end table by the living-room couch, set it on the bookcase in the hall, and found the outlet was too far for the cord to reach. She brought the lamp as close to him as she could, setting it on the floor about three feet from him, and then plugged in the plug. The light glared across the pages of his book. "Oh, hey, great," he said, smiling, and turned a page. She went on upstairs to her room. Walls and ceiling were white, the bedspreads on the two narrow beds were blue. A picture of blue mountains she had painted in ninth-grade art class was pinned to the closet door, and she reconfirmed with a long look at it that it was beautiful. It was the only good picture she had ever painted, and she marveled at it, the gift that had given itself to her, undeserved, no strings attached. She opened the backpack she had dumped on one bed, got out a geology textbook and a high-lighter, lay down on the other bed, and began to reread for the midterm examination. At the end of a section on subduction, she turned her head to look at the picture of blue mountains again, and thought, I wonder what would it be like?—or those are the words she might have used to express the feelings of curiosity, pleasure, and awe which accompanied the images in her mind of small figures scattered among great lava cliffs on the field trip in September, of journeys, of levels stretching to the horizon, high deserts under which lay fossils folded like tissue paper; of moraines; of long veins of ore and crystals in the darkness underground. Intent and careful, she turned the page and started the next section.

Sue Shepard fussed with her little computer thing. Her face was plump, pink, round-eyed, and Rita had to make the interpretation "intellectual" consciously. It would not arise of itself from the pink face, the high voice, the girlish manner, as it would from the pink face, high voice, and boyish manner of a male counterpart. She knew that she still so identified mind and masculinity that only women who imitated men were immediately recognizable to her as intellectuals, even after all these years, even after Mag. Also, Sue Shepard might be disguising her intellect, as Mag didn't. And the jargon of the Education Department was a pretty good disguise in itself. But she was keen, it was a keen mind, and perhaps Professor Whozis didn't like to be reminded of it, so young, so bright, so close behind. Probably he liked flutter and butter, as Amory used to call it, in his graduate-student women. But fluttery buttery little Sue had already set aside a whole sheaf of the professor's questions as time-wasting, and was asking, intently and apparently on her own hook, about Rita's girl-hood.

"Well, when I was born we lived on a ranch out from Prineville, in the high country. The sagebrush, you know. But I don't remember much that's useful. I think Father must have been keeping books for the ranch. It was a big operation—huge—all the way to the John Day River, I think. When I was nine, he took over managing a mill in Ultimate, in the Coast Range. A lumber mill. Nothing left of all that now. There isn't even a gravel road in to Ultimate any more. Half the state's like that, you know. It's very strange. Easterners come and think it's this wild pristine wilderness and actually it's all Indian graveyards underfoot and old homesteads and second growth and towns nobody even remembers were there. It's just that the trees and the weeds grow back so fast. Like ivy. Where are you from?"

"Seattle," said Sue Shepard, friendly, but not to be misled as to who was
interviewing whom.

"Well, I'm glad. I seem to have more and more trouble talking with
Easterners."

Sue Shepard laughed, probably not understanding, and pursued; "So
you went to school in Ultimate?"

"Yes, until high school. Then I came to live with Aunt Josie in Portland
and went to old Lincoln High. The nearest high school to Ultimate was
thirty miles on logging roads, and anyhow it wasn't good enough for
Father. He was afraid I'd grow up to be a roughneck, or marry one. . . ."
Sue Shepard clicketed on her little machine, and Rita thought, But what
did Mother think? Did she want to send me away at age thirteen to live
in the city with her sister-in-law? The question opened on a blank area
that she gazed into, fascinated. I know what Father wanted, but why
don't I know what she wanted? Did she cry? No, of course not. Did I? I
don't think so. I can't even remember talking about it with Mother. We
made my clothes that summer. That's when she taught me how to cut out
a pattern. And then we came up to Portland the first time, and stayed
at the old Multnomah Hotel, and we bought shoes for me for school—
and the oyster silk ones for dressing up, the little undercut heel and one
strap, I wish they still made them. I was already wearing Mother's size.
And we ate lunch in that restaurant, the cut-glass water goblets, the two
of us, where was Father? But I never even wondered what she thought,
I never knew. I never know what Mag really thinks, either. They don't
say. Rocks. Look at Mag's mouth, just like Mother's, like a seam in a
rock. Why did Mag go into teaching, talk, talk, talk all day, when she
really hates talking? Although she never was quite as gruff as Gret is, but
that's because Amory wouldn't have stood for it. But why didn't Mother
and I say anything to each other? She was so stoical. Rock. And then I
was happy in Portland, and there she was in Ultimate. . . . "Oh, yes, I
loved it," she answered Sue Shepard. "The twenties were a nice time to

be a teenager, we really were very spoiled, not like now, poor things. It's terribly hard to be thirteen or fourteen now, isn't it? We went to dancing school, they've got AIDS and the atomic bomb. My granddaughter's twice as old as I was at eighteen. In some ways. She's amazingly young for her age in others. It's so complicated. After all, think of Juliet! It's never *really* simple, is it? But I think I had a very nice, innocent time in high school, and right on into college. Until the crash. The mill closed in '32, my second year. But actually we went right on having a good time. But it was terribly depressing for my parents and my brothers. The mill shut right down, and they all came up to Portland looking for work, everybody did. And then I left school after my junior year, because I'd got a summer job bookkeeping in the University accounting office, and they wanted me to stay on, and so I did, since everybody else in the family was out of work, except Mother finally got a job in a bakery, nights. It was terrible for men, the Depression, you know. It killed my father. He looked and looked for work and couldn't find anything, and there I was, doing what he was qualified to do, only of course at a very low level, and terrible pay—sixty dollars a month, can you imagine?"

"A week?"

"No, a month. But still, I was making it. And men of his generation were brought up to be depended on, which is a wonderful thing, but then they weren't allowed ever *not* to be depended on, when they had to depend on other people, which everybody actually does. It was terribly unrealistic, I think, a real whatdyoucallit. Double time?"

"Double bind," said young Sue, sharp as tacks, clicketing almost inaudibly away on her little lap computer, while the tape recorder tape went silently round and round, recording Rita's every maunder and meander. Rita sighed. "I'm sure that's why he died so young," she said. "He was only fifty."

But Mother hadn't died young, though her husband had, and her elder son had drifted off to Texas to be swallowed alive so far as his mother was concerned by a jealous wife, and her younger son had poured whiskey onto diabetes and died at thirty-one. Men did seem to be so fragile. But what had kept Margaret Jamison Holz going? Her independence? But she had been brought up to be dependent, hadn't she? Anyhow, nobody could keep going long on mere independence; when they tried to they ended up pushing shopping carts full of stuff and sleeping in doorways. Mother hadn't done that. She had sat here on the deck looking out at the dunes, a small, tough, old woman. No retirement pension, of course, and a tiny little dribble of insurance money, and she did let Amory pay the rent on her two-room apartment in Portland, but she was independent to the end, visiting them only once or twice a year at the University, and then always for a full month here, in summer. Gret's room now had been Mother's room then. How strange it was, how it changed! But recently Rita had wakened in the deep night or when it was just beginning to get light and had lain there in bed thinking, not with fear but with a kind of frightened, lively thrill, It is so strange, all of it is so *strange*!

"When were you able to go back to college?" Sue Shepard asked, and she answered, "In '35," resolving to stick to the point and stop babbling.

"And then you met Dr. Inman when you took his class."

"No. I never took a class in Education."

"Oh," Sue Shepard said, blank.

"I met him in the accounting office. I was still clerking there halftime, paying my way. And he came in because he hadn't been paid his salary for three months. People used to be just as good at mistakes like that as computers are now. It took days and days to find out how they'd managed to lose him from the faculty payroll. Did he tell somebody that I'd taken his class and that's how we met?" Sue Shepard wasn't going to admit it; she was discreet. "How funny. It was one of the other women he went out with, and he got his memories crossed. Students were always falling in love with him. He was *extremely* attractive—I used to think Charles Boyer without the French accent—"

Mag heard them laughing on the front deck as she came through the hall, edging around her husband. A gooseneck lamp standing on the floor near him glared in his eyes, but he was holding his book so that its pages were in shadow.

"Phil."

"Mm."

"Get up and go read in the living room."

He smiled, reading. "Found this . . ."

"The interviewer's here. She'll be staying for lunch. You're in the way. You've been in the way for two hours. You're in the dark. There's daylight six feet away. Get up and go read in the living room."

"People . . ."

"Nobody's there! People come through *here*. Are you—" The wave of hatred and compassion set free by her words carried her on past him, though she had checked the words. In silence, she turned the corner and climbed the stairs. She went into the southwest bedroom and looked for a decent shirt in the crowded closet; the cotton sweater she had worn from Portland was too warm for this mild coastal weather. The search led her into a rummage-out of summer clothes. She sorted, rehung, folded her clothes, then Phil's. From the depths she pulled out paint-stiff, knee-frayed blue jeans, a madras shirt with four buttons gone which had been stuffed into the closet unwashed. Even here at the beach house, her father's clothes had always been clean, smelled clean, smelled of virtue, *virtú*. With a violent swing she threw the madras shirt at the wastebasket. It draped itself half in, half out, a short sleeve sticking up pitifully. Not waving but drowning . . . But to go on drowning for twenty-five years?

The window was ajar, and she could hear the sea and her mother's voice down on the front deck answering questions about her husband the eminent educator, the clean-bodied man: How had he written his books? When had he broken with John Dewey's theories? Where had the UNICEF work taken him? Now, little apple-cheeked handmaiden of success, ask me about my husband the eminent odd-job man: how did he quit halfway through graduate school, when had he broken with the drywalling contractor, where had his graveyard shift at the Copy Shop taken him? Phil the Failure, he called himself, with the charming honesty that concealed a hideous smugness that probably but not certainly concealed despair. What was certain was that nobody else in the world knew the depth of Phil's contempt for them, his absolute lack of admiration or sympathy for anything anybody did or was. If that indifference was originally a defense, it had consumed what it had once defended. He was invulnerable, by now. And people were so careful not to hurt him. Finding that she was Dr. Rilow and he was an unemployed drywaller, they assumed it was hard for him; and then when they found that it wasn't, they admired him for being so secure, so unmacho, taking it so easily, handling it so well. Indeed he handled it well, cherished it, his dear failure, his great success at doing what he wanted to do and nothing else. No wonder he was so sweet, so serene, so unstrained. No wonder she had blown up, teaching *Bleak House* last week, at the mooncalf student who couldn't see what was supposed to be wrong with Harold Skimpole. "Don't you see that his behavior is totally irresponsible?" she had demanded in righteous wrath, and the mooncalf had replied with aplomb, "I don't see why *everybody* is supposed to be responsible." It was a kind of Taoist koan, actually. For Taoist wives. It was hard to be married to a man who lived in a perpetual condition of *wu wei* and not to end up totally *wei*, you had to be very careful or you ended up washing the ten thousand shirts.

But then of course Mother had looked after Father's shirts.

The jeans weren't even good for rags, even if they would sell in the Soviet Union for a hundred dollars; she threw them after the shirt, and knocked the wastebasket over. Faintly ashamed, she retrieved them and the shirt and stuffed them into a plastic bag that had been squirreled away in a cranny of the closet. An advantage of Phil's indifference was that he would never come downstairs demanding to know where his wonderful old jeans and madras shirt were. He never got attached to clothes; he wore whatever was provided. "Distrust all occasions that require new clothes." What a prig Thoreau was. Ten to one he meant weddings but hadn't had the guts to say so, let alone get married. Actually Phil liked new clothes, liked to get them for Christmas and birthdays, accepted all presents, cherished none. "Phil is a saint, Mag," his mother had said to her shortly before they were married, and she had agreed, laughing, thinking the exaggeration quite forgivable; but it had not been a burble of mother love. It had been a warning.

She knew that her father had hoped that the marriage wouldn't last. He had never quite said so. By now the matter of her marriage, between her and her mother, was buried miles deep. Between her and her daughter it was an unaskable question. Everybody protecting everybody. It was stupid. It kept her and Gret from saying much to each other. And it wasn't really the right question, the one that needed asking, anyhow. They were married. But there was a question. No one had asked it and she did not know what it was. Possibly, if she found out, her life would change. The headless torso of Apollo would speak: *Du musst dein Leben ändern*. Meanwhile, did she particularly want her life to change? "I will never desert Mr. Micawber," she said under her breath, reaching into yet another cranny of the closet and discovering there yet another plastic bag, which when opened disclosed rust-colored knitted wool: a sweater, which she stared at dumbly till she recognized it as one she had bought on sale for Gret for Christmas several years ago and had utterly forgotten ever since. "Gret! Look here!" she cried, crossing the hall, knocking, opening the door of her daughter's room. "Merry Christmas!"

After explanations, Gret pulled the sweater on. Her dark, thin face emerged from the beautiful color with a serious expression. She looked at the sweater seriously in the mirror. She was very hard to please, preferred to buy her own clothes, and wore the ones she liked till they fell apart. She kept them moderately clean. "Are the sleeves kind of short, a little?" she asked, in the mother tongue.

"Kind of. Probably why it was on sale. It was incredibly cheap, I remember, at the Sheep Tree. Years ago. I liked the color."

"It's neat," Gret said, still judging. She pushed up the sleeves. "Thanks," she said. Her face was a little flushed. She smiled and glanced around at the book lying open on the bed. Something was unsaid, almost said. She did not know how to say it and Mag did not know how to allow her to say it; they both had trouble with their native language. Awkward, intrusive, the mother retreated, saying, "Lunch about one-thirty."

"Need help?"

"Not really. Picnic on the deck. With the interviewer."

"When's she leaving?"

"Before dinner, I hope. It's a good color on you." She went out, closing the door behind her, as she had been taught to do.

Gret took off the orange sweater. It was too hot for the mild day, and she wasn't sure she liked it yet. It would take a while. It would have to sit around a while till she got used to it, and then she would know. She thought she liked it; it felt like she'd worn it before. She put it into a drawer so her mother wouldn't get hurt. Last year when her mother had come into her room at home and stared around, Gret had suddenly realized that the stare wasn't one of disapproval but of pain. Disorder, dirt, disrespect for objects caused her pain, like being shoved or hit. It must be hard for her, living, in general. Knowing that, Gret tried to put stuff away; but it didn't make much difference. She was mostly at college now. Mother went on nagging and ordering and enduring, and Daddy and the boys didn't let it worry them. Just like some goddamn sitcom. Everything about families and people was exactly like some goddamn sitcom. Waiting for David to call, just like a soap opera. Everything the same as it was for everybody else, the same things happening over and over and over, all petty and trivial and stupid, and you couldn't ever get free. It clung to you, held on, pinioned you. Like the dream she used to have of the room with wallpaper that caught and stuck to you, the Velcro dream. She reopened the textbook and read about the nature of gabbro, the origins of slate.

The boys came back from the beach just in time for lunch. They always did. Still. Just as when her milk would spurt and the baby in the next room cried at the exact same moment. Their clomping in to go to the bathroom finally got Phil off the hall floor. He carried out platters to the table on the front porch and talked with whatsername the interviewer, who got quite pink and pleased. Phil looked so thin and short and hairy and vague and middle-aged that they never expected it till whammy! right between the eyes. Wooed and won. Go it, Phil. She looked like an intelligent girl, actually, overserious, and Phil wouldn't hurt her. Wouldn't hurt a fly, would old Phil. St. Philip, bestower of sexual favors. She smiled at them and said, "Come and get it."

Sue Student was being nice to Daddy, talking with him about forest fires or something. Daddy had his little company smile and was being nice to Sue Student. She didn't sound too stupid, actually. She was a vegetarian. "So is Gret," Gran said. "What is it about the U these days? They used to live on raw elk." Why did she always have to disapprove of everything Gret did? She never said stuff like that about the boys. They were scarfing up salami. Mother watched them all loading their plates and making their sandwiches with that brooding hawk expression. Filling her niche. That was the trouble with biology, it was the sitcom. All niches. Mother provides. Better the dark slate levels, the basalt plains. Anything could happen, there.

She was worn out. She went for the wine bottle; food later. She must get by herself for a while, that bit of a nap in the morning hadn't helped. Such a long, long morning, with the drive over from Portland. And talking about old times was a most terrible thing to do. All the lost things, lost chances, all the dead people. The town with no road to it any more. She had had to say ten times, "He's dead now," "No, she's dead." What a strange thing to say, after all! You couldn't *be* dead. You couldn't *be* anything but alive. If you weren't alive, you weren't—you had been. You shouldn't have to say "He's dead now," as if it was just some other way of being, but "He isn't now," or "He was." Keep the past in the past tense. And the present in the present, where it belongs. Because you didn't live on in others, as people said. You changed them, yes. She was entirely different because Amory had lived. But he didn't live on in her, in her memory, or in his books, or anywhere. He had gone. He was gone. Maybe "passed away" wasn't such a whatdyoucallit, after all. At least it was in the passed tense, the past tense, not the present. He had come to her and she had come to him and they had made each other's life what it had been, and then he had gone. Passed away. It wasn't a euphemism, that's what it wasn't. Her mother . . . There was a pause in her thoughts. She drank the wine. Her mother was different, how? She came back to the rock. Of course she was dead, but it did not seem that she had passed away, the way he had. She went back to the table, refilled her glass with the red wine, laid salami, cheese, and green onions on brown bread.

She was beautiful now. In the tight, short, ugly fashions of the sixties, when Mag had first looked at her from any distance and with any judgment, she had looked too big, and for a while after Amory's death and when she had the bone marrow thing she had been gaunt, but now she was extraordinary: the line of the cheek, the long, soft lips, the long-lidded eyes with their fine wrinkle-pleating. What had she said about raw elk? The interviewer hadn't heard and wouldn't understand if she had heard, wouldn't know that she had just been told what Mrs. Amory Inman thought of the institution of which her husband had been the luminary, what indeed she thought, in her increasing aloofness, her oldwomanhood, of most human institutions. Poor little whatsername, trapped in the works and dark machinations of that toughest survivor of the Middle Ages, the university, ground in the mills of assistantships, grants, competitions, examinations, dissertations, all set up to separate the men from the boys and both from the rest of the world, she wouldn't have time for years yet to look up, to look out, to learn that there were such bare, airy places as the place where Rita Inman lived.

"Yes, it is nice, isn't it? We bought it in '55, when things over here were still pretty cheap. We haven't even asked you indoors, how terrible! After lunch you must look round the house. I think I'm going to have a little lie-down, after lunch. Or perhaps you'd like to go down on the beach then—the children will take you walking as far as you'd like, if you like. Mag, Sue says she needs an hour or two more with me. She hasn't asked all . . ." a pause, "the professor's questions yet. I'm afraid I kept wandering off the subject." How sternly beautiful Mag was, her rock-seam mouth, her dark-waterfall hair going silver. Managing everything, as usual, seeing to everything, the good lunch. No, definitely her mother was not dead in the same way Father was dead, or Amory, or Clyde, or Polly, or Jim and Jean; there was something different there. She really must get by herself and think about it.

"Geology." The word came out. Spoken. Mother's ears went up like a cat's, eyebrows flickering, eyes and mouth impassive. Daddy acted like he'd known her decision all along, maybe he had, he couldn't have. Sue Student had to keep asking who was in the Geo department and what you did with geology. She only knew a couple of the professors' names and felt stupid not knowing more. She said, "Oh, you get hired by oil companies, mining companies, all kinds of land-rape companies. Find uranium under Indian reservations." Oh, shut up. Sue Student meant well. Everybody meant well. It spoiled everything. Softened everything. "The grizzled old prospector limps in from twenty years alone in the desert, swearing at her mule," Daddy said, and she laughed, it was funny, Daddy was funny, but she was for a moment, a flash, afraid of him. He was so quick. He knew that this was something important, and did he mean well? He loved her, he liked her, he was like her, but when she wasn't like him did he like it? Mother was saying how geology had been all cut-and-dried when she was in college and how it was all changed now by these new theories. "Plate tectonics isn't exactly new," oh, shut up, shut up. Mother meant well. Sue Student and Mother talked about academic careers in science and got interested comparing, colleaguing. Sue was at the U but she was younger and only a grad student; Mother was only at a community college but she was older and had a Ph.D. from Berkeley. And Daddy was out of it. And Gran half asleep, and Tom and Sam cleaning up the platters. She said, "It's funny. I was thinking. All of us—the family, I mean—nobody will ever know any of us ever existed. Except for Granddaddy. He's the only real one."

Sue gazed mildly. Daddy nodded in approval. Mother stared, the hawk at bay. Gran said in a curious, distant tone, "Oh I don't think so at all." Tom was throwing bread to a seagull, but Sam, finishing the salami, said, in his mother's voice, "Fame is the spur!" At that, the hawk blinked and stooped to the prey: "Whatever do you mean, Gret? Reality is being a dean of the School of Education?"

"He was important. He has a biography. None of us will."

"Thank goodness," Gran said, getting up. "I do hope you don't mind, if I have just a bit of a lie-down now I'll be much brighter later, I hope."

Everybody moved.

"Boys. You do the dishes. Tom!"

He came. They obeyed. She felt a tremendous, a ridiculous surge, as warm and irresistible as tears or milk, of pride—in them, in herself. They were lovely. Lovely boys. Grumbling, coltish, oafish, gangling, redhanded, they unloaded the table with efficiency and speed, Sam insulting Tom steadily in his half-broken voice, Tom replying on two sweet notes at intervals like a thrush, "Ass-sole. . . . Ass-sole. . . ."

"Who's for a walk on the beach?"

Mag was, the interviewer was, Phil was, Gret surprisingly was.

They crossed Searoad and went single file between the dunes. Down
on the beach she looked back to see the front windows and the roof
above the dune grass, always remembering the pure delight of seeing
it so the first time, the first time ever. To Gret and the boys the beach
house was coeval with existence, but to her it was connected with joy.
When she was a child they had stayed in other people's beach houses,
places in Gearhart and Neskowin, summerhouses of deans and provosts
and the rich people who clung to university administrators under the
impression that they were intellectuals; or else, as she got older, Dean
Inman had taken her and her mother along to his ever more exotic con-
ferences, to Botswana, Brasilia, Bangkok, until she had rebelled at last.
"But they are interesting *places*," her mother had said, deprecating, "you
really don't enjoy going?" And she had howled, "I'm sick of feeling like
a white giraffe, why can't I ever stay home where people are the same
size?" And at some indefinite but not long interval after that, they had
driven over to look at this house. "What do you think?" her father had
asked, standing in the small living room, a smiling sixty-year-old public
man, kindly rhetorical. There was no need to ask. They had all three
been mad for it from the moment they saw it at the end of the long
sand road between the marshes and the sea. "My room, OK?" Mag had
said, coming out of the southwest bedroom. She and Phil had had their
honeymoon summer there.

She looked across the sand at him. He was walking at the very edge of
the water, moving crabwise east when a wave came washing farther in,
following the outwash back west, absorbed as a child, slight, stooped,
elusive. She veered her way to intersect with his. "Phildog," she said.

"Magdog."

"You know, she was right. What made her say it, do you think?"

"Defending me."

How easily he said it. How easy his assumption. It had not occurred
to her.

"Could be. And herself? And me? . . . And then geology! Is she just in love with the course, or is she serious?"

"Never anything but."

"It might be a good major for her. Unless it's all labs now. I don't know, it's just a section of Intro Sci at CC. I'll ask Benjie what geologists do these days. I hope still those little hammers. And khaki shorts."

"That Priestley novel in the bookcase," Phil said, and went on to talk about it, and novelists contemporary with Priestley, and she listened attentively as they walked along the hissing fringes of the continent. If Phil had not quit before the prelims, he would have got much farther in his career than she in hers, because men got farther easier then, of course, but mainly because he was such a natural; he had the right temperament, the necessary indifference and passion of the scholar. He was drawn to early twentieth century English fiction with the perfect combination of detachment and fascination, and could have written a fine study of Priestley, Galsworthy, Bennett, that lot, a book worth a good professorship at a good school. Or worth at least a sense of self-respect. But self-respect wasn't a saint's business, was it? Dean Inman had had plenty of self-respect, and plenty of respect, too. Had she been escaping the various manifestations of respect when she fell for Phil? No. She still missed it, in fact, and supplied it when she could. She had fallen for Phil because she was strong, because of the awful need strength has for weakness. If you're not weak how can I be strong? Years it had taken her, years, until now, to learn that strength, like the lovely boys washing the dishes, like Gret saying that terrible thing at lunch, was what strength needed, craved, rested in. Rested and grew weak in, with the true weakness, the fecundity. Without self-defense. Gret had not been defending Phil, or anybody. Phil had to see it that way. But Gret had been speaking out of the true weakness. Dean Inman wouldn't have understood it, but it wouldn't have worried him; he would have seen that Gret respected him, and that to him would have meant that she respected herself. And Rita? She could not remember what Rita had said, when Gret said that about their not being real. Something not disapproving, but remote. Moving away. Rita was moving away. Like the gulls there ahead of them, always moving away as they advanced towards them, curved wings and watchful, indifferent eyes. Airborne, with hollow bones. She looked back down the sands. Gret and the interviewer were walking slowly, talking, far behind, so that she and Phil kept moving away from them, too. A tongue of the tide ran up the sand between them, cross-currents drawing lines across it, and hissed softly out again. The horizon was a blue murk, but the sunlight was hot. "Ha!" Phil said, and picked up a fine white sand dollar. He always saw the invaluable treasures, the dollars of no currency; he went on finding Japanese glass netfloats every winter on this beach, years after the Japanese had given up glass floats for plastic, years after anyone else had found one. Some of the floats he found had limpets growing on them. Bearded with moss and in garments green, they had floated for years on the great waves, tiny unburst bubbles, green, translucent earthlets in foam galaxies, moving away, drawing near. "But how much Maupassant is there in *The Old Wives' Tale*?" she asked. "I mean, that kind of summing-up-women thing?" And Phil, pocketing his sea-paid salary, answered, as her father had answered her questions, and she listened to him and to the sea.

Sue's mother had died of cancer of the womb. Sue had gone home to stay with her before college was out last spring. It had taken her four months to die, and Sue had to talk about it. Gret had to listen. An honor, an imposition, an initiation. From time to time, barely enduring, Gret lifted her head to look out across the grey level of the sea, or up at Breton Head towering closer, or ahead at Mother and Daddy going along like slow sandpipers at the foam-fringe, or down at the damp brown sand and her grotty sneakers making footprints. But she bent her head again to Sue, confining herself. Sue had to tell and she had to listen, to learn all the instruments, the bonds, the knives, the racks and pinions, and how you became part of the torture, complicit with it, and whether in the end the truth, after such efforts to obtain it, would be spoken.

"My father hated the male nurses to touch her," Sue said. "He said it was woman's work, he tried to make them send women nurses in."

She talked about catheters, metastases, transfusions, each word an iron maiden, a toothed vagina. Women's work. "The oncologist said it would get better when he put her on morphine, when her mind would get confused. But it got worse. It was the worst. The last week was the worst thing I will ever go through." She knew what she was saying, and it was tremendous. To be able to say that meant that you need not be afraid again. But it seemed like you had to lose a good deal for that gain.

Gret's escaping gaze passed her mother and father, who had halted at the foot of Breton Head, and followed the breakers on out to where the sea went level. Somebody had told her in high school that if you jumped from a height like Breton Head, hitting the water would be just like hitting rock.

"I didn't mean to go on telling you all that. I'm sorry. I just haven't got through it yet. I have to keep working through it."

"Sure," Gret said.

"Your grandmother is so—she's a beautiful person. And your whole family. You all just seem so real. I really appreciate being here with you."

She stopped walking, and Gret had to stop, too.

"What you said at lunch, about your grandfather being famous."

Gret nodded.

"When I suggested to Professor Nabe about talking to Dean Inman's family, you know, maybe getting some details that weren't just public knowledge, some insights on how his educational theories and his life went together, and his family, and so on—you know what he said? He said, 'But they're all quite unimportant people, aren't they?'"

The two young women walked on side by side.

"That's funny," Gret said, with a grin. She stooped for a black pebble.

It was basalt, of course; there was nothing but basalt this whole stretch of the coast, outflow from the great shield volcanoes up the Columbia, or pillow basalts from undersea vents; that's what Mother and Daddy were clambering on now, big, hard pillows from under the sea. The hard sea.

"What did you find?" Sue asked, over-intense about everything, strung out. Gret showed her the dull black pebble, then flipped it at the breakers.

"*Everyone* is important," Sue said. "I learned that this summer."

Was that the truth that the croaking voice had gasped at torture's end? She didn't believe it. Nobody was important. But she couldn't say that. It would sound as cheap, as stupid, as the stupid professor. But the pebble wasn't important, neither was she, neither was Sue. Neither was the sea. Important wasn't the point. Things didn't have rank.

"Want to go on up the Head a ways? There's a sort of path."

Sue consulted her watch. "I don't want to keep your grandmother waiting when she wakes up. I'd better go back. I could listen to her talk forever. She's just amazing." She was going to say, "You're so lucky!" She did.

"Yeah," Gret said. "Some Greek, I think it was some Greek said don't say that to anybody until they're dead." She raised her voice. "Ma! Dad! Yo!" She gestured to them that she and Sue were returning. The small figures on the huge black pillows nodded and waved, and her mother's voice cried something, like a hawk's cry or a gull's, the sea drowning out all consonants, all sense.

Crows cawed and carked over the marshes inland. It was the only sound but the sound of the sea coming in the open window and filling the room and the whole house full as a shell is full of sound that sounds like the sea but is something else, your blood running in your veins, they said, but how could it be that you could hear that in a shell but never in your own ear or your cupped hand? In a coffee cup there was a sound like it, but less, not coming and going like the sea-sound. She had tried it as a child, the hand, the cup, the shell. Caw, cark, caw! Black heavy swoopers, queer. The light like no other on the white ceiling boards.

Tongue and groove, tongue in cheek. What had the child said that for, that Amory was the only real one of them? An awful thing to say about reality. The child would have to be very careful, she was so strong. Stronger even than Maggie. Because her father was so weak. Of course that was all backwards, but it was so hard to think the things straight that the words had all backwards. Only she knew that the child would have to be very careful, not to be caught. Cark, ark, caw! the crows cried far over the marshes. What was the sound that kept going on? The wind, it must be the wind across the sagebrush plains. But that was far away. What was it she had wanted to think about when she lay down?

ETHER, OR

For the Narrative Americans

Edna

I NEVER GO IN THE TWO BLUE MOONS ANY MORE. I THOUGHT about that when I was arranging the grocery window today and saw Corrie go in across the street and open up. Never did go into a bar alone in my life. Sook came by for a candy bar and I said that to her, said I wonder if I ought to go have a beer there sometime, see if it tastes different on your own. Sook said Oh Ma you always been on your own. I said I seldom had a moment to myself and four husbands, and she said You know that don't count. Sook's fresh. Breath of fresh air. I saw Needless looking at her with that kind of dog look men get. I was surprised to find it gave me a pang, I don't know what of. I just never saw Needless look that way. What did I expect, Sook is twenty and the man is human. He just always seemed like he did fine on his own. Independent. That's why he's restful. Silvia died years and years and years ago, but I never thought of it before as a long time. I wonder if I have mistaken him. All this time working for him. That would be a strange thing. That was what the pang felt like, like when you know you've made some kind of mistake, been stupid, sewn the seam inside out, left the burner on.

They're all strange, men are. I guess if I understood them I wouldn't find them so interesting. But Toby Walker, of them all he was the

strangest. The stranger. I never knew where he was coming from. Roger
came out of the desert, Ady came out of the ocean, but Toby came from
farther. But he was here when I came. A lovely man, dark all through,
dark as forests. I lost my way in him. I loved to lose my way in him.
How I wish it was then, not now! Seems like I can't get lost any more.
There's only one way to go. I have to keep plodding along it. I feel like
I was walking across Nevada, like the pioneers, carrying a lot of stuff I
need, but as I go along I have to keep dropping off things. I had a piano
once but it got swamped at a crossing of the Platte. I had a good frypan
but it got too heavy and I left it in the Rockies. I had a couple ovaries
but they wore out around the time we were in the Carson Sink. I had
a good memory but pieces of it keep dropping off, have to leave them
scattered around in the sagebrush, on the sand hills. All the kids are
still coming along, but I don't have them. I had them, it's not the same
as having them. They aren't with me any more, even Archie and Sook.
They're all walking along back where I was years ago. I wonder will they
get any nearer than I have to the west side of the mountains, the valleys
of the orange groves? They're years behind me. They're still in Iowa.
They haven't even thought about the Sierras yet. I didn't either till I got
here. Now I begin to think I'm a member of the Donner Party.

Thos. Sunn

THE WAY YOU CAN'T COUNT ON ETHER IS A HINDRANCE SOME-
times, like when I got up in the dark this morning to catch the minus
tide and stepped out the door in my rubber boots and plaid jacket with
my clam spade and bucket, and overnight she'd gone inland again. The
damn desert and the damn sagebrush. All you could dig up there with
your damn spade would be a God damn fossil. Personally I blame it on
the Indians. I do not believe that a fully civilised country would allow

these kind of irregularities in a town. However as I have lived here since 1949 and could not sell my house and property for chicken feed, I intend to finish up here, like it or not. That should take a few more years, ten or fifteen most likely. Although you can't count on anything these days anywhere let alone a place like this. But I like to look after myself, and I can do it here. There is not so much Government meddling and interference and general hindering in Ether as you would find in the cities. This may be because it isn't usually where the Government thinks it is, though it is, sometimes.

When I first came here I used to take some interest in a woman, but it is my belief that in the long run a man does better not to. A woman is a worse hindrance to a man than anything else, even the Government.

I have read the term "a crusty old bachelor" and would be willing to say that that describes me so long as the crust goes all the way through. I don't like things soft in the center. Softness is no use in this hard world. I am like one of my mother's biscuits.

My mother, Mrs. J. J. Sunn, died in Wichita, KS, in 1944, at the age of 79. She was a fine woman and my experience of women in general does not apply to her in particular.

Since they invented the kind of biscuits that come in a tube which you hit on the edge of the counter and the dough explodes out of it under pressure, that's the kind I buy, and by baking them about one half hour they come out pretty much the way I like them, crust clear through. I used to bake the dough all of a piece, but then discovered that you can break it apart into separate biscuits. I don't hold with reading directions and they are always printed in small, fine print on the damn foil which gets torn when you break open the tube. I use my mother's glasses. They are a good make.

The woman I came here after in 1949 is still here. That was during my brief period of infatuation. Fortunately I can say that she did not get her hooks onto me in the end. Some other men have not been as lucky. She has married or as good as several times and was pregnant and pushing a baby carriage for decades. Sometimes I think everybody under forty in this town is one of Edna's. I had a very narrow escape. I have had a dream about Edna several times. In this dream I am out on the sea fishing for salmon from a small boat, and Edna swims up from the sea waves and tries to climb into the boat. To prevent this I hit her hands with the gutting knife and cut off the fingers, which fall into the water and turn into some kind of little creatures that swim away. I never can tell if they are babies or seals. Then Edna swims after them making a strange noise, and I see that in actuality she is a kind of seal or sea lion, like the big ones in the cave on the south coast, light brown and very large and fat and sleek in the water.

This dream disturbs me, as it is unfair. I am not the kind of man who would do such a thing. It causes me discomfort to remember the strange noise she makes in the dream, when I am in the grocery store and Edna is at the cash register. To make sure she rings it up right and I get the right change, I have to look at her hands opening and shutting the drawers and her fingers working on the keys. What's wrong with women is that you can't count on them. They are not fully civilised.

Roger Hiddenstone

I ONLY COME INTO TOWN SOMETIMES. IT'S A NOW AND THEN THING. If the road takes me there, fine, but I don't go hunting for it. I run a two hundred thousand acre cattle ranch, which gives me a good deal to do. I'll look up sometimes and the moon is new that I saw full last night. One summer comes after another like steers through a chute. In the winters, though, sometimes the weeks freeze like the creek water, and things hold still for a while. The air can get still and clear in the winter here in the high desert. I have seen the mountain peaks from Baker and

Rainier in the north, Hood and Jefferson, Three-Fingered Jack and the
Sisters east of here, on south to Shasta and Lassen, all standing up in the
sunlight for eight hundred or a thousand miles. That was when I was
flying. From the ground you can't see that much of the ground, though
you can see the rest of the universe, nights.

I traded in my two-seater Cessna for a quarterhorse mare, and I generally keep a Ford pickup, though at times I've had a Chevrolet. Any one
of them will get me in to town so long as there isn't more than a couple feet
of snow on the road. I like to come in now and then and have a Denver
omelette at the café for breakfast, and a visit with my wife and son. I have
a drink at the Two Blue Moons, and spend the night at the motel. By the
next morning I'm ready to go back to the ranch to find out what went
wrong while I was gone. It's always something.

Edna was only out to the ranch once while we were married. She
spent three weeks. We were so busy in the bed I don't recall much else about
it, except the time she tried to learn to ride. I put her on Sally, the cutting
horse I traded the Cessna plus fifteen hundred dollars for, a highly reliable
horse and more intelligent than most Republicans. But Edna had that mare
morally corrupted within ten minutes. I was trying to explain how she'd
interpret what you did with your knees, when Edna started yipping and
raking her like a bronc rider. They lit out of the yard and went halfway
to Ontario at a dead run. I was riding the old roan gelding and only met
them coming back. Sally was unrepentant, but Edna was sore and delicate that evening. She claimed all the love had been jolted out of her. I
guess that this was true, in the larger sense, since it wasn't long after that
that she asked to go back to Ether. I thought she had quit her job at the
grocery, but she had only asked for a month off, and she said Needless
would want her for the extra business at Christmas. We drove back to town,
finding it a little west of where we had left it, in a very pretty location
near the Ochoco Mountains, and we had a happy Christmas season in
Edna's house with the children.

I don't know whether Archie was begotten there or at the ranch. I'd like to think it was at the ranch so that there would be that in him drawing him to come back some day. I don't know who to leave all this to. Charlie Echeverria is good with the stock, but can't think ahead two days and couldn't deal with the buyers, let alone the corporations. I don't want the corporations profiting from this place. The hands are nice young fellows, but they don't stay put, or want to. Cowboys don't want land. Land owns you. You have to give in to that. I feel sometimes like all the stones on two hundred thousand acres were weighing on me, and my mind's gone to rimrock. And the beasts wandering and calling across all that land. The cows stand with their young calves in the wind that blows March snow like frozen sand across the flats. Their patience is a thing I try to understand.

Gracie Fane

I SAW THAT OLD RANCHER ON MAIN STREET YESTERDAY, MR. Hiddenstone, was married to Edna once. He acted like he knew where he was going, but when the street ran out onto the sea cliff he sure did look foolish. Turned round and came back in those high-heel boots, long legs, putting his feet down like a cat the way cowboys do. He's a skinny old man. He went into the Two Blue Moons. Going to try to drink his way back to eastern Oregon, I guess. I don't care if this town is east or west. I don't care if it's anywhere. It never is anywhere anyway. I'm going to leave here and go to Portland, to the Intermountain, the big trucking company, and be a truck driver. I learned to drive when I was five on my grandpa's tractor. When I was ten I started driving my dad's Dodge Ram, and I've driven pickups and delivery vans for Mom and Mr. Needless ever since I got my license. Jase gave me lessons on his eighteen-wheeler last summer. I did real good. I'm a natural. Jase said so. I never got to get out onto the I–5 but only once or twice, though. He kept saying

I needed more practice pulling over and parking and shifting up and down. I didn't mind practicing, but then when I got her stopped he'd want to get me into this bed thing he fixed up behind the seats and pull my jeans off, and we had to screw some before he'd go on teaching me anything. My own idea would be to drive a long way and learn a lot and then have some sex and coffee and then drive back a different way, maybe on hills where I'd have to practice braking and stuff. But I guess men have different priorities. Even when I was driving he'd have his arm around my back and be petting my boobs. He has these huge hands can reach right across both boobs at once. It felt good, but it interfered with his concentration teaching me. He would say *Oh baby you're so great* and I would think he meant I was driving great but then he'd start making those sort of groaning noises and I'd have to shift down and find a place to pull out and get in the bed thing again. I used to practice changing gears in my mind when we were screwing and it helped. I could shift him right up and down again. I used to yell *Going eighty!* when I got him really shifted up. *Fuzz on your tail!* And make these sireen noises. That's my CB name: Sireen. Jase got his route shifted in August. I made my plans then. I'm driving for the grocery and saving money till I'm seventeen and go to Portland to work for the Intermountain Company. I want to drive the I–5 from Seattle to LA, or get a run to Salt Lake City. Till I can buy my own truck. I got it planned out.

Tobinye Walker

THE YOUNG PEOPLE ALL WANT TO GET OUT OF ETHER. YOUNG Americans in a small town want to get up and go. And some do, and some come to a time when they stop talking about where they're going to go when they go. They have come to where they are. Their problem, if it's a problem, isn't all that different from mine. We have a window of opportunity; it closes. I used to walk across the years as easy as a child here crosses the street, but I went lame, and had to stop walking. So this is my time, my heyday, my floruit.

When I first knew Edna she said a strange thing to me; we had been talking, I don't remember what about, and she stopped and gazed at me. "You have a look on you like an unborn child," she said. "You look at things like an unborn child." I don't know what I answered, and only later did I wonder how she knew how an unborn child looks, and whether she meant a fetus in the womb or a child that never came to be conceived. Maybe she meant a newborn child. But I think she used the word she meant to use.

When I first stopped by here, before my accident, there was no town, of course, no settlement. Several peoples came through and sometimes encamped for a season, but it was a range without boundary, though it had names. At that time people didn't have the expectation of stability they have now; they knew that so long as a river keeps running it's a river. Nobody but the beavers built dams, then. Ether always covered a lot of territory, and it has retained that property. But its property is not continuous.

The people I used to meet coming through generally said they came down Humbug Creek from the river in the mountains, but Ether itself never has been in the Cascades, to my knowledge. Fairly often you can see them to the west of it, though usually it's west of them, and often west of the Coast Range in the timber or the dairy country, sometimes right on the sea. It has a broken range. It's an unusual place. I'd like to go back to the center to tell about it, but I can't walk any more. I have to do my flourishing here.

J. Needless

PEOPLE THINK THERE ARE NO CALIFORNIANS. NOBODY CAN COME from the promise land. You have to be going to it. Die in the desert, grave by the wayside. I come from California, born there, think about it some. I was born in the Valley of San Arcadio. Orchards. Like a white bay of orange flowers under bare blue-brown mountains. Sunlight like air, like clear water, something you lived in, an element. Our place was a little farmhouse up in the foothills, looking out over the valley. My father was a manager for one of the companies. Oranges flower white, with a sweet, fine scent. Outskirts of Heaven, my mother said once, one morning when she was hanging out the wash. I remember her saying that. We live on the outskirts of Heaven.

She died when I was six and I don't remember a lot but that about her. Now I have come to realise that my wife has been dead so long that I have lost her too. She died when our daughter Corrie was six. Seemed like there was some meaning in it at the time, but if there was I didn't find it.

Ten years ago when Corrie was twenty-one she said she wanted to go to Disneyland for her birthday. With me. Damn if she didn't drag me down there. Spent a good deal to see people dressed up like mice with water on the brain and places made to look like places they weren't. I guess that is the point there. They clean dirt till it is a sanitary substance and spread it out to look like dirt so you don't have to touch dirt. You and Walt are in control there. You can be in any kind of place, space or the ocean or castles in Spain, all sanitary, no dirt. I would have liked it as a boy, when I thought the idea was to run things. Changed my ideas, settled for a grocery.

Corrie wanted to see where I grew up, so we drove over to San Arcadio. It wasn't there, not what I meant by it. Nothing but roofs, houses, streets and houses. Smog so thick it hid the mountains and the sun looked green. God damn, get me out of here, I said, they have changed the color of the sun. Corrie wanted to look for the house but I was serious. Get me out of here, I said, this is the right place but the wrong year. Walt Disney can get rid of the dirt on his property if he likes, but this is going too far. This is my property.

I felt like that. Like I thought it was something I had, but they scraped all the dirt off and underneath was cement and some electronic wiring. I'd as soon not have seen that. People come through here say how can you stand living in a town that doesn't stay in the same place all the time, but have they been to Los Angeles? It's anywhere you want to say it is.

Well, since I don't have California what have I got? A good enough business. Corrie's still here. Good head on her. Talks a lot. Runs that bar like a bar should be run. Runs her husband pretty well too. What do I mean when I say I had a mother, I had a wife? I mean remembering what orange flowers smell like, whiteness, sunlight. I carry that with me. Corinna and Silvia, I carry their names. But what do I have?

What I don't have is right within hand's reach every day. Every day but Sunday. But I can't reach out my hand. Every man in town gave her a child and all I ever gave her was her week's wages. I know she trusts me. That's the trouble. Too late now. Hell, what would she want me in her bed for, the Medicare benefits?

Emma Bodely

EVERYTHING IS SERIAL KILLERS NOW. THEY SAY EVERYONE IS naturally fascinated by a man planning and committing one murder after another without the least reason and not even knowing who he kills personally. There was the man up in the city recently who tortured and tormented three tiny little boys and took photographs of them while he tortured them and of their corpses after he killed them. Authorities are talking now about what they ought to do with these photographs. They could make a lot of money from a book of them. He was apprehended by the police as he lured yet another tiny boy to come with him, as in a nightmare. There were men in California and Texas and I believe Chicago who dismembered and buried innumerably. Then of course it goes back in history to Jack the Ripper who killed poor women and was supposed to be a member of the Royal Family of England, and no doubt before his time there were many other serial killers, many of them members of Royal Families or Emperors and Generals who killed thousands and thousands of people. But in wars they kill people more or less simultaneously, not one by one, so that they are mass murderers, not serial killers, but I'm not sure I see the difference, really. Since for the person being murdered it only happens once.

I should be surprised if we had a serial killer in Ether. Most of the men were soldiers in one of the wars, but they would be mass murderers, unless they had desk jobs. I can't think who here would be a serial killer. No doubt I would be the last to find out. I find being invisible works both ways. Often I don't see as much as I used to when I was visible. Being invisible however I'm less likely to become a serial victim.

It's odd how the natural fascination they talk about doesn't include the serial victims. I suppose it is because I taught young children for thirty-five years, but perhaps I am unnatural, because I think about those three little boys. They were three or four years old. How strange that their whole life was only a few years, like a cat. In their world suddenly instead of their mother there was a man who told them how he was going to hurt them and then did it, so that there was nothing in their life at all but fear and pain. So they died in fear and pain. But all the reporters tell is the nature of the mutilations and how decomposed they were, and that's all about them. They were little boys not men. They are not fascinating. They are just dead. But the serial killer they tell all about over and over and discuss his psychology and how his parents caused him to be so fascinating, and he lives forever, as witness Jack the Ripper and Hitler the Ripper. Everyone around here certainly remembers the name of the man who serially raped and photographed the tortured little boys before he serially murdered them. He was named Westley Dodd but what were their names?

Of course we the people murdered him back. That was what he wanted. He wanted us to murder him. I cannot decide if hanging him was a mass murder or a serial murder. We all did it, like a war, so it is a mass murder, but we each did it, democratically, so I suppose it is serial, too. I would as soon be a serial victim as a serial murderer, but I was not given the choice.

My choices have become less. I never had a great many, as my sexual impulses were not appropriate to my position in life, and no one I fell in love with knew it. I am glad when Ether turns up in a different place as it is kind of like a new choice of where to live, only I didn't have to make it. I am capable only of very small choices. What to eat for breakfast, oatmeal or corn flakes, or perhaps only a piece of fruit? Kiwi fruits were fifteen cents apiece at the grocery and I bought half a dozen. A while ago they were the most exotic thing, from New Zealand I think and a dollar each, and now they raise them all over the Willamette Valley. But then, the Willamette Valley may be quite exotic to a person in New Zealand. I like the way they're cool in your mouth, the same way the flesh of them looks cool, a smooth green you can see into, like jade stone. I still see things like that perfectly clearly. It's only with people that my eyes are more and more transparent, so that I don't always see what they're doing, and so that they can look right through me as if my eyes were air and say, "Hi, Emma, how's life treating you?"

Life's treating me like a serial victim, thank you.

I wonder if she sees me or sees through me. I don't dare look. She is shy and lost in her crystal dreams. If only I could look after her. She needs looking after. A cup of tea. Herbal tea, echinacea maybe, I think her immune system needs strengthening. She is not a practical person. I am a very practical person. Far below her dreams.

Lo still sees me. Of course Lo is a serial killer as far as birds are concerned, and moles, but although it upsets me when the bird's not dead yet it's not the same as the man taking photographs. Mr. Hiddenstone once told me that cats have the instinct to let a mouse or bird stay alive awhile in order to take it to the kittens and train them to hunt, so what seems to be cruelty is thoughtfulness. Now I know that some tom cats kill kittens, and I don't think any tom ever raised kittens and trained them thoughtfully to hunt. The queen cat does that. A tom cat is the Jack the Ripper of the Royal Family. But Lo is neutered, so he might behave like a queen or at least like a kind of uncle if there were kittens around, and bring them his birds to hunt. I don't know. He doesn't mix with other cats much. He stays pretty close to home, keeping an eye on the birds and moles and me. I know that my invisibility is not universal when I wake up in the middle of the night and Lo is sitting on the bed right beside my pillow purring and looking very intently at me. It's a strange thing to do, a little uncanny. His eyes wake me, I think. But it's a good waking, knowing that he can see me, even in the dark.

Edna

ALL RIGHT NOW, I WANT AN ANSWER. ALL MY LIFE SINCE I WAS fourteen I have been making my soul. I don't know what else to call it, that's what I called it then, when I was fourteen and came into the possession of my life and the knowledge of my responsibility. Since then I have not had time to find a better name for it. The word responsible means that you have to answer. You can't not answer. You'd might rather not answer, but you have to. When you answer you are making your soul, so that it has a shape to it, and size, and some staying power. I understood that, I came into that knowledge, when I was thirteen and early fourteen, that long winter in the Siskiyous. All right, so ever since then, more or less, I have worked according to that understanding. And I have worked. I have done what came into my hands to do, and I've done it the best I could and with all the mind and strength I had to give to it. There have been jobs, waitressing and clerking, but first of all and always the ordinary work of raising the children and keeping the house so that people can live decently and in health and some degree of peace of mind. Then there is responding to the needs of men. That seems like it should come first. People might say I never thought of anything but answering what men asked, pleasing men and pleasing myself, and goodness knows such questions are a joy to answer if asked by a pleasant man. But in the order of my mind, the children come before the fathers of the children. Maybe I see it that way because I was the eldest daughter and there were four younger than me and my father had gone off. Well, all right then, those are my responsibilities as I see them, those are the questions I have tried always to answer: can people live in this house, and how does a child grow up rightly, and how to be trustworthy.

But now I have my own question. I never asked questions, I was so busy answering them, but am sixty years old this winter and think I should have time for a question. But it's hard to ask. Here it is. It's like all the time I was working keeping house and raising the kids and making love and earning our keep I thought there was going to come a time or there would be some place where all of it all came together. Like it was words I was saying, all my life, all the kinds of work, just a word here and a word there, but finally all the words would make a sentence, and I could read the sentence. I would have made my soul and know what it was for.

But I have made my soul and I don't know what to do with it. Who wants it? I have lived sixty years. All I'll do from now on is the same as what I have done only less of it, while I get weaker and sicker and smaller all the time, shrinking and shrinking around myself, and die. No matter what I did, or made, or know. The words don't mean anything. I ought to talk with Emma about this. She's the only one who doesn't say stuff like, "You're only as old as you think you are," "Oh Edna you'll never be old," rubbish like that. Toby Walker wouldn't talk that way either, but he doesn't say much at all any more. Keeps his sentence to himself. My kids that still live here, Archie and Sook, they don't want to hear anything about it. Nobody young can afford to believe in getting old.

So is all the responsibility you take only useful then, but no use later—disposable? What's the use, then? All the work you did is just gone. It doesn't make anything. But I may be wrong. I hope so, I would like to have more trust in dying. Maybe it's worth while, like some kind of answering, coming into another place. Like I felt that winter in the Siskiyous, walking on the snow road between black firs under all the stars, that I was the same size as the universe, the same thing as the universe. And if I kept on walking ahead there was this glory waiting for me. In time I would come into glory. I knew that. So that's what I made my soul for. I made it for glory.

And I have known a good deal of glory. I'm not ungrateful. But it doesn't last. It doesn't come together to make a place where you can live, a house. It's gone and the years go. What's left? Shrinking and forgetting and thinking about aches and acid indigestion and cancers and pulse rates and bunions until the whole world is a room that smells like urine, is that what all the work comes to, is that the end of the babies' kicking legs, the children's eyes, the loving hands, the wild rides, the light on water, the stars over the snow? Somewhere inside it all there has to still be the glory.

Ervin Muth

I HAVE BEEN WATCHING MR. "TOBY" WALKER FOR A GOOD WHILE, checking up on things, and if I happened to be called upon to I could state with fair certainty that this "Mr. Walker" is *not an American*. My research has taken me considerably farther afield than that. But there are these "gray areas" or some things which many people as a rule are unprepared to accept. It takes training.

My attention was drawn to these kind of matters in the first place by scrutinizing the town records on an entirely different subject of research. Suffice it to say that I was checking the title on the Fane place at the point in time when Mrs. Osey Jean Fane put the property into the hands of Ervin Muth Realty, of which I am proprietor. There had been a dispute concerning the property line on the east side of the Fane property in 1939 into which, due to being meticulous concerning these kind of detailed responsibilities, I checked. To my surprise I was amazed to discover that the adjoining lot, which had been developed in 1906, had been in the name of Tobinye Walker since that date, 1906! I naturally assumed at that point in time that this "Tobinye Walker" was "Mr. Toby Walker's" father and thought little more about the issue until my researches into another matter, concerning the Essel/Emmer lots, in the town records indicated that the name "Tobinye Walker" was shown as purchaser of a livery stable on that site (on Main St. between Rash St. and Goreman Ave.) in 1880.

While purchasing certain necessaries in the Needless Grocery Store soon after, I encountered Mr. Walker in person. I remarked in a jocular vein that I had been meeting his father and grandfather. This was of course a mere pleasantry. Mr. "Toby" Walker responded in what struck me as a suspicious fashion. There was some taking aback going on. Although with laughter. His exact words, to which I can attest, were the following: "I had no idea that you were capable of travelling in time!"

This was followed by my best efforts to seriously inquire concerning the persons of his same name which my researches in connection with my work as a relator had turned up. These were only met with facetious remarks such as, "I've lived here quite a while, you see," and, "Oh, I remember when Lewis and Clark came through," a statement in reference to the celebrated explorers of the Oregon Trail, who I ascertained later to have been in Oregon in 1806.

Soon after, Mr. Toby Walker *"walked"* away, thus ending the conversation.

I am convinced by evidence that "Mr. Walker" is an illegal immigrant from a foreign country who has assumed the name of a Founding Father of this fine community, that is to wit the Tobinye Walker who purchased the livery stable in 1880. I have my reasons.

My research shows conclusively that the Lewis and Clark Expedition sent by President Thos. Jefferson did not pass through any of the localities which our fine community of Ether has occupied over the course of its history. Ether never got that far north.

If Ether is to progress to fulfill its destiny as a Destination Resort on the beautiful Oregon Coast and Desert as I visualize it with a complete downtown entertainment center and entrepreneurial business community, including hub motels, RV facilities, and a Theme Park, the kind of thing that is represented by "Mr." Walker will have to go. It is the American way to buy and sell houses and properties continually in the course of moving for the sake of upward mobility and self-improvement. Stagnation is the enemy of the American way. The same person owning the same property since 1906 is unnatural and Unamerican. Ether is an American town and moves all the time. That is its destiny. I can call myself an expert.

Starra Walinow Amethyst

I KEEP PRACTICING LOVE. I WAS IN LOVE WITH THAT FRENCH actor Gerard but it's really hard to say his last name. Frenchmen attract me. When I watch *Star Trek The Next Generation* reruns I'm in love with Captain Jean-Luc Picard, but I can't stand Commander Riker. I used to be in love with Heathcliff when I was twelve and Miss Freff gave me *Wuthering Heights* to read. And I was in love with Sting for a while before he got weirder. Sometimes I think I am in love with Lieutenant Worf but that is pretty weird, with all those sort of wrinkles and horns

on his forehead, since he's a Klingon, but that's not really what's weird. I
mean it's just in the TV that he's an alien. Really he is a human named
Michael Dorn. That is so weird to me. I mean I never have seen a real
black person except in movies and TV. Everybody in Ether is white. So
a black person would actually be an alien here. I thought what it would
be like if somebody like that came into like the drug store, really tall,
with that dark brown skin and dark eyes and those very soft lips that
look like they could get hurt so easily, and asked for something in that
really, really deep voice. Like, "Where would I find the aspirin?" And I
would show him where the aspirin kind of stuff is. He would be standing beside me in front of the shelf, really big and tall and dark, and I'd
feel warmth coming out of him like out of an iron woodstove. He'd say
to me in a very low voice, "I don't belong in this town," and I'd say back,
"I don't either," and he'd say, "Do you want to come with me?" only really
really nicely, not like a come-on but like two prisoners whispering how
to get out of prison together. I'd nod, and he'd say, "Back of the gas station,
at dusk."

At dusk.

I love that word. Dusk. It sounds like his voice.

Sometimes I feel weird thinking about him like this. I mean because
he is actually real. If it was just Worf, that's OK, because Worf is just this
alien in some old reruns of a show. But there is actually Michael Dorn.
So thinking about him in a sort of story that way makes me uncomfortable
sometimes, because it's like I was making him a toy, something I can do
anything with, like a doll. That seems like it was unfair to him. And it
makes me sort of embarrassed when I think about how he actually has
his own life with nothing to do with this dumb girl in some hick town
he never heard of. So I try to make up somebody else to make that kind
of stories about. But it doesn't work.

I really tried this spring to be in love with Morrie Stromberg, but
it didn't work. He's really beautiful-looking. It was when I saw him

shooting baskets that I thought maybe I could be in love with him. His legs and arms are long and smooth and he moves smooth and looks kind of like a mountain lion, with a low forehead and short dark blond hair, tawny colored. But all he ever does is hang out with Joe's crowd and talk about sport scores and cars, and once in class he was talking with Joe about me so I could hear, like, "Oh yeah Starra, wow, *she* reads *books*," not really mean, but kind of like I was like an alien from another planet, just totally absolutely strange. Like Worf or Michael Dorn would feel here. Like he meant OK, it's OK to be like that only not here. Somewhere else, OK? As if Ether wasn't already somewhere else. I mean, didn't it use to be the Indians that lived here, and now there aren't any of them either? So who belongs here and where does it belong?

About a month ago Mom told me the reason she left my father. I don't remember anything like that. I don't remember any father. I don't remember anything before Ether. She says we were living in Seattle and they had a store where they sold crystals and oils and New Age stuff, and when she got up one night to go to the bathroom he was in my room holding me. She wanted to tell me everything about how he was holding me and stuff, but I just went, "So, like, he was molesting me." And she went, "Yeah," and I said, "So what did you do?" I thought they would have had a big fight. But she said she didn't say anything, because she was afraid of him. She said, "See, to him it was like he owned me and you. And when I didn't go along with that, he would get real crazy." I think they were into a lot of pot and heavy stuff, she talks about that sometimes. So anyway next day when he went to the store she just took some of the crystals and stuff they kept at home, we still have them, and got some money they kept in a can in the kitchen just like she does here, and got on the bus to Portland with me. Somebody she met there gave us a ride here. I don't remember any of that. It's like I was born here. I asked did he ever try to look for her, and she said she didn't know but if he did he'd have a hard time finding her here. She changed her last name to Amethyst, which is her favorite stone. Walinow was her real name. She says it's Polish.

I don't know what his name was. I don't know what he did. I don't care. It's like nothing happened. I'm never going to belong to anybody.

What I know is this, I am going to love people. They will never know it. But I am going to be a great lover. I know how. I have practiced. It isn't when you belong to somebody or they belong to you or stuff. That's like Chelsey getting married to Tim because she wanted to have the wedding and the husband and a no-wax kitchen floor. She wanted stuff to belong to.

I don't want stuff, but I want practice. Like we live in this shack with no kitchen let alone a no-wax floor, and we cook on a trashburner, with a lot of crystals around, and cat pee from the strays Mom takes in, and Mom does stuff like sweeping out for Myrella's beauty parlor, and gets zits because she eats Hostess Twinkies instead of food. Mom needs to get it together. But I need to give it away.

I thought maybe the way to practice love was to have sex so I had sex with Danny last summer. Mom bought us condoms and made me hold hands with her around a bayberry candle and talk about the Passage Into Womanhood. She wanted Danny to be there too but I talked her out of it. The sex was OK but what I was really trying to do was be in love. It didn't work. Maybe it was the wrong way. He just got used to getting sex and so he kept coming around all fall, going "Hey Starra baby you know you need it." He wouldn't even say that it was him that needed it. If I need it, I can do it a lot better myself than he can. I didn't tell him that. Although I nearly did when he kept not letting me alone after I told him to stop. If he hadn't finally started going with Dana I might would have told him.

I don't know anybody else here I can be in love with. I wish I could practice on Archie but what's the use while there's Gracie Fane? It would just be dumb. I thought about asking Archie's father Mr. Hiddenstone if I could work on his ranch, next time we get near it. I could still come see Mom, and maybe there would be like ranch hands or cowboys. Or Archie would come out sometimes and there wouldn't be Gracie. Or actually there's Mr. Hiddenstone. He looks like Archie. Actually handsomer. But I guess is too old. He has a face like the desert. I noticed his eyes are the same color as Mom's turquoise ring. But I don't know if he needs a cook or anything and I suppose fifteen is too young.

J. Needless

NEVER HAVE FIGURED OUT WHERE THE HOHOVARS COME FROM. Somebody said White Russia. That figures. They're all big and tall and heavy with hair so blond it's white and those little blue eyes. They don't look at you. Noses like new potatoes. Women don't talk. Kids don't talk. Men talk like, "Vun case yeast peggets, tree case piggle beet." Never say hello, never say good-bye, never say thanks. But honest. Pay right up in cash. When they come in town they're all dressed head to foot, the women in these long dresses with a lot of fancy stuff around the bottom and sleeves, the little girls just the same as the women, even the babies in the same long stiff skirts, all of them with bonnet things that hide their hair. Even the babies don't look up. Men and boys in long pants and shirt and coat even when it's desert here and a hundred and five in July. Something like those ammish folk on the east coast, I guess. Only the Hohovars have buttons. A lot of buttons. The vest things the women wear have about a thousand buttons. Men's flies the same. Must slow 'em down getting to the action. But everybody says buttons are no problem when they get back to their community. Everything off. Strip naked to go to their church. Tom Sunn swears to it, and Corrie says she used to sneak out there more than once on Sunday with a bunch of other kids to see the Hohovars all going over the hill buck naked, singing in their language. That would be some sight, all those tall, heavy-fleshed, white-skinned, big-ass, big-tit women parading over the hill. Barefoot, too. What the hell they do in church I don't know. Tom says they commit fornication but Tom Sunn don't know shit from a hole in the ground. All talk. Nobody I know has ever been over that hill.

Some Sundays you can hear them singing.

Now religion is a curious thing in America. According to the Christians there is only one of anything. On the contrary there seems to me to be one or more of everything. Even here in Ether we have, that I know of, Baptists of course, Methodists, Church of Christ, Lutheran, Presbyterian, Catholic though no church in town, a Quaker, a lapsed Jew, a witch, the Hohovars, and the gurus or whatever that lot in the grange are. This is not counting most people, who have no religious affiliation except on impulse.

That is a considerable variety for a town this size. What's more, they try out each other's churches, switch around. Maybe the nature of the town makes us restless. Anyhow people in Ether generally live a long time, though not as long as Toby Walker. We have time to try out different things. My daughter Corrie has been a Baptist as a teenager, a Methodist while in love with Jim Fry, then had a go at the Lutherans. She was married Methodist but is now the Quaker, having read a book. This may change, as lately she has been talking to the witch, Pearl W. Amethyst, and reading another book, called *Crystals and You.*

Edna says the book is all tosh. But Edna has a harder mind than most.

Edna is my religion, I guess. I was converted years ago.

As for the people in the grange, the guru people, they caused some stir when they arrived ten years ago, or is it twenty now. Maybe it was in the sixties. Seems like they've been there a long time when I think about it. My wife was still alive. Anyhow, that's a case of religion mixed up some way with politics, not that it isn't always.

When they came to Ether they had a hell of a lot of money to throw around, though they didn't throw much my way. Bought the old grange and thirty acres of pasture adjacent. Put a fence right round and God damn if they didn't electrify that fence. I don't mean the little jolt you might run in for steers but a kick would kill an elephant. Remodeled the old grange and built on barns and barracks and even a generator. Everybody inside the fence was to share everything in common with everybody else inside the fence. Though from outside the fence it looked like the guru shared a lot more of it than the rest of 'em. That was the political part. Socialism. The bubonic socialism. Rats carry it and there is no vaccine. I tell you people here were upset. Thought the whole population behind the iron curtain plus all the hippies in California were moving in next Tuesday. Talked about bringing in the National Guard to defend the rights of citizens. Personally I'd of preferred the hippies over the National Guard. Hippies were unarmed. They killed by smell alone, as people said. But at the time there was a siege mentality here. A siege inside the grange, with their electric fence and their socialism, and a siege outside the grange, with their rights of citizens to be white and not foreign and not share anything with anybody.

At first the guru people would come into the town in their orange color T-shirts, doing a little shopping, talking politely. Young people got invited into the grange. They were calling it the osh rom by then. Corrie told me about the altar with the marigolds and the big photograph of Guru Jaya Jaya Jaya. But they weren't really friendly people and they didn't get friendly treatment. Pretty soon they never came into town, just drove in and out the road gate in their orange Buicks. Sometime along in there the Guru Jaya Jaya Jaya was supposed to come from India to visit the osh rom. Never did. Went to South America instead and founded an osh rom for old Nazis, they say. Old Nazis probably have more money to share with him than young Oregonians do. Or maybe he came to find his osh rom and it wasn't where they told him.

It has been kind of depressing to see the T-shirts fade and the Buicks break down. I don't guess there's more than two Buicks and ten, fifteen people left in the osh rom. They still grow garden truck, eggplants, all kinds of peppers, greens, squash, tomatoes, corn, beans, blue and rasp and straw and marion berries, melons. Good quality stuff. Raising crops takes some skill here where the climate will change overnight. They do beautiful irrigation and don't use poisons. Seen them out there picking bugs off the plants by hand. Made a deal with them some years ago to supply my produce counter and have not regretted it. Seems like Ether is meant to be a self-sufficient place. Every time I'd get a routine set up with a supplier in Cottage Grove or Prineville, we'd switch. Have to call up and say sorry, we're on the other side of the mountains again this week, cancel those cantaloupes. Dealing with the guru people is easier. They switch along with us.

What they believe in aside from organic gardening I don't know. Seems like the Guru Jaya Jaya Jaya would take some strenuous believing, but people can put their faith in anything, I guess. Hell, I believe in Edna.

Archie Hiddenstone

DAD GOT STRANDED IN TOWN AGAIN LAST WEEK. HE HUNG around awhile to see if the range would move back east, finally drove his old Ford over to Eugene and up the McKenzie River highway to get back to the ranch. Said he'd like to stay but Charlie Echeverria would be getting into some kind of trouble if he did. He just doesn't like to stay away from the place more than a night or two. It's hard on him when we turn up way over here on the coast like this.

I know he wishes I'd go back with him. I guess I ought to. I ought to live with him. I could see Mama every time Ether was over there. It isn't that. I ought to get it straight in my mind what I want to do. I ought to go to college. I ought to get out of this town. I ought to get away.

I don't think Gracie ever actually has seen me. I don't do anything she can see. I don't drive a semi.

I ought to learn. If I drove a truck she'd see me. I could come through Ether off the 1–5 or down from 84, wherever. Like that shit kept coming here last summer she was so crazy about. Used to come into the Seven-Eleven all the time for Gatorade. Called me Boy. Hey boy gimme the change in quarters. She'd be sitting up in his eighteen-wheeler playing with the gears. She never came in. Never even looked. I used to think maybe she was sitting there with her jeans off. Bareass on that truck seat. I don't know why I thought that. Maybe she was.

I don't want to drive a God damn stinking semi or try to feed a bunch of steers in a God damn desert either or sell God damn Hostess Twinkies to crazy women with purple hair either. I ought to go to college. Learn something. Drive a sports car. A Miata. Am I going to sell Gatorade to shits all my life? I ought to be somewhere that is somewhere.

I dreamed the moon was paper and I lit a match and set fire to it. It flared up just like a newspaper and started dropping down fire on the roofs, scraps of burning. Mama came out of the grocery and said, "That'll take the ocean." Then I woke up. I heard the ocean where the sagebrush hills had been.

I wish I could make Dad proud of me anywhere but the ranch. But that's the only place he lives. He won't ever ask me to come live there. He knows I can't. I ought to.

Edna

OH HOW MY CHILDREN TUG AT MY SOUL JUST AS THEY TUGGED at my breasts, so that I want to yell Stop! I'm dry! You drank me dry years ago! Poor sweet stupid Archie. What on earth to do for him. His father found the desert he needed. All Archie's found is a tiny little oasis he's scared to leave.

I dreamed the moon was paper, and Archie came out of the house with a box of matches and tried to set it afire, and I was frightened and ran into the sea.

Ady came out of the sea. There were no tracks on that beach that morning except his, coming up towards me from the breaker line. I keep thinking about the men lately. I keep thinking about Needless. I don't know why. I guess because I never married him. Some of them I wonder why I did, how it came about. There's no reason in it. Who'd ever have thought I'd ever sleep with Tom Sunn? But how could I go on saying no to a need like that? His fly bust every time he saw me across the street. Sleeping with him was like sleeping in a cave. Dark, uncomfortable, echoes, bears farther back in. Bones. But a fire burning. Tom's true soul is that fire burning, but he'll never know it. He starves the fire and smothers it with wet ashes, he makes himself the cave where he sits on cold ground gnawing bones. Women's bones.

But Mollie is a brand snatched from his burning. I miss Mollie. Next time we're over east again I'll go up to Pendleton and see her and the grandbabies. She doesn't come. Never did like the way Ether ranges. She's a stayputter. Says all the moving around would make the children insecure. It didn't make her insecure in any harmful way that I can see. It's her Eric that would disapprove. He's a snob. Prison clerk. What a job. Walk out of a place every night where the others are all locked in, how's that for a ball and chain? Sink you if you ever tried to swim.

Where did Ady swim up from I wonder? Somewhere deep. Once he said he was Greek, once he said he worked on an Australian ship, once he said he had lived on an island in the Philippines where they speak a language nobody else anywhere speaks, once he said he was born in a canoe at sea. It could all have been true. Or not. Maybe Archie should go to sea. Join the Navy or the Coast Guard. But no, he'd drown.

Tad knows he'll never drown. He's Ady's son, he can breathe water. I wonder where Tad is now. That is a tugging too, that not knowing, not knowing where the child is, an aching pull you stop noticing because it never stops. But sometimes it turns you, you find you're facing another direction, like your body was caught by the thorn of a blackberry, by an undertow. The way the moon pulls the tides.

I keep thinking about Archie, I keep thinking about Needless. Ever since I saw him look at Sook. I know what it is, it's that other dream I had. Right after the one with Archie. I dreamed something, it's hard to get hold of, something about being on this long long beach, like I was beached, yes, that's it, I was stranded, and I couldn't move. I was drying up and I couldn't get back to the water. Then I saw somebody walking towards me from way far away down the beach. His tracks in the sand were ahead of him. Each time he stepped in one, in the footprint, it was gone when he lifted his foot. He kept coming straight to me and I knew if he got to me I could get back in the water and be all right. When he got close up I saw it was him. It was Needless. That's an odd dream.

If Archie went to sea he'd drown. He's a drylander, like his father.

Sookie, now, Sook is Toby Walker's daughter. She knows it. She told me, once, I didn't tell her. Sook goes her own way. I don't know if he knows it. I don't think so. She has my eyes and hair. And there were some other possibilities. And I never felt it was the right thing to tell a man unless he asked. Toby didn't ask, because of what he believed about himself. But I knew the night, I knew the moment she was conceived. I felt the child-to-be leap in me like a fish leaping in the sea, a salmon coming up the river, leaping the rocks and rapids, shining. Toby had told me he couldn't have children—"not with any woman born," he said, with a sorrowful look. He came pretty near telling me where he came from, that night. But I didn't ask. Maybe because of what I believe about myself, that I only have the one life and no range, no freedom to walk in the hidden places.

Anyhow, I told him that that didn't matter, because if I felt like it I could conceive by taking thought. And for all I know that's what happened. I thought Sookie and out she came, red as a salmon, quick and shining. She is the most beautiful child, girl, woman. What does she want to stay here in Ether for? Be an old maid teacher like Emma? Pump gas, give perms, clerk in the grocery? Who'll she meet here? Well, God knows I met enough. I like it, she says, I like not knowing where I'll wake up. She's like me. But still there's the tug, the dry longing. Oh, I guess I had too many children. I turn this way, that way, like a compass with forty Norths. Yet always going on the same way in the end. Fitting my feet into my footprints that disappear behind me.

It's a long way down from the mountains. My feet hurt.

Tobinye Walker

MAN IS THE ANIMAL THAT BINDS TIME, THEY SAY. I WONDER. We're bound by time, bounded by it. We move from a place to another place, but from a time to another time only in memory and intention, dream and prophecy. Yet time travels us. Uses us as its road, going on never stopping always in one direction. No exits off this freeway.

I say *we* because I am a naturalized citizen. I didn't use to be a citizen at all. Time once was to me what my back yard is to Emma's cat. No fences mattered, no boundaries. But I was forced to stop, to settle, to join. I am an American. I am a castaway. I came to grief.

I admit I've wondered if it's my doing that Ether ranges, doesn't stay put. An effect of my accident. When I lost the power to walk straight, did I impart a twist to the locality? Did it begin to travel because my travelling had ceased? If so, I can't work out the mechanics of it. It's logical, it's neat, yet I don't think it's the fact. Perhaps I'm just dodging my responsibility. But to the best of my memory, ever since Ether was a town it's always been a real American town, a place that isn't where you left it. Even when you live there it isn't where you think it is. It's missing. It's restless. It's off somewhere over the mountains, making up in one dimension what it lacks in another. If it doesn't keep moving the malls will catch it. Nobody's surprised it's gone. The white man's his own burden. And nowhere to lay it down. You can leave town easy enough, but coming back is tricky. You come back to where you left it and there's nothing but the parking lot for the new mall and a giant yellow grinning clown made of balloons. Is that all there was to it? Better not believe it, or that's all you'll ever have: blacktop and cinder-block and a blurred photograph of a little boy smiling. The child was murdered along with many others. There's more to it than that, there is an old glory in it, but it's hard to locate, except by accident. Only Roger Hiddenstone can come back when he wants to, riding his old Ford or his old horse, because Roger owns nothing but the desert and a true heart. And of course wherever Edna is, it is. It's where she lives.

I'll make my prophecy. When Starra and Roger lie in each other's tender arms, she sixteen he sixty, when Gracie and Archie shake his pickup truck to pieces making love on the mattress in the back on the road out to the Hohovars, when Ervin Muth and Thomas Sunn get drunk with the farmers in the ashram and dance and sing and cry all night, when Emma Bodely and Pearl Amethyst gaze long into each other's shining eyes among the cats, among the crystals—that same night Needless the grocer will come at last to Edna. To him she will bear no child but joy. And orange trees will blossom in the streets of Ether.

HALF PAST FOUR

A NEW LIFE

STEPHEN BLUSHED. A FAIR-SKINNED MAN, BALD TO THE CROWN, he blushed clear pink. He hugged Ann with one arm as she kissed his cheek. "Good to see you, honey," he said, freeing himself, glancing past her, and smiling rather desperately. "Ella just went out. Just ten minutes ago. She had to take some typing over to Bill Hoby. Stay around till she gets back, she'd be real sorry to miss you."

"Sure," Ann said. "Mother's fine, she had this flu, but not as bad as some people. You all been OK?"

"Oh, yeah, sure. You want some coffee? Coke? Come on in." He stood aside and followed her through the small living room crowded with blond furniture to the kitchen where yellow metal slat blinds directed sunlight in molten strips onto the counters.

"Hey, it's hot," Ann said.

"Want some coffee? There's this cinnamon and mocha decaf that Ella and I drink a lot. It sure is. Glad it's Saturday. It's up here somewhere."

"I don't want anything."

"Coke?" He closed the cupboard, opened the refrigerator.

"Oh, sure, OK. Diet if you've got it."

She stood by the counter and watched him get the glass and the ice and the bottle, a plastic half-gallon of cola. She did not want to open doors in this kitchen as if prying, as if entitled, or to change the angle of the slat blinds, as she would have done at home, to shut the hot light out. He fixed her a tall red plastic glass of cola, and she drank off half of it. "Oh, yeah!" she said. "OK!"

"Come on outside."

"No ball game?"

"Been doing some gardening. With Toddie."

Ann had assumed that the boy was with his mother, or rather her imagination had linked him to his mother so that if Ella wasn't here Toddie wasn't here; now she felt betrayed.

Indicating where she should go but making her go first, as when he had brought her through the house, her father ushered her to the back-porch door, and stood aside and followed her as she went past the washer and dryer and the mop bucket and some brooms to the screen door and down the single cement step into the back yard.

He batted the screen door shut with one foot and stood beside her on a brick path, two bricklengths wide, that ran along dividing the flower-beds under the house wall from the small, shrub-circled lawn. Two small iron chairs painted white, with rust stains where the paint had come off, faced each other across a matching table at one side of the grass plot. Beyond them Toddie crouched, turned away, near a big flowering abelia in the shade of the mirrorplant hedge that enclosed the garden.

Toddie was bigger than she had remembered, as broad-backed as a grown man.

"Hey, Toddie. Here's ah, here's Ann!" Stephen said. His fair, tanned face was still pink. Maybe he wasn't blushing, maybe it was the heat. In the enclosed garden the sunlight glaring from the white house wall burned on the skin like an open fire. Had he been going to say, "your sister"? His voice was loud and jovial. Toddie did not respond in any way.

Ann looked around at the garden. It was an airless, grass-floored room with high green walls and a ceiling of brightness. Beautiful pale-colored poppies swayed by the hose rack, growing in clean, weeded dirt. She looked back at them, away from the stocky figure crouched in the shade across the lawn. She did not want to look at him, and her father had no right to make her be with him and look at him, even if it was superstitious, he should think of protecting the baby, but that was stupid, that was superstitious. "Those are really neat," she said, touching the loose, soft petal of an open poppy. "Terrific colors. This is a nice garden, Daddy. You must have been working hard on it."

"Haven't you ever been out back here?"

She shook her head. She had never even been in the bedrooms. She had been three or four times to this house since Stephen and Ella married. Once for Sunday brunch. Ella had served on trays in the living room, and Toddie had watched TV the whole time. The first time she had been in the house was when Ella was one of Stephen's salesgirls, not his wife. They had stopped by her house for her father to leave off some papers or something. Ann had been in high school, she had stood around in the living room while her father and Ella talked about shoe orders. Knowing that Ella had a retarded child, she had hoped that it wouldn't come into the room but all the same had wanted to see it. When Ella's husband died suddenly of something, Ann's father had said solemnly at the dinner table, "Lucky thing they had that house of theirs paid off," and Ann's mother had said, "Poor thing, with that poor child of theirs, what is it, a mongoloid?" and then they had talked about how mongoloids usually died and it was a mercy. But here he was still alive and Stephen was living in his house.

"I need some shade," Ann said, heading for the iron chairs. "Come and talk with me, Daddy."

He followed her. While she sat down and slipped off her sandals to cool her bare feet in the grass, he stood there. She looked up at him. The curve of his bald forehead shone in the sunlight, open and noble as a high hill standing bare above a crowded subdivision. His face was suburban, crowded with features, chin and long lips and nostrils and fleshy nose and the small, clear, anxious blue eyes. Only the forehead that looked like a big California hill had room. "Oh, Daddy," she said, "how you *been*?"

"Just fine. Just fine," he said, half turned away from her. "The Walnut Creek store is going just great. Walking shoes." He bent to uproot a small dandelion from the short, coarse grass. "Walking shoes outsell running shoes two to one at the Mall. So, you been job hunting? You ever talk to Krim?"

"Oh, yeah, couple weeks ago." Ann yawned. The still heat and the smell of newly turned earth made her sleepy. Everything made her sleepy. Waking up made her sleepy. She yawned again. "Excuse me! He said, oh, he said something might would open up in May."

"Good. Good. Good outfit," Stephen said, looking around the garden, and moving a few steps away. "Good contacts."

"But I'll have to stop working in July because of the baby, so I don't know if it's worth it."

"Get to know people, get started," Stephen said indistinctly. He went to the edge of the lawn nearest the abelia and said in a cheerful, loud voice, "Hey, great work there, Toddie! Hey, look at that! That's my boy. All right!"

A blurred, whitish face under dark hair turned up to him for a moment in shadow.

"Look at that. Diggin' up a storm there. You're a real farmer." Stephen turned and spoke to Ann from shade across the white molten air to her strip of shade: "Toddie's going to put in some more flowers here. Bulbs and stuff for fall."

Ann drank her melted-ice water and got up from the dwarf chair that had already stained her white T-shirt with rust. She came over nearer her father and looked at the strip of upturned earth. The big boy crouched motionless, trowel in hand, head sunk.

"Look, why not sort of round off that corner, see," Stephen said to him, going forward to point. "Dig to here, maybe. Think so?"

The boy nodded and began digging, slowly and forcefully. His hands were white and thick, with very short, wide nails rimmed with black dirt.

"What do you think, maybe dig it up clear over to that rose bush. Space out the bulbs better. Think it'd look good?"

Toddie looked up at him again. Ann looked at the blurred mouth, the dark-haired upper lip. "Yeah, uh-huh," Toddie said, and bent to work again.

"Kind of curve it off there at the rose bush," Stephen said. He glanced round at Ann. His face was relaxed, uncrowded. "This guy's a natural farmer," he said. "Get anything to grow. Teachin' me. Isn't that right, Toddie? Teachin' me!"

"I guess," the low voice said. The head stayed bowed, the thick fingers groped in earth.

Stephen smiled at Ann. "Teachin' me," he said.

"That's neat," she said. The sides of her mouth felt very stiff and her throat ached. "Listen, Daddy, I just looked in to say hi on the way to Permanente, I'm supposed to have a check-up. No, look, I'll just leave this in the kitchen and go out the gate there. It's real good to see you, Daddy."

"Got to go already," he said.

"Yeah, I just wanted to say hi since I was over this way. Say hi to Ella for me. I'm sorry I missed her." She had slipped her sandals back on; she took her empty glass into the kitchen, set it in the sink and ran water into it, came out again to her father standing on the brick path, bald to the sun. She put one foot up on the cement step to refasten the sandal. "My ankles were all swelled up," she said. "Dr. Schell took me off salt. I can't put salt on anything, not even eggs."

"Yeah, they say we should all cut down on salt," Stephen said.

"Yeah, that's right." After a pause Ann said, "Only this is because of being pregnant, that I have high blood pressure and this edema stuff. Unless I'm careful." She looked at her father. He was looking across the lawn.

"You know, Daddy, even if the baby doesn't have a father it can have a grandfather," she said. She laughed, and blushed, feeling the red heat mask her face and tingle in her scalp.

"Yeah, well, sure," he said, "I guess, you know," and if he finished the sentence she did not understand it. "We all got to take care," he said.

"Sure. Well, you take care too, Daddy," she said. She came to him to kiss his cheek. She tasted the faint salt of his sweat on her lips as she went along the brick path to the gate next to the trash cans, and let herself out onto the sidewalk under a purple jacaranda in full flower, and fastened the gate behind her.

UNBREAKING

"MY BACK ITCHES."

Ann reached out the garden fork and lightly raked its clawed tines down her brother's spine.

"Not there. There." He wrapped an arm round himself trying to show her the spot, his thick fingers with dirt-caked nails scrabbling in the air.

She hitched forward and scratched his back vigorously with her own fingertips. "That got it?"

"Uh-huh."

"I want some lemonade."

"Uh-huh," Todd said as she got up, whacking dirt off her bare knees. She had to bend at the knees, not at the waist, to reach them.

The yellow kitchen was hot and close like the inside of a room in a beehive, a cell full of yellow light, smelling of sweet wax, airless. A grub would love it. Ann mixed up instant lemonade, poured it over ice in tall plastic glasses, and carried them out, kicking the screen door shut behind her.

"Here you go, Todd."

He straightened up kneeling and took the glass in his left hand without putting down the trowel in his right. He drank off half the lemonade and then stooped to dig again, still holding the glass.

"Put it down there," Ann said, "by the bush."

He put the glass down carefully on the weedy dirt, and went on digging.

"Hey that's good!" Ann said, sucking at her lemonade, her mouth squirting saliva like a lawn sprinkler. She sat down on the grass with her head in the shade and her legs in the sun, and chewed ice slowly.

"You aren't digging," Todd said after a while.

"Nope."

After a while she told him, "Drink your lemonade. The ice is all melting."

He put down the trowel and picked up the glass. After drinking the lemonade he put the empty glass where it had been before.

"Hey, Ann," he said, not digging, but kneeling there with his bare, thick, pale back to her.

"Hey, Todd."

"Is Daddy coming home at Christmas?"

She tried for a moment to figure this one out. She was too sleepy. "No," she said. "He isn't coming home at all. You know that."

"I thought at Christmas," her brother said, barely audible.

"At Christmas he'll be with his new wife, with Marie. That's where he lives now, that's where his home is, in Riverside."

"I thought he might visit. At Christmas."

"No. He won't do that."

Todd was silent. He picked up the trowel and laid it down again. Ann knew he was unsatisfied but she could not figure out what his problem was and did not want any problems. She got her back against the trunk of the camphor tree and sat feeling the sun on her legs and the prickling grass under them and a sweat-drop trickle down between her breasts and the baby move once softly deep in and over on the left side of the universe.

"Maybe we could ask him to come at Christmas," Todd said.

"Honey," Ann said, "we can't do that. He and Mama got divorced so he could marry Marie. Right? And he'll have Christmas with her now. With Marie. And we'll have our Christmas here like always. Right?" She waited for his nod. She was not sure she got one, but went on anyhow. "If you're missing him a lot, Todd, we can write him and tell him that."

"Maybe we could visit him."

Oh, yeah, dandy. Hi Daddy, here's your moron son and your unwed pregnant daughter on welfare, hi Marie! It struck her funny but not enough to laugh. "We can't," she said. "Hey, look. If you dig over to the end there, in front of the roses, we could put in those canna bulbs Mama got, too. They'd look real good there. They'll be red, big red lilies."

Todd picked up the trowel, and then laid it down again in the same place.

"After Christmas he has to come," he said.

"What for? Why does he have to?"

"For the baby," her brother said, very low and blurry.

"Oh," Ann said. "Oh, shit. OK. Well. Listen, Toddie. Look. I'm having the baby, right?"

"After Christmas."

"Right. And it will be mine. Ours. You and Mama are going to help me bring it up. Right? And that's all I need. All I want. All the baby wants. Just you and Mama. All right?" She waited for his nod. "You're going to help me with the baby. Tell me when it cries. Play with it. Like that little girl at school, Sandy, that you help with. OK, Toddie?"

"Yeah. Sure," her brother said in the voice he had sometimes, masculine and matter-of-fact, as if a man spoke through him from somewhere else. He knelt erect, his hands splayed on his bluejeaned thighs, his face and torso in shadow illuminated by the glare of sunlight on the grass. "But he's an older parent," he said.

He's an ex-parent, Ann stopped herself from saying. "Right. So what?"

"Older parents often have Down children."

"Older mothers do. Right. So?"

She looked at Todd's round, heavy face, the sparse mustache at the ends of the upper lip, the dark eyes. He looked away.

"So your baby could be a Down baby," he said.

"Sure, it could. But I'm not an older parent, honey."

"But Daddy is."

"Oh," Ann said, and after a pause, "Right." She hitched herself heavily into the shade, with her bare feet in the fresh dirt Todd had been digging up. "OK, listen, Todd. Daddy is your father. And my father. But *not* the *baby's* father. Right?" No nod. "The baby has a different father. You don't know the baby's father. He doesn't live here. He lives in Davis, where I was. And Daddy is—Daddy isn't anything. He isn't interested. He has a new family. A new wife. Maybe they'll have a baby. They can be older parents. But they can't have this baby. I'm having this baby. It's our baby. It doesn't *have* any father. It doesn't have any *grandfather*. It's got me and Mama and you. Right? You're going to be its uncle. Did you know that? Will you be the baby's Uncle Todd?"

"Yeah," Todd said unhappily. "Sure."

A couple of months ago when she was crying all the time she would have cried, but now the universe inside her surrounded her with distance, through which all emotions travelled so far to reach her that they became quiet and smooth, deep and soft, like the big unbreaking waves out in mid-ocean. Instead of crying she thought about crying, the salty ache. She picked up the three-tined garden fork and reached over, trying to scratch Todd's head with it. He had shifted out of reach.

"Hey, kids," their mother said, the screen door banging behind her.

"Hey, Ella," Ann said.

"Hi, Mama," Todd said, turning away, bending to dig.

"Lemonade in the fridge," Ann said.

"What are you doing? Planting those old bulbs? I dug them up I don't know when, I bet they won't grow now. The cannas ought to. Oh I'm so hot! It's so hot downtown!" She came across the lawn in her high-heeled sandals, pantyhose, yellow cotton shirt dress, silk scarf, makeup, nail polish, sprayed set dyed hair, full secretarial uniform, complete armor. She bent over to kiss the top of her son's head, and kicked the sole of Ann's bare foot with the toe of her sandal. "Dirty children," she said. "Oh! It's so hot! I'm going to have a shower!" She went back across the lawn. The screen door banged. Ann imagined the soft folds released from under the girdle, the makeup sluiced away under warm spraying water running down over her first universe, that soft distance where she lived now, joined.

THE TIGER

ELLA HAD ON HER YELLOW SLEEVELESS DRESS WITH THE BLACK patent belt and black jet costume earrings. She had sprayed her hair. "Who's coming?" Ann asked from the couch.

"I told you yesterday. Stephen Sandies." Ella clipped past on her high wedge-heeled sandals like a circus pony on stilts, leaving a faint wake of hairspray smell and perfume.

"What are you wearing?"

"My yellow dress from the boteek."

"I mean perfume, dummy."

"I can't pronounce it," Ella called from the kitchen.

"Jardins de Bagatelle."

"That's it. The bagatelle part is OK. I used to play bagatelle. But I just pointed and said, 'That one.' I was trying testers at Krim's. Do you like it?"

"Yes. I stole some last night."

"What?"

"Never mind."

Ann raised a leg languidly and looked up along it as if sighting. She spread out her toes fanwise to make sights, closed them together, spread them. "Exercises, exercises, *always do* your *ex*ercises," she chanted, raising the other leg. "Zhardang, zhardang it all to bagatelle."

"What?"

"Nothing, Ma!"

Ella clipped back into the living room with a vase of red cannas. "I see London, I see France," she observed.

"I'm exercising. When Stephen Sandman comes I'll lie here and do breathing exercises, ha-ah-ha-ah-ha-ah-ha-ah. Who is he?"

"Sandies. He's in Accounting. I asked him to come in for a drink before we go out."

"Go out where?"

"The new Vietnamese place. They only have a beer and wine license."

"Is he nice? Stephen Sandpiper?"

"I don't know him well," Ella said primly. "That is, of course we've known each other at the office slightly for years. He and his wife were divorced a couple of years ago now."

"Ha-ah-ha-ah-ha-ah," Ann said.

Ella stood back from the arrangement of cannas. "Do they look all right?"

"Terrific. What do you want to do about me? Shall I lie here showing my underpants and doing puppy breathing?"

"We'll sit out on the patio, I thought."

"Then the cannas are just for the walk-through."

"And you're very welcome to join us, dear."

"We could impress this guy," Ann said, sitting up and assuming half-lotus position. "I could put on an apron and be the maid. Do we have an apron? One of those little white cap things. I could serve the canapés. Canapé, Mr. Sandpuppy? Canopee, Mr. Sandpoopoo?"

"Oh, hush," her mother said. "You're silly. I hope it'll be warm enough on the patio." She clipped back to the kitchen.

"If you really want to impress him," Ann called, "you'd better hide me."

Ella appeared instantly in the doorway, her mouth drawn in, her small blue eyes burning like the lights on airfields. "I will not listen to you talk that way, Ann!"

"I meant, I'm such a slob, my panties show, I haven't washed my hair, and look at the bottoms of my feet, God."

Ella continued to glare for a moment, then turned and went back into the kitchen. Ann hauled herself out of half-lotus and onto her feet. She came to the kitchen doorway.

"I just thought maybe you'd rather be alone. You know."

"I would like him to meet my daughter," Ella said, fiercely mashing cream cheese.

"I'll get dressed. You smell terrific. He'll die, you know." Ann snuffled around the base of her mother's neck, the creamy, slightly freckled skin in which two soft, round creases appeared when she turned her head, weakly crying, "Don't, don't, it tickles!"

"Vamp," Ann whispered hotly behind her mother's ear.

"Stop!"

Ann went off to the bathroom and showered. Enjoying the sound and the steam and the sluicing of the hot water, she took a long time about it. As she came naked out into the hallway she heard a man's voice and leaped back into the bathroom, pulling the door shut, then reopening it slightly to listen. They had got about as far as the cannas. She slipped out of the bathroom and down the hall to her room. She pulled on bikinis and the T-shirt dress that slithered pleasantly on her skin and embraced her rounded belly in forgiving shapelessness. She blowdried her hair on hot while she teased it with her fingers, put on lipstick and wiped it off, checked in the long mirror, and went sedate and barefoot down the hall, past the cannas, out onto the little flagged terrace.

Stephen Sandies, wearing a cool grey canvas sports coat and white shirt without tie, stood up and gave her a firm handshake. His smile was white but not too. Dark hair greying nicely. Trim, tan, fit, around fifty, stern mouth but not pursy, everything under control. Cool, but not sweating to keep cool. Would do. Good going, Ma, pour on the Zhardang de Big Hotel! Ann winked at her mother, who recrossed her ankles and said, "I forgot the lemonade, dear, if that's what you want? It's in the icebox." Ella was the last person in the Western Industrial Hegemony who said icebox, or canapé, or crossed her legs at the ankles. When Ann returned with a glass of lemonade, Stephen was talking. She sat down in a white webbed chair. Quietly, like a good girl. She sipped. They were on their second margaritas. Stephen's voice was soft, with a kind of burring or slight huskiness in it, very sexy, a kind voice. Drink your lemonade now like a good girl and slope off. Slope off where? The belly telly in the bedroom? Shit. Forget it. Hang on, it's been a nice day. Keep playing tag in Bagatelle Gardens. Can't catch me. What was he saying about his son?

"Well," he said, and fetched a sigh. Fetched it from deep inside, a long haul. He looked up at Ella with the wry, dry grin appropriate to the question, "Do you really want to hear all this?"

She's supposed to say no?

"Yes," Ella said.

"Well, it's a long, dull story, really. Legal battles are dull. Not like Hollywood courtroom scenes. To put it as briefly as possible, when Marie and I separated I was so angry and so . . . bewildered, really, that I agreed to several arrangements too hastily. To put it briefly, I've been forced to the conclusion that she's not fit to bring up my son. So we're into the classic custody battle. I'd rather, frankly, that she didn't even have visiting rights, but I'll compromise if I have to. Judges favor the mother, of course. But I intend to win. And I will. My lawyers are very good. If only the process were faster. It's very painful to me to wait through the delays and procedures. Every day he's with her will have to be undone. It's as if it were a disease for which there is a cure, and I have the cure. But they won't let me have him to begin the cure." Wow. So much conviction, and so quiet. So certain. Ann studied his face briefly sidelong. Handsome, stern, kind, sad, like God. Was he possibly very very very conceited? Was he possibly right?

"Is it—Is she drinking?" Ella hazarded, sounding weak, and setting down her glass.

"Not to the point of alcoholism," Stephen replied in his gently measured way. He looked down into his margarita-slush. "You know, I don't like to say these things. We were married for eleven years. There were good times."

"Oh, yes," Ella murmured pathetically, squirming with the pain his understatement concealed. But why didn't he squirm?

"But," he said. "Well. Far be it from me! God knows. No job, but a credit card—Where my child-support payments go I don't know. Three schools for Todd in two years. Disorder, bohemianism—but if that were all—it isn't that. It's the exposure of my child to immorality."

Ann was terrified. She had not expected this. Debt, dirt, disorder, OK, but immorality—her child would be exposed, exposed to immorality. Naked, soft, helpless, exposed. She would expose it by giving birth to it. By being its mother she would expose it to the dirt, the disorder, the immorality of a woman's life, her life. Its father would come from Riverside with a court order on clean, white paper. It would be taken from her, taken into custody. She would never see it. No visiting rights. No birth rights. It would be stillborn, it would die of immorality even before she could expose it.

Ella's mouth was drawn in, her eyes cast down. Stephen had just said a word to her that explained all. And Ann had not been listening. Had the word been "woman"?

"You see why I can't leave the boy there," Stephen said, and though not squirming he was in pain, no doubt of it, his hand tight on the arm of the chair.

Ella shook her head in agreement.

"And this—woman's friends. All—the same kind. Flaunting it."

Ann saw the monstrous regiment.

Stephen's head moved in tiny, rigid spasms as he spoke. "And the boy alone, in that. With them. Eight years old. A good kid. Straight as an arrow. I can't. I can't stand. To think of him. With them. Learning. That."

Each staccato burst hit Ann like machine-gun fire. She set down her lemonade glass on the flagstone, got carefully to her feet, and slipped away from Margaritaville with a vague smile, bleeding, bleeding evil monthly blood, nine months' worth bleeding from the holes he had shot in her. Behind her, her mother's voice said something consolatory to the man and then was raised, thin and weak, to cry, "Ann?"

"Back in a minute, Mama."

Passing the cannas flaming in twilight, she heard Ella say, "Ann is taking a year off from college. She's five months pregnant." She spoke in a strange tone, warning, boastful. Flaunting.

Ann went on to the bathroom. She had left her old underpants and shorts and T-shirt all over the bathroom when she showered, and he would have come to pee before they left and seen them and then her mother would have too and died. She picked things up. The bullet holes had been closed by her mother's voice. The blood had sublimated and ethe-realised into tears. She snivelled as she dropped dirty clothes and wet towels into the dirty-clothes hamper, she cried gratefully, she washed her face and opened the bottle of Jardins de Bagatelle, the perfume of the mother tiger, and put it on her hands and on her face where she could smell it.

LIVING IN YINLAND

DUFFY SLUNG ON HER KNAPSACK AND WENT OUT, SAYING OVER her shoulder, "Back around seven."

Her motorcycle revving and roaring off left silence behind. The Sunday paper was all over the living room. Nobody had got up till after noon.

"God, you know," Ella said, dropping the comics, "we get our periods exactly the same time now, within a day?"

"Hey, yeah? I've heard of that. That's kind of neat."

"Yeah, only I was beginning to stop having periods most of the time. Oh well. Tit for tat, as they say." Ella snorted. "I want some more coffee." She got up and shuffled off to the kitchen. "You want some?" she called.

"Not now."

Ella shuffled back in. She wore pink feather mules with low heels that flopped off if she lifted her foot.

"Those are really frivolous, El. I mean seriously frivolous."

"Duffy ordered them for me from some mail order catalogue." Ella sat down on the couch again, set her coffee cup on the table, and lifted one leg to look at the slipper. "She thought they'd suit me. Actually it's kind of like the things Stephen used to buy me sometimes. Mistakes."

"Like the stuff you make at school and then your parents have to use them."

"Like women buying men ties, it really is true. I love paisley and Stephen hated it, he thought paisley looked like bugs, those curvy sort of shapes, you know, and I didn't realise it and I always bought him these beautiful paisley ties."

"Isn't it weird how . . ."

"How what?"

"I don't know, how we don't get through to each other, you know, only we sort of do, only not where we thought we were. I mean, like you're *wearing* those. Well, and like both of us thinking the other one would like disapprove, and all that stuff you went through psyching yourself up to call me about selling Mother's house. Everything backwards. But it works. Sometimes."

"Yeah," Ella said. "Sometimes." She had put both pink-feathered feet up on the edge of the coffee table, and gazed at them, her small, bright, light-blue eyes stern, judgmental. Her half-sister Ann, a much larger woman fifteen years younger, sat on the floor amidst the comics and classifieds and coffee cups, wearing purple sweatpants and a red sweatshirt with an expressionless yellow circle-face on it labelled, "Have A Day."

"Mom used that chicken ashtray I made in fourth grade till she died," Ella said.

"Even after she quit smoking. El, did you like my dad?"

Ella gazed at her feet. "Yeah," she said. "I liked him. You know, I didn't ever remember a whole lot about my own father. I was only six when he got killed and he'd been overseas a year. I don't think I even cried except because Mom cried. So I wasn't comparing, or anything. I guess what I didn't like when Mom and Bill married was I missed her and me being together. Like this, you know, slopping around. Women slopping around. That's partly why I like it with Duffy. Only Duffy's more, well, it has to do with sex, not gender, I guess. With Duffy it's not so easy, you have to watch it. With Mom it was so easy. With you it's easy."

"Too easy, sort of?"

"I don't know. Maybe. I like it, though. Anyhow. I wasn't ever jealous of Bill or anything. He was a sweet guy. I guess in fact I had a crush on him for a while. Trying to compete with Mom. Practicing . . ."

Ella's smile, which was infrequent, curved her long, thin lips into a charming half-circle.

"I got a crush on everybody. My math teacher. The bus driver. The paper boy. God, I used to get up in the dark and wait at the window to see the paper boy."

"Always men?"

Ella nodded. "They hadn't invented women yet, then," she said.

Ann stretched out flat on the floor and raised first one purple leg, pointing her toes at the ceiling, then the other.

"What were you when you got married? Nineteen?" she asked.

"Nineteen. Young. Younger than, Christ, fresh eggs. But you know, I wasn't really dumb. I mean Stephen was a really good guy, I mean a prince. You probably only remember him after he was drinking."

"I remember your wedding."

"Oh Christ yes, when you were flower girl."

"And that little fart son of Aunt Marie's was ring bearer, and we got into a fight."

"Oh God yes, and Marie started crying and saying she never thought to have people in the *family* who were *minorities*, and Mom got mad and said why not call Bill a spick straight out then, and Marie did, she started yelling, 'A spick then! A spick then!' And she had hysterics, and Bill's brother the vet got her squiffed in the vestry. No wonder things went wrong with a start like that. But I did want to say about Steve, he was a really, really bright, lovely guy. See, I can't say that to Duffy. It would just hurt her for no reason. She isn't very secure. But sometimes I need to say it, to be fair to him, and to myself. Because it was so unfair what being alcoholic did to him. And you know, I had to finally just get out and run. And for me that was OK, it's worked out fine. But I think of how he started out and how he ended up, and it, I don't know, it isn't fair."

"You ever hear from him any more?"

Ella shook her head. "I've been thinking the last year or so he's probably dead," she said in the same quiet voice. "He was down so far. But I won't ever know."

"Was he the only guy you went with seriously?"

Ella nodded one nod.

After a while, looking at her pink-feathered feet, she said, "Sex with a drunk is not the biggest turn-on. I don't guess anybody but Duffy could of got through to me, maybe." She blushed, a delicate but vivid pink appearing suddenly in her rather sallow cheeks and fading slowly. "Duffy's a very kind person," she said.

"I like her," Ann said.

Ella sighed. She slid her feet out of the feathered mules, letting them drop to the floor, and curled herself up on the couch. "What is this, true confession time?" she said. "I was wanting to ask you how come you didn't want to stay with the baby's father, was he a jerk or something."

"Oh God."

"I'm sorry."

"No. It's just embarrassing to say. Todd's seventeen. Eighteen by now, I guess. One of my Computer Programming students." Ann sat up and bowed her head down to her knees, stretching tension out of her back and hiding her face, then sat up straight; she was smiling.

"Does he know?"

"Nope."

"Did you think about an abortion at all?"

"Oh, yeah. But see. It was me that was careless. So I wondered, why was I careless? And I wanted to quit teaching anyhow. And get out of Riverside. I want to stay around the Bay here and get work. Temping to start with, till I find what I want. I can always find a job, that's no problem for me. I want to get into programming eventually, and maybe consulting. I can have the baby and then go back part time. And I want to live alone with the baby and kind of take my time. Because I kept sort of rushing into everything, you know? But what I think is I'm a maternal type, actually, more than a wife type or a lover type."

"Could take some finding out," Ella said.

"Well, that's why I want to sort of slow down. But I'll tell you my long-range plans. I'll find this executive, fifty, fifty up, maybe sixty up, and marry him. Mommy marries Daddy, see?" She bowed her head to her knees again and came up smiling.

"Dumb, dumb, dumb," Ella said. "Dumb shit sister. You can leave the baby here on your honeymoon."

"With Auntie Ella."

"And Uncle Duffy. Christ. I haven't seen Duffy with a baby."

"Is Duffy her real name?"

"She'd kill me if she knew I told you. Marie."

"Cross my heart."

They unfolded and refolded various sections of the paper, leafed slowly. Ann looked at pictures of resorts in the Northern Coast Range, read advertisements from travel agencies, fly to Hawaii, cruise Alaska.

"What ever happened to that little fart son of Aunt Marie's, anyhow?"

"Wayne. He got some degree in Business Administration at UCLA."

"It figures."

"What are you? Pisces?"

"I think so."

"It says this is a good day for you to make long-range plans, and look out for an important Scorpio. That's your sugar daddy, I guess."

"No, what's November, is that Scorpio?"

"Yeah. Till the twenty-fourth, it says."

"OK, that's this long-range plan in here. I'll look out for it. . . ."

After a pause Ella, reading, said, "Seventeen."

"*All* right," Ann said, reading.

MIRRORING

THE LOWER EDGE OF THE LAWN ABOVE THE RIVERBANK WAS planted in red cannas. Beyond that intense color the river was gunbarrel blue. Both the red line and the blue reflected in Stephen's mirror-finish sunglasses, moving up and down across the surface and seeming to change the expression of his face incomprehensibly. Todd looked away from this display with an irritable turn of the head. Stephen asked at once, "What's wrong?"

"I wish you didn't wear mirror shades."

"See yourself reflected in them?" Smiling, Stephen slowly took the glasses off. "Is that so bad?"

"What I see is all these colors running across your face like some robot in the movies. Mirror shades are like aggressive, you know? Black dudes coming on cool. Hank Williams Junior."

"If you're behind them, they're defensive. Soft-bodied animal hiding. Protective mimicry. I bought them for this trip." Stephen's face without the glasses did look soft, not doughy or rubbery but soft-finished like stone or wood long used, worn down to fineness. All the lines that etched his face were fine, and the cut of lip and nostril and eyelid was delicate but blurred by that softening, that abrasion of years. Todd looked down at his own big, smooth hands and knees and thighs with a sense of self-consciousness that sharpened to discomfort. He looked back at Stephen's hands holding the sunglasses.

"No, you're right," Stephen said, "they're aggressive." He was holding them so that the curved, insectile planes reflected his own face and behind it the white facade of the hotel against the dark mountain. "I see you—you don't see me. . . . But I want to look at you all the time. And with these on, I can do just that. And you don't have to see as much of me."

"I like seeing you," Todd said, but Stephen was fitting the glasses back across his face.

"Now I can be contemplating the river, for all *they* know, while all the time inside here I'm actually staring, staring, staring at you, trying to get my fill. . . . I don't believe you. I can't believe you. That you came. That you wanted to come. That you wanted to give me this incredible gift. I have to wear these when I look at you. You are nineteen years old. I could go blind. You don't have to say anything. Letting me say these things is your gift to me. Part of your gift to me." When he wore the mirroring glasses his voice was smoother, softer, deflecting answers.

Todd said doggedly, "The giving goes the other way too. Mostly, in fact."

"No, no, no," Stephen murmured. "Nothing. Nothing."

"All this?" Todd looked around at the red cannas, the white hotel, the dark ridges, the river.

"All this," Stephen repeated. "Plus Miz Gertrude and Miz Alice B. My God, those women follow us like reflections in a funnyhouse. Don't look!"

Todd was already looking over his shoulder to see the two women coming up the path between the lawns from the river. The old one was in the lead and the young one a good ways behind her, carrying fishing poles. Seeing him turn, the old one held up a couple of good-sized trout and called out something ending with "breakfast!"

Todd nodded and made a V for Victory sign.

"They catch fish," Stephen murmured. "They beach whales. They play five-card stud. They fell giant sequoias. They deploy missiles. They gut bears. Only please God let them stay busy and leave us alone! A fish-waving bull dyke is more than I can cope with just now. Tell me that they're going away."

"They're going away."

"Good. Good." The curved black surfaces turned again, canna-red flashing across them. "They'll have vacated the rowboat we were hoping for, presumably. Shall we go on the river?"

"Sure." Todd stood up.

"Do you want to, Tadziu?"

Todd nodded.

"You do whatever I ask or suggest. You should do what *you* like. Your pleasure is my pleasure."

"Let's go."

"Let's go," Stephen repeated, smiling, standing up.

On the lazy water of the lake above the dam, Todd shipped the oars and slid down to lie with his back against the seat.

Behind him Stephen's husky voice sang in a whisper, *"Dans les jardins de mon père . . ."* and then, after a silence, spoke softly aloud:

> *"Âme, te souvient-il, au fond du paradis,*
> *De la gare d'Auteuil, et des trains de jadis?"*

"No assignments on spring break," Todd said.

"No one could translate it in any case."

Todd felt Stephen's finger like a feather caress the outer rim of his left ear, once.

It was completely silent on the water. On his lips Todd tasted the salt of his sweat from rowing. Behind him Stephen sitting in the prow made no sound, said nothing.

"One of them left a fly box under the seat here," Todd said, looking down at it.

"Under no circumstances take it to them. I'll turn it in at the hotel desk. Or drop it overboard. It's the excuse they've been waiting for. It's a plant. Oh how kind of you we've just been dying to talk to you and your father and I'm Alice B and this is Gertie and isn't this place just bully for all us boys? It's called the dyke bursting."

Todd laughed. Again the feather touch went round his ear, and he laughed again, repressing a shudder of pleasure.

All he could see as he half lay in the boat was colorless sky and one long sunlit ridge.

"You know," he said, "I think actually you've got them wrong. The girl was talking last night to that girl Marie that cooks, you know? On the terrace, when I went out to smoke a joint, last night late, you know. And she was telling her she came here with her mother, because her brother died, and her mother had been nursing him, or something, like he was sick for a long time or like brain damaged or something. So when he died she wanted to bring her mother up here for a rest and like a change.

So actually they'd be mother and daughter. I looked in the registration book when I came in and it said Ella Sanderson and Ann Sanderson."

The silence behind him continued. He tipped his head back and back till he could see Stephen's face upside down, the black sunglasses mirroring the sky.

"Does it matter?" Stephen's voice said, terribly melancholy.

"No."

Todd lifted his head and looked across the colorless water at the colorless sky beyond where the ridges narrowed in the dam.

"It doesn't matter at all," he said.

"I could sink the boat now," the sorrowful, tender voice behind him said. "Like a stone."

"OK."

"You understand . . . ?"

"Sure. This is the center. Like which is water and which is sky. So sinking's flying. It doesn't matter. At the center. Go on."

After a long time Todd sat back up on the seat, reset the oars, and began rowing in long, quiet strokes away from the lip of the dam. He did not look around.

EARTHWORKS

ANN'S FATHER HAD RECENTLY MADE A POND FROM A SPRING BELOW the ranch house, and after lunch they walked down to see it. Horses grazed on the high, bare, golden hill on the far side of the water. From the rainy-season highwater line the banks were bare and muddy down to the summer level, making a reddish rim. A rowboat, looking oversized, was pulled up beside the tiny dock. They sat on the dock, in bathing suits, dangling their feet in the tepid water. They were too full of food and wine to want to swim yet. Although the baby did not yet crawl and was sound asleep anyhow, the knowledge that he was sleeping with water a foot or two away on either side of him was a dim unease in Ann's mind, making her look round at him quite frequently and keep one hand touching the flannel blanket he lay on. To hide her overprotectiveness or to excuse it from herself, each time she looked round at the baby she readjusted the cotton shirt which she had taken off and tented up over him to protect his head from the sun.

"Now," said her father, "I want to know about your life. The place you live. The woman you live with. Start there."

"Ground floor of an old house in San Pablo. Two bedrooms, and a walk-in closet for Toddie's room. Old Japanese couple have the upstairs. The neighborhood's a little rough but there's a lot of nice people, and our block is OK. OK? Then Marie. She's gay, but we're not living together. It's actually Toddie she was interested in."

"Jesus!"

"I mean, she wanted to help parent a baby." Ann broke into a laugh that was both genuine and nervous. "She does computer programming and counselling, so she works at home a lot. It works out really well for care-sharing. The way it works out with her and me, we each have a wife."

"Great," Stephen said.

"I mean, you know, a person you can count on to sort of take over if you can't. And do the shitwork, and you know."

"Not my experience of wives," her father said. "So you've given up on men, then."

"No. Like I said, Marie and I aren't together. She has lesbian friends, a lot of my friends are straight, but just now, I don't know, I'm just not into that a whole lot. I will again, you know. It's not like I'm bitter or anything. I wanted to have the baby. I just want to be with him mainly at this point. The job's weird hours, but that means when I'm out Marie's there, and mostly when he's awake, I'm there. So it's real good now. And later it'll change. . . ."

As she spoke she felt in her father, sitting a foot or two from her, a physical resistance, a great impatience; she felt it physically as a high, hard, slanting blade, like the blade of a bulldozer. The owner of the land had the right to clear it, to clear out this underbrush of odd jobs, half-couplings, rented closets, hiding places, makeshifts. The blade advanced.

"Since Penny and I divorced I've done a lot of stock-taking. Sitting right here. Or riding Dolly over there around the ranch." Her father was looking across the pond at the high hill as he spoke, watching the grazing mare and colt and the white gelding. "Thinking about both my marriages. Especially about the first one, strangely enough. I began to see that I didn't ever work through the whole thing before I married Penny. I never really handled the pain your mother caused me. I denied it. Macho, tough guy—real men don't feel pain. You can keep up that crap for years. But it finally catches up with you. And then you realise all you've done is save your shit to drown in. So I've been doing the work I should have done ten, twelve years ago. And some of it's almost too late. I have to face the fact that I wasted a lot of those years, wasted a marriage. Started it and ended it in all the unfinished business from the first marriage. Well, OK. Win one, lose one. What I'm doing now is establishing priorities. What's important. What comes first. And doing that, I've been able to see what my mistake, my one real mistake, was. You know what it was?"

He looked at her so keenly with his clear, light-blue eyes that she flinched. He waited, smiling slightly, alert.

"Divorcing Mama, I guess," she said, looking down and swallowing the words because she knew they were wrong. He did not speak, and she looked back at him. He was still smiling, and she thought what a handsome man he was, looking like a Roman general now with his short-cropped hair and silver-blue eyes, long lips and eagle nose, but wearing a Plains Indian beaded talisman on a rawhide cord about his neck. He was very deeply tanned. On his ranch in summer he wore nothing but shorts and thong sandals, or went naked.

"That was no mistake," he said. "That was one of the right things I did. And buying this place. I had to move *on*. And Ella isn't willing, isn't able to go on, to act, move, develop. Her strength is in staying put. God, what strength! But it's all in that. So the shit piles up around her, and she never clears it away. Hell, she builds walls of it! Fecal fortifications. Defending her from, God forbid, change. From, God forbid, freedom . . . I had to break out of her fortress. I was suffocating. Buried alive. I tried to take her with me. She wouldn't come. Wouldn't move. Ella never had any use for freedom, her own or anybody else's. And I was so desperate for it by then that I'd take it on any terms. So that's where I made my mistake."

She felt remiss at still not understanding what his mistake had been, but he said nothing, and she was obliged to admit it: "I guess I don't know what mistake," she said, feeling as she said it that it must have something to do with her, and oppressed by the feeling. She glanced over her shoulder at the sleeping baby.

"Leaving you," her father said quietly. "Not putting up a fight for custody."

She knew that this was very important to him and ought to be so to her, but all she felt was that she was being crowded, pushed along by the slanting, uprooting blade, and she looked back again at the baby and moved the shirttail unnecessarily to shade his legs.

"A little late to think about that, she thinks," her father's voice said gently.

"Oh, I don't know. Anyhow we got to see each other every summer," she said, blushing red.

The blade moved forward, levelling and making clear. "I needed freedom in order to go on living, and I saw you as part of the jail. Part of Ella. I *literally* didn't separate you from her—you see? She didn't allow that possibility even as an idea. You were her, you were her motherhood, and she was the Great Mother. She had you built right into the walls. And I bought that. Maybe if you'd been a boy I'd have seen what was going on sooner. I'd have felt my part in you, my claim—my right to

get you out of the shitfort, the earthworks. *My* right to assert *your* right
to freedom. You see? But I didn't see it. I didn't look. I just got loose and
left you as hostage. It's taken me twelve years to be able to admit that. I
want you to know that I do admit it now."

Ann picked a foxtail from the corner of the baby's blanket by her hip.
"Yeah, well," she said. "I guess it worked out OK, anyhow, you know, Mom
and me, and anyhow Penny didn't want some teenage stepdaughter
around all the time."

"If I'd fought for you and won custody—and if I'd fought I'd have
won—what Penny wanted or didn't want would have been a matter of
supreme indifference. I probably wouldn't have married her. One mistake
leads to the next one. You'd have lived here. All your summers here. Gone
to a good school. And a four-year college, maybe an Eastern school, Smith
or Vassar. And you wouldn't be living with a lesbian in San Pablo, working nights for a phone company. I'm not blaming you, I'm blaming myself.
I can't believe how true to form Ella is, how unchangingly unchanging—
how she dug you in, walled you into the same dirt, the same futureless
trap. What kind of future does your life spell for your kid, Ann?"

But I was really lucky to get the job, Ann thought, but what's neat is
that for a while things aren't changing all the time, but you haven't even
seen Mom for ten years so how do you know? All these thoughts were mere
shadows and underbrush, among which her mind hopped like a rabbit.

"Well," she said, "things are really OK the way they worked out," and,
unable to control her increasing anxiety about Toddie, she turned away
from her father and knelt above the sleeping baby, pretending that he
had waked up. "All right then! Up you come! Hey, baby bunny boy.
Hey, you sleepy bunny." The baby's head wobbled, his eyes looked in
different directions, and as soon as she settled him on her lap he fell
fast asleep again. His small, warm, neat weight gave her substance. She
stirred the lake with her toes and said, "You shouldn't worry about it,
Daddy. I'm really happy. I just wish you were, if you aren't."

"You're happy," he said, with one glance of his light eyes, the almost scornfully accurate touch she remembered, that reversed the poles.

"Yes, I am," she said. "But there's one thing I wanted to tell you about."

While she summoned up words, Stephen said, with satisfaction in his acuteness, "I thought so. The father's back in the picture."

"No," Ann said vaguely, not heeding. "Well, see, they think at the clinic that Toddie had some brain damage, probably at birth. That's why he's slow developing in some ways. We noticed it pretty soon. They can't tell how much yet, and they think it isn't real severe. But they know there's some impairment." She drew her fingertip very lightly around the tiny pink curve of the baby's ear. "So. That's taken some, you know, thinking. Getting used to. It's not as big a deal as I thought. But it is, in some ways."

"What are you doing about it?"

"There isn't anything to do. Now. Sort of wait and see. And watch. He's only five months. They noticed a—"

"What are you doing about correcting it?"

"There isn't anything like that to do."

"You're just going to take this?"

She was silent.

"Ann, this is my grandson."

She nodded.

"Don't cut me out. You may be angry at the father, but don't take it out on men, don't join the castraters, for God's sake! Let me help. Let me get some competent doctors, let's get some light on this. Don't dig down into a hole with all these fears and old wives' tales, and smother the kid with them. I don't accept this. Not on the word of some midwife at this women's clinic that botched the kid's birth! My God, Ann! You can't take this out on *him!* There are things that can be done!"

"I've taken him to Permanente," Ann said.

"Shit! Permanente! You need first-class doctors, specialists, neurologists— Bill can give us some recommendations. I'll get onto it when we go back

to the house. I'll call him. My God. This is what I meant! This is it.
This is what I left you in—the mud—My God! how could you sit here
all day with him and me and *not tell me?*"

"It isn't your fault, Daddy."

"Yes," he said, "it is. Exactly. If I—"

She interrupted. "It's the way he is. And there's a best way for him to be,
like anybody. And that's what we can do, is find that. So please don't talk
shit about 'correcting.' Look, I'd like to have a swim now, I think. Will
you hold him?"

She saw that he was startled, even frightened, but he said nothing.
She carefully transferred the rosy, sweaty, silky baby onto his thin thighs
covered with sparse sun-bleached hairs. She saw his large, fine hand cup
the small head. She got up then and went three steps to the end of the
little dock and stood on the weather-gnawed grey planks. The water was
shallow, and she did not dive but splashed down in, her feet tangling
for a moment in slimy weeds. She swam. Ten or fifteen yards out she
turned, floated awhile, trod water to look back at the dock. Stephen
sat motionless in the flood of sunlight, his head bowed over the baby,
whom she could not even see in the shadow of her father's body.

THE PHOTOGRAPH

As she was scrubbing out the kitchen sink, where she had
let bleaching powder stand to whiten the old rust stains, Ella saw that the
girl from the complex was talking with Stephen. She rinsed out the sink,
got her dark glasses from the kitchen oddments drawer, polished them
a bit with the dishtowel, put them on, and went out into the back yard.

Stephen was weeding the vegetable plot by the fence, and the girl was
standing on the other side of the fence, just her head and shoulders showing. She had her baby in one of those kangaroo things that mashed it up

against its mother's front. It was asleep, nothing visible but the tiny sleek head like a kitten's back. Stephen was working, his head bent down as usual, and didn't seem to be paying attention to the girl, but just as she came out, before the screen door banged, Ella heard him say, "Green beans."

The girl looked up and said, "Oh, hi, Mrs. Hoby!" in a bright voice. Stephen kept his head bent down at his weeding.

Ella came over to the laundry roundabout and felt the clothes she had hung out earlier in the afternoon. Stephen's T-shirts and her yellow wash dress were dry already, but Stephen's jeans were still damp, as she had expected; feeling them was nothing but an excuse for coming out.

"You sure have a nice garden," the girl said.

The complex of eight apartments they had built next door ten years ago had nothing but cement and garages behind it where the Pannis's garden with the big jacaranda had been. There was no place for a child to play there. But before the baby was old enough the girl would have moved on, the welfare-and-food-stamp people never stayed, the men with no jobs and the girls with no husbands, playing their big radio-tape machines loud and smoking dope at night in those hot little apartments.

"Stephen and I know each other from the store," the girl said. "He carried my groceries home for me last week. That was a nice thing to do. I had the baby, and my arms were just about falling off."

Stephen laughed his "huh-huh," not looking up.

"Have you lived here for a long time?" the girl asked. Ella was rehanging the jeans, for something to do. She answered after she had got the seams matched. "My brother has lived here all his life. This is his house."

"It is? That's neat," the girl said. "All his *life*? That's amazing! How old are you, Stephen?"

Ella thought he would not answer, and it might serve the girl right, but after a considerable pause he said, "Four. Forty-four."

"Forty-four years right here? That's wonderful. It's a nice house, too."

"It was," Ella said. "It was all single-family houses when we were children

here." She spoke dryly, but she had to admit that the girl did not mean to
patronise, and was pleasant, the way she talked right to Stephen instead
of across him the way most people did, or else they shouted at him as if
he were deaf, which he was only slightly, in the right ear.

Stephen stood up, dusted off his knees carefully, and went across the
grass and into the house, hooking the screen door shut behind him with
his foot.

Ella had sat down on the small cement base of the laundry round-about
to pull at a dandelion clump in the grass. It had been there for years,
always coming back. You had to get every single piece of root of a dandelion, and the roots went under the cement.

"Did I hurt his feelings?" the girl asked, shifting the baby in its carrier.

"No," Ella said. "He's probably getting a photograph to show you. Of
the house."

"I really like him," the girl said. Her voice was low and a little husky,
with a break in it, like some children's voices. What they used to call a
whiskey voice, only childlike. The poor thing was not much more than
a child. Babies having babies, they had said on the television.

"Have you always lived here too, Mrs. Hoby?"

Ella worked at the dandelion root, loosening it, then took off her
sunglasses and looked round at the girl. "My husband and I ran a resort
hotel," she said. "Up in the redwood country, on a river. A very old
place, built in the eighteen eighties, quite well known. We owned it
for twenty-seven years. When my husband passed away I ran it for two
more years. Then when my mother passed away and left the house to
Stephen, I decided to retire and come live here with him. He has never
lived with strangers. He's fifty-four, not forty-four. Numbers confuse
him sometimes."

The girl listened intently. "Did you have to sell the resort? Do you
still own it?"

"I sold it," Ella said.

"What was it like?"

"A big country hotel, up north. Twenty-six rooms. High ceilings. A terraced dining room over the river. We had to modernise the kitchens and the plumbing entirely when we bought it. There used to be places like that. Elegant. Before the motels. People came for a week, or a month. Some people, families and single people, came every summer or fall for years. They made their reservation for the next year before they left. We offered fishing, good trout fishing, and horseback riding, and mountain walks. It was called The Old River Inn. It's mentioned in several books. The present owners call it a 'bed and breakfast.'" Ella dug her fingers in under the dandelion root, sinewy there in its dirt darkness, and pried. It broke. She should have got the weeder or the garden fork.

"What an amazing kind of thing to do," the girl said, "running a place like that." Ella could have told her that they had never had a vacation themselves for a quarter of a century and that the hotel had worn her out and finally killed Bill and eaten up their lives for nothing, mortgaged and remortgaged and the payments from the bed and breakfast people not even enough to live on here, but because there was a break or a catch in the girl's voice that sounded as if she saw the forest ridges and the Inn on its lawns above the river as Ella saw it, as the old, noble, beautiful, remote thing, she said only, "It was hard work," but smiled a little as she said it.

Stephen came out of the house and straight across the grass, glancing up once at the girl and then down again at the picture he held. It was the framed photograph of Mama and Papa on the porch of the house, the year they bought it, and Ella in her pinafore dress sitting on the top front step, and Baby Stephen sitting in the pram. The girl took it and looked at it for quite a time.

"That's Mama. That's Papa. That's Ella. That's me, the baby," he said, and laughed quietly, "huh-huh!"

The girl laughed too and sniffled and wiped her nose and her eyes quite openly. "Look how little all the trees are!" she said. "You've been doing a lot of gardening since they took that picture, I guess." She handed it carefully back across the fence to Stephen. "Thank you for showing it to me," she said, and her little whiskey voice was so sad that Ella turned her head away and scraped her nails in the dirt trying to seize the broken root, in vain, till the girl had gone, because there was nothing to say to her but what she knew already.

THE STORY

ANN SAT ERECT IN THE WHITE-PAINTED IRON CHAIR ON THE little flagged terrace behind the house. She wore white, and was barefoot. The old abelia bushes behind her, above the terrace, were in full flower. Her child sat among scattered plastic toys on the edge of the terrace where it met the lawn, near her. Ella looked at them from the kitchen window, through the yellow metal blinds that were slanted to send the hot afternoon light upward to the ceiling, making the low room glow like the wax of a lighted beeswax candle. Todd moved the toys about, but she could not see a pattern in the way he moved or placed them; they did not seem to relate to each other. He did not talk when he picked up one or another. There was no story being told. He dropped an animal figure and picked up a broken-off dandelion flower, dropped it. Only from time to time he made a humming or droning noise, loud enough that Ella could hear it pretty clearly, a rhythmic, nasal sound, "Anh-hanh, anh-hanh, hanh . . ."When he was making this music of his he swayed or rocked a little and his face, half hidden by thick glasses, brightened and relaxed. He was a pretty child.

His mother, Ann, was very beautiful there in the sunlight, her pale skin shining with sweat, her dark hair loose and bright against the shadow and the small, pale, creamy flowers of the abelia. Had she given promise of such beauty? Ella had thought her rather plain as a child, but then she had held herself back from the child, not looking for her beauty, knowing that if she found it all it meant was losing it, since Stephen and Marie came West so seldom, and after the divorce Marie never wanted to send the child alone. Three or four years would pass when she never saw Ann. And a grandchild's life goes by so fast, faster than a child's.

Stephen had been a pretty child, now! People had stopped her to admire him in his little blue and white suit in the pram, or when he was walking and held her hand and walked with her down to the old Cash and Carry Market. His blue eyes were so bright and clear, and his fair hair curled all over his head. And that innocent look some little boys have, that trusting look, he had kept that so long, right into his teens, really. And how Stephen had told stories when he was this child's age! From morning till night there had been some tale going, till it drove her crazy sometimes, Stephen babbling softly away at table, anywhere, telling his unending saga about the Wood Dog and what was it?—the Puncha. The Puncha, and other characters he had made up out of his head. They didn't have the TV then, or the bright plastic toys, soldiers and tanks and monsters. While they lived up on the ranch, Stephen had had no playmates at all, unless Shirley brought her girls over for the day. So he told his endless adventures, which Ella could never understand, playing with a toy car or two and bits of mill ends for blocks, or an old spool, wooden the way spools were, and wooden clothespins, and the little husky monotone voice: "So they went up there rrrrrm, rrrrrm, rrrrrm, and they were waiting there, so they went along there, rrrrrm, rrrrrm, so then the road stopped and they fell off, they fell down, down, down, help help where's Puncha?" And so on and on like that, even in his bed at night.

"Stephen?"

"Yes, Mama!"

"Hush now and go to sleep!"

"I *am* asleep, Mama!" Virtuous indignation. She hid her laugh. She tiptoed to the door, and in a minute the little voice would begin to whisper again: "So then they said Let's go to the, to the lake. So there was this boat on the lake and so then Wood Dog started sinking, crash, splash, help help where's Puncha? Here I am Wood Dog. . . ." Then at last a small yawn. Then silence.

Where did all that go? What happened to it? The funny little boy making everything in the world into his story, he never would have understood any story about a telephone company executive recently married for the third time whose only child by his first marriage was sitting now in the white chair watching her only child by no marriage rock back and forth restlessly and endlessly, droning his music of one nasal syllable.

"Ann," Ella said, lifting the slatted blind, "diet cola or lemonade?"

"Lemonade, Grandmother."

What became of it? she asked again, getting the ice out of the refrigerator, getting the glasses down from the cupboard. Why didn't the story make sense? Such hope she had had for Stephen, so sure he would do something noble. Not a word people used, and of course it was silly to expect a happy ending. Would it have been better to be like poor young Ann, who had no hope or pride beyond the most austere realism—"He won't be fully self-sufficient, but his dependence level can be reduced a good deal. . . ." Was it better, more honest, to tell only very short stories, like that? Were all the others mere lies, romances?

She put the two tall tumblers and the plastic cup on a tray, filled them with ice and lemonade, then clicked her tongue at herself in disgust, took the ice out of Todd's cup, and refilled it with plain lemonade. She put four animal crackers in a row on the tray and carried it out, batting the screen door shut behind her with her foot. Ann stood up and took the tray from her and set it down on the wobbly iron table, its curlicues clogged solid with years of repainting with white enamel, but still rusting through in spots.

"Can someone have the cookies?" Ella inquired softly.

"Oh, yes," Ann said. "Oh, very much yes. Todd. Look what's here. Look what Grandmother brought you!"

The thick little glasses peered round. The child got up and came to the table.

"Grandmother will give you a cookie, Todd," the young mother said, clear and serious.

The child stood still.

Ella picked up an animal cracker. "Here you are, sweetie," she said. "It's a tiger, I do believe. Here comes the tiger, walking to you." She walked the cracker across the tray, hopped it over the edge of the tray, and walked it onto the table's edge. She was not sure the four-year-old was watching.

"Take it, Todd," the mother said.

Slowly the child raised his open hand towards the table.

"Hop!" Ella said, hopping the tiger into the hand.

Todd looked at the tiger and then at his mother.

"Eat it, Todd. It's very good."

The child stood still, the cracker lying on his palm. He looked at it again. "Hop," he said.

"That's right! It went Hop! right to Toddie!" Ella said. Tears came into her eyes. She walked the next cracker across the tray. "This one is a pig. It can go Hop! too, Toddie. Do you want it to go Hop?"

"Hop!" the child said.

It was better than no story at all.

"Hop!" said the great-grandmother.

PART II:

OUTER SPACE, INNER LANDS

INTRODUCTION

The Obligatory Bit about Science Fiction, Fantasy, and Genre

THERE ARE DOZENS OF DEFINITIONS OF WHAT "SCIENCE FICTION" is; few are useful and none is definitive. Variations on the term, such as "speculative fiction," complicate the discussion more than they clarify it.

Nobody—for good reason—has ever been able to say exactly where "fantasy" begins and ends. It is immensely larger than the current commercial category of books labelled Fantasy. It cannot be limited to "the impossible," or "magic," or "the supernatural." The origins of fantastic literature are lost to sight, because it is worldwide, and if myth and legend are included in it, it long predates history and literacy. It's permanent, it thrives, because it's infinitely adaptable. Magic realism was a brilliant modern use of fantasy to record a reality not accessible to the techniques of realism. Science fiction can be seen as a brilliant modern development of fantasy to use the imagination within the parameters of the rationally possible, or at least the plausible.

Genre, a concept which could have served as a useful distinction of various kinds of fiction, has been degraded into a disguise for mere value-judgment. The various "genres" are now mainly commercial product-labels to make life easy for lazy readers, lazy critics, and the Sales Departments of publishers.

It's not my job as a writer to make life easy for anybody. Including myself.

Three stories from my 1996 story collection *Unlocking the Air* are in the first volume of this collection. On my web site you can find a table of contents for that book. You want genre? I'll give you genre. I described each story, not in such crude, vague terms as "realism" or "fantasy," but accurately: Miniaturized Realism, Geriatric Realism, Californian Realism, Oregonian Realism, and Uncompromising Realism; Surrealism; Mythological Fantasy, Temporal Fantasy, Vegetable Fantasy, Visionary Fantasy, Revisionary Fantasy, Real Fantasy. . . . You won't find any of the various subgenres of Science Fiction (Hard, Soft, Crunchy, Peanut-Free, Social, Slipstream, etc.), however, because *Unlocking the Air* doesn't include any science fiction at all.

The Stories in this Volume

FOR A WRITER, THERE IS A GENUINE DIFFERENCE BETWEEN FANTASY and science fiction, which has nothing to do with the commercial branding of books as "genre" or the categorical imperatives of critics. The difference is in how you write it—what you are doing as a writer. In fantasy you get to make it all up, even the rules of how things work, and then follow your rules absolutely. In science fiction you get to make it up, but you have to follow most of the rules of science, or at least not ignore them.

Nine of the stories in this second volume are what I'd call science fiction, partly because they use familiar tropes—imaginary other planets reached by human beings in space ships, or imaginary other planets inhabited by human-like species, or Space Aliens visiting Earth—and also because they make some effort not to violate physical possibility, though stretching scientific ideas much farther than a scientist would.

"Semley's Necklace" has a good many elements of myth (Norse) and fantasy mixed into the space-ship-alien-planet business. I think this mixture is now called science fantasy, but I only did it because I didn't know any better yet. By the time I wrote "Nine Lives" I had a clearer idea of what I wanted to do with science fiction and how to do it.

"Mazes" does something I find myself doing fairly often: it speaks from the point of view of someone who has traditionally not been allowed a point of view at all.

As a matter of fact, so does "The First Contact with the Gorgonids," a story that Harlan Ellison asked me to write, but then he didn't like it, so I sold it to somebody else for a whole lot more money, but he and I have long since forgiven each other; we always do.

"The Shobies' Story" is part of a semi-suite of stories in the collection *A Fisherman of the Inland Sea*. It's essentially a story about what stories do, or can do. Bringing people together on a space ship from several of my "Hainish" worlds of earlier books and stories gave me a good deal of pleasure.

"Betrayals" is from the book *Four Ways to Forgiveness*, which (with a later, fifth story, "Old Music and the Slave Women") is about a great slave uprising on the planets Werel and O. Sometimes a character comes into my mind with a story to tell. I learned that if I listen, carefully, with some patience, and write what I'm told, the story will come to be. As I grew older, more and more stories have been given me in that way, as gifts.

But not all. "The Matter of Seggri" started very differently, with my own questions. A scientific question, not yet fully and satisfactorily answered: When a few males would serve to procreate a species, why are there so many? And a social question, not yet answered adequately at all: Why, in almost all societies, do men dominate women? What's the Darwinian profit in having equal numbers of the two genders but making them unequal in power? What if the situation were reversed? . . . A lot of science fiction starts out that way.

"Solitude" was written because I wanted to write about an introvert who finds a good place for introverts to live. Clearly it had to be on another world, because the World As We Know It is filled almost solid with extraverts, who refuse to learn how to spell "extravert" because they're too busy rushing around in crowds shouting and cellphoning and texting and friending and joining groups and being outgoing and sociable to pay any attention to stuff like Latin prefixes, or silence, or introverts.

"The Wild Girls" is science fiction in that the caste system it depicts is modelled on historical observations of certain societies of the Mississippi Valley peoples. It's one of the last stories I wrote, and a dark one.

"The Fliers of Gy" and "The Silence of the Asonu" come from *Changing Planes*, in which travel to other worlds is accomplished not on space ships, but by sitting too long in airports. Does space travel fueled by enforced misery and boredom rate as science fiction? Anyhow, the stories are less science-fictional or fantastic than satirical in intent.

If you're getting bored with this classifying, I'm sorry—I'm doing it to show that the whole vocabulary—"realism" "science fiction," "genre fiction," and the rest of it—doesn't give even a remotely adequate description of what I write. Or of what many other serious writers are writing. We need a whole new discourse on fiction.

Fantasy is still a valid term, if used carefully. "The Poacher" is pure fantasy: a riff on the folk tale of The Sleeping Beauty. "The Rule of Names" is also a fantasy, an early voyage to Earthsea. (I excluded stories closely associated with novels, but this one's here because my editors wanted it, and how could I say no to Ursula's mother and father?) "Small Change" and "The Wife's Story" belong, I suppose, to the subgenres of ghost story, sort of, and werewolf story, sort of, only backwards.

"Omelas" (which is pronounced OH-meh-lahss) is a fable, I think. Its premise was stolen from the philosopher William James. You can find it also in Dostoevsky's *The Brothers Karamazov,* being told by the Grand Inquisitor, with a somewhat different purpose. My version of it has had a long and happy career of being used by teachers to upset students and make them argue fiercely about morality.

The first draft of "She Unnames Them" was written down on a cocktail napkin during a bourbon on the rocks on an airplane flying home alone from New York to Oregon after getting an award. I was feeling good. I was feeling like rewriting the Bible. That story and "Sur" are probably my favorites in this volume, which is why I put them last.

I LEAVE IT ENTIRELY UP YOU, O READER, TO DECIDE WHICH volume of these two is the Real and which is the Unreal. I believe the science of deciding such questions is called Ontology, but I never learned it. I am strictly an amateur. I don't know anything about reality, but I know what I like.

—Ursula K. Le Guin. August 2012.

THE ONES
WHO WALK AWAY
FROM OMELAS

(Variations on a theme by William James)

WITH A CLAMOR OF BELLS THAT SET THE SWALLOWS SOARING, the Festival of Summer came to the city Omelas, bright-towered by the sea. The rigging of the boats in harbor sparkled with flags. In the streets between houses with red roofs and painted walls, between old moss-grown gardens and under avenues of trees, past great parks and public buildings, processions moved. Some were decorous: old people in long stiff robes of mauve and grey, grave master workmen, quiet, merry women carrying their babies and chatting as they walked. In other streets the music beat faster, a shimmering of gong and tambourine, and the people went dancing, the procession was a dance. Children dodged in and out, their high calls rising like the swallows' crossing flights over the music and the singing. All the processions wound towards the north side of the city, where on the great water-meadow called the Green Fields boys and girls, naked in the bright air, with mud-stained feet and ankles and long, lithe arms, exercised their restive horses before the race. The horses wore no gear at all but a halter without bit. Their manes were braided with streamers of silver, gold, and green. They flared their nostrils and pranced and boasted to one another; they were vastly excited, the horse being the only animal who has adopted our ceremonies as his own.

Far off to the north and west the mountains stood up half encircling Omelas on her bay. The air of morning was so clear that the snow still crowning the Eighteen Peaks burned with white-gold fire across the miles of sunlit air, under the dark blue of the sky. There was just enough wind to make the banners that marked the racecourse snap and flutter now and then. In the silence of the broad green meadows one could hear the music winding through the city streets, farther and nearer and ever approaching, a cheerful faint sweetness of the air that from time to time trembled and gathered together and broke out into the great joyous clanging of the bells.

Joyous! How is one to tell about joy? How describe the citizens of Omelas?

They were not simple folk, you see, though they were happy. But we do not say the words of cheer much any more. All smiles have become archaic. Given a description such as this one tends to make certain assumptions. Given a description such as this one tends to look next for the King, mounted on a splendid stallion and surrounded by his noble knights, or perhaps in a golden litter borne by a great-muscled slave. But there was no king. They did not use swords, or keep slaves. They were not barbarians. I do not know the rules and laws of their society, but I suspect that they were singularly few. As they did without monarchy and slavery, so they also got on without the stock exchange, the advertisement, the secret police, and the bomb. Yet I repeat that these were not simple folk, not dulcet shepherds, noble savages, bland utopians. They were not less complex than us. The trouble is that we have a bad habit, encouraged by pedants and sophisticates, of considering happiness as something rather stupid. Only pain is intellectual, only evil interesting. This is the treason of the artist: a refusal to admit the banality of evil and the terrible boredom of pain. If you can't lick 'em, join 'em. If it hurts, repeat it. But to praise despair is to condemn delight, to embrace violence is to lose hold of everything else. We have almost lost hold; we can no longer describe a happy man, nor make any celebration of joy. How can I tell you about the people of Omelas? They were not naïve and happy children—though their children were, in fact, happy. They were mature, intelligent, passionate adults whose lives were not wretched. O miracle! but I wish I could describe it better. I wish I could convince you. Omelas sounds in my words like a city in a fairy tale, long ago and far away, once upon a time. Perhaps it would be best if you imagined it as your own fancy bids, assuming it will rise to the occasion, for certainly I cannot suit you all. For instance, how about technology? I think that there would be no cars or helicopters in and above the streets; this follows from the fact that the people of Omelas are happy people. Happiness is based on a just discrimination of what is necessary, what is neither necessary nor destructive, and what is destructive. In the middle category, however—that of the unnecessary but undestructive, that of comfort, luxury, exuberance, etc.—they could perfectly well have central heating, subway trains, washing machines, and all kinds of marvelous devices not yet invented here, floating light-sources, fuelless power, a cure for the common cold. Or they could have none of that: it doesn't matter. As you like it. I incline to think that people from towns up and down the coast have been coming in to Omelas during the last days before the Festival on very fast little trains and double-decked trams, and that the train station of Omelas is actually the handsomest building in town, though plainer than the magnificent Farmers' Market. But even granted trains, I fear that Omelas so far strikes some of you as goody-goody. Smiles, bells, parades, horses, bleh. If so, please add an orgy. If an orgy would help, don't hesitate. Let us not, however, have temples from which issue beautiful nude priests and priestesses already half in ecstasy and ready to copulate with any man or woman, lover or stranger, who desires union with the deep godhead of the blood, although that was my first idea. But really it would be better not to have temples in Omelas—at least, not manned temples. Religion yes, clergy no. Surely the beautiful nudes can just wander about, offering themselves like divine soufflés to the hunger of the needy and the rapture of the flesh. Let them join the processions. Let tambourines be struck above the copulations, and the glory of desire be proclaimed upon the gongs, and (a not unimportant point) let the offspring of these delightful rituals be beloved and looked after by all. One thing I know there is none of in Omelas is guilt. But what else should there be? I thought at first there were no drugs, but that is puritanical. For those who like it, the faint insistent sweetness of *drooz* may perfume the ways of the city, *drooz* which first brings a great lightness and brilliance to the mind and limbs, and then after some hours a dreamy langour, and wonderful visions at last of the very arcana and inmost secrets of the Universe, as well as exciting the pleasure of sex beyond all belief; and it is not habit-forming. For more modest tastes I think there ought to be beer. What else, what else belongs in the joyous city? The sense of victory, surely, the celebration of courage. But as we did without clergy, let us do without soldiers. The joy built upon successful slaughter is not the right kind of joy; it will not do; it is fearful and it is trivial. A boundless and generous contentment, a magnanimous triumph felt not against some outer enemy but in communion with the finest and fairest in the souls of all men everywhere and the splendor of the world's summer: this is what swells the hearts of the people of Omelas, and the victory they celebrate is that of life. I really don't think many of them need to take *drooz*.

Most of the processions have reached the Green Fields by now. A marvelous smell of cooking goes forth from the red and blue tents of the provisioners. The faces of small children are amiably sticky; in the benign grey beard of a man a couple of crumbs of rich pastry are entangled. The youths and girls have mounted their horses and are beginning to group around the starting line of the course. An old woman, small, fat, and laughing, is passing out flowers from a basket, and tall young men wear her flowers in their shining hair. A child of nine or ten sits at the edge of the crowd, alone, playing on a wooden flute. People pause to listen, and they smile, but they do not speak to him, for he never ceases playing and never sees them, his dark eyes wholly rapt in the sweet, thin magic of the tune.

He finishes, and slowly lowers his hands holding the wooden flute.

As if that little private silence were the signal, all at once a trumpet sounds from the pavilion near the starting line: imperious, melancholy, piercing. The horses rear on their slender legs, and some of them neigh in answer. Sober-faced, the young riders stroke the horses' necks and soothe them, whispering, "Quiet, quiet, there my beauty, my hope. . . ." They begin to form in rank along the starting line. The crowds along the racecourse are like a field of grass and flowers in the wind. The Festival of Summer has begun.

Do you believe? Do you accept the festival, the city, the joy? No? Then let me describe one more thing.

In a basement under one of the beautiful public buildings of Omelas, or perhaps in the cellar of one of its spacious private homes, there is a room. It has one locked door, and no window. A little light seeps in dustily between cracks in the boards, secondhand from a cobwebbed window somewhere across the cellar. In one corner of the little room a couple of mops, with stiff, clotted, foul-smelling heads, stand near a rusty bucket. The floor is dirt, a little damp to the touch, as cellar dirt usually is. The room is about three paces long and two wide: a mere broom closet or disused tool room. In the room a child is sitting. It could be a boy or a girl. It looks about six, but actually is nearly ten. It is feeble-minded. Perhaps it was born defective, or perhaps it has become imbecile through fear, malnutrition, and neglect. It picks its nose and occasionally fumbles vaguely with its toes or genitals, as it sits hunched in the corner farthest from the bucket and the two mops. It is afraid of the mops. It finds them horrible. It shuts its eyes, but it knows the mops are still standing there; and the door is locked; and nobody will come. The door is always locked; and nobody ever comes, except that sometimes—the child has no understanding of time or interval—sometimes the door rattles terribly and opens, and a person, or several people, are there. One of them may come in and kick the child to make it stand up. The others never come close, but peer in at it with frightened, disgusted eyes. The food bowl and the water jug are hastily filled, the door is locked, the eyes disappear. The people at the door never say anything, but the child, who has not always lived in the tool room, and can remember sunlight and its mother's voice, sometimes speaks. "I will be good," it says. "Please let me out. I will be good!" They never answer. The child used to scream for help at night, and cry a good deal, but now it only makes a kind of whining, "eh-haa, eh-haa," and it speaks less and less often: It is so thin there are no calves to its legs; its belly protrudes; it lives on a half-bowl of corn meal and grease a day. It is naked. Its buttocks and thighs are a mass of festered sores, as it sits in its own excrement continually.

They all know it is there, all the people of Omelas. Some of them have come to see it, others are content merely to know it is there. They all know that it has to be there. Some of them understand why, and some do not, but they all understand that their happiness, the beauty of their city, the tenderness of their friendships, the health of their children, the wisdom of their scholars, the skill of their makers, even the abundance of their harvest and the kindly weathers of their skies, depend wholly on this child's abominable misery.

This is usually explained to children when they are between eight and twelve, whenever they seem capable of understanding; and most of those who come to see the child are young people, though often enough an adult comes, or comes back, to see the child. No matter how well the matter has been explained to them, these young spectators are always shocked and sickened at the sight. They feel disgust, which they had thought themselves superior to. They feel anger, outrage, impotence, despite all the explanations. They would like to do something for the child. But there is nothing they can do. If the child were brought up into the sunlight out of that vile place, if it were cleaned and fed and comforted, that would be a good thing, indeed; but if it were done, in that day and hour all the prosperity and beauty and delight of Omelas would wither and be destroyed. Those are the terms. To exchange all the goodness and grace of every life in Omelas for that single, small improvement: to throw away the happiness of thousands for the chance of the happiness of one: that would be to let guilt within the walls indeed.

The terms are strict and absolute; there may not even be a kind word spoken to the child.

Often the young people go home in tears, or in a tearless rage, when they have seen the child and faced this terrible paradox. They may brood over it for weeks or years. But as time goes on they begin to realize that even if the child could be released, it would not get much good of its freedom: a little vague pleasure of warmth and food, no doubt, but little more. It is too degraded and imbecile to know any real joy. It has been afraid too long ever to be free of fear. Its habits are too uncouth for it to respond to humane treatment. Indeed, after so long it would probably be wretched without walls about it to protect it, and darkness for its eyes, and its own excrement to sit in. Their tears at the bitter injustice dry when they begin to perceive the terrible justice of reality, and to accept it. Yet it is their tears and anger, the trying of their generosity and the acceptance of their helplessness, which are perhaps the true source of the splendor of their lives. Theirs is no vapid, irresponsible happiness. They know that they, like the child, are not free. They know compassion. It is the existence of the child, and their knowledge of its existence, that makes possible the nobility of their architecture, the poignancy of their music, the profundity of their science. It is because of the child that they are so gentle with children. They know that if the wretched one were not there snivelling in the dark, the other one, the flute-player, could make no joyful music as the young riders line up in their beauty for the race in the sunlight of the first morning of summer.

Now do you believe in them? Are they not more credible? But there is one more thing to tell, and this is quite incredible.

At times one of the adolescent girls or boys who go to see the child does not go home to weep or rage, does not, in fact, go home at all. Sometimes also a man or woman much older falls silent for a day or two, and then leaves home. These people go out into the street, and walk down the street alone. They keep walking, and walk straight out of the city of Omelas, through the beautiful gates. They keep walking across the farmlands of Omelas. Each one goes alone, youth or girl, man or woman. Night falls; the traveler must pass down village streets, between the houses with yellow-lit windows, and on out into the darkness of the fields. Each alone, they go west or north, towards the mountains. They go on. They leave Omelas, they walk ahead into the darkness, and they do not come back. The place they go towards is a place even less imaginable to most of us than the city of happiness. I cannot describe it at all. It is possible that it does not exist. But they seem to know where they are going, the ones who walk away from Omelas.

SEMLEY'S
NECKLACE

HOW CAN YOU TELL THE LEGEND FROM THE FACT ON THESE worlds that lie so many years away?—planets without names, called by their people simply The World, planets without history, where the past is the matter of myth, and a returning explorer finds his own doings of a few years back have become the gestures of a god. Unreason darkens that gap of time bridged by our lightspeed ships, and in the darkness uncertainty and disproportion grow like weeds.

In trying to tell the story of a man, an ordinary League scientist, who went to such a nameless half-known world not many years ago, one feels like an archaeologist amid millennial ruins, now struggling through choked tangles of leaf, flower, branch and vine to the sudden bright geometry of a wheel or a polished cornerstone, and now entering some commonplace, sunlit doorway to find inside it the darkness, the impossible flicker of a flame, the glitter of a jewel, the half-glimpsed movement of a woman's arm.

How can you tell fact from legend, truth from truth?

Through Rocannon's story the jewel, the blue glitter seen briefly, returns. With it let us begin, here:

GALACTIC AREA 8, NO. 62: FOMALHAUT II.
HIGH-INTELLIGENCE LIFE FORMS: SPECIES CONTACTED:

SPECIES I.

A. Gdemiar (singular Gdem): Highly intelligent, fully hominoid nocturnal troglodytes, 120–135 cm. in height, light skin, dark head-hair. When contacted these cave-dwellers possessed a rigidly stratified oligarchic urban society modified by partial colonial telepathy, and a technologically oriented Early Steel culture. Technology enhanced to Industrial, Point C, during League Mission of 252–254. In 254 an Automatic Drive ship (to-from New South Georgia) was presented to oligarchs of the Kiriensea Area community. Status C-Prime.

B. Fiia (singular Fian): Highly intelligent, fully hominoid, diurnal, av. ca. 130 cm. in height, observed individuals generally light in skin and hair. Brief contacts indicated village and nomadic communal societies, partial colonial telepathy, also some indication of short-range TK. The race appears a-technological and evasive, with minimal and fluid culture-patterns. Currently untaxable. Status E-Query.

SPECIES II.

Liuar (singular Liu): Highly intelligent, fully hominoid, diurnal, av. height above 170 cm., this species possesses a fortress/village, clan-descent society, a blocked technology (Bronze), and feudal-heroic culture. Note horizontal social cleavage into 2 pseudo-races: (a) Olgyior, "midmen," light-skinned and dark-haired; (b) Angyar, "lords," very tall, dark-skinned, yellow-haired—

"That's her," said Rocannon, looking up from the *Abridged Handy Pocket Guide to Intelligent Life-forms* at the very tall, dark-skinned, yellow-haired woman who stood halfway down the long museum hall. She stood still and erect, crowned with bright hair, gazing at something in a display case. Around her fidgeted four uneasy and unattractive dwarves.

"I didn't know Fomalhaut II had all those people besides the trogs," said Ketho, the curator.

"I didn't either. There are even some 'Unconfirmed' species listed here, that they never contacted. Sounds like time for a more thorough survey mission to the place. Well, now at least we know what she is."

"I wish there were some way of knowing *who* she is. . . ."

SHE WAS OF AN ANCIENT FAMILY, A DESCENDANT OF THE FIRST kings of the Angyar, and for all her poverty her hair shone with the pure, steadfast gold of her inheritance. The little people, the Fiia, bowed when she passed them, even when she was a barefoot child running in the fields, the light and fiery comet of her hair brightening the troubled winds of Kirien.

She was still very young when Durhal of Hallan saw her, courted her, and carried her away from the ruined towers and windy halls of her childhood to his own high home. In Hallan on the mountainside there was no comfort either, though splendor endured. The windows were unglassed, the stone floors bare; in coldyear one might wake to see the night's snow in long, low drifts beneath each window. Durhal's bride stood with narrow bare feet on the snowy floor, braiding up the fire of her hair and laughing at her young husband in the silver mirror that hung in their room. That mirror, and his mother's bridal-gown sewn with a thousand tiny crystals, were all his wealth. Some of his lesser kinfolk of Hallan still possessed wardrobes of brocaded clothing, furniture of gilded wood, silver harness for their steeds, armor and silver mounted swords, jewels and jewelry—and on these last Durhal's bride looked enviously, glancing back at a gemmed coronet or a golden brooch even when the wearer of the ornament stood aside to let her pass, deferent to her birth and marriage-rank.

Fourth from the High Seat of Hallan Revel sat Durhal and his bride Semley, so close to Hallanlord that the old man often poured wine for Semley with his own hand, and spoke of hunting with his nephew and heir Durhal, looking on the young pair with a grim, unhopeful love. Hope came hard to the Angyar of Hallan and all the Western Lands, since the Starlords had appeared with their houses that leaped about on pillars of fire and their awful weapons that could level hills. They had interfered with all the old ways and wars, and though the sums were small there was terrible shame to the Angyar in having to pay a tax to them, a tribute for the Starlords' war that was to be fought with some strange enemy, somewhere in the hollow places between the stars, at the end of years. "It will be your war too," they said, but for a generation now the Angyar had sat in idle shame in their revel-halls, watching their double swords rust, their sons grow up without ever striking a blow in battle, their daughters marry poor men, even midmen, having no dowry of heroic loot to bring a noble husband. Hallanlord's face was bleak when he watched the fair-haired couple and heard their laughter as they drank bitter wine and joked together in the cold, ruinous, resplendent fortress of their race.

Semley's own face hardened when she looked down the hall and saw, in seats far below hers, even down among the halfbreeds and the midmen, against white skins and black hair, the gleam and flash of precious stones. She herself had brought nothing in dowry to her husband, not even a silver hairpin. The dress of a thousand crystals she had put away in a chest for the wedding-day of her daughter, if daughter it was to be.

It was, and they called her Haldre, and when the fuzz on her little brown skull grew longer it shone with steadfast gold, the inheritance of the lordly generations, the only gold she would ever possess. . . .

Semley did not speak to her husband of her discontent. For all his gentleness to her, Durhal in his pride had only contempt for envy, for vain wishing, and she dreaded his contempt. But she spoke to Durhal's sister Durossa.

"My family had a great treasure once," she said. "It was a necklace all of gold, with the blue jewel set in the center—sapphire?"

Durossa shook her head, smiling, not sure of the name either. It was late in warmyear, as these Northern Angyar called the summer of the eight-hundred-day year, beginning the cycle of months anew at each equinox; to Semley it seemed an outlandish calendar, a midmannish reckoning. Her family was at an end, but it had been older and purer than the race of any of these northwestern marchlanders, who mixed too freely with the Olgyior. She sat with Durossa in the sunlight on a stone windowseat high up in the Great Tower, where the older woman's apartment was. Widowed young, childless, Durossa had been given in second marriage to Hallanlord, who was her father's brother. Since it was a kinmarriage and a second marriage on both sides she had not taken the title of Hallanlady, which Semley would some day bear; but she sat with the old lord in the High Seat and ruled with him his domains. Older than her brother Durhal, she was fond of his young wife, and delighted in the bright-haired baby Haldre.

"It was bought," Semley went on, "with all the money my forebear Leynen got when he conquered the Southern Fiefs—all the money from a whole kingdom, think of it, for one jewel! Oh, it would outshine anything here in Hallan, surely, even those crystals like koob-eggs your cousin Issar wears. It was so beautiful they gave it a name of its own; they called it the Eye of the Sea. My great-grandmother wore it."

"You never saw it?" the older woman asked lazily, gazing down at the green mountainslopes where long, long summer sent its hot and restless winds straying among the forests and whirling down white roads to the seacoast far away.

"It was lost before I was born."

"The Starlords took it for tribute?"

"No, my father said it was stolen before the Starlords ever came to our realm. He wouldn't talk of it, but there was an old midwoman full of tales who always told me the Fiia would know where it was."

"Ah, the Fiia I should like to see!" said Durossa. "They're in so many songs and tales; why do they never come to the Western Lands?"

"Too high, too cold in winter, I think. They like the sunlight of the valleys of the south."

"Are they like the Clayfolk?"

"Those I've never seen; they keep away from us in the south. Aren't they white like midmen, and misformed? The Fiia are fair; they look like children, only thinner, and wiser. Oh, I wonder if they know where the necklace is, who stole it and where he hid it! Think, Durossa—if I could come into Hallan Revel and sit down by my husband with the wealth of a kingdom round my neck, and outshine the other women as he outshines all men!"

Durossa bent her head above the baby, who sat studying her own brown toes on a fur rug between her mother and aunt. "Semley is foolish," she murmured to the baby; "Semley who shines like a falling star, Semley whose husband loves no gold but the gold of her hair. . . ."

And Semley, looking out over the green slopes of summer toward the distant sea, was silent.

But when another coldyear had passed, and the Starlords had come again to collect their taxes for the war against the world's end—this time using a couple of dwarfish Clayfolk as interpreters, and so leaving all the Angyar humiliated to the point of rebellion—and another warmyear too was gone, and Haldre had grown into a lovely, chattering child, Semley brought her one morning to Durossa's sunlit room in the tower. Semley wore an old cloak of blue, and the hood covered her hair.

"Keep Haldre for me these few days, Durossa," she said, quick and calm. "I'm going south to Kirien."

"To see your father?"

"To find my inheritance. Your cousins of Harget Fief have been taunting Durhal. Even that halfbreed Parna can torment him, because

Parna's wife has a satin coverlet for her bed, and a diamond earring, and three gowns, the dough-faced black-haired trollop! while Durhal's wife must patch her gown—"

"Is Durhal's pride in his wife, or what she wears?"

But Semley was not to be moved. "The Lords of Hallan are becoming poor men in their own hall. I am going to bring my dowry to my lord, as one of my lineage should."

"Semley! Does Durhal know you're going?"

"My return will be a happy one—that much let him know," said young Semley, breaking for a moment into her joyful laugh; then she bent to kiss her daughter, turned, and before Durossa could speak, was gone like a quick wind over the floors of sunlit stone.

Married women of the Angyar never rode for sport, and Semley had not been from Hallan since her marriage; so now, mounting the high saddle of a windsteed, she felt like a girl again, like the wild maiden she had been, riding half-broken steeds on the north wind over the fields of Kirien. The beast that bore her now down from the hills of Hallan was of finer breed, striped coat fitting sleek over hollow, buoyant bones, green eyes slitted against the wind, light and mighty wings sweeping up and down to either side of Semley, revealing and hiding, revealing and hiding the clouds above her and the hills below.

On the third morning she came to Kirien and stood again in the ruined courts. Her father had been drinking all night, and, just as in the old days, the morning sunlight poking through his fallen ceilings annoyed him, and the sight of his daughter only increased his annoyance. "What are you back for?" he growled, his swollen eyes glancing at her and away. The fiery hair of his youth was quenched, grey strands tangled on his skull. "Did the young Halla not marry you, and you've come sneaking home?"

"I am Durhal's wife. I came to get my dowry, father."

The drunkard growled in disgust; but she laughed at him so gently that he had to look at her again, wincing.

"Is it true, father, that the Fiia stole the necklace Eye of the Sea?"

"How do I know? Old tales. The thing was lost before I was born, I think. I wish I never had been. Ask the Fiia if you want to know. Go to them, go back to your husband. Leave me alone here. There's no room at Kirien for girls and gold and all the rest of the story. The story's over here; this is the fallen place, this is the empty hall. The sons of Leynen all are dead, their treasures are all lost. Go on your way, girl."

Grey and swollen as the web-spinner of ruined houses, he turned and went blundering toward the cellars where he hid from daylight.

Leading the striped windsteed of Hallan, Semley left her old home and walked down the steep hill, past the village of the midmen, who greeted her with sullen respect, on over fields and pastures where the great, wing-clipped, half-wild herilor grazed, to a valley that was green as a painted bowl and full to the brim with sunlight. In the deep of the valley lay the village of the Fiia, and as she descended leading her steed the little, slight people ran up toward her from their huts and gardens, laughing, calling out in faint, thin voices.

"Hail Halla's bride, Kirienlady, Windborne, Semley the Fair!"

They gave her lovely names and she liked to hear them, minding not at all their laughter; for they laughed at all they said. That was her own way, to speak and laugh. She stood tall in her long blue cloak among their swirling welcome.

"Hail Lightfolk, Sundwellers, Fiia friends of men!"

They took her down into the village and brought her into one of their airy houses, the tiny children chasing along behind. There was no telling the age of a Fian once he was grown; it was hard even to tell one from another and be sure, as they moved about quick as moths around a candle, that she spoke always to the same one. But it seemed that one of them talked with her for a while, as the others fed and petted her steed, and brought water for her to drink, and bowls of fruit from their gardens of little trees. "It was never the Fiia that stole the necklace of the Lords of Kirien!" cried the little man. "What would the Fiia do with gold, Lady? For us there is sunlight in warmyear, and in coldyear the remembrance of sunlight; the yellow fruit, the yellow leaves in endseason, the yellow hair of our lady of Kirien; no other gold."

"Then it was some midman stole the thing?"

Laughter rang long and faint about her. "How would a midman dare? O Lady of Kirien, how the great jewel was stolen no mortal knows, not man nor midman nor Fian nor any among the Seven Folk. Only dead minds know how it was lost, long ago when Kireley the Proud whose great-granddaughter is Semley walked alone by the caves of the sea. But it may be found perhaps among the Sunhaters."

"The Clayfolk?"

A louder burst of laughter, nervous.

"Sit with us, Semley, sunhaired, returned to us from the north." She sat with them to eat, and they were as pleased with her graciousness as she with theirs. But when they heard her repeat that she would go to the Clayfolk to find her inheritance, if it was there, they began not to laugh; and little by little there were fewer of them around her. She was alone at last with perhaps the one she had spoken with before the meal. "Do not go among the Clayfolk, Semley," he said, and for a moment her heart failed her. The Fian, drawing his hand down slowly over his eyes, had darkened all the air about them. Fruit lay ash-white on the plate; all the bowls of clear water were empty.

"In the mountains of the far land the Fiia and the Gdemiar parted. Long ago we parted," said the slight, still man of the Fiia. "Longer ago we were one. What we are not, they are. What we are, they are not. Think of the sunlight and the grass and the trees that bear fruit, Semley; think that not all roads that lead down lead up as well."

"Mine leads neither down nor up, kind host, but only straight on to my inheritance. I will go to it where it is, and return with it."

The Fian bowed, laughing a little.

Outside the village she mounted her striped windsteed, and, calling farewell in answer to their calling, rose up into the wind of afternoon and flew southwestward toward the caves down by the rocky shores of Kiriensea.

She feared she might have to walk far into those tunnel-caves to find the people she sought, for it was said the Clayfolk never came out of their caves into the light of the sun, and feared even the Greatstar and the moons. It was a long ride; she landed once to let her steed hunt tree-rats while she ate a little bread from her saddle-bag. The bread was hard and dry by now and tasted of leather, yet kept a faint savor of its making, so that for a moment, eating it alone in a glade of the southern forests, she heard the quiet tone of a voice and saw Durhal's face turned to her in the light of the candles of Hallan. For a while she sat daydreaming of that stern and vivid young face, and of what she would say to him when she came home with a kingdom's ransom around her neck: "I wanted a gift worthy of my husband, Lord. . . ." Then she pressed on, but when she reached the coast the sun had set, with the Greatstar sinking behind it. A mean wind had come up from the west, starting and gusting and veering, and her windsteed was weary fighting it. She let him glide down on the sand. At once he folded his wings and curled his thick, light limbs under him with a thrum of purring. Semley stood holding her cloak close at her throat, stroking the steed's neck so that he flicked his ears and purred again. The warm fur comforted her hand, but all that met her eyes was grey sky full of smears of cloud, grey sea, dark sand. And then running over the sand a low, dark creature—another—a group of them, squatting and running and stopping.

She called aloud to them. Though they had not seemed to see her, now in a moment they were all around her. They kept a distance from her windsteed; he had stopped purring, and his fur rose a little under Semley's hand. She took up the reins, glad of his protection but afraid of the nervous ferocity he might display. The strange folk stood silent, staring, their thick bare feet planted in the sand. There was no mistaking them: they were the height of the Fiia and in all else a shadow, a black image of those laughing people. Naked, squat, stiff, with lank hair and grey-white skins, dampish-looking like the skins of grubs; eyes like rocks.

"You are the Clayfolk?"

"Gdemiar are we, people of the Lords of the Realms of Night." The voice was unexpectedly loud and deep, and rang out pompous through the salt, blowing dusk; but, as with the Fiia, Semley was not sure which one had spoken.

"I greet you, Nightlords. I am Semley of Kirien, Durhal's wife of Hallan. I come to you seeking my inheritance, the necklace called Eye of the Sea, lost long ago."

"Why do you seek it here, Angya? Here is only sand and salt and night."

"Because lost things are known of in deep places," said Semley, quite ready for a play of wits, "and gold that came from earth has a way of going back to the earth. And sometimes the made, they say, returns to the maker." This last was a guess; it hit the mark.

"It is true the necklace Eye of the Sea is known to us by name. It was made in our caves long ago, and sold by us to the Angyar. And the blue stone came from the Clayfields of our kin to the east. But these are very old tales, Angya."

"May I listen to them in the places where they are told?"

The squat people were silent a while, as if in doubt. The grey wind blew by over the sand, darkening as the Greatstar set; the sound of the sea loudened and lessened. The deep voice spoke again: "Yes, lady of the Angyar. You may enter the Deep Halls. Come with us now." There was a changed note in his voice, wheedling. Semley would not hear it. She followed the Claymen over the sand, leading on a short rein her sharp-taloned steed.

At the cave-mouth, a toothless, yawning mouth from which a stinking warmth sighed out, one of the Claymen said, "The air-beast cannot come in."

"Yes," said Semley.

"No," said the squat people.

"Yes. I will not leave him here. He is not mine to leave. He will not harm you, so long as I hold his reins."

"No," deep voices repeated; but others broke in, "As you will," and after a moment of hesitation they went on. The cave-mouth seemed to snap shut behind them, so dark was it under the stone. They went in single file, Semley last.

The darkness of the tunnel lightened, and they came under a ball of weak white fire hanging from the roof. Farther on was another, and another; between them long black worms hung in festoons from the rock. As they went on these fire-globes were set closer, so that all the tunnel was lit with a bright, cold light.

Semley's guides stopped at a parting of three tunnels, all blocked by doors that looked to be of iron. "We shall wait, Angya," they said, and eight of them stayed with her, while three others unlocked one of the doors and passed through. It fell to behind them with a clash.

Straight and still stood the daughter of the Angyar in the white, blank light of the lamps; her windsteed crouched beside her, flicking the tip of his striped tail, his great folded wings stirring again and again with the checked impulse to fly. In the tunnel behind Semley the eight Claymen squatted on their hams, muttering to one another in their deep voices, in their own tongue.

The central door swung clanging open. "Let the Angya enter the Realm of Night!" cried a new voice, booming and boastful. A Clayman who wore some clothing on his thick grey body stood in the doorway, beckoning to her. "Enter and behold the wonders of our lands, the marvels made by hands, the works of the Nightlords!"

Silent, with a tug at her steed's reins, Semley bowed her head and followed him under the low doorway made for dwarfish folk. Another glaring tunnel stretched ahead, dank walls dazzling in the white light,

but, instead of a way to walk upon, its floor carried two bars of polished
iron stretching off side by side as far as she could see. On the bars rested
some kind of cart with metal wheels. Obeying her new guide's gestures,
with no hesitation and no trace of wonder on her face, Semley stepped
into the cart and made the windsteed crouch beside her. The Clayman
got in and sat down in front of her, moving bars and wheels about. A
loud grinding noise arose, and a screaming of metal on metal, and then
the walls of the tunnel began to jerk by. Faster and faster the walls slid
past, till the fireglobes overhead ran into a blur, and the stale warm air
became a foul wind blowing the hood back off her hair.

The cart stopped. Semley followed the guide up basalt steps into a
vast anteroom and then a still vaster hall, carved by ancient waters or
by the burrowing Clayfolk out of the rock, its darkness that had never
known sunlight lit with the uncanny cold brilliance of the globes. In
grilles cut in the walls huge blades turned and turned, changing the
stale air. The great closed space hummed and boomed with noise, the
loud voices of the Clayfolk, the grinding and shrill buzzing and vibra-
tion of turning blades and wheels, the echoes and re-echoes of all this
from the rock. Here all the stumpy figures of the Claymen were clothed
in garments imitating those of the Starlords—divided trousers, soft
boots, and hooded tunics—though the few women to be seen, hurrying servile dwarves, were naked. Of the males many were soldiers, bearing at their sides weapons shaped like the terrible light-throwers of the
Starlords, though even Semley could see these were merely shaped iron
clubs. What she saw, she saw without looking. She followed where she
was led, turning her head neither to left nor right. When she came
before a group of Claymen who wore iron circlets on their black hair her
guide halted, bowed, boomed out, "The High Lords of the Gdemiar!"

There were seven of them, and all looked up at her with such arrogance on their lumpy grey faces that she wanted to laugh.

"I come among you seeking the lost treasure of my family, O Lords of the Dark Realm," she said gravely to them. "I seek Leynen's prize, the Eye of the Sea." Her voice was faint in the racket of the huge vault.

"So said our messengers, Lady Semley." This time she could pick out the one who spoke, one even shorter than the others, hardly reaching Semley's breast, with a white, fierce face. "We do not have this thing you seek."

"Once you had it, it is said."

"Much is said, up there where the sun blinks."

"And words are borne off by the winds, where there are winds to blow. I do not ask how the necklace was lost to us and returned to you, its makers of old. Those are old tales, old grudges. I only seek to find it now. You do not have it now; but it may be you know where it is."

"It is not here."

"Then it is elsewhere."

"It is where you cannot come to it. Never, unless we help you."

"Then help me. I ask this as your guest."

"It is said, *The Angyar take; the Fiia give; the Gdemiar give and take.* If we do this for you, what will you give us?"

"My thanks, Nightlord."

She stood tall and bright among them, smiling. They all stared at her with a heavy, grudging wonder, a sullen yearning.

"Listen, Angya, this is a great favor you ask of us. You do not know how great a favor. You cannot understand. You are of a race that will not understand, that cares for nothing but wind-riding and crop-raising and sword-fighting and shouting together. But who made your swords of the bright steel? We, the Gdemiar! Your lords come to us here and in the Clayfields and buy their swords and go away, not looking, not understanding. But you are here now, you will look, you can see a few of our endless marvels, the lights that burn forever, the car that pulls itself, the machines that make our clothes and cook our food and sweeten our air and serve us in all things. Know that all these things are beyond your understanding. And know this: we, the Gdemiar, are the friends of those you call the Starlords! We came with them to Hallan, to Reohan, to Hul-Orren, to all your castles, to help them speak to you. The lords to whom you, the proud Angyar, pay tribute, are our friends. They do us favors as we do them favors! Now, what do your thanks mean to us?"

"That is your question to answer," said Semley, "not mine. I have asked my question. Answer it, Lord."

For a while the seven conferred together, by word and silence. They would glance at her and look away, and mutter and be still. A crowd grew around them, drawn slowly and silently, one after another till Semley was encircled by hundreds of the matted black heads, and all the great booming cavern floor was covered with people, except a little space directly around her. Her windsteed was quivering with fear and irritation too long controlled, and his eyes had gone very wide and pale, like the eyes of a steed forced to fly at night. She stroked the warm fur of his head, whispering, "Quietly now, brave one, bright one, windlord. . . ."

"Angya, we will take you to the place where the treasure lies." The Clayman with the white face and iron crown had turned to her once more. "More than that we cannot do. You must come with us to claim the necklace where it lies, from those who keep it. The air-beast cannot come with you. You must come alone."

"How far a journey, Lord?"

His lips drew back and back. "A very far journey, Lady. Yet it will last only one long night."

"I thank you for your courtesy. Will my steed be well cared for this night? No ill must come to him."

"He will sleep till you return. A greater windsteed you will have ridden, when you see that beast again! Will you not ask where we take you?"

"Can we go soon on this journey? I would not stay long away from my home."

"Yes. Soon." Again the grey lips widened as he stared up into her face.

What was done in those next hours Semley could not have retold;

it was all haste, jumble, noise, strangeness. While she held her steed's head a Clayman stuck a long needle into the golden-striped haunch. She nearly cried out at the sight, but her steed merely twitched and then, purring, fell asleep. He was carried off by a group of Clayfolk who clearly had to summon up their courage to touch his warm fur. Later on she had to see a needle driven into her own arm—perhaps to test her courage, she thought, for it did not seem to make her sleep; though she was not quite sure. There were times she had to travel in the rail-carts, passing iron doors and vaulted caverns by the hundred and hundred; once the rail-cart ran through a cavern that stretched off on either hand measureless into the dark, and all that darkness was full of great flocks of herilor. She could hear their cooing, husky calls, and glimpse the flocks in the front-lights of the cart; then she saw some more clearly in the white light, and saw that they were all wingless, and all blind. At that she shut her eyes. But there were more tunnels to go through, and always more caverns, more grey lumpy bodies and fierce faces and booming boasting voices, until at last they led her suddenly out into the open air. It was full night; she raised her eyes joyfully to the stars and the single moon shining, little Heliki brightening in the west. But the Clayfolk were all about her still, making her climb now into some new kind of cart or cave; she did not know which. It was small, full of little blinking lights like rushlights, very narrow and shining after the great dank caverns and the starlit night. Now another needle was stuck in her, and they told her she would have to be tied down in a sort of flat chair, tied down head and hand and foot.

"I will not," said Semley.

But when she saw that the four Claymen who were to be her guides let themselves be tied down first, she submitted. The others left. There was a roaring sound, and a long silence; a great weight that could not be seen pressed upon her. Then there was no weight; no sound; nothing at all.

"Am I dead?" asked Semley.

"Oh no, Lady," said a voice she did not like.

Opening her eyes, she saw the white face bent over her, the wide lips pulled back, the eyes like little stones. Her bonds had fallen away from her, and she leaped up. She was weightless, bodiless; she felt herself only a gust of terror on the wind.

"We will not hurt you," said the sullen voice or voices. "Only let us touch you, Lady. We would like to touch your hair. Let us touch your hair. . . ."

The round cart they were in trembled a little. Outside its one window lay blank night, or was it mist, or nothing at all? One long night, they had said. Very long. She sat motionless and endured the touch of their heavy grey hands on her hair. Later they would touch her hands and feet and arms, and once her throat: at that she set her teeth and stood up, and they drew back.

"We have not hurt you, Lady," they said. She shook her head.

When they bade her, she lay down again in the chair that bound her down; and when light flashed golden, at the window, she would have wept at the sight, but fainted first.

"WELL," SAID ROCANNON, "NOW AT LEAST WE KNOW WHAT SHE IS."

"I wish there were some way of knowing *who* she is," the curator mumbled. "She wants something we've got here in the Museum, is that what the trogs say?"

"Now, don't call 'em trogs," Rocannon said conscientiously; as a hilfer, an ethnologist of the High Intelligence Life-forms, he was supposed to resist such words. "They're not pretty, but they're Status C Allies. . . . I wonder why the Commission picked them to develop? Before even contacting all the HILF species? I'll bet the survey was from Centaurus—Centaurans always like nocturnals and cave dwellers. I'd have backed Species II, here, I think."

"The troglodytes seem to be rather in awe of her."

"Aren't you?"

Ketho glanced at the tall woman again, then reddened and laughed. "Well, in a way. I never saw such a beautiful alien type in eighteen years here on New South Georgia. I never saw such a beautiful woman anywhere, in fact. She looks like a goddess." The red now reached the top of his bald head, for Ketho was a shy curator, not given to hyperbole. But Rocannon nodded soberly, agreeing.

"I wish we could talk to her without those tr—Gdemiar as interpreters. But there's no help for it." Rocannon went toward their visitor, and when she turned her splendid face to him he bowed down very deeply, going right down to the floor on one knee, his head bowed and his eyes shut. This was what he called his All-Purpose Intercultural Curtsey, and he performed it with some grace. When he came erect again the beautiful woman smiled and spoke.

"She say, Hail, Lord of Stars," growled one of her squat escorts in Pidgin-Galactic.

"Hail, Lady of the Angyar," Rocannon replied. "In what way can we of the Museum serve the lady?"

Across the troglodytes' growling her voice ran like a brief silver wind.

"She say, Please give her necklace which treasure her blood-kin-forebears long long."

"Which necklace?" he asked, and understanding him, she pointed to the central display of the case before them, a magnificent thing, a chain of yellow gold, massive but very delicate in workmanship, set with one big hot-blue sapphire. Rocannon's eyebrows went up, and Ketho at his shoulder murmured, "She's got good taste. That's the Fomalhaut Necklace—famous bit of work."

She smiled at the two men, and again spoke to them over the heads of the troglodytes.

"She say, O Starlords, Elder and Younger Dwellers in House of Treasures, this treasure her one. Long long time. Thank you."

"How did we get the thing, Ketho?"

"Wait; let me look it up in the catalogue. I've got it here. Here. It came from these trogs—trolls—whatever they are: Gdemiar. They have a bargain-obsession, it says; we had to let 'em buy the ship they came here on, an AD-4. This was part payment. It's their own handiwork."

"And I'll bet they can't do this kind of work any more, since they've been steered to Industrial."

"But they seem to feel the thing is hers, not theirs or ours. It must be important, Rocannon, or they wouldn't have given up this time-span to her errand. Why, the objective lapse between here and Fomalhaut must be considerable!"

"Several years, no doubt," said the hilfer, who was used to starjumping. "Not very far. Well, neither the *Handbook* nor the *Guide* gives me enough data to base a decent guess on. These species obviously haven't been properly studied at all. The little fellows may be showing her simple courtesy. Or an interspecies war may depend on this damn sapphire. Perhaps her desire rules them, because they consider themselves totally inferior to her. Or despite appearances she may be their prisoner, their decoy. How can we tell? . . . Can you give the thing away, Ketho?"

"Oh, yes. All the Exotica are technically on loan, not our property, since these claims come up now and then. We seldom argue. Peace above all, until the War comes. . . ."

"Then I'd say give it to her."

Ketho smiled. "It's a privilege," he said. Unlocking the case, he lifted out the great golden chain; then, in his shyness, he held it out to Rocannon, saying, "You give it to her."

So the blue jewel first lay, for a moment, in Rocannon's hand.

His mind was not on it; he turned straight to the beautiful, alien woman, with his handful of blue fire and gold. She did not raise her hands to take it, but bent her head, and he slipped the necklace over her hair. It lay like a burning fuse along her golden-brown throat. She looked up from it with such pride, delight, and gratitude in her face, that Rocannon stood wordless, and the little curator murmured hurriedly in his own language, "You're welcome, you're very welcome." She bowed her golden head to him and to Rocannon. Then, turning, she nodded to her squat guards—or captors?—and, drawing her worn blue cloak about her, paced down the long hall and was gone. Ketho and Rocannon stood looking after her.

"What I feel . . ." Rocannon began.

"Well?" Ketho inquired hoarsely, after a long pause.

"What I feel sometimes is that I . . . meeting these people from worlds we know so little of, you know, sometimes . . . that I have as it were blundered through the corner of a legend, or a tragic myth, maybe, which I do not understand. . . ."

"Yes," said the curator, clearing his throat. "I wonder . . . I wonder what her name is."

Semley the Fair, Semley the Golden, Semley of the Necklace. The Clayfolk had bent to her will, and so had even the Starlords in that terrible place where the Clayfolk had taken her, the city at the end of the night. They had bowed to her, and given her gladly her treasure from amongst their own.

But she could not yet shake off the feeling of those caverns about her where rock lowered overhead, where you could not tell who spoke or what they did, where voices boomed and grey hands reached out—Enough of that. She had paid for the necklace; very well. Now it was hers. The price was paid, the past was the past.

Her windsteed had crept out of some kind of box, with his eyes filmy and his fur rimed with ice, and at first when they had left the caves of the Gdemiar he would not fly. Now he seemed all right again, riding a smooth south wind through the bright sky toward Hallan. "Go quick, go quick," she told him, beginning to laugh as the wind cleared away her mind's darkness. "I want to see Durhal soon, soon. . . ."

And swiftly they flew, coming to Hallan by dusk of the second day. Now the caves of the Clayfolk seemed no more than last year's nightmare, as the steed swooped with her up the thousand steps of Hallan and across the Chasmbridge where the forests fell away for a thousand feet. In the gold light of evening in the flightcourt she dismounted and walked up the last steps between the stiff carven figures of heroes and the two gatewards, who bowed to her, staring at the beautiful, fiery thing around her neck.

In the Forehall she stopped a passing girl, a very pretty girl, by her looks one of Durhal's close kin, though Semley could not call to mind her name. "Do you know me, maiden? I am Semley, Durhal's wife. Will you go tell the Lady Durossa that I have come back?"

For she was afraid to go on in and perhaps face Durhal at once, alone; she wanted Durossa's support.

The girl was gazing at her, her face very strange. But she murmured, "Yes, Lady," and darted off toward the Tower.

Semley stood waiting in the gilt, ruinous hall. No one came by; were they all at table in the Revel-hall? The silence was uneasy. After a minute Semley started toward the stairs to the Tower. But an old woman was coming to her across the stone floor, holding her arms out, weeping.

"O Semley, Semley!"

She had never seen the grey-haired woman, and shrank back.

"But Lady, who are you?"

"I am Durossa, Semley."

She was quiet and still, all the time that Durossa embraced her and wept, and asked if it were true the Clayfolk had captured her and kept her under a spell all these long years, or had it been the Fiia with their strange arts? Then, drawing back a little, Durossa ceased to weep.

"You're still young, Semley. Young as the day you left here. And you wear round your neck the necklace. . ."

"I have brought my gift to my husband Durhal. Where is he?"

"Durhal is dead."

Semley stood unmoving.

"Your husband, my brother, Durhal Hallanlord was killed seven years ago in battle. Nine years you had been gone. The Starlords came no more. We fell to warring with the Eastern Halls, with the Angyar of Log and Hul-Orren. Durhal, fighting, was killed by a midman's spear, for he had little armor for his body, and none at all for his spirit. He lies buried in the fields above Orren Marsh."

Semley turned away. "I will go to him, then," she said, putting her hand on the gold chain that weighed down her neck. "I will give him my gift."

"Wait, Semley! Durhal's daughter, your daughter, see her now, Haldre the Beautiful!"

It was the girl she had first spoken to and sent to Durossa, a girl of nineteen or so, with eyes like Durhal's eyes, dark blue. She stood beside Durossa, gazing with those steady eyes at this woman Semley who was her mother and was her own age. Their age was the same, and their gold hair, and their beauty. Only Semley was a little taller, and wore the blue stone on her breast.

"Take it, take it. It was for Durhal and Haldre that I brought it from the end of the long night!" Semley cried this aloud, twisting and bowing her head to get the heavy chain off, dropping the necklace so it fell on the stones with a cold, liquid clash. "O take it, Haldre!" she cried again, and then, weeping aloud, turned and ran from Hallan, over the bridge and down the long, broad steps, and, darting off eastward into the forest of the mountainside like some wild thing escaping, was gone.

NINE LIVES

SHE WAS ALIVE INSIDE BUT DEAD OUTSIDE, HER FACE A BLACK and dun net of wrinkles, tumors, cracks. She was bald and blind. The tremors that crossed Libra's face were mere quiverings of corruption. Underneath, in the black corridors, the halls beneath the skin, there were crepitations in darkness, ferments, chemical nightmares that went on for centuries. "O the damned flatulent planet," Pugh murmured as the dome shook and a boil burst a kilometer to the southwest, spraying silver pus across the sunset. The sun had been setting for the last two days. "I'll be glad to see a human face."

"Thanks," said Martin.

"Yours is human to be sure," said Pugh, "but I've seen it so long I can't see it."

Radvid signals cluttered the communicator which Martin was operating, faded, returned as face and voice. The face filled the screen, the nose of an Assyrian king, the eyes of a samurai, skin bronze, eyes the color of iron: young, magnificent. "Is that what human beings look like?" said Pugh with awe. "I'd forgotten."

"Shut up, Owen, we're on."

"Libra Exploratory Mission Base, come in please, this is *Passerine* launch."

"Libra here. Beam fixed. Come on down, launch."

"Expulsion in seven E-seconds. Hold on." The screen blanked and sparkled.

"Do they all look like that? Martin, you and I are uglier men than I thought."

"Shut up, Owen. . . ."

For twenty-two minutes Martin followed the landing craft down by signal and then through the cleared dome they saw it, small star in the blood-colored east, sinking. It came down neat and quiet, Libra's thin atmosphere carrying little sound. Pugh and Martin closed the head-pieces of their swimsuits, zipped out of the dome airlocks, and ran with soaring strides, Nijinsky and Nureyev, toward the boat. Three equipment modules came floating down at four-minute intervals from each other and hundred-meter intervals east of the boat. "Come on out," Martin said on his suit radio, "we're waiting at the door."

"Come on in, the methane's fine," said Pugh.

The hatch opened. The young man they had seen on the screen came out with one athletic twist and leaped down onto the shaky dust and clinkers of Libra. Martin shook his hand, but Pugh was staring at the hatch, from which another young man emerged with the same neat twist and jump, followed by a young woman who emerged with the same neat twist, ornamented by a wriggle, and the jump. They were all tall, with bronze skin, black hair, high-bridged noses, epicanthic fold, the same face. They all had the same face. The fourth was emerging from the hatch with a neat twist and jump. "Martin bach," said Pugh, "we've got a clone."

"Right," said one of them, "we're a tenclone. John Chow's the name. You're Lieutenant Martin?"

"I'm Owen Pugh."

"Alvaro Guillen Martin," said Martin, formal, bowing slightly. Another girl was out, the same beautiful face; Martin stared at her and his eye rolled like a nervous pony's. Evidently he had never given any thought to cloning and was suffering technological shock. "Steady," Pugh said in the Argentine dialect, "it's only excess twins." He stood close by Martin's elbow. He was glad himself of the contact.

It is hard to meet a stranger. Even the greatest extravert meeting even the meekest stranger knows a certain dread, though he may not know he knows it. Will he make a fool of me wreck my image of myself invade me destroy me change me? Will he be different from me? Yes, that he will. There's the terrible thing: the strangeness of the stranger.

After two years on a dead planet, and the last half year isolated as a team of two, oneself and one other, after that it's ever harder to meet a stranger, however welcome he may be. You're out of the habit of difference, you've lost the touch; and so the fear revives, the primitive anxiety, the old dread.

The clone, five males and five females, had got done in a couple of minutes what a man might have got done in twenty: greeted Pugh and Martin, had a glance at Libra, unloaded the boat, made ready to go. They went, and the dome filled with them, a hive of golden bees. They hummed and buzzed quietly, filled up all silences, all spaces with a honey-brown swarm of human presence. Martin looked bewildered at the long-limbed girls, and they smiled at him, three at once. Their smile was gentler than that of the boys, but no less radiantly self-possessed.

"Self-possessed," Owen Pugh murmured to his friend, "that's it. Think of it, to be oneself ten times over. Nine seconds for every motion, nine ayes on every vote. It would be glorious." But Martin was asleep. And the John Chows had all gone to sleep at once. The dome was filled with their quiet breathing. They were young, they didn't snore. Martin sighed and snored, his Hershey-bar-colored face relaxed in the dim afterglow of Libra's primary, set at last. Pugh had cleared the dome and stars looked in, Sol among them, a great company of lights, a clone of splendors. Pugh slept and dreamed of a one-eyed giant who chased him through the shaking halls of Hell.

FROM HIS SLEEPING BAG PUGH WATCHED THE CLONE'S AWAKEN-
ing. They all got up within one minute except for one pair, a boy and a
girl, who lay snugly tangled and still sleeping in one bag. As Pugh saw this
there was a shock like one of Libra's earthquakes inside him, a very deep
tremor. He was not aware of this and in fact thought he was pleased at
the sight; there was no other such comfort on this dead hollow world.
More power to them, who made love. One of the others stepped on the
pair. They woke and the girl sat up flushed and sleepy, with bare golden
breasts. One of her sisters murmured something to her; she shot a glance
at Pugh and disappeared in the sleeping bag; from another direction came
a fierce stare, from still another direction a voice: "Christ, we're used to
having a room to ourselves. Hope you don't mind, Captain Pugh."

"It's a pleasure," Pugh said half truthfully. He had to stand up then
wearing only the shorts he slept in, and he felt like a plucked rooster,
all white scrawn and pimples. He had seldom envied Martin's compact
brownness so much. The United Kingdom had come through the Great
Famines well, losing less than half its population: a record achieved by
rigorous food control. Black marketeers and hoarders had been executed.
Crumbs had been shared. Where in richer lands most had died and a
few had thrived, in Britain fewer died and none throve. They all got lean.
Their sons were lean, their grandsons lean, small, brittle-boned, easily
infected. When civilization became a matter of standing in lines, the
British had kept queue, and so had replaced the survival of the fittest
with the survival of the fair-minded. Owen Pugh was a scrawny little
man. All the same, he was there.

At the moment he wished he wasn't.

At breakfast a John said, "Now if you'll brief us, Captain Pugh—"

"Owen, then."

"Owen, we can work out our schedule. Anything new on the mine since your last report to your Mission? We saw your reports when *Passerine* was orbiting Planet V, where they are now."

Martin did not answer, though the mine was his discovery and project, and Pugh had to do his best. It was hard to talk to them. The same faces, each with the same expression of intelligent interest, all leaned toward him across the table at almost the same angle. They all nodded together.

Over the Exploitation Corps insigne on their tunics each had a name-band, first name John and last name Chow of course, but the middle names different. The men were Aleph, Kaph, Yod, Gimel, and Samedh; the women Sadhe, Daleth, Zayin, Beth, and Resh. Pugh tried to use the names but gave it up at once; he could not even tell sometimes which one had spoken, for all the voices were alike.

Martin buttered and chewed his toast, and finally interrupted: "You're a team. Is that it?"

"Right," said two Johns.

"God, what a team! I hadn't seen the point. How much do you each know what the others are thinking?"

"Not at all, properly speaking," replied one of the girls, Zayin. The others watched her with the proprietary, approving look they had. "No ESP, nothing fancy. But we think alike. We have exactly the same equipment. Given the same stimulus, the same problem, we're likely to be coming up with the same reactions and solutions at the same time. Explanations are easy—don't even have to make them, usually. We seldom misunderstand each other. It does facilitate our working as a team."

"Christ yes," said Martin. "Pugh and I have spent seven hours out of ten for six months misunderstanding each other. Like most people. What about emergencies, are you as good at meeting the unexpected problem as a nor . . . an unrelated team?"

"Statistics so far indicate that we are," Zayin answered readily. Clones must be trained, Pugh thought, to meet questions, to reassure and reason. All they said had the slightly bland and stilted quality of answers furnished to the Public. "We can't brainstorm as singletons can, we as a team don't profit from the interplay of varied minds; but we have a compensatory advantage. Clones are drawn from the best human material, individuals of IIQ ninety-ninth percentile, Genetic Constitution alpha double A, and so on. We have more to draw on than most individuals do."

"And it's multiplied by a factor of ten. Who is—who was John Chow?"

"A genius surely," Pugh said politely. His interest in cloning was not so new and avid as Martin's.

"Leonardo Complex type," said Yod. "Biomath, also a cellist and an undersea hunter, and interested in structural engineering problems and so on. Died before he'd worked out his major theories."

"Then you each represent a different facet of his mind, his talents?"

"No," said Zayin, shaking her head in time with several others. "We share the basic equipment and tendencies, of course, but we're all engineers in Planetary Exploitation. A later clone can be trained to develop other aspects of the basic equipment. It's all training; the genetic substance is identical. We *are* John Chow. But we are differently trained."

Martin looked shell-shocked. "How old are you?"

"Twenty-three."

"You say he died young—had they taken germ cells from him beforehand or something?"

Gimel took over: "He died at twenty-four in an air car crash. They couldn't save the brain, so they took some intestinal cells and cultured them for cloning. Reproductive cells aren't used for cloning, since they have only half the chromosomes. Intestinal cells happen to be easy to despecialize and reprogram for total growth."

"All chips off the old block," Martin said valiantly. "But how can . . . some of you be women . . . ?"

Beth took over: "It's easy to program half the clonal mass back to the female. Just delete the male gene from half the cells and they revert to the basic, that is, the female. It's trickier to go the other way, have to hook in artificial Y chromosomes. So they mostly clone from males, since clones function best bisexually."

Gimel again: "They've worked these matters of technique and function out carefully. The taxpayer wants the best for his money, and of course clones are expensive. With the cell manipulations, and the incubation in Ngama Placentae, and the maintenance and training of the foster-parent groups, we end up costing about three million apiece."

"For your next generation," Martin said, still struggling, "I suppose you . . . you breed?"

"We females are sterile," said Beth with perfect equanimity. "You remember that the Y chromosome was deleted from our original cell. The males can interbreed with approved singletons, if they want to. But to get John Chow again as often as they want, they just reclone a cell from this clone."

Martin gave up the struggle. He nodded and chewed cold toast. "Well," said one of the Johns, and all changed mood, like a flock of starlings that change course in one wingflick, following a leader so fast that no eye can see which leads. They were ready to go. "How about a look at the mine? Then we'll unload the equipment. Some nice new models in the roboats; you'll want to see them. Right?" Had Pugh or Martin not agreed they might have found it hard to say so. The Johns were polite but unanimous; their decisions carried. Pugh, Commander of Libra Base 2, felt a qualm. Could he boss around this superman/woman-entity-of-ten? and a genius at that? He stuck close to Martin as they suited for outside. Neither said anything.

Four apiece in the three large airjets, they slipped off north from the dome, over Libra's dun rugose skin, in starlight.

"Desolate," one said.

It was a boy and girl with Pugh and Martin. Pugh wondered if these were the two that had shared a sleeping bag last night. No doubt they wouldn't mind if he asked them. Sex must be as handy as breathing to them. Did you two breathe last night?

"Yes," he said, "it is desolate."

"This is our first time off, except training on Luna." The girl's voice was definitely a bit higher and softer.

"How did you take the big hop?"

"They doped us. I wanted to experience it." That was the boy; he sounded wistful. They seemed to have more personality, only two at a time. Did repetition of the individual negate individuality?

"Don't worry," said Martin, steering the sled, "you can't experience no-time because it isn't there."

"I'd just like to once," one of them said. "So we'd know."

The Mountains of Merioneth showed leprotic in starlight to the east, a plume of freezing gas trailed silvery from a vent-hole to the west, and the sled tilted groundward. The twins braced for the stop at one moment, each with a slight protective gesture to the other. Your skin is my skin, Pugh thought, but literally, no metaphor. What would it be like, then, to have someone as close to you as that? Always to be answered when you spoke; never to be in pain alone. Love your neighbor as you love yourself. . . . That hard old problem was solved. The neighbor was the self: the love was perfect.

And here was Hellmouth, the mine.

Pugh was the Exploratory Mission's E.T. geologist, and Martin his technician and cartographer; but when in the course of a local survey Martin had discovered the U-mine, Pugh had given him full credit, as well as the onus of prospecting the lode and planning the Exploitation Team's job. These kids had been sent out from Earth years before Martin's reports got there and had not known what their job would be until they got here. The Exploitation Corps simply sent out teams regularly and blindly as a dandelion sends out its seed, knowing there would be a job for them on Libra or the next planet out or one they hadn't even heard about yet. The government wanted uranium too urgently to wait while reports drifted home across the lightyears. The stuff was like gold,

old-fashioned but essential, worth mining extraterrestrially and shipping interstellar. Worth its weight in people, Pugh thought sourly, watching the tall young men and women go one by one, glimmering in starlight, into the black hole Martin had named Hellmouth.

As they went in their homeostatic forehead-lamps brightened. Twelve nodding gleams ran along the moist, wrinkled walls. Pugh heard Martin's radiation counter peeping twenty to the dozen up ahead. "Here's the drop-off," said Martin's voice in the suit intercom, drowning out the peeping and the dead silence that was around them. "We're in a side-fissure, this is the main vertical vent in front of us." The black void gaped, its far side not visible in the headlamp beams. "Last vulcanism seems to have been a couple of thousand years ago. Nearest fault is twenty-eight kilos east, in the Trench. This area seems to be as safe seismically as anything in the area. The big basalt-flow overhead stabilizes all these substructures, so long as it remains stable itself. Your central lode is thirty-six meters down and runs in a series of five bubble caverns northeast. It is a lode, a pipe of very high-grade ore. You saw the percentage figures, right? Extraction's going to be no problem. All you've got to do is get the bubbles topside."

"Take off the lid and let 'em float up." A chuckle. Voices began to talk, but they were all the same voice and the suit radio gave them no location in space. "Open the thing right up.—Safer that way.—But it's a solid basalt roof, how thick, ten meters here?—Three to twenty, the report said.—Blow good ore all over the lot.—Use this access we're in, straighten it a bit and run slider rails for the robos.—Import burros.—Have we got enough propping material?—What's your estimate of total payload mass, Martin?"

"Say over five million kilos and under eight."

"Transport will be here in ten E-months.—It'll have to go pure.—No, they'll have the mass problem in NAFAL shipping licked by now, remember it's been sixteen years since we left Earth last Tuesday.—Right, they'll send the whole lot back and purify it in Earth orbit.—Shall we go down, Martin?"

"Go on. I've been down."

The first one—Aleph? (Heb., the ox, the leader)—swung onto the ladder and down; the rest followed. Pugh and Martin stood at the chasm's edge. Pugh set his intercom to exchange only with Martin's suit, and noticed Martin doing the same. It was a bit wearing, this listening to one person think aloud in ten voices, or was it one voice speaking the thoughts of ten minds?

"A great gut," Pugh said, looking down into the black pit, its veined and warted walls catching stray gleams of headlamps far below. "A cow's bowel. A bloody great constipated intestine."

Martin's counter peeped like a lost chicken. They stood inside the dead but epileptic planet, breathing oxygen from tanks, wearing suits impermeable to corrosives and harmful radiations, resistant to a 200-degree range of temperatures, tear-proof, and as shock-resistant as possible given the soft vulnerable stuff inside.

"Next hop," Martin said, "I'd like to find a planet that has nothing whatever to exploit."

"You found this."

"Keep me home next time."

Pugh was pleased. He had hoped Martin would want to go on working with him, but neither of them was used to talking much about their feelings, and he had hesitated to ask. "I'll try that," he said.

"I hate this place. I like caves, you know. It's why I came in here. Just spelunking. But this one's a bitch. Mean. You can't ever let down in here. I guess this lot can handle it, though. They know their stuff."

"Wave of the future, whatever," said Pugh.

The wave of the future came swarming up the ladder, swept Martin to the entrance, gabbled at and around him: "Have we got enough material for supports?—If we convert one of the extractor servos to anneal, yes.—Sufficient if we miniblast?—Kaph can calculate stress." Pugh had switched his intercom back to receive them; he looked at them, so many thoughts jabbering in an eager mind, and at Martin standing silent among them, and at Hellmouth and the wrinkled plain. "Settled! How does that strike you as a preliminary schedule, Martin?"

"It's your baby," Martin said.

WITHIN FIVE E-DAYS THE JOHNS HAD ALL THEIR MATERIAL AND equipment unloaded and operating and were starting to open up the mine. They worked with total efficiency. Pugh was fascinated and frightened by their effectiveness, their confidence, their independence. He was no use to them at all. A clone, he thought, might indeed be the first truly stable, self-reliant human being. Once adult it would need nobody's help. It would be sufficient to itself physically, sexually, emotionally, intellectually. Whatever he did, any member of it would always receive the support and approval of his peers, his other selves. Nobody else was needed.

Two of the clone stayed in the dome doing calculations and paper-work, with frequent sled trips to the mine for measurements and tests. They were the mathematicians of the clone, Zayin and Kaph. That is, as Zayin explained, all ten had had thorough mathematical training from age three to twenty-one, but from twenty-one to twenty-three she and Kaph had gone on with math while the others intensified study in other specialties, geology, mining, engineering, electronic engineering, equip-ment robotics, applied atomics, and so on. "Kaph and I feel," she said, "that we're the element of the clone closest to what John Chow was in his singleton lifetime. But of course he was principally in biomath, and they didn't take us far in that."

"They needed us most in this field," Kaph said, with the patriotic priggishness they sometimes evinced.

Pugh and Martin soon could distinguish this pair from the others,

Zayin by gestalt, Kaph only by a discolored left fourth fingernail, got from an ill-aimed hammer at the age of six. No doubt there were many such differences, physical and psychological, among them; nature might be identical, nurture could not be. But the differences were hard to find. And part of the difficulty was that they never really talked to Pugh and Martin. They joked with them, were polite, got along fine. They gave nothing. It was nothing one could complain about; they were very pleasant, they had the standardized American friendliness. "Do you come from Ireland, Owen?"

"Nobody comes from Ireland, Zayin."

"There are lots of Irish-Americans."

"To be sure, but no more Irish. A couple of thousand in all the island, the last I knew. They didn't go in for birth control, you know, so the food ran out. By the Third Famine there were no Irish left at all but the priesthood, and they all celibate, or nearly all."

Zayin and Kaph smiled stiffly. They had no experience of either bigotry or irony. "What are you then, ethnically?" Kaph asked, and Pugh replied, "A Welshman."

"Is it Welsh that you and Martin speak together?"

None of your business, Pugh thought, but said, "No, it's his dialect, not mine: Argentinean. A descendant of Spanish."

"You learned it for private communication?"

"Whom had we here to be private from? It's just that sometimes a man likes to speak his native language."

"Ours is English," Kaph said unsympathetically. Why should they have sympathy? That's one of the things you give because you need it back.

"Is Wells quaint?" asked Zayin.

"Wells? Oh, Wales, it's called. Yes, Wales is quaint." Pugh switched on his rock-cutter, which prevented further conversation by a synapse-destroying whine, and while it whined he turned his back and said a profane word in Welsh.

That night he used the Argentine dialect for private communication. "Do they pair off in the same couples or change every night?"

Martin looked surprised. A prudish expression, unsuited to his features, appeared for a moment. It faded. He too was curious. "I think it's random."

"Don't whisper, man, it sounds dirty. I think they rotate."

"On a schedule?"

"So nobody gets omitted."

Martin gave a vulgar laugh and smothered it. "What about us? Aren't we omitted?"

"That doesn't occur to them."

"What if I proposition one of the girls?"

"She'd tell the others and they'd decide as a group."

"I am not a bull," Martin said, his dark, heavy face heating up. "I will not be judged—"

"Down, down, *machismo*," said Pugh. "Do you mean to proposition one?"

Martin shrugged, sullen. "Let 'em have their incest."

"Incest is it, or masturbation?"

"I don't care, if they'd do it out of earshot!"

The clone's early attempts at modesty had soon worn off, unmotivated by any deep defensiveness of self or awareness of others. Pugh and Martin were daily deeper swamped under the intimacies of its constant emotional-sexual-mental interchange: swamped yet excluded.

"Two months to go," Martin said one evening.

"To what?" snapped Pugh. He was edgy lately, and Martin's sullenness got on his nerves.

"To relief."

In sixty days the full crew of their Exploratory Mission were due back from their survey of the other planets of the system. Pugh was aware of this.

"Crossing off the days on your calendar?" he jeered.

"Pull yourself together, Owen."

"What do you mean?"

"What I say."

They parted in contempt and resentment.

PUGH CAME IN AFTER A DAY ALONE ON THE PAMPAS, A VAST LAVA plain the nearest edge of which was two hours south by jet. He was tired but refreshed by solitude. They were not supposed to take long trips alone but lately had often done so. Martin stooped under bright lights, drawing one of his elegant masterly charts. This one was of the whole face of Libra, the cancerous face. The dome was otherwise empty, seeming dim and large as it had before the clone came. "Where's the golden horde?"

Martin grunted ignorance, cross-hatching. He straightened his back to glance round at the sun, which squatted feebly like a great red toad on the eastern plain, and at the clock, which said 18:45. "Some big quakes today," he said, returning to his map. "Feel them down there? Lots of crates were falling around. Take a look at the seismo."

The needle jigged and wavered on the roll. It never stopped dancing here. The roll had recorded five quakes of major intensity back in mid-afternoon; twice the needle had hopped off the roll. The attached computer had been activated to emit a slip reading, "Epicenter 61' N by 42' 4" E."

"Not in the Trench this time."

"I thought it felt a bit different from usual. Sharper."

"In Base One I used to lie awake all night feeling the ground jump. Queer how you get used to things."

"Go spla if you didn't. What's for dinner?"

"I thought you'd have cooked it."

"Waiting for the clone."

Feeling put upon, Pugh got out a dozen dinnerboxes; stuck two in the Instobake, pulled them out. "All right, here's dinner."

"Been thinking," Martin said, coming to table. "What if some clone cloned itself? Illegally. Made a thousand duplicates—ten thousand. Whole army. They could make a tidy power grab, couldn't they?"

"But how many millions did this lot cost to rear? Artificial placentae and all that. It would be hard to keep secret, unless they had a planet to themselves. . . . Back before the Famines when Earth had national governments, they talked about that: clone your best soldiers, have whole regiments of them. But the food ran out before they could play that game."

They talked amicably, as they used to do.

"Funny," Martin said, chewing. "They left early this morning, didn't they?"

"All but Kaph and Zayin. They thought they'd get the first payload above ground today. What's up?"

"They weren't back for lunch."

"They won't starve, to be sure."

"They left at seven."

"So they did." Then Pugh saw it. The air tanks held eight hours' supply.

"Kaph and Zayin carried out spare cans when they left. Or they've got a heap out there."

"They did, but they brought the whole lot in to recharge." Martin stood up, pointing to one of the stacks of stuff that cut the dome into rooms and alleys.

"There's an alarm signal on every imsuit."

"It's not automatic."

Pugh was tired and still hungry. "Sit down and eat, man. That lot can look after themselves."

Martin sat down but did not eat. "There was a big quake, Owen. The first one. Big enough it scared me."

After a pause Pugh sighed and said, "All right."

Unenthusiastically, they got out the two-man sled that was always left for them and headed it north. The long sunrise covered everything in poisonous red jello. The horizontal light and shadow made it hard to see, raised walls of fake iron ahead of them which they slid through, turned the convex plain beyond Hellmouth into a great dimple full of bloody water. Around the tunnel entrance a wilderness of machinery stood, cranes and cables and servos and wheels and diggers and robocarts and sliders and control huts, all slanting and bulking incoherently in the red light. Martin jumped from the sled, ran into the mine. He came out again, to Pugh. "Oh God, Owen, it's down," he said. Pugh went in and saw, five meters from the entrance, the shiny moist, black wall that ended the tunnel. Newly exposed to air, it looked organic, like visceral tissue. The tunnel entrance, enlarged by blasting and double-tracked for robocarts, seemed unchanged until he noticed thousands of tiny spiderweb cracks in the walls. The floor was wet with some sluggish fluid.

"They were inside," Martin said.

"They may be still. They surely had extra air cans—"

"Look, Owen, look at the basalt flow, at the roof, don't you see what the quake did, look at it."

The low hump of land that roofed the caves still had the unreal look of an optical illusion. It had reversed itself, sunk down, leaving a vast dimple or pit. When Pugh walked on it he saw that it too was cracked with many tiny fissures. From some a whitish gas was seeping, so that the sunlight on the surface of the gas pool was shafted as if by the waters of a dim red lake.

"The mine's not on the fault. There's no fault here!"

Pugh came back to him quickly. "No, there's no fault, Martin—Look, they surely weren't all inside together."

Martin followed him and searched among the wrecked machines dully, then actively. He spotted the airsled. It had come down heading south, and stuck at an angle in a pothole of colloidal dust. It had carried two riders. One was half sunk in the dust, but his suit meters registered normal functioning; the other hung strapped onto the tilted sled. Her imsuit had burst open on the broken legs, and the body was frozen hard as any rock. That was all they found. As both regulation and custom demanded, they cremated the dead at once with the laser guns they carried by regulation and had never used before. Pugh, knowing he was going to be sick, wrestled the survivor onto the two-man sled and sent Martin off to the dome with him. Then he vomited and flushed the waste out of his suit, and finding one four-man sled undamaged, followed after Martin, shaking as if the cold of Libra had got through to him.

The survivor was Kaph. He was in deep shock. They found a swelling on the occiput that might mean concussion, but no fracture was visible.

Pugh brought two glasses of food concentrate and two chasers of aquavit. "Come on," he said. Martin obeyed, drinking off the tonic. They sat down on crates near the cot and sipped the aquavit.

Kaph lay immobile, face like beeswax, hair bright black to the shoulders, lips stiffly parted for faintly gasping breaths.

"It must have been the first shock, the big one," Martin said. "It must have slid the whole structure sideways. Till it fell in on itself. There must be gas layers in the lateral rocks, like those formations in the Thirty-first Quadrant. But there wasn't any sign—" As he spoke the world slid out from under them. Things leaped and clattered, hopped and jigged, shouted Ha! Ha! Ha! "It was like this at fourteen hours," said Reason shakily in Martin's voice, amidst the unfastening and ruin of the world. But Unreason sat up, as the tumult lessened and things ceased dancing, and screamed aloud.

Pugh leaped across his spilt aquavit and held Kaph down. The muscular body flailed him off. Martin pinned the shoulders down. Kaph screamed, struggled, choked; his face blackened. "Oxy," Pugh said, and his hand found the right needle in the medical kit as if by homing instinct; while Martin held the mask he struck the needle home to the vagus nerve, restoring Kaph to life.

"Didn't know you knew that stunt," Martin said, breathing hard.

"The Lazarus Jab, my father was a doctor. It doesn't often work,"

Pugh said. "I want that drink I spilled. Is the quake over? I can't tell."

"Aftershocks. It's not just you shivering."

"Why did he suffocate?"

"I don't know, Owen. Look in the book."

Kaph was breathing normally and his color was restored; only the lips were still darkened. They poured a new shot of courage and sat down by him again with their medical guide. "Nothing about cyanosis or asphyxiation under 'Shock' or 'Concussion.' He can't have breathed in anything with his suit on. I don't know. We'd get as much good out of *Mother Mog's Home Herbalist* . . . 'Anal Hemorrhoids,' fy!" Pugh pitched the book to a crate table. It fell short, because either Pugh or the table was still unsteady.

"Why didn't he signal?"

"Sorry?"

"The eight inside the mine never had time. But he and the girl must have been outside. Maybe she was in the entrance and got hit by the first slide. He must have been outside, in the control hut maybe. He ran in, pulled her out, strapped her onto the sled, started for the dome. And all that time never pushed the panic button in his imsuit. Why not?"

"Well, he'd had that whack on his head. I doubt he ever realized the girl was dead. He wasn't in his senses. But if he had been I don't know if he'd have thought to signal us. They looked to one another for help."

Martin's face was like an Indian mask, grooves at the mouth corners, eyes of dull coal. "That's so. What must he have felt, then, when the quake came and he was outside, alone—"

In answer Kaph screamed.

He came off the cot in the heaving convulsions of one suffocating, knocked Pugh right down with his flailing arm, staggered into a stack of crates and fell to the floor, lips blue, eyes white. Martin dragged him back onto the cot and gave him a whiff of oxygen, then knelt by Pugh, who was sitting up, and wiped at his cut cheekbone. "Owen, are you all right, are you going to be all right, Owen?"

"I think I am," Pugh said. "Why are you rubbing that on my face?"

It was a short length of computer tape, now spotted with Pugh's blood. Martin dropped it. "Thought it was a towel. You clipped your cheek on that box there."

"Is he out of it?"

"Seems to be."

They stared down at Kaph lying stiff, his teeth a white line inside dark parted lips.

"Like epilepsy. Brain damage maybe?"

"What about shooting him full of meprobamate?"

Pugh shook his head. "I don't know what's in that shot I already gave him for shock. Don't want to overdose him."

"Maybe he'll sleep it off now."

"I'd like to myself. Between him and the earthquake I can't seem to keep on my feet."

"You got a nasty crack there. Go on, I'll sit up a while."

Pugh cleaned his cut cheek and pulled off his shirt, then paused.

"Is there anything we ought to have done—have tried to do—"

"They're all dead," Martin said heavily, gently.

Pugh lay down on top of his sleeping bag and one instant later was wakened by a hideous, sucking, struggling noise. He staggered up, found the needle, tried three times to jab it in correctly and failed, began to massage over Kaph's heart. "Mouth-to-mouth," he said, and Martin obeyed. Presently Kaph drew a harsh breath, his heartbeat steadied, his rigid muscles began to relax.

"How long did I sleep?"

"Half an hour."

They stood up sweating. The ground shuddered, the fabric of the dome sagged and swayed. Libra was dancing her awful polka again, her

Totentanz. The sun, though rising, seemed to have grown larger and redder; gas and dust must have been stirred up in the feeble atmosphere.

"What's wrong with him, Owen?"

"I think he's dying with them."

"Them—But they're all dead, I tell you."

"Nine of them. They're all dead, they were crushed or suffocated. They were all him, he is all of them. They died, and now he's dying their deaths one by one."

"Oh, pity of God," said Martin.

The next time was much the same. The fifth time was worse, for Kaph fought and raved, trying to speak but getting no words out, as if his mouth were stopped with rocks or clay. After that the attacks grew weaker, but so did he. The eighth seizure came at about four-thirty; Pugh and Martin worked till five-thirty doing all they could to keep life in the body that slid without protest into death. They kept him, but Martin said, "The next will finish him." And it did; but Pugh breathed his own breath into the inert lungs, until he himself passed out.

He woke. The dome was opaqued and no light on. He listened and heard the breathing of two sleeping men. He slept, and nothing woke him till hunger did.

The sun was well up over the dark plains, and the planet had stopped dancing. Kaph lay asleep. Pugh and Martin drank tea and looked at him with proprietary triumph.

When he woke Martin went to him: "How do you feel, old man?" There was no answer. Pugh took Martin's place and looked into the brown, dull eyes that gazed toward but not into his own. Like Martin he quickly turned away. He heated food concentrate and brought it to Kaph. "Come on, drink."

He could see the muscles in Kaph's throat tighten. "Let me die," the young man said.

"You're not dying."

Kaph spoke with clarity and precision: "I am nine-tenths dead. There is not enough of me left alive."

That precision convinced Pugh, and he fought the conviction. "No," he said, peremptory. "They are dead. The others. Your brothers and sisters. You're not them, you're alive. You are John Chow. Your life is in your own hands."

The young man lay still, looking into a darkness that was not there.

Martin and Pugh took turns taking the Exploitation hauler and a spare set of robos over to Hellmouth to salvage equipment and protect it from Libra's sinister atmosphere, for the value of the stuff was, literally, astronomical. It was slow work for one man at a time, but they were unwilling to leave Kaph by himself. The one left in the dome did paperwork, while Kaph sat or lay and stared into his darkness and never spoke. The days went by, silent.

The radio spat and spoke: the Mission calling from the ship. "We'll be down on Libra in five weeks, Owen. Thirty-four E-days nine hours I make it as of now. How's tricks in the old dome?"

"Not good, chief. The Exploit team were killed, all but one of them, in the mine. Earthquake. Six days ago."

The radio crackled and sang starsong. Sixteen seconds' lag each way; the ship was out around Planet II now. "Killed, all but one? You and Martin were unhurt?"

"We're all right, chief."

Thirty-two seconds.

"*Passerine* left an Exploit team out here with us. I may put them on the Hellmouth project then, instead of the Quadrant Seven project. We'll settle that when we come down. In any case you and Martin will be relieved at Dome Two. Hold tight. Anything else?"

"Nothing else."

Thirty-two seconds.

"Right then. So long, Owen."

Kaph had heard all this, and later on Pugh said to him, "The chief may ask you to stay here with the other Exploit team. You know the ropes here." Knowing the exigencies of Far Out life, he wanted to warn the young man. Kaph made no answer. Since he had said, "There is not enough of me left alive," he had not spoken a word.

"Owen," Martin said on suit intercom, "he's spla. Insane. Psycho."

"He's doing very well for a man who's died nine times."

"Well? Like a turned-off android is well? The only emotion he has left is hate. Look at his eyes."

"That's not hate, Martin. Listen, it's true that he has, in a sense, been dead. I cannot imagine what he feels. But it's not hatred. He can't even see us. It's too dark."

"Throats have been cut in the dark. He hates us because we're not Aleph and Yod and Zayin."

"Maybe. But I think he's alone. He doesn't see us or hear us, that's the truth. He never had to see anyone else before. He never was alone before. He had himself to see, talk with, live with, nine other selves all his life. He doesn't know how you go it alone. He must learn. Give him time."

Martin shook his heavy head. "Spla," he said. "Just remember when you're alone with him that he could break your neck one-handed."

"He could do that," said Pugh, a short, soft-voiced man with a scarred cheekbone; he smiled. They were just outside the dome airlock, programming one of the servos to repair a damaged hauler. They could see Kaph sitting inside the great half-egg of the dome like a fly in amber.

"Hand me the insert pack there. What makes you think he'll get any better?"

"He has a strong personality, to be sure."

"Strong? Crippled. Nine-tenths dead, as he put it."

"But he's not dead. He's a live man: John Kaph Chow. He had a jolly queer upbringing, but after all every boy has got to break free of his family. He will do it."

"I can't see it."

"Think a bit, Martin bach. What's this cloning for? To repair the human race. We're in a bad way. Look at me. My IIQ and GC are half this John Chow's. Yet they wanted me so badly for the Far Out Service that when I volunteered they took me and fitted me out with an artificial lung and corrected my myopia. Now if there were enough good sound lads about would they be taking one-lunged short-sighted Welshmen?"

"Didn't know you had an artificial lung."

"I do then. Not tin, you know. Human, grown in a tank from a bit of somebody, cloned, if you like. That's how they make replacement organs, the same general idea as cloning, but bits and pieces instead of whole people. It's my own lung now, whatever. But what I am saying is this, there are too many like me these days and not enough like John Chow. They're trying to raise the level of the human genetic pool, which is a mucky little puddle since the population crash. So then if a man is cloned, he's a strong and clever man. It's only logic, to be sure."

Martin grunted; the servo began to hum.

Kaph had been eating little; he had trouble swallowing his food, choking on it, so that he would give up trying after a few bites. He had lost eight or ten kilos. After three weeks or so, however, his appetite began to pick up, and one day he began to look through the clone's possessions, the sleeping bags, kits, papers which Pugh had stacked neatly in a far angle of a packing-crate alley. He sorted, destroyed a heap of papers and oddments, made a small packet of what remained, then relapsed into his walking coma.

Two days later he spoke. Pugh was trying to correct a flutter in the tape-player and failing; Martin had the jet out, checking their maps of the Pampas. "Hell and damnation!" Pugh said, and Kaph said in a toneless voice, "Do you want me to do that?"

Pugh jumped, controlled himself, and gave the machine to Kaph. The young man took it apart, put it back together, and left it on the table.

"Put on a tape," Pugh said with careful casualness, busy at another table.

Kaph put on the topmost tape, a chorale. He lay down on his cot. The sound of a hundred human voices singing together filled the dome. He lay still, his face blank.

In the next days he took over several routine jobs, unasked. He undertook nothing that wanted initiative, and if asked to do anything he made no response at all.

"He's doing well," Pugh said in the dialect of Argentina.

"He's not. He's turning himself into a machine. Does what he's programmed to do, no reaction to anything else. He's worse off than when he didn't function at all. He's not human any more."

Pugh sighed. "Well, good night," he said in English. "Good night, Kaph."

"Good night," Martin said; Kaph did not.

Next morning at breakfast Kaph reached across Martin's plate for the toast. "Why don't you ask for it?" Martin said with the geniality of repressed exasperation. "I can pass it."

"I can reach it," Kaph said in his flat voice.

"Yes, but look. Asking to pass things, saying good night or hello, they're not important, but all the same when somebody says something a person ought to answer. . . ."

The young man looked indifferently in Martin's direction; his eyes still did not seem to see clear through to the person he looked toward. "Why should I answer?"

"Because somebody has said something to you."

"Why?"

Martin shrugged and laughed. Pugh jumped up and turned on the rock-cutter.

Later on he said, "Lay off that, please, Martin."

"Manners are essential in small isolated crews, some kind of manners, whatever you work out together. He's been taught that, everybody in Far Out knows it. Why does he deliberately flout it?"

"Do you tell yourself good night?"

"So?"

"Don't you see Kaph's never known anyone but himself?"

Martin brooded and then broke out. "Then by God this cloning business is all wrong. It won't do. What are a lot of duplicate geniuses going to do for us when they don't even know we exist?"

Pugh nodded. "It might be wiser to separate the clones and bring them up with others. But they make such a grand team this way."

"Do they? I don't know. If this lot had been ten average inefficient E.T. engineers, would they all have got killed? What if, when the quake came and things started caving in, what if all those kids ran the same way, farther into the mine, maybe, to save the one who was farthest in? Even Kaph was outside and went in. . . . It's hypothetical. But I keep thinking, out of ten ordinary confused guys, more might have got out."

"I don't know. It's true that identical twins tend to die at about the same time, even when they have never seen each other. Identity and death, it is very strange. . . ."

The days went on, the red sun crawled across the dark sky, Kaph did not speak when spoken to, Pugh and Martin snapped at each other more frequently each day. Pugh complained of Martin's snoring. Offended, Martin moved his cot clear across the dome and also ceased speaking to Pugh for some while. Pugh whistled Welsh dirges until Martin complained, and then Pugh stopped speaking for a while.

The day before the Mission ship was due, Martin announced he was going over to Merioneth.

"I thought at least you'd be giving me a hand with the computer to finish the rock analyses," Pugh said, aggrieved.

"Kaph can do that. I want one more look at the Trench. Have fun," Martin added in dialect, and laughed, and left.

"What is that language?"

"Argentinean. I told you that once, didn't I?"

"I don't know." After a while the young man added, "I have forgotten a lot of things, I think."

"It wasn't important, to be sure," Pugh said gently, realizing all at once how important this conversation was. "Will you give me a hand running the computer, Kaph?"

He nodded.

Pugh had left a lot of loose ends, and the job took them all day. Kaph was a good coworker, quick and systematic, much more so than Pugh himself. His flat voice, now that he was talking again, got on the nerves; but it didn't matter, there was only this one day left to get through and then the ship would come, the old crew, comrades and friends.

During tea break Kaph said, "What will happen if the Explore ship crashes?"

"They'd be killed."

"To you, I mean."

"To us? We'd radio SOS signals and live on half rations till the rescue cruiser from Area Three Base came. Four and a half E-years away it is. We have life support here for three men for, let's see, maybe between four and five years. A bit tight, it would be."

"Would they send a cruiser for three men?"

"They would."

Kaph said no more.

"Enough cheerful speculations," Pugh said cheerfully, rising to get back to work. He slipped sideways and the chair avoided his hand; he did a sort of half-pirouette and fetched up hard against the dome hide. "My goodness," he said, reverting to his native idiom, "what is it?"

"Quake," said Kaph.

The teacups bounced on the table with a plastic cackle, a litter of papers slid off a box, the skin of the dome swelled and sagged. Underfoot there was a huge noise, half sound, half shaking, a subsonic boom.

Kaph sat unmoved. An earthquake does not frighten a man who died in an earthquake.

Pugh, white-faced, wiry black hair sticking out, a frightened man, said, "Martin is in the Trench."

"What trench?"

"The big fault line. The epicenter for the local quakes. Look at the seismograph." Pugh struggled with the stuck door of a still-jittering locker.

"Where are you going?"

"After him."

"Martin took the jet. Sleds aren't safe to use during quakes. They go out of control."

"For God's sake man, shut up."

Kaph stood up, speaking in a flat voice as usual. "It's unnecessary to go out after him now. It's taking an unnecessary risk."

"If his alarm goes off, radio me," Pugh said, shut the head-piece of his suit, and ran to the lock. As he went out Libra picked up her ragged skirts and danced a belly dance from under his feet clear to the red horizon.

Inside the dome, Kaph saw the sled go up, tremble like a meteor in the dull red daylight, and vanish to the northeast. The hide of the dome quivered, the earth coughed. A vent south of the dome belched up a slow-flowing bile of black gas.

A bell shrilled and a red light flashed on the central control board. The sign under the light read Suit 2 and scribbled under that, A.G.M. Kaph did not turn the signal off. He tried to radio Martin, then Pugh, but got no reply from either.

When the aftershocks decreased he went back to work and finished up Pugh's job. It took him about two hours. Every half hour he tried to contact Suit 1 and got no reply, then Suit 2 and got no reply. The red light had stopped flashing after an hour.

It was dinnertime. Kaph cooked dinner for one and ate it. He lay down on his cot.

The aftershocks had ceased except for faint rolling tremors at long intervals. The sun hung in the west, oblate, pale red, immense. It did not sink visibly. There was no sound at all.

Kaph got up and began to walk about the messy, half-packed-up, overcrowded, empty dome. The silence continued. He went to the player and put on the first tape that came to hand. It was pure music, electronic, without harmonies, without voices. It ended. The silence continued.

Pugh's uniform tunic, one button missing, hung over a stack of rock samples. Kaph stared at it a while.

The silence continued.

The child's dream: There is no one else alive in the world but me. In all the world.

Low, north of the dome, a meteor flickered.

Kaph's mouth opened as if he were trying to say something, but no sound came. He went hastily to the north wall and peered out into the gelatinous red light.

The little star came in and sank. Two figures blurred the airlock. Kaph stood close beside the lock as they came in. Martin's imsuit was covered with some kind of dust so that he looked raddled and warty like the surface of Libra. Pugh had him by the arm.

"Is he hurt?"

Pugh shucked his suit, helped Martin peel off his. "Shaken up," he said, curt.

"A piece of cliff fell onto the jet," Martin said, sitting down at the table and waving his arms. "Not while I was in it though. I was parked, see, and poking about that carbon-dust area when I felt things humping. So I went out onto a nice bit of early igneous I'd noticed from above, good footing and out from under the cliffs. Then I saw this bit of the planet fall off onto the flyer, quite a sight it was, and after a while it occurred to me the spare aircans were in the flyer, so I leaned on the panic button.

But I didn't get any radio reception, that's always happening here during quakes, so I didn't know if the signal was getting through either. And things went on jumping around and pieces of the cliff coming off. Little rocks flying around, and so dusty you couldn't see a meter ahead. I was really beginning to wonder what I'd do for breathing in the small hours, you know, when I saw old Owen buzzing up the Trench in all that dust and junk like a big ugly bat—"

"Want to eat?" said Pugh.

"Of course I want to eat. How'd you come through the quake here, Kaph? No damage? It wasn't a big one actually, was it, what's the seismo say? My trouble was I was in the middle of it. Old Epicenter Alvaro. Felt like Richter fifteen there—total destruction of planet—"

"Sit down," Pugh said. "Eat."

After Martin had eaten a little his spate of talk ran dry. He very soon went off to his cot, still in the remote angle where he had removed it when Pugh complained of his snoring. "Good night, you one-lunged Welshman," he said across the dome.

"Good night."

There was no more out of Martin. Pugh opaqued the dome, turned the lamp down to a yellow glow less than a candle's light, and sat doing nothing, saying nothing, withdrawn.

The silence continued.

"I finished the computations."

Pugh nodded thanks.

"The signal from Martin came through, but I couldn't contact you or him."

Pugh said with effort, "I should not have gone. He had two hours of air left even with only one can. He might have been heading home when I left. This way we were all out of touch with one another. I was scared."

The silence came back, punctuated now by Martin's long, soft snores.

"Do you love Martin?"

Pugh looked up with angry eyes: "Martin is my friend. We've worked together, he's a good man." He stopped. After a while he said, "Yes, I love him. Why did you ask that?"

Kaph said nothing, but he looked at the other man. His face was changed, as if he were glimpsing something he had not seen before; his voice too was changed. "How can you . . . How do you . . ."

But Pugh could not tell him. "I don't know," he said, "it's practice, partly. I don't know. We're each of us alone, to be sure. What can you do but hold your hand out in the dark?"

Kaph's strange gaze dropped, burned out by its own intensity.

"I'm tired," Pugh said. "That was ugly, looking for him in all that black dust and muck, and mouths opening and shutting in the ground. . . . I'm going to bed. The ship will be transmitting to us by six or so." He stood up and stretched.

"It's a clone," Kaph said. "The other Exploit Team they're bringing with them."

"Is it then?"

"A twelveclone. They came out with us on the *Passerine.*"

Kaph sat in the small yellow aura of the lamp seeming to look past it at what he feared: the new clone, the multiple self of which he was not part. A lost piece of a broken set, a fragment, inexpert at solitude, not knowing even how you go about giving love to another individual, now he must face the absolute, closed self-sufficiency of the clone of twelve; that was a lot to ask of the poor fellow, to be sure. Pugh put a hand on his shoulder in passing. "The chief won't ask you to stay here with a clone. You can go home. Or since you're Far Out maybe you'll come on farther out with us. We could use you. No hurry deciding. You'll make out all right."

Pugh's quiet voice trailed off. He stood unbuttoning his coat, stooped a little with fatigue. Kaph looked at him and saw the thing he had never seen before, saw him: Owen Pugh, the other, the stranger who held his hand out in the dark.

"Good night," Pugh mumbled, crawling into his sleeping bag and half asleep already, so that he did not hear Kaph reply after a pause, repeating, across darkness, benediction.

MAZES

I HAVE TRIED HARD TO USE MY WITS AND KEEP UP MY COURAGE, but I know now that I will not be able to withstand the torture any longer. My perceptions of time are confused, but I think it has been several days since I realized I could no longer keep my emotions under aesthetic control, and now the physical breakdown is also nearly complete. I cannot accomplish any of the greater motions. I cannot speak. Breathing, in this heavy foreign air, grows more difficult. When the paralysis reaches my chest I shall die: probably tonight.

The alien's cruelty is refined, yet irrational. If it intended all along to starve me, why not simply withhold food? But instead of that it gave me plenty of food, mountains of food, all the greenbud leaves I could possibly want. Only they were not fresh. They had been picked; they were dead; the element that makes them digestible to us was gone, and one might as well eat gravel. Yet there they were, with all the scent and shape of greenbud, irresistible to my craving appetite. Not at first, of course. I told myself, I am not a child, to eat picked leaves! But the belly gets the better of the mind. After a while it seemed better to be chewing something, anything, that might still the pain and craving in the gut. So I ate, and ate, and starved. It is a relief, now, to be so weak I cannot eat.

The same elaborately perverse cruelty marks all its behavior. And the worst thing of all is just the one I welcomed with such relief and delight at first: the maze. I was badly disoriented at first, after the trapping, being handled by a giant, being dropped into a prison; and this place around the prison is disorienting, spatially disquieting, the strange, smooth, curved wall-ceiling is of an alien substance and its lines are meaningless to me. So when I was taken up and put down, amidst all this strangeness, in a maze, a recognizable, even familiar maze, it was a moment of strength and hope after great distress. It seemed pretty clear that I had been put in the maze as a kind of test or investigation, that a first approach toward communication was being attempted. I tried to cooperate in every way. But it was not possible to believe for very long that the creature's purpose was to achieve communication.

It is intelligent, highly intelligent, that is clear from a thousand evidences. We are both intelligent creatures, we are both maze-builders: surely it would be quite easy to learn to talk together! If that were what the alien wanted. But it is not. I do not know what kind of mazes it builds for itself. The ones it made for me were instruments of torture.

The mazes were, as I said, of basically familiar types, though the walls were of that foreign material much colder and smoother than packed clay. The alien left a pile of picked leaves in one extremity of each maze, I do not know why; it may be a ritual or superstition. The first maze it put me in was babyishly short and simple. Nothing expressive or even interesting could be worked out from it. The second, however, was a kind of simple version of the Ungated Affirmation, quite adequate for the reassuring, outreaching statement I wanted to make. And the last, the long maze, with seven corridors and nineteen connections, lent itself surprisingly well to the Maluvian mode, and indeed to almost all the New Expressionist techniques. Adaptations had to be made to the alien spatial understanding, but a certain quality of creativity arose precisely from the adaptations. I worked hard at the problem of that maze, planning all night long, reimagining the lines and spaces, the feints and pauses, the erratic, unfamiliar, and yet beautiful course of the True Run. Next day when I was placed in the long maze and the alien began to observe, I performed the Eighth Maluvian in its entirety.

It was not a polished performance. I was nervous, and the spatio-temporal parameters were only approximate. But the Eighth Maluvian survives the crudest performance in the poorest maze. The evolutions in the ninth encatenation, where the "cloud" theme recurs so strangely transposed into the ancient spiraling motif, are indestructibly beautiful. I have seen them performed by a very old person, so old and stiff-jointed that he could only suggest the movements, hint at them, a shadow-gesture, a dim reflection of the themes: and all who watched were inexpressibly moved. There is no nobler statement of our being. Performing, I myself was carried away by the power of the motions and forgot that I was a prisoner, forgot the alien eyes watching me; I transcended the errors of the maze and my own weakness, and danced the Eighth Maluvian as I have never danced it before.

When it was done, the alien picked me up and set me down in the first maze—the short one, the maze for little children who have not yet learned how to talk.

Was the humiliation deliberate? Now that it is all past, I see that there is no way to know. But it remains very hard to ascribe its behavior to ignorance.

After all, it is not blind. It has eyes, recognizable eyes. They are enough like our eyes that it must see somewhat as we do. It has a mouth, four legs, can move bipedally, has grasping hands, etc.; for all its gigantism and strange looks, it seems less fundamentally different from us, physically, than a fish. And yet, fish school and dance and, in their own stupid way, communicate! The alien has never once attempted to talk with me. It has been with me, watched me, touched me, handled me, for days: but all its motions have been purposeful, not communicative. It is evidently a solitary creature, totally self-absorbed.

This would go far to explain its cruelty.

I noticed early that from time to time it would move its curious horizontal mouth in a series of fairly delicate, repetitive gestures, a little like someone eating. At first I thought it was jeering at me; then I wondered if it was trying to urge me to eat the indigestible fodder; then I wondered if it could be communicating *labially*. It seemed a limited and unhandy language for one so well provided with hands, feet, limbs, flexible spine, and all; but that would be like the creature's perversity, I thought. I studied its lip-motions and tried hard to imitate them. It did not respond. It stared at me briefly and then went away.

In fact, the only indubitable *response* I ever got from it was on a pitifully low level of interpersonal aesthetics. It was tormenting me with knob-pushing, as it did once a day. I had endured this grotesque routine pretty patiently for the first several days. If I pushed one knob I got a nasty sensation in my feet, if I pushed a second I got a nasty pellet of dried-up food, if I pushed a third I got nothing whatever. Obviously, to demonstrate my intelligence I was to push the third knob. But it appeared that my intelligence irritated my captor, because it removed the neutral knob after the second day. I could not imagine what it was trying to establish or accomplish, except the fact that I was its prisoner and a great deal smaller than it. When I tried to leave the knobs, it forced me physically to return. I must sit there pushing knobs for it, receiving punishment from one and mockery from the other. The deliberate outrageousness of the situation, the insufferable heaviness and thickness of this air, the feeling of being forever watched yet never understood, all combined to drive me into a condition for which we have no description at all. The nearest thing I can suggest is the last interlude of the Ten Gate Dream, when all the feintways are closed and the dance narrows in and in until it bursts terribly into the vertical. I cannot say what I felt, but it was a little like that. If I got my feet stung once more, or got pelted once more with a lump of rotten food, I would go vertical forever . . . I took the

knobs off the wall (they came off with a sharp tug, like flowerbuds), laid
them in the middle of the floor, and defecated on them.

The alien took me up at once and returned to my prison. It had got
the message, and had acted on it. But how unbelievably primitive the
message had had to be! And the next day, it put me back in the knob
room, and there were the knobs as good as new, and I was to choose
alternate punishments for its amusement . . . Until then I had told myself
that the creature was alien, therefore incomprehensible and uncomprehending, perhaps not intelligent in the same *manner* as we, and so on.
But since then I have known that, though all that may remain true, it is
also unmistakably and grossly cruel.

When it put me into the baby maze yesterday, I could not move. The
power of speech was all but gone (I am dancing this, of course, in my
mind; "the best maze is the mind," the old proverb goes) and I simply
crouched there, silent. After a while it took me out again, gently enough.
There is the ultimate perversity of its behavior: it has never once touched
me cruelly.

It set me down in the prison, locked the gate, and filled up the trough
with inedible food. Then it stood two-legged, looking at me for a while.

Its face is very mobile, but if it speaks with its face I cannot understand it, that is too foreign a language. And its body is always covered
with bulky, binding mats, like an old widower who has taken the Vow
of Silence. But I had become accustomed to its great size, and to the
angular character of its limb-positions, which at first had seemed to
be saying a steady stream of incoherent and mispronounced phrases, a
horrible nonsense-dance like the motions of an imbecile, until I realized
that they were strictly purposive movements. Now I saw something a
little beyond that, in its position. There were no words, yet there was
communication. I saw, as it stood watching me, a clear signification of
angry sadness—as clear as the Sembrian Stance. There was the same lax
immobility, the bentness, the assertion of defeat. Never a word came clear,

and yet it told me that it was filled with resentment, pity, impatience, and frustration. It told me it was sick of torturing me, and wanted me to help it. I am sure I understood it. I tried to answer. I tried to say, "What is it you want of me? Only tell me what it is you want." But I was too weak to speak clearly, and it did not understand. It has never understood.

And now I have to die. No doubt it will come in to watch me die; but it will not understand the dance I dance in dying.

THE
FIRST CONTACT
WITH THE
GORGONIDS

MRS. JERRY DEBREE, THE HEROINE OF GRONG CROSSING, LIKED to look pretty. It was important to Jerry in his business contacts, of course, and also it made her feel more confident and kind of happy to know that her cellophane was recent and her eyelashes really well glued on and that the highlighter blush was bringing out her cheekbones like the nice girl at the counter had said. But it was beginning to be hard to feel fresh and look pretty as this desert kept getting hotter and hotter and redder and redder until it looked, really, almost like what she had always thought the Bad Place would look like, only not so many people. In fact none.

"Could we have passed it, do you think?" she ventured at last, and received without surprise the exasperation she had safety-valved from him: "How the fuck could we have *passed* it when we haven't *passed* one fucking *thing* except those fucking *bushes* for ninety miles? *Christ* you're dumb."

Jerry's language was a pity. And sometimes it made it so hard to talk to him. She had had the least little tiny sort of feeling, woman's intuition maybe, that the men that had told him how to get to Grong Crossing were teasing him, having a little joke. He had been talking so loud in the hotel bar about how disappointed he had been with the Corroboree after flying all the way out from Adelaide to see it. He kept comparing it to the Indian dance they had seen at Taos. Actually he had been very bored and restless at Taos and they had had to leave in the middle so he could have a drink and she never had got to see the people with the masks come, but now he talked about how they really knew how to put on a native show in the U.S.A. He said a few scruffy abos jumping around weren't going to give tourists from the real world anything to write home about. The Aussies ought to visit Disney World and find out how to do the real thing, he said.

She agreed with that; she loved Disney World. It was the only thing in Florida, where they had to live now that Jerry was ACEO, that she liked much. One of the Australian men at the bar had seen Disneyland and agreed that it was amazing, or maybe he meant amusing; what he said was amizing. He seemed to be a nice man. Bruce, he said his name was, and his friend's name was Bruce too. "Common sort of name here," he said, only he said nime, but he meant name, she was quite sure. When Jerry went on complaining about the Corroboree, the first Bruce said, "Well, mite, you might go out to Grong Crossing, if you really want to see the real thing—right, Bruce?"

At first the other Bruce didn't seem to know what he meant, and that was when her woman's intuition woke up. But pretty soon both Bruces were talking away about this place, Grong Crossing, way out in "the bush," where they were certain to meet real abos really living in the desert. "Near Alice Springs," Jerry said knowledgeably, but it wasn't, they said; it was still farther west from here. They gave directions so precisely that it was clear they knew what they were talking about. "Few hours' drive, that's all," Bruce said, "but y'see most tourists want to keep on the beaten path. This is a bit more on the inside track."

"Bang-up shows," said Bruce. "Nightly Corroborees."

"Hotel any better than this dump?" Jerry asked, and they laughed. No hotel, they explained. "It's like a safari, see—tents under the stars. Never rines," said Bruce.

"Marvelous food, though," Bruce said. "Fresh kangaroo chops. Kangaroo hunts daily, see. Witchetty grubs along with the drinks before dinner. Roughing it in luxury, I'd call it; right, Bruce?"

"Absolutely," said Bruce.

"Friendly, are they, these abos?" Jerry asked.

"Oh, salt of the earth. Treat you like kings. Think white men are sort of gods, y'know," Bruce said. Jerry nodded.

So Jerry wrote down all the directions, and here they were driving and driving in the old station wagon that was all there was to rent in the small town they'd been at for the Corroboree, and by now you only knew the road was a road because it was perfectly straight forever. Jerry had been in a good humor at first. "This'll be something to shove up that bastard Thiel's ass," he said. His friend Thiel was always going to places like Tibet and having wonderful adventures and showing videos of himself with yaks. Jerry had bought a very expensive camcorder for this trip, and now he said, "Going to shoot me some abos. Show that fucking Thiel and his musk-oxes!" But as the morning went on and the road went on and the desert went on— did they call it "the bush" because there was one little thorny bush once a mile or so?—he got hotter and hotter and redder and redder, just like the desert. And she began to feel depressed and like her mascara was caking.

She was wondering if after another forty miles (four was her lucky number) she could say, "Maybe we ought to turn back?" for the first time, when he said, "There!"

There was something ahead, all right.

"There hasn't been any sign," she said, dubious. "They didn't say anything about a hill, did they?"

"Hell, that's no hill, that's a rock—what do they call it—some big fucking red rock—"

"Ayers Rock?" She had read the Welcome to Down Under flyer in the hotel in Adelaide while Jerry was at the plastics conference. "But that's in the middle of Australia, isn't it?"

"So where the fuck do you think we are? In the middle of Australia! What do you think this is, fucking East Germany?" He was shouting, and he speeded up. The terribly straight road shot them straight at the hill, or rock, or whatever it was. It *wasn't* Ayers Rock, she *knew* that, but there wasn't any use irritating Jerry, especially when he started shouting.

It was reddish, and shaped kind of like a huge VW bug, only lumpier; and there were certainly people all around it, and at first she was very glad to see them. Their utter isolation—they hadn't seen another car or farm or anything for two hours—had scared her. Then as they got closer she thought the people looked rather funny. Funnier than the ones at the Corroboree even. "I guess they're natives," she said aloud.

"What the shit did you expect, Frenchmen?" Jerry said, but he said it like a joke, and she laughed. But—"Oh! goodness!" she said involuntarily, getting her first clear sight of one of the natives.

"Big fellows, huh," he said. "Bushmen, they call 'em."

That didn't seem right, but she was still getting over the shock of seeing that tall, thin, black-and-white, weird person. It had been just standing looking at the car, only she couldn't see its eyes. Heavy brows and thick, hairy eyebrows hid them. Black, ropy hair hung over half its face and stuck out from behind its ears.

"Are they—are they painted?" she asked weakly.

"They always paint 'emselves up like that." His contempt for her ignorance was reassuring.

"They almost don't look human," she said, very softly so as not to hurt their feelings, if they spoke English, since Jerry had stopped the car and flung the doors open and was rummaging out the video camera.

"Hold this!"

She held it. Five or six of the tall black-and-white people had sort of turned their way, but they all seemed to be busy with something at the foot of the hill or rock or whatever it was. There were some things that might be tents. Nobody came to welcome them or anything, but she was actually just as glad they didn't.

"Hold this! Oh for Chrissake what did you do with the—All right, just give it here."

"Jerry, I wonder if we should ask them," she said.

"Ask who what?" he growled, having trouble with the cassette thing.

"The people here—if it's all right to photograph. Remember at Taos they said that when the—"

"For fuck sake you don't need fucking *permission* to photograph a bunch of *natives!* God! Did you ever *look* at the fucking *National Geographic?* Shit! *Permission!*"

It really wasn't any use when he started shouting. And the people didn't seem to be interested in what he was doing. Although it was quite hard to be sure what direction they were actually looking.

"Aren't you going to get out of the fucking *car?*"

"It's so hot," she said.

He didn't really mind it when she was afraid of getting too hot or sunburned or anything, because he liked being stronger and tougher. She probably could even have said that she was afraid of the natives, because he liked to be braver than her, too; but sometimes he got angry when she was afraid, like the time he made her eat that poisonous fish, or a fish that might or might not be poisonous, in Japan, because she said she was afraid to, and she threw up and embarrassed everybody. So she just sat in the car and kept the engine on and the air-conditioning on, although the window on her side was open.

Jerry had his camera up on his shoulder now and was panning the scene—the faraway hot red horizon, the queer rock-hill-thing with shiny places in it like glass, the black, burned-looking ground around it, and the people swarming all over. There were forty or fifty of them at least. It only dawned on her now that if they were wearing any clothes at all, she didn't know which was clothes and which was skin, because they were so strange-shaped, and painted or colored all in stripes and spots of white on black, not like zebras but more complicated, more like skeleton suits but not exactly. And they must be eight feet tall, but their arms were short, almost like kangaroos'. And their hair was like black ropes standing up all over their heads. It was embarrassing to look at people without clothes on, but you couldn't really see anything like *that*. In fact she couldn't tell, actually, if they were men or women.

They were all busy with their work or ceremony or whatever it was. Some of them were handling some things like big, thin, golden leaves, others were doing something with cords or wires. They didn't seem to be talking, but there was all the time in the air a soft, drumming, droning, rising and falling, deep sound, like cats purring or voices far away.

Jerry started walking towards them.

"Be careful," she said faintly. He paid no attention, of course.

They paid no attention to him either, as far as she could see, and he kept filming, swinging the camera around. When he got right up close to a couple of them, they turned towards him. She couldn't see their eyes at all, but what happened was their *hair* sort of stood up and bent towards Jerry—each thick, black rope about a foot long moving around and bending down exactly as if it were peering at him. At that, her own hair tried to stand up, and the blast of the air conditioner ran like ice down her sweaty arms. She got out of the car and called his name.

He kept filming.

She went towards him as fast as she could on the cindery, stony soil in her high-heeled sandals.

"Jerry, come back. I think—"

"Shut up!" he yelled so savagely that she stopped short for a moment. But she could see the hair better now, and she could see that it did have eyes, and mouths too, with little red tongues darting out.

"Jerry, come back," she said. "They're not natives, they're Space Aliens.

That's their saucer." She knew from the *Sun* that there had been sightings down here in Australia.

"Shut the fuck up," he said. "Hey, big fella, give me a little action, huh? Don't just stand there. Dancee-dancee, OK?" His eye was glued to the camera.

"Jerry," she said, her voice sticking in her throat, as one of the Space Aliens pointed with its little weak-looking arm and hand at the car. Jerry shoved the camera right up close to its head, and at that it put its hand over the lens. That made Jerry mad, of course, and he yelled, "Get the fuck off that!" And he actually looked at the Space Alien, not through the camera but face to face. "Oh, gee," he said.

And his hand went to his hip. He always carried a gun, because it was an American's right to bear arms and there were so many drug addicts these days. He had smuggled it through the airport inspection the way he knew how. Nobody was going to disarm *him*.

She saw perfectly clearly what happened. The Space Alien opened its eyes. There were eyes under the dark, shaggy brows; they had been kept closed till now. Now they were open and looked once straight at Jerry, and he turned to stone. He just stood there, one hand on the camera and one reaching for his gun, motionless.

Several more Space Aliens had gathered round. They all had their eyes shut, except for the ones at the ends of their hair. Those glittered and shone, and the little red tongues flickered in and out, and the humming, droning sound was much louder. Many of the hair-snakes writhed to look at her. Her knees buckled and her heart thudded in her throat, but she had to get to Jerry.

She passed right between two huge Space Aliens and reached him and patted him—"Jerry, wake up!" she said. He was just like stone, paralyzed. "Oh," she said, and tears ran down her face. "Oh, what should I do, what can I do?" She looked around in despair at the tall, thin, black-and-white faces looming above her, white teeth showing, eyes tight shut, hairs staring and stirring and murmuring. The murmur was soft, almost like music, not angry, soothing. She watched two tall Space Aliens pick up Jerry quite gently, as if he were a tiny little boy—a stiff one—and carry him carefully to the car.

They poked him into the back seat lengthwise, but he didn't fit. She ran to help. She let down the back seat so there was room for him in the back. The Space Aliens arranged him and tucked the video camera in beside him, then straightened up, their hairs looking down at her with little twinkly eyes. They hummed softly, and pointed with their childish arms back down the road.

"Yes," she said. "Thank you. Good-bye!"

They hummed.

She got in and closed the window and turned the car around there on a wide place in the road—and there *was* a signpost, Grong Crossing, although she didn't see any crossroad.

She drove back, carefully at first because she was shaky, then faster and faster because she should get Jerry to the doctor, of course, but also because she loved driving on long straight roads very fast, like this. Jerry never let her drive except in town.

The paralysis was total and permanent, which would have been terrible, except that she could afford full-time, round-the-clock, first-class care for poor Jerry, because of the really good deals she made with the TV people and then with the rights people for the video. First it was shown all over the world as "Space Aliens Land in Australian Outback," but then it became part of real science and history as "Grong Crossing, South Australia: The First Contact With the Gorgonids." In the voice-over they told how it was her, Annie Laurie Debree, who had been the first human to talk with our friends from Outer Space, even before they sent the ambassadors to Canberra and Reykjavik. There was only one good shot of her on the film, and Jerry had been sort of shaking, and her high-lighter was kind of streaked, but that was all right. She was the heroine.

THE
SHOBIES' STORY

THEY MET AT VE PORT MORE THAN A MONTH BEFORE THEIR FIRST flight together, and there, calling themselves after their ship as most crews did, became the Shobies. Their first consensual decision was to spend their isyeye in the coastal village of Liden, on Hain, where the negative ions could do their thing.

Liden was a fishing port with an eighty-thousand-year history and a population of four hundred. Its fisherfolk farmed the rich shoal waters of their bay, shipped the catch inland to the cities, and managed the Liden Resort for vacationers and tourists and new space crews on isyeye (the word is Hainish and means "making a beginning together," or "beginning to be together," or, used technically, "the period of time and area of space in which a group forms if it is going to form." A honeymoon is an isyeye of two). The fisher-women and fishermen of Liden were as weathered as driftwood and about as talkative. Six-year-old Asten, who had misunderstood slightly, asked one of them if they were all eighty thousand years old. "Nope," she said.

Like most crews, the Shobies used Hainish as their common language. So the name of the one Hainish crew member, Sweet Today, carried its meaning as words as well as name, and at first seemed a silly thing to call a big, tall, heavy woman in her late fifties, imposing of carriage and almost as taciturn as the villagers. But her reserve proved to be a deep well of congeniality and tact, to be called upon as needed, and her name soon began to sound quite right. She had family—all Hainish have family—kinfolk of all denominations, grandchildren and cross-cousins, affines and cosines, scattered all over the Ekumen, but no relatives in this crew. She asked to be Grandmother to Rig, Asten, and Betton, and was accepted.

The only Shoby older than Sweet Today was the Terran Lidi, who was seventy-two EYs and not interested in grandmothering. Lidi had been navigating for fifty years, and there was nothing she didn't know about NAFAL ships, although occasionally she forgot that their ship was the *Shoby* and called it the *Soso* or the *Alterra.* And there were things she didn't know, none of them knew, about the *Shoby.*

They talked, as human beings do, about what they didn't know.

Churten theory was the main topic of conversation, evenings at the driftwood fire on the beach after dinner. The adults had read whatever there was to read about it, of course, before they ever volunteered for the test mission. Gveter had more recent information and presumably a better understanding of it than the others, but it had to be pried out of him. Only twenty-five, the only Cetian in the crew, much hairier than the others, and not gifted in language, he spent a lot of time on the defensive. Assuming that as an Anarresti he was more proficient at mutual aid and more adept at cooperation than the others, he lectured them about their propertarian habits; but he held tight to his knowledge, because he needed the advantage it gave him. For a while he would speak only in negatives: don't call it the churten "drive," it isn't a drive, don't call it the churten "effect," it isn't an effect. What is it, then? A long lecture ensued, beginning with the rebirth of Cetian physics since the revision of Shevekian temporalism by the Intervalists, and ending with the general conceptual framework of the churten. Everyone listened very carefully, and finally Sweet Today spoke, carefully. "So the ship will be moved," she said, "by ideas?"

"No, no, no, no," said Gveter. But he hesitated for the next word so long that Karth asked a question: "Well, you haven't actually talked about any physical, material events or effects at all." The question was characteristically indirect. Karth and Oreth, the Gethenians who with their two children were the affective focus of the crew, the "hearth" of it, in their terms, came from a not very theoretically minded subculture, and knew it. Gveter could run rings round them with his Cetian physico-philosophico-techno-natter. He did so at once. His accent did not make his explanations any clearer. He went on about coherence and meta-intervals, and at last demanded, with gestures of despair, "Khow can I say it in Khainish? No! It is not physical, it is not not physical, these are the categories our minds must discard entirely, this is the khole point!"

"Buth-buth-buth-buth-buth-buth," went Asten, softly, passing behind the half circle of adults at the driftwood fire on the wide, twilit beach. Rig followed, also going, "Buth-buth-buth-buth," but louder. They were being spaceships, to judge from their maneuvers around a dune and their communications—"Locked in orbit, Navigator!"—But the noise they were imitating was the noise of the little fishing boats of Liden putt-putting out to sea.

"I crashed!" Rig shouted, flailing in the sand. "Help! Help! I crashed!"

"Hold on, Ship Two!" Asten cried. "I'll rescue you! Don't breathe! Oh, oh, trouble with the Churten Drive! Buth-buth-ack! Ack! Brrrrmmm-ack-ack-ack-rrrrrmm-mmm, buth-buth-buth-buth. . . ."

They were six and four EYs old. Tai's son Betton, who was eleven, sat at the driftwood fire with the adults, though at the moment he was watching Rig and Asten as if he wouldn't mind taking off to help rescue Ship Two. The little Gethenians had spent more time on ships than on planet, and Asten liked to boast about being "actually fifty-eight," but this was Betton's first crew, and his only NAFAL flight had been from

Terra to Hain. He and his biomother, Tai, had lived in a reclamation commune on Terra. When she had drawn the lot for Ekumenical service, and requested training for ship duty, he had asked her to bring him as family. She had agreed; but after training, when she volunteered for this test flight, she had tried to get Betton to withdraw, to stay in training or go home. He had refused. Shan, who had trained with them, told the others this, because the tension between the mother and son had to be understood to be used effectively in group formation. Betton had requested to come, and Tai had given in, but plainly not with an undivided will. Her relationship to the boy was cool and mannered. Shan offered him fatherly-brotherly warmth, but Betton accepted it sparingly, coolly, and sought no formal crew relation with him or anyone.

Ship Two was being rescued, and attention returned to the discussion. "All right," said Lidi. "We know that anything that goes faster than light, any *thing* that goes faster than light, by so doing transcends the material/immaterial category—that's how we got the ansible, by distinguishing the message from the medium. But if we, the crew, are going to travel as messages, I want to understand *how*."

Gveter tore his hair. There was plenty to tear. It grew fine and thick, a mane on his head, a pelt on his limbs and body, a silvery nimbus on his hands and face. The fuzz on his feet was, at the moment, full of sand. "Khow!" he cried. "I'm trying to tell you khow! Message, information, no no no, that's old, that's ansible technology. This is transilience! Because the field is to be conceived as the virtual field, in which the unreal interval becomes virtually effective through the mediary coherence—don't you see?"

"No," Lidi said. "What do you mean by mediary?"

After several more bonfires on the beach, the consensus opinion was that churten theory was accessible only to minds very highly trained in Cetian temporal physics. There was a less freely voiced conviction that the engineers who had built the *Shoby's* churten apparatus did not entirely understand how it worked. Or, more precisely, what it did when it worked. That it worked was certain. The *Shoby* was the fourth ship it had been tested with, using robot crew; so far sixty-two instantaneous trips, or transiliences, had been effected between points from four hundred kilometers to twenty-seven light-years apart, with stopovers of varying lengths. Gveter and Lidi steadfastly maintained that this proved that the engineers knew perfectly well what they were doing, and that for the rest of them the seeming difficulty of the theory was only the difficulty human minds had in grasping a genuinely new concept.

"Like the circulation of the blood," said Tai. "People went around with their hearts beating for a long time before they understood why." She did not look satisfied with her own analogy, and when Shan said, "The heart has its reasons, which reason does not know," she looked offended. "Mysticism," she said, in the tone of voice of one warning a companion about dog-shit on the path.

"Surely there's nothing *beyond* understanding in this process," Oreth said, somewhat tentatively. "Nothing that can't be understood, and reproduced."

"And quantified," Gveter said stoutly.

"But, even if people understand the process, nobody knows the human response to it—the *experience* of it. Right? So we are to report on that."

"Why shouldn't it be just like NAFAL flight, only even faster?" Betton asked.

"Because it is totally different," said Gveter.

"What could happen to us?"

Some of the adults had discussed possibilities, all of them had considered them; Karth and Oreth had talked it over in appropriate terms with their children; but evidently Betton had not been included in such discussions.

"We don't know," Tai said sharply. "I told you that at the start, Betton."

"Most likely it will be like NAFAL flight," said Shan, "but the first people who flew NAFAL didn't know what it would be like, and had to find out the physical and psychic effects—"

"The worst thing," said Sweet Today in her slow, comfortable voice, "would be that we would die. Other living beings have been on some of the test flights. Crickets. And intelligent ritual animals on the last two *Shoby* tests. They were all right." It was a very long statement for Sweet Today, and carried proportional weight.

"We are almost certain," said Gveter, "that no temporal rearrangement is involved in churten, as it is in NAFAL. And mass is involved only in terms of needing a certain core mass, just as for ansible transmission, but not in itself. So maybe even a pregnant person could be a transilient."

"They can't go on ships," Asten said. "The unborn dies if they do."

Asten was half lying across Oreth's lap; Rig, thumb in mouth, was asleep on Karth's lap.

"When we were Oneblins," Asten went on, sitting up, "there were ritual animals with our crew. Some fish and some Terran cats and a whole lot of Hainish gholes. We got to play with them. And we helped thank the ghole that they tested for lithovirus. But it didn't die. It bit Shapi. The cats slept with us. But one of them went into kemmer and got pregnant, and then the *Oneblin* had to go to Hain, and she had to have an abortion, or all her unborns would have died inside her and killed her too. Nobody knew a ritual for her, to explain to her. But I fed her some extra food. And Rig cried."

"Other people I know cried too," Karth said, stroking the child's hair.

"You tell good stories, Asten," Sweet Today observed. "So we're sort of ritual humans," said Betton.

"Volunteers," Tai said.

"Experimenters," said Lidi.

"Experiencers," said Shan.

"Explorers," Oreth said.

"Gamblers," said Karth.

The boy looked from one face to the next.

"You know," Shan said, "back in the time of the League, early in NAFAL flight, they were sending out ships to really distant systems—trying to explore everything—crews that wouldn't come back for centuries. Maybe some of them are still out there. But some of them came back after four, five, six hundred years, and they were all mad. Crazy!" He paused dramatically. "But they were all crazy when they started. Unstable people. They had to be crazy to volunteer for a time dilation like that. What a way to pick a crew, eh?" He laughed.

"Are we stable?" said Oreth. "I like instability. I like this job. I like the risk, taking the risk together. High stakes! That's the edge of it, the sweetness of it."

Karth looked down at their children, and smiled.

"Yes. Together," Gveter said. "You aren't crazy. You are good. I love you. We are ammari."

"Ammar," the others said to him, confirming this unexpected declaration. The young man scowled with pleasure, jumped up, and pulled off his shirt. "I want to swim. Come on, Betton. Come on swimming!" he said, and ran off towards the dark, vast waters that moved softly beyond the ruddy haze of their fire. The boy hesitated, then shed his shirt and sandals and followed. Shan pulled up Tai, and they followed; and finally the two old women went off into the night and the breakers, rolling up their pants legs, laughing at themselves.

To Gethenians, even on a warm summer night on a warm summer world, the sea is no friend. The fire is where you stay. Oreth and Asten moved closer to Karth and watched the flames, listening to the faint voices out in the glimmering surf, now and then talking quietly in their own tongue, while the little sisterbrother slept on.

AFTER THIRTY LAZY DAYS AT LIDEN THE SHOBIES CAUGHT THE fish train inland to the city, where a Fleet lander picked them up at the train station and took them to the spaceport on Ve, the next planet out from Hain. They were rested, tanned, bonded, and ready to go.

One of Sweet Today's hemi-affiliate cousins once removed was on ansible duty in Ve Port. She urged the Shobies to ask the inventors of the churten on Urras and Anarres any questions they had about churten operation. "The purpose of the experimental flight is understanding," she insisted, "and your full intellectual participation is essential. They've been very anxious about that."

Lidi snorted.

"Now for the ritual," said Shan, as they went to the ansible room in the sunward bubble. "They'll explain to the animals what they're going to do and why, and ask them to help."

"The animals don't understand that," Betton said in his cold, angelic treble. "It's just to make the humans feel better."

"The humans understand?" Sweet Today asked.

"We all use each other," Oreth said. "The ritual says: we have no right to do so; therefore, we accept the responsibility for the suffering we cause."

Betton listened and brooded.

Gveter addressed the ansible first and talked to it for half an hour, mostly in Pravic and mathematics. Finally, apologizing, and looking a little unnerved, he invited the others to use the instrument. There was a pause. Lidi activated it, introduced herself, and said, "We have agreed that none of us, except Gveter, has the theoretical background to grasp the principles of the churten."

A scientist twenty-two light-years away responded in Hainish via the rather flat auto-translator voice, but with unmistakable hopefulness, "The churten, in lay terms, may be seen as displacing the virtual field in order to realize relational coherence in terms of the transiliential experientiality."

"Quite," said Lidi.

"As you know, the material effects have been nil, and negative effect on low-intelligence sentients also nil; but there is considered to be a possibility that the participation of high intelligence in the process might affect the displacement in one way or another. And that such displacement would reciprocally affect the participant."

"What has the level of our intelligence got to do with how the churten functions?" Tai asked.

A pause. Their interlocutor was trying to find the words, to accept the responsibility.

"We have been using 'intelligence' as shorthand for the psychic complexity and cultural dependence of our species," said the translator voice at last. "The presence of the transilient as conscious mind nonduring transilience is the untested factor."

"But if the process is instantaneous, how can we be conscious of it?" Oreth asked.

"Precisely," said the ansible, and after another pause continued: "As the experimenter is an element of the experiment, so we assume that the transilient may be an element or agent of transilience. This is why we asked for a crew to test the process, rather than one or two volunteers. The psychic interbalance of a bonded social group is a margin of strength against disintegrative or incomprehensible experience, if any such occurs. Also, the separate observations of the group members will mutually interverify."

"Who programs this translator?" Shan snarled in a whisper. "Interverify! Shit!"

Lidi looked around at the others, inviting questions.

"How long will the trip actually take?" Betton asked.

"No long," the translator voice said, then self-corrected: "No time."

Another pause.

"Thank you," said Sweet Today, and the scientist on a planet twenty-two years of time-dilated travel from Ve Port answered, "We are grateful for your generous courage, and our hope is with you."

They went directly from the ansible room to the *Shoby*.

THE CHURTEN EQUIPMENT, WHICH WAS NOT VERY SPACE-CONSUMING and the controls of which consisted essentially of an on-off switch, had been installed alongside the Nearly As Fast As Light motivators and controls of an ordinary interstellar ship of the Ekumenical Fleet. The *Shoby* had been built on Hain about four hundred years ago, and was thirty-two years old. Most of its early runs had been exploratory, with a Hainish-Chiffewarian crew. Since in such runs a ship might spend years in orbit in a planetary system, the Hainish and Chiffewarians, feeling that it might as well be lived in rather than endured, had arranged and furnished it like a very large, very comfortable house. Three of its residential modules had been disconnected and left in the hangars on Ve, and still there was more than enough room for a crew of only ten. Tai, Betton, and Shan, new from Terra, and Gveter from Anarres, accustomed to the barracks and the communal austerities of their marginally habitable worlds, stalked about the *Shoby*, disapproving it. "Excremental," Gveter growled. "Luxury!" Tai sneered. Sweet Today, Lidi, and the Gethenians, more used to the amenities of shipboard life, settled right in and made themselves at home. And Gveter and the younger Terrans found it hard to maintain ethical discomfort in the spacious, high-ceilinged, well-furnished, slightly shabby living rooms and bedrooms, studies, high- and low-G gyms, the dining room, library, kitchen, and bridge of the *Shoby*. The carpet in the bridge was a genuine Henyekaulil, soft deep blues and purples woven in the patterns of the constellations of the Hainish sky. There was a large, healthy plantation of Terran bamboo in the meditation gym, part of the ship's self-contained vegetal/respiratory system. The windows of any room could be programmed by the homesick to a view of Abbenay or New Cairo or the beach at Liden, or cleared to look out on the suns nearer and farther and the darkness between the suns.

Rig and Asten discovered that as well as the elevators there was a stately staircase with a curving banister, leading from the reception hall up to the library. They slid down the banister shrieking wildly, until Shan threatened to apply a local gravity field and force them to slide up it, which they besought him to do. Betton watched the little ones with a superior gaze, and took the elevator; but the next day he slid down the banister, going a good deal faster than Rig and Asten because he could push off harder and had greater mass, and nearly broke his tailbone. It was Betton who organized the tray-sliding races, but Rig generally won them, being small enough to stay on the tray all the way down the stairs. None of the children had had any lessons at the beach, except in swimming and being Shobies; but while they waited through an unexpected five-day delay at Ve Port, Gveter did physics with Betton and math with all three daily in the library, and they did some history with Shan and Oreth, and danced with Tai in the low-G gym.

When she danced, Tai became light, free, laughing. Rig and Asten loved her then, and her son danced with her like a colt, like a kid, awkward and blissful. Shan often joined them; he was a dark and elegant dancer, and she would dance with him, but even then was shy, would not touch. She had been celibate since Betton's birth. She did not want Shan's patient, urgent desire, did not want to cope with it, with him. She would turn from him to Betton, and son and mother would dance wholly absorbed in the steps, the airy pattern they made together. Watching them, the afternoon before the test flight, Sweet Today began to wipe tears from her eyes, smiling, never saying a word.

"Life is good," said Gveter very seriously to Lidi.

"It'll do," she said.

Oreth, who was just coming out of female kemmer, having thus triggered Karth's male kemmer, all of which, by coming on unexpectedly early, had delayed the test flight for these past five days, enjoyable days for all—Oreth watched Rig, whom she had fathered, dance with

Asten, whom she had borne, and watched Karth watch them, and said in Karhidish, "Tomorrow . . ." The edge was very sweet.

ANTHROPOLOGISTS SOLEMNLY AGREE THAT WE MUST NOT ATTRI-bute "cultural constants" to the human population of any planet; but certain cultural traits or expectations do seem to run deep. Before dinner that last night in port, Shan and Tai appeared in black-and-silver uni-forms of the Terran Ekumen, which had cost them—Terra also still had a money economy—a half-year's allowance.

Asten and Rig clamored at once for equal grandeur. Karth and Oreth suggested their party clothes, and Sweet Today brought out silver lace scarves, but Asten sulked, and Rig imitated. The idea of a *uniform,* Asten told them, was that it was the *same.*

"Why?" Oreth inquired.

Old Lidi answered sharply: "So that no one is responsible."

She then went off and changed into a black velvet evening suit that wasn't a uniform but that didn't leave Tai and Shan sticking out like sore thumbs. She had left Terra at age eighteen and never been back nor wanted to, but Tai and Shan were shipmates.

Karth and Oreth got the idea and put on their finest fur-trimmed hiebs, and the children were appeased with their own party clothes plus all of Karth's hereditary and massive gold jewelry. Sweet Today appeared in a pure white robe which she claimed was in fact ultra-violet. Gveter braided his mane. Betton had no uniform, but needed none, sitting beside his mother at table in a visible glory of pride.

Meals, sent up from the Port kitchens, were very good, and this one was superb: a delicate Hainish iyanwi with all seven sauces, followed by a pudding flavored with Terran chocolate. A lively evening ended quietly at the big fireplace in the library. The logs were fake, of course, but good fakes; no use having a fireplace on a ship and then burning plastic in it. The neocellulose logs and kindling smelled right, resisted catching, caught with spits and sparks and smoke billows, flared up bright. Oreth had laid the fire, Karth lit it. Everybody gathered round.

"Tell bedtime stories," Rig said.

Oreth told about the Ice Caves of Kerm Land, how a ship sailed into the great blue sea-cave and disappeared and was never found by the boats that entered the caves in search; but seventy years later that ship was found drifting—not a living soul aboard nor any sign of what had become of them—off the coast of Osemyet, a thousand miles overland from Kerm. . . .

Another story?

Lidi told about the little desert wolf who lost his wife and went to the land of the dead for her, and found her there dancing with the dead, and nearly brought her back to the land of the living, but spoiled it by trying to touch her before they got all the way back to life, and she vanished, and he could never find the way back to the place where the dead danced, no matter how he looked, and howled, and cried. . . .

Another story!

Shan told about the boy who sprouted a feather every time he told a lie, until his commune had to use him for a duster.

Another!

Gveter told about the winged people called gluns, who were so stupid that they died out because they kept hitting each other head-on in midair. "They weren't real," he added conscientiously. "Only a story."

Another—No. Bedtime now.

Rig and Asten went round as usual for a good-night hug, and this time Betton followed them. When he came to Tai he did not stop, for she did not like to be touched; but she put out her hand, drew the child to her, and kissed his cheek. He fled in joy.

"Stories," said Sweet Today. "Ours begins tomorrow, eh?"

A CHAIN OF COMMAND IS EASY TO DESCRIBE; A NETWORK OF response isn't. To those who live by mutual empowerment, "thick" description, complex and open-ended, is normal and comprehensible, but to those whose only model is hierarchic control, such description seems a muddle, a mess, along with what it describes. Who's in charge here? Get rid of all these petty details. How many cooks spoil a soup? Let's get this perfectly clear now. Take me to your leader!

The old navigator was at the NAFAL console, of course, and Gveter at the paltry churten console; Oreth was wired into the AI; Tai, Shan, and Karth were their respective Support, and what Sweet Today did might be called supervising or overseeing if that didn't suggest a hierarchic function. Interseeing, maybe, or subvising. Rig and Asten always naffled (to use Rig's word) in the ship's library, where, during the boring and disorienting experience of travel at near lightspeed, Asten could try to look at pictures or listen to a music tape, and Rig could curl up on and under a certain furry blanket and go to sleep. Betton's crew function during flight was Elder Sib; he stayed with the little ones, provided himself with a barf bag since he was one of those whom NAFAL flight made queasy, and focused the intervid on Lidi and Gveter so he could watch what they did.

So they all knew what they were doing, as regards NAFAL flight. As regards the churten process, they knew that it was supposed to effectuate their transilience to a solar system seventeen light-years from Ve Port without temporal interval; but nobody, anywhere, knew what they were doing.

So Lidi looked around, like the violinist who raises her bow to poise the chamber group for the first chord, a flicker of eye contact, and sent the *Shoby* into NAFAL mode, as Gveter, like the cellist whose bow comes down in that same instant to ground the chord, sent the *Shoby* into churten mode. They entered unduration. They churtened. No long, as the ansible had said.

"What's wrong?" Shan whispered.

"By damn!" said Gveter.

"What?" said Lidi, blinking and shaking her head.

"That's it," Tai said, flicking readouts.

"That's not A-sixty-whatsit," Lidi said, still blinking.

Sweet Today was gestalting them, all ten at once, the seven on the bridge and by intervid the three in the library. Betton had cleared a window, and the children were looking out at the murky, brownish convexity that filled half of it. Rig was holding a dirty, furry blanket. Karth was taking the electrodes off Oreth's temples, disengaging the AI link. "There was no interval," Oreth said.

"We aren't anywhere," Lidi said.

"There was no interval," Gveter repeated, scowling at the console. "That's right."

"Nothing happened," Karth said, skimming through the AI flight report.

Oreth got up, went to the window, and stood motionless looking out.

"That's it. M-60-340-nolo," Tai said.

All their words fell dead, had a false sound.

"Well! We did it, Shobies!" said Shan.

Nobody answered.

"Buzz Ve Port on the ansible," Shan said with determined jollity. "Tell 'em we're all here in one piece."

"All where?" Oreth asked.

"Yes, of course," Sweet Today said, but did nothing.

"Right," said Tai, going to the ship's ansible. She opened the field, centered to Ve, and sent a signal. Ships' ansibles worked only in the visual mode; she waited, watching the screen. She resignaled. They were all watching the screen.

"Nothing going through," she said.

Nobody told her to check the centering coordinates; in a network system nobody gets to dump their anxieties that easily. She checked the coordinates. She signaled; rechecked, reset, resignaled; opened the field and centered to Abbenay on Anarres and signaled. The ansible screen was blank.

"Check the—" Shan said, and stopped himself.

"The ansible is not functioning," Tai reported formally to her crew.

"Do you find malfunction?" Sweet Today asked.

"No. Nonfunction."

"We're going back now," said Lidi, still seated at the NAFAL console.

Her words, her tone, shook them, shook them apart.

"No, we're not!" Betton said on the intervid while Oreth said, "Back where?"

Tai, Lidi's Support, moved towards her as if to prevent her from activating the NAFAL drive, but then hastily moved back to the ansible to prevent Gveter from getting access to it. He stopped, taken aback, and said, "Perhaps the churten affected ansible function?"

"*I'm* checking it out," Tai said. "Why should it? Robot-operated ansible transmission functioned in all the test flights."

"Where are the AI reports?" Shan demanded.

"I told you, there are none," Karth answered sharply.

"Oreth was plugged in."

Oreth, still at the window, spoke without turning. "Nothing happened."

Sweet Today came over beside the Gethenian. Oreth looked at her and said, slowly, "Yes. Sweet Today. We cannot . . . do this. I think. I can't think."

Shan had cleared a second window, and stood looking out it. "Ugly," he said.

"What is?" said Lidi.

Gveter said, as if reading from the Ekumenical Atlas, "Thick, stable atmosphere, near the bottom of the temperature window for life. Micro-organisms. Bacterial clouds, bacterial reefs."

"Germ stew," Shan said. "Lovely place to send us."

"So that if we arrived as a neutron bomb or a black hole event we'd only take bacteria with us," Tai said. "But we didn't."

"Didn't what?" said Lidi.

"Didn't arrive?" Karth asked.

"Hey," Betton said, "is everybody going to stay on the bridge?"

"I want to come there," said Rig's little pipe, and then Asten's voice, clear but shaky, "Maba, I'd like to go back to Liden now."

"Come on," Karth said, and went to meet the children. Oreth did not turn from the window, even when Asten came close and took Oreth's hand.

"What are you looking at, Maba?"

"The planet, Asten."

"What planet?"

Oreth looked at the child then.

"There isn't anything," Asten said.

"That brown color—that's the surface, the atmosphere of a planet."

"There isn't any brown color. There isn't *anything*. I want to go back to Liden. You said we could when we were done with the test."

Oreth looked around, at last, at the others.

"Perception variation," Gveter said.

"I think," Tai said, "that we must establish that we are—that we got here—and then get here."

"You mean, go back," Betton said.

"The readings are perfectly clear," Lidi said, holding on to the rim of her seat with both hands and speaking very distinctly. "Every coordinate in order. That's M-60-Etcetera down there. What more do you want? Bacteria samples?"

"Yes," Tai said. "Instrument function's been affected, so we can't rely on instrumental records."

"Oh, shitsake!" said Lidi. "What a farce! All right. Suit up, go down, get some goo, and then let's get out. Go home. By NAFAL."

"By NAFAL?" Shan and Tai echoed, and Gveter said, "But we would spend seventeen years, Ve time, and no ansible to explain why."

"Why, Lidi?" Sweet Today asked.

Lidi stared at the Hainishwoman. "You want to churten again?" she demanded, raucous. She looked round at them all. "Are you people made of stone?" Her face was ashy, crumpled, shrunken. "It doesn't bother you, seeing through the walls?"

No one spoke, until Shan said cautiously, "How do you mean?"

"I can see the stars through the walls!" She stared round at them again, pointing at the carpet with its woven constellations. "You can't?" When no one answered, her jaw trembled in a little spasm, and she said, "All right. All right. I'm off duty. Sorry. Be in my room." She stood up. "Maybe you should lock me in," she said.

"Nonsense," said Sweet Today.

"If I fall through . . ." Lidi began, and did not finish. She walked to the door, stiffly and cautiously, as if through a thick fog. She said something they did not understand, "Cause," or perhaps, "Gauze."

Sweet Today followed her.

"I can see the stars too!" Rig announced.

"Hush," Karth said, putting an arm around the child.

"I can! I can see all the stars everywhere. And I can see Ve Port. And I can see anything I want!"

"Yes, of course, but hush now," the mother murmured, at which the child pulled free, stamped, and shrilled, "I can! I can too! I can see *everything*! And Asten can't! And there *is* a planet, there is too! No, don't hold me! Don't! Let me go!"

Grim, Karth carried the screaming child off to their quarters. Asten turned around to yell after Rig, "There is *not* any planet! You're just making it up!"

Grim, Oreth said, "Go to our room, please, Asten."

Asten burst into tears and obeyed. Oreth, with a glance of apology to the others, followed the short, weeping figure across the bridge and out into the corridor.

The four remaining on the bridge stood silent.

"Canaries," Shan said.

"Khallucinations?" Gveter proposed, subdued. "An effect of the churten on extrasensitive organisms—maybe?"

Tai nodded.

"Then is the ansible not functioning, or are we hallucinating non-function?" Shan asked after a pause.

Gveter went to the ansible; this time Tai walked away from it, leaving it to him. "I want to go down," she said.

"No reason not to, I suppose," Shan said unenthusiastically.

"Khwat reason to?" Gveter asked over his shoulder.

"It's what we're here for, isn't it? It's what we volunteered to do, isn't it? To test instantaneous—transilience—prove that it worked, that we are here! With the ansible out, it'll be seventeen years before Ve gets our radio signal!"

"We can just churten back to Ve and *tell* them," Shan said. "If we did that now, we'd have been . . . here . . . about eight minutes."

"Tell them—tell them what? What kind of evidence is that?"

"Anecdotal," said Sweet Today, who had come back quietly to the bridge; she moved like a big sailing ship, imposingly silent.

"Is Lidi all right?" Shan asked.

"No," Sweet Today answered. She sat down where Lidi had sat, at the NAFAL console.

"I ask a consensus about going down onplanet," Tai said.

"I'll ask the others," Gveter said, and went out, returning presently with Karth. "Go down, if you want," the Gethenian said. "Oreth's staying with the children for a bit. They are—We are extremely disoriented."

"I will come down," Gveter said.

"Can I come?" Betton asked, almost in a whisper, not raising his eyes to any adult face.

"No," Tai said, as Gveter said, "Yes."

Betton looked at his mother, one quick glance.

"Khwy not?" Gveter asked her.

"We don't know the risks."

"The planet was surveyed."

"By robot ships—"

"We'll wear suits." Gveter was honestly puzzled.

"I don't want the responsibility," Tai said through her teeth.

"Khwy is it yours?" Gveter asked, more puzzled still. "We all share it; Betton is crew. I don't understand."

"I know you don't understand," Tai said, turned her back on them both, and went out. The man and the boy stood staring, Gveter after Tai, Betton at the carpet.

"I'm sorry," Betton said.

"Not to be," Gveter told him.

"What is . . . what is going on?" Shan asked in an overcontrolled voice. "Why are we—We keep crossing, we keep—coming and going—"

"Confusion due to the churten experience," Gveter said.

Sweet Today turned from the console. "I have sent a distress signal," she said. "I am unable to operate the NAFAL system. The radio—" She cleared her throat. "Radio function seems erratic."

There was a pause.

"This is not happening," Shan said, or Oreth said, but Oreth had stayed with the children in another part of the ship, so it could not have been Oreth who said, "This is not happening," it must have been Shan.

A CHAIN OF CAUSE AND EFFECT IS AN EASY THING TO DESCRIBE; a cessation of cause and effect is not. To those who live in time, sequency is the norm, the only model, and simultaneity seems a muddle, a mess, a hopeless confusion, and the description of that confusion hopelessly confusing. As the members of the crew network no longer perceived the network steadily and were unable to communicate their perceptions, an individual perception is the only clue to follow through the labyrinth of their dislocation. Gveter perceived himself as being on the bridge with Shan, Sweet Today, Betton, Karth, and Tai. He perceived himself as methodically checking out the ship's systems. The NAFAL he found dead, the radio functioning in erratic bursts, the internal electrical and mechanical systems of the ship all in order. He sent out a lander unmanned and brought it back, and perceived it as functioning normally. He perceived himself discussing with Tai her determination to go down onplanet. Since he admitted his unwillingness to trust any instrumental reading on the ship, he had to admit her point that only material evidence would show that they had actually arrived at their destination, M-60-340-nolo. If they were going to have to spend the next seventeen years traveling back to Ve in real time, it would be nice to have something to show for it, even if only a handful of slime.

He perceived this discussion as perfectly rational.

It was, however, interrupted by outbursts of egoizing not characteristic of the crew.

"If you're going, go!" Shan said.

"Don't give me orders," Tai said.

"Somebody's got to stay in control here," Shan said.

"Not the men!" Tai said.

"Not the Terrans," Karth said. "Have you people no self-respect?"

"Stress," Gveter said. "Come on, Tai, Betton, all right, let's go, all right?"

In the lander, everything was clear to Gveter. One thing happened after another just as it should. Lander operation is very simple, and he asked Betton to take them down. The boy did so. Tai sat, tense and compact as always, her strong fists clenched on her knees. Betton managed the little ship with aplomb, and sat back, tense also, but dignified: "We're down," he said.

"No, we're not," Tai said.

"It—it says contact," Betton said, losing his assurance.

"An excellent landing," Gveter said. "Never even felt it." He was running the usual tests. Everything was in order. Outside the lander ports pressed a brownish darkness, a gloom. When Betton put on the outside lights the atmosphere, like a dark fog, diffused the light into a useless glare.

"Tests all tally with survey reports," Gveter said. "Will you go out, Tai, or use the servos?"

"Out," she said.

"Out," Betton echoed.

Gveter, assuming the formal crew role of Support, which one of them would have assumed if he had been going out, assisted them to lock their helmets and decontaminate their suits; he opened the hatch series for them, and watched them on the vid and from the port as they climbed down from the outer hatch. Betton went first. His slight figure, elongated by the whitish suit, was luminous in the weak glare of the lights. He walked a few steps from the ship, turned, and waited. Tai was stepping off the ladder. She seemed to grow very short—did she kneel down? Gveter looked from the port to the vid screen and back. She was shrinking? sinking—she must be sinking into the surface—which could not be solid, then, but bog, or some suspension like quicksand—but Betton had walked on it and was walking back to her, two steps, three steps, on the ground which Gveter could not see clearly but which must be solid, and which must be holding Betton up because he was lighter—but no, Tai must have stepped into a hole, a trench of some kind, for he could see her only from the waist up now, her legs hidden in the dark bog or fog, but she was moving, moving quickly, going right away from the lander and from Betton.

"Bring them back," Shan said, and Gveter said on the suit intercom, "Please return to the lander, Betton and Tai." Betton at once started up the ladder, then turned to look for his mother. A dim blotch that might be her helmet showed in the brown gloom, almost beyond the suffusion of light from the lander.

"Please come in, Betton. Please return, Tai."

The whitish suit flickered up the ladder, while Betton's voice in the intercom pleaded, "Tai—Tai, come back—Gveter, should I go after her?"

"No. Tai, please return at once to lander."

The boy's crew-integrity held; he came up into the lander and watched from the outer hatch, as Gveter watched from the port. The vid had lost her. The pallid blotch sank into the formless murk.

Gveter perceived that the instruments recorded that the lander had sunk 3.2 meters since contact with planet surface and was continuing to sink at an increasing rate.

"What is the surface, Betton?"

"Like muddy ground—Where is she?"

"Please return at once, Tai!"

"Please return to *Shoby*, Lander One and all crew," said the ship intercom; it was Tai's voice. "This is Tai," it said. "Please return at once to ship, lander and all crew."

"Stay in suit, in decon, please, Betton," Gveter said. "I'm sealing the hatch."

"But—All right," said the boy's voice.

Gveter took the lander up, decontaminating it and Betton's suit on the way. He perceived that Betton and Shan came with him through the hatch series into the *Shoby* and along the halls to the bridge, and that Karth, Sweet Today, Shan, and Tai were on the bridge.

Betton ran to his mother and stopped; he did not put out his hands to her. His face was immobile, as if made of wax or wood.

"Were you frightened?" she asked. "What happened down there?" And she looked to Gveter for an explanation.

Gveter perceived nothing. Unduring a nonperiod of no long, he perceived nothing was had happening happened that had not happened. Lost, he groped, lost, he found the word, the word that saved—"You—" he said, his tongue thick, dumb—"You called us."

It seemed that she denied, but it did not matter. What mattered? Shan was talking. Shan could tell. "Nobody called, Gveter," he said.

"You and Betton went out, I was Support; when I realized I couldn't get the lander stable, that there's something funny about that surface, I called you back into the lander, and we came up."

All Gveter could say was, "Insubstantial . . ."

"But Tai came—" Betton began, and stopped. Gveter perceived that the boy moved away from his mother's denying touch. What mattered?

"Nobody went down," Sweet Today said. After a silence and before it, she said, "There is no down to go to."

Gveter tried to find another word, but there was none. He perceived outside the main port a brownish, murky convexity, through which, as he looked intently, he saw small stars shining.

He found a word then, the wrong word. "Lost," he said, and speaking perceived how the ship's lights dimmed slowly into a brownish murk, faded, darkened, were gone, while all the soft hum and busyness of the ship's systems died away into the real silence that was always there. But there was nothing there. Nothing had happened. We are at Ve Port! he tried with all his will to say; but there was no saying.

The suns burn through my flesh, Lidi said.

I am the suns, said Sweet Today. Not I, all is.

Don't breathe! cried Oreth.

It is death, Shan said. What I feared, is: nothing.

Nothing, they said.

Unbreathing, the ghosts flitted, shifted, in the ghost shell of a cold, dark hull floating near a world of brown fog, an unreal planet. They spoke, but there were no voices. There is no sound in vacuum, nor in nontime.

In her cabined solitude, Lidi felt the gravity lighten to the half-G of the ship's core-mass; she saw them, the nearer and the farther suns, burn through the dark gauze of the walls and hulls and the bedding and her body. The brightest, the sun of this system, floated directly under her navel. She did not know its name.

I am the darkness between the suns, one said.

I am nothing, one said.

I am you, one said.

You—one said—You—

And breathed, and reached out, and spoke: "Listen!" Crying out to the other, to the others, "Listen!"

"We have always known this. This is where we have always been, will always be, at the hearth, at the center. There is nothing to be afraid of, after all."

"I can't breathe," one said.

"I am not breathing," one said.

"There is nothing to breathe," one said.

"You are, you are breathing, please breathe!" said another.

"We're here, at the hearth," said another.

Oreth had laid the fire, Karth lit it. As it caught they both said softly, in Karhidish, "Praise also the light, and creation unfinished."

The fire caught with spark-spits, crackles, sudden flares. It did not go out. It burned. The others grouped round.

They were nowhere, but they were nowhere together; the ship was dead, but they were in the ship. A dead ship cools off fairly quickly, but not immediately. Close the doors, come in by the fire; keep the cold night out, before we go to bed.

Karth went with Rig to persuade Lidi from her starry vault. The navigator would not get up. "It's my fault," she said.

"Don't egoize," Karth said mildly. "How could it be?"

"I don't know. I want to stay here," Lidi muttered. Then Karth begged her: "Oh, Lidi, not alone!"

"How else?" the old woman asked, coldly.

But she was ashamed of herself, then, and ashamed of her guilt trip, and growled, "Oh, all right." She heaved herself up and wrapped a blanket around her body and followed Karth and Rig. The child carried a little biolume; it glowed in the black corridors, just as the plants of the aerobic tanks lived on, metabolizing, making an air to breathe, for a while. The light moved before her like a star among the stars through darkness to the room full of books, where the fire burned in the stone hearth. "Hello, children," Lidi said. "What are we doing here?"

"Telling stories," Sweet Today replied.

Shan had a little voice-recorder notebook in his hand.

"Does it work?" Lidi inquired.

"Seems to. We thought we'd tell . . . what happened," Shan said, squinting the narrow black eyes in his narrow black face at the firelight. "Each of us. What we—what it seemed like, seems like, to us. So that . . ."

"As a record, yes. In case . . . How funny that it works, though, your notebook. When nothing else does."

"It's voice-activated," Shan said absently. "So. Go on, Gveter."

Gveter finished telling his version of the expedition to the planet's surface. "We didn't even bring back samples," he ended. "I never thought of them."

"Shan went with you, not me," Tai said.

"You did go, and I did," the boy said with a certainty that stopped her. "And we did go outside. And Shan and Gveter were Support, in the lander. And I took samples. They're in the Stasis closet."

"I don't know if Shan was in the lander or not," Gveter said, rubbing his forehead painfully.

"Where would the lander have gone?" Shan said. "Nothing is out there—we're nowhere—outside time, is all I can think—But when one of you tells how they saw it, it seems as if it was that way, but then the next one changes the story, and I . . ."

Oreth shivered, drawing closer to the fire.

"I never believed this damn thing would work," said Lidi, bearlike in the dark cave of her blanket.

"Not understanding it was the trouble," Karth said. "None of us understood how it would work, not even Gveter. Isn't that true?"

"Yes," Gveter said.

"So that if our psychic interaction with it affected the process—"

"Or *is* the process," said Sweet Today, "so far as we're concerned."

"Do you mean," Lidi said in a tone of deep existential disgust, "that we have to *believe* in it to make it work?"

"You have to believe in yourself in order to act, don't you?" Tai said.

"No," the navigator said. "Absolutely not. I don't believe in myself. I *know* some things. Enough to go on."

"An analogy," Gveter offered. "The effective action of a crew depends on the members perceiving themselves as a crew—you could call it believing in the crew, or just *being* it—Right? So, maybe, to churten, we—we conscious ones—maybe it depends on our consciously perceiving ourselves as . . . as transilient—as being in the other place—the destination?"

"We lost our crewness, certainly, for a—Are there whiles?" Karth said. "We fell apart."

"We lost the thread," Shan said.

"Lost," Oreth said meditatively, laying another massive, half-weightless log on the fire, volleying sparks up into the chimney, slow stars.

"We lost—what?" Sweet Today asked.

No one answered for a while.

"When I can see the sun through the carpet . . ." Lidi said.

"So can I," Betton said, very low.

"I can see Ve Port," said Rig. "And everything. I can tell you what I can see. I can see Liden if I look. And my room on the *Oneblin*. And—"

"First, Rig," said Sweet Today, "tell us what happened."

"All right," Rig said agreeably. "Hold on to me harder, maba, I start floating. Well, we went to the liberry, me and Asten and Betton, and Betton was Elder Sib, and the adults were on the bridge, and I was going to go to sleep like I do when we naffle-fly, but before I even lay down there was the brown planet and Ve Port and both the suns and everywhere else, and you could see through everything, but Asten couldn't. But I can."

"We never went *anywhere*," Asten said. "Rig tells stories all the time."

"We all tell stories all the time, Asten," Karth said.

"Not dumb ones like Rig's!"

"Even dumber," said Oreth. "What we need . . . What we need is . . ."

"We need to know," Shan said, "what transilience is, and we don't, because we never did it before, nobody ever did it before."

"Not in the flesh," said Lidi.

"We need to know what's—real—what happened, *whether* anything happened—" Tai gestured at the cave of firelight around them and the dark beyond it. "Where are we? Are we here? Where is here? What's the story?"

"We have to tell it," Sweet Today said. "Recount it. Relate it. . . . Like Rig. Asten, how does a story begin?"

"A thousand winters ago, a thousand miles away," the child said; and Shan murmured, "Once upon a time . . ."

"There was a ship called the *Shoby*," said Sweet Today, "on a test flight, trying out the churten, with a crew of ten.

"Their names were Rig, Asten, Betton, Karth, Oreth, Lidi, Tai, Shan, Gveter, and Sweet Today. And they related their story, each one and together. . . ."

There was silence, the silence that was always there, except for the stir and crackle of the fire and the small sounds of their breathing, their movements, until one of them spoke at last, telling the story.

"The boy and his mother," said the light, pure voice, "were the first human beings ever to set foot on that world."

Again the silence; and again a voice.

"Although she wished . . . she realized that she really hoped the thing wouldn't work, because it would make her skills, her whole life, obsolete . . . all the same she really wanted to learn how to use it, too, if she could, if she wasn't too old to learn. . . ."

A long, softly throbbing pause, and another voice.

"They went from world to world, and each time they lost the world they left, lost it in time dilation, their friends getting old and dying while they were in NAFAL flight. If there were a way to live in one's own time, and yet move among the worlds, they wanted to try it. . . ."

"Staking everything on it," the next voice took up the story, "because nothing works except what we give our souls to, nothing's safe except what we put at risk."

A while, a little while; and a voice.

"It was like a game. It was like we were still in the *Shoby* at Ve Port just waiting before we went into NAFAL flight. But it was like we were at the brown planet too. At the same time. And one of them was just pretend, and the other one wasn't, but I didn't know which. So it was like when you pretend in a game. But I didn't want to play. I didn't know how."

Another voice.

"If the churten principle were proved to be applicable to actual transilience of living, conscious beings, it would be a great event in the mind of his people—for all people. A new understanding. A new partnership. A new way of being in the universe. A wider freedom. . . . He wanted that very much. He wanted to be one of the crew that first formed that partnership, the first people to be able to think this thought, and to . . . to relate it. But also he was afraid of it. Maybe it wasn't a true relation, maybe false, maybe only a dream. He didn't know."

It was not so cold, so dark, at their backs, as they sat round the fire. Was it the waves of Liden, hushing on the sand?

Another voice.

"She thought a lot about her people, too. About guilt, and expiation, and sacrifice. She wanted a lot to be on this flight that might give people—more freedom. But it was different from what she thought it would be. What happened—What *happened* wasn't what mattered. What mattered was that she came to be with people who gave *her* freedom. Without guilt. She wanted to stay with them, to be crew with them. . . . And with her son. Who was the first human being to set foot on an unknown world."

A long silence; but not deep, only as deep as the soft drum of the ship's systems, steady and unconscious as the circulation of the blood.

Another voice.

"They were thoughts in the mind; what else had they ever been? So they could be in Ve and at the brown planet, and desiring flesh and entire spirit, and illusion and reality, all at once, as they'd always been. When he remembered this, his confusion and fear ceased, for he knew that they couldn't be lost."

"They got lost. But they found the way," said another voice, soft above the hum and hushing of the ship's systems, in the warm fresh air and light inside the solid walls and hulls.

Only nine voices had spoken, and they looked for the tenth; but the tenth had gone to sleep, thumb in mouth.

"That story was told and is yet to be told," the mother said. "Go on. I'll churten here with Rig."

They left those two by the fire, and went to the bridge, and then to the hatches to invite on board a crowd of anxious scientists, engineers, and officials of Ve Port and the Ekumen, whose instruments had been assuring them that the *Shoby* had vanished, forty-four minutes ago, into non-existence, into silence. "What happened?" they asked. "What happened?" And the Shobies looked at one another and said, "Well, it's quite a story. . . ."

BETRAYALS

"ON THE PLANET O THERE HAS NOT BEEN A WAR FOR FIVE THOU-sand years," she read, "and on Gethen there has never been a war." She stopped reading, to rest her eyes and because she was trying to train herself to read slowly, not gobble words down in chunks the way Tikuli gulped his food. "There has never been a war:" in her mind the words stood clear and bright, surrounded by and sinking into an infinite, dark, soft incredulity. What would that world be, a world without war? It would be the real world. Peace was the true life, the life of working and learn-ing and bringing up children to work and learn. War, which devoured work, learning, and children, was the denial of reality. But my people, she thought, know only how to deny. Born in the dark shadow of power misused, we set peace outside our world, a guiding and unattainable light. All we know to do is fight. Any peace one of us can make in our life is only a denial that the war is going on, a shadow of the shadow, a doubled unbelief.

So as the cloud-shadows swept over the marshes and the page of the book open on her lap, she sighed and closed her eyes, thinking, "I am a liar." Then she opened her eyes and read more about the other worlds, the far realities.

Tikuli, sleeping curled up around his tail in the weak sunshine, sighed as if imitating her, and scratched a dreamflea. Gubu was out in the reeds, hunting; she could not see him, but now and then the plume of a reed quivered, and once a marsh hen flew up cackling in indignation.

Absorbed in a description of the peculiar social customs of the Ithsh, she did not see Wada till he was at the gate letting himself in. "Oh, you're here already," she said, taken by surprise and feeling unready, incompetent, old, as she always felt with other people. Alone, she only felt old when she was overtired or ill. Maybe living alone was the right thing for her after all. "Come on in," she said, getting up and dropping her book and picking it up and feeling her back hair where the knot was coming loose. "I'll just get my bag and be off, then."

"No hurry," the young man said in his soft voice. "Eyid won't be here for a while yet."

Very kind of you to tell me I don't have to hurry to leave my own house, Yoss thought, but said nothing, obedient to the insufferable, adorable selfishness of the young. She went in and got her shopping bag, reknotted her hair, tied a scarf over it, and came out onto the little open porch. Wada had sat down in her chair; he jumped up when she came out. He was a shy boy, the gentler, she thought, of the two lovers. "Have fun," she said with a smile, knowing she embarrassed him. "I'll be back in a couple of hours—before sunset." She went down to her gate, let herself out, and set off the way Wada had come, along the path up to the winding wooden causeway across the marshes to the village.

She would not meet Eyid on the way. The girl would be coming from the north on one of the bog-paths, having left the village at a different time and in a different direction than Wada, so that nobody would notice that for a few hours every week or so the two young people were gone at the same time. They were madly in love, had been in love for three years, and would have lived in partnership long since if Wada's father and Eyid's father's brother hadn't quarreled over a piece of reallocated Corporation land and set up a feud between the families that had so far stopped short of bloodshed, but put a love match out of the question. The land was valuable; the families, though poor, each aspired to be leaders of the village. Nothing would heal the grudge. The whole village took sides in it. Eyid and Wada had nowhere to go, no skills to keep them alive in the cities, no tribal relations in another village who might take them in. Their passion was trapped in the hatred of the old. Yoss had come on them, a year ago now, in each other's arms on the cold ground of an island in the marshes—blundering onto them as once she had blundered onto a pair of fendeer fawns holding utterly still in the nest of grass where the doe had left them. This pair had been as frightened, as beautiful and vulnerable as the fawns, and they had begged her "not to tell" so humbly, what could she do? They were shivering with cold, Eyid's bare legs were muddy, they clung to each other like children. "Come to my house," she said sternly. "For mercy sake!" She stalked off. Timidly, they followed her. "I will be back in an hour or so," she said when she had got them indoors, into her one room with the bed alcove right beside the chimney. "Don't get things muddy!"

That time she had roamed the paths keeping watch, in case anybody was out looking for them. Nowadays she mostly went into the village while "the fawns" were in her house having their sweet hour.

They were too ignorant to think of any way to thank her. Wada, a peat-cutter, might have supplied her fire without anyone being suspicious, but they never left so much as a flower, though they always made up the bed very neat and tight. Perhaps indeed they were not very grateful. Why should they be? She gave them only what was their due: a bed, an hour of pleasure, a moment of peace. It wasn't their fault, or her virtue, that nobody else would give it to them.

Her errand today took her in to Eyid's uncle's shop. He was the village sweets-seller. All the holy abstinence she had intended when she came here two years ago, the single bowl of unflavored grain, the draft of pure water, she'd given that up in no time. She got diarrhea from a cereal diet, and the water of the marshes was undrinkable. She ate every fresh vegetable she could buy or grow, drank wine or bottled water or fruit juice from the city, and kept a large supply of sweets—dried fruits, raisins, sugar-brittle, even the cakes Eyid's mother and aunts made, fat disks with a nutmeat squashed onto the top, dry, greasy, tasteless, but curiously satisfying. She bought a bagful of them and a brown wheel of sugar-brittle, and gossiped with the aunts, dark, darting-eyed little women who had been at old Uad's wake last night and wanted to talk about it. "Those people"—Wada's family, indicated by a glance, a shrug, a sneer—had misbehaved as usual, got drunk, picked fights, boasted, got sick, and vomited all over the place, greedy upstart louts that they were. When she stopped by the newsstand to pick up a paper (another vow long since broken; she had been going to read only the *Arkamye* and learn it by heart), Wada's mother was there, and she heard how "those people"—Eyid's family—had boasted and picked fights and vomited all over the place at the wake last night. She did not merely hear; she asked for details, she drew the gossip out; she loved it.

What a fool, she thought, starting slowly home on the causeway path, what a fool I was to think I could ever drink water and be silent! I'll never, never be able to let anything go, anything at all. I'll never be free, never be worthy of freedom. Even old age can't make me let go. Even losing Safnan can't make me let go.

Before the Five Armies they stood. Holding up his sword, Enar said to Kamye: My hands hold your death, my Lord! Kamye answered: Brother, it is your death they hold.

She knew those lines, anyway. Everybody knew those lines. And so then Enar dropped his sword, because he was a hero and a holy man, the Lord's younger brother. But I can't drop my death. I'll hold it to the end, I'll cherish it, hate it, eat it, drink it, listen to it, give it my bed, mourn it, everything but let it go.

She looked up out of her thoughts into the afternoon on the marshes: the sky a cloudless misty blue, reflected in one distant curving channel of water, and the sunlight golden over the dun levels of the reedbeds and among the stems of the reeds. The rare, soft west wind blew. A perfect day. The beauty of the world, the beauty of the world! A sword in my hand, turned against me. Why do you make beauty to kill us, my Lord?

She trudged on, pulling her headscarf tighter with a little dissatisfied jerk. At this rate she would soon be wandering around the marshes shouting aloud, like Abberkam.

And there he was, the thought had summoned him: lurching along in the blind way he had as if he never saw anything but his thoughts, striking at the roadway with his big stick as if he was killing a snake. Long grey hair blowing around his face. He wasn't shouting, he only shouted at night, and not for a long time now, but he was talking, she saw his lips move; then he saw her, and shut his mouth, and drew himself into himself, wary as a wild animal. They approached each other on the narrow causeway path, not another human being in all the wilderness of reeds and mud and water and wind.

"Good evening, Chief Abberkam," Yoss said when there were only a few paces between them. What a big man he was; she never could believe how tall and broad and heavy he was till she saw him again, his dark skin still smooth as a young man's, but his head stooped and his hair grey and wild. A huge hook nose and the mistrustful, unseeing eyes. He muttered some kind of greeting, hardly slowing his gait.

The mischief was in Yoss today; she was sick of her own thoughts and sorrows and shortcomings. She stopped, so that he had to stop or else run right into her, and said, "Were you at the wake last night?"

He stared down at her; she felt he was getting her into focus, or part of her; he finally said, "Wake?"

"They buried old Uad last night. All the men got drunk, and it's a mercy the feud didn't finally break out."

"Feud?" he repeated in his deep voice.

Maybe he wasn't capable of focusing any more, but she was driven to talk to him, to get through to him. "The Dewis and Kamanners. They're quarreling over that arable island just north of the village. And the two poor children, they want to be partners, and their fathers threaten to kill them if they look at each other. What idiocy! Why don't they divide the island and let the children pair and let their children share it? It'll come to blood one of these days, I think."

"To blood," the Chief said, repeating again like a half-wit, and then slowly, in that great, deep voice, the voice she had heard crying out in agony in the night across the marshes, "Those men. Those shopkeepers. They have the souls of owners. They won't kill. But they won't share. If it's property, they won't let go. Never."

She saw again the lifted sword.

"Ah," she said with a shudder. "So then the children must wait . . . till the old people die . . ."

"Too late," he said. His eyes met hers for one instant, keen and strange; then he pushed back his hair impatiently, growled something by way of good-bye, and started on so abruptly that she almost crouched aside to make way for him. That's how a chief walks, she thought wryly, as she went on. Big, wide, taking up space, stamping the earth down. And this, this is how an old woman walks, narrowly, narrowly.

There was a strange noise behind her—gunshots, she thought, for city usages stay in the nerves—and she turned sharp round. Abberkam had stopped and was coughing explosively, tremendously, his big frame hunched around the spasms that nearly wracked him off his feet. Yoss knew that kind of coughing. The Ekumen was supposed to have medicine for it, but she'd left the city before any of it came. She went to Abberkam and when the paroxysm was over and he stood gasping, grey-faced, she said, "That's berlot: are you getting over it or are you getting it?"

He shook his head.

She waited.

While she waited she thought, what do I care if he's sick or not? Does he care? He came here to die. I heard him howling out on the marshes in the dark, last winter. Howling in agony. Eaten out with shame, like a man with cancer who's been all eaten out by the cancer but can't die.

"It's all right," he said, hoarse, angry, wanting her only to get away from him; and she nodded and went on her way. Let him die. How could he want to live knowing what he'd lost, his power, his honor, and what he'd done? Lied, betrayed his supporters, embezzled. The perfect politician. Big Chief Abberkam, hero of the Liberation, leader of the World Party, who had destroyed the World Party by his greed and folly.

She glanced back once. He was moving very slowly or perhaps had stopped, she was not sure. She went on, taking the righthand way where the causeway forked, going down onto the bog-path that led to her little house.

Three hundred years ago these marshlands had been a vast, rich agricultural valley, one of the first to be irrigated and cultivated by the Agricultural Plantation Corporation when they brought their slaves from Werel to the Yeowe Colony. Too well irrigated, too well cultivated; fertilizing chemicals and salts of the soil had accumulated till nothing would grow, and the Owners went elsewhere for their profit. The banks of the irrigation canals slumped here and there and the waters of the river wandered free again, pooling and meandering, slowly washing the lands clean. The reeds grew, miles and miles of reeds bowing a little under the wind, under the cloud-shadows and the wings of long-legged birds. Here and there on an island of rockier soil a few fields and a slave-village remained, a few sharecroppers left behind, useless people on useless land. The freedom of desolation. And all through the marshes there were lonely houses.

Growing old, the people of Werel and Yeowe might turn to silence, as their religion recommended them to do: when their children were

grown, when they had done their work as house-holder and citizen, when
as their body weakened their soul might make itself strong, they left
their life behind and came empty-handed to lonely places. Even on the
Plantations, the Bosses had let old slaves go out into the wilderness, go
free. Here in the North, freedmen from the cities had come out to the
marshlands and lived as recluses in the lonely houses. Now, since the
Liberation, even women came.

Some of the houses were derelict, and any soulmaker might claim
them; most, like Yoss's thatched cabin, were owned by villagers who
maintained them and gave them to a recluse rent-free as a religious duty,
a means of enriching the soul. Yoss liked knowing that she was a source
of spiritual profit to her landlord, a grasping man whose account with
Providence was probably otherwise all on the debit side. She liked to feel
useful. She took it for another sign of her incapacity to let the world go,
as the Lord Kamye bade her do. *You are no longer useful,* he had told her
in a hundred ways, over and over, since she was sixty; but she would not
listen. She left the noisy world and came out to the marshes, but she let
the world go on chattering and gossiping and singing and crying in her
ears. She would not hear the low voice of the Lord.

Eyid and Wada were gone when she got home; the bed was made up
very tight, and the foxdog Tikuli was sleeping on it, curled up around
his tail. Gubu the spotted cat was prancing around asking about dinner.
She picked him up and petted his silken, speckled back while he nuzzled
under her ear, making his steady roo-roo-roo of pleasure and affection;
then she fed him. Tikuli took no notice, which was odd. Tikuli was
sleeping too much. She sat on the bed and scratched the roots of his stiff,
red-furred ears. He woke and yawned and looked at her with soft amber
eyes, his red plume of tail stirring. "Aren't you hungry?" she asked him.
I will eat to please you, Tikuli answered, getting down off the bed rather
stiffly. "Oh, Tikuli, you're getting old," Yoss said, and the sword stirred
in her heart. Her daughter Safnan had given her Tikuli, a tiny red cub, a

scurry of paws and plume-tail—how long ago? Eight years. A long time. A lifetime for a foxdog.

More than a lifetime for Safnan. More than a lifetime for her children, Yoss's grandchildren, Enkamma and Uye.

If I am alive, they are dead, Yoss thought, as she always thought; if they are alive, I am dead. They went on the ship that goes like light; they are translated into the light. When they return into life, when they step off the ship on the world called Hain, it will be eighty years from the day they left, and I will be dead, long dead; I am dead. They left me and I am dead. Let them be alive, Lord, sweet Lord, let them be alive, I will be dead. I came here to be dead. For them. I cannot, I cannot let them be dead for me.

Tikuli's cold nose touched her hand. She looked intently at him. The amber of his eyes was dimmed, bluish. She stroked his head, scratched the roots of his ears, silent.

He ate a few bites to please her, and climbed back up onto the bed. She made her own dinner, soup and rewarmed soda cakes, and ate it, not tasting it. She washed the three dishes she had used, made up the fire, and sat by it trying to read her book slowly, while Tikuli slept on the bed and Gubu lay on the hearth gazing into the fire with round golden eyes, going roo-roo-roo very softly. Once he sat up and made his battlecall, "Hoooo!" at some noise he heard out in the marshes, and stalked about a bit; then he settled down again to staring and roo-ing. Later, when the fire was out and the house utterly dark in the starless darkness, he joined Yoss and Tikuli in the warm bed, where earlier the young lovers had had their brief, sharp joy.

SHE FOUND SHE WAS THINKING ABOUT ABBERKAM, THE NEXT couple of days, as she worked in her little vegetable garden, cleaning it up for the winter. When the Chief first came, the villagers had been all abuzz with excitement about his living in a house that belonged to the headman of their village. Disgraced, dishonored, he was still a very famous man. An elected Chief of the Heyend, one of the principal Tribes of Yeowe, he had come to prominence during the last years of the War of Liberation, leading a great movement for what he called Racial Freedom. Even some of the villagers had embraced the main principle of the World Party: No one was to live on Yeowe but its own people. No Werelians, the hated ancestral colonizers, the Bosses and Owners. The War had ended slavery; and in the last few years the diplomats of the Ekumen had negotiated an end to Werel's economic power over its former colony-planet. The Bosses and Owners, even those whose families had lived on Yeowe for centuries, had all withdrawn to Werel, the Old World, next outward from the sun. They had run, and their soldiers had been driven after them. They must never return, said the World Party. Not as traders, not as visitors, they would never again pollute the soil and soul of Yeowe. Nor would any other foreigner, any other Power. The Aliens of the Ekumen had helped Yeowe free itself; now they too must go. There was no place for them here. "This is our world. This is the free world. Here we will make our souls in the image of Kamye the Swordsman," Abberkam had said over and over, and that image, the curved sword, was the symbol of the World Party.

And blood had been shed. From the Uprising at Nadami on, thirty years of fighting, rebellions, retaliations, half her lifetime, and even after Liberation, after all the Werelians were gone, the fighting went on. Always, always, the young men were ready to rush out and kill whoever the old men told them to kill, each other, women, old people, children; always there was a war to be fought in the name of Peace, Freedom, Justice, the Lord. Newly freed tribes fought over land, the city chiefs fought for power. All Yoss had worked for all her life as an educator in the capital had come to pieces not only during the War of Liberation but after it, as the city disintegrated in one ward-war after another.

In all fairness, she thought, despite his waving Kamye's sword,

Abberkam, in leading the World Party, had tried to avoid war and had partly succeeded. His preference was for the winning of power by policy and persuasion, and he was a master of it. He had come very near success. The curved sword was everywhere, the rallies cheering his speeches were immense. ABBERKAM AND RACIAL FREEDOM! said huge posters stretched across the city avenues. He was certain to win the first free election ever held on Yeowe, to be Chief of the World Council. And then, nothing much at first, the rumors. The defections. His son's suicide. His son's mother's accusations of debauchery and gross luxury. The proof that he had embezzled great sums of money given his party for relief of districts left in poverty by the withdrawal of Werelian capital. The revelation of the secret plan to assassinate the Envoy of the Ekumen and put the blame on Abberkam's old friend and supporter Demeye. . . . That was what brought him down. A chief could indulge himself sexually, misuse power, grow rich off his people and be admired for it, but a chief who betrayed a companion was not forgiven. It was, Yoss thought, the code of the slave.

Mobs of his own supporters turned against him, attacking the old APCY Manager's Residency, which he had taken over. Supporters of the Ekumen joined with forces still loyal to him to defend him and restore order to the capital city. After days of street warfare, hundreds of men killed fighting and thousands more in riots around the continent, Abberkam surrendered. The Ekumen supported a provisional government in declaring amnesty. Their people walked him through the bloodstained, bombed-out streets in absolute silence. People watched, people who had trusted him, people who had revered him, people who had hated him, watched him walk past in silence, guarded by the foreigners, the Aliens he had tried to drive from their world.

She had read about it in the paper. She had been living in the marshes for over a year then. "Serve him right," she had thought, and not much more. Whether the Ekumen was a true ally or a new set of Owners in disguise, she didn't know, but she liked to see any chief go down. Werelian Bosses, strutting tribal headmen, or ranting demagogues, let them taste dirt. She'd eaten enough of their dirt in her life.

When a few months later they told her in the village that Abberkam was coming to the marshlands as a recluse, a soulmaker, she had been surprised and for a moment ashamed at having assumed his talk had all been empty rhetoric. Was he a religious man, then?—Through all the luxury, the orgies, the thefts, the powermongering, the murders? No! Since he'd lost his money and power, he'd stay in view by making a spectacle of his poverty and piety. He was utterly shameless. She was surprised at the bitterness of her indignation. The first time she saw him she felt like spitting at the big, thick-toed, sandaled feet, which were all she saw of him; she refused to look at his face.

But then in the winter she had heard the howling out on the marshes, at night, in the freezing wind. Tikuli and Gubu had pricked an ear but been unfrightened by the awful noise. That led her after a minute to recognize it as a human voice—a man shouting aloud, drunk? mad?— howling, beseeching, so that she had got up to go to him, despite her terror; but he was not calling out for human aid. "Lord, my Lord, Kamye!" he shouted, and looking out her door she saw him up on the causeway, a shadow against the pale night clouds, striding and tearing at his hair and crying like an animal, like a soul in pain.

After that night she did not judge him. They were equals. When she next met him she looked him in the face and spoke, forcing him to speak to her.

That was not often; he lived in true seclusion. No one came across the marshes to see him. People in the village often enriched their souls by giving her food, harvest surplus, leftovers, sometimes at the holy days a dish cooked for her; but she saw no one take anything out to Abberkam's house. Maybe they had offered and he was too proud to take. Maybe they were afraid to offer.

She dug up her root bed with the miserable short-handled spade Em Dewi had given her, and thought about Abberkam howling, and about the way he had coughed. Safnan had nearly died of the berlot when she was four. Yoss had heard that terrible cough for weeks. Had Abberkam been going to the village to get medicine, the other day? Had he got there, or turned back?

She put on her shawl, for the wind had turned cold again, the autumn was getting on. She went up to the causeway and took the right-hand turn.

Abberkam's house was of wood, riding a raft of tree trunks sunk in the peaty water of the marsh. Such houses were very old, going back two hundred years or more to when there had been trees growing in the valley. It had been a farmhouse and was much larger than her hut, a rambling, dark place, the roof in ill repair, some windows boarded over, planks on the porch loose as she stepped up on it. She said his name, then said it again louder. The wind whined in the reeds. She knocked, waited, pushed the heavy door open. It was dark indoors. She was in a kind of vestibule. She heard him talking in the next room. "Never down to the adit, in the intent, take it out, take it out," the deep, hoarse voice said, and then he coughed. She opened the door; she had to let her eyes adjust to the darkness for a minute before she could see where she was. It was the old front room of the house. The windows were shuttered, the fire dead. There was a sideboard, a table, a couch, but a bed stood near the fireplace. The tangled covers had slid to the floor, and Abberkam was naked on the bed, writhing and raving in fever. "Oh, Lord!" Yoss said. That huge, black, sweat-oiled breast and belly whorled with grey hair, those powerful arms and groping hands, how was she going to get near him?

She managed it, growing less timid and cautious as she found him weak in his fever, and, when he was lucid, obedient to her requests. She got him covered up, piled up all the blankets he had and a rug from the floor of an unused room on top; she built up the fire as hot as she could make it; and after a couple of hours he began to sweat, sweat pouring out of him till the sheets and mattress were soaked. "You are immoderate," she railed at him in the depths of the night, shoving and hauling at him, making him stagger over to the decrepit couch and lie there wrapped in the rug so she could get his bedding dry at the fire. He shivered and coughed, and she brewed up the herbals she had brought, and drank the scalding tea along with him. He fell suddenly asleep and slept like death, not wakened even by the cough that wracked him. She fell as suddenly asleep and woke to find herself lying on bare hearthstones, the fire dying, the day white in the windows.

Abberkam lay like a mountain range under the rug, which she saw now to be filthy; his breath wheezed but was deep and regular. She got up piece by piece, all ache and pain, made up the fire and got warm, made tea, investigated the pantry. It was stocked with essentials; evidently the Chief ordered in supplies from Veo, the nearest town of any size. She made herself a good breakfast, and when Abberkam roused, got some more herbal tea into him. The fever had broken. The danger now was water in the lungs, she thought; they had warned her about that with Safnan, and this was a man of sixty. If he stopped coughing, that would be a danger sign. She made him lie propped up. "Cough," she told him.

"Hurts," he growled.

"You have to," she said, and he coughed, hak-hak.

"More!" she ordered, and he coughed till his body was shaken with the spasms.

"Good," she said. "Now sleep." He slept.

Tikuli, Gubu would be starving! She fled home, fed her pets, petted them, changed her underclothes, sat down in her own chair by her own fireside for half an hour with Gubu going roo-roo under her ear. Then she went back across the marshes to the Chief's house.

She got his bed dried out by nightfall and moved him back into it. She stayed that night, but left him in the morning, saying, "I'll be back in the evening." He was silent, still very sick, indifferent to his own plight or hers.

The next day he was clearly better: the cough was phlegmy and rough, a good cough; she well remembered when Safnan had finally begun coughing a good cough. He was fully awake from time to time, and when she brought him the bottle she had made serve as a bedpan he took it from her and turned away from her to piss in it. Modesty, a good sign in a Chief, she thought. She felt pleased with him and with herself. She had been useful. "I'm going to leave you tonight; don't let the covers slip off. I'll be back in the morning," she told him, pleased with herself, her decisiveness, her unanswerability.

But when she got home in the clear, cold evening, Tikuli was curled up in a corner of the room where he had never slept before. He would not eat, and crept back to his corner when she tried to move him, pet him, make him sleep on the bed. Let me be, he said, looking away from her, turning his eyes away, tucking his dry, black, sharp nose into the curve of his foreleg. Let me be, he said patiently, let me die, that is what I am doing now.

She slept, because she was very tired. Gubu stayed out in the marshes all night. In the morning Tikuli was just the same, curled up on the floor in the place where he had never slept, waiting.

"I have to go," she told him, "I'll be back soon—very soon. Wait for me, Tikuli."

He said nothing, gazing away from her with dim amber eyes. It was not her he waited for.

She strode across the marshes, dry-eyed, angry, useless. Abberkam was much the same as he had been; she fed him some grain pap, looked to his needs, and said, "I can't stay. My kit is sick, I have to go back."

"Kit," the big man said in his rumble of voice.

"A foxdog. My daughter gave him to me." Why was she explaining, excusing herself? She left; when she got home Tikuli was where she had

left him. She did some mending, cooked up some food she thought
Abberkam might eat, tried to read the book about the worlds of the
Ekumen, about the world that had no war, where it was always winter,
where people were both men and women. In the middle of the afternoon
she thought she must go back to Abberkam, and was just getting up when
Tikuli too stood up. He walked very slowly over to her. She sat down
again in her chair and stooped to pick him up, but he put his sharp
muzzle into her hand, sighed, and lay down with his head on his paws.
He sighed again.

She sat and wept aloud for a while, not long; then she got up and
got the gardening spade and went outdoors. She made the grave at the
corner of the stone chimney, in a sunny nook. When she went in and
picked Tikuli up she thought with a thrill like terror, "He is not dead!"
He was dead, only he was not cold yet; the thick red fur kept the body's
warmth in. She wrapped him in her blue scarf and took him in her arms,
carried him to his grave, feeling that faint warmth still through the
cloth, and the light rigidity of the body, like a wooden statue. She filled
the grave and set a stone that had fallen from the chimney on it. She
could not say anything, but she had an image in her mind like a prayer,
of Tikuli running in the sunlight somewhere.

She put out food on the porch for Gubu, who had kept out of the
house all day, and set off up the causeway. It was a silent, overcast evening. The reeds stood grey and the pools had a leaden gleam.

Abberkam was sitting up in bed, certainly better, perhaps with a
touch of fever but nothing serious; he was hungry, a good sign. When
she brought him his tray he said, "The kit, it's all right?"

"No," she said and turned away, able only after a minute to say, "Dead."

"In the Lord's hands," said the hoarse, deep voice, and she saw Tikuli in
the sunlight again, in some presence, some kind presence like the sunlight.

"Yes," she said. "Thank you." Her lips quivered and her throat closed
up. She kept seeing the design on her blue scarf, leaves printed in a darker

blue. She made herself busy. Presently she came back to see to the fire and sit down beside it. She felt very tired.

"Before the Lord Kamye took up the sword, he was a herdsman," Abberkam said. "And they called him Lord of the Beasts, and Deer-Herd, because when he went into the forest he came among the deer, and lions also walked with him among the deer, offering no harm. None were afraid."

He spoke so quietly that it was a while before she realised he was saying lines from the *Arkamye*.

She put another block of peat on the fire and sat down again.

"Tell me where you come from, Chief Abberkam," she said.

"Gebba Plantation."

"In the east?"

He nodded.

"What was it like?"

The fire smouldered, making its pungent smoke. The night was intensely silent. When she first came out here from the city the silence had wakened her, night after night.

"What was it like," he said almost in a whisper. Like most people of their race, the dark iris filled his eyes, but she saw the white flash as he glanced over at her. "Sixty years ago," he said. "We lived in the Plantation compound. The canebrakes; some of us worked there, cut cane, worked in the mill. Most of the women, the little children. Most men and the boys over nine or ten went down the mines. Some of the girls, too, they wanted them small, to work the shafts a man couldn't get into. I was big. They sent me down the mines when I was eight years old."

"What was it like?"

"Dark," he said. Again she saw the flash of his eyes. "I look back and think how did we live? how did we stay living in that place? The air down the mine was so thick with the dust that it was black. Black air. Your lantern light didn't go five feet into that air. There was water in most of the workings, up to a man's knees. There was one shaft where a soft-coal face had caught fire and was burning so the whole system was full of smoke. They went on working it, because the lodes ran behind that coke. We wore masks, filters. They didn't do much good. We breathed the smoke. I always wheeze some like I do now. It's not just the berlot. It's the old smoke. The men died of the black lung. All the men. Forty, forty-five years old, they died. The Bosses gave your tribe money when a man died. A death bonus. Some men thought that made it worthwhile dying."

"How did you get out?"

"My mother," he said. "She was a chief's daughter from the village. She taught me. She taught me religion and freedom."

He has said that before, Yoss thought. It has become his stock answer, his standard myth.

"How? What did she say?"

A pause. "She taught me the Holy Word," Abberkam said. "And she said to me, 'You and your brother, you are the true people, you are the Lord's people, his servants, his warriors, his lions: only you. Lord Kamye came with us from the Old World and he is ours now, he lives among us.' She named us Abberkam, Tongue of the Lord, and Domerkam, Arm of the Lord. To speak the truth and fight to be free."

"What became of your brother?" Yoss asked after a time.

"Killed at Nadami," Abberkam said, and again both were silent for a while.

Nadami had been the first great outbreak of the Uprising which finally brought the Liberation to Yeowe. At Nadami plantation slaves and city freedpeople had first fought side by side against the owners. If the slaves had been able to hold together against the owners, the Corporations, they might have won their freedom years sooner. But the liberation movement had constantly splintered into tribal rivalries, chiefs vying for power in the newly freed territories, bargaining with the Bosses to consolidate their gains. Thirty years of war and destruction before the vastly outnumbered Werelians were defeated, driven offworld, leaving the Yeowans free to turn upon one another.

"Your brother was lucky," said Yoss.

Then she looked across at the Chief, wondering how he would take this challenge. His big, dark face had a softened look in the firelight. His grey, coarse hair had escaped from the loose braid she had made of it to keep it from his eyes, and straggled around his face. He said slowly and softly, "He was my younger brother. He was Enar on the Field of the Five Armies."

Oh, so then you're the Lord Kamye himself? Yoss retorted in her mind, moved, indignant, cynical. What an ego!—But, to be sure, there was another implication. Enar had taken up his sword to kill his Elder Brother on that battlefield, to keep him from becoming Lord of the World. And Kamye had told him that the sword he held was his own death; that there is no lordship and no freedom in life, only in the letting go of life, of longing, of desire. Enar had laid down his sword and gone into the wilderness, into the silence, saying only, "Brother, I am thou." And Kamye had taken up that sword to fight the Armies of Desolation, knowing there is no victory.

So who was he, this man? this big fellow? this sick old man, this little boy down in the mines in the dark, this bully, thief, and liar who thought he could speak for the Lord?

"We're talking too much," Yoss said, though neither of them had said a word for five minutes. She poured a cup of tea for him and set the kettle off the fire, where she had kept it simmering to keep the air moist. She took up her shawl. He watched her with that same soft look in his face, an expression almost of confusion.

"It was freedom I wanted," he said. "Our freedom."

His conscience was none of her concern. "Keep warm," she said.

"You're going out now?"

"I can't get lost on the causeway."

It was a strange walk, though, for she had no lantern, and the night was very black. She thought, feeling her way along the causeway, of that black air he had told her of down in the mines, swallowing light. She thought of Abberkam's black, heavy body. She thought how seldom she had walked alone at night. When she was a child on Banni Plantation, the slaves were locked in the compound at night. Women stayed on the women's side and never went alone. Before the War, when she came to the city as a freedwoman, studying at the training school, she'd had a taste of freedom; but in the bad years of the War and even since the Liberation a woman couldn't go safely in the streets at night. There were no police in the working quarters, no streetlights; district warlords sent their gangs out raiding; even in daylight you had to look out, try to stay in the crowd, always be sure there was a street you could escape by.

She grew anxious that she would miss her turning, but her eyes had grown used to the dark by the time she came to it, and she could even make out the blot of her house down in the formlessness of the reed-beds. The Aliens had poor night vision, she had heard. They had little eyes, little dots with white all round them, like a scared calf. She didn't like their eyes, though she liked the colors of their skin, mostly dark brown or ruddy brown, warmer than her greyish-brown slave skin or the blue-black hide Abberkam had got from the owner who had raped his mother. Cyanid skins, the Aliens said politely, and ocular adaptation to the radiation spectrum of the Werelian System sun.

Gubu danced about her on the pathway down, silent, tickling her legs with his tail. "Look out," she scolded him, "I'm going to walk on you." She was grateful to him, picked him up as soon as they were indoors. No dignified and joyous greeting from Tikuli, not this night, not ever. Roo-roo-roo, Gubu went under her ear, listen to me, I'm here, life goes on, where's dinner?

THE CHIEF GOT A TOUCH OF PNEUMONIA AFTER ALL, AND SHE went into the village to call the clinic in Veo. They sent out a practitioner, who said he was doing fine, just keep him sitting up and coughing, the herbal teas were fine, just keep an eye on him, that's right, and went away, thanks very much. So she spent her afternoons with him. The house without Tikuli seemed very drab, the late autumn days seemed very cold, and anyhow what else did she have to do? She liked the big, dark raft-house. She wasn't going to clean house for the Chief or any man who didn't do it for himself, but she poked about in it, in rooms Abberkam evidently hadn't used or even looked at. She found one upstairs, with long low windows all along the west wall, that she liked. She swept it out and cleaned the windows with their small, greenish panes. When he was asleep she would go up to that room and sit on a ragged wool rug, its only furnishing. The fireplace had been sealed up with loose bricks, but heat came up it from the peat fire burning below, and with her back against the warm bricks and the sunlight slanting in, she was warm. She felt a peacefulness there that seemed to belong to the room, the shape of its air, the greenish, wavery glass of the windows. There she would sit in silence, unoccupied, content, as she had never sat in her own house.

The Chief was slow to get his strength back. Often he was sullen, dour, the uncouth man she had first thought him, sunk in a stupor of self-centered shame and rage. Other days he was ready to talk; even to listen, sometimes.

"I've been reading a book about the worlds of the Ekumen," Yoss said, waiting for their bean-cakes to be ready to turn and fry on the other side. For the last several days she had made and eaten dinner with him in the late afternoon, washed up, and gone home before dark. "It's very interesting. There isn't any question that we're descended from the people of Hain, all of us. Us and the Aliens too. Even our animals have the same ancestors."

"So they say," he grunted.

"It isn't a matter of who says it," she said. "Anybody who will look at the evidence sees it; it's a genetic fact. That you don't like it doesn't alter it."

"What is a 'fact' a million years old?" he said. "What has it to do with you, with me, with us? This is our world. We are ourselves. We have nothing to do with them."

"We do now," she said rather fliply, flipping the bean-cakes.

"Not if I had had my way," he said.

She laughed. "You don't give up, do you?"

"No," he said.

After they were eating, he in bed with his tray, she at a stool on the hearth, she went on, with a sense of teasing a bull, daring the avalanche to fall; for all he was still sick and weak, there was that menace in him, his size, not of body only. "Is that what it was all about, really?" she asked. "The World Party. Having the planet for ourselves, no Aliens? Just that?"

"Yes," he said, the dark rumble.

"Why? The Ekumen has so much to share with us. They broke the Corporations' hold over us. They're on our side."

"We were brought to this world as slaves," he said, "but it is our world to find our own way in. Kamye came with us, the Herdsman, the Bondsman, Kamye of the Sword. This is his world. Our earth. No one can give it to us. We don't need to share other peoples' knowledge or follow their gods. This is where we live, this earth. This is where we die to rejoin the Lord."

After a while she said, "I have a daughter, and a grandson and granddaughter. They left this world four years ago. They're on a ship that is going to Hain. All these years I live till I die are like a few minutes, an hour to them. They'll be there in eighty years—seventy-six years, now. On that other earth. They'll live and die there. Not here."

"Were you willing for them to go?"

"It was her choice."

"Not yours."

"I don't live her life."

"But you grieve," he said.

The silence between them was heavy.

"It is wrong, wrong, wrong!" he said, his voice strong and loud. "We had our own destiny, our own way to the Lord, and they've taken it from us—we're slaves again! The wise Aliens, the scientists with all their great knowledge and inventions, our ancestors, they say they are—'Do this!' they say, and we do it. 'Do that!' and we do it. 'Take your children on the wonderful ship and fly to our wonderful worlds!' And the children are taken, and they'll never come home. Never know their home. Never know who they are. Never know whose hands might have held them."

He was orating; for all she knew it was a speech he had made once or a hundred times, ranting and magnificent; there were tears in his eyes. There were tears in her eyes also. She would not let him use her, play on her, have power over her.

"If I agreed with you," she said, "still, still, why did you cheat, Abberkam? You lied to your own people, you stole!"

"Never," he said. "Everything I did, always, every breath I took, was for the World Party. Yes, I spent money, all the money I could get, what was it for except the cause? Yes, I threatened the Envoy, I wanted to drive him and all the rest of them off this world! Yes, I lied to them, because they want to control us, to own us, and I will do anything to save my people from slavery—anything!"

He beat his great fists on the mound of his knees, and gasped for breath, sobbing.

"And there is nothing I can do, O Kamye!" he cried, and hid his face in his arms.

She sat silent, sick at heart.

After a long time he wiped his hands over his face, like a child, wiping the coarse, straggling hair back, rubbing his eyes and nose. He picked up the tray and set it on his knees, picked up the fork, cut a piece of bean-cake, put it in his mouth, chewed, swallowed. If he can, I can, Yoss thought, and did the same. They finished their dinner. She got up and came to take his tray. "I'm sorry," she said.

"It was gone then," he said very quietly. He looked up at her directly, seeing her, as she felt he seldom did.

She stood, not understanding, waiting.

"It was gone then. Years before. What I believed at Nadami. That all we needed was to drive them out and we would be free. We lost our way as the war went on and on. I knew it was a lie. What did it matter if I lied more?"

She understood only that he was deeply upset and probably somewhat mad, and that she had been wrong to goad him. They were both old, both defeated, they had both lost their child. Why did she want to hurt him? She put her hand on his hand for a moment, in silence, before she picked up his tray.

As she washed up the dishes in the scullery, he called her, "Come here, please!" He had never done so before, and she hurried into the room.

"Who were you?" he asked.

She stood staring.

"Before you came here," he said impatiently.

"I went from the plantation to education school," she said. "I lived in the city. I taught physics. I administered the teaching of science in the schools. I brought up my daughter."

"What is your name?"

"Yoss. Seddewi Tribe, from Banni."

He nodded, and after a moment more she went back to the scullery. He didn't even know my name, she thought.

EVERY DAY SHE MADE HIM GET UP, WALK A LITTLE, SIT IN A CHAIR; he was obedient, but it tired him. The next afternoon she made him walk about a good while, and when he got back to bed he closed his eyes at once. She slipped up the rickety stairs to the west-window room and sat there a long time in perfect peace.

She had him sit up in the chair while she made their dinner. She talked to cheer him up, for he never complained at her demands, but he looked gloomy and bleak, and she blamed herself for upsetting him yesterday. Were they not both here to leave all that behind them, all their mistakes and failures as well as their loves and victories? She told him about Wada and Eyid, spinning out the story of the star-crossed lovers, who were, in fact, in bed in her house that afternoon. "I didn't use to have anywhere to go when they came," she said. "It could be rather inconvenient, cold days like today. I'd have to hang around the shops in the village. This is better, I must say. I like this house."

He only grunted, but she felt he was listening intently, almost that he was trying to understand, like a foreigner who did not know the language.

"You don't care about the house, do you?" she said, and laughed, serving up their soup. "You're honest, at least. Here I am pretending to be holy, to be making my soul, and I get fond of things, attached to them, I love things." She sat down by the fire to eat her soup. "There's a beautiful room upstairs," she said, "the front corner room, looking west. Something good happened in that room, lovers lived there once, maybe. I like to look out at the marshes from there."

When she made ready to go he asked, "Will they be gone?"

"The fawns? Oh yes. Long since. Back to their hateful families. I suppose if they could live together, they'd soon be just as hateful. They're very ignorant. How can they help it? The village is narrow-minded, they're so poor. But they cling to their love for each other, as if they knew it . . . it was their truth . . ."

" 'Hold fast to the noble thing,' " Abberkam said. She knew the quotation.

"Would you like me to read to you?" she asked. "I have the *Arkamye,* I could bring it."

He shook his head, with a sudden, broad smile. "No need," he said, "I know it."

"All of it?"

He nodded.

"I meant to learn it—part of it anyway—when I came here," she said, awed. "But I never did. There never seems to be time. Did you learn it here?"

"Long ago. In the jail, in Gebba City," he said. "Plenty of time there. . . . These days, I lie here and say it to myself." His smile lingered as he looked up at her. "It gives me company in your absence."

She stood wordless.

"Your presence is sweet to me," he said.

She wrapped herself in her shawl and hurried out with scarcely a word of good-bye.

She walked home in a crowd of confused, conflicted feelings. What a monster the man was! He had been flirting with her: there was no doubt about it. Coming on to her, was more like it. Lying in bed like a great felled ox, with his wheezing and his grey hair! That soft, deep voice, that smile, he knew the uses of that smile, he knew how to keep it rare. He knew how to get round a woman, he'd got round a thousand if the stories were true, round them and into them and out again, here's a little semen to remember your Chief by, and bye-bye, baby. Lord!

So, why had she taken it into her head to tell him about Eyid and Wada being in her bed? Stupid woman, she told herself, striding into the mean east wind that scoured the greying reeds. Stupid, stupid, old, old woman.

Gubu came to meet her, dancing and batting with soft paws at her legs and hands, waving his short, end-knotted, black-spotted tail. She had left the door unlatched for him, and he could push it open. It was ajar. Feathers of some kind of small bird were strewn all over the room and there was a little blood and a bit of entrail on the hearthrug. "Monster," she told him. "Murder outside!" He danced his battle dance and cried Hoo! Hoo! He slept all night curled up in the small of her back, obligingly getting up, stepping over her, and curling up on the other side each time she turned over.

She turned over frequently, imagining or dreaming the weight and heat of a massive body, the weight of hands on her breasts, the tug of lips at her nipples, sucking life.

SHE SHORTENED HER VISITS TO ABBERKAM. HE WAS ABLE TO GET up, see to his needs, get his own breakfast; she kept his peatbox by the chimney filled and his larder supplied, and she now brought him dinner but did not stay to eat it with him. He was mostly grave and silent, and she watched her tongue. They were wary with each other. She missed her hours upstairs in the western room; but that was done with, a kind of dream, a sweetness gone.

Eyid came to Yoss's house alone one afternoon, sullen-faced. "I guess I won't come back out here," she said.

"What's wrong?"

The girl shrugged.

"Are they watching you?"

"No. I don't know. I might, you know. I might get stuffed." She used the old slave word for pregnant.

"You used the contraceptives, didn't you?" She had bought them for the pair in Veo, a good supply.

Eyid nodded vaguely. "I guess it's wrong," she said, pursing her mouth.

"Making love? Using contraceptives?"

"I guess it's wrong," the girl repeated, with a quick, vengeful glance.

"All right," Yoss said.

Eyid turned away.

"Good-bye, Eyid."

Without speaking, Eyid went off by the bog-path.

"Hold fast to the noble thing," Yoss thought, bitterly.

She went round the house to Tikuli's grave, but it was too cold to stand outside for long, a still, aching, midwinter cold. She went in and shut the door. The room seemed small and dark and low. The dull peat fire smoked and smouldered. It made no noise burning. There was no noise outside the house. The wind was down, the ice-bound reeds were still.

I want some wood, I want a wood fire, Yoss thought. A flame leaping and crackling, a story-telling fire, like we used to have in the grandmothers' house on the plantation.

The next day she went off one of the bog-paths to a ruined house half a mile away and pulled some loose boards off the fallen-in porch. She had a roaring blaze in her fireplace that night. She took to going to the ruined house once or more daily, and built up a sizeable woodpile next to the stacked peat in the nook on the other side of the chimney from her bed nook. She was no longer going to Abberkam's house; he was recovered, and she wanted a goal to walk to. She had no way to cut the longer boards, and so shoved them into the fireplace a bit at a time; that way one would last all the evening. She sat by the bright fire and tried to learn the First Book of the *Arkamye*. Gubu lay on the hearthstone sometimes watching the flames and whispering roo, roo, sometimes asleep. He hated so to go out into the icy reeds that she made him a little dirt-box in the scullery, and he used it very neatly.

The deep cold continued, the worst winter she had known on the marshes. Fierce drafts led her to cracks in the wood walls she had not known about; she had no rags to stuff them with and used mud and wadded reeds. If she let the fire go out, the little house grew icy within an hour. The peat fire, banked, got her through the nights. In the daytime often she put on a piece of wood for the flare, the brightness, the company of it.

She had to go into the village. She had put off going for days, hoping that the cold might relent, and had run out of practically everything. It was colder than ever. The peat blocks now on the fire were earthy and burned poorly, smouldering, so she put a piece of wood in with them to keep the fire lively and the house warm. She wrapped every jacket and shawl she had around her and set off with her sack. Gubu blinked at her from the hearth. "Lazy lout," she told him. "Wise beast."

The cold was frightening. If I slipped on the ice and broke a leg, no one might come by for days, she thought. I'd lie here and be frozen dead in a few hours. Well, well, well, I'm in the Lord's hands, and dead in a few years one way or the other. Only, dear Lord, let me get to the village and get warm!

She got there, and spent a good while at the sweet-shop stove catching up on gossip, and at the news vendor's woodstove, reading old newspapers about a new war in the eastern province. Eyid's aunts and Wada's father, mother, and aunts all asked her how the Chief was. They also all told her to go by her landlord's house, Kebi had something for her. He had a packet of cheap nasty tea for her. Perfectly willing to let him enrich his soul, she thanked him for the tea. He asked her about Abberkam. The Chief had been ill? He was better now? He pried; she replied indifferently. It's easy to live in silence, she thought; what I could not do is live with these voices.

She was loath to leave the warm room, but her bag was heavier than she liked to carry, and the icy spots on the road would be hard to see as the light failed. She took her leave and set off across the village again and up onto the causeway. It was later than she had thought. The sun was quite low, hiding behind one bar of cloud in an otherwise stark sky, as if grudging even a half hour's warmth and brightness. She wanted to get home to her fire, and stepped right along.

Keeping her eyes on the way ahead for fear of ice, at first she only heard the voice. She knew it, and she thought, Abberkam has gone mad again! For he was running towards her, shouting. She stopped, afraid of him, but it was her name he was shouting. "Yoss! Yoss! It's all right!" he shouted, coming up right on her, a huge wild man, all dirty, muddy, ice and mud in his grey hair, his hands black, his clothes black, and she could see the whites all round his eyes.

"Get back!" she said, "get away, get away from me!"

"It's all right," he said, "but the house, but the house—"

"What house?"

"Your house, it burned. I saw it, I was coming to the village, I saw the smoke down in the marsh—"

He went on, but Yoss stood paralysed, unhearing. She had shut the door, let the latch fall. She never locked it, but she had let the latch fall, and Gubu would not be able to get out. He was in the house. Locked in: the bright, desperate eyes: the little voice crying—

She started forward. Abberkam blocked her way.

"Let me get by," she said. "I have to get by." She set down her bag and began to run.

Her arm was caught, she was stopped as if by a sea wave, swung right round. The huge body and voice were all around her. "It's all right, the kit is all right, it's in my house," he was saying. "Listen, listen to me, Yoss! The house burned. The kit is all right."

"What happened?" she said, shouting, furious. "Let me go! I don't understand! What happened?"

"Please, please be quiet," he begged her, releasing her. "We'll go by there. You'll see it. There isn't much to see."

Very shakily, she walked along with him while he told her what had happened. "But how did it start?" she said, "how could it?"

"A spark; you left the fire burning? Of course, of course you did, it's cold. But there were stones out of the chimney, I could see that. Sparks, if there was any wood on the fire—maybe a floorboard caught—the thatch, maybe. Then it would all go, in this dry weather, everything dried out, no rain. Oh my Lord, my sweet Lord, I thought you were in there. I thought you were in the house. I saw the fire, I was up on the causeway—then I was down at the door of the house, I don't know how, did I fly, I don't know—I pushed, it was latched, I pushed it in, and I saw the whole back wall and ceiling burning, blazing. There was so much smoke, I couldn't tell if you were there, I went in, the little animal was hiding in a corner—I thought how you cried when the other one died, I tried to catch it, and it went out the door like a flash, and I saw no one was there, and made for the door, and the roof fell in." He laughed, wild, triumphant. "Hit me on the head, see?" He stooped, but she still was not tall enough to see the top of his head. "I saw your bucket and tried to throw water on the front wall, to save something, then I saw that was crazy, it was all on fire, nothing left. And I went up the path, and the little animal, your pet, was waiting there, all shaking. It let me pick it up, and I didn't know what to do with it, so I ran back to my house, and left it there. I shut the door. It's safe there. Then I thought you must be in the village, so I came back to find you."

They had come to the turnoff. She went to the side of the causeway and looked down. A smear of smoke, a huddle of black. Black sticks. Ice. She shook all over and felt so sick she had to crouch down, swallowing cold saliva. The sky and the reeds went from left to right, spinning, in her eyes; she could not stop them spinning.

"Come, come on now, it's all right. Come on with me." She was aware of the voice, the hands and arms, a large warmth supporting her. She walked along with her eyes shut. After a while she could open them and look down at the road, carefully.

"Oh, my bag—I left it—It's all I have," she said suddenly with a kind of laugh, turning around and nearly falling over because the turn started the spinning again.

"I have it here. Come on, it's just a short way now." He carried the bag oddly, in the crook of his arm. The other arm was around her, helping her stand up and walk. They came to his house, the dark raft-house. It faced a tremendous orange-and-yellow sky, with pink streaks going up the sky from where the sun had set; the sun's hair, they used to call that, when she was a child. They turned from the glory, entering the dark house.

"Gubu?" she said.

It took a while to find him. He was cowering under the couch. She had to haul him out, he would not come to her. His fur was full of dust and came out in her hands as she stroked it. There was a little foam on his mouth, and he shivered and was silent in her arms. She stroked and stroked the silvery, speckled back, the spotted sides, the silken white belly fur. He closed his eyes finally; but the instant she moved a little, he leapt, and ran back under the couch.

She sat and said, "I'm sorry, I'm sorry, Gubu, I'm sorry."

Hearing her speak, the Chief came back into the room. He had been in the scullery. He held his wet hands in front of him and she wondered why he didn't dry them. "Is he all right?" he asked.

"It'll take a while," she said. "The fire. And a strange house. They're . . . cats are territorial. Don't like strange places."

She could not arrange her thoughts or words, they came in pieces, unattached.

"That is a cat, then?"

"A spotted cat, yes."

"Those pet animals, they belonged to the Bosses, they were in the Bosses' houses," he said. "We never had any around."

She thought it was an accusation. "They came from Werel with the Bosses," she said, "yes. So did we." After the sharp words were out she thought that maybe what he had said was an apology for ignorance.

He still stood there holding out his hands stiffly. "I'm sorry," he said. "I need some kind of bandage, I think."

She focused slowly on his hands.

"You burned them," she said.

"Not much. I don't know when."

"Let me see." He came nearer and turned the big hands palm up: a fierce red blistered bar across the bluish inner skin of the fingers of one, and a raw bloody wound in the base of the thumb of the other.

"I didn't notice till I was washing," he said. "It didn't hurt."

"Let me see your head," she said, remembering; and he knelt and presented her a matted shaggy sooty object with a red-and-black burn right across the top of it, "Oh, Lord," she said.

His big nose and eyes appeared under the grey tangle, close to her, looking up at her, anxious. "I know the roof fell onto me," he said, and she began to laugh.

"It would take more than a roof falling onto you!" she said. "Have you got anything—any clean cloths—I know I left some clean dish towels in the scullery closet—Any disinfectant?"

She talked as she cleaned the head wound. "I don't know anything about burns except try to keep them clean and leave them open and dry. We should call the clinic in Veo. I can go into the village, tomorrow."

"I thought you were a doctor or a nurse," he said.

"I'm a school administrator!"

"You looked after me."

"I knew what you had. I don't know anything about burns. I'll go into the village and call. Not tonight, though."

"Not tonight," he agreed. He flexed his hands, wincing. "I was going to make us dinner," he said. "I didn't know there was anything wrong with my hands. I don't know when it happened."

"When you rescued Gubu," Yoss said in a matter-of-fact voice, and then began crying. "Show me what you were going to eat, I'll put it on," she said through tears.

"I'm sorry about your things," he said.

"Nothing mattered. I'm wearing almost all my clothes," she said, weeping. "There wasn't anything. Hardly any food there even. Only the *Arkamye*. And my book about the worlds." She thought of the pages blackening and curling as the fire read them. "A friend sent me that from the city, she never approved of me coming here, pretending to drink water and be silent. She was right, too, I should go back, I should never have come. What a liar I am, what a fool! Stealing wood! Stealing wood so I could have a nice fire! So I could be warm and cheerful! So I set the house on fire, so everything's gone, ruined, Kebi's house, my poor little cat, your hands, it's my fault. I forgot about sparks from wood fires, the chimney was built for peat fires, I forgot. I forget everything, my mind betrays me, my memory lies, I lie. I dishonor my Lord, pretending to turn to him when I can't turn to him, when I can't let go the world. So I burn it! So the sword cuts your hands." She took his hands in hers and bent her head over them. "Tears are disinfectant," she said. "Oh I'm sorry, I am sorry!"

His big, burned hands rested in hers. He leaned forward and kissed her hair, caressing it with his lips and cheek. "I will say you the *Arkamye,*" he said. "Be still now. We need to eat something. You feel very cold. I think you have some shock, maybe. You sit there. I can put a pot on to heat, anyhow."

She obeyed. He was right, she felt very cold. She huddled closer to the fire. "Gubu?" she whispered. "Gubu, it's all right. Come on, come on, little one." But nothing moved under the couch.

Abberkam stood by her, offering her something: a glass: it was wine, red wine.

"You have wine?" she said, startled.

"Mostly I drink water and am silent," he said. "Sometimes I drink wine and talk. Take it."

She took it humbly. "I wasn't shocked," she said.

"Nothing shocks a city woman," he said gravely. "Now I need you to open up this jar."

"How did you get the wine open?" she asked as she unscrewed the lid of a jar of fish stew.

"It was already open," he said, deep-voiced, imperturbable.

They sat across the hearth from each other to eat, helping themselves from the pot hung on the firehook. She held bits of fish down low so they could be seen from under the couch and whispered to Gubu, but he would not come out.

"When he's very hungry, he will," she said. She was tired of the teary quaver in her voice, the knot in her throat, the sense of shame. "Thank you for the food," she said. "I feel better."

She got up and washed the pot and the spoons; she had told him not to get his hands wet, and he did not offer to help her, but sat on by the fire, motionless, like a great dark lump of stone.

"I'll go upstairs," she said when she was done. "Maybe I can get hold of Gubu and take him with me. Let me have a blanket or two."

He nodded. "They're up there. I lighted the fire," he said. She did not know what he meant; she had knelt to peer under the couch. She knew as she did so that she was grotesque, an old woman bundled up in shawls with her rear end in the air, whispering, "Gubu, Gubu!" to a piece of furniture. But there was a little scrabbling, and then Gubu came straight into her hands. He clung to her shoulder with his nose hidden under her ear. She sat up on her heels and looked at Abberkam, radiant. "Here he is!" she said. She got to her feet with some difficulty, and said, "Good night."

"Good night, Yoss," he said. She dared not try to carry the oil lamp, and made her way up the stairs in the dark, holding Gubu close with both hands till she was in the west room and had shut the door. Then she stood staring. Abberkam had unsealed the fireplace, and some time this evening he had lighted the peat laid ready in it; the ruddy glow flickered in the long, low windows black with night, and the scent of it was sweet. A bedstead that had been in another unused room now stood in this one, made up, with mattress and blankets and a new white wool rug thrown over it. A jug and basin stood on the shelf by the chimney. The old rug she had used to sit on had been beaten and scrubbed, and lay clean and threadbare on the hearth.

Gubu pushed at her arms; she set him down, and he ran straight under the bed. He would be all right there. She poured a little water from the jug into the basin and set it on the hearth in case he was thirsty. He could use the ashes for his box. Everything we need is here, she thought, still looking with a sense of bewilderment at the shadowy room, the soft light that struck the windows from within.

She went out, closing the door behind her, and went downstairs.

Abberkam sat still by the fire. His eyes flashed at her. She did not know what to say.

"You liked that room," he said.

She nodded.

"You said maybe it was a lovers' room once. I thought maybe it was a lovers' room to be."

After a while she said, "Maybe."

"Not tonight," he said, with a low rumble: a laugh, she realised. She had seen him smile once, now she had heard him laugh.

"No. Not tonight," she said stiffly.

"I need my hands," he said, "I need everything, for that, for you."

She said nothing, watching him.

"Sit down, Yoss, please," he said. She sat down in the hearth-seat facing him.

"When I was ill I thought about these things," he said, always a touch of the orator in his voice. "I betrayed my cause, I lied and stole in its name, because I could not admit I had lost faith in it. I feared the Aliens because I feared their gods. So many gods! I feared that they would diminish my Lord. Diminish him!" He was silent for a minute, and drew breath; she could hear the deep rasp in his chest. "I betrayed my son's mother many times, many times. Her, other women, myself. I did not hold to the one noble thing." He opened up his hands, wincing a little, looking at the burns across them. "I think you did," he said.

After a while she said, "I only stayed with Safnan's father a few years. I had some other men. What does it matter, now?"

"That's not what I mean," he said. "I mean that you did not betray your men, your child, yourself. All right, all that's past. You say, what does it matter now, nothing matters. But you give me this chance even now, this beautiful chance, to me, to hold you, hold you fast."

She said nothing.

"I came here in shame," he said, "and you honored me."

"Why not? Who am I to judge you?"

"'Brother, I am thou."

She looked at him in terror, one glance, then looked into the fire. The peat burned low and warm, sending up one faint curl of smoke. She thought of the warmth, the darkness of his body.

"Would there be any peace between us?" she said at last.

"Do you need peace?"

After a while she smiled a little.

"I will do my best," he said. "Stay in this house a while."

She nodded.

THE MATTER

OF

SEGGRI

*The first recorded contact with Seggri was in year 242 of
Hainish Cycle 93. A Wandership six generations out from
Iao (4-Taurus) came down on the planet, and the captain
entered this report in his ship's log.*

CAPTAIN AOLAO-OLAO'S REPORT

WE HAVE SPENT NEAR FORTY DAYS ON THIS WORLD THEY CALL
Se-ri or Ye-ha-ri, well entertained, and leave with as good an esti-
mation of the natives as is consonant with their unregenerate state.
They live in fine great buildings they call castles, with large parks all
about. Outside the walls of the parks lie well-tilled fields and abun-
dant orchards, reclaimed by diligence from the parched and arid desert
of stone that makes up the greatest part of the land. Their women
live in villages and towns huddled outside the walls. All the common
work of farm and mill is performed by the women, of whom there is
a vast superabundance. They are ordinary drudges, living in towns
which belong to the lords of the castle. They live amongst the cattle
and brute animals of all kinds, who are permitted into the houses,
some of which are of fair size. These women go about drably clothed,

always in groups and bands. They are never allowed within the walls of the park, leaving the food and necessaries with which they provide the men at the outer gate of the castle. They evinced great fear and distrust of us. A few of my men following some girls on the road, women rushed from the town like a pack of wild beasts, so that the men thought it best to return forthwith to the castle. Our hosts advised us that it were best for us to keep away from their towns, which we did.

The men go freely about their great parks, playing at one sport or another. At night they go to certain houses which they own in the town, where they may have their pick among the women and satisfy their lust upon them as they will. The women pay them, we were told, in their money, which is copper, for a night of pleasure, and pay them yet more if they get a child on them. Their nights thus are spent in carnal satisfaction as often as they desire, and their days in a diversity of sports and games, notably a kind of wrestling, in which they throw each other through the air so that we marveled that they seemed never to take hurt, but rose up and returned to the combat with wonderful dexterity of hand and foot. Also they fence with blunt swords, and combat with long light sticks. Also they play a game with balls on a great field, using the arms to catch or throw the ball and the legs to kick the ball and trip or catch or kick the men of the other team, so that many are bruised and lamed in the passion of the sport, which was very fine to see, the teams in their contrasted garments of bright colors much gauded out with gold and finery seething now this way, now that, up and down the field in a mass, from which the balls were flung up and caught by runners breaking free of the struggling crowd and fleeting towards the one or the other goal with all the rest in hot pursuit. There is a "battlefield" as they call it of this game lying without the walls of the castle park, near to the town, so that the women may come watch and cheer, which they do heartily, calling out the names of favorite players and urging them with many uncouth cries to victory.

Boys are taken from the women at the age of eleven and brought to the castle to be educated as befits a man. We saw such a child brought into the castle with much ceremony and rejoicing. It is said that the women find it difficult to bring a pregnancy of a manchild to term, and that of those born many die in infancy despite the care lavished upon them, so that there are far more women than men. In this we see the curse of GOD laid upon this race as upon all those who acknowledge HIM not, unrepentant heathens whose ears are stopped to true discourse and blind to the light.

These men know little of art, only a kind of leaping dance, and their science is little beyond that of savages. One great man of a castle to whom I talked, who was dressed out in cloth of gold and crimson and whom all called Prince and Grandsire with much respect and deference, yet was so ignorant he believed the stars to be worlds full of people and beasts, asking us from which star we descended. They have only vessels driven by steam along the surface of the land and water, and no notion of flight either in the air or in space, nor any curiosity about such things, saying with disdain, "That is all women's work," and indeed I found that if I asked these great men about matters of common knowledge such as the working of machinery, the weaving of cloth, the transmission of holovision, they would soon chide me for taking interest in womanish things as they called them, desiring me to talk as befit a man.

In the breeding of their fierce cattle within the parks they are very knowledgeable, as in the sewing up of their clothing, which they make from cloth the women weave in their factories. The men vie in the ornamentation and magnificence of their costumes to an extent which we might indeed have thought scarcely manly, were they not withal such proper men, strong and ready for any game or sport, and full of pride and a most delicate and fiery honor.

The log including Captain Aolao-olao's entries was (after a 12-generation journey) returned to the Sacred Archives of the Universe on Iao, which were dispersed during the period called The Tumult, and eventually preserved in fragmentary form on Hain. There is no record of further contact with Seggri until the First Observers were sent by the Ekumen in 93/1333: an Alterran man and a Hainish woman, Kaza Agad and G. Merriment. After a year in orbit mapping, photographing, recording and studying broadcasts, and analysing and learning a major regional language, the Observers landed. Acting upon a strong persuasion of the vulnerability of the planetary culture, they presented themselves as survivors of the wreck of a fishing boat, blown far off course, from a remote island. They were, as they had anticipated, separated at once, Kaza Agad being taken to the Castle and Merriment into the town. Kaza kept his name, which was plausible in the native context; Merriment called herself Yude. We have only her report, from which three excerpts follow.

FROM MOBILE GERINDU'UTTAHAYUDETWE'MENRADE
MERRIMENT'S NOTES FOR A REPORT TO THE EKUMEN, 93/1334

34/223. THEIR NETWORK OF TRADE AND INFORMATION, HENCE their awareness of what goes on elsewhere in their world, is too sophisticated for me to maintain my Stupid Foreign Castaway act any longer. Ekhaw called me in today and said, "If we had a sire here who was worth buying or if our teams were winning their games, I'd think you were a spy. Who are you, anyhow?"

I said, "Would you let me go to the College at Hagka?"

She said, "Why?"

"There are scientists there, I think? I need to talk with them."

This made sense to her; she made their "Mh" noise of assent.

"Could my friend go there with me?"

"Shask, you mean?"

We were both puzzled for a moment. She didn't expect a woman to call a man "friend," and I hadn't thought of Shask as a friend. She's very young, and I haven't taken her very seriously.

"I mean Kaza, the man I came with."

"A man—to the college?" she said, incredulous. She looked at me and said, "Where *do* you come from?"

It was a fair question, not asked in enmity or challenge. I wish I could have answered it, but I am increasingly convinced that we can do great damage to these people; we are facing Resehavanar's Choice here, I fear.

Ekhaw paid for my journey to Hagka, and Shask came along with me. As I thought about it I saw that of course Shask was my friend. It was she who brought me into the motherhouse, persuading Ekhaw and Azman of their duty to be hospitable; it was she who had looked out for me all along. Only she was so conventional in everything she did and said that I hadn't realised how radical her compassion was. When I tried to thank her, as our little jitney-bus purred along the road to Hagka, she said things like she always says—"Oh, we're all family," and "People have to help each other," and "Nobody can live alone."

"Don't women ever live alone?" I asked her, for all the ones I've met belong to a motherhouse or a daughterhouse, whether a couple or a big family like Ekhaw's, which is three generations: five older women, three of their daughters living at home, and four children—the boy they all coddle and spoil so, and three girls.

"Oh yes," Shask said. "If they don't want wives, they can be single-women. And old women, when their wives die, sometimes they just live alone till they die. Usually they go live at a daughterhouse. In the colleges, the *vev* always have a place to be alone." Conventional she may be, but Shask always tries to answer a question seriously and completely; she thinks about her answer. She has been an invaluable informant. She has also made life easy for me by not asking questions about where I come from. I took this for the incuriosity of a person securely embedded in an unquestioned way of life, and for the self-centeredness of the young. Now I see it as delicacy.

"A vev is a teacher?"

"Mh."

"And the teachers at the college are very respected?"

"That's what vev means. That's why we call Eckaw's mother Vev Kakaw. She didn't go to college, but she's a thoughtful person, she's learned from life, she has a lot to teach us."

So respect and teaching are the same thing, and the only term of respect I've heard women use for women means teacher. And so in teaching me, young Shask respects herself? And/or earns my respect? This casts a different light on what I've been seeing as a society in which wealth is the important thing. Zadedr, the current mayor of Reha, is certainly admired for her very ostentatious display of possessions; but they don't call her Vev.

I said to Shask, "You have taught me so much, may I call you Vev Shask?"

She was equally embarrassed and pleased, and squirmed and said, "Oh no no no no." Then she said, "If you ever come back to Reha I would like very much to have love with you, Yude."

"I thought you were in love with Sire Zadr!" I blurted out.

"Oh, I am," she said, with that eye-roll and melted look they have when they speak of the sires, "aren't you? Just think of him fucking you, oh! Oh, I get all wet thinking about it!" She smiled and wriggled. I felt embarrassed in my turn and probably showed it. "Don't you like him?" she inquired with a naivety I found hard to bear. She was acting like a silly adolescent, and I know she's not a silly adolescent. "But I'll never be able to afford him," she said, and sighed.

So you want to make do with me, I thought nastily.

"I'm going to save my money," she announced after a minute. "I think I want to have a baby next year. Of course I can't afford Sire Zadr, he's a Great Champion, but if I don't go to the Games at Kadaki this year I can save up enough for a really good sire at our fuckery, maybe Master Rosra. I wish, I know this is silly, I'm going to say it anyway, I've been wishing you could be its lovemother. I know you can't, you have to go to the college. I just wanted to tell you. I love you." She took my hands, drew them to her face, pressed my palms on her eyes for a moment, and then released me. She was smiling, but her tears were on my hands.

"Oh, Shask," I said, floored.

"It's all right!" she said. "I have to cry a minute." And she did. She wept openly, bending over, wringing her hands, and wailing softly. I patted her arm and felt unutterably ashamed of myself. Other passengers looked round and made little sympathetic grunting noises. One old woman said, "That's it, that's right, lovey!" In a few minutes Shask stopped crying, wiped her nose and face on her sleeve, drew a long, deep breath, and said, "All right." She smiled at me. "Driver," she called, "I have to piss, can we stop?"

The driver, a tense-looking woman, growled something, but stopped the bus on the wide, weedy roadside; and Shask and another woman got off and pissed in the weeds. There is an enviable simplicity to many acts in a society which has, in all its daily life, only one gender. And which, perhaps—I don't know this but it occurred to me then, while I was ashamed of myself—has no shame?

34/245. (DICTATED) STILL NOTHING FROM KAZA. I THINK I WAS right to give him the ansible. I hope he's in touch with somebody. I wish it was me. I need to know what goes on in the castles.

Anyhow I understand better now what I was seeing at the Games in Reha. There are sixteen adult women for every adult man. One conception in six or so is male, but a lot of nonviable male fetuses and defective male births bring it down to one in sixteen by puberty. My ancestors must have really had fun playing with these people's chromosomes. I feel guilty, even if it was a million years ago. I have to learn to do without shame but had better not forget the one good use of guilt. Anyhow. A fairly small town like Reha shares its castle with other towns. That confusing spectacle I was taken to on my tenth day down was Awaga Castle trying to keep its place in the Maingame against a castle from up north, and losing. Which means Awaga's team can't play in the big game this year in Fadrga, the city south of here, from which the winners go on to compete in the *big* big game at Zask, where people come from all over the continent—hundreds of contestants and thousands of spectators. I saw some holos of last year's Maingame at Zask. There were 1,280 players, the comment said, and forty balls in play. It looked to me like a total mess, my idea of a battle between two unarmed armies, but I gather that great skill and strategy is involved. All the members of the winning team get a special title for the year, and another one for life, and bring glory back to their various castles and the towns that support them.

I can now get some sense of how this works, see the system from outside it, because the college doesn't support a castle. People here aren't obsessed with sports and athletes and sexy sires the way the young women in Reha were, and some of the older ones. It's a kind of obligatory obsession. Cheer your team, support your brave men, adore your local hero. It makes sense. Given their situation, they need strong, healthy men at their fuckery; it's social selection reinforcing natural selection. But I'm glad to get away from the rah-rah and the swooning and the posters of fellows with swelling muscles and huge penises and bedroom eyes.

I have made Resehavanar's Choice. I chose the option: Less than the truth. Shoggrad and Skodr and the other teachers, professors we'd call them, are intelligent, enlightened people, perfectly capable of understanding the concept of space travel, etc., making decisions about technological innovation, etc. I limit my answers to their questions to technology. I let them assume, as most people naturally assume, particularly people from a monoculture, that our society is pretty much like theirs. When they find how it differs, the effect will be revolutionary, and I have no mandate, reason, or wish to cause such a revolution on Seggri.

Their gender imbalance has produced a society in which, as far as I can tell, the men have all the privilege and the women have all the power. It's obviously a stable arrangement. According to their histories, it's lasted at least two millennia, and probably in some form or another much longer than that. But it could be quickly and disastrously destabilised by contact with us, by their experiencing the human norm. I don't know if the men would cling to their privileged status or demand freedom, but surely the women would resist giving up their power, and their sexual system and affectional relationships would break down. Even if they learned to undo the genetic program that was inflicted on them, it would take several generations to restore normal gender distribution. I can't be the whisper that starts that avalanche.

34/266. (DICTATED) SKODR GOT NOWHERE WITH THE MEN OF Awaga Castle. She had to make her inquiries very cautiously, since it would endanger Kaza if she told them he was an alien or in any way unique. They'd take it as a claim of superiority, which he'd have to defend in trials of strength and skill. I gather that the hierarchies within the castles are a rigid framework, within which a man moves up or down issuing challenges and winning or losing obligatory and optional trials. The sports and games the women watch are only the showpieces of an endless series of competitions going on inside the castles. As an untrained, grown man Kaza would be at a total disadvantage in such trials. The only way he might get out of them, she said, would be by feigning illness or idiocy. She thinks he must have done so, since he is at least alive; but that's all she could find out—"The man who was cast away at Taha-Reha is alive."

Although the women feed, house, clothe, and support the lords of the castle, they evidently take their noncooperation for granted. She seemed glad to get even that scrap of information. As I am.

But we have to get Kaza out of there. The more I hear about it from Skodr the more dangerous it sounds. I keep thinking "spoiled brats!" but actually these men must be more like soldiers in the training camps that militarists have. Only the training never ends. As they win trials they gain all kinds of titles and ranks you could translate as "generals" and the other names militarists have for all their power-grades. Some of the "generals," the Lords and Masters and so on, are the sports idols, the darlings of the fuckeries, like the one poor Shask adored; but as they get older apparently they often trade glory among the women for power among the men, and become tyrants within their castle, bossing the "lesser" men around, until they're overthrown, kicked out. Old sires often live alone, it seems, in little houses away from the main castle, and are considered crazy and dangerous—rogue males.

It sounds like a miserable life. All they're allowed to do after age eleven is compete at games and sports inside the castle, and compete in the fuckeries, after they're fifteen or so, for money and number of fucks and so on. Nothing else. No options. No trades. No skills of making. No travel unless they play in the big games. They aren't allowed into the colleges to gain any kind of freedom of mind. I asked Skodr why an intelligent man couldn't at least come study in the college, and she told me that learning was very bad for men: it weakens a man's sense of honor, makes his muscles flabby, and leaves him impotent. "'What goes to the brain takes from the testicles,'" she said. "Men have to be sheltered from education for their own good."

I tried to "be water," as I was taught, but I was disgusted. Probably she felt it, because after a while she told me about "the secret college." Some women in colleges do smuggle information to men in castles. The poor things meet secretly and teach each other. In the castles, homosexual relationships are encouraged among boys under fifteen, but not officially tolerated among grown men; she says the "secret colleges" often are run by the homosexual men. They have to be secret because if they're caught reading or talking about ideas they may be punished by their Lords and Masters. There have been some interesting works from the "secret colleges," Skodr said, but she had to think to come up with examples. One was a man who had smuggled out an interesting mathematical theorem, and one was a painter whose landscapes, though primitive in technique, were admired by professionals of the art. She couldn't remember his name.

Arts, sciences, all learning, all professional techniques, are *haggyad*, skilled work. They're all taught at the colleges, and there are no divisions and few specialists. Teachers and students cross and mix fields all the time, and being a famous scholar in one field doesn't keep you from being a student in another. Skodr is a vev of physiology, writes plays, and is currently studying history with one of the history vevs. Her thinking is informed and lively and fearless. My School on Hain could learn from this college. It's a wonderful place, full of free minds. But only minds of one gender. A hedged freedom.

I hope Kaza has found a secret college or something, some way to fit in at the castle. He's strong, but these men have trained for years for the games they play. And a lot of the games are violent. The women say don't worry, we don't let the men kill each other, we protect them, they're our treasures. But I've seen men carried off with concussions, on the holos of their martial-art fights, where they throw each other around spectacularly. "Only inexperienced fighters get hurt." Very reassuring.

And they wrestle bulls. And in that melee they call the Maingame they break each other's legs and ankles deliberately. "What's a hero without a limp?" the women say. Maybe that's the safe thing to do, get your leg broken so you don't have to prove you're a hero any more. But what else might Kaza have to prove?

I asked Shask to let me know if she ever heard of him being at the Reha fuckery. But Awaga Castle services (that's their word, the same word they use for their bulls) four towns, so he might get sent to one of the others. But probably not, because men who don't win at things aren't allowed to go to the fuckeries. Only the champions. And boys between fifteen and nineteen, the ones the older women call *dippida*, baby animals— puppy, kitty, lamby. They use the dippida for pleasure. They only pay for a champion when they go to the fuckery to get pregnant. But Kaza's thirty-six, he isn't a puppy or a kitten or a lamb. He's a man, and this is a terrible place to be a man.

Kaza Agad had been killed; the Lords of Awaga Castle finally disclosed the fact, but not the circumstances. A year later, Merriment radioed her lander and left Seggri for Hain. Her recommendation was to observe and avoid. The Stabiles, however, decided to send another pair of observers; these were both women, Mobiles Alee Iyoo and Zerin Wu. They lived for eight years on Seggri, after the third year as First Mobiles; Iyoo stayed as Ambassador another fifteen years. They made Resehavanar's Choice as "all the truth slowly." A limit of two hundred visitors from offworld was set. During the next several generations the people of Seggri, becoming accustomed to the alien presence, considered their own options as members of the Ekumen. Proposals for a planetwide referendum on genetic alteration were abandoned, since the men's vote

*would be insignificant unless the women's vote were
handicapped. As of the date of this report the Seggri
have not undertaken major genetic alteration, though
they have learned and applied various repair techniques,
which have resulted in a higher proportion of full-term
male infants; the gender balance now stands at about 12:1.
    The following is a memoir given to Ambassador Eritho
te Ves in 93/1569 by a woman in Ush on Seggri.*

YOU ASKED ME, DEAR FRIEND, TO TELL YOU ANYTHING I MIGHT like people on other worlds to know about my life and my world. That's not easy! Do I want anybody anywhere else to know anything about my life? I know how strange we seem to all the others, the half-and-half races; I know they think us backward, provincial, even perverse. Maybe in a few more decades we'll decide that we should remake ourselves. I won't be alive then; I don't think I'd want to be. I like my people. I like our fierce, proud, beautiful men, I don't want them to become like women. I like our trustful, powerful, generous women, I don't want them to become like men. And yet I see that among you each man has his own being and nature, each woman has hers, and I can hardly say what it is I think we would lose.

When I was a child I had a brother a year and a half younger than me. His name was Ittu. My mother had gone to the city and paid five years' savings for my sire, a Master Champion in the Dancing. Ittu's sire was an old fellow at our village fuckery; they called him "Master Fallback." He'd never been a champion at anything, hadn't sired a child for years, and was only too glad to fuck for free. My mother always laughed about it—she was still suckling me, she didn't even use a preventive, and she tipped him two coppers! When she found herself pregnant she was furious. When they tested and found it was a male fetus she was even more disgusted at having, as they say, to wait for the miscarriage. But when Ittu was born sound and healthy, she gave the old sire two hundred coppers, all the cash she had.

He wasn't delicate like so many boy babies, but how can you keep from protecting and cherishing a boy? I don't remember when I wasn't looking after Ittu, with it all very clear in my head what Little Brother should do and shouldn't do and all the perils I must keep him from. I was proud of my responsibility, and vain, too, because I had a brother to look after. Not one other motherhouse in my village had a son still living at home.

Ittu was a lovely child, a star. He had the fleecy soft hair that's common in my part of Ush, and big eyes; his nature was sweet and cheerful, and he was very bright. The other children loved him and always wanted to play with him, but he and I were happiest playing by ourselves, long elaborate games of make-believe. We had a herd of twelve cattle an old woman of the village had carved from gourd-shell for Ittu—people always gave him presents—and they were the actors in our dearest game. Our cattle lived in a country called Shush, where they had great adventures, climbing mountains, discovering new lands, sailing on rivers, and so on. Like any herd, like our village herd, the old cows were the leaders; the bull lived apart; the other males were gelded; and the heifers were the adventurers. Our bull would make ceremonial visits to service the cows, and then he might have to go fight with men at Shush Castle. We made the castle of clay and the men of sticks, and the bull always won, knocking the stick-men to pieces. Then sometimes he knocked the castle to pieces too. But the best of our stories were told with two of the heifers. Mine was named Op and my brother's was Utti. Once our hero heifers were having a great adventure on the stream that runs past our village, and their boat got away from us. We found it caught against a log far downstream where the stream was deep and quick. My heifer was still in it. We both dived and dived, but we never found Utti. She had drowned. The Cattle of Shush had a great funeral for her, and Ittu cried very bitterly.

He mourned his brave little toy cow so long that I asked Djerdji the cattleherd if we could work for her, because I thought being with the real cattle might cheer Ittu up. She was glad to get two cowhands for free (when Mother found out we were really working, she made Djerdji pay us a quarter-copper a day). We rode two big, goodnatured old cows, on saddles so big Ittu could lie down on his. We took a herd of two-year-old calves out onto the desert every day to forage for the *edta* that grows best when it's grazed. We were supposed to keep them from wandering off and from trampling streambanks, and when they wanted to settle down and chew the cud we were supposed to gather them in a place where their droppings would nourish useful plants. Our old mounts did most of the work. Mother came out and checked on what we were doing and decided it was all right, and being out in the desert all day was certainly keeping us fit and healthy.

We loved our riding cows, but they were serious-minded and responsible, rather like the grown-ups in our motherhouse. The calves were something else; they were all riding breed, not fine animals of course, just villagebred; but living on edta they were fat and had plenty of spirit. Ittu and I rode them bareback with a rope rein. At first we always ended up on our own backs watching a calf's heels and tail flying off. By the end of a year we were good riders, and took to training our mounts to tricks, trading mounts at a full run, and hornvaulting. Ittu was a marvelous hornvaulter. He trained a big three-year-old roan ox with lyre horns, and the two of them danced like the finest vaulters of the great castles that we saw on the holos. We couldn't keep our excellence to ourselves out in the desert; we started showing off to the other children, inviting them to come out to Salt Springs to see our Great Trick Riding Show. And so of course the adults got to hear of it.

My mother was a brave woman, but that was too much for even her, and she said to me in cold fury, "I trusted you to look after Ittu. You let me down."

All the others had been going on and on about endangering the precious life of a boy, the Vial of Hope, the Treasurehouse of Life, and so on, but it was what my mother said that hurt.

"I do look after Ittu, and he looks after me," I said to her, in that passion of justice that children know, the birthright we seldom honor. "We both know what's dangerous and we don't do stupid things and we know our cattle and we do everything together. When he has to go to the castle he'll have to do lots more dangerous things, but at least he'll already know how to do one of them. And there he has to do them alone, but we did everything together. And I didn't let you down."

My mother looked at us. I was nearly twelve, Ittu was ten. She burst into tears, she sat down on the dirt and wept aloud. Ittu and I both went to her and hugged her and cried. Ittu said, "I won't go. I won't go to the damned castle. They can't make me!"

And I believed him. He believed himself. My mother knew better.

Maybe some day it will be possible for a boy to choose his life. Among your peoples a man's body does not shape his fate, does it? Maybe some day that will be so here.

Our Castle, Hidjegga, had of course been keeping their eye on Ittu ever since he was born; once a year Mother would send them the doctor's report on him, and when he was five Mother and her wives took him out there for the ceremony of Confirmation. Ittu had been embarrassed, disgusted, and flattered. He told me in secret, "There were all these old *men* that smelled funny and they made me take off my clothes and they had these measuring things and they measured my peepee! And they said it was very good. They said it was a good one. What happens when you descend?" It wasn't the first question he had ever asked me that I couldn't answer, and as usual I made up the answer. "Descend means you can have babies," I said, which, in a way, wasn't so far off the mark.

Some castles, I am told, prepare boys of nine and ten for the Severance, woo them with visits from older boys, tickets to games, tours of the park and the buildings, so that they may be quite eager to go to the castle when they turn eleven. But we "outyonders," villagers of the edge of the desert, kept to the harsh old-fashioned ways. Aside from Confirmation, a boy had no contact at all with men until his eleventh birthday. On that day everybody he had ever known brought him to the Gate and gave him to the strangers with whom he would live the rest of his life. Men and women alike believed and still believe that this absolute severance makes the man.

Vev Ushiggi, who had borne a son and had a grandson, and had been mayor five or six times, and was held in great esteem even though she'd never had much money, heard Ittu say that he wouldn't go to the damned Castle. She came next day to our motherhouse and asked to talk to him. He told me what she said. She didn't do any wooing or sweetening. She told him that he was born to the service of his people and had one responsibility, to sire children when he got old enough; and one duty, to be a strong, brave man, stronger and braver than other men, so that women would choose him to sire their children. She said he had to live in the Castle because men could not live among women. At this, Ittu asked her, "Why can't they?"

"You did?" I said, awed by his courage, for Vev Ushiggi was a formidable old woman.

"Yes. And she didn't really answer. She took a long time. She looked at me and then she looked off somewhere and then she stared at me for a long time and then finally she said, 'Because we would destroy them.'"

"But that's crazy," I said. "Men are our treasures. What did she say that for?"

Ittu, of course, didn't know. But he thought hard about what she had said, and I think nothing she could have said would have so impressed him.

After discussion, the village elders and my mother and her wives decided that Ittu could go on practicing hornvaulting, because it really would be a useful skill for him in the Castle; but he could not herd cattle any longer, nor go with me when I did, nor join in any of the work children of the village did, nor their games. "You've done everything together with Po," they told him, "but she should be doing things together with the other girls, and you should be doing things by yourself, the way men do."

They were always very kind to Ittu, but they were stern with us girls; if they saw us even talking with Ittu they'd tell us to go on about our work, leave the boy alone. When we disobeyed—when Ittu and I sneaked off and met at Salt Springs to ride together, or just hid out in our old playplace down in the draw by the stream to talk—he got treated with cold silence to shame him, but I got punished. A day locked in the cellar of the old fiber-processing mill, which was what my village used for a jail; next time it was two days; and the third time they caught us alone together, they locked me in that cellar for ten days. A young woman called Fersk brought me food once a day and made sure I had enough water and wasn't sick, but she didn't speak; that's how they always used to punish people in the villages. I could hear the other children going by up on the street in the evening. It would get dark at last and I could sleep. All day I had nothing to do, no work, nothing to think about except the scorn and contempt they held me in for betraying their trust, and the injustice of my getting punished when Ittu didn't.

When I came out, I felt different. I felt like something had closed up inside me while I was closed up in that cellar.

When we ate at the motherhouse they made sure Ittu and I didn't sit near each other. For a while we didn't even talk to each other. I went back to school and work. I didn't know what Ittu was doing all day. I didn't think about it. It was only fifty days to his birthday.

One night I got into bed and found a note under my clay pillow: *in the draw to-nt.* Ittu never could spell; what writing he knew I had taught him in secret. I was frightened and angry, but I waited an hour till everybody was asleep, and got up and crept outside into the windy, starry night, and ran to the draw. It was late in the dry season and the stream was barely running. Ittu was there, hunched up with his arms round his knees, a little lump of shadow on the pale, cracked clay at the waterside.

The first thing I said was, "You want to get me locked up again? They said next time it would be thirty days!"

"They're going to lock me up for fifty years," Ittu said, not looking at me.

"What am I supposed to do about it? It's the way it has to be! You're a man. You have to do what men do. They won't lock you up, anyway, you get to play games and come to town to do service and all that. You don't even know what being locked up is!"

"I want to go to Seradda," Ittu said, talking very fast, his eyes shining as he looked up at me. "We could take the riding cows to the bus station in Redang, I saved my money, I have twenty-three coppers, we could take the bus to Seradda. The cows would come back home if we turned them loose."

"What do you think you'd do in Seradda?" I asked, disdainful but curious. Nobody from our village had ever been to the capital.

"The Ekkamen people are there," he said.

"The Ekumen," I corrected him. "So what?"

"They could take me away," Ittu said.

I felt very strange when he said that. I was still angry and still disdainful but a sorrow was rising in me like dark water. "Why would they do that? What would they talk to some little boy for? How would you find them? Twenty-three coppers isn't enough anyway. Seradda's way far off. That's a really stupid idea. You can't do that."

"I thought you'd come with me," Ittu said. His voice was softer, but didn't shake.

"I wouldn't do a stupid thing like that," I said furiously.

"All right," he said. "But you won't tell. Will you?"

"No, I won't tell!" I said. "But you can't run away, Ittu. You can't. It would be—it would be dishonorable."

This time when he answered his voice shook. "I don't care," he said. "I don't care about honor. I want to be free!"

We were both in tears. I sat down by him and we leaned together the way we used to, and cried a while; not long; we weren't used to crying.

"You can't do it," I whispered to him. "It won't work, Ittu."

He nodded, accepting my wisdom.

"It won't be so bad at the Castle," I said.

After a minute he drew away from me very slightly.

"We'll see each other," I said.

He said only, "When?"

"At games. I can watch you. I bet you'll be the best rider and horn-vaulter there. I bet you win all the prizes and get to be a Champion."

He nodded, dutiful. He knew and I knew that I had betrayed our love and our birthright of justice. He knew he had no hope.

That was the last time we talked together alone, and almost the last time we talked together.

Ittu ran away about ten days after that, taking the riding cow and heading for Redang; they tracked him easily and had him back in the village before nightfall. I don't know if he thought I had told them where he would be going. I was so ashamed of not having gone with him that I could not look at him. I kept away from him; they didn't have to keep me away any more. He made no effort to speak to me.

I was beginning my puberty, and my first blood was the night before Ittu's birthday. Menstruating women are not allowed to come near the Gates at conservative castles like ours, so when Ittu was made a man I stood far back among a few other girls and women, and could not see much of the ceremony. I stood silent while they sang, and looked down at the dirt and my new sandals and my feet in the sandals, and felt the ache and tug of my womb and the secret movement of the blood, and grieved. I knew even then that this grief would be with me all my life.

Ittu went in and the Gates closed.

He became a Young Champion Hornvaulter, and for two years, when he was eighteen and nineteen, came a few times to service in our village, but I never saw him. One of my friends fucked with him and started to tell me about it, how nice he was, thinking I'd like to hear, but I shut her up and walked away in a blind rage which neither of us understood.

He was traded away to a castle on the east coast when he was twenty. When my daughter was born I wrote him, and several times after that, but he never answered my letters.

I don't know what I've told you about my life and my world. I don't know if it's what I want you to know. It is what I had to tell.

> *The following is a short story written in 93/1586 by a popular writer of the city of Adr, Sem Gridji. The classic literature of Seggri was the narrative poem and the drama. Classical poems and plays were written collaboratively, in the original version and also by re-writers of subsequent generations, usually anonymous. Small value was placed on preserving a "true" text, since the work was seen as an ongoing process. Probably under Ekumenical influence, individual writers in the late sixteenth century began writing short prose narratives, historical and fictional. The genre became popular, particularly in the cities, though it never obtained the immense audience of the great classical epics and plays. Literally everyone knew the plots and many quotations from the epics and plays, from books and holo, and almost every adult woman had seen or participated in a staged performance of several of them.*

They were one of the principal unifying influences of
the Seggrian monoculture. The prose narrative, read
in silence, served rather as a device by which the
culture might question itself, and a tool for individual
moral self-examination. Conservative Seggrian
women disapproved of the genre as antagonistic to the
intensely cooperative, collaborative structure of their
society. Fiction was not included in the curriculum of
the literature departments of the colleges, and was often
dismissed contemptuously—"fiction is for men."
   Sem Gridji published three books of stories. Her bare,
blunt style is characteristic of the Seggrian short story.

Love Out of Place by Sem Gridji

AZAK GREW UP IN A MOTHERHOUSE IN THE DOWNRIVER QUARTER,
near the textile mills. She was a bright girl, and her family and neighborhood were proud to gather the money to send her to college. She came
back to the city as a starting manager at one of the mills. Azak worked
well with other people; she prospered. She had a clear idea of what she
wanted to do in the next few years: to find two or three partners with
whom to found a daughterhouse and a business.

   A beautiful woman in the prime of youth, Azak took great pleasure in
sex, especially liking intercourse with men. Though she saved money for
her plan of founding a business, she also spent a good deal at the fuckery,
going there often, sometimes hiring two men at once. She liked to see
how they incited each other to prowess beyond what they would have
achieved alone, and shamed each other when they failed. She found a
flaccid penis very disgusting, and did not hesitate to send away a man
who could not penetrate her three or four times an evening.

   The castle of her district bought a Young Champion at the Southeast

Castles Dance Tournament, and soon sent him to the fuckery. Having seen him dance in the finals on the holovision and been captivated by his flowing, graceful style and his beauty, Azak was eager to have him service her. His price was twice that of any other man there, but she did not hesitate to pay it. She found him handsome and amiable, eager and gentle, skillful and compliant. In their first evening they came to orgasm together five times. When she left she gave him a large tip. Within the week she was back, asking for Toddra. The pleasure he gave her was exquisite, and soon she was quite obsessed with him.

"I wish I had you all to myself," she said to him one night as they lay still conjoined, languorous and fulfilled.

"That is my heart's desire," he said. "I wish I were your servant. None of the other women that come here arouse me. I don't want them. I want only you."

She wondered if he was telling the truth. The next time she came, she inquired casually of the manager if Toddra were as popular as they had hoped. "No," the manager said. "Everybody else reports that he takes a lot of arousing, and is sullen and careless towards them."

"How strange," Azak said.

"Not at all," said the manager. "He's in love with you."

"A man in love with a woman?" Azak said, and laughed.

"It happens all too often," the manager said.

"I thought only women fell in love," said Azak.

"Women fall in love with a man, sometimes, and that's bad too," said the manager. "May I warn you, Azak? Love should be between women. It's out of place here. It can never come to any good end. I hate to lose the money, but I wish you'd fuck with some of the other men and not always ask for Toddra. You're encouraging him, you see, in something that does harm to him."

"But he and you are making lots of money from me!" said Azak, still taking it as a joke.

"He'd make more from other women if he wasn't in love with you," said the manager. To Azak that seemed a weak argument against the pleasure she had in Toddra, and she said, "Well, he can fuck them all when I've done with him, but for now, I want him."

After their intercourse that evening, she said to Toddra, "The manager here says you're in love with me."

"I told you I was," Toddra said. "I told you I wanted to belong to you, to serve you, you alone. I would die for you, Azak."

"That's foolish," she said.

"Don't you like me? Don't I please you?"

"More than any man I ever knew," she said, kissing him. "You are beautiful and utterly satisfying, my sweet Toddra."

"You don't want any of the other men here, do you?" he asked.

"No. They're all ugly fumblers, compared to my beautiful dancer."

"Listen, then," he said, sitting up and speaking very seriously. He was a slender man of twenty-two, with long, smooth-muscled limbs, wide-set eyes, and a thin-lipped, sensitive mouth. Azak lay stroking his thigh, thinking how lovely and lovable he was. "I have a plan," he said. "When I dance, you know, in the story-dances, I play a woman, of course; I've done it since I was twelve. People always say they can't believe I really am a man, I play a woman so well. If I escaped—from here, from the Castle—as a woman—I could come to your house as a servant—"

"What?" cried Azak, astounded.

"I could live there," he said urgently, bending over her. "With you. I would always be there. You could have me every night. It would cost you nothing, except my food. I would serve you, service you, sweep your house, do anything, anything, Azak, please, my beloved, my mistress, let me be yours!" He saw that she was still incredulous, and hurried on, "You could send me away when you got tired of me—"

"If you tried to go back to the Castle after an escapade like that they'd whip you to death, you idiot!"

"I'm valuable," he said. "They'd punish me, but they wouldn't damage me."

"You're wrong. You haven't been dancing, and your value here has slipped because you don't perform well with anybody but me. The manager told me so."

Tears stood in Toddra's eyes. Azak disliked giving him pain, but she was genuinely shocked at his wild plan. "And if you were discovered, my dear," she said more gently, "I would be utterly disgraced. It is a very childish plan, Toddra. Please never dream of such a thing again. But I am truly, truly fond of you, I adore you and want no other man but you. Do you believe that, Toddra?"

He nodded. Restraining his tears, he said, "For now."

"For now and for a long, long, long time! My dear, sweet, beautiful dancer, we have each other as long as we want, years and years! Only do your duty by the other women that come, so that you don't get sold away by your Castle, please! I couldn't bear to lose you, Toddra." And she clasped him passionately in her arms, and arousing him at once, opened to him, and soon both were crying out in the throes of delight.

Though she could not take his love entirely seriously, since what could come of such a misplaced emotion, except such foolish schemes as he had proposed?—still he touched her heart, and she felt a tenderness towards him that greatly enhanced the pleasure of their intercourse. So for more than a year she spent two or three nights a week with him at the fuckery, which was as much as she could afford. The manager, trying still to discourage his love, would not lower Toddra's fee, even though he was unpopular among the other clients of the fuckery; so Azak spent a great deal of money on him, although he would never, after the first night, accept a tip from her.

Then a woman who had not been able to conceive with any of the sires at the fuckery tried Toddra, and at once conceived, and being tested found the fetus to be male. Another woman conceived by him, again a male fetus. At once Toddra was in demand as a sire. Women began coming from all over the city to be serviced by him. This meant, of course, that he must be free during their period of ovulation. There were now many evenings that he could not meet Azak, for the manager was not to be bribed. Toddra disliked his popularity, but Azak soothed and reassured him, telling him how proud she was of him, and how his work would never interfere with their love. In fact, she was not altogether sorry that he was so much in demand, for she had found another person with whom she wanted to spend her evenings.

This was a young woman named Zedr, who worked in the mill as a machine-repair specialist. She was tall and handsome; Azak noticed first how freely and strongly she walked and how proudly she stood. She found a pretext to make her acquaintance. It seemed to Azak that Zedr admired her; but for a long time each behaved to the other as a friend only, making no sexual advances. They were much in each other's company, going to games and dances together, and Azak found that she enjoyed this open and sociable life better than always being in the fuckery alone with Toddra. They talked about how they might set up a machine-repair service in partnership. As time went on, Azak found that Zedr's beautiful body was always in her thoughts. At last, one evening in her singlewoman's flat, she told her friend that she loved her, but did not wish to burden their friendship with an unwelcome desire.

Zedr replied, "I have wanted you ever since I first saw you, but I didn't want to embarrass you with my desire. I thought you preferred men."

"Until now I did, but I want to make love with you," Azak said.

She found herself quite timid at first, but Zedr was expert and subtle, and could prolong Azak's orgasms till she found such consummation as she had not dreamed of. She said to Zedr, "You have made me a woman."

"Then let's make each other wives," said Zedr joyfully.

They married, moved to a house in the west of the city, and left the mill, setting up in business together.

All this time, Azak had said nothing of her new love to Toddra, whom she had seen less and less often. A little ashamed of her cowardice, she reassured herself that he was so busy performing as a sire that he would not really miss her. After all, despite his romantic talk of love, he was a man, and to a man fucking is the most important thing, instead of being merely one element of love and life as it is to a woman.

When she married Zedr, she sent Toddra a letter, saying that their lives had drifted apart, and she was now moving away and would not see him again, but would always remember him fondly.

She received an immediate answer from Toddra, a letter begging her to come and talk with him, full of avowals of unchanging love, badly spelled and almost illegible. The letter touched, embarrassed, and shamed her, and she did not answer it.

He wrote again and again, and tried to reach her on the holonet at her new business. Zedr urged her not to make any response, saying, "It would be cruel to encourage him."

Their new business went well from the start. They were home one evening busy chopping vegetables for dinner when there was a knock at the door. "Come in," Zedr called, thinking it was Chochi, a friend they were considering as a third partner. A stranger entered, a tall, beautiful woman with a scarf over her hair. The stranger went straight to Azak, saying in a strangled voice, "Azak, Azak, please, please let me stay with you." The scarf fell back from his long hair. Azak recognised Toddra.

She was astonished and a little frightened, but she had known Toddra a long time and been very fond of him, and this habit of affection made her put out her hands to him in greeting. She saw fear and despair in his face, and was sorry for him.

But Zedr, guessing who he was, was both alarmed and angry. She kept the chopping knife in her hand. She slipped from the room and called the city police.

When she returned she saw the man pleading with Azak to let him stay hidden in their household as a servant. "I will do anything," he said. "Please, Azak, my only love, please! I can't live without you. I can't service those women, those strangers who only want to be impregnated. I can't dance any more. I think only of you, you are my only hope. I will be a woman, no one will know. I'll cut my hair, no one will know!" So he went on, almost threatening in his passion, but pitiful also. Zedr listened coldly, thinking he was mad. Azak listened with pain and shame. "No, no, it is not possible," she said over and over, but he would not hear.

When the police came to the door and he realised who they were, he bolted to the back of the house seeking escape. The policewomen caught him in the bedroom; he fought them desperately, and they subdued him brutally. Azak shouted at them not to hurt him, but they paid no heed, twisting his arms and hitting him about the head till he stopped resisting. They dragged him out. The chief of the troop stayed to take evidence. Azak tried to plead for Toddra, but Zedr stated the facts and added that she thought he was insane and dangerous.

After some days, Azak inquired at the police office and was told that Toddra had been returned to his Castle with a warning not to send him to the fuckery again for a year or until the Lords of the Castle found him capable of responsible behavior. She was uneasy thinking of how he might be punished. Zedr said, "They won't hurt him, he's too valuable," just as he himself had said. Azak was glad to believe this. She was, in fact, much relieved to know that he was out of the way.

She and Zedr took Chochi first into their business and then into their household. Chochi was a woman from the dockside quarter, tough and humorous, a hard worker and an undemanding, comfortable lovemaker. They were happy with one another, and prospered.

A year went by, and another year. Azak went to her old quarter to arrange a contract for repair work with two women from the mill where she had first worked. She asked them about Toddra. He was back at the fuckery from time to time, they told her. He had been named the year's Champion Sire of his Castle, and was much in demand, bringing an even higher price, because he impregnated so many women and so many of the conceptions were male. He was not in demand for pleasure, they said, as he had a reputation for roughness and even cruelty. Women asked for him only if they wanted to conceive. Thinking of his gentleness with her, Azak found it hard to imagine him behaving brutally. Harsh punishment at the Castle, she thought, must have altered him. But she could not believe that he had truly changed.

Another year passed. The business was doing very well, and Azak and Chochi both began talking seriously about having children. Zedr was not interested in bearing, though happy to be a mother.

Chochi had a favorite man at their local fuckery to whom she went now and then for pleasure; she began going to him at ovulation, for he had a good reputation as a sire.

Azak had not been to a fuckery since she and Zedr married. She honored fidelity highly, and made love with no one but Zedr and Chochi. When she thought of being impregnated, she found that her old interest in fucking with men had quite died out or even turned to distaste. She did not like the idea of self-impregnation from the sperm bank, but the idea of letting a strange man penetrate her was even more repulsive. Thinking what to do, she thought of Toddra, whom she had truly loved and had pleasure with. He was again a Champion Sire, known throughout the city as a reliable impregnator. There was certainly no other man with whom she could take any pleasure. And he had loved her so much he had put his career and even his life in danger, trying to be with her. That irresponsibility was over and done with. He had never written to her again, and the Castle and the managers of the fuckery would never have let him service women if they thought him mad or untrustworthy. After all this time, she thought, she could go back to him and give him the pleasure he had so desired.

She notified the fuckery of the expected period of her next ovulation, requesting Toddra. He was already engaged for that period, and they offered her another sire; but she preferred to wait till the next month.

Chochi had conceived, and was elated. "Hurry up, hurry up!" she said to Azak. "We want twins!"

Azak found herself looking forward to being with Toddra. Regretting the violence of their last encounter and the pain it must have given him, she wrote the following letter to him:

> *"My dear, I hope our long separation and the distress of our last meeting will be forgotten in the joy of being together again, and that you still love me as I still love you. I shall be very proud to bear your child, and let us hope it may be a son! I am impatient to see you again, my beautiful dancer. Your Azak."*

There had not been time for him to answer this letter when her ovulation period began. She dressed in her best clothes. Zedr still distrusted Toddra and had tried to dissuade her from going to him; she bade her "Good luck!" rather sulkily. Chochi hung a mother-charm around her neck, and she went off.

There was a new manager on duty at the fuckery, a coarse-faced young woman who told her, "Call out if he gives you any trouble. He may be a Champion but he's rough, and we don't let him get away with hurting anybody."

"He won't hurt me," Azak said, smiling, and went eagerly into the familiar room where she and Toddra had enjoyed each other so often. He was standing waiting at the window just as he had used to stand. When he turned he looked just as she remembered, long-limbed, his silky hair flowing like water down his back, his wide-set eyes gazing at her.

"Toddra!" she said, coming to him with outstretched hands.

He took her hands and said her name.

"Did you get my letter? Are you happy?"

"Yes," he said, smiling.

"And all that unhappiness, all that foolishness about love, is it over? I am so sorry you were hurt, Toddra, I don't want any more of that. Can we just be ourselves and be happy together as we used to be?"

"Yes, all that is over," he said. "And I am happy to see you." He drew her gently to him. Gently he began to undress her and caress her body, just as he had used to, knowing what gave her pleasure, and she remembering what gave him pleasure. They lay down naked together. She was fondling his erect penis, aroused and yet a little reluctant to be penetrated after so long, when he moved his arm as if uncomfortable. Drawing away from him a little, she saw that he had a knife in his hand, which he must have hidden in the bed. He was holding it concealed behind his back.

Her womb went cold, but she continued to fondle his penis and testicles, not daring to say anything and not able to pull away, for he was holding her close with the other hand.

Suddenly he moved onto her and forced his penis into her vagina with a thrust so painful that for an instant she thought it was the knife. He ejaculated instantly. As his body arched she writhed out from under him, scrambled to the door, and ran from the room crying for help.

He pursued her, striking with the knife, stabbing her in the shoulder-blade before the manager and other women and men seized him. The men were very angry and treated him with a violence which the manager's protests did not lessen. Naked, bloody, and half-conscious, he was bound and taken away immediately to the Castle.

Everyone now gathered around Azak, and her wound, which was slight, was cleaned and covered. Shaken and confused, she could ask only, "What will they do to him?"

"What do you think they do to a murdering rapist? Give him a prize?" the manager said. "They'll geld him."

"But it was my fault," Azak said.

The manager stared at her and said, "Are you mad? Go home."

She went back into the room and mechanically put on her clothes. She looked at the bed where they had lain. She stood at the window where Toddra had stood. She remembered how she had seen him dance long ago in the contest where he had first been made champion. She thought, "My life is wrong." But she did not know how to make it right.

> *Alteration in Seggrian social and cultural institutions did not take the disastrous course Merriment feared. It has been slow and its direction is not clear. In 93/1602 Terhada College invited men from two neighboring castles to apply as students, and three men did so. In the next decades, most colleges opened their doors to men. Once they were graduated, male students had to return to their castle, unless they left the planet, since native men were not allowed to live anywhere but as students in a college or in a castle, until the Open Gate Law was passed in 93/1662.*
>
> *Even after passage of that law, the castles remained closed to women; and the exodus of men from the castles was much slower than opponents of the measure feared. Social adjustment to the Open Gate Law has been slow. In several regions programs to train men in basic skills such as farming and construction have met with moderate success; the men work in competitive teams, separate from and managed by the women's companies. A good many Seggri have come to Hain to study in recent years—more men than women, despite the great numerical imbalance that still exists.*
>
> *The following autobiographical sketch by one of these*

men is of particular interest, since he was involved in the
event which directly precipitated the Open Gate Law.

AUTOBIOGRAPHICAL SKETCH
BY MOBILE ARDAR DEZ

I WAS BORN IN EKUMENICAL CYCLE 93, YEAR 1641, IN RAKEDR
on Seggri. Rakedr was a placid, prosperous, conservative town, and I
was brought up in the old way, the petted boychild of a big motherhouse.
Altogether there were seventeen of us, not counting the kitchen staff—a
great-grandmother, two grandmothers, four mothers, nine daughters,
and me. We were well off; all the women were or had been managers
or skilled workers in the Rakedr Pottery, the principal industry of the
town. We kept all the holidays with pomp and energy, decorating the
house from roof to foundation with banners for Hillalli, making fantastic costumes for the Harvest Festival, and celebrating somebody's
birthday every few weeks with gifts all round. I was petted, as I said,
but not, I think, spoiled. My birthday was no grander than my sisters',
and I was allowed to run and play with them just as if I were a girl.
Yet I was always aware, as were they, that our mothers' eyes rested on
me with a different look, brooding, reserved, and sometimes, as I grew
older, desolate.

After my Confirmation, my birthmother or her mother took me to
Rakedr Castle every spring on Visiting Day. The gates of the park, which
had opened to admit me alone (and terrified) for my Confirmation,
remained shut, but rolling stairs were placed against the park walls. Up
these I and a few other little boys from the town climbed, to sit on top
of the park wall in great state, on cushions, under awnings, and watch
demonstration dancing, bull-dancing, wrestling, and other sports on
the great gamefield inside the wall. Our mothers waited below, outside,

in the bleachers of the public field. Men and youths from the Castle sat with us, explaining the rules of the games and pointing out the fine points of a dancer or wrestler, treating us seriously, making us feel important. I enjoyed that very much, but as soon as I came down off the wall and started home it all fell away like a costume shrugged off, a part played in a play; and I went on with my work and play in the motherhouse with my family, my real life.

When I was ten I went to Boys' Class downtown. The class had been set up forty or fifty years before as a bridge between the motherhouses and the Castle, but the Castle, under increasingly reactionary gover-nance, had recently withdrawn from the project. Lord Fassaw forbade his men to go anywhere outside the walls but directly to the fuckery, in a closed car, returning at first light; and so no men were able to teach the class. The townswomen who tried to tell me what to expect when I went to the Castle did not really know much more than I did. However well-meaning they were, they mostly frightened and confused me. But fear and confusion were an appropriate preparation.

I cannot describe the ceremony of Severance. I really cannot describe it. Men on Seggri, in those days, had this advantage: they knew what death is. They had all died once before their body's death. They had turned and looked back at their whole life, every place and face they had loved, and turned away from it as the gate closed.

At the time of my Severance, our small Castle was internally divided into "collegials" and "traditionals," a liberal faction left from the regime of Lord Ishog and a younger, highly conservative faction. The split was already disastrously wide when I came to the Castle. Lord Fassaw's rule had grown increasingly harsh and irrational. He governed by corrup-tion, brutality, and cruelty. All of us who lived there were of course infected, and would have been destroyed if there had not been a strong, constant, moral resistance, centered around Ragaz and Kohadrat, who had been protégés of Lord Ishog. The two men were open partners; their followers were all the homosexuals in the Castle, and a good number of other men and older boys.

My first days and months in the Scrubs' dormitory were a bewildering alternation: terror, hatred, shame, as the boys who had been there a few months or years longer than I were incited to humiliate and abuse the newcomer, in order to make a man of him—and comfort, gratitude, love, as boys who had come under the influence of the collegials offered me secret friendship and protection. They helped me in the games and competitions and took me into their beds at night, not for sex but to keep me from the sexual bullies. Lord Fassaw detested adult homosexuality and would have reinstituted the death penalty if the Town Council had allowed it. Though he did not dare punish Ragaz and Kohadrat, he punished consenting love between older boys with bizarre and appalling physical mutilations—ears cut into fringes, fingers branded with red-hot iron rings. Yet he encouraged the older boys to rape the eleven- and twelve-year-olds, as a manly practice. None of us escaped. We particularly dreaded four youths, seventeen or eighteen years old when I came there, who called themselves the Lordsmen. Every few nights they raided the Scrubs' dormitory for a victim, whom they raped as a group. The collegials protected us as best they could by ordering us to their beds, where we wept and protested loudly, while they pretended to abuse us, laughing and jeering. Later, in the dark and silence, they comforted us with candy, and sometimes, as we grew older, with a desired love, gentle and exquisite in its secrecy.

There was no privacy at all in the Castle. I have said that to women who asked me to describe life there, and they thought they understood me. "Well, everybody shares everything in a motherhouse," they would say, "everybody's in and out of the rooms all the time. You're never really alone unless you have a singlewoman's flat." I could not tell them how different the loose, warm commonality of the motherhouse was from the rigid, deliberate publicity of the forty-bed, brightly-lighted Castle dormitories. Nothing in Rakedr was private: only secret, only silent. We ate our tears.

I grew up; I take some pride in that, along with my profound gratitude to the boys and men who made it possible. I did not kill myself, as several boys did during those years, nor did I kill my mind and soul, as some did so their body could survive. Thanks to the maternal care of the collegials—the resistance, as we came to call ourselves—I grew up.

Why do I say maternal, not paternal? Because there were no fathers in my world. There were only sires. I knew no such word as father or paternal. I thought of Ragaz and Kohadrat as my mothers. I still do.

Fassaw grew quite mad as the years went on, and his hold over the Castle tightened to a deathgrip. The Lordsmen now ruled us all. They were lucky in that we still had a strong Maingame team, the pride of Fassaw's heart, which kept us in the First League, as well as two Champion Sires in steady demand at the town fuckeries. Any protest the resistance tried to bring to the Town Council could be dismissed as typical male whining, or laid to the demoralising influence of the aliens. From the outside Rakedr Castle seemed all right. Look at our great team! Look at our champion studs! The women looked no further.

How could they abandon us?—the cry every Seggrian boy must make in his heart. How could she leave me here? Doesn't she know what it's like? Why doesn't she know? Doesn't she want to know?

"Of course not," Ragaz said to me when I came to him in a passion of righteous indignation, the Town Council having denied our petition to be heard. "Of course they don't want to know how we live. Why do they never come into the castles? Oh, we keep them out, yes; but do you think we could keep them out if they wanted to enter? My dear, we collude with them and they with us in maintaining the great foundation of ignorance and lies on which our civilisation rests."

"Our own mothers abandon us," I said.

"Abandon us? Who feeds us, clothes us, houses us, pays us? We're utterly dependent on them. If ever we made ourselves independent, perhaps we could rebuild society on a foundation of truth."

Independence was as far as his vision could reach. Yet I think his mind groped further, towards what he could not see, the body's obscure, inalterable dream of mutuality.

Our effort to make our case heard at the Council had no effect except within the Castle. Lord Fassaw saw his power threatened. Within a few days Ragaz was seized by the Lordsmen and their bully boys, accused of repeated homosexual acts and treasonable plots, arraigned, and sentenced by the Lord of the Castle. Everyone was summoned to the Gamefield to witness the punishment. A man of fifty with a heart ailment—he had been a Maingame racer in his twenties and had overtrained—Ragaz was tied naked across a bench and beaten with "Lord Long," a heavy leather tube filled with lead weights. The Lordsman Berhed, who wielded it, struck repeatedly at the head, the kidneys, and the genitals. Ragaz died an hour or two later in the infirmary.

The Rakedr Mutiny took shape that night. Kohadrat, older than Ragaz and devastated by his loss, could not restrain or guide us. His vision had been of a true resistance, longlasting and nonviolent, through which the Lordsmen would in time destroy themselves. We had been following that vision. Now we let it go. We dropped the truth and grabbed weapons. "How you play is what you win," Kohadrat said, but we had heard all those old saws. We would not play the patience game any more. We would win, now, once for all.

And we did. We won. We had our victory. Lord Fassaw, the Lordsmen and their bullies had been slaughtered by the time the police got to the Gate.

I remember how those tough women strode in among us, staring at the rooms of the Castle which they had never seen, staring at the mutilated bodies, eviscerated, castrated, headless—at Lordsman Berhed, who had been nailed to the floor with "Lord Long" stuffed down his throat—at us, the rebels, the victors, with our bloody hands and defiant faces—at Kohadrat, whom we thrust forward as our leader, our spokesman.

He stood silent. He ate his tears.

The women drew closer to one another, clutching their guns, staring around. They were appalled, they thought us all insane. Their utter incomprehension drove one of us at last to speak—a young man, Tarsk, who wore the iron ring that had been forced onto his finger when it was red-hot. "They killed Ragaz," he said. "They were all mad. Look." He held out his crippled hand.

The chief of the troop, after a pause, said, "No one will leave here till this is looked into," and marched her women out of the Castle, out of the park, locking the gate behind them, leaving us with our victory.

The hearings and judgments on the Rakedr Mutiny were all broadcast, of course, and the event has been studied and discussed ever since. My own part in it was the murder of the Lordsman Tatiddi. Three of us set on him and beat him to death with exercise-clubs in the gymnasium where we had cornered him.

How we played was what we won.

We were not punished. Men were sent from several castles to form a government over Rakedr Castle. They learned enough of Fassaw's behavior to see the cause of our rebellion, but the contempt of even the most liberal of them for us was absolute. They treated us not as men, but as irrational, irresponsible creatures, untamable cattle. If we spoke they did not answer.

I do not know how long we could have endured that cold regime of shame. It was only two months after the Mutiny that the World Council enacted the Open Gate Law. We told one another that that was our victory, we had made that happen. None of us believed it. We told one another we were free. For the first time in history, any man who wanted to leave his castle could walk out the gate. We were free!

What happened to the free man outside the gate? Nobody had given it much thought.

I was one who walked out the gate, on the morning of the day the law came into force. Eleven of us walked into town together.

Several of us, men not from Rakedr, went to one or another of the fuckeries, hoping to be allowed to stay there; they had nowhere else to go. Hotels and inns of course would not accept men. Those of us who had been children in the town went to our motherhouses.

What is it like to return from the dead? Not easy. Not for the one who returns, nor for his people. The place he occupied in their world has closed up, ceased to be, filled with accumulated change, habit, the doings and needs of others. He has been replaced. To return from the dead is to be a ghost: a person for whom there is no room.

Neither I nor my family understood that, at first. I came back to them at twenty-one as trustingly as if I were the eleven-year-old who had left them, and they opened their arms to their child. But he did not exist. Who was I?

For a long time, months, we refugees from the Castle hid in our motherhouses. The men from other towns all made their way home, usually by begging a ride with teams on tour. There were seven or eight of us in Rakedr, but we scarcely ever saw one another. Men had no place on the street; for hundreds of years a man seen alone on the street had been arrested immediately. If we went out, women ran from us, or reported us, or surrounded and threatened us—"Get back into your Castle where you belong! Get back to the fuckery where you belong! Get out of our city!" They called us drones, and in fact we had no work, no function at all in the community. The fuckeries would not accept us for service, because we had no guarantee of health and good behavior from a castle.

This was our freedom: we were all ghosts, useless, frightened, frightening intruders, shadows in the corners of life. We watched life going on around us—work, love, childbearing, childrearing, getting and spending, making and shaping, governing and adventuring—the women's world, the bright, full, real world—and there was no room in it for us.

All we had ever learned to do was play games and destroy one another.

My mothers and sisters racked their brains, I know, to find some place and use for me in their lively, industrious household. Two old live-in cooks had run our kitchen since long before I was born, so cooking, the one practical art I had been taught in the Castle, was superfluous. They found household tasks for me, but they were all make-work, and they and I knew it. I was perfectly willing to look after the babies, but one of the grandmothers was very jealous of that privilege, and also some of my sisters' wives were uneasy about a man touching their baby. My sister Pado broached the possibility of an apprenticeship in the clay-works, and I leaped at the chance; but the managers of the Pottery, after long discussion, were unable to agree to accept men as employees. Their hormones would make male workers unreliable, and female workers would be uncomfortable, and so on.

The holonews was full of such proposals and discussions, of course, and orations about the unforeseen consequences of the Open Gate Law, the proper place of men, male capacities and limitations, gender as destiny. Feeling against the Open Gate policy ran very strong, and it seemed that every time I watched the holo there was a woman talking grimly about the inherent violence and irresponsibility of the male, his biological unfitness to participate in social and political decision-making. Often it was a man saying the same things. Opposition to the new law had the fervent support of all the conservatives in the castles, who pleaded eloquently for the gates to be closed and men to return to their proper station, pursuing the true, masculine glory of the games and the fuckeries.

Glory did not tempt me, after the years at Rakedr Castle; the word itself had come to mean degradation to me. I ranted against the games and competitions, puzzling most of my family, who loved to watch the Maingames and wrestling, and complained only that the level of excellence of most of the teams had declined since the gates were opened.

And I ranted against the fuckeries, where, I said, men were used as cattle, stud bulls, not as human beings. I would never go there again.

"But my dear boy," my mother said at last, alone with me one evening, "will you live the rest of your life celibate?"

"I hope not," I said.

"Then . . . ?"

"I want to get married."

Her eyes widened. She brooded a bit, and finally ventured, "To a man."

"No. To a woman. I want a normal, ordinary marriage. I want to have a wife and be a wife."

Shocking as the idea was, she tried to absorb it. She pondered, frowning.

"All it means," I said, for I had had a long time with nothing to do but ponder, "is that we'd live together just like any married pair. We'd set up our own daughterhouse, and be faithful to each other, and if she had a child I'd be its lovemother along with her. There isn't any reason why it wouldn't work!"

"Well, I don't know—I don't know of any," said my mother, gentle and judicious, and never happy at saying no to me. "But you do have to find the woman, you know."

"I know," I said glumly.

"It's such a problem for you to meet people," she said. "Perhaps if you went to the fuckery . . . ? I don't see why your own motherhouse couldn't guarantee you just as well as a castle. We could try—?"

But I passionately refused. Not being one of Fassaw's sycophants, I had seldom been allowed to go to the fuckery; and my few experiences there had been unfortunate. Young, inexperienced, and without recommendation, I had been selected by older women who wanted a plaything. Their practiced skill at arousing me had left me humiliated and enraged. They patted and tipped me as they left. That elaborate, mechanical excitation and their condescending coldness were vile to me, after the tenderness of my lover-protectors in the Castle. Yet women attracted me physically as men never had; the beautiful bodies of my sisters and their wives, all around me constantly now, clothed and naked, innocent and sensual, the wonderful heaviness and strength and softness of women's bodies, kept me continually aroused. Every night I masturbated, fantasising my sisters in my arms. It was unendurable. Again I was a ghost, a raging, yearning impotence in the midst of untouchable reality.

I began to think I would have to go back to the Castle. I sank into a deep depression, an inertia, a chill darkness of the mind.

My family, anxious, affectionate, busy, had no idea what to do for me or with me. I think most of them thought in their hearts that it would be best if I went back through the gate.

One afternoon my sister Pado, with whom I had been closest as a child, came to my room—they had cleared out a dormer attic for me, so that I had room at least in the literal sense. She found me in my now constant lethargy, lying on the bed doing nothing at all. She breezed in, and with the indifference women often show to moods and signals, plumped down on the foot of the bed and said, "Hey, what do you know about the man who's here from the Ekumen?"

I shrugged and shut my eyes. I had been having rape fantasies lately. I was afraid of her.

She talked on about the offworlder, who was apparently in Rakedr to study the Mutiny. "He wants to talk to the resistance," she said. "Men like you. The men who opened the gates. He says they won't come forward, as if they were ashamed of being heroes."

"Heroes!" I said. The word in my language is gendered female. It refers to the semi-divine, semi-historic protagonists of the Epics.

"It's what you are," Pado said, intensity breaking through her assumed breeziness. "You took responsibility in a great act. Maybe you did it wrong. Sassume did it wrong in the *Founding of Emmo*, didn't she, she let Faradr get killed. But she was still a hero. She took the responsibility. So did you. You ought to go talk to this Alien. Tell him what happened.

Nobody really knows what happened at the Castle. You owe us the story."

That was a powerful phrase, among my people. "The untold story mothers the lie," was the saying. The doer of any notable act was held literally *accountable* for it to the community.

"So why should I tell it to an Alien?" I said, defensive of my inertia.

"Because he'll listen," my sister said drily. "We're all too damned busy."

It was profoundly true. Pado had seen a gate for me and opened it; and I went through it, having just enough strength and sanity left to do so.

Mobile Noem was a man in his forties, born some centuries earlier on Terra, trained on Hain, widely travelled; a small, yellow-brown, quick-eyed person, very easy to talk to. He did not seem at all masculine to me, at first; I kept thinking he was a woman, because he acted like one. He got right to business, with none of the maneuvering to assert his authority or jockeying for position that men of my society felt obligatory in any relationship with another man. I was used to men being wary, indirect, and competitive. Noem, like a woman, was direct and receptive. He was also as subtle and powerful as any man or woman I had known, even Ragaz. His authority was in fact immense; but he never stood on it. He sat down on it, comfortably, and invited you to sit down with him.

I was the first of the Rakedr mutineers to come forward and tell our story to him. He recorded it, with my permission, to use in making his report to the Stabiles on the condition of our society, "the matter of Seggri," as he called it. My first description of the Mutiny took less than an hour. I thought I was done. I didn't know, then, the inexhaustible desire to learn, to understand, to hear *all* the story, that characterises the Mobiles of the Ekumen. Noem asked questions, I answered; he speculated and extrapolated, I corrected; he wanted details, I furnished them—telling the story of the Mutiny, of the years before it, of the men of the Castle, of the women of the Town, of my people, of my life—little by little, bit by bit, all in fragments, a muddle. I talked to Noem daily for a month. I learned that the story has no beginning, and no story has an end. That the story is all muddle, all middle. That the story is never true, but that the lie is indeed a child of silence.

By the end of the month I had come to love and trust Noem, and of course to depend on him. Talking to him had become my reason for being. I tried to face the fact that he would not stay in Rakedr much longer. I must learn to do without him. Do what? There were things for men to do, ways for men to live, he proved it by his mere existence; but could I find them?

He was keenly aware of my situation, and would not let me withdraw, as I began to do, into the lethargy of fear again; he would not let me be silent. He asked me impossible questions. "What would you be if you could be anything?" he asked me, a question children ask each other.

I answered at once, passionately—"A wife!"

I know now what the flicker that crossed his face was. His quick, kind eyes watched me, looked away, looked back.

"I want my own family," I said. "Not to live in my mothers' house, where I'm always a child. Work. A wife, wives—children—to be a mother. I want life, not games!"

"You can't bear a child," he said gently.

"No, but I can mother one!"

"We gender the word," he said. "I like it better your way. . . . But tell me, Ardar, what are the chances of your marrying—meeting a woman willing to marry a man? It hasn't happened, here, has it?"

I had to say no, not to my knowledge.

"It will happen, certainly, I think," he said (his certainties were always uncertain). "But the personal cost, at first, is likely to be high. Relationships formed against the negative pressure of a society are under terrible strain; they tend to become defensive, over-intense, unpeaceful. They have no room to grow."

"Room!" I said. And I tried to tell him my feeling of having no room in my world, no air to breathe.

He looked at me, scratching his nose; he laughed. "There's plenty of room in the galaxy, you know," he said.

"Do you mean . . . I could . . . That the Ekumen . . ." I didn't even know what the question I wanted to ask was. Noem did. He began to answer it thoughtfully and in detail. My education so far had been so limited, even as regards the culture of my own people, that I would have to attend a college for at least two or three years, in order to be ready to apply to an offworld institution such as the Ekumenical Schools on Hain. Of course, he went on, where I went and what kind of training I chose would depend on my interests, which I would go to a college to discover, since neither my schooling as a child nor my training at the Castle had really given me any idea of what there was to be interested in. The choices offered me had been unbelievably limited, addressing neither the needs of a normally intelligent person nor the needs of my society. And so the Open Gate Law instead of giving me freedom had left me "with no air to breathe but airless Space," said Noem, quoting some poet from some planet somewhere. My head was spinning, full of stars. "Hagka College is quite near Rakedr," Noem said, "did you never think of applying? If only to escape from your terrible Castle?"

I shook my head. "Lord Fassaw always destroyed the application forms when they were sent to his office. If any of us had tried to apply . . ."

"You would have been punished. Tortured, I suppose. Yes. Well, from the little I know of your colleges, I think your life there would be better than it is here, but not altogether pleasant. You will have work to do, a place to be; but you will be made to feel marginal, inferior. Even highly educated, enlightened women have difficulty accepting men as their intellectual equals. Believe me, I have experienced it myself! And because you were trained at the Castle to compete, to want to excel, you may find it hard to be among people who either believe you incapable of excellence, or to whom the concept of competition, of winning and defeating, is valueless. But just there, there is where you will find air to breathe."

Noem recommended me to women he knew on the faculty of Hagka College, and I was enrolled on probation. My family were delighted to pay my tuition. I was the first of us to go to college, and they were genuinely proud of me.

As Noem had predicted, it was not always easy, but there were enough other men there that I found friends and was not caught in the paralysing isolation of the motherhouse. And as I took courage, I made friends among the women students, finding many of them unprejudiced and companionable. In my third year, one of them and I managed, tentatively and warily, to fall in love. It did not work very well or last very long, yet it was a great liberation for both of us, our liberation from the belief that the only communication or commonality possible between us was sexual, that an adult man and woman had nothing to join them but their genitals. Emadr loathed the professionalism of the fuckery as I did, and our lovemaking was always shy and brief. Its true significance was not as a consummation of desire, but as proof that we could trust each other. Where our real passion broke loose was when we lay together talking, telling each other what our lives had been, how we felt about men and women and each other and ourselves, what our nightmares were, what our dreams were. We talked endlessly, in a communion that I will cherish and honor all my life, two young souls finding their wings, flying together, not for long, but high. The first flight is the highest.

Emadr has been dead two hundred years; she stayed on Seggri, married into a motherhouse, bore two children, taught at Hagka, and died in her seventies. I went to Hain, to the Ekumenical Schools, and later to Werel and Yeowe as part of the Mobile's staff; my record is herewith enclosed. I have written this sketch of my life as part of my application to return to Seggri as a Mobile of the Ekumen. I want very much to live among my people, to learn who they are, now that I know with at least an uncertain certainty who I am.

SOLITUDE

*An addition to "POVERTY: The Second Report on
Eleven-Soro" by Mobile Entselenne'temharyonoterregwis
Leaf, by her daughter, Serenity.*

MY MOTHER, A FIELD ETHNOLOGIST, TOOK THE DIFFICULTY OF
learning anything about the people of Eleven-Soro as a personal challenge.
The fact that she used her children to meet that challenge might be seen
as selfishness or as selflessness. Now that I have read her report I know
that she finally thought she had done wrong. Knowing what it cost her, I
wish she knew my gratitude to her for allowing me to grow up as a person.

Shortly after a robot probe reported people of the Hainish Descent
on the eleventh planet of the Soro system, she joined the orbital crew
as backup for the three First Observers down on-planet. She had spent
four years in the tree-cities of nearby Huthu. My brother In Joy Born
was eight years old and I was five; she wanted a year or two of ship duty
so we could spend some time in a Hainish-style school. My brother
had enjoyed the rainforests of Huthu very much, but though he could
brachiate he could barely read, and we were all bright blue with skin
fungus. While Borny learned to read and I learned to wear clothes and
we all had anti-fungus treatments, my mother became as intrigued by
Eleven-Soro as the Observers were frustrated by it.

All this is in her report, but I will say it as I learned it from her, which
helps me remember and understand. The language had been recorded

by the probe and the Observers had spent a year learning it. The many dialectical variations excused their accents and errors, and they reported that language was not a problem. Yet there was a communication problem. The two men found themselves isolated, faced with suspicion or hostility, unable to form any connection with the native men, all of whom lived in solitary houses as hermits, or in pairs. Finding communities of adolescent males, they tried to make contact with them, but when they entered the territory of such a group the boys either fled or rushed desperately at them trying to kill them. The women, who lived in what they called "dispersed villages," drove them away with volleys of stones as soon as they came anywhere near the houses. "I believe," one of them reported, "that the only community activity of the Sorovians is throwing rocks at men."

Neither of them succeeded in having a conversation of more than three exchanges with a man. One of them mated with a woman who came by his camp; he reported that though she made unmistakable and insistent advances, she seemed disturbed by his attempts to converse, refused to answer his questions, and left him, he said, "as soon as she got what she came for."

The woman Observer was allowed to settle in an unused house in a "village" (auntring) of seven houses. She made excellent observations of daily life, insofar as she could see any of it, and had several conversations with adult women and many with children; but she found that she was never asked into another woman's house, nor expected to help or ask for help in any work. Conversation concerning normal activities was unwelcome to the other women; the children, her only informants, called her Aunt Crazy-Jabber. Her aberrant behavior caused increasing distrust and dislike among the women, and they began to keep their children away from her. She left. "There's no way," she told my mother, "for an adult to learn anything. They don't ask questions, they don't answer questions. Whatever they learn, they learn when they're children."

Aha! said my mother to herself, looking at Borny and me. And she requested a family transfer to Eleven-Soro with Observer status. The Stabiles interviewed her extensively by ansible, and talked with Borny and even with me—I don't remember it, but she told me I told the Stabiles all about my new stockings—and agreed to her request. The ship was to stay in close orbit, with the previous Observers in the crew, and she was to keep radio contact with it, daily if possible.

I have a dim memory of the tree-city, and of playing with what must have been a kitten or a ghole-kit on the ship; but my first clear memories are of our house in the auntring. It is half underground, half aboveground, with wattle-and-daub walls. Mother and I are standing outside it in the warm sunshine. Between us is a big mud puddle, into which Borny pours water from a basket; then he runs off to the creek to get more water. I muddle the mud with my hands, deliciously, till it is thick and smooth. I pick up a big double handful and slap it onto the walls where the sticks show through. Mother says, "That's good! That's right!" in our new language, and I realise that this is work, and I am doing it. I am repairing the house. I am making it right, doing it right. I am a competent person.

I have never doubted that, so long as I lived there.

We are inside the house at night, and Borny is talking to the ship on the radio, because he misses talking the old language, and anyway he is supposed to tell them stuff. Mother is making a basket and swearing at the split reeds. I am singing a song to drown out Borny so nobody in the auntring hears him talking funny, and anyway I like singing. I learned this song this afternoon in Hyuru's house. I play every day with Hyuru. "Be aware, listen, listen, be aware," I sing. When Mother stops swearing she listens, and then she turns on the recorder. There is a little fire still left from cooking dinner, which was lovely pigi root, I never get tired of pigi. It is dark and warm and smells of pigi and of burning duhur, which is a strong, sacred smell to drive out magic and bad feelings, and as I sing "Listen, be aware," I get sleepier and sleepier and lean against Mother, who is dark and warm and smells like Mother, strong and sacred, full of good feelings.

Our daily life in the auntring was repetitive. On the ship, later, I learned that people who live in artificially complicated situations call such a life "simple." I never knew anybody, anywhere I have been, who found life simple. I think a life or a time looks simple when you leave out the details, the way a planet looks smooth, from orbit.

Certainly our life in the auntring was easy, in the sense that our needs came easily to hand. There was plenty of food to be gathered or grown and prepared and cooked, plenty of temas to pick and rett and spin and weave for clothes and bedding, plenty of reeds to make baskets and thatch with; we children had other children to play with, mothers to look after us, and a great deal to learn. None of this is simple, though it's all easy enough, when you know how to do it, when you are aware of the details.

It was not easy for my mother. It was hard for her, and complicated. She had to pretend she knew the details while she was learning them, and had to think how to report and explain this way of living to people in another place who didn't understand it. For Borny it was easy until it got hard because he was a boy. For me it was all easy. I learned the work and played with the children and listened to the mothers sing.

The First Observer had been quite right: there was no way for a grown woman to learn how to make her soul. Mother couldn't go listen to another mother sing, it would have been too strange. The aunts all knew she hadn't been brought up well, and some of them taught her a good deal without her realising it. They had decided her mother must have been irresponsible and had gone on scouting instead of settling in an auntring, so that her daughter didn't get educated properly. That's why even the most aloof of the aunts always let me listen with their children, so that I could become an educated person. But of course they couldn't ask another adult into their houses. Borny and I had to tell her all the songs and stories we learned, and then she would tell them to the radio, or we told them to the radio while she listened to us. But she never got it right, not really. How could she, trying to learn it after she'd grown up, and after she'd always lived with magicians?

"Be aware!" She would imitate my solemn and probably irritating imitation of the aunts and the big girls. "Be aware! How many times a day do they say that? Be aware of what? They aren't aware of *what* the ruins are, their own history—they aren't aware of each other! They don't even talk to each other! Be aware, indeed!"

When I told her the stories of the Before Time that Aunt Sadne and Aunt Noyit told their daughters and me, she often heard the wrong things in them. I told her about the People, and she said, "Those are the ancestors of the people here now." When I said, "There aren't any people here now," she didn't understand. "There are persons here now," I said, but she still didn't understand.

Borny liked the story about the Man Who Lived with Women, how he kept some women in a pen, the way some persons keep rats in a pen for eating, and all of them got pregnant, and they each had a hundred babies, and the babies grew up as horrible monsters and ate the man and the mothers and each other. Mother explained to us that that was a parable of the human overpopulation of this planet thousands of years ago. "No, it's not," I said, "it's a moral story."—"Well, yes," Mother said. "The moral is, don't have too many babies."—"No, it's not," I said. "Who could have a hundred babies even if they wanted to? The man was a sorcerer. He did magic. The women did it with him. So their children were monsters."

The key, of course, is the word "tekell," which translates so nicely into the Hainish word "magic," an art or power that violates natural law. It was hard for Mother to understand that some persons truly consider most human relationships unnatural; that marriage, for instance, or government, can be seen as an evil spell woven by sorcerers. It is hard for her people to believe magic.

The ship kept asking if we were all right, and every now and then a

Stabile would hook up the ansible to our radio and grill Mother and us. She always convinced them that she wanted to stay, for despite her frustrations, she was doing the work the First Observers had not been able to do, and Borny and I were happy as mudfish, all those first years. I think Mother was happy too, once she got used to the slow pace and the indirect way she had to learn things. She was lonely, missing other grown-ups to talk to, and told us that she would have gone crazy without us. If she missed sex she never showed it. I think, though, that her report is not very complete about sexual matters, perhaps because she was troubled by them. I know that when we first lived in the auntring, two of the aunts, Hedimi and Behyu, used to meet to make love, and Behyu courted my mother; but Mother didn't understand, because Behyu wouldn't talk the way Mother wanted to talk. She couldn't understand having sex with a person whose house you wouldn't enter.

Once when I was nine or so, and had been listening to some of the older girls, I asked her why didn't she go out scouting. "Aunt Sadne would look after us," I said hopefully. I was tired of being the uneducated woman's daughter. I wanted to live in Aunt Sadne's house and be just like the other children.

"Mothers don't scout," she said, scornfully, like an aunt.

"Yes, they do, sometimes," I insisted. "They have to, or how could they have more than one baby?"

"They go to settled men near the auntring. Behyu went back to the Red Knob Hill Man when she wanted a second child. Sadne goes and sees Downriver Lame Man when she wants to have sex. They know the men around here. None of the mothers scout."

I realised that in this case she was right and I was wrong, but I stuck to my point. "Well, why don't you go see Downriver Lame Man? Don't you ever want sex? Migi says she wants it all the time."

"Migi is seventeen," Mother said drily. "Mind your own nose." She sounded exactly like all the other mothers.

Men, during my childhood, were a kind of uninteresting mystery to me. They turned up a lot in the Before Time stories, and the singing-circle girls talked about them; but I seldom saw any of them. Sometimes I'd glimpse one when I was foraging, but they never came near the auntring. In summer the Downriver Lame Man would get lonesome waiting for Aunt Sadne and would come lurking around, not very far from the auntring—not in the bush or down by the river, of course, where he might be mistaken for a rogue and stoned—but out in the open, on the hillsides, where we could all see who he was. Hyuru and Didsu, Aunt Sadne's daughters, said she had had sex with him when she went out scouting the first time, and always had sex with him and never tried any of the other men of the settlement.

She had told them, too, that the first child she bore was a boy, and she drowned it, because she didn't want to bring up a boy and send him away. They felt queer about that and so did I, but it wasn't an uncommon thing. One of the stories we learned was about a drowned boy who grew up underwater, and seized his mother when she came to bathe, and tried to hold her under till she too drowned; but she escaped.

At any rate, after the Downriver Lame Man had sat around for several days on the hillsides, singing long songs and braiding and unbraiding his hair, which was long too, and shone black in the sun, Aunt Sadne always went off for a night or two with him, and came back looking cross and self-conscious.

Aunt Noyit explained to me that Downriver Lame Man's songs were magic; not the usual bad magic, but what she called the great good spells. Aunt Sadne never could resist his spells. "But he hasn't half the charm of some men I've known," said Aunt Noyit, smiling reminiscently.

Our diet, though excellent, was very low in fat, which Mother thought might explain the rather late onset of puberty; girls seldom menstruated before they were fifteen, and boys often weren't mature till they were considerably older than that. But the women began looking askance at boys as soon as they showed any signs at all of adolescence. First Aunt Hedimi, who was always grim, then Aunt Noyit, then even Aunt Sadne began to turn away from Borny, to leave him out, not answering when he spoke. "What are you doing playing with the children?" old Aunt Dnemi asked him so fiercely that he came home in tears. He was not quite fourteen.

Sadne's younger daughter Hyuru was my soulmate, my best friend, you would say. Her elder sister Didsu, who was in the singing circle now, came and talked to me one day, looking serious. "Borny is very handsome," she said. I agreed proudly.

"Very big, very strong," she said, "stronger than I am."

I agreed proudly again, and then I began to back away from her.

"I'm not doing magic, Ren," she said.

"Yes you are," I said. "I'll tell your mother!"

Didsu shook her head. "I'm trying to speak truly. If my fear causes your fear, I can't help it. It has to be so. We talked about it in the singing circle. I don't like it," she said, and I knew she meant it; she had a soft face, soft eyes, she had always been the gentlest of us children. "I wish he could be a child," she said. "I wish I could. But we can't."

"Go be a stupid old woman, then," I said, and ran away from her. I went to my secret place down by the river and cried. I took the holies out of my soulbag and arranged them. One holy—it doesn't matter if I tell you—was a crystal that Borny had given me, clear at the top, cloudy purple at the base. I held it a long time and then I gave it back. I dug a hole under a boulder, and wrapped the holy in duhur leaves inside a square of cloth I tore out of my kilt, beautiful, fine cloth Hyuru had woven and sewn for me. I tore the square right from the front, where it would show. I gave the crystal back, and then sat a long time there near it. When I went home I said nothing of what Didsu had said. But Borny was very silent, and my mother had a worried look. "What have you done to your kilt, Ren?" she asked. I raised my head a little and did not answer; she started to speak again, and then did not. She had finally learned not to talk to a person who chose to be silent.

Borny didn't have a soulmate, but he had been playing more and more often with the two boys nearest his age, Ednede who was a year or two older, a slight, quiet boy, and Bit who was only eleven, but boisterous and reckless. The three of them went off somewhere all the time. I hadn't paid much attention, partly because I was glad to be rid of Bit. Hyuru and I had been practising being aware, and it was tiresome to always have to be aware of Bit yelling and jumping around. He never could leave anyone quiet, as if their quietness took something from him. His mother, Hedimi, had educated him, but she wasn't a good singer or storyteller like Sadne and Noyit, and Bit was too restless to listen even to them. Whenever he saw me and Hyuru trying to slow-walk or sitting being aware, he hung around making noise till we got mad and told him to go, and then he jeered, "Dumb girls!"

I asked Borny what he and Bit and Ednede did, and he said, "Boy stuff."

"Like what?"

"Practising."

"Being aware?"

After a while he said, "No."

"Practising what, then?"

"Wrestling. Getting strong. For the boygroup." He looked gloomy, but after a while he said, "Look," and showed me a knife he had hidden under his mattress. "Ednede says you have to have a knife, then nobody will challenge you. Isn't it a beauty?" It was metal, old metal from the People, shaped like a reed, pounded out and sharpened down both edges, with a sharp point. A piece of polished flintshrub wood had been bored and fitted on the handle to protect the hand. "I found it in an empty man's-house," he said. "I made the wooden part." He brooded over it lovingly. Yet he did not keep it in his soulbag.

"What do you *do* with it?" I asked, wondering why both edges were sharp, so you'd cut your hand if you used it.

"Keep off attackers," he said.

"Where was the empty man's-house?"

"Way over across Rocky Top."

"Can I go with you if you go back?"

"No," he said, not unkindly, but absolutely.

"What happened to the man? Did he die?"

"There was a skull in the creek. We think he slipped and drowned."

He didn't sound quite like Borny. There was something in his voice like a grown-up; melancholy; reserved. I had gone to him for reassurance, but came away more deeply anxious. I went to Mother and asked her, "What do they do in the boygroups?"

"Perform natural selection," she said, not in my language but in hers, in a strained tone. I didn't always understand Hainish any more and had no idea what she meant, but the tone of her voice upset me; and to my horror I saw she had begun to cry silently. "We have to move, Serenity," she said—she was still talking Hainish without realising it. "There isn't any reason why a family can't move, is there? Women just move in and move out as they please. Nobody cares what anybody does. Nothing is anybody's business. Except hounding the boys out of town!"

I understood most of what she said, but got her to say it in my language; and then I said, "But anywhere we went, Borny would be the same age, and size, and everything."

"Then we'll leave," she said fiercely. "Go back to the ship."

I drew away from her. I had never been afraid of her before: she had never used magic on me. A mother has great power, but there is nothing unnatural in it, unless it is used against the child's soul.

Borny had no fear of her. He had his own magic. When she told him she intended leaving, he persuaded her out of it. He wanted to go join the boygroup, he said; he'd been wanting to for a year now. He didn't belong in the auntring any more, all women and girls and little kids. He wanted to go live with other boys. Bit's older brother Yit was a member of the boygroup in the Four Rivers Territory, and would look after a boy from his auntring. And Ednede was getting ready to go. And Borny and Ednede and Bit had been talking to some men, recently. Men weren't all ignorant and crazy, the way Mother thought. They didn't talk much, but they knew a lot.

"What do they know?" Mother asked grimly.

"They know how to be men," Borny said. "It's what I'm going to be."

"Not that kind of man—not if I can help it! In Joy Born, you must remember the men on the ship, real men—nothing like these poor, filthy hermits. I can't let you grow up thinking that that's what you have to be!"

"They're not like that," Borny said. "You ought to go talk to some of them, Mother."

"Don't be naive," she said with an edgy laugh. "You know perfectly well that women don't go to men to *talk*."

I knew she was wrong; all the women in the auntring knew all the settled men for three days' walk around. They did talk with them, when they were out foraging. They only kept away from the ones they didn't trust; and usually those men disappeared before long. Noyit had told me, "Their magic turns on them." She meant the other men drove them away or killed them. But I didn't say any of this, and Borny said only, "Well, Cave Cliff Man is really nice. And he took us to the place where I found those People things"—some ancient artifacts that Mother had been excited about. "The men know things the women don't," Borny went on. "At least I could go to the boygroup for a while, maybe. I ought to. I could learn a lot! We don't have any solid information on them at all. All we know anything about is this auntring. I'll go and stay long enough to get material for our report. I can't ever come back to either the auntring or the boygroup once I leave them. I'll have to go to the ship, or else try to be a man. So let me have a real go at it, please, Mother?"

"I don't know why you think you have to learn how to be a man," she said after a while. "You know how already."

He really smiled then, and she put her arm around him.

What about me? I thought. I don't even know what the ship is. I want to be here, where my soul is. I want to go on learning to be in the world.

But I was afraid of Mother and Borny, who were both working magic, and so I said nothing and was still, as I had been taught.

Ednede and Borny went off together. Noyit, Ednede's mother, was as glad as Mother was about their keeping company, though she said nothing. The evening before they left, the two boys went to every house in the auntring. It took a long time. The houses were each just within sight or hearing of one or two of the others, with bush and gardens and irrigation ditches and paths in between. In each house the mother and the children were waiting to say good-bye, only they didn't say it; my language has no word for hello or good-bye. They asked the boys in and gave them something to eat, something they could take with them on the way to the Territory. When the boys went to the door everybody in the household came and touched their hand or cheek. I remembered when Yit had gone around the auntring that way. I had cried then, because even though I didn't much like Yit, it seemed so strange for somebody to leave forever, like they were dying. This time I didn't cry; but I kept waking and waking again, until I heard Borny get up before the first light and pick up his things and leave quietly. I know Mother was awake too, but we did as we should do, and lay still while he left, and for a long time after.

I have read her description of what she calls "An Adolescent Male leaves the Auntring: a Vestigial Survival of Ceremony."

She had wanted him to put a radio in his soulbag and get in touch with her at least occasionally. He had been unwilling. "I want to do it right, Mother. There's no use doing it if I don't do it right."

"I simply can't handle not hearing from you at all, Borny," she had said in Hainish.

"But if the radio got broken or taken or something, you'd worry a lot more, maybe with no reason at all."

She finally agreed to wait half a year, till the first rain; then she would go to a landmark, a huge ruin near the river that marked the southern end of the Territory, and he would try and come to her there. "But only wait ten days," he said. "If I can't come, I can't." She agreed. She was like a mother with a little baby, I thought, saying yes to everything. That seemed wrong to me; but I thought Borny was right. Nobody ever came back to their mother from boygroup.

But Borny did.

Summer was long, clear, beautiful. I was learning to starwatch; that is when you lie down outside on the open hills in the dry season at night, and find a certain star in the eastern sky, and watch it cross the sky till it sets. You can look away, of course, to rest your eyes, and doze, but you try to keep looking back at the star and the stars around it, until you feel the earth turning, until you become aware of how the stars and the world and the soul move together. After the certain star sets you sleep until dawn wakes you. Then as always you greet the sunrise with aware silence. I was very happy on the hills those warm great nights, those clear dawns. The first time or two Hyuru and I starwatched together, but after that we went alone, and it was better alone.

I was coming back from such a night, along the narrow valley between Rocky Top and Over Home Hill in the first sunlight, when a man came crashing through the bush down onto the path and stood in front of me. "Don't be afraid," he said. "Listen!" He was heavyset, half-naked; he stank. I stood still as a stick. He had said "Listen!" just as the aunts did, and I listened. "Your brother and his friend are all right. Your mother shouldn't go there. Some of the boys are in a gang. They'd rape her. I and some others are killing the leaders. It takes a while. Your brother is with the other gang. He's all right. Tell her. Tell me what I said."

I repeated it word for word, as I had learned to do when I listened.

"Right. Good," he said, and took off up the steep slope on his short, powerful legs, and was gone.

Mother would have gone to the Territory right then, but I told the man's message to Noyit, too, and she came to the porch of our house to speak to Mother. I listened to her, because she was telling things I didn't know well and Mother didn't know at all. Noyit was a small, mild woman, very like her son Ednede; she liked teaching and singing, so the children were always around her place. She saw Mother was getting ready for a journey. She said, "House on the Skyline Man says the boys are all right." When she saw Mother wasn't listening, she went on; she pretended to be talking to me, because women don't teach women: "He says some of the men are breaking up the gang. They do that, when the boygroups get wicked. Sometimes there are magicians among them, leaders, older boys, even men who want to make a gang. The settled men will kill the magicians and make sure none of the boys gets hurt. When gangs come out of the Territories, nobody is safe. The settled men don't like that. They see to it that the auntring is safe. So your brother will be all right."

My mother went on packing pigi-roots into her net.

"A rape is a very, very bad thing for the settled men," said Noyit to me. "It means the women won't come to them. If the boys raped some woman, probably the men would kill *all* the boys."

My mother was finally listening.

She did not go to the rendezvous with Borny, but all through the rainy season she was utterly miserable. She got sick, and old Dnemi sent Didsu over to dose her with gagberry syrup. She made notes while she was sick, lying on her mattress, about illnesses and medicines and how the older girls had to look after sick women, since grown women did not enter one another's houses. She never stopped working and never stopped worrying about Borny.

Late in the rainy season, when the warm wind had come and the yellow honey-flowers were in bloom on all the hills, the Golden World time,

Noyit came by while Mother was working in the garden. "House on the Skyline Man says things are all right in the boygroup," she said, and went on.

Mother began to realise then that although no adult ever entered another's house, and adults seldom spoke to one another, and men and women had only brief, often casual relationships, and men lived all their lives in real solitude, still there was a kind of community, a wide, thin, fine network of delicate and certain intention and restraint: a social order. Her reports to the ship were filled with this new understanding. But she still found Sorovian life impoverished, seeing these persons as mere survivors, poor fragments of the wreck of something great.

"My dear," she said, in Hainish; there is no way to say "my dear" in my language. She was speaking Hainish with me in the house so that I wouldn't forget it entirely. "My dear, the explanation of an uncomprehended technology as magic *is* primitivism. It's not a criticism, merely a description."

"But technology isn't magic," I said.

"Yes, it is, in their minds; look at the story you just recorded. Before-Time sorcerers who could fly in the air and undersea and underground in magic boxes!"

"In *metal* boxes," I corrected.

"In other words, airplanes, tunnels, submarines; a lost technology explained as supernatural."

"The *boxes* weren't magic," I said. "The *people* were. They were sorcerers. They used their power to get power over other persons. To live rightly a person has to keep away from magic."

"That's a cultural imperative, because a few thousand years ago uncontrolled technological expansion led to disaster. Exactly. There's a perfectly rational reason for the irrational taboo."

I did not know what "rational" and "irrational" meant in my language; I could not find words for them. "Taboo" was the same as "poisonous."

I listened to my mother because a daughter must learn from her mother, and my mother knew many, many things no other person knew; but my education was very difficult, sometimes. If only there were more stories and songs in her teaching, and not so many words, words that slipped away from me like water through a net!

The Golden Time passed, and the beautiful summer; the Silver Time returned, when the mists lie in the valleys between the hills, before the rains begin; and the rains began, and fell long and slow and warm, day after day after day. We had heard nothing of Borny and Ednede for over a year. Then in the night the soft thrum of rain on the reed roof turned into a scratching at the door and a whisper, "Shh—it's all right—it's all right."

We wakened the fire and crouched at it in the dark to talk. Borny had got tall and very thin, like a skeleton with the skin dried on it. A cut across his upper lip had drawn it up into a kind of snarl that bared his teeth, and he could not say *p, b,* or *m.* His voice was a man's voice. He huddled at the fire trying to get warmth into his bones. His clothes were wet rags. The knife hung on a cord around his neck. "It was all right," he kept saying. "I don't want to go on there, though."

He would not tell us much about the year and a half in the boygroup, insisting that he would record a full description when he got to the ship. He did tell us what he would have to do if he stayed on Soro. He would have to go back to the Territory and hold his own among the older boys, by fear and sorcery, always proving his strength, until he was old enough to walk away—that is, to leave the Territory and wander alone till he found a place where the men would let him settle. Ednede and another boy had paired, and were going to walk away together when the rains stopped. It was easier for a pair, he said, if their bond was sexual; so long as they offered no competition for women, settled men wouldn't challenge them. But a new man in the region anywhere within three days' walk of an auntring had to prove himself against the settled men there. "It would 'e three or four years of the sa'e thing," he said, "challenging, fighting, always watching the others, on guard, showing how strong you are, staying alert all night, all day. To go on living alone your whole life. I can't do it." He looked at me. "I'ne not a 'erson," he said. "I want to go ho'e."

"I'll radio the ship now," Mother said quietly, with infinite relief.

"No," I said.

Borny was watching Mother, and raised his hand when she turned to speak to me.

"I'll go," he said. "She doesn't have to. Why should she?" Like me, he had learned not to use names without some reason to.

Mother looked from him to me and finally gave a kind of laugh. "I can't leave her here, Borny!"

"Why should you go?"

"Because I want to," she said. "I've had enough. More than enough. We've got a tremendous amount of material on the women, over seven years of it, and now you can fill the information gaps on the men's side. That's enough. It's time, past time, that we all got back to our own people. All of us."

"I have no people," I said. "I don't belong to people. I am trying to be a person. Why do you want to take me away from my soul? You want me to do magic! I won't. I won't do magic. I won't speak your language. I won't go with you!"

My mother was still not listening; she started to answer angrily. Borny put up his hand again, the way a woman does when she is going to sing, and she looked at him.

"We can talk later," he said. "We can decide. I need to sleep."

He hid in our house for two days while we decided what to do and how to do it. That was a miserable time. I stayed home as if I were sick so that I would not lie to the other persons, and Borny and Mother and I talked and talked. Borny asked Mother to stay with me; I asked her to leave me with Sadne or Noyit, either of whom would certainly take me into their household. She refused. She was the mother and I the child and her power was sacred. She radioed the ship and arranged for a lander to pick us up in a barren area two days' walk from the auntring. We left at night, sneaking away. I carried nothing but my soulbag. We walked all next day, slept a little when it stopped raining, walked on and came to the desert. The ground was all lumps and hollows and caves, Before-Time ruins; the soil was tiny bits of glass and hard grains and fragments, the way it is in the deserts. Nothing grew there. We waited there.

The sky broke open and a shining thing fell down and stood before us on the rocks, bigger than any house, though not as big as the ruins of the Before Time. My mother looked at me with a queer, vengeful smile. "Is it magic?" she said. And it was very hard for me not to think that it was. Yet I knew it was only a thing, and there is no magic in things, only in minds. I said nothing. I had not spoken since we left my home.

I HAD RESOLVED NEVER TO SPEAK TO ANYBODY UNTIL I GOT home again; but I was still a child, used to listening and obeying. In the ship, that utterly strange new world, I held out only for a few hours, and then began to cry and ask to go home. Please, please, can I go home now.

Everyone on the ship was very kind to me.

Even then I thought about what Borny had been through and what I was going through, comparing our ordeals. The difference seemed total. He had been alone, without food, without shelter, a frightened boy trying to survive among equally frightened rivals against the brutality of older youths intent on having and keeping power, which they saw as manhood. I was cared for, clothed, fed so richly I got sick, kept so warm I felt feverish, guided, reasoned with, praised, befriended by citizens of a very great city, offered a share in their power, which they saw as humanity. He and I had both fallen among sorcerers. Both he and I could see the good in the people we were among, but neither he nor I could live with them.

Borny told me he had spent many desolate nights in the Territory crouched in a fireless shelter, telling over the stories he had learned from the aunts, singing the songs in his head. I did the same thing every night on the ship. But I refused to tell the stories or sing to the people there. I would not speak my language, there. It was the only way I had to be silent.

My mother was enraged, and for a long time unforgiving. "You owe your knowledge to our people," she said. I did not answer, because all I had to say was that they were not my people, that I had no people. I was a person. I had a language that I did not speak. I had my silence. I had nothing else.

I went to school; there were children of different ages on the ship, like an auntring, and many of the adults taught us. I learned Ekumenical history and geography, mostly, and Mother gave me a report to learn about the history of Eleven-Soro, what my language calls the Before Time. I read that the cities of my world had been the greatest cities ever built on any world, covering two of the continents entirely, with small areas set aside for farming; there had been 120 billion people living in the cities, while the animals and the sea and the air and the dirt died, until the people began dying too. It was a hideous story. I was ashamed of it and wished nobody else on the ship or in the Ekumen knew about it. And yet, I thought, if they knew the stories I knew about the Before Time, they would understand how magic turns on itself, and that it must be so.

After less than a year, Mother told us we were going to Hain. The ship's doctor and his clever machines had repaired Borny's lip; he and Mother had put all the information they had into the records; he was old enough to begin training for the Ekumenical Schools, as he wanted to do. I was not flourishing, and the doctor's machines were not able to repair me. I kept losing weight, I slept badly, I had terrible headaches. Almost as soon as we came aboard the ship, I had begun to menstruate; each time the cramps were agonizing. "This is no good, this ship life," Mother said. "You need to be outdoors. On a planet. On a civilised planet."

"If I went to Hain," I said, "when I came back, the persons I know would all be dead hundreds of years ago."

"Serenity," she said, "you must stop thinking in terms of Soro. We have left Soro. You must stop deluding and tormenting yourself, and look forward, not back. Your whole life is ahead of you. Hain is where you will learn to live it."

I summoned up my courage and spoke in my own language: "I am not a child now. You have no power over me. I will not go. Go without me. You have no power over me!"

Those are the words I had been taught to say to a magician, a sorcerer. I don't know if my mother fully understood them, but she did understand that I was deathly afraid of her, and it struck her into silence.

After a long time she said in Hainish, "I agree. I have no power over you. But I have certain rights; the right of loyalty; of love."

"Nothing is right that puts me in your power," I said, still in my language.

She stared at me. "You are like one of them," she said. "You are one of them. You don't know what love is. You're closed into yourself like a rock. I should never have taken you there. People crouching in the ruins of a society—brutal, rigid, ignorant, superstitious—each one in a terrible solitude—and I let them make you into one of them!"

"You educated me," I said, and my voice began to tremble and my mouth to shake around the words, "and so does the school here, but my aunts educated me, and I want to finish my education." I was weeping, but I kept standing with my hands clenched. "I'm not a woman yet. I want to be a woman."

"But Ren, you will be!—ten times the woman you could ever be on Soro—you must try to understand, to believe me—"

"You have no power over me," I said, shutting my eyes and putting my hands over my ears. She came to me then and held me, but I stood stiff, enduring her touch, until she let me go.

The ship's crew had changed entirely while we were on-planet. The First Observers had gone on to other worlds; our backup was now a

Gethenian archeologist named Arrem, a mild, watchful person, not young. Arrem had gone down on-planet only on the two desert continents, and welcomed the chance to talk with us, who had "lived with the living," as heshe said. I felt easy when I was with Arrem, who was so unlike anybody else. Arrem was not a man—I could not get used to having men around all the time—yet not a woman; and so not exactly an adult, yet not a child: a person, alone, like me. Heshe did not know my language well, but always tried to talk it with me. When this crisis came, Arrem came to my mother and took counsel with her, suggesting that she let me go back down on-planet. Borny was in on some of these talks, and told me about them.

"Arrem says if you go to Hain you'll probably die," he said. "Your soul will. Heshe says some of what we learned is like what they learn on Gethen, in their religion. That kind of stopped Mother from ranting about primitive superstition. . . . And Arrem says you could be useful to the Ekumen, if you stay and finish your education on Soro. You'll be an invaluable resource." Borny sniggered, and after a minute I did too. "They'll mine you like an asteroid," he said. Then he said, "You know, if you stay and I go, we'll be dead."

That was how the young people of the ships said it, when one was going to cross the lightyears and the other was going to stay. Good-bye, we're dead. It was the truth.

"I know," I said. I felt my throat get tight, and was afraid. I had never seen an adult at home cry, except when Sut's baby died. Sut howled all night. Howled like a dog, Mother said, but I had never seen or heard a dog; I heard a woman terribly crying. I was afraid of sounding like that. "If I can go home, when I finish making my soul, who knows, I might come to Hain for a while," I said, in Hainish.

"Scouting?" Borny said in my language, and laughed, and made me laugh again.

Nobody gets to keep a brother. I knew that. But Borny had come back from being dead to me, so I might come back from being dead to him; at least I could pretend I might.

My mother came to a decision. She and I would stay on the ship for another year while Borny went to Hain. I would keep going to school; if at the end of the year I was still determined to go back on-planet, I could do so. With me or without me, she would go on to Hain then and join Borny. If I ever wanted to see them again, I could follow them. It was a compromise that satisfied no one, but it was the best we could do, and we all consented.

When he left, Borny gave me his knife.

After he left, I tried not to be sick. I worked hard at learning everything they taught me in the ship school, and I tried to teach Arrem how to be aware and how to avoid witchcraft. We did slow walking together in the ship's garden, and the first hour of the Untrance movements from the Handdara of Karhide on Gethen. We agreed that they were alike.

The ship was staying in the Soro system not only because of my family, but because the crew was now mostly zoologists who had come to study a sea animal on Eleven-Soro, a kind of cephalopod that had mutated towards high intelligence, or maybe it already was highly intelligent; but there was a communication problem. "Almost as bad as with the local humans," said Steadiness, the zoologist who taught and teased us mercilessly. She took us down twice by lander to the uninhabited islands in the Northern Hemisphere where her station was. It was very strange to go down to my world and yet be a world away from my aunts and sisters and my soulmate; but I said nothing.

I saw the great, pale, shy creature come slowly up out of the deep waters with a running ripple of colors along its long coiling tentacles and a ringing shimmer of sound, all so quick it was over before you could follow the colors or hear the tune. The zoologist's machine produced a pink glow and a mechanically speeded-up twitter, tinny and feeble in the immensity of the sea. The cephalopod patiently responded in its beautiful silvery shadowy language. "CP," Steadiness said to us, ironic—Communication Problem. "We don't know what we're talking about."

I said, "I learned something in my education here. In one of the songs, it says," and I hesitated, trying to translate it into Hainish, "it says, thinking is one way of doing, and words are one way of thinking."

Steadiness stared at me, in disapproval I thought, but probably only because I had never said anything to her before except "Yes." Finally she said, "Are you suggesting that it doesn't speak in words?"

"Maybe it's not speaking at all. Maybe it's thinking."

Steadiness stared at me some more and then said, "Thank you." She looked as if she too might be thinking. I wished I could sink into the water, the way the cephalopod was doing.

The other young people on the ship were friendly and mannerly. Those are words that have no translation in my language. I was unfriendly and unmannerly, and they let me be. I was grateful. But there was no place to be alone on the ship. Of course we each had a room; though small, the *Heyho* was a Hainish-built explorer, designed to give its people room and privacy and comfort and variety and beauty while they hung around in a solar system for years on end. But it was designed. It was all human-made—everything was human. I had much more privacy than I had ever had at home in our one-room house; yet there I had been free and here I was in a trap. I felt the pressure of people all around me, all the time. People around me, people with me, people pressing on me, pressing me to be one of them, to be one of them, one of the people. How could I make my soul? I could barely cling to it. I was in terror that I would lose it altogether.

One of the rocks in my soulbag, a little ugly grey rock that I had picked up on a certain day in a certain place in the hills above the river in the Silver Time, a little piece of my world, that became my world. Every night I took it out and held it in my hand while I lay in bed waiting to sleep, thinking of the sunlight on the hills above the river, listening to the soft hushing of the ship's systems, like a mechanical sea.

The doctor hopefully fed me various tonics. Mother and I ate breakfast together every morning. She kept at work, making our notes from all the years on Eleven-Soro into her report to the Ekumen, but I knew the work did not go well. Her soul was in as much danger as mine was.

"You will never give in, will you, Ren?" she said to me one morning out of the silence of our breakfast. I had not intended the silence as a message. I had only rested in it.

"Mother, I want to go home and you want to go home," I said. "Can't we?"

Her expression was strange for a moment, while she misunderstood me; then it cleared to grief, defeat, relief.

"Will we be dead?" she asked me, her mouth twisting.

"I don't know. I have to make my soul. Then I can know if I can come."

"You know I can't come back. It's up to you."

"I know. Go see Borny," I said. "Go home. Here we're both dying." Then noises began to come out of me, sobbing, howling. Mother was crying. She came to me and held me, and I could hold my mother, cling to her and cry with her, because her spell was broken.

FROM THE LANDER APPROACHING I SAW THE OCEANS OF ELEVEN-Soro, and in the greatness of my joy I thought that when I was grown and went out alone I would go to the sea shore and watch the sea-beasts shimmering their colors and tunes till I knew what they were thinking. I would listen, I would learn, till my soul was as large as the shining world. The scarred barrens whirled beneath us, ruins as wide as the continent, endless desolations. We touched down. I had my soulbag, and Borny's knife around my neck on its string, a communicator implant behind my right earlobe, and a medicine kit Mother had made for me. "No use dying of an infected finger, after all," she had said. The people on the lander said good-bye, but I forgot to. I set off out of the desert, home.

It was summer; the night was short and warm; I walked most of it.

I got to the auntring about the middle of the second day. I went to my house cautiously, in case somebody had moved in while I was gone; but it was just as we had left it. The mattresses were moldy, and I put them and the bedding out in the sun, and started going over the garden to see what had kept growing by itself. The pigi had got small and seedy, but there were some good roots. A little boy came by and stared; he had to be Migi's baby. After a while Hyuru came by. She squatted down near me in the garden in the sunshine. I smiled when I saw her, and she smiled, but it took us a while to find something to say.

"Your mother didn't come back," she said.

"She's dead," I said.

"I'm sorry," Hyuru said.

She watched me dig up another root.

"Will you come to the singing circle?" she asked.

I nodded.

She smiled again. With her rose-brown skin and wide-set eyes, Hyuru had become very beautiful, but her smile was exactly the same as when we were little girls. "Hi, ya!" she sighed in deep contentment, lying down on the dirt with her chin on her arms. "This is good!"

I went on blissfully digging.

That year and the next two, I was in the singing circle with Hyuru and two other girls. Didsu still came to it often, and Han, a woman who settled in our auntring to have her first baby, joined it too. In the singing circle the older girls pass around the stories, songs, knowledge they learned from their own mother, and young women who have lived in other auntrings teach what they learned there; so women make each other's souls, learning how to make their children's souls.

Han lived in the house where old Dnemi had died. Nobody in the auntring except Sut's baby had died while my family lived there. My mother had complained that she didn't have any data on death and burial. Sut had gone away with her dead baby and never came back, and nobody talked about it. I think that turned my mother against the others more than anything else. She was angry and ashamed that she could not go and try to comfort Sut and that nobody else did. "It is not human," she said. "It is pure animal behavior. Nothing could be clearer evidence that this is a broken culture—not a society, but the remains of one. A terrible, an appalling poverty."

I don't know if Dnemi's death would have changed her mind. Dnemi was dying for a long time, of kidney failure I think; she turned a kind of dark orange color, jaundice. While she could get around, nobody helped her. When she didn't come out of her house for a day or two, the women would send the children in with water and a little food and fire-wood. It went on so through the winter; then one morning little Rashi told his mother Aunt Dnemi was "staring." Several of the women went to Dnemi's house, and entered it for the first and last time. They sent for all the girls in the singing circle, so that we could learn what to do. We took turns sitting by the body or in the porch of the house, singing soft songs, child-songs, giving the soul a day and a night to leave the body and the house; then the older women wrapped the body in the bedding, strapped it on a kind of litter, and set off with it towards the barren lands. There it would be given back, under a rock cairn or inside one of the ruins of the ancient city. "Those are the lands of the dead," Sadne said. "What dies stays there."

Han settled down in that house a year later. When her baby began to be born she asked Didsu to help her, and Hyuru and I stayed in the porch and watched, so that we could learn. It was a wonderful thing to see, and quite altered the course of my thinking, and Hyuru's too. Hyuru said, "I'd like to do that!" I said nothing, but thought, So do I, but not for a long time, because once you have a child you're never alone.

And though it is of the others, of relationships, that I write, the heart of my life has been my being alone.

I think there is no way to write about being alone. To write is to tell something to somebody, to communicate to others. CP, as Steadiness would say. Solitude is noncommunication, the absence of others, the presence of a self sufficient to itself.

A woman's solitude in the auntring is, of course, based firmly on the presence of others at a little distance. It is a contingent, and therefore human, solitude. The settled men are connected as stringently to the women, though not to one another; the settlement is an integral though distant element of the auntring. Even a scouting woman is part of the society—a moving part, connecting the settled parts. Only the isolation of a woman or man who chooses to live outside the settlements is absolute. They are outside the network altogether. There are worlds where such persons are called saints, holy people. Since isolation is a sure way to prevent magic, on my world the assumption is that they are sorcerers, outcast by others or by their own will, their conscience.

I knew I was strong with magic, how could I help it? and I began to long to get away. It would be so much easier and safer to be alone. But at the same time, and increasingly, I wanted to know something about the great harmless magic, the spells cast between men and women.

I preferred foraging to gardening, and was out on the hills a good deal; and these days, instead of keeping away from the man's-houses, I wandered by them, and looked at them, and looked at the men if they were outside. The men looked back. Downriver Lame Man's long, shining hair was getting a little white in it now, but when he sat singing his long, long songs I found myself sitting down and listening, as if my legs had lost their bones. He was very handsome. So was the man I remembered as a boy named Tret in the auntring, when I was little, Behyu's son. He had come back from the boygroup and from wandering, and had built a house and made a fine garden in the valley of Red Stone Creek. He had a big nose and big eyes, long arms and legs, long hands; he moved very quietly, almost like Arrem doing the Untrance. I went often to pick lowberries in Red Stone Creek valley.

He came along the path and spoke. "You were Borny's sister," he said. He had a low voice, quiet.

"He's dead," I said.

Red Stone Man nodded. "That's his knife."

In my world, I had never talked with a man. I felt extremely strange. I kept picking berries.

"You're picking green ones," Red Stone Man said.

His soft, smiling voice made my legs lose their bones again.

"I think nobody's touched you," he said. "I'd touch you gently. I think about it, about you, ever since you came by here early in the summer. Look, here's a bush full of ripe ones. Those are green. Come over here."

I came closer to him, to the bush of ripe berries.

When I was on the ship, Arrem told me that many languages have a single word for sexual desire and the bond between mother and child and the bond between soulmates and the feeling for one's home and worship of the sacred; they are all called love. There is no word that great in my language. Maybe my mother is right, and human greatness perished in my world with the people of the Before Time, leaving only small, poor, broken things and thoughts. In my language, love is many different words. I learned one of them with Red Stone Man. We sang it together to each other.

We made a brush house on a little cove of the creek, and neglected our gardens, but gathered many, many sweet berries.

Mother had put a lifetime's worth of nonconceptives in the little medicine kit. She had no faith in Sorovian herbals. I did, and they worked.

But when a year or so later, in the Golden Time, I decided to go out scouting, I thought I might go places where the right herbs were scarce; and so I stuck the little noncon jewel on the back of my left earlobe. Then I wished I hadn't, because it seemed like witchcraft. Then I told myself I was being superstitious; the noncon wasn't any more witchcraft than the herbs were, it just worked longer. I had promised my mother in my soul that I would never be superstitious. The skin grew over the noncon, and I took my soulbag and Borny's knife and the medicine kit, and set off across the world.

I had told Hyuru and Red Stone Man I would be leaving. Hyuru and I sang and talked together all one night down by the river. Red Stone Man said in his soft voice, "Why do you want to go?" and I said, "To get away from your magic, sorcerer," which was true in part. If I kept going to him I might always go to him. I wanted to give my soul and body a larger world to be in.

Now to tell of my scouting years is more difficult than ever. CP! A woman scouting is entirely alone, unless she chooses to ask a settled man for sex, or camps in an auntring for a while to sing and listen with the singing circle. If she goes anywhere near the territory of a boygroup, she is in danger; and if she comes on a rogue she is in danger; and if she hurts herself or gets into polluted country, she is in danger. She has no responsibility except to herself, and so much freedom is very dangerous.

In my right earlobe was the tiny communicator; every forty days, as I had promised, I sent a signal to the ship that meant "all well." If I wanted to leave, I would send another signal. I could have called for the lander to rescue me from a bad situation, but though I was in bad situations a couple of times I never thought of using it. My signal was the mere fulfilment of a promise to my mother and her people, the network I was no longer part of, a meaningless communication.

Life in the auntring, or for a settled man, is repetitive, as I said; and so it can be dull. Nothing new happens. The mind always wants new happenings. So for the young soul there is wandering and scouting, travel, danger, change. But of course travel and danger and change have their own dullness. It is finally always the same otherness over again; another hill, another river, another man, another day. The feet begin to turn in a long, long circle. The body begins to think of what it learned back home, when it learned to be still. To be aware. To be aware of the grain of dust beneath the sole of the foot, and the skin of the sole of the foot, and the touch and scent of the air on the cheek, and the fall and motion of the light across the air, and the color of the grass on the high hill across the river, and the thoughts of the body, of the soul, the shimmer and ripple of colors and sounds in the clear darkness of the depths, endlessly moving, endlessly changing, endlessly new.

So at last I came back home. I had been gone about four years.

Hyuru had moved into my old house when she left her mother's house. She had not gone scouting, but had taken to going to Red Stone Creek valley; and she was pregnant. I was glad to see her living there. The only house empty was an old half-ruined one too close to Hedimi's. I decided to make a new house. I dug out the circle as deep as my chest; the digging took most of the summer. I cut the sticks, braced and wove them, and then daubed the framework solidly with mud inside and out. I remembered when I had done that with my mother long, long ago, and how she had said, "That's right. That's good." I left the roof open, and the hot sun of late summer baked the mud into clay. Before the rains came, I thatched the house with reeds, a triple thatching, for I'd had enough of being wet all winter.

My auntring was more a string than a ring, stretching along the north bank of river for about three kilos; my house lengthened the string a good bit, upstream from all the others. I could just see the smoke from Hyuru's fireplace. I dug the house into a sunny slope with good drainage. It is still a good house.

I settled down. Some of my time went to gathering and gardening and mending and all the dull, repetitive actions of primitive life, and some went to singing and thinking the songs and stories I had learned here at home and while scouting, and the things I had learned on the ship, also. Soon enough I found why women are glad to have children come to listen to them, for songs and stories are meant to be heard, listened to. "Listen!" I would say to the children. The children of the auntring came and went, like the little fish in the river, one or two or five of them, little ones, big ones. When they came, I sang or told stories to them. When they left, I went on in silence. Sometimes I joined the singing circle to give what I had learned travelling to the older girls. And that was all I did; except that I worked, always, to be aware of all I did.

By solitude the soul escapes from doing or suffering magic; it escapes from dullness, from boredom, by being aware. Nothing is boring if you are aware of it. It may be irritating, but it is not boring. If it is pleasant the pleasure will not fail so long as you are aware of it. Being aware is the hardest work the soul can do, I think.

I helped Hyuru have her baby, a girl, and played with the baby. Then after a couple of years I took the noncon out of my left earlobe. Since it left a little hole, I made the hole go all the way through with a burnt needle, and when it healed I hung in it a tiny jewel I had found in a ruin when I was scouting. I had seen a man on the ship with a jewel hung in his ear that way. I wore it when I went out foraging. I kept clear of Red Stone Valley. The man there behaved as if he had a claim on me, a right to me. I liked him still, but I did not like that smell of magic about him, his imagination of power over me. I went up into the hills, northward.

A pair of young men had settled in old North House about the time I came home. Often boys got through boygroup by pairing, and often they stayed paired when they left the Territory. It helped their chances of survival. Some of them were sexually paired, others weren't; some stayed paired, others didn't. One of this pair had gone off with another man last summer. The one that stayed wasn't a handsome man, but I had noticed him. He had a kind of solidness I liked. His body and hands were short and strong. I had courted him a little, but he was very shy. This day, a day in the Silver Time when the mist lay on the river, he saw the jewel swinging in my ear, and his eyes widened.

"It's pretty, isn't it?" I said.

He nodded.

"I wore it to make you look at me," I said.

He was so shy that I finally said, "If you only like sex with men, you know, just tell me." I really was not sure.

"Oh, no," he said, "no. No." He stammered and then bolted back down the path. But he looked back; and I followed him slowly, still not certain whether he wanted me or wanted to be rid of me.

He waited for me in front of a little house in a grove of redroot, a lovely little bower, all leaves outside, so that you would walk within arm's length of it and not see it. Inside he had laid sweet grass, deep and dry and soft, smelling of summer. I went in, crawling because the door was very low, and sat in the summer-smelling grass. He stood outside. "Come in," I said, and he came in very slowly.

"I made it for you," he said.

"Now make a child for me," I said.

And we did that; maybe that day, maybe another.

Now I will tell you why after all these years I called the ship, not knowing even if it was still there in the space between the planets, asking for the lander to meet me in the barren land.

When my daughter was born, that was my heart's desire and the fulfilment of my soul. When my son was born, last year, I knew there is no fulfilment. He will grow towards manhood, and go, and fight and endure, and live or die as a man must. My daughter, whose name is Yedneke, Leaf, like my mother, will grow to womanhood and go or stay as she chooses. I will live alone. This is as it should be, and my desire. But I am of two worlds; I am a person of this world, and a woman of my mother's people. I owe my knowledge to the children of her people. So I asked the lander to come, and spoke to the people on it. They gave me my mother's report to read, and I have written my story in their machine, making a record for those who want to learn one of the ways to make a soul. To them, to the children I say: Listen! Avoid magic! Be aware!

THE
WILD GIRLS

BELA TEN BELEN WENT ON A FORAY WITH FIVE COMPANIONS. There had been no nomad camps near the City for several years, but harvesters in the Eastern Fields reported seeing smoke of fires beyond the Dayward Hills, and the six young men announced that they'd go see how many camps there were. They took with them as guide Bidh Handa, who had guided forays against the nomad tribes before. Bidh and his sister had been captured from a nomad village as children and grew up in the City as slaves. Bidh's sister Nata was famous for her beauty, and Bela's brother Alo had given her owner a good deal of the Belen family wealth to get her for his wife.

Bela and his companions walked and ran all day following the course of the East River up into the hills. In the evening they came to the crest of the hills and saw on the plains below them, among watermeadows and winding streams, three circles of the nomads' skin huts, strung out quite far apart.

"They came to the marshes to gather mudroots," the guide said. "They're not planning a raid on the Fields of the City. If they were, the three camps would be close together."

"Who gathers the roots?" Bela ten Belen asked.

"Men and women. Old people and children stay in the camps."

"When do the people go to the marshes?"

"Early in the morning."

"We'll go down to that nearest camp tomorrow after the gatherers are gone."

"It would be better to go to the second village, the one on the river," Bidh said.

Bela ten Belen turned to his soldiers and said, "Those are this man's people. We should shackle him."

They agreed, but none of them had brought shackles. Bela began to tear his cape into strips.

"Why do you want to tie me up, lord?" the Dirt man asked with his fist to his forehead to show respect. "Have I not guided you, and others before you, to the nomads? Am I not a man of the City? Is not my sister your brother's wife? Is not my nephew your nephew, and a god? Why would I run away from our City to those ignorant people who starve in the wilderness, eating mudroots and crawling things?" The Crown men did not answer the Dirt man. They tied his legs with the lengths of twisted cloth, pulling the knots in the silk so tight they could not be untied but only cut open. Bela appointed three men to keep watch in turn that night.

Tired from walking and running all day, the young man on watch before dawn fell asleep. Bidh put his legs into the coals of their fire and burned through the silken ropes and stole away.

When he woke in the morning and found the slave gone, Bela ten Belen's face grew heavy with anger, but he said only, "He'll have warned that nearest camp. We'll go to the farthest one, off there on the high ground."

"They'll see us crossing the marshes," said Dos ten Han.

"Not if we walk in the rivers," Bela ten Belen said.

And once they were out of the hills on the flat lands they walked along streambeds, hidden by the high reeds and willows that grew on the banks. It was autumn, before the rains, so the water was shallow enough that they could make their way along beside it or wade in it. Where the reeds grew thin and low and the stream widened out into the marshes, they crouched down and found what cover they could.

By midday they came near the farthest of the camps, which was on a low grassy rise like an island among the marshes. They could hear the voices of people gathering mudroot on the eastern side of the island. They crept up through the high grass and came to the camp from the south. No one was in the circle of skin huts but a few old men and women and a little swarm of children. The children were spreading out long yellow-brown roots on the grass, the old people cutting up the largest roots and putting them on racks over low fires to hasten the drying. The six Crown men came among them suddenly with their swords drawn. They cut the throats of the old men and women. Some children ran away down into the marshes. Others stood staring, uncomprehending.

Young men on their first foray, the soldiers had made no plans—Bela ten Belen had said to them, "I want to go out there and kill some thieves and bring home slaves," and that was all the plan they wanted. To his friend Dos ten Han he had said, "I want to get some new Dirt girls, there's not one in the City I can stand to look at." Dos ten Han knew he was thinking about the beautiful nomad-born woman his brother had married. All the young Crown men thought about Nata Belenda and wished they had her or a girl as beautiful as her.

"Get the girls," Bela shouted to the others, and they all ran at the children, seizing one or another. The older children had mostly fled at once, it was the young ones who stood staring or began too late to run. Each soldier caught one or two and dragged them back to the center of the village where the old men and women lay in their blood in the sunlight.

Having no ropes to tie the children with, the men had to keep hold of them. One little girl fought so fiercely, biting and scratching, that the soldier dropped her, and she scrabbled away screaming shrilly for help. Bela ten Belen ran after her, took her by the hair, and cut her throat to silence her screaming. His sword was sharp and her neck was soft and thin; her body dropped away from her head, held on only by the bones at the back of the neck. He dropped the head and came running back to his men. "Take one you can carry and follow me," he shouted at them.

"Where? The people down there will be coming," they said. For the children who had escaped had run down to the marsh where their parents were.

"Follow the river back," Bela said, snatching up a girl of about five years old. He seized her wrists and slung her on his back as if she were a sack. The other men followed him, each with a child, two of them babies a year or two old.

The raid had occurred so quickly that they had a long lead on the nomads who came straggling up round the hill following the children who had run to them. The soldiers were able to get down into the river-course, where the banks and reeds hid them from people looking for them even from the top of the island.

The nomads scattered out through the reedbeds and meadows west of the island, looking to catch them on their way back to the City. But Bela had led them not west but down a branch of the river that led off southeast. They trotted and ran and walked as best they could in the water and mud and rocks of the riverbed. At first they heard voices far behind them. The heat and light of the sun filled the world. The air above the reeds was thick with stinging insects. Their eyes soon swelled almost closed with bites and burned with salt sweat. Crown men, unused to carrying burdens, they found the children heavy, even the little ones. They struggled to go fast but went slower and slower along the winding channels of the water, listening for the nomads behind them. When a child made any noise, the soldiers slapped or shook it till it was still. The girl Bela ten Belen carried hung like a stone on his back and never made any sound.

When at last the sun sank behind the Dayward Hills, that seemed strange to them, for they had always seen the sun rise behind those hills.

They were now a long way south and east of the hills. They had heard no sound of their pursuers for a long time. The gnats and mosquitoes growing even thicker with dusk drove them at last up onto a drier meadowland, where they could sink down in a place where deer had lain, hidden by the high grasses. There they all lay while the light died away. The great herons of the marsh flew over with heavy wings. Birds down in the reeds called. The men heard each other's breathing and the whine and buzz of insects. The smaller children made tiny whimpering noises, but not often, and not loud. Even the babies of the nomad tribes were used to fear and silence.

As soon as the soldiers had let go of them, making threatening gestures to them not to try to run away, the six children crawled together and huddled up into a little mound, holding one another. Their faces were swollen with insect bites and one of the babies looked dazed and feverish. There was no food, but none of the children complained.

The light sank away from the marshes, and the insects grew silent. Now and then a frog croaked, startling the men as they sat silent, listening.

Dos ten Han pointed northward: he had heard a sound, a rustling in the grasses, not far away.

They heard the sound again. They unsheathed their swords as silently as they could.

Where they were looking, kneeling, straining to see through the high grass without revealing themselves, suddenly a ball of faint light rose up and wavered in the air above the grasses, fading and brightening. They heard a voice, shrill and faint, singing. The hair stood up on their heads and arms as they stared at the bobbing blur of light and heard the meaningless words of the song.

The child that Bela had carried suddenly called out a word. The oldest, a thin girl of eight or so who had been a heavy burden to Dos ten Han, hissed at her and tried to make her be still, but the younger child called out again, and an answer came.

Singing, talking, and babbling shrilly, the voice came nearer. The marsh fire faded and burned again. The grasses rustled and shook so much that the men, gripping their swords, looked for a whole group of people, but only one head appeared among the grasses. A single child came walking towards them. She kept talking, stamping, waving her hands so that they would know she was not trying to surprise them. The soldiers stared at her, holding their heavy swords.

She looked to be nine or ten years old. She came closer, hesitating all the time but not stopping, watching the men all the time but talking to the children. Bela's girl got up and ran to her and they clung to each other. Then, still watching the men, the new girl sat down with the other children. She and Dos ten Han's girl talked a little in low voices. She held Bela's girl in her arms, on her lap, and the little girl fell asleep almost at once.

"It must be that one's sister," one of the men said.

"She must have tracked us from the beginning," said another.

"Why didn't she call the rest of her people?"

"Maybe she did."

"Maybe she was afraid to."

"Or they didn't hear."

"Or they did."

"What was that light?"

"Marsh fire."

"Maybe it's them."

They were all silent, listening, watching. It was almost dark. The lamps of the City of Heaven were being lighted, reflecting the lights of the City of Earth, making the soldiers think of that city, which seemed as far away as the one above them in the sky. The faint bobbing light had died away. There was no sound but the sigh of the night wind in the reeds and grasses.

The soldiers argued in low voices about how to keep the children from running off during the night. Each may have thought that he would be glad enough to wake and find them gone, but did not say so. Dos ten Han said the smaller ones could hardly go any distance in the dark. Bela ten Belen said nothing, but took out the long lace from one of his sandals and tied one end around the neck of the little girl he had taken and the other end around his own wrist; then he made the child lie down, and lay down to sleep next to her. Her sister, the one who had followed them, lay down by her on the other side. Bela said, "Dos, keep watch first, then wake me."

So the night passed. The children did not try to escape, and no one came on their trail.

The next day they kept going south but mainly west, so that by mid-afternoon they reached the Dayward Hills. The children walked, even the five-year-old, and the men passed the two babies from one to another, so their pace was steady if not fast. Along in the morning, the marsh-fire girl pulled at Bela's tunic and kept pointing left, to a swampy place, making gestures of pulling up roots and eating. Since they had eaten nothing for two days, they followed her. The older children waded out into the water and pulled up certain wide-leaved plants by the roots. They began to cram what they pulled up into their mouths, but the soldiers waded after them and took the muddy roots and ate them till they had had enough. Dirt people do not eat before Crown people eat. The children did not seem surprised.

When she had finally got and eaten a root for herself, the marsh-fire girl pulled up another, chewed some and spat it out into her hand for the babies to eat. One of them ate eagerly from her hand, but the other would not; she lay where she had been put down, and her eyes did not seem to see. Dos ten Han's girl and the marsh-fire girl tried to make her drink water. She would not drink.

Dos stood in front of them and said, pointing to the elder girl, "Vui Handa," naming her Vui and saying she belonged to his family. Bela named the marsh-fire girl Modh Belenda, and her little sister, the one he had carried off, he named Mal Belenda. The other men named their prizes, but when Ralo ten Bal pointed at the sick baby to name her, the marsh-fire girl, Modh, got between him and the baby, vigorously gesturing no, no, and putting her hand to her mouth for silence.

"What's she up to?" Ralo asked. He was the youngest of the men, sixteen.

Modh kept up her pantomime: she lay down, lolled her head, and half opened her eyes, like a dead person; she leapt up with her hands held like claws and her face distorted, and pretended to attack Vui; she pointed at the sick baby.

The young men stood staring. It seemed she meant the baby was dying. The rest of her actions they did not understand.

Ralo pointed at the baby and said, "Groda," which is a name given to Dirt people who have no owner and work in the field teams—Nobody's.

"Come on," Bela ordered, and they made ready to go on. Ralo walked off, leaving the sick child lying.

"Aren't you bringing your Dirt?" one of the others asked him.

"What for?" he said.

Modh picked up the sick baby, Vui picked up the other baby, and they went on. After that the soldiers let the older girls carry the sick baby, though they themselves passed the well one about so as to make better speed.

When they got up on higher ground away from the clouds of stinging insects and the wet and heavy heat of the marshlands, the young men were glad, feeling they were almost safe now; they wanted to move fast and get back to the City. But the children, worn out, struggled to climb the steep hills. Vui, who was carrying the sick baby, straggled along slower and slower. Dos, her owner, slapped her legs with the flat of his sword to make her go faster. "Ralo, take your Dirt, we have to keep going," he said.

Ralo turned back angrily. He took the sick baby from Vui. The baby's face had gone greyish and its eyes were half closed, like Modh's in her pantomime. Its breath whistled a little. Ralo shook the child. Its head flopped. Ralo threw it away into the high bushes. "Come on, then," he said, and set off walking fast uphill.

Vui tried to run to the baby, but Dos kept her away from it with his sword, stabbing at her legs, and drove her on up the hill in front of him.

Modh dodged back to the bushes where the baby was, but Bela got in front of her and herded her along with his sword. As she kept dodging and trying to go back, he seized her by the arm, slapped her hard, and dragged her after him by the wrist. Little Mal stumbled along behind them.

When the place of the high bushes was lost from sight behind a hillslope, Vui began to make a shrill long-drawn cry, a keening, and so did Modh and Mal. The keening grew louder. The soldiers shook and beat them till they stopped but soon they started again, all the children, even the baby. The soldiers did not know if they were far enough from the nomads and near enough the Fields of the City that they need not fear pursuers hearing the sound. They hurried on, carrying or dragging or driving the children, and the shrill keening cry went with them like the sound of the insects in the marshlands.

It was almost dark when they got to the crest of the Dayward Hills. Forgetting how far south they had gone, the men expected to look down on the Fields and the City. They saw only dusk falling lands, and the dark west, and the lights of the City of the Sky beginning to shine.

They settled down in a clearing, for all were very tired. The children huddled together and were asleep almost at once. Bela forbade the men to make fire. They were hungry, but there was a creek down the hill to drink from. Bela set Ralo ten Bal on first watch. Ralo was the one who had gone to sleep, their first night out, allowing Bidh to escape.

Bela woke in the night, cold, missing his cape, which he had torn up to make bonds. He saw that someone had made a small fire and was sitting cross-legged beside it. He sat up and said "Ralo!" furiously, and then saw that the man was not Ralo but the guide, Bidh.

Ralo lay motionless near the fire.

Bela drew his sword.

"He fell asleep again," the Dirt man said, grinning at Bela.

Bela kicked Ralo, who snorted and sighed and did not wake. Bela leapt up and went round to the others, fearing Bidh had killed them in their sleep, but they had their swords and were sleeping soundly. The children slept in a little heap. He returned to the fire and stamped it out.

"Those people are miles away," Bidh said. "They won't see the fire. They never found your track."

"Where did you go?" Bela asked him after a while, puzzled and suspicious. He did not understand why the Dirt man had come back.

"To see my people in the village."

"Which village?"

"The one nearest the hills. My people are the Allulu. I saw my grandfather's hut from up in the hills. I wanted to see the people I used to know. My mother's still alive, but my father and brother have gone to the Sky City. I talked with my people and told them a foray was coming. They waited for you in their huts. They would have killed you, but you would have killed some of them. I was glad you went on to the Tullu village."

It is fitting that a Crown ask a Dirt person questions, but not that he converse or argue with him. Bela, however, was so disturbed that he said sharply, "Dead Dirt does not go to the Sky City. Dirt goes to dirt."

"So it is," Bidh said politely, as a slave should, with his fist to his forehead. "My people foolishly believe that they go to the sky, but even if they did, no doubt they wouldn't go to the palaces there. No doubt they wander in the wild, dirty parts of the sky." He poked at the fire to see if he could start a flame, but it was dead. "But you see, they can only go up there if they have been buried. If they're not buried, their soul stays down here on earth. It is likely to turn into a very bad thing then. A bad spirit. A ghost."

"Why did you follow us?" Bela demanded.

Bidh looked puzzled, and put his fist to his forehead. "I belong to Lord ten Han," he said. "I eat well, and live in a fine house. I'm respected in the City because of my sister and being a guide. I don't want to stay with the Allulu. They're very poor."

"But you ran away!"

"I wanted to see my family," Bidh said. "And I didn't want them to be killed. I only would have shouted to them to warn them. But you tied my legs. That made me so sad. You failed to trust me. I could think only about my people, and so I ran away. I am sorry, my lord."

"You would have warned them. They would have killed us!"

"Yes," Bidh said, "if you'd gone there. But if you'd let me guide you, I would have taken you to the Bustu or the Tullu village and helped you catch children. Those are not my people. I was born an Allulu and am a man of the City. My sister's child is a god. I am to be trusted."

Bela ten Belen turned away and said nothing.

He saw the starlight in the eyes of a child, her head raised a little, watching and listening. It was the marsh-fire girl, Modh, who had followed them to be with her sister.

"That one," Bidh said. "That one, too, will mother gods."

II

CHERGO'S DAUGHTER AND DEAD AYU'S FIRST DAUGHTER, WHO were now named Vui and Modh, whispered in the grey of the morning before the men woke.

"Do you think she's dead?" Vui whispered.

"I heard her crying. All night."

They both lay listening.

"That one named her," Vui whispered very low. "So she can follow us."

"She will."

The little sister, Mal, was awake, listening. Modh put her arm around her and whispered, "Go back to sleep."

Near them, Bidh suddenly sat up, scratching his head. The girls stared wide-eyed at him.

"Well, Daughters of Tullu," he said in their language, spoken the way the Allulu spoke it, "you're Dirt people now."

They stared and said nothing.

"You're going to live in heaven on earth," he said. "A lot of food. Big, rich huts to live in. And you don't have to carry your house around on your back across the world! You'll see. Are you virgins?"

After a while they nodded.

"Stay that way if you can," he said. "Then you can marry gods. Big, rich husbands! These men are gods. But they can only marry Dirt women. So look after your little cherrystones, keep them from Dirt boys and men like me, and then you can be a god's wife and live in a golden hut." He grinned at their staring faces and stood up to piss on the cold ashes of the fire.

While the Crown men were rousing, Bidh took the older girls into the forest to gather berries from a tangle of bushes nearby; he let them eat some, but made them put most of what they picked into his cap. He brought the cap full of berries back to the soldiers and offered them, his knuckles to his forehead. "See," he said to the girls, "this is how you must do. Crown people are like babies and you must be their mothers."

Modh's little sister Mal and the younger children were silently weeping with hunger. Modh and Vui took them to the stream to drink. "Drink all you can, Mal," Modh told her sister. "Fill up your belly. It helps." Then she said to Vui, "Man-babies!" and spat. "Men who take food from children!"

"Do as the Allulu says," said Vui.

Their captors now ignored them, leaving Bidh to look after them.

It was some comfort to have a man who spoke their language with them. He was kind enough, carrying the little ones, sometimes two at a time, for he was strong. He told Vui and Modh stories about the place where they were going. Vui began to call him Uncle. Modh would not let him carry Mal, and did not call him anything.

Modh was eleven. When she was six, her mother had died in child-birth, and she had always looked after the little sister.

When she saw the golden man pick up her sister and run down the hill, she ran after them with nothing in her mind but that she must not lose the little one. The men went so fast at first that she could not keep up, but she did not lose their trace, and kept after them all that day. She had seen her grandmothers and grandfathers slaughtered like pigs. She thought everybody she knew in the world was dead. Her sister was alive and she was alive. That was enough. That filled her heart.

When she held her little sister in her arms again, that was more than enough.

But then, in the hills, the cruel man named Sio's Daughter and then threw her away, and the golden man kept her from going to pick her up. She tried to look back at the high bushes where the baby lay, she tried to see the place so she could remember it, but the golden man hit her so she was dizzy and drove and dragged her up the hill so fast her breath burned in her chest and her eyes clouded with pain. Sio's Daughter was lost. She would lie dead there in the bushes. Foxes and wild dogs would eat her flesh and break her bones. A terrible emptiness came into Modh, a hollow, a hole of fear and anger that everything else fell into. She would never be able to go back and find the baby and bury her. Children before they are named have no ghosts, even if they are unburied, but the cruel one had named Sio's Daughter. He had pointed and named her: Groda. Groda would follow them. Modh had heard the thin cry in the night. It came from the hollow place. What could fill that hollow? What could be enough?

III

BELA TEN BELEN AND HIS COMPANIONS DID NOT RETURN TO THE City in triumph, since they had not fought with other men; but neither did they have to creep in by back ways at night as an unsuccessful foray. They had not lost a man, and they brought back six slaves, all female. Only Ralo ten Bal brought nothing, and the others joked about him losing his catch and falling asleep on watch. And Bela ten Belen joked about his own luck in catching two fish on one hook, telling how the marsh-fire girl had followed them of her own will to be with her sister.

As he thought about his foray, he realised that they had been lucky indeed, and that their success was due not to him, but to Bidh. If Bidh had told them to do so, the Allulu would have ambushed and killed the soldiers before they ever reached the farther village. The slave had saved them. His loyalty seemed natural and expectable to Bela, but he honored it. He knew Bidh and his sister Nata were fond of each other, but could rarely see each other, since Bidh belonged to the Hans and Nata to the Belens. When the opportunity arose, he traded two of his own house-slaves for Bidh and made him overseer of the Belen House slave compound.

Bela had gone slave-catching because he wanted a girl to bring up in the house with his mother and sister and his brother's wife: a young girl, to be trained and formed to his desire until he married her.

Some Crown men were content to take their Dirt wife from the dirt, from the slave quarters of their own compound or the barracks of the city, to get children on her, keep her in the hanan, and have nothing else to do with her. Others were more fastidious. Bela's mother Hehum had been brought up from birth in a Crown hanan, trained to be a Crown's wife. Nata, four years old when she was caught, had lived at first in the slave barracks, but within a few years a Root merchant, speculating on the child's beauty, had traded five male slaves for her and kept her in his hanan so that she would not be raped or lie with a man till she could be sold as a wife. Nata's beauty became famous, and many Crown men sought to marry her. When she was fifteen, the Belens traded the produce of their best field and the use of a whole building in Copper Street for her. Like her mother-in-law, she was treated with honor in the Belen household.

Finding no girl in the barracks or hanans he was willing to look at as a wife, Bela had resolved to go catch a wild one. He had succeeded doubly.

At first he thought to keep Mal and send Modh to the barracks. But though Mal was charming, with a plump little body and big, long-lashed eyes, she was only five years old. He did not want sex with a baby, as some men did. Modh was eleven, still a child, but not for long. She was not always beautiful, but always vivid. Her courage in following her sister had impressed him. He brought both sisters to the hanan of the Belen house and asked his mother, his sister-in-law, and his sister to see that they were properly brought up.

It was strange to the wild girls to hear Nata Belenda speak words of their language, for to them she seemed a creature of another order, as did Hehum Belenda, the mother of Bela and Alo, and Tudju Belen, the sister. All three women were tall and clean and soft-skinned, with soft hands and long lustrous hair. They wore garments of cobweb colored like spring flowers, like sunset clouds. They were goddesses. But Nata Belenda smiled and was gentle and tried to talk to the children in their own tongue, though she remembered little of it. The grandmother Hehum Belenda was grave and stern-looking, but quite soon she took Mal onto her lap to play with Nata's baby boy. Tudju, the daughter of the house, was the one who most amazed them. She was not much older than Modh, but a head taller, and Modh thought she was wearing moonlight. Her robes were cloth of silver, which only Crown women could wear. A heavy silver belt slanted from her waist to her hip, with a marvelously worked silver sheath hanging from it. The sheath was empty, but she pretended to draw a sword from it, and flourished the sword of air, and lunged with it, and laughed to see little Mal still looking for the sword. But she showed the girls that they must not touch her; she was sacred, that day. They understood that.

Living with these women in the great house of the Belens, they began to understand many more things. One was the language of the City. It was not so different from theirs as it seemed at first, and within a few weeks they were babbling along in it.

After three months they attended their first ceremony at the Great Temple: Tudju's coming of age. They all went in procession to the Great Temple. To Modh it was wonderful to be out in the open air again, for she was weary of walls and ceilings. Being Dirt women, they sat behind the yellow curtain, but they could see Tudju chose her sword from the row of swords hanging behind the altar. She would wear it the rest of her life whenever she went out of the house. Only women born to the Crown wore swords. No one else in the City was allowed to carry any weapon, except Crown men when they served as soldiers. Modh and Mal knew that, now. They knew many things, and also knew there was much more to learn—everything one had to know to be a woman of the City.

It was easier for Mal. She was young enough that to her the City rules and ways soon became the way of the world. Modh had to unlearn the rules and ways of the Tullu people. But as with the language, some things were more familiar than they first seemed. Modh knew that when a Tullu man was elected chief of the village, even if he already had a wife he had to marry a slave woman. Here, the Crown men were all chiefs. And they all had to marry Dirt women—slaves. It was the same rule, only, like everything in the City, made greater and more complicated.

In the village, there had been two kinds of person, Tullu and slaves. Here there were three kinds; and you could not change your kind, and you could not marry your kind. There were the Crowns, who owned land and slaves, and were all chiefs, priests, gods on earth. And the Dirt people, who were slaves. Even though a Dirt woman who married a Crown might be treated almost like a Crown herself—like the Nata and Hehum— still, they were Dirt. And there were the other people, the Roots.

Modh knew little about the Roots. There was nobody like them in her village. She asked Nata about them and observed what she could from the seclusion of the hanan. Root people were rich. They oversaw planting and harvest, the storehouses and marketplaces. Root women were in charge of housebuilding, and all the marvelous clothes the Crowns wore were made by Root women.

Crown men had to marry Dirt women, but Crown women, if they married, had to marry Root men. When she got her sword, Tudju also acquired several suitors—Root men who came with packages of sweets and stood outside the hanan curtain and said polite things, and then went and talked to Alo and Bela, who were the lords of Belen since their father had died in a foray years ago.

Root women had to marry Dirt men. There was a Root woman who wanted to buy Bidh and marry him. Alo and Bela told him they would sell him or keep him, as he chose. He had not decided yet.

Root people owned slaves and crops, but they owned no land, no houses. All real property belonged to Crowns. "So," said Modh, "Crowns let the Root people live in the City, let them have this house or that, in exchange for the work they do and what their slaves grow in the fields—is that right?"

"As a *reward* for working," Nata corrected her, always gentle, never scolding. "The Sky Father made the City for his sons, the Crowns. And they reward good workers by letting them live in it. As our owners, Crowns and Roots, reward us for work and obedience by letting us live, and eat, and have shelter."

Modh did not say, "But—"

It was perfectly clear to her that it was a system of exchange, and that it was not fair exchange. She came from just far enough outside it to be able to look at it. And, being excluded from reciprocity, any slave can see the system with an undeluded eye. But Modh did not know of any other system, any possibility of another system, which would have allowed her to say "But." Neither did Nata know of that alternative, that possible even when unattainable space in which there is room for justice, in which the word "But" can be spoken and have meaning.

Nata had undertaken to teach the wild girls how to live in the City, and she did so with honest care. She taught them the rules. She taught them what was believed. The rules did not include justice, so she did not teach them justice. If she did not herself believe what was believed, yet she taught them how to live with those who did. Modh was self-willed and bold when she came, and Nata could easily have let her think she had rights, encouraged her to rebel, and then watched her be whipped or mutilated or sent to the fields to be worked to death. Some slave women would have done so. Nata, kindly treated most of her life, treated others kindly. Warm-hearted, she took the girls to her heart. Her own baby boy was a Crown, she was proud of her godling, but she loved the wild girls too. She liked to hear Bidh and Modh talk in the language of the nomads, as they did sometimes. Mal had forgotten it by then.

Mal soon grew out of her plumpness and became as thin as Modh. After a couple of years in the City both girls were very different from the tough little wildcats Bela ten Belen's foray had caught. They were slender, delicate-looking. They ate well and lived soft. These days, they might not have been able to keep up the cruel pace of their captors' flight to the City. They got little exercise but dancing, and had no work to do. Conservative Crown families like the Belens did not let their slave wives do work that was beneath them, and all work was beneath a Crown.

Modh would have gone mad with boredom if the grandmother had not let her run and play in the courtyard of the compound, and if Tudju had not taught her to sword-dance and to fence. Tudju loved her sword and the art of using it, which she studied daily with an older priestess. Equipping Modh with a blunted bronze practice sword, she passed along all she learned, so as to have a partner to practice with. Tudju's sword was extremely sharp, but she already used it skillfully and never once hurt Modh.

Tudju had not yet accepted any of the suitors who came and murmured at the yellow curtain of the hanan. She imitated the Root men mercilessly after they left, so that the hanan rocked with laughter. She claimed she could smell each one coming—the one that smelled like boiled chard, the one that smelled like cat-dung, the one that smelled like old men's feet. She told Modh, in secret, that she did not intend to marry, but to be a priestess and a judge-councillor. But she did not tell her brothers that. Bela and Alo were expecting to make a good profit in food-supply or clothing from Tudju's marriage; they lived expensively, as Crowns should. The Belen larders and clothes-chests had been supplied too long by bartering rentals for goods. Nata alone had cost twenty years' rent on their best property.

Modh made friends among the Belenda slaves and was very fond of Tudju, Nata, and old Hehum, but she loved no one as she loved Mal. Mal was all she had left of her old life, and she loved in her all that she had lost for her. Perhaps Mal had always been the only thing she had: her sister, her child, her charge, her soul.

She knew now that most of her people had not been killed, that her father and the rest of them were no doubt following their annual round across the plains and hills and waterlands; but she never seriously thought of trying to escape and find them. Mal had been taken, she had followed Mal. There was no going back. And as Bidh had said to them, it was a big, rich life here.

She did not think of the grandmothers and grandfathers lying slaughtered, or Dua's Daughter who had been beheaded. She had seen all that yet not seen it; it was her sister she had seen. Her father and the others would have buried all those people and sung the songs for them. They were here no longer. They were going on the bright roads and the dark roads of the sky, dancing in the bright hut-circles up there.

She did not hate Bela ten Belen for leading the raid, killing Dua's Daughter, stealing her and Mal and the others. Men did that, nomads as well as City men. They raided, killed people, took food, took slaves. That was the way men were. It would be as stupid to hate them for it as to love them for it.

But there was one thing that should not have been, that should not be and yet continued endlessly to be, the small thing, the nothing that when she remembered it made the rest, all the bigness and richness of life, shrink up into the shriveled meat of a bad walnut, the yellow smear of a crushed fly.

It was at night that she knew it, she and Mal, in their soft bed with cobweb sheets, in the safe darkness of the warm, high-walled house: Mal's indrawn breath, the cold chill down her own arms, *do you hear it?*

They clung together, listening, hearing.

Then in the morning Mal would be heavy-eyed and listless, and if Modh tried to make her talk or play she would begin to cry, and Modh would sit down at last and hold her and cry with her, endless, useless, dry, silent weeping. There was nothing they could do. The baby followed them because she did not know whom else to follow.

Neither of them spoke of this to anyone in the household. It had nothing to do with these women. It was theirs. Their ghost.

Sometimes Modh would sit up in the dark and whisper aloud, "Hush, Groda! Hush, be still!" And there might be silence for a while. But the thin wailing would begin again.

Modh had not seen Vui since they came to the City. Vui belonged to the Hans, but she had not been treated as Modh and Mal had. Dos ten Han bargained for a pretty girl from a Root wife-broker, and Vui was one of the slaves he bartered for that wife. If she was still alive, she did not live where Modh could reach her or hear of her. Seen from the hills, as she had seen it that one time, the City did not look very big in the great slant and distance of the fields and meadows and forests stretching on to the west; but if you lived in it, it was as endless as the plains. You could be lost in it. Vui was lost in it.

Modh was late coming to womanhood, by City standards: fourteen. Hehum and Tudju held the ceremony for her in the worship-room of the house, a full day of rituals and singing. She was given new clothes. When it was over Bidh came to the yellow curtain of the hanan, called to her, and put into her hands a little deerskin pouch, crudely stitched.

She looked at it puzzled. Bidh said, "You know, in the village, a girl's uncle gives her a *delu*," and turned away. She caught his hand and thanked him, touched, half-remembering the custom and fully knowing the risk he had run in making his gift. Dirt people were forbidden to do any sewing. Sewing was a Root prerogative. A slave found with a needle and thread could have a hand cut off. Like his sister Nata, Bedh was warm-hearted. Both Modh and Mal had called him Uncle for years now.

Alo ten Belen had three sons from Nata by now to be priests and soldiers of the House of Belen. Alo came most nights to play with the little boys and take Nata off to his rooms, but they saw little of Bela in the hanan. His friend Dos ten Han had given him a concubine, a pretty, teasing, experienced woman who kept him satisfied for a long time. He had forgotten about the nomad sisters, lost interest in his plans of educating them. Their days passed peacefully and cheerfully. As the years went by, their nights too grew more peaceful. The crying now came seldom to Modh, and only in a dream, from which she could waken.

But always, when she wakened so, she saw Mal's eyes wide open in the darkness. They said nothing, but held each other till they slept again.

In the morning, Mal would seem quite herself; and Modh would say nothing, fearing to upset her sister, or fearing to make the dream no dream.

Then things changed.

Tudju's brothers Bela and Alo called for her. She was gone all day, and came back to the hanan looking fierce and aloof, fingering the hilt of her silver sword. When her mother went to embrace her, Tudju made the gesture that put her aside. All these years with Tudju in the hanan, it had been easy to forget that she was a Crown woman, the only Crown among them; that the yellow curtain was to separate them, not her, from the sacred parts of the house; that she was herself a sacred being. But now she had to take up her birthright.

"They want me to marry that fat Root man, so we can get his shop and looms in Silk Street," she said. "I will not. I am going to live at the Great Temple." She looked around at them all, her mother, her sister-in-law, Mal, Modh, the other slave women. "Everything I'm given there, I'll send here," she said. "But I told Bela that if he gives one finger's width of land for that woman he wants now, I'll send nothing home from the Temple. He can go slave-catching again to feed her. And you." She looked again at Mal and Modh. "Keep an eye on him," she said. "It is time he married."

Bela had recently traded his concubine and the Dirt son she had borne him, making a good bargain in cropland, and then promptly offered almost the whole amount for another woman he had taken a fancy to. It was not a question of marriage, for a Dirt woman, to marry, must be a virgin, and the woman he wanted had been owned by several men. Alo and Tudju had prevented the bargain, which he could not make without their consent. It was, as Tudju said, time for Bela to consider his sacred obligation to marry and beget children of the sky on a woman of the dirt.

So Tudju left the hanan and the house to serve in the Great Temple, only returning sometimes on formal visits. She was replaced, evenings, by her brother Bela. Dour and restless, like a dog on a chain, he would stalk in after Alo, and watch the little boys running about and the slaves' games and dances.

He was a tall man, handsome, lithe and well-muscled. From the day she first saw him in the horror and carnage of the foray, to Modh he had been the golden man. She had seen many other golden men in the City since then, but he was the first, the model.

She had no fear of him, other than the guardedness a slave must feel towards the master; he was spoilt, of course, but not capricious or cruel; even when he was sulky he did not take out his temper on his slaves. Mal, however, shrank from him in uncontrollable dread. Modh told her she was foolish. Bela was nearly as good-natured as Alo, and Mal trusted Alo completely. Mal just shook her head. She never argued, and grieved bitterly when she disagreed with her sister on anything, but she could not even try not to fear Bela.

Mal was thirteen. She had her ceremony (and to her too Bidh secretly gave a crude little "soulbag"). In the evening of that day she wore her new clothing. Dirt people even when they lived with Crowns could not wear sewn garments, only lengths of cloth; but there are many graceful ways of draping and gathering unshaped material, and though the spider-silk could not be hemmed, it could be delicately fringed and tasseled. Mal's garments were undyed silk, with a blue-green overveil so fine it was transparent.

When she came in, Bela looked up, and looked at her, and went on looking.

Modh stood up suddenly without plan or forethought and said, "Lords, Masters! May I dance for my sister's festival?" She scarcely waited for their consent, but spoke to Lui, who played the tablet-drums for dancers, and ran to her room for the bronze sword Tudju had given her and the pale flame-colored veil that had been given her at her festival. She ran back with the veil flowing about her. Lui drummed, and Modh danced. She had never danced so well. She had never danced the way she did now, with all the fierce formal precision of the sword-dance, but also with a wildness, a hint of threat in her handling of the blade, a sexual syncopation to the drumbeat that made Lui's drumming grow ever faster and fiercer in response, so that the dance gathered and gathered like a flame, hotter and brighter, the translucent veil flowing, whirling at the watchers' faces. Bela sat motionless, fixed, gazing, and did not flinch even when the veil struck its spiderweb blow across his eyes.

When she was done he said, "When did you learn to dance like that?"

"Under your eyes," she said.

He laughed, a little uneasy. "Let Mal dance now," he said, looking around for her.

"She's too tired to dance," Modh said. "The rites were long. She tires easily. But I will dance again."

He motioned her to go on dancing with a flick of his hand. She nodded to Lui, who grinned widely and began the hesitant, insinuating beat of the slow dance called mimei. Modh put on the ankle-bells Lui kept with her drums; she arranged her veil so that it covered her face and body and arms, baring only her ankles with the jingling anklets and her naked feet. The dance began, her feet moving slightly and constantly, her body swaying, the beat and the movements slowly becoming more intense.

She could see through the gauzy silk; she could see the stiff erection under Bela's silk tunic; she could see his heart beat in his chest.

After that night Bela hung around Modh so closely that her problem was not to draw his attention but to prevent his getting her alone and raping her. Hehum and the other women made sure she was never alone, for they were eager for Bela to marry her. They all liked her, and she would cost the House of Belen nothing. Within a few days Bela declared his intention to marry Modh. Alo gave his approval gladly, and Tudju came from the Temple to officiate at the marriage rites.

All Bela's friends came to the wedding. The yellow curtain was moved back from the dancing room, hiding only the sleeping rooms of the women.

For the first time in seven years Modh saw the men who had been on the foray. The man she remembered as *the big one* was Dos ten Han; Ralo ten Bal was *the cruel one*. She tried to keep away from Ralo, for the sight of him disturbed her. The youngest of the men, he had changed more than the others, yet he acted boyish and petulant. He drank a lot and danced with all the slave girls.

Mal hung back as always, and even more than usual; she was frightened without the yellow curtain to hide behind, and the sight of the men from the foray made her tremble. She tried to stay close to Hehum. But the old woman teased her gently and pushed her forward to let the Crown men see her, for this was a rare chance to show her off. She was marriageable now, and these Crown men might pay to marry her rather than merely use her. She was very pretty, and might bring back a little wealth to the Belens.

Modh pitied her misery, but did not worry about her safety even among drunken men. Hehum and Alo would not let anybody have her virginity, which was her value as a bride.

Bela stayed close beside Modh every moment except when she danced. She danced two of the sword dances and then the mimei. The men watched her breathlessly, while Bela watched her and them, tense and triumphant. "Enough!" he said aloud just before the end of the veiled dance, perhaps to prove he was master even of this flame of a woman, perhaps because he could not restrain himself. She stopped instantly and stood still, though the drum throbbed on for a few beats.

"Come," he said. She put out her hand from the veil, and he took it and led her out of the great hall, to his apartments. Behind them was laughter, and a new dance began.

It was a good marriage. They were well matched. She was wise enough to obey any order he gave immediately and without any resistance, but she never forestalled his orders by anticipating his wishes, babying him, coddling him, as most slave women he knew had done. He felt in her an unyieldingness that allowed her to be obedient yet never slavish. It was as if in her soul she were indifferent to him, no matter what their bodies did; he could bring her to sexual ecstasy or, if he liked, he could have had her tortured, but nothing he did would change her, would touch her; she was like a wildcat or a fox, not tameable.

This impassibility, this distance kept him drawn to her, trying to lessen it. He was fascinated by her, his little fox, his vixen. In time they became friends as well. Their lives were boring; they found each other good company.

In the daytime, he was off, of course, still sometimes playing in the ballcourts with his friends, performing his priestly duties at the temples, and increasingly often going to the Great Temple. Tudju wanted him to join the Council. She had a considerable influence over Bela, because she knew what she wanted and he did not. He never had known what he wanted. There was not much for a Crown man to want. He had imagined himself a soldier until he led the foray over the Dayward Hills. Successful as it had been, in that they had caught slaves and come home safe, he could not bear to recall the slaughter, the hiding, the proof of his own ineptitude, the days and nights of fear, confusion, disgust, exhaustion, and shame. So there was nothing to do but play in the ballcourts, officiate at rites, and drink, and dance. And now there was Modh. And sons of his own to come. And maybe, if Tudju kept at him, he would become a councillor. It was enough.

For Modh, it was hard to get used to sleeping beside the golden man and not beside her sister. She would wake in darkness, and the weight of the bed and the smell and everything was wrong. She would want Mal then, not him. But in the daytime she would go back to the hanan and be with Mal and the others just as before, and then he would be there in the evening, and it would have been all right, it would have been good, except for Ralo ten Bal.

Ralo had noticed Mal on the wedding night, cowering near Hehum, in her blue veil that was like a veil of rain. He had come up to her and tried to make her talk or dance; she had shrunk, quailed, shivered. She would not speak or look up. He put his thumb under her chin to make her raise her face, and at that Mal retched as if about to vomit and staggered where she stood. Hehum had interfered: "Lord Master ten Bal, she is untouched," she said, with the stern dignity of her position as Mother of Gods. Ralo laughed and withdrew his hand, saying foolishly, "Well, I've touched her now."

Within a few days an offer for her had come from the Bals. It was not a good one. She was asked for as a slave girl, as if she were not marriageable, and the barter was to be merely the produce of one of the Bal grain-plots. Given the Bals' wealth and the relative poverty of the Belens, it was an insulting offer. Alo and Bela refused it without explanation or apology, haughtily. It was a great relief to Modh when Bela told her that. When the offer came, she had been stricken. Had she seduced Bela away from Mal only to leave her prey to a man Mal feared even more than Bela, and with better reason? Trying to protect her sister, had she exposed her to far greater harm? She rushed to Mal to tell her they had turned down the Bals' offer, and telling her burst into tears of guilt and relief. Mal did not weep; she took the good news quietly. She had been terribly quiet since the wedding.

She and Modh were together all day, as they had always been. But it was not the same; it could not be. The husband came between the sisters. They could not share their sleep.

Days and festivals passed. Modh had put Ralo ten Bal out of mind, when he came home with Bela after a game at the ball courts. Bela did not seem comfortable about bringing him into the house, but had no reason to turn him away. Bela came into the hanan and said to Modh, "He hopes to see you dance again."

"You aren't bringing him behind the curtain?"

"Only into the dancing room."

He saw her frown, but was not accustomed to reading expressions. He waited for a reply.

"I will dance for him," Modh said.

She told Mal to stay back in the sleeping rooms in the hanan. Mal nodded. She looked small, slender, weary. She put her arms around her sister. "Oh Modh," she said. "You're brave, you're kind."

Modh felt frightened and hateful, but she said nothing, only hugged Mal hard, smelling the sweet smell of her hair, and went back to the dancing room.

She danced, and Ralo praised her dancing. Then he said what she knew he had been waiting to say from the moment he came: "Where's your wife's sister, Bela?"

"Not well," Modh said, though it was not for a Dirt woman to answer a question one Crown asked another Crown.

"Not very well tonight," Bela said, and Modh could have kissed him from eyes to toes for hearing her, for saying it.

"Ill?"

"I don't know," Bela said, weakening, glancing at Modh.

"Yes," Modh said.

"But perhaps she could just come show me her pretty eyebrows."

Bela glanced at Modh again. She said nothing.

"I had nothing to do with that stupid message my father sent you about her," Ralo said. He looked from Bela to Modh and back at Bela, smirking, conscious of his power. "Father heard me talking about her. He just wanted to give me a treat. You must forgive him. He was thinking of her as an ordinary Dirt girl." He looked at Modh again. "Bring your little sister out just for a moment, Modh Belenda," he said, bland, vicious.

Bela nodded to her. She rose and went behind the yellow curtain.

She stood some minutes in the empty hall that led to the sleeping rooms, then came back to the dancing room. "Forgive me, Lord Master Bal," she said in her softest voice, "the girl has a fever and cannot rise to obey your summons. She has been unwell a long time. I am so sorry. May I send one of the other girls?"

"No," Ralo said. "I want that one." He spoke to Bela, ignoring Modh. "You brought two home from that raid we went on. I didn't get one. I shared the danger, it's only fair you share the catch." He had evidently rehearsed this sentence.

"You got one," Bela said.

"What are you talking about?"

Bela looked uncomfortable. "You had one," he said, in a less decisive voice.

"I came home with nothing!" Ralo cried, his voice rising, accusing. "And you kept two! Listen, I know you've brought them up all these years, I know it's expensive rearing girls. I'm not asking for a gift."

"You very nearly did," Bela said, stiffly, in a low voice.

Ralo put this aside with a laugh. "Just keep in mind, Bela, we were soldiers together," he said, cajoling, boyish, putting his arm round Bela's shoulders. "You were my captain. I don't forget that! We were brothers in arms. Listen, I'm not talking about just buying the girl. You married one sister, I'll marry the other. Hear that? We'll be brothers in the dirt, how's that?" He laughed and slapped his hand on Bela's shoulder. "How's that?" he said. "You won't be the poorer for it, Captain!"

"This is not the time to talk about it," Bela said, awkward and dignified.

Ralo smiled and said, "But soon, I hope."

Bela stood, and Ralo had to take his leave. "Please send to tell me when Pretty Eyebrows is feeling better," he said to Modh, with his smirk and his piercing glance. "I'll come at once."

When he was gone Modh could not be silent. "Lord Husband, don't give Mal to him. Please don't give Mal to him."

"I don't want to," he said.

"Then don't! Please don't!"

"It's all his talk. He boasts."

"Maybe. But if he makes an offer?"

"Wait till he makes an offer," Bela said, a little heavily, but smiling. He drew her to him and stroked her hair. "How you fret over Mal. She's not really ill, is she?"

"I don't know. She isn't well."

"Girls," he said, shrugging. "You danced well tonight."

"I danced badly. I would not dance well for that scorpion."

That made him laugh. "You did leave out the best part of the amei."

"Of course I did. I want to dance that only for you."

"Lui has gone to bed, or I'd ask you to."

"Oh, I don't need a drummer. Here, here's my drum." She took his hands and put them on her full breasts. "Feel the beat?" she said. She stood, struck the pose, raised her arms, and began the dance, there right in front of him, till he seized her, burying his face between her thighs, and she sank down on him laughing.

Hehum came out into the dancing room; she drew back, seeing them, but Modh untangled herself from her husband and went to the old woman.

"Mal is ill," Hehum began, with a worried face.

"Oh I knew it, I knew it!" Modh cried, instantly certain that it was her fault, that her lie had made itself truth. She ran to Mal's room, which she shared with her so long.

Hehum followed her. "She hides her ears," she said, "I think she has the earache. She cries and hides her ears."

Mal sat up when Modh came into the room. She looked wild and haggard. "You hear it, you hear it, don't you?" she cried, taking Modh's hands.

"No," Modh murmured, "no, I don't hear it. I hear nothing. There is nothing, Mal."

Mal stared up at her. "When he comes," she whispered.

"No," Modh said.

"Groda comes with him."

"No. It was years ago, years ago. You have got to be strong, Mal, you have got to put all that away."

Mal let out a piteous, loud moan and put Modh's hands up over her own ears. "I don't want to hear it!" she cried, and began to sob violently.

"Tell my husband I will spend this night with Mal," Modh said to Hehum. She held her sister in her arms till she slept at last, and then she slept too, though not easily, waking often, listening always.

In the morning she went to Bidh and asked him if he knew what people—their people, the villagers—did about ghosts.

He thought about it. "I think if there was a ghost somewhere they didn't go there. Or they moved away. What kind of ghost?"

"An unburied person."

Bidh made a face. "They would move away," he said with certainty.

"What if it followed them?"

Bidh held out his hands. "I don't know! The priest, the yegug, would do something, I guess. Some spell. The yegug knew all about things like that. These priests here, these temple people, they don't know anything but their dances and singing and talk-talk-talk. So, what is this? Is it Mal?"

"Yes."

He made a face again. "Poor little one," he said. Then, brightening, "Maybe it would be good if she left this house."

Several days passed. Mal was feverish and sleepless, hearing the ghost cry or fearing to hear it every night. Modh spent the nights with her, and Bela made no objection. But one evening when he came home he talked some while with Alo, and then the brothers came to the hanan. Hehum and Nata were there with the children. The brothers sent the children away, and asked that Modh come. Mal stayed in her room.

"Ralo ten Bal wants Mal for his wife," Alo said. He looked at Modh, forestalling whatever she might say. "We said she is very young, and has not been well. He says he will not sleep with her until she is fifteen. He will have her looked after with every attention. He wants to marry her now so that no other man may compete with him for her."

"And so raise her price," Nata said, with unusual sharpness. She had been the object of such a bidding war, which was why the Belens had all but beggared themselves to buy her.

"The price the Bals offer now could not be matched by any house in the City," Alo said gravely. "Seeing we were unwilling, they at once increased what they offered, and increased it again. It is the largest bride-bargain

I ever heard of. Larger than yours, Nata." He looked with a strange smile at his wife, half pride half shame, rueful, intimate. Then he looked at his mother and at Modh. "They offer all the fields of Nuila. Their western orchards. Five Root houses on Wall Street. The new silk factory. And gifts—jewelry, fine garments, gold." He looked down. "It is impossible for us to refuse," he said.

"We will be nearly as wealthy as we used to be," Bela said.

"Nearly as wealthy as the Bals," Alo said, with the same rueful twist to his mouth.

"They thought we were bargaining. It was ridiculous. Every time I began to speak, old Loho ten Bal would hold up his hand to stop me and add something to the offer!" He glanced at Bela, who nodded and laughed.

"Have you spoken to Tudju?" Modh said.

"Yes," Bela answered.

"She agrees?" The question was unnecessary. Bela nodded.

"Ralo will not mistreat your sister, Modh," Alo said seriously. "Not after paying such a price for her. He'll treat her like a golden statue. They all will. He is sick with desire for her. I never saw a man so infatuated. It's odd, he's barely seen her, only at your wedding. But he's enthralled."

"He wants to marry her right away?" Nata asked.

"Yes. But he won't touch her till she's fifteen. If we'd asked him he might have promised never to touch her at all!"

"Promises are easy," Nata said.

"If he does lie with her it won't kill her," Bela said. "It might do her good. She's been spoiled here. You spoil her, Modh. A man in her bed may be what she needs."

"But—*that* man—" Modh said, her mouth dry, her ears ringing.

"Ralo's a bit spoiled himself. There's nothing wrong with him."

"He—" She bit her lip. She could not say the words.

Bela was keeping her from turning back to pick up the baby, jabbing his sword at her, dragging her by the arm. Mal was crying and stumbling behind them in the dust, up the steep hill, among the trees.

They all sat in uncomfortable silence.

"So," Alo said, louder than necessary, "there will be another wedding."

"When?"

"Before the Sacrifice."

Another silence.

"We mean no harm to come to Mal," Alo said to Modh. "Be sure of that, Modh. Tell her that."

She sat unable to move or speak.

"Neither of you has ever been mistreated," Bela said, resentfully, as if answering an accusation. His mother frowned at him and clicked her tongue. He reddened and fidgeted.

"Go speak to your sister, Modh," Hehum said. Modh got up. As she stood she saw the walls and tapestries and faces grow small and bright, sparkling with little lights. She walked slowly and stopped in the doorway.

"I am not the one to tell her," she said, hearing her own voice far away.

"Bring her here then," Alo said.

She nodded; but when she nodded the walls kept turning around her, and reaching out for support, she fell in a half-faint.

Bela came to her and cradled her in his arms. "Little fox, little fox," he murmured. She heard him say angrily to Alo, "The sooner the better."

He carried Modh to their bedroom, sat with her till she pretended to sleep, then left her quietly.

She knew that by her concern, by the nights she had spent with Mal, she had let her husband become jealous of her sister.

It was for her sake I came to you! she cried to him in her heart.

But there was nothing she could say now that would not cause more harm.

When she got up she went to Mal's room. Mal ran to her weeping, but Modh only held her, not speaking, till the girl grew quieter. Then she said, "Mal, there is nothing I can do. You must endure this. So must I."

Mal drew back a little and said nothing for a while. "It cannot happen," she said then, with a kind of certainty. "It will not be allowed. The child will not allow it."

Modh was bewildered for a moment. She had for some days been fairly sure she was pregnant. Now she thought for a moment that Mal was pregnant. Then she understood.

"You must not think about that child," she said. "She was not yours or mine. She was not daughter or sister of ours. Her death was not our death."

"No. It is his," Mal said, and almost smiled. She stroked Modh's arms and turned away. "I will be good, Modh," she said. "You must not let this trouble you—you and your husband. It's not your trouble. Don't worry. What must happen will happen."

Cowardly, Modh let herself accept Mal's reassurance. More cowardly still, she let herself be glad that it was only a few days until the wedding. Then what must happen would have happened. It would be done, it would be over.

She was pregnant; she told Hehum and Nata of the signs. They both smiled and said, "A boy."

There was a flurry of getting ready for the wedding. The ceremony was to be in Belen House, and the Belens refused to let the Bals provide food or dancers or musicians or any of the luxuries they offered. Tudju was to be the marriage priestess. She came a couple of days early to stay in her old home, and she and Modh played at sword-practice the way they had done as girls, while Mal looked on and applauded as she had used to do. Mal was thin and her eyes looked large, but she went through the days serenely. What her nights were, Modh did not know. Mal did not send for her. In the morning, she would smile at Modh's questions about the night and say, "It passed."

But the night before the wedding, Modh woke in the deep night, hearing a baby cry.

She felt Bela awake beside her.

"Where is that child?" he said, his voice rough and deep in the darkness.

She said nothing.

"Nata should quiet her brat," he said.

"It is not Nata's."

It was a thin, strange cry, not the bawling of Nata's healthy boys. They heard it first to the left, as if in the hanan. Then after a silence the thin wail came from their right, in the public rooms of the house.

"Maybe it's my child," Modh said.

"What child?"

"Yours."

"What do you mean?"

"I carry your child. Nata and Hehum say it's a boy. I think it's a girl, though."

"But why is it crying?" Bela whispered, holding her.

She shuddered and held him. "It's not our baby, it's not our baby," she cried.

All night the baby wailed. People rose up and lighted lanterns and walked the halls and corridors of Belen House. They saw nothing but each other's frightened faces. Sometimes the weak, sickly crying ceased for a long time, then it would begin again. Mostly it was faint, as if far away, even when it was heard in the next room. Nata's little boys heard it, and shouted, "Make it stop!" Tudju burned incense in the prayer room and chanted all night long. To her the faint wailing seemed to be under the floor, under her feet.

When the sun rose the people of Belen House ceased to hear the ghost. They made ready for the wedding festival as best they could.

The people of Bal House came. Mal was brought out from behind the yellow curtain, wearing voluminous unsewn brocaded silks and golden jewellery, her transparent veil like rain about her head. She looked very small in the elaborate draperies, straight-backed, her gaze held down. Ralo ten Bal was resplendent in puffed and sequined velvet. Tudju lighted the wedding fire and began the rites.

Modh listened, listened, not to the words Tudju chanted. She heard nothing.

The wedding party was brief, strained, everything done with the utmost formality. The guests left soon after the ceremony, following the bride and groom to Bal House, where there was to be more dancing and music. Tudju and Hehum, Alo and Nata went with them for civility's sake. Bela stayed home. He and Modh said almost nothing to each other. They took off their finery and lay silent in their bed, taking comfort in each other's warmth, trying not to listen for the wail of the child. They heard nothing, only the others returning, and then silence.

Tudju was to return to the Temple the next day. Early in the morning she came to Bela and Modh's apartments. Modh had just risen.

"Where is my sword, Modh?"

"You put it in the box in the dancing room."

"Your bronze one is there, not mine."

Modh looked at her in silence. Her heart began to beat heavily.

There was a noise, shouting, beating at the doors of the house.

Modh ran to the hanan, to the room she and Mal had slept in, and hid in the corner, her hands over her ears.

Bela found her there later. He raised her up, holding her wrists gently. She remembered how he had dragged her by the wrists up the hill through the trees. "Mal killed Ralo," he said. "She had Tudju's sword hidden under her dress. They strangled her."

"Where did she kill him?"

"On her bed," Bela said bleakly. "He never did keep his promises."

"Who will bury her?"

"No one," Bela said, after a long pause. "She was a Dirt woman. She murdered a Crown. They'll throw her body in the butcher's pit for the wild dogs."

"Oh, no," Modh said. She slipped her wrists from his grip. "No," she said. "She will be buried."

Bela shook his head.

"Will you throw everything away, Bela?"

"There is nothing I can do," he said.

She leaped up, but he caught and held her.

HE TOLD THE OTHERS THAT MODH WAS MAD WITH GRIEF. They kept her locked in the house, and kept watch over her.

Bedh knew what troubled her. He lied to her, trying to give her comfort; he said he had gone to the butcher's pit at night, found Mal's body, and buried it out past the Fields of the City. He said he had spoken what words he could remember that might be spoken to a spirit. He described Mal's grave vividly, the oak trees, the flowering bushes. He promised to take Modh there when she was well. She listened and smiled and thanked him. She knew he lied. Mal came to her every night and lay in the silence beside her.

Bela knew she came. He did not try to come to that bed again.

All through her pregnancy Modh was locked in Belen House. She did not go into labor until almost ten months had passed. The baby was too large; it would not be born, and with its death killed her.

Bela ten Belen buried his wife and unborn son with the Belen dead in the holy grounds of the Temple, for though she was only a Dirt woman, she had a dead god in her womb.

THE
FLIERS OF GY

THE PEOPLE OF GY LOOK PRETTY MUCH LIKE PEOPLE FROM OUR plane except that they have plumage, not hair. A fine, fuzzy down on the heads of infants becomes a soft, short coat of speckled dun on the fledglings, and with adolescence this grows out into a full head of feathers. Most men have ruffs at the back of the neck, shorter feathers all over the head, and tall, erectile crests. The head plumage of males is brown or black, barred and marked variously with bronze, red, green, and blue. Women's plumes usually grow long, sometimes sweeping down the back almost to the floor, with soft, curling, trailing edges, like the tails of ostriches; the colors of the feathers of women are vivid— purple, scarlet, coral, turquoise, gold. Gyr men and women are downy in the pubic region and pit of the arm and often have short, fine plumage over the whole body. People with brightly colored body feathers are a cheerful sight when naked, but they are much troubled by lice and nits.

Moulting is a continuous process, not seasonal. As people age, not all the moulted feathers grow back, and patchy baldness is common among both men and women over forty. Most people, therefore, save the best of their head feathers as they moult out, to make into wigs or false crests as needed. Those whose plumage is scanty or dull can also buy feather wigs at special shops. There are fads for bleaching one's feathers or spraying them gold or curling them, and wig shops in the cities will bleach, dye, spray, or crimp one's plumage and sell headdresses in whatever the current fashion is. Poor women with specially long, splendid head feathers often sell them to the wig shops for a fairly good price.

The Gyr write with quill pens. It is traditional for a father to give a set of his own stiff ruff quills to a child beginning to learn to write. Lovers exchange feathers with which they write love letters to one another, a pretty custom, referred to in a famous scene in the play *The Misunderstanding* by Inuinui:

> *O my betraying plume, that wrote his love*
> *To her! His love—my feather, and my blood!*

The Gyr are a staid, steady, traditional people, uninterested in innovation, shy of strangers. They are resistant to technological invention and novelty; attempts to sell them ballpoint pens or airplanes, or to induce them to enter the wonderful world of electronics, have failed. They continue writing letters to one another with quill pens, calculating with their heads, walking afoot or riding in carriages pulled by large, doglike animals called ugnunu, learning a few words in foreign languages when absolutely necessary, and watching classic stage plays written in traditional meters. No amount of exposure to the useful technologies, the marvelous gadgets, the advanced scientific knowledge of other planes—for Gy is a fairly popular tourist stop—seems to rouse envy or greed or a sense of inferiority in the Gyran bosom. They go on doing exactly as they have always done, not stodgily, exactly, but with a kind of dullness, a polite indifference and impenetrability, behind which may lie supreme self-satisfaction, or something quite different.

The crasser kind of tourists from other planes refer to the Gyr, of course, as birdies, birdbrains, featherheads, and so on. Many visitors from livelier planes visit the small, placid cities, take rides out into the country in ugnunu chaises, attend sedate but charming balls (for the Gyr like to dance), and enjoy an old-fashioned evening at the theater, without losing one degree of their contempt for the natives. "Feathers but no wings" is the conventional judgment that sums it up.

Such patronising visitors may spend a week in Gy without ever seeing a winged native or learning that what they took for a bird or a jet was a woman on her way across the sky.

The Gyr don't talk about their winged people unless asked. They don't conceal them or lie about them, but they don't volunteer information. I had to ask questions fairly persistently to be able to write the following description.

Wings never develop before late adolescence. There is no sign at all of the propensity until suddenly a girl of eighteen, a boy of nineteen, wakes up with a slight fever and an ache in the shoulder blades.

After that comes a year or more of great physical stress and pain, during which the subject must be kept quiet, warm, and well-fed. Nothing gives comfort but food—the nascent fliers are terribly hungry most of the time—and being wrapped or swaddled in blankets, while the body restructures, remakes, rebuilds itself. The bones lighten and become porous, the whole upper body musculature changes, and bony protuberances, developing rapidly from the shoulder blades, grow out into immense alar processes. The final stage is the growth of the wing feathers, which is not painful. The primaries are, as feathers go, massive, and may be a meter long. The wingspread of an adult male Gyr is about four meters, that of a woman usually about a half meter less. Stiff feathers sprout from the calves and ankles, to be spread wide in flight.

Any attempt to interfere, to prevent or halt the growth of wings, is useless and harmful or fatal. If the wings are not allowed to develop, the bones and muscles begin to twist and shrivel, causing unendurable, unceasing pain. Amputation of the wings or the flight feathers, at any stage, results in a slow, agonising death.

Among some of the most conservative, archaic peoples of the Gyr, the tribal societies living along the icy coasts of the north polar regions and the herdsfolk of the cold, barren steppes of the far south, this vulnerability of the winged people is incorporated into religion and ritual behavior. In the north, as soon as a youth shows the fatal signs, he or she is captured and handed over to the tribal elders. With rituals similar to their funeral rites, they fasten heavy stones to the victim's hands and feet, then go in procession to a cliff high above the sea and push the victim over, shouting, "Fly! Fly for us!"

Among the steppe tribes, the wings are allowed to develop completely, and the youth is carefully, worshipfully attended all that year. Let us say that it is a girl who has shown the fatal symptoms. In her feverish trances she functions as a shaman and soothsayer. The priests listen and interpret all her sayings to the people. When her wings are full grown, they are bound down to her back. Then the whole tribe set out to walk with her to the nearest high place, cliff or crag—often a journey of weeks in that flat, desolate country.

On the heights, after days of dancing and imbibing hallucinatory smoke from smudge fires of byubyu wood, the priests go with the young woman, all of them drugged, dancing and singing, to the edge of the cliff. There her wings are freed. She lifts them for the first time, and then like a young falcon leaving the nest, leaps stumbling off the cliff into the air, wildly beating those huge, untried wings. Whether she flies or falls, all the men of the tribe, screaming with excitement, shoot at her with bow and arrow or throw their razor-pointed hunting spears. She falls, pierced by dozens of spears and arrows. The women scramble down the cliff, and if there is any life left in her, they beat it out with stones. They then throw and heap stones over the body till it is buried under a cairn.

There are many cairns at the foot of every steep hill or crag in all the steppe country. Ancient cairns furnish stones for the new ones.

Such young people may try to escape their fate by running away from their people, but the weakness and fever that attend the development of wings cripple them, and they never get far.

There is a folktale in the South Marches of Merm of a winged man who leapt up into the air from the sacrificial crag and flew so strongly that he escaped the spears and arrows and disppeared into the sky. The original story ends there. The playwright Norwer used it as the basis of a romantic tragedy. In his play *Transgression,* the young man has appointed a tryst with his beloved and flies there to meet with her; but she has unwittingly betrayed him to another suitor, who lies in wait. As the lovers embrace, the suitor hurls his spear and kills the winged one. The maiden pulls out her own knife and kills the murderer and then— after exchanging anguished farewells with the not quite expired winged one—stabs herself. It is melodramatic but, if well staged, very moving; everybody has tears in their eyes when the hero first descends like an eagle, and when, dying, he enfolds his beloved in his great bronze wings.

A version of *Transgression* was performed a few years ago on my plane, in Chicago, at the Actual Reality Theater. It was probably inevitably, but unfortunately, translated as *Sacrifice of the Angels.* There is absolutely no mythology or lore concerning anything like our angels among the Gyr. Sentimental pictures of sweet little cherubs with baby wings, hovering guardian spirits, or grander images of divine messengers would strike them as a hideous mockery of something every parent and every adolescent dreads: a rare but fearful deformity, a curse, a death sentence.

Among the urbanised Gyr, that dread is mitigated to some degree, since the winged ones are treated not as sacrificial scapegoats but with tolerance and even sympathy, as people with a most unfortunate handicap.

We may find this odd. To soar over the heads of the earthbound, to race with eagles and soar with condors, to dance on air, to ride the wind, not in a noisy metal box or on a contraption of plastic and fabric and straps but on one's own vast, strong, splendid, outstretched wings—how could that be anything but a joy, a freedom? How stodgy, sullen-hearted, leaden-souled the Gyr must be, to think that people who can fly are cripples!

But they do have their reasons. The fact is that the winged Gyr can't trust their wings.

No fault can be found in the actual design of the wings. They serve admirably, with a little practice, for short flights, for effortless gliding and soaring on updrafts and, with more practice, for stunts and tumbling, aerial acrobatics. When winged people are fully mature, if they fly regularly they may achieve great stamina. They can stay aloft almost indefinitely. Many learn to sleep on the wing. Flights of over two thousand miles have been recorded, with only brief hover-stops to eat. Most of these very long flights were made by women, whose lighter bodies and bone structure give them the advantage over distance. Men, with their more powerful musculature, would take the speed-flying awards, if there were any. But the Gyr, at least the wingless majority, are not interested in records or awards, certainly not in competitions that involve a high risk of death.

The problem is that fliers' wings are liable to sudden, total, disastrous failure. Flight engineers and medical investigators on Gyr and elsewhere have not been able to account for it. The design of the wings has no detectable fault; their failure must be caused by an as yet unidentified physical or psychological factor, an incompatibility of the alar processes with the rest of the body. Unfortunately no weakness shows up beforehand; there is no way to predict wing failure. It occurs without warning. A flier who has flown his entire adult life without a shadow of trouble takes off one morning and, having attained altitude, suddenly, appallingly, finds his wings will not obey him—they are shuddering, closing, clapping down along his sides, paralysed. And he falls from the sky like a stone.

The medical literature states that as many as one flight in twenty ends in failure. Fliers I talked to believe that wing failure is not nearly as frequent as that, citing cases of people who have flown daily for decades. But it is not a matter they want to talk about with me, or perhaps even with one another. They seem to have no preventive precautions or rituals, accepting it as truly random. Failure may come on the first flight or the thousandth. No cause has been found for it—heredity, age, inexperience, fatigue, diet, emotion, physical condition. Every time a flier goes up, the chance of wing failure is the same.

Some survive the fall. But they never fall again, because they can never fly again. Once the wings have failed, they are useless. They remain paralysed, dragging along beside and behind their owner like a huge, heavy feather cape.

Foreigners ask why fliers don't carry parachutes in case of wing failure. No doubt they could. It is a question of temperament. Winged people who fly are those willing to take the risk of wing failure. Those who do not want the risk, do not fly. Or perhaps those who consider it a risk do not fly, and those who fly do not consider it a risk.

As amputation of the wings is invariably fatal, and surgical removal of any part of them causes acute, incurable, crippling pain, the fallen fliers and those who choose not to fly must drag their wings about all their lives, through the streets, up and down the stairs. Their changed bone structure is not well suited to ground life. They tire easily walking and suffer many fractures and muscular injuries. Few nonflying fliers live to sixty.

Those who do fly face their death every time they take off. Some of them, however, are still alive and still flying at eighty.

It is a quite wonderful sight, takeoff. Human beings aren't as awkward as I would have expected, having seen the graceless flapping of such masters of the air as pelicans and swans getting airborne. Of course it is easiest to launch from a perch or height, but if there's no such convenience handy, all they need is a run of twenty or twenty-five meters, enough for a couple of lifts and downbeats of the great extended wings, and then a step that doesn't touch the ground, and then they're up, aloft, soaring—maybe circling back overhead to smile and wave down at uplifted faces before arrowing off above the roofs or over the hills.

They fly with the legs close together, the body arched a little backward, the leg feathers fanning out into a hawklike tail as needed. As the arms have no integral muscular connection to the wings—winged Gyr are six-limbed creatures—the hands may be kept down along the sides to reduce air resistance and increase speed. In a leisurely flight, they may do anything hands do—scratch the head, peel a fruit, sketch an aerial view of the landscape, hold a baby. Though the last I saw only once, and it troubled me.

I talked several times with a winged Gyr named Ardiadia; what follows is all in his own words, recorded, with his permission, during our conversations.

OH, YES, WHEN I FIRST FOUND OUT—WHEN IT STARTED HAPPENING to me, you know—I was floored. Terrified! I couldn't believe it. I'd been so sure it wouldn't happen to me. When we were kids, you know, we used to joke about so-and-so being "flighty," or say, "He'll be taking off one of these days." But me? Me grow wings? It wasn't going to happen to me. So when I got this headache, and then my teeth ached for a while, and then my back began to hurt, I kept telling myself it was a toothache, I had an infection, an abscess . . . But when it really began, there was no more fooling myself. It was terrible. I really can't remember much about it. It was bad. It hurt. First like knives running back and forth between my shoulders, and claws digging up and down my spine. And then all over, my arms, my legs, my fingers, my face . . . And I was so weak I couldn't stand up. I got out of bed and fell down on the floor and I couldn't get up. I lay there calling my mother, "Mama! Mama, please come!" She was asleep. She worked late, waiting in a restaurant, and didn't get home till way after midnight, and so she slept hard. And I could feel the floor getting hot underneath me, I was so hot with fever, and I'd try to move my face to a cooler place on the floor . . .

Well, I don't know if the pain eased off or I just got used to it, but it was a bit better after a couple of months. It was hard, though. And long, and dull, and strange. Lying there. But not on my back. You can't lie on your back, ever, you know. Hard to sleep at night. When it hurt, it always hurt most at night. Always a little fevery, thinking strange thoughts, having funny ideas. And never able to think a thought through, never able quite to hold on to an idea. I felt as if I myself really couldn't think any more. Thoughts just came into me and went through me and I watched them. And no plans for the future any more, because what was my future now? I'd thought of being a schoolteacher. My mother had been so excited about that, she'd encouraged me to stay in school the extra year, to qualify for teachers' college . . . Well. I had my nineteenth birthday lying there in my little room in our three-room flat over the grocery on Lacemakers Lane. My mother brought some fancy food from the restaurant and a bottle of honey wine, and we tried to have a celebration, but I couldn't drink the wine, and she couldn't eat because she was crying. But I could eat, I was always starving hungry, and that cheered her up . . . Poor Mama!

Well, so, I came out of that, little by little, and the wings grew in, great ugly dangling naked things, disgusting, to start with, and even worse when they started to fledge, with the pinfeathers like great pimples. But when the primaries and secondaries came out, and I began to feel the muscles there, and to be able to shudder my wings, shake them, raise them a little—and I wasn't feverish any more, or I'd got used to running a fever all the time, I'm not really sure which it is—and I was able to get up and walk around, and feel how light my body was now, as if gravity couldn't affect me, even with the weight of those huge wings dragging after me . . . but I could lift them, get them up off the floor . . .

Not myself, though. I was earthbound. My body felt light, but I wore out even trying to walk, got weak and shaky. I used to be pretty good at the broad jump, but now I couldn't get both feet off the ground at once.

I was feeling a lot better, but it bothered me to be so weak, and I felt closed in. Trapped. Then a flier came by, a man from uptown, who'd heard about me. Fliers look after kids going through the change. He'd looked in a couple of times to reassure my mother and make sure I was doing all right. I was grateful for that. Now he came and talked to me for a long time, and showed me the exercises I could do. And I did them, every day, all the time—hours and hours. What else did I have to do? I used to like reading, but it didn't seem to hold my attention any more. I used to like going to the theater, but I couldn't do that, I still wasn't strong enough. And places like theaters, they don't have room for people with unbound wings. You take up too much space, you cause a fuss. I'd been good at mathematics in school, but I couldn't fix my attention on the problems any more. They didn't seem to matter. So I had nothing to do but the exercises the flier taught me. And I did them. All the time.

The exercises helped. There really wasn't enough room even in our sitting room, I never could do a vertical stretch fully, but I did what I could. I felt better, I got stronger. I finally began to feel like my wings were mine. Were part of me. Or I was part of them.

Then one day I couldn't stand being inside any more. Thirteen months I'd been inside, in those three little rooms, most of them just in the one room, thirteen months! Mama was out at work. I went downstairs. I walked the first ten steps down and then I lifted my wings. Even though the staircase was way too narrow, I could lift them some, and I stepped off and floated down the last six steps. Well, sort of. I hit pretty hard at the bottom, and my knees buckled, but I didn't really fall. It wasn't flying, but it wasn't quite falling.

I went outside. The air was wonderful. I felt like I hadn't had any air for a year. Actually, I felt like I'd never known what air was in my whole life. Even in that narrow little street, with the houses hanging over it, there was wind, there was the sky, not a ceiling. The sky overhead. The air. I started walking. I hadn't planned anything. I wanted to get out of the lanes and alleys, to somewhere open, a big plaza or square or park, anything open to the sky. I saw people staring at me but I didn't care. I'd stared at people with wings, when I didn't have them. Not meaning anything, just curious. Wings aren't all that common. I used to wonder a little about what it felt like to have them, you know. Just ignorance. So I didn't care if people looked at me now. I was too eager to get out from under the roofs. My legs were weak and shaky but they kept going, and sometimes, where the street wasn't crowded with people, I'd lift my wings a little, loft them, get a feel of the air under the feathers, and for a little I'd be lighter on my feet.

So I got to the Fruit Market. The market had shut down, it was evening, the booths were all shoved back, so there was a big space in the middle, cobblestones. I stood there under the Assay Office for a while doing exercises, lifts and stretches—I could do a vertical all the way for the first time, and it felt wonderful. Then I began to trot a little as I lofted, and my feet would get off the ground for a moment, and so I couldn't resist, I couldn't help it, I began to run and to loft my wings, and then beat down, and loft again, and I was up! But there was the Weights and Measures Building right in front of me, this grey stone facade right in my face, and I actually had to fend off, push myself away from it with my hands, and drop down to the pavement. But I turned around and there I had the full run ahead of me, clear across the marketplace to the Assay Office. And I ran, and I took off.

I swooped around the marketplace for a while, staying low, learning how to turn and bank, and how to use my tail feathers. It comes pretty natural, you feel what to do, the air tells you . . . but the people down below were looking up, and ducking when I banked too steep, or stalled . . . I didn't care. I flew for over an hour, till after dark, after all the people had gone. I'd got way up over the roofs by then. But I realised my wing muscles were getting tired and I'd better come down. That was hard. I mean, landing was hard because I didn't know how to land. I came down like a sack of rocks, bam! Nearly sprained my ankle, and the soles of my feet stung like fire. If anybody saw it they must have laughed. But I didn't care. It was just hard to be on the ground. I hated being down. Limping home, dragging my wings that weren't any good here, feeling weak, feeling heavy.

It took me quite a while to get home, and Mama came in just a little after me. She looked at me and said, "You've been out," and I said, "I flew, Mama," and she burst into tears.

I was sorry for her but there wasn't much I could say.

She didn't even ask me if I was going to go on flying. She knew I would. I don't understand the people who have wings and don't use them. I suppose they're interested in having a career. Maybe they were already in love with somebody on the ground. But it seems . . . I don't know. I can't really understand it. *Wanting* to stay down. *Choosing* not to fly. Wingless people can't help it, it's not their fault they're grounded. But if you have wings . . .

Of course they may be afraid of wing failure. Wing failure doesn't happen if you don't fly. How can it? How can something fail that never worked?

I suppose being safe is important to some people. They have a family or commitments or a job or something. I don't know. You'd have to talk to one of them. I'm a flier.

I ASKED ARDIADIA HOW HE MADE HIS LIVING. LIKE MANY FLIERS, he worked part-time for the postal service. He mostly carried government correspondence and dispatches on long flights, even overseas. Evidently he was considered a gifted and reliable employee. For particularly important dispatches, he told me that two fliers were always sent, in case one suffered wing failure.

He was thirty-two. I asked him if he was married, and he told me that fliers never married; they considered it, he said, beneath them. "Affairs on the wing," he said, with a slight smile. I asked if the affairs were always with other fliers, and he said, "Oh, yes, of course," unintentionally revealing his surprise or disgust at the idea of making love to a nonflier. His manners were pleasant and civil, he was most obliging, but he could not quite hide his sense of being apart from, different from the wingless, having nothing really to do with them. How could he help but look down on us?

I pressed him a little about this feeling of superiority, and he tried to explain. "When I said it was as if I was my wings, you know?—that's it. Being able to fly makes other things seem uninteresting. What people do seems so trivial. Flying is complete. It's enough. I don't know if you can understand. It's one's whole body, one's whole self, up in the whole sky. On a clear day, in the sunlight, with everything lying down there below, far away . . . Or in a high wind, in a storm—out over the sea, that's where I like best to fly. Over the sea in stormy weather. When the fishing boats run for land, and you have it all to yourself, the sky full of rain and lightning, and the clouds under your wings. Once off Emer Cape I danced with the waterspouts . . . It takes everything to fly. Everything you are, everything you have. And so if you go down, you go down whole. And over the sea, if you go down, that's it, who's to know, who cares? I don't want to be buried in the ground." The idea made him shiver a little. I could see the shudder in his long, heavy, bronze-and-black wing feathers.

I asked if the affairs on the wing sometimes resulted in children, and he said with indifference that of course they did. I pressed him a little about it, and he said that a baby was a great bother to a flying mother, so that as soon as it was weaned it was usually left "on the ground," as he put it, to be brought up by relatives. Sometimes the winged mother got so attached to the child that she grounded herself to look after it. He told me this with some disdain.

The children of fliers are no more likely to grow wings than other children. The phenomenon has no genetic factor but is a developmental pathology shared by all Gyr, which appears in less than one out of a thousand.

I think Ardiadia would not accept the word *pathology*.

I talked also with a nonflying winged Gyr, who let me record our conversation but asked that I not use his name. He is a member of a respectable law firm in a small city in Central Gy.

He said, "I never flew, no. I was twenty when I got sick. I'd thought I was past the age, safe. It was a terrible blow. My parents had already spent a good deal of money, made sacrifices to get me into college. I was doing well in college. I liked learning. I had an intellect. To lose a year was bad enough. I wasn't going to let this business eat up my whole life. To me the wings are simply excrescences. Growths. Impediments to walking, dancing, sitting in a civilised manner on a normal chair, wearing decent clothing. I refused to let something like that get in the way of my education, my life. Fliers are stupid, their brains go all to feathers. I wasn't going to trade in my mind for a chance to flitter about over rooftops. I'm more interested in what goes on *under* the roofs. I don't care for scenery. I prefer people. And I wanted a normal life. I wanted to marry, to have children. My father was a kind man; he died when I was sixteen, and I'd always thought that if I could be as good to my children as he was to us, it would be a way of thanking him, of honoring his memory . . . I was fortunate enough to meet a beautiful woman who refused to let my handicap frighten her. In fact she won't let me call it that. She insists that all this"—he indicated his wings with a slight gesture of his head—"was what she first saw in me. Claims that when we first met, she thought I was quite a boring, stuffy young fellow, till I turned around."

His head feathers were black with a blue crest. His wings, though flattened, bound, and belted down, as nonfliers' wings always are, to keep them out of the way and as unnoticeable as possible, were splendidly feathered in patterns of dark blue and peacock blue with black bars and edges.

"At any rate, I was determined to keep my feet on the ground, in every sense. If I'd ever had any youthful notions about flitting off for a while, which I really never did, once I was through with the fever and delirium and had made peace with the whole painful, wasteful process—if I had ever thought of flying, once I was married, once we had a child, nothing, nothing could induce me to yearn for even a taste of that life, to consider it even for a moment. The utter irresponsibility of it, the arrogance—the arrogance of it is very distasteful to me."

We then talked for some time about his law practice, which was an admirable one, devoted to representing poor people against swindlers and profiteers. He showed me a charming portrait of his two children, eleven and nine years old, which he had drawn with one of his own quills. The chances that either child would grow wings was, as for every Gyr, a thousand to one.

Shortly before I left, I asked him, "Do you ever dream of flying?"

Lawyerlike, he was slow to answer. He looked away, out the window. "Doesn't everyone?" he said.

THE
SILENCE
OF THE
ASONU

THE SILENCE OF THE ASONU IS PROVERBIAL. THE FIRST VISITORS believed that these gracious, gracile people were mute, lacking any language other than that of gesture, expression, and gaze. Later, hearing Asonu children chatter, the visitors suspected that among themselves the adults spoke, keeping silence only with strangers. We know now that the Asonu are not dumb, but that once past early childhood they speak only very rarely, to anyone, under any circumstances. They do not write; and unlike mutes, or monks under vows of silence, they do not use any signs or other devices in place of speaking.

This nearly absolute abstinence from language makes them fascinating.

People who live with animals value the charm of muteness. It can be a real pleasure to know when the cat walks into the room that he won't mention any of your shortcomings, or that you can tell your grievances to your dog without his repeating them to the people who caused them.

And those who can talk, but don't, have the great advantage over the rest of us that they never say anything stupid. This may be why we are convinced that if they spoke they would have something wise to say.

Thus there has come to be considerable tourist traffic to the Asonu. Having a strong tradition of hospitality, the Asonu entertain their visitors courteously, though without modifying their own customs.

Some people go there simply in order to join the natives in their silence, grateful to spend a few weeks where they do not have to festoon and obscure every human meeting with verbiage. Many such visitors, having been accepted into a household as a paying guest, return year after year, forming bonds of unspoken affection with their quiet hosts.

Others follow their Asonu guides or hosts about, talking to them continually, confiding their whole life stories to them, in rapture at having at last found a listener who won't interrupt or comment or mention that his cousin had an even larger tumor than that. As such people usually know little Asonu and speak mostly or entirely in their own language, they evidently aren't worried by the question that vexes some visitors: Since the Asonu don't talk, do they, in fact, listen?

They certainly hear and understand what is said to them in their own language, since they're prompt to respond to their children, to indicate directions by gesture to inquiring tourists, and to leave a building at the cry of "Fire!" But the question remains, do they listen to discursive speech and sociable conversation, or do they merely hear it, while keeping silently attentive to something beyond speech? Their amiable and apparently easy manner seems to some observers the placid surface of a deep preoccupation, a constant alertness, like that of a mother who while entertaining her guests or seeing to her husband's comfort yet is listening every moment for the cry of her baby in another room.

To perceive the Asonu thus is almost inevitably to interpret their silence as a concealment. As they grow up, it seems, they cease to speak because they are listening to something we do not hear, a secret which their silence hides.

Some visitors to their world are convinced that the lips of these quiet people are locked upon a knowledge which, in proportion as it is hidden, must be valuable—a spiritual treasure, a speech beyond speech, possibly even that ultimate revelation promised by so many religions, and indeed frequently delivered, but never in a wholly communicable form. The transcendent knowledge of the mystic cannot be expressed in language. It may be that the Asonu avoid language for this very reason. It may be that they keep silence because if they spoke everything of importance would have been said.

To some, the utterances of the Asonu do not seem to be as momentous as one might expect from their rarity. They might even be described as banal. But believers in the Wisdom of the Asonu have followed individuals about for years, waiting for the rare words they speak, writing them down, saving them, studying them, arranging and collating them, finding arcane meanings and numerical correspondences in them, in search of the hidden message.

There is no written form of the Asonu language, and translation of speech is considered to be so uncertain that translatomats aren't issued to the tourists, most of whom don't want them anyway. Those who wish to learn Asonu can do so only by listening to and imitating children, who by six or seven years old are already becoming unhappy when asked to talk.

Here are the "Eleven Sayings of the Elder of Isu," collected over four years by a devotee from Ohio, who had already spent six years learning the language from the children of the Isu Group. Months of silence occurred between most of these statements, and two years between the fifth and sixth.

1. Not there.
2. It is almost ready [or] Be ready for it soon.
3. Unexpected!
4. It will never cease.
5. Yes.
6. When?
7. It is very good.

8. Perhaps.

9. Soon.

10. Hot! [or] Very warm!

11. It will not cease.

The devotee wove these eleven sayings into a coherent spiritual statement or testament which he understood the Elder to have been making, little by little, during the last four years of his life. The Ohio Reading of the Sayings of the Elder of Isu is as follows:

> "(1)What we seek is not there in any object or experience of our mortal life. We live among appearances, on the verge of the Spiritual Truth. (2) We must be ready for it as it is ready for us, for (3) it will come when we least expect it. Our perception of the Truth is sudden as a lightning-flash, but (4) the Truth itself is eternal and unchanging. (5) Indeed we must positively and hopefully, in a spirit of affirmation, (6) continually ask when, when shall we find what we seek? (7) For the Truth is the medicine for our soul, the knowledge of absolute goodness. (8, 9) It may come very soon. Perhaps it is coming even now in this moment. (10) Its warmth and brightness are as those of the sun, but the sun will perish (11) and the Truth will not perish. Never will the warmth, the brightness, the goodness of the Truth cease or fail us."

Another interpretation of the Sayings may be made by referring to the circumstances in which the Elder spoke, faithfully recorded by the devotee from Ohio, whose patience was equalled only by the Elder's:

1. Spoken in an undertone as the Elder looked through a chest of clothing and ornaments.

2. Spoken to a group of children on the morning of a ceremony.

3. Said with a laugh in greeting the Elder's younger sister, returned from a long trip.

4. Spoken the day after the burial of the Elder's sister.

5. Said while embracing the Elder's brother-in-law some days after the funeral.

6. Asked of an Asonu "doctor" who was making a "spirit-body" drawing in white and black sand for the Elder. These drawings seem to be both curative and diagnostic, but we know very little about them. The observer states that the doctor's answer was a short curving line drawn outward from the navel of the "spirit-body" figure. This, however, may be only the observer's reading of what was not an answer at all.

7. Said to a child who had woven a reed mat.

8. Spoken in answer to a young grandchild who asked, "Will you be at the big feast, Grandmother?"

9. Spoken in answer to the same child, who asked, "Are you going to be dead like Great-Auntie?"

10. Said to a baby who was toddling towards a firepit where the flames were invisible in the sunlight.

11. Last words, spoken the day before the Elder's death.

The last six Sayings were all spoken in the last half-year of the Elder's life, as if the approach of death had made the Elder positively loquacious. Five of the Sayings were spoken to, or at least in the presence of, young children who were still at the talking stage.

Speech from an adult must be very impressive to an Asonu child. But, like the foreign linguists, Asonu babies must learn the language by listening to older children. The mother and other parents encourage the child to speak only by attentive listening and prompt, affectionate, wordless response.

The Asonu live in close-knit extended-family groups, in frequent contact with other groups. Their pasturing life, following the great flocks of anamanu which furnish them wool, leather, milk, and meat, leads them on a ceaseless seasonal nomadic circuit within a vast shared territory of mountains and foothills. Families frequently leave their family group to go wandering and visiting. At the great festivals and ceremonies of healing and renewal many groups come together for days or weeks, exchanging hospitality. No hostile relations between groups are apparent, and in fact no observer has reported seeing adult Asonu fight or quarrel. Arguments, evidently, are out of the question.

Children from two to six years old chatter to each other constantly; they argue, wrangle, and bicker, and sometimes come to blows. As they come to be six or seven they begin to speak less and to quarrel less. By the time they are eight or nine most of them are very shy of words and reluctant to answer a question except by gesture. They have learned to quietly evade inquiring tourists and linguists with notebooks and recording devices. By adolescence they are as silent and as peaceable as the adults.

Children between eight and twelve do most of the looking after the younger ones. All the children of the family group go about together, and in such groups the two-to-six-year-olds provide language models for the babies. Older children shout wordlessly in the excitement of a game or tag or hide-and-seek, and sometimes scold an errant toddler with a "Stop!" or "No!"—just as the Elder of Isu murmured "Hot!" as a child approached an invisible fire; though of course the Elder may have used that circumstance as a parable, in order to make a statement of profound spiritual meaning, as appears in the Ohio Reading.

Even songs lose their words as the singers grow older. A game rhyme sung by little children has words:

> *Look at us tumbledown*
> *Stumbledown tumbledown*

> *All of us tumbledown*
> *All in a heap!*

Older children cheerfully play the game with the little ones, falling into wriggling piles with yells of joy, but they do not sing the words, only the tune, vocalised on a neutral syllable.

Adult Asonu often hum or sing at work, while herding, while rocking the baby. Some of the tunes are traditional, others improvised. Many employ motifs based on the whistles of the anamanu. None have words; all are hummed or vocalised. At the meetings of the clans and at marriages and funerals the ceremonial choral music is rich in melody and harmonically complex and subtle. No instruments are used, only the voice. The singers practice many days for the ceremonies. Some students of Asonu music believe that their particular spiritual wisdom or insight finds its expression in these great wordless chorales.

I am inclined to agree with others who, having lived a long time among the Asonu, believe that their choral singing is an element of a sacred occasion, and certainly an art, a festive communal act, and a pleasurable release of feeling, but no more. What is sacred to them remains in silence.

The little children call people by relationship words, mother, uncle, clan-sister, friend, etc. If the Asonu have names, we do not know them.

ABOUT TEN YEARS AGO A ZEALOUS BELIEVER IN THE SECRET Wisdom of the Asonu kidnapped a child of four from one of the mountain clans in the dead of winter. He had obtained a zoo collector's permit, and smuggled her back to his home world in an animal cage marked "Anamanu." Believing that the Asonu enforce silence on their children, his plan was to encourage the little girl to keep talking as she grew up. When adult, he thought, she would thus be able to speak the innate Wisdom which her people would have obliged her to keep secret.

For the first year or so it appears that she would talk to her kidnapper, who, aside from the abominable cruelty of his action, seems to have begun by treating her kindly enough. His knowledge of the Asonu language was limited, and she saw no one else but a small group of sectarians who came to gaze worshipfully at her and listen to her talk. Her vocabulary and syntax gained no enlargement, and began to atrophy. She became increasingly silent.

Frustrated, the zealot tried to teach her his own language so that she would be able to express her innate Wisdom in a different tongue. We have only his report, which is that she "refused to learn," was silent or spoke almost inaudibly when he tried to make her repeat words, and "did not obey." He ceased to let other people see her. When some members of the sect finally notified the civil authorities, the child was about seven. She had spent three years hidden in a basement room, and for a year or more had been whipped and beaten regularly "to teach her to talk," her captor explained, "because she's stubborn." She was dumb, cowering, undernourished, and brutalized.

She was promptly returned to her family, who for three years had mourned her, believing she had wandered off and been lost on the glacier. They received her with tears of joy and grief. Her condition since then is not known, because the Interplanary Agency closed the entire area to all visitors, tourist or scientist, at the time she was brought back. No foreigner has been up in the Asonu mountains since. We may well imagine that her people were resentful; but nothing was ever said.

THE
ASCENT
OF THE
NORTH FACE

From the diary of Simon Interthwaite of the First *Lovejoy Street Expedition*

2/21. Robert has reached Base Camp with five Sherbets. He brought several copies of the *Times* from last month, which we devoured eagerly. Our team is now complete. Tomorrow the Advance Party goes up. Weather holds.

2/22. Accompanied Advance Party as far as the col below The Verandah before turning back. Winds up to 40 mph in gusts, but weather holds. Tonight Peter radioed all well at Verandah Camp.

The Sherbets are singing at their campfires.

2/23. Making ready. Tightened gossels. Weather holds.

2/24. Reached Verandah Camp easily in one day's climb. Tricky bit where the lattice and tongue and groove join, but Advance Party had left rope in place and we negotiated the overhang without real difficulty. Omu Ba used running jump and arrived earlier than rest of party. Inventive but undisciplined. Bad example to other Sherbets. Verandah Camp is level, dry, sheltered, far more comfortable than Base. Glad to be out of the endless rhododendrons. Snowing tonight.

2/25. IMMOBILIZED BY SNOW.

2/26. SAME.

2/27. SAME. FINISHED LAST SHEETS OF *TIMES* (ADVERTS).

2/28. DEREK, NIGEL, COLIN, AND I WENT UP IN BLINDING SNOW and wind to plot course and drive pigils. Visibility very poor. Nigel whined. Turned back at noon, reached Verandah Camp at 3 pip emma.

2/29. DRIVING RAIN AND WIND. OMU BA DRUNK SINCE 2/27. What on? Stove alcohol found to be low. Inventive but undisciplined. Chastisement difficult in circumstances.

2/30. ROBERT ROPED RIGHT UP TO THE NORTH-EAST OVERHANG. Forced to turn back by Sherbets' dread of occupants. Insuperable superstition. We must eliminate plans for that route and go straight for the Drain Pipe. We cannot endure much longer here crowded up in this camp without newspapers. There is not room for six men in our tent, and we hear the sixteen Sherbets fighting continually in theirs. I see now that the group is unnecessarily numerous even if some are under 5 foot 2 inches in height. Ten men, handpicked, would be enough. Visibility zero all day. Snow, rain, wind.

2/31. HAIL, SLEET, FOG. THREE SHERBETS HAVE GONE MISSING.

3/1. OUT OF BOVRIL. DEREK VERY LOW.

3/4. MISSED ENTRIES DURING BLIZZARD. TODAY BRIGHT SUN, no wind. Snow dazzling on lower elevations; from here we cannot see the heights. Sherbets returned from unexplained absence with Ovaltine. Spirits high. Digging out and making ready all day for ascent (two groups) tomorrow.

3/5. SUCCESS! WE ARE ON THE VERANDAH ROOF! VIEW overwhelming. Unattained summit of 2618 clearly visible in the SE. Second Party (Peter, Robert, eight Sherbets) not here yet. Windy and exposed campsite on steep slope. Shingles slippery with rain and sleet.

3/6. NIGEL AND TWO SHERBETS WENT BACK DOWN TO THE North Edge to meet Second Party. Returned 4 pip emma without having sighted them. They must have been delayed at Verandah Camp. Anxiety. Radio silent. Wind rising.

3/7. COLIN STRAINED SHOULDER ON ROPE CLIMBING UP TO THE Window. Stupid, childish prank. Whether or not there are occupants, the Sherbets are very strong on not disturbing them. No sign of Second Party. Radio messages enigmatic, constant interference from KWJJ Country Music Station. Windy, but clear weather holds.

3/8. RESOLVED TO GO UP TOMORROW IF WEATHER HOLDS. MENDED doggles, replaced worn pigil-holders. Sherbets noncommittal.

3/9. I AM ALONE ON THE HIGH ROOF.
No one else willing to continue ascent. Cohn and Nigel will wait for me three days at Verandah Roof Camp; Derek and four Sherbets began descent to Base. I set off with two Sherbets at 5 ack emma. Fine sunrise, in East, at 7.04 ack emma. Climbed steadily all day. Tricky bit at last overhang. Sherbets very plucky. Omu Ba while swinging on rope said,

"Observe fine view, sah!" Exhausted at arrival at High Roof Camp, but the three advance Sherbets had tents set up and Ovaltine ready. Slope so steep here I feel I may roll off in my sleep!

Sherbets singing in their tent.

Above me the sharp Summit, and the Chimney rising sheer against the stars.

That is the last entry in Simon Interthwaite's journal. Four of the five Sherbets with him at the High Roof Camp returned after three days to the Base Camp. They brought the journal, two clean vests, and a tube of anchovy paste back with them. Their report of his fate was incoherent. The Interthwaite Party abandoned the attempt to scale the North Face of 2647 Lovejoy Street and returned to Calcutta.

In 1980 a Japanese party of Izutsu employees with four Sherbet guides attained the summit by a North Face route, rappelling across the study windows and driving pitons clear up to the eaves. Occupant protest was ineffective.

No one has yet climbed the Chimney.

THE AUTHOR
OF THE
ACACIA SEEDS

AND OTHER EXTRACTS FROM THE
Journal of the Association of Therolinguistics

MS. FOUND IN AN ANTHILL

THE MESSAGES WERE FOUND WRITTEN IN TOUCH-GLAND EXU-
dation on degerminated acacia seeds laid in rows at the end of a narrow,
erratic tunnel leading off from one of the deeper levels of the colony. It
was the orderly arrangement of the seeds that first drew the investigator's
attention.

The messages are fragmentary, and the translation approximate and
highly interpretative; but the text seems worthy of interest if only for its
striking lack of resemblance to any other Ant texts known to us.

Seeds 1–13

[I will] not touch feelers. [I will] not stroke. [I will] spend
on dry seeds [my] soul's sweetness. It may be found when [I
am] dead. Touch this dry wood! [I] call! [I am] here!

Alternatively, this passage may be read:

[Do] not touch feelers. [Do] not stroke. Spend on dry seeds
[your] soul's sweetness. [Others] may find it when [you are]
dead. Touch this dry wood! Call: [I am] here!

No known dialect of Ant employs any verbal person except the third person singular and plural and the first person plural. In this text, only the root forms of the verbs are used; so there is no way to decide whether the passage was intended to be an autobiography or a manifesto.

> *Seeds 14–22*
> Long are the tunnels. Longer is the untunneled. No tunnel reaches the end of the untunneled. The untunneled goes on farther than we can go in ten days [*i.e.*, forever]. Praise!

The mark translated "Praise!" is half of the customary salutation "Praise the Queen!" or "Long live the Queen!" or "Huzza for the Queen!"—but the word/mark signifying "Queen" has been omitted.

> *Seeds 23–29*
> As the ant among foreign-enemy ants is killed, so the ant without ants dies, but being without ants is as sweet as honeydew.

An ant intruding in a colony not its own is usually killed. Isolated from other ants, it invariably dies within a day or so. The difficulty in this passage is the word/mark "without ants," which we take to mean "alone"—a concept for which no word/mark exists in Ant.

> *Seeds 30–31*
> Eat the eggs! Up with the Queen!

There has already been considerable dispute over the interpretation of the phrase on Seed 31. It is an important question, since all the preceding seeds can be fully understood only in the light cast by this ultimate exhortation. Dr. Rosbone ingeniously argues that the author, a wingless neuter-female worker, yearns hopelessly to be a winged male, and to found a new colony, flying upward in the nuptial flight with a new Queen. Though the text certainly permits such a reading, our conviction is that nothing in the text *supports* it—least of all the text of the immediately preceding seed, No. 30: "Eat the eggs!" This reading, though shocking, is beyond disputation.

We venture to suggest that the confusion over Seed 31 may result from an ethnocentric interpretation of the word "up." To us, "up" is a "good" direction. Not so, or not necessarily so, to an ant. "Up" is where the food comes from, to be sure; but "down" is where security, peace, and home are to be found. "Up" is the scorching sun; the freezing night; no shelter in the beloved tunnels; exile; death. Therefore we suggest that this strange author, in the solitude of her lonely tunnel, sought with what means she had to express the ultimate blasphemy conceivable to an ant, and that the correct reading of Seeds 30–31, in human terms, is:

Eat the eggs! Down with the Queen!

The desiccated body of a small worker was found beside Seed 31 when the manuscript was discovered. The head had been severed from the thorax, probably by the jaws of a soldier of the colony. The seeds, carefully arranged in a pattern resembling a musical stave, had not been disturbed. (Ants of the soldier caste are illiterate; thus the soldier was presumably not interested in the collection of useless seeds from which the edible germs had been removed.) No living ants were left in the colony, which was destroyed in a war with a neighboring anthill at some time subsequent to the death of the Author of the Acacia Seeds.

—*G. D'Arbay, T. R. Bardol*

ANNOUNCEMENT OF AN EXPEDITION

THE EXTREME DIFFICULTY OF READING PENGUIN HAS BEEN VERY much lessened by the use of the underwater motion-picture camera. On film it is at least possible to repeat, and to slow down, the fluid sequences of the script, to the point where, by constant repetition and patient study, many elements of this most elegant and lively literature may be grasped, though the nuances, and perhaps the essence, must forever elude us.

It was Professor Duby who, by pointing out the remote affiliation of the script with Low Greylag, made possible the first tentative glossary of Penguin. The analogies with Dolphin which had been employed up to that time never proved very useful, and were often quite misleading.

Indeed it seemed strange that a script written almost entirely in wings, neck, and air should prove the key to the poetry of short-necked, flipper-winged water-writers. But we should not have found it so strange if we had kept in mind the fact that penguins are, despite all evidence to the contrary, birds.

Because their script resembles Dolphin in *form*, we should never have assumed that it must resemble Dolphin in *content*. And indeed it does not. There is, of course, the same extraordinary wit, the flashes of crazy humor, the inventiveness, and the inimitable grace. In all the thousands of literatures of the Fish stock, only a few show any humor at all, and that usually of a rather simple, primitive sort; and the superb gracefulness of Shark or Tarpon is utterly different from the joyous vigor of all Cetacean scripts. The joy, the vigor, and the humor are all shared by Penguin authors; and, indeed, by many of the finer Seal *auteurs*. The temperature of the blood is a bond. But the construction of the brain, and of the womb, makes a barrier! Dolphins do not lay eggs. A world of difference lies in that simple fact.

Only when Professor Duby reminded us that penguins are birds, that they do not swim but *fly in water*, only then could the therolinguist begin to approach the sea literature of the penguin with understanding; only then could the miles of recordings already on film be restudied and, finally, appreciated.

But the difficulty of translation is still with us.

A satisfying degree of promise has already been made in Adélie. The difficulties of recording a group kinetic performance in a stormy ocean as thick as pea soup with plankton at a temperature of 31° Fahrenheit are considerable; but the perseverance of the Ross Ice Barrier Literary Circle has been fully rewarded with such passages as "Under the Iceberg," from the *Autumn Song*—a passage now world famous in the rendition by Anna Serebryakova of the Leningrad Ballet. No verbal rendering can approach the felicity of Miss Serebryakova's version. For, quite simply, there is no way to reproduce in writing the all-important *multiplicity* of the original text, so beautifully rendered by the full chorus of the Leningrad Ballet company.

Indeed, what we call "translations" from the Adélie—or from any group kinetic text—are, to put it bluntly, mere notes—libretto without the opera. The ballet version is the true translation. Nothing in words can be complete.

I therefore suggest, though the suggestion may well be greeted with frowns of anger or with hoots of laughter, that *for the therolinguist*—as opposed to the artist and the amateur—the kinetic sea writings of Penguin are the *least* promising field of study: and, further, that Adélie, for all its charm and relative simplicity, is a less promising field of study than is Emperor.

Emperor!—I anticipate my colleagues' response to this suggestion. Emperor! The most difficult, the most remote, of all the dialects of Penguin! The language of which Professor Duby himself remarked, "The literature of the emperor penguin is as forbidding, as inaccessible, as the frozen heart of Antarctica itself. Its beauties may be unearthly, but they are not for us."

Maybe. I do not underestimate the difficulties: not least of which is the imperial temperament, so much more reserved and aloof than that of any other penguin. But, paradoxically, it is just in this reserve that I place my hope. The emperor is not a solitary, but a social bird, and while on land for the breeding season dwells in colonies, as does the adélie; but these colonies are very much smaller and very much quieter than those of the adélie. The bonds between the members of an emperor colony are rather personal than social. The emperor is an individualist. Therefore I think it almost certain that the literature of the emperor will prove to be composed by single authors, instead of chorally; and therefore it will be translatable into human speech. It will be a kinetic literature, but how different from the spatially extensive, rapid, multiplex choruses of sea writing! Close analysis, and genuine transcription, will at last be possible.

What! say my critics—Should we pack up and go to Cape Crozier, to the dark, to the blizzards, to the -60° cold, in the mere hope of recording the problematic poetry of a few strange birds who sit there, in the midwinter dark, in the blizzards, in the -60° cold, on the eternal ice, with an egg on their feet?

And my reply is, Yes. For, like Professor Duby, my instinct tells me that the beauty of that poetry is as unearthly as anything we shall ever find on earth.

To those of my colleagues in whom the spirit of scientific curiosity and aesthetic risk is strong, I say, Imagine it: the ice, the scouring snow, the darkness, the ceaseless whine and scream of wind. In that black desolation a little band of poets crouches. They are starving; they will not eat for weeks. On the feet of each one, under the warm belly feathers, rests one large egg, thus preserved from the mortal touch of the ice. The poets cannot hear one another; they cannot see one another. They can only feel the other's *warmth*. That is their poetry, that is their art. Like all kinetic literatures, it is silent; unlike other kinetic literatures, it is all but immobile, ineffably subtle. The ruffling of a feather; the shifting of a wing; the touch, the slight, faint, warm touch of the one beside you. In unutterable, miserable, black solitude, the affirmation. In absence, presence. In death, life.

I have obtained a sizable grant from UNESCO and have stocked an expedition. There are still four places open. We leave for Antarctica on Thursday. If anyone wants to come along, welcome!

—*D. Petri*

EDITORIAL. BY THE PRESIDENT OF THE THEROLINGUISTICS ASSOCIATION

WHAT IS LANGUAGE?

This question, central to the science of therolinguistics, has been answered—heuristically—by the very existence of the science. Language is communication. That is the axiom on which all our theory and research rest, and from which all our discoveries derive; and the success of the discoveries testifies to the validity of the axiom. But to the related, yet not identical question, What is Art? we have not yet given a satisfactory answer.

Tolstoy, in the book whose title is that very question, answered it firmly and clearly: Art, too, is communication. This answer has, I believe, been accepted without examination or criticism by therolinguistics. For example: Why do therolinguists study only animals?

Why, because plants do not communicate.

Plants do not communicate; that is a fact. Therefore plants have no language; very well; that follows from our basic axiom. Therefore, also, plants have no art. But stay! That does *not* follow from the basic axiom, but only from the unexamined Tolstoyan corollary.

What if art is not communicative?

Or, what if some art is communicative, and some art is not?

Ourselves animals, active, predators, we look (naturally enough) for an active, predatory, communicative art; and when we find it, we recognise it. The development of this power of recognition and the skills of appreciation is a recent and glorious achievement.

But I submit that, for all the tremendous advances made by therolinguistics during the last decades, we are only at the beginning of our age of discovery. We must not become slaves to our own axioms. We have not yet lifted our eyes to the vaster horizons before us. We have not faced the almost terrifying challenge of the Plant.

If a non-communicative, vegetative art exists, we must rethink the very elements of our science, and learn a whole new set of techniques.

For it is simply not possible to bring the critical and technical skills appropriate to the study of Weasel murder mysteries, or Batrachian erotica, or the tunnel sagas of the earthworm, to bear on the art of the redwood or the zucchini.

This is proved conclusively by the failure—a noble failure—of the efforts of Dr. Srivas, in Calcutta, using time-lapse photography, to produce a lexicon of Sunflower. His attempt was daring, but doomed to failure. For his approach was kinetic—a method appropriate to the *communicative* arts of the tortoise, the oyster, and the sloth. He saw the extreme slowness of the kinesis of plants, and only that, as the problem to be solved.

But the problem was far greater. The art he sought, if it exists, is a non-communicative art: and probably a non-kinetic one. It is possible that Time, the essential element, matrix, and measure of all known animal art, does not enter into vegetable art at all. The plants may use the meter of eternity. We do not know.

We do not know. All we can guess is that the putative Art of the Plant is *entirely different* from the Art of the Animal. What it is, we cannot say; we have not yet discovered it. Yet I predict with some certainty that it exists, and that when it is found it will prove to be, not an action, but a reaction: not a communication, but a reception. It will be exactly the opposite of the art we know and recognise. It will be the first *passive* art known to us.

Can we, in fact, know it? Can we ever understand it?

It will be immensely difficult. That is clear. But we should not despair. Remember that so late as the mid-twentieth century, most scientists, and many artists, did not believe that even Dolphin would ever be comprehensible to the human brain—or worth comprehending! Let another century pass, and we may seem equally laughable. "Do you realise," the phytolinguist will say to the aesthetic critic, "that they couldn't even read Eggplant?" And they will smile at our ignorance, as they pick up their rucksacks and hike on up to read the newly deciphered lyrics of the lichen on the north face of Pike's Peak.

And with them, or after them, may there not come that even bolder adventurer—the first geolinguist, who, ignoring the delicate, transient lyrics of the lichen, will read beneath it the still less communicative, still more passive, wholly atemporal, cold, volcanic poetry of the rocks: each one a word spoken, how long ago, by the earth itself, in the immense solitude, the immenser community, of space.

THE

WIFE'S STORY

HE WAS A GOOD HUSBAND, A GOOD FATHER. I DON'T UNDERSTAND it. I don't believe in it. I don't believe that it happened. I saw it happen but it isn't true. It can't be. He was always gentle. If you'd have seen him playing with the children, anybody who saw him with the children would have known that there wasn't any bad in him, not one mean bone. When I first met him he was still living with his mother, over near Spring Lake, and I used to see them together, the mother and the sons, and think that any young fellow that was that nice with his family must be one worth knowing. Then one time when I was walking in the woods I met him by himself coming back from a hunting trip. He hadn't got any game at all, not so much as a field mouse, but he wasn't cast down about it. He was just larking along enjoying the morning air. That's one of the things I first loved about him. He didn't take things hard, he didn't grouch and whine when things didn't go his way. So we got to talking that day. And I guess things moved right along after that, because pretty soon he was over here pretty near all the time. And my sister said—see, my parents had moved out the year before and gone south, leaving us the place— my sister said, kind of teasing but serious, "Well! If he's going to be here every day and half the night, I guess there isn't room for me!" And she moved out—just down the way. We've always been real close, her and me. That's the sort of thing doesn't ever change. I couldn't ever have got through this bad time without my sis.

Well, so he come to live here. And all I can say is, it was the happy year of my life. He was just purely good to me. A hard worker and never lazy, and so big and fine-looking. Everybody looked up to him, you know, young as he was. Lodge Meeting nights, more and more often they had him to lead the singing. He had such a beautiful voice, and he'd lead off strong, and the others following and joining in, high voices and low. It brings the shivers on me now to think of it, hearing it, nights when I'd stayed home from meeting when the children was babies—the singing coming up through the trees there, and the moonlight, summer nights, the full moon shining. I'll never hear anything so beautiful. I'll never know a joy like that again.

It was the moon, that's what they say. It's the moon's fault, and the blood. It was in his father's blood. I never knew his father, and now I wonder what become of him. He was from up Whitewater way, and had no kin around here. I always thought he went back there, but now I don't know. There was some talk about him, tales, that come out after what happened to my husband. It's something runs in the blood, they say, and it may never come out, but if it does, it's the change of the moon that does it. Always it happens in the dark of the moon. When everybody's home and asleep. Something comes over the one that's got the curse in his blood, they say, and he gets up because he can't sleep, and goes out into the glaring sun, and goes off all alone—drawn to find those like him.

And it may be so, because my husband would do that. I'd half rouse and say, "Where you going to?" and he'd say, "Oh, hunting, be back this evening," and it wasn't like him, even his voice was different. But I'd be so sleepy, and not wanting to wake the kids, and he was so good and responsible, it was no call of mine to go asking "Why?" and "Where?" and all like that.

So it happened that way maybe three times or four. He'd come back late, and worn out, and pretty near cross for one so sweet-tempered—not wanting to talk about it. I figured everybody got to bust out now and then, and nagging never helped anything. But it did begin to worry me. Not so much that he went, but that he come back so tired and strange. Even, he smelled strange. It made my hair stand up on end. I could not endure it and I said, "What is that—those smells on you? All over you!" And he said, "I don't know," real short, and made like he was sleeping. But he went down when he thought I wasn't noticing, and washed and washed himself. But those smells stayed in his hair, and in our bed, for days.

And then the awful thing. I don't find it easy to tell about this. I want to cry when I have to bring it to my mind. Our youngest, the little one, my baby, she turned from her father. Just overnight. He come in and she got scared-looking, stiff, with her eyes wide, and then she begun to cry and try to hide behind me. She didn't yet talk plain but she was saying over and over, "Make it go away! Make it go away!"

The look in his eyes, just for one moment, when he heard that. That's what I don't want ever to remember. That's what I can't forget. The look in his eyes looking at his own child.

I said to the child, "Shame on you, what's got into you!"—scolding, but keeping her right up close to me at the same time, because I was frightened too. Frightened to shaking.

He looked away then and said something like, "Guess she just waked up dreaming," and passed it off that way. Or tried to. And so did I. And I got real mad with my baby when she kept on acting crazy scared of her own dad. But she couldn't help it and I couldn't change it.

He kept away that whole day. Because he knew, I guess. It was just beginning dark of the moon.

It was hot and close inside, and dark, and we'd all been asleep some while, when something woke me up. He wasn't there beside me. I heard a little stir in the passage, when I listened. So I got up, because I could bear it no longer. I went out into the passage, and it was light there, hard sunlight coming in from the door. And I saw him standing just outside, in the tall grass by the entrance. His head was hanging. Presently he sat down, like he felt weary, and looked down at his feet. I held still, inside, and watched—I didn't know what for.

And I saw what he saw. I saw the changing. In his feet, it was, first. They got long, each foot got longer, stretching out, the toes stretching out and the foot getting long, and fleshy, and white. And no hair on them.

The hair begun to come away all over his body. It was like his hair fried away in the sunlight and was gone. He was white all over, then, like a worm's skin. And he turned his face. It was changing while I looked. It got flatter and flatter, the mouth flat and wide, and the teeth grinning flat and dull, and the nose just a knob of flesh with nostril holes, and the ears gone, and the eyes gone blue—blue, with white rims around the blue—staring at me out of that flat, soft, white face.

He stood up then on two legs.

I saw him, I had to see him, my own dear love, turned into the hateful one.

I couldn't move, but as I crouched there in the passage staring out into the day I was trembling and shaking with a growl that burst out into a crazy, awful howling. A grief howl and a terror howl and a calling howl. And the others heard it, even sleeping, and woke up.

It stared and peered, that thing my husband had turned into, and shoved its face up to the entrance of our house. I was still bound by mortal fear, but behind me the children had waked up, and the baby was whimpering. The mother anger come into me then, and I snarled and crept forward.

The man thing looked around. It had no gun, like the ones from the man places do. But it picked up a heavy fallen tree branch in its long white foot, and shoved the end of that down into our house, at me. I snapped the end of it in my teeth and started to force my way out, because I knew the man would kill our children if it could. But my sister was already coming. I saw her running at the man with her head low and her mane high and her eyes yellow as the winter sun. It turned on her and raised up that branch to hit her. But I come out of the doorway, mad with the mother anger, and the others all were coming answering my call, the whole pack gathering, there in that blind glare and heat of the sun at noon.

The man looked round at us and yelled out loud, and brandished the branch it held. Then it broke and ran, heading for the cleared fields and plowlands, down the mountainside. It ran, on two legs, leaping and weaving, and we followed it.

I was last, because love still bound the anger and the fear in me. I was running when I saw them pull it down. My sister's teeth were in its throat. I got there and it was dead. The others were drawing back from the kill, because of the taste of the blood, and the smell. The younger ones were cowering and some crying, and my sister rubbed her mouth against her forelegs over and over to get rid of the taste. I went up close because I thought if the thing was dead the spell, the curse must be done, and my husband could come back—alive, or even dead, if I could only see him, my true love, in his true form, beautiful. But only the dead man lay there white and bloody. We drew back and back from it, and turned and ran, back up into the hills, back to the woods of the shadows and the twilight and the blessed dark.

THE
RULE OF NAMES

MR. UNDERHILL CAME OUT FROM UNDER HIS HILL, SMILING AND breathing hard. Each breath shot out of his nostrils as a double puff of steam, snow-white in the morning sunshine. Mr. Underhill looked up at the bright December sky and smiled wider than ever, showing snow-white teeth. Then he went down to the village.

"Morning, Mr. Underhill," said the villagers as he passed them in the narrow street between houses with conical, overhanging roofs like the fat red caps of toadstools. "Morning, morning!" he replied to each. (It was of course bad luck to wish anyone a *good* morning; a simple statement of the time of day was quite enough, in a place so permeated with Influences as Sattins Island, where a careless adjective might change the weather for a week.) All of them spoke to him, some with affection, some with affectionate disdain. He was all the little island had in the way of a wizard, and so deserved respect—but how could you respect a little fat man of fifty who waddled along with his toes turned in, breathing steam and smiling? He was no great shakes as a workman either. His fireworks were fairly elaborate but his elixirs were weak. Warts he charmed off frequently reappeared after three days; tomatoes he enchanted grew no bigger than canteloupes; and those rare times when a strange ship

stopped at Sattins Harbor, Mr. Underhill always stayed under his hill—
for fear, he explained, of the evil eye. He was, in other words, a wizard
the way walleyed Gan was a carpenter: by default. The villagers made
do with badly-hung doors and inefficient spells, for this generation, and
relieved their annoyance by treating Mr. Underhill quite familiarly, as
a mere fellow-villager. They even asked him to dinner. Once he asked
some of them to dinner, and served a splendid repast, with silver, crystal,
damask, roast goose, sparkling Andrades '639, and plum pudding with
hard sauce; but he was so nervous all through the meal that it took the
joy out of it, and besides, everybody was hungry again half an hour
afterward. He did not like anyone to visit his cave, not even the anteroom, beyond which in fact nobody had ever got. When he saw people
approaching the hill he always came trotting out to meet them. "Let's sit
out here under the pine trees!" he would say, smiling and waving towards
the fir grove, or if it was raining, "Let's go have a drink at the inn, eh?"
though everybody knew he drank nothing stronger than well-water.

Some of the village children, teased by that locked cave, poked and
pried and made raids while Mr. Underhill was away; but the small door
that led into the inner chamber was spell-shut, and it seemed for once
to be an effective spell. Once a couple of boys, thinking the wizard was
over on the West Shore curing Mrs. Ruuna's sick donkey, brought a
crowbar and a hatchet up there, but at the first whack of the hatchet on
the door there came a roar of wrath from inside, and a cloud of purple
steam. Mr. Underhill had got home early. The boys fled. He did not
come out, and the boys came to no harm, though they said you couldn't
believe what a huge hooting howling hissing horrible bellow that little
fat man could make unless you'd heard it.

His business in town this day was three dozen fresh eggs and a pound
of liver; also a stop at Seacaptain Fogeno's cottage to renew the seeing-
charm on the old man's eyes (quite useless when applied to a case of
detached retina, but Mr. Underhill kept trying), and finally a chat with

old Goody Guld, the concertina-maker's widow. Mr. Underhill's friends were mostly old people. He was timid with the strong young men of the village, and the girls were shy of him. "He makes me nervous, he smiles so much," they all said, pouting, twisting silky ringlets round a finger. "Nervous" was a newfangled word, and their mothers all replied grimly, "Nervous my foot, silliness is the word for it. Mr. Underhill is a very respectable wizard!"

After leaving Goody Guld, Mr. Underhill passed by the school, which was being held this day out on the common. Since no one on Sattins Island was literate, there were no books to learn to read from and no desks to carve initials on and no blackboards to erase, and in fact no schoolhouse. On rainy days the children met in the loft of the Communal Barn, and got hay in their pants; on sunny days the schoolteacher, Palani, took them anywhere she felt like. Today, surrounded by thirty interested children under twelve and forty uninterested sheep under five, she was teaching an important item on the curriculum: the Rules of Names. Mr. Underhill, smiling shyly, paused to listen and watch. Palani, a plump, pretty girl of twenty, made a charming picture there in the wintry sunlight, sheep and children around her, a leafless oak above her, and behind her the dunes and sea and clear, pale sky. She spoke earnestly, her face flushed pink by wind and words. "Now you know the Rules of Names already, children. There are two, and they're the same on every island in the world. What's one of them?"

"It ain't polite to ask anybody what his name is," shouted a fat, quick boy, interrupted by a little girl shrieking, "You can't never tell your own name to nobody my ma says!"

"Yes, Suba. Yes, Popi dear, don't screech. That's right. You never ask anybody his name. You never tell your own. Now think about that a minute and then tell me why we call our wizard Mr. Underhill." She smiled across the curly heads and the woolly backs at Mr. Underhill, who beamed, and nervously clutched his sack of eggs.

"'Cause he lives under a hill!" said half the children.

"But is it his truename?"

"No!" said the fat boy, echoed by little Popi shrieking, "No!"

"How do you know it's not?"

"'Cause he came here all alone and so there wasn't anybody knew his truename so they couldn't tell us, and *he* couldn't—"

"Very good, Suba. Popi, don't shout. That's right. Even a wizard can't tell his truename. When you children are through school and go through the Passage, you'll leave your childnames behind and keep only your truenames, which you must never ask for and never give away. Why is that the rule?"

The children were silent. The sheep bleated gently. Mr. Underhill answered the question: "Because the name is the thing," he said in his shy, soft, husky voice, "and the truename is the true thing. To speak the name is to control the thing. Am I right, Schoolmistress?"

She smiled and curtseyed, evidently a little embarrassed by his participation. And he trotted off towards his hill, clutching his eggs to his bosom. Somehow the minute spent watching Palani and the children had made him very hungry. He locked his inner door behind him with a hasty incantation, but there must have been a leak or two in the spell, for soon the bare anteroom of the cave was rich with the smell of frying eggs and sizzling liver.

The wind that day was light and fresh out of the west, and on it at noon a little boat came skimming the bright waves into Sattins Harbor. Even as it rounded the point a sharp-eyed boy spotted it, and knowing, like every child on the island, every sail and spar of the forty boats of the fishing fleet, he ran down the street calling out, "A foreign boat, a foreign boat!" Very seldom was the lonely isle visited by a boat from some equally lonely isle of the East Reach, or an adventurous trader from the Archipelago. By the time the boat was at the pier half the village was there to greet it, and fishermen were following it homewards, and cowherds and clam-diggers and herb-hunters were puffing up and down all the rocky hills, heading towards the harbor.

But Mr. Underhill's door stayed shut.

There was only one man aboard the boat. Old Seacaptain Fogeno, when they told him that, drew down a bristle of white brows over his unseeing eyes. "There's only one kind of man," he said, "that sails the Outer Reach alone. A wizard, or a warlock, or a Mage . . ."

So the villagers were breathless hoping to see for once in their lives a Mage, one of the mighty White Magicians of the rich, towered, crowded inner islands of the Archipelago. They were disappointed, for the voyager was quite young, a handsome black-bearded fellow who hailed them cheerfully from his boat, and leaped ashore like any sailor glad to have made port. He introduced himself at once as a sea-peddlar. But when they told Seacaptain Fogeno that he carried an oaken walking-stick around with him, the old man nodded. "Two wizards in one town," he said. "Bad!" And his mouth snapped shut like an old carp's.

As the stranger could not give them his name, they gave him one right away: Blackbeard. And they gave him plenty of attention. He had a small mixed cargo of cloth and sandals and piswi feathers for trimming cloaks and cheap incense and levity stones and fine herbs and great glass beads from Venway—the usual peddlar's lot. Everyone on Sattins Island came to look, to chat with the voyager, and perhaps to buy something—"Just to remember him by!" cackled Goody Guld, who like all the women and girls of the village was smitten with Blackbeard's bold good looks. All the boys hung round him too, to hear him tell of his voyages to far, strange islands of the Reach or describe the great rich islands of the Archipelago, the Inner Lanes, the roadsteads white with ships, and the golden roofs of Havnor. The men willingly listened to his tales; but some of them wondered why a trader should sail alone, and kept their eyes thoughtfully upon his oaken staff.

But all this time Mr. Underhill stayed under his hill.

"This is the first island I've ever seen that had no wizard," said Blackbeard one evening to Goody Guld, who had invited him and her nephew and Palani in for a cup of rushwash tea. "What do you do when you get a toothache, or the cow goes dry?"

"Why, we've got Mr. Underhill!" said the old woman.

"For what that's worth," muttered her nephew Birt, and then blushed purple and spilled his tea. Birt was a fisherman, a large, brave, wordless young man. He loved the schoolmistress, but the nearest he had come to telling her of his love was to give baskets of fresh mackerel to her father's cook.

"Oh, you do have a wizard?" Blackbeard asked. "Is he invisible?"

"No, he's just very shy," said Palani. "You've only been here a week, you know, and we see so few strangers here. . . ." She also blushed a little, but did not spill her tea.

Blackbeard smiled at her. "He's a good Sattinsman, then, eh?"

"No," said Goody Guld, "no more than you are. Another cup, nevvy? keep it in the cup this time. No, my dear, he came in a little bit of a boat, four years ago was it? just a day after the end of the shad run, I recall, for they was taking up the nets over in East Creek, and Pondi Cowherd broke his leg that very morning—five years ago it must be. No, four. No, five it is, 'twas the year the garlic didn't sprout. So he sails in on a bit of a sloop loaded full up with great chests and boxes and says to Seacaptain Fogeno, who wasn't blind then, though old enough goodness knows to be blind twice over, 'I hear tell,' he says, 'you've got no wizard nor warlock at all, might you be wanting one?' 'Indeed, if the magic's white!' says the Captain, and before you could say cuttlefish Mr. Underhill had settled down in the cave under the hill and was charming the mange off Goody Beltow's cat. Though the fur grew in grey, and 'twas an orange cat. Queer-looking thing it was after that. It died last winter in the cold spell. Goody Beltow took on so at that cat's death, poor thing, worse than when her man was drowned on the Long Banks, the year of the long herring-runs, when nevvy Birt here was but a babe in petticoats." Here Birt spilled his tea again, and Blackbeard grinned, but Goody Guld proceeded undismayed, and talked on till nightfall.

Next day Blackbeard was down at the pier, seeing after the sprung board in his boat which he seemed to take a long time fixing, and as usual drawing the taciturn Sattinsmen into talk. "Now which of these is your wizard's craft?" he asked. "Or has he got one of those the Mages fold up into a walnut shell when they're not using it?"

"Nay," said a stolid fisherman. "She's oop in his cave, under hill."

"He carried the boat he came in up to his cave?"

"Aye. Clear oop. I helped. Heavier as lead she was. Full oop with great boxes, and they full oop with books o' spells, he says. Heavier as lead she was." And the stolid fisherman turned his back, sighing stolidly. Goody Guld's nephew, mending a net nearby, looked up from his work and asked with equal stolidity, "Would ye like to meet Mr. Underhill, maybe?"

Blackbeard returned Birt's look. Clever black eyes met candid blue ones for a long moment; then Blackbeard smiled and said, "Yes. Will you take me up to the hill, Birt?"

"Aye, when I'm done with this," said the fisherman. And when the net was mended, he and the Archipelagan set off up the village street towards the high green hill above it. But as they crossed the common Blackbeard said, "Hold on a while, friend Birt. I have a tale to tell you, before we meet your wizard."

"Tell away," says Birt, sitting down in the shade of a live-oak.

"It's a story that started a hundred years ago, and isn't finished yet—though it soon will be, very soon. . . . In the very heart of the Archipelago, where the islands crowd thick as flies on honey, there's a little isle called Pendor. The sealords of Pendor were mighty men, in the old days of war before the League. Loot and ransom and tribute came pouring into Pendor, and they gathered a great treasure there, long ago. Then from somewhere away out in the West Reach, where dragons breed on the lava isles, came one day a very mighty dragon. Not one of those over-grown lizards most of you Outer Reach folk call dragons, but a big, black, winged, wise, cunning monster, full of strength and subtlety, and like all dragons loving gold and precious stones above all things. He killed the Sealord and his soldiers, and the people of Pendor fled in their ships by night. They all fled away and left the dragon coiled up in Pendor Towers. And there he stayed for a hundred years, dragging his scaly belly over the emerald sand sapphires and coins of gold, coming forth only once in a year or two when he must eat. He'd raid nearby islands for his food. You know what dragons eat?"

Birt nodded and said in a whisper, "Maidens."

"Right," said Blackbeard. "Well, that couldn't be endured forever, nor the thought of him sitting on all that treasure. So after the League grew strong, and the Archipelago wasn't so busy with wars and piracy, it was decided to attack Pendor, drive out the dragon, and get the gold and jewels for the treasury of the League. They're forever wanting money, the League is. So a huge fleet gathered from fifty islands, and seven Mages stood in the prows of the seven strongest ships, and they sailed towards Pendor. . . . They got there. They landed. Nothing stirred. The houses all stood empty, the dishes on the tables full of a hundred years' dust. The bones of the old Sealord and his men lay about in the castle courts and on the stairs. And the Tower rooms reeked of dragon. But there was no dragon. And no treasure, not a diamond the size of a poppyseed, not a single silver bead . . . Knowing that he couldn't stand up to seven Mages, the dragon had skipped out. They tracked him, and found he'd flown to a deserted island up north called Udrath; they followed his trail there, and what did they find? Bones again. His bones—the dragon's. But no treasure. A wizard, some unknown wizard from somewhere, must have met him singlehanded, and defeated him—and then made off with the treasure, right under the League's nose!"

The fisherman listened, attentive and expressionless.

"Now that must have been a powerful wizard and a clever one, first to kill a dragon, and second to get off without leaving a trace. The lords and Mages of the Archipelago couldn't track him at all, neither where he'd come from nor where he'd made off to. They were about to give up. That was last spring; I'd been off on a three-year voyage up in the North Reach, and got back about that time. And they asked me to help them find the unknown wizard. That was clever of them. Because I'm not only a wizard myself, as I think some of the oafs here have guessed, but I am also a descendant of the Lords of Pendor. That treasure is mine. It's mine, and knows that it's mine. Those fools of the League couldn't find it, because it's not theirs. It belongs to the House of Pendor, and the great emerald, the star of the hoard, Inalkil the Greenstone, knows its master. Behold!" Blackbeard raised his oaken staff and cried aloud, "Inalkil!" The tip of the staff began to glow green, a fiery green radiance, a dazzling haze the color of April grass, and at the same moment the staff tipped in the wizard's hand, leaning, slanting till it pointed straight at the side of the hill above them.

"It wasn't so bright a glow, far away in Havnor," Blackbeard murmured, "but the staff pointed true. Inalkil answered when I called. The jewel knows its master. And I know the thief, and I shall conquer him. He's a mighty wizard, who could overcome a dragon. But I am mightier. Do you want to know why, oaf? Because I know his name!"

As Blackbeard's tone got more arrogant, Birt had looked duller and duller, blanker and blanker; but at this he gave a twitch, shut his mouth, and stared at the Archipelagan. "How did you . . . learn it?" he asked very slowly.

Blackbeard grinned, and did not answer.

"Black magic?"

"How else?"

Birt looked pale, and said nothing.

"I am the Sealord of Pendor, oaf, and I will have the gold my fathers won, and the jewels my mothers wore, and the Greenstone! For they are mine.—Now, you can tell your village boobies the whole story after I have defeated this wizard and gone. Wait here. Or you can come and watch, if you're not afraid. You'll never get the chance again to see a great wizard in all his power." Blackbeard turned, and without a backward glance strode off up the hill towards the entrance to the cave.

Very slowly, Birt followed. A good distance from the cave he stopped, sat down under a hawthorn tree, and watched. The Archipelagan had stopped; a stiff, dark figure alone on the green swell of the hill before the gaping cavemouth, he stood perfectly still. All at once he swung his staff up over his head, and the emerald radiance shone about him as he shouted, "Thief, thief of the Hoard of Pendor, come forth!"

There was a crash, as of dropped crockery, from inside the cave, and a lot of dust came spewing out. Scared, Birt ducked. When he looked again he saw Blackbeard still standing motionless, and at the mouth of the cave, dusty and dishevelled, stood Mr. Underhill. He looked small and pitiful, with his toes turned in as usual, and his little bowlegs in black tights, and no staff—he never had had one, Birt suddenly thought. Mr. Underhill spoke. "Who are you?" he said in his husky little voice.

"I am the Sealord of Pendor, thief, come to claim my treasure!"

At that, Mr. Underhill slowly turned pink, as he always did when people were rude to him. But he then turned something else. He turned yellow. His hair bristled out, he gave a coughing roar—and was a yellow lion leaping down the hill at Blackbeard, white fangs gleaming.

But Blackbeard no longer stood there. A gigantic tiger, color of night and lightning, bounded to meet the lion. . . .

The lion was gone. Below the cave all of a sudden stood a high grove of trees, black in the winter sunshine. The tiger, checking himself in midleap just before he entered the shadow of the trees, caught fire in the air, became a tongue of flame lashing out at the dry black branches. . . .

But where the trees had stood a sudden cataract leaped from the hillside, an arch of silvery crashing water, thundering down upon the fire. But the fire was gone. . . .

For just a moment before the fisherman's staring eyes two hills rose—the green one he knew, and a new one, a bare, brown hillock ready to drink up the rushing waterfall. That passed so quickly it made Birt blink, and after blinking he blinked again, and moaned, for what he saw now was a great deal worse. Where the cataract had been there hovered a dragon. Black wings darkened all the hill, steel claws reached groping, and from the dark, scaly, gaping lips fire and steam shot out.

Beneath the monstrous creature stood Blackbeard, laughing.

"Take any shape you please, little Mr. Underhill!" he taunted. "I can match you. But the game grows tiresome. I want to look upon my treasure, upon Inalkil. Now, big dragon, little wizard, take your true shape. I command you by the power of your true name—Yevaud!"

Birt could not move at all, not even to blink. He cowered, staring whether he would or not. He saw the black dragon hang there in the air above Blackbeard. He saw the fire lick like many tongues from the scaly mouth, the steam jet from the red nostrils. He saw Blackbeard's face grow white, white as chalk, and the beard-fringed lips trembling.

"Your name is Yevaud!"

"Yes," said a great, husky, hissing voice. "My truename is Yevaud, and my true shape is this shape."

"But the dragon was killed—they found dragon bones on Udrath Island—"

"That was another dragon," said the dragon, and then stooped like a hawk, talons outstretched. And Birt shut his eyes.

When he opened them the sky was clear, the hillside empty, except for a reddish-blackish trampled spot, and a few talon-marks in the grass.

Birt the fisherman got to his feet and ran. He ran across the common, scattering sheep to right and left, and straight down the village street to Palani's father's house. Palani was out in the garden weeding the nasturtiums. "Come with me!" Birt gasped. She stared. He grabbed her wrist and dragged her with him. She screeched a little, but did not resist. He ran with her straight to the pier, pushed her into his fishing-sloop the *Queenie,* untied the painter, took up the oars and set off rowing like a demon. The last that Sattins Island saw of him and Palani was the *Queenie*'s sail vanishing in the direction of the nearest island westward.

The villagers thought they would never stop talking about it, how Goody Guld's nephew Birt had lost his mind and sailed off with the schoolmistress on the very same day that the peddlar Blackbeard disappeared without a trace, leaving all his feathers and beads behind. But they did stop talking about it, three days later. They had other things to talk about, when Mr. Underhill finally came out of his cave.

Mr. Underhill had decided that since his truename was no longer a secret, he might as well drop his disguise. Walking was a lot harder than flying, and besides, it was a long, long time since he had had a real meal.

SMALL
CHANGE

"SMALL CHANGE," MY AUNT SAID AS I PUT THE OBOL ON HER tongue. "I'll need more than that where I'm going."

It is true that the change was very small. She looked exactly as she had looked a few hours before, except that she was not breathing.

"Good-bye, Aunt," I said.

"I'm not going yet!" she snapped. I always tried her patience. "There are rooms in this house I've never even opened the door of!"

I did not know what she was talking about. Our house has two rooms.

"This obol tastes funny," she said after a long silence. "Where did you get it?"

I did not want to tell her that it was a good-luck piece, a copper sequin, not money though it was round like a coin, which I had carried for a year or more in my pocket, ever since I picked it up by the gate of the bricklayer's yard. I had rubbed it clean, of course, but my aunt had a keen tongue, and it was trodden mud, dog turds, brick dust, and the inside of my pocket that she was tasting, along with the dry-blood taste of copper. I pretended that I had not understood her question.

"A wonder you had it at all," my aunt said. "If you have a penny in your pocket after a month without me, I'll be surprised. Poor thing!"

She would have sighed if she had been breathing. I had not known that she would continue to worry about me after she died. I began to cry.

"That's good," my aunt said with satisfaction. "Just don't keep it up too long. I'm not going far, now. I just want very much to find out what room that door leads to."

She looked younger when she got up, younger than she was when I was born. She went across the room lightly and opened a door I had not known was there.

I heard her say in a pleased, surprised voice, "Lila!" Lila was the name of her sister, my mother.

"For goodness' sake, Lila," my aunt said, "you haven't been waiting in here for eleven years?"

I could not hear what my mother said.

"I'm very sorry about leaving the girl," my aunt said. "I did what I could, I tried my best. She's a good girl. But what will become of her now!"

My aunt never cried, and now she had no tears; but her anxiety over me made me cry again in alarm and self-pity.

My mother came out of that new room in the form of a lacewing fly and saw me crying. Tears taste salt to the living but sweet to the dead, and they have a taste for sweets, at first. I did not know all that, then. I was just glad to have my mother with me even as a tiny fly. It was a gladness the size of a fly.

That was all there was left of my mother in the house, and she had got what she wanted; so my aunt went on.

The room she was in was large and rather shadowy, lighted only by a skylight, like a storeroom. Along one wall stood distaffs full of spun flax, in a row, and in the place where the light fell from the skylight stood a loom. My aunt had been a notable spinster and weaver all her life, and was sorely tempted now by those rolls of fine, even thread, as well spun as any she had ever spun herself; the loom was warped, and there lay the shuttle ready. But linen weaving is a careful art. If she began a shroud now she would be at it for a long time, and much as she wanted a proper shroud, she never had been one to start a job and then drop it unfinished. So it was that she kept worrying about what would become of me. But she had already made up her mind to leave the housework undone (since housework is never done anyhow), and now she admitted that she must let other people see to her winding sheet. She hoped she could trust me to choose a clean sheet, at least, and a well-patched one. But she could not resist picking up the end thread of one of the distaffs and feeding out a length between her thumb and finger to test it for evenness and strength; and she kept the thread running between thumb and finger as she walked on.

It was well that she did so, as the new room opened onto a corridor along which were many doorways, each one leading to other halls and rooms, a maze in which she would certainly have lost her way but for the thread of flax.

The rooms were clean, a little dusty, and unfurnished. In one of them my aunt found a toy lying on the floor, a wooden horse. It was crudely carved, the forelegs all of a piece and the hind legs the same, a kind of a two-legged horse with round, flat eyes, which she thought she remembered, though she was not sure.

In another long, narrow room many unused kitchen tools and pans lay on a counter, and three horn buttons in a row.

At the end of a long corridor into which she was drawn by a gleam or a reflection at the far end, there stood an engine of some kind, which was certainly nothing my aunt had ever seen before.

In one small room with no skylight an intense, pungent smell hung in the air, filling up the room like a living creature caught in it. My aunt left that room hurriedly, upset.

Though her curiosity had been roused by finding all these rooms she had not known in her house, her explorations, and the silence, brought on her a sense of oppression and unease. She stood for a moment outside the door of the room where the strong smell was, making up her mind.

That never took her long. She began to follow the thread back, winding it about the fingers of her left hand as she took it up. This process needed more attention than the paying out, and lifting her eyes from a tangle in the thread she was puzzled to find herself in a room which she did not recall passing through, but could hardly have crossed without noticing, for it was very large. The walls were of a beautiful fine-grained stone of a pale grey hue, in which certain figures like astrologers' charts of the constellations, fine lines connecting stars or clusters of stars, were inlaid in gold wire. The ceiling was light and high, the floor of worn, dark marble. It was like a church, my aunt thought, but not a religious church (that is what she thought). The patterns on the walls were like the illustrations in books of learning, and the room itself was like the hall of the great library in the city; there were no books, but the place was majestic and reposeful, having about it a collected stillness very pleasant to the spirit of my aunt. She was tired of walking, and decided to rest there.

She sat down, since there was no furniture, on the floor in the corner nearest the door to which the thread had led her. My aunt was a woman who liked a wall at her back. The invasions had left her uneasy in open spaces, always looking over her shoulder. Though who could hurt her now? as she said to herself, sitting down. But, as she said to herself, you never can be sure.

The lines of gold wire on the walls led her eye along them as she sat resting. Some of the figures they made seemed familiar. She began to think that these figures or patterns were a map of the maze which she was in, the wires representing passages and the stars, rooms; or perhaps the stars represented the doors into rooms, the walls of which were not outlined. She could pretty certainly retrace the first corridor back to the room of the distaffs; but on the far side of that, where the old part of our house ought to be, the patterns continued, looking a good deal more like the familiar constellations of the sky in early winter. She was not certain she understood the map at all, but she continued to study it, to let her mind follow the lines from star to star, until she began to see her way. She got up then, and went back, pursuing the flaxen thread and taking it up in her left hand, till she came back.

There I was in the same room still crying. My mother was gone. Lacewing flies wait years to be born, but they live only a day. The undertaker's men were just leaving, and I had to follow them, so my aunt came along to her funeral, though she did not want to leave the house. She tried to bring her ball of thread with her, but it broke as she crossed the threshold. I could hear her swear under her breath, the way she always did when she broke a thread or spilled the sugar—"Damn!" in a whisper.

Neither of us enjoyed the funeral at all. My aunt grew panicky as they began to throw the dirt back into the grave. She cried aloud, "I can't breathe! I can't breathe!"—which frightened me so much that I thought it was myself speaking, myself suffocating, and I fell down. People had to help me get up, and help me get home. I was so ashamed and confused among them that I lost my aunt.

One of the neighbors, who had never been particularly pleasant to us, took pity on me, and behaved with much kindness. She talked so wisely to me that I got up the courage to ask her, "Where is my aunt? Will she come back?" But she did not know, and only said things meant to comfort me. I am not as clever as most people, but I knew there was no comfort for me.

The neighbor made sure I could look after myself, and that evening she sent one of her children over with dinner in a dish for me. I ate it, and it was very good. I had not eaten anything while my aunt was away in the other part of the house.

At night, after dark, I lay down all alone in the bedroom. At first I felt well and cheerful, because of the food I had eaten, and I pretended my aunt was there sleeping in the same room, the way it had always been. Then I got frightened, and the fright grew in the darkness.

My aunt came up out of the floor in the middle of the room. The red tiles humped up and cracked apart. Her hair and her head pushed through the tiles, and then her body. She looked very dark, like dirt, and she was much smaller than she had been.

"Let me be!" she said.

I was too terrified to speak.

"Let me go!" my aunt said. But it was not truly my aunt; it was only an old part of her that had come back underground from the graveyard, because I had been wanting her. I did not like that part of her, or want it there. I cried, "Go away! Go back!" and hid my head in my arms.

My aunt made a little creaking sound like a wicker basket. I kept my eyes hidden so long that I nearly fell asleep. When I looked, no one was there, or only a kind of darker place in the air, and the tiles were not cracked apart. I went to sleep.

Next morning when I woke up the sunlight was in the window and things were all right, but I could not walk across that part of the floor where my aunt had come up through the tiles.

I was afraid to cry after that night, since crying might bring her back to taste the sweetness or to scold me. But it was lonely in the house now that she was buried and gone. I had no idea what to do without her. The neighbor came in and talked about finding me work, and gave me food again; but the next day a man came, who said he had been sent by a creditor. He took away the chest of clothes and bedding. Later that day, in the evening, he came back, because he had seen that I was alone there. I kept the door locked this time. He spoke smoothly at first, trying to make me let him in, and then he began saying in a low voice that he would hurt me, but I kept the door locked and never answered. The next day somebody else came, but I had pushed the bedstead up against the door. It may have been the neighbor's child that came, but I was afraid to look. I felt safe staying in the back room. Other people came and knocked, but I never answered, and they went away again.

I stayed in the back room until at last I saw the door that my aunt had gone through, that day. I went and opened it. I was sure she would be there. But the room was empty. The loom was gone, and the distaffs were gone, and no one was there.

I went on to the corridor beyond, but no farther. I could never find my way by myself through all those halls and rooms, or understand the patterns of the stars. I was so afraid and wretched that I went back, and crawled into my own mouth, and hid there.

My aunt came to fetch me. She was very cross. I always tried her patience. All she said was, "Come on!" And she pulled me along by the hand. Once she said, "Shame on you!" When we got to the riverbank she looked me over very sternly. She washed my face with the dark water of that river, and pressed my hair down with the palms of her hands. She said, "I should have known."

"I'm sorry, Aunt," I said.

"Oh, yes," she said. "Come along, now. Look sharp!"

For the boat had come across the river and was tying up at the wharf. We walked down to the wharf among the reeds in the twilight. It was after sunset, and there was no moon or stars, and no wind blowing. The river was so wide I could not see the other shore.

My aunt dickered with the ferryman. I let her do that, since people always cheated me. She had taken the obol off her tongue, and was talking fast. "My niece, can't you see how it is? Of course they didn't give her the fare! She's not responsible! I came along with her to look after her. Here's the fare. Yes, it's for us both. No, you don't," and she drew back her hand, having merely shown him a glimpse of the bit of copper. "Not till we're both safe across!"

The ferryman glowered, but began to loosen the painter.

"Come along, then!" my aunt said. She stepped into the boat, and held out her hand to me. So I followed her.

THE
POACHER

. . . And must one kiss
Revoke the silent house, the birdsong wilderness?
—Sylvia Townsend Warner

I WAS A CHILD WHEN I CAME TO THE GREAT HEDGE FOR THE FIRST time. I was hunting mushrooms, not for sport, as I have read ladies and gentlemen do, but in earnest. To hunt without need is the privilege, they say, of noblemen. I should say that it is one of the acts that makes a man a nobleman, that constitutes privilege itself. To hunt because one is hungry is the lot of the commoner. All it generally makes of him is a poacher. I was poaching mushrooms, then, in the King's Forest.

My father had sent me out that morning with a basket and the command, "Don't come sneaking back here till it's full!" I knew he would beat me if I didn't come back with the basket full of something to eat—mushrooms at best, at this time of year, or the fiddleheads of ferns that were just beginning to poke through the cold ground in a few places. He would hit me across the shoulders with the hoe handle or a switch, and send me to bed supperless, because he was hungry and disappointed. He could feel that he was at least better off than somebody, if he made me hungrier than himself, and sore and ashamed as well. After a while my stepmother would pass silently by my corner of the hut and leave on my pallet or in my hand some scrap she had contrived or saved from her own scant supper—half a crust, a lump of pease pudding. Her eyes told

me eloquently, Don't say anything! I said nothing. I never thanked her.
I ate the food in darkness.

Often my father would beat her. It was my fate, fortunate or misfor-
tunate, not to feel better off than her when I saw her beaten. Instead I felt
more ashamed than ever, worse off even than the weeping, wretched woman.
She could do nothing, and I could do nothing for her. Once I tried to
sweep out the hut when she was working in our field, so that things would
be in order when she came back, but my sweeping only stirred the dirt
around. When she came in from hoeing, filthy and weary, she noticed
nothing, but set straight to building up the fire, fetching water, and so
on, while my father, as filthy and weary as she, sat down in the one chair
we had with a great sigh. And I was angry because I had, after all, done
nothing at all.

I remembered that when my father first married her, when I was quite
small, she had played with me like another child. She knew knife-toss
games, and taught me them. She taught me the ABC from a book she
had. The nuns had brought her up, and she knew her letters, poor thing.
My father had a notion that I might be let into the friary if I learned to
read, and make the family rich. That came to nothing, of course. She
was little and weak and not the help to him at work my mother had been,
and things did not prosper for us. My lessons in reading ended soon.

It was she who found I was a clever hunter and taught me what to look
for—the golden and brown mushrooms, woodmasters and morels and
other fungi, the wild shoots, roots, berries, and hips in their seasons,
the cresses in the streams; she taught me to make fishtraps; my father
showed me how to set snares for rabbits. They soon came to count on
me for a good portion of our food, for everything we grew on our field
went to the Baron, who owned it, and we were allowed to cultivate only
a mere patch of kitchen garden, lest our labors there detract from our
work for the Baron. I took pride in my foraging, and went willingly into
the forest, and fearlessly. Did we not live on the very edge of the forest,

almost in it? Did I not know every path and glade and grove within a mile of our hut? I thought of it as my own domain. But my father still ordered me to go, every morning, as if I needed his command, and he laced it with distrust—"Don't come sneaking back until the basket's full!"

That was no easy matter sometimes—in early spring, when nothing was up yet—like the day I first saw the great hedge. Old snow still lay greyish in the shadows of the oaks. I went on, finding not a mushroom nor a fiddlehead. Mummied berries hung on the brambles, tasting of decay. There had been no fish in the trap, no rabbit in the snares, and the crayfish were still hiding in the mud. I went on farther than I had yet gone, hoping to discover a new fernbrake, or trace a squirrel's nuthoard by her tracks on the glazed and porous snow. I was trudging along easily enough, having found a path almost as good as a road, like the avenue that led to the Baron's hall. Cold sunlight lay between the tall beechtrees that stood along it. At the end of it was something like a hedgerow, but high, so high I had taken it at first for clouds. Was it the end of the forest? the end of the world?

I stared as I walked, but never stopped walking. The nearer I came the more amazing it was—a hedge taller than the ancient beeches, and stretching as far as I could see to left and right. Like any hedgerow, it was made of shrubs and trees that laced and wove themselves together as they grew, but they were immensely tall, and thick, and thorny. At this time of the year the branches were black and bare, but nowhere could I find the least gap or hole to let me peer through to the other side. From the huge roots up, the thorns were impenetrably tangled. I pressed my face up close, and got well scratched for my pains, but saw nothing but an endless dark tangle of gnarled stems and fierce branches.

Well, I thought, if they're brambles, at least I've found a lot of berries, come summer!—for I didn't think about much but food, when I was a child. It was my whole business and chief interest.

All the same, a child's mind will wander. Sometimes when I'd had enough to eat for supper, I'd lie watching our tiny hearthfire dying down, and wonder what was on the other side of the great hedge of thorns.

The hedge was indeed a treasury of berries and haws, so that I was often there all summer and autumn. It took me half the morning to get there, but when the great hedge was bearing, I could fill my basket and sack with berries or haws in no time at all, and then I had all the middle of the day to spend as I pleased, alone. Oftenest what pleased me was to wander along beside the hedge, eating a particularly fine blackberry here and there, dreaming formless dreams. I knew no tales then, except the terribly simple one of my father, my stepmother, and myself, and so my daydreams had no shape or story to them. But all the time I walked, I had half an eye for any kind of gap or opening that might be a way through the hedge. If I had a story to tell myself, that was it: There is a way through the great hedge, and I discover it.

Climbing it was out of the question. It was the tallest thing I had ever seen, and all up that great height the thorns of the branches were as long as my fingers and sharp as sewing needles. If I was careless picking berries from it, my clothes got caught and ripped, and my arms were a net of red and black scratches every summer.

Yet I liked to go there, and to walk beside it. One day of early summer, some years after I first found the hedge, I went there. It was too soon for berries, but when the thorns blossomed the flowered sprays rose up and up one above the other like clouds into the sky, and I liked to see that, and to smell their scent, as heavy as the smell of meat or bread, but sweet. I set off to the right. The walking was easy, all along the hedge, as if there might have been a road there once. The sun-dappling arms of the old beeches of the forest did not quite reach to the thorny wall that bore its highest sprays of blossom high above their crowns. It was shady under the wall, smelling heavily of blackberry flowers, and windlessly hot. It was always very silent there, a silence that came through the hedge.

I had noticed long ago that I never heard a bird sing on the other side, though their spring songs might be ringing down every aisle of the forest. Sometimes I saw birds fly over the hedge, but I never was sure I saw the same one fly back.

So I wandered on in the silence, on the springy grass, keeping an eye out for the little russet-brown mushrooms that were my favorites, when I began to feel something queer about the grass and the woods and the flowering hedge. I thought I had never walked this far before, and yet it all looked as if I had seen it many times. Surely I knew that clump of young birches, one bent down by last winter's long snow? Then I saw, not far from the birches, under a currant bush beside the grassy way, a basket and a knotted sack. Someone else was here, where I had never met another soul. Someone was poaching in my domain.

People in the village feared the forest. Because our hut was almost under the trees of the forest, people feared us. I never understood what they were afraid of. They talked about wolves. I had seen a wolf's track once, and sometimes heard the lonely voices, winter nights, but no wolf came near the houses or fields. People talked about bears. Nobody in our village had ever seen a bear or a bear's track. People talked about dangers in the forest, perils and enchantments, and rolled their eyes and whispered, and I thought them all great fools. I knew nothing of enchantments. I went to and fro in the forest and up and down in it as if it were my kitchen garden, and never yet had I found anything to fear.

So whenever I had to go the half-mile from our hut and enter the village, people looked askance at me, and called me the wild boy. And I took pride in being called wild. I might have been happier if they had smiled at me and called me by my name, but as it was, I had my pride, my domain, my wilderness, where no one but I dared go.

So it was with fear and pain that I gazed at the signs of an intruder, an interloper, a rival—until I recognised the bag and basket as my own. I had walked right round the great hedge. It was a circle. My forest was all outside it. The other side of it was—whatever it was—inside.

From that afternoon, my lazy curiosity about the great hedge grew to a desire and resolve to penetrate it and see for myself that hidden place within, that secret. Lying watching the dying embers at night, I thought now about the tools I would need to cut through the hedge, and how I could get such tools. The poor little hoes and mattocks we worked our field with would scarcely scratch those great stems and branches. I needed a real blade, and a good stone to whet it on.

So began my career as a thief.

An old woodcutter down in the village died; I heard of his death at market that day. I knew he had lived alone, and was called a miser. He might have what I needed. That night when my father and stepmother slept, I crept out of the hut and went back by moonlight to the village. The door of the cottage was open. A fire smoldered in the hearth under the smokehole. In the sleeping end of the house, to the left of the fire, a couple of women had laid out the corpse. They were sitting up by it, chatting, now and then putting up a howl or two of keening when they thought about it. I went softly in to the stall end of the cottage; the fire was between us, and they did not see or hear me. The cow chewed her cud, the cat watched me, the women across the fire mumbled and laughed, and the old man lay stark on his pallet in his windingsheet. I looked through his tools, quietly, but without hurrying. He had a fine hatchet, a crude saw, and a mounted, circular grindstone—a treasure to me. I could not take the mounting, but stuck the handle in my shirt, took the tools under my arm and the stone in both hands, and walked out again. "Who's there?" said one of the women, without interest, and sent up a perfunctory wail.

The stone all but pulled my arms out before I got it up the road to our hut, where I hid it and the tools and the handle a little way inside the forest under a bit of brushwood. I crept back into the windowless blackness of the hut and felt my way over to my pallet, for the fire was dead. I lay a long time, my heart beating hard, telling my story: I had stolen my weapons, now I would lay my siege on the great thorn hedge. But I did not use those words. I knew nothing of sieges, wars, victories, all such matters of great history. I knew no story but my own.

It would be a very dull one to read in a book. I cannot tell much of it. All that summer and autumn, winter and spring, and the next summer, and the next autumn, and the next winter, I fought my war, I laid my siege: I chopped and hewed and hacked at the thicket of bramble and thorn. I cut through a thick, tough trunk, but could not pull it free till I had cut through fifty branches tangled in its branches. When it was free I dragged it out and then I began to cut at the next thick trunk. My hatchet grew dull a thousand times. I had made a mount for the grindstone, and on it I sharpened the hatchet a thousand times, till the blade was worn down into the thickness of the metal and would not hold an edge. In the first winter, the saw shivered against a rootstock hard as flint. In the second summer, I stole an ax and a handsaw from a party of travelling woodcutters camped a little way inside the forest near the road to the Baron's hall. They were poaching wood from my domain, the forest. In return, I poached tools from them. I felt it was a fair trade.

My father grumbled at my long absences, but I kept up my foraging, and had so many snares out that we had rabbit as often as we wanted it. In any case, he no longer dared strike me. I was sixteen or seventeen years old, I suppose, and though I was by no means well grown, or tall, or very strong, I was stronger than he, a worn-out old man, forty years old or more. He struck my stepmother as often as he liked. She was a little, toothless, red-eyed, old woman now. She spoke very seldom. When she spoke my father would cuff her, railing at women's chatter, women's nagging. "Will you never be quiet?" he would shout, and she would shrink away, drawing her head down in her hunched shoulders like a turtle. And yet sometimes when she washed herself at night with a rag and a basin of water warmed in the ashes, her blanket would slip down, and I saw her body was fine-skinned, with soft breasts and rounded hips shadowy in the firelight. I would turn away, for she was frightened and ashamed when she saw me looking at her. She called me "son," though I was not her son. Long ago she had called me by my name.

Once I saw her watching me as I ate. It had been a good harvest, that first autumn, and we had turnips right through the winter. She watched me with a look on her face, and I knew she wanted to ask me then, while my father was out of the house, what it was I did all day in the forest, why my shirt and vest and trousers were forever ripped and shredded, why my hands were callused on the palms and crosshatched with a thousand scratches on the backs. If she had asked I would have told her. But she did not ask. She turned her face down into the shadows, silent.

Shadows and silence filled the passage I had hacked into the great hedge. The thorn trees stood so tall and thickly branched above it that no light at all made its way down through them.

As the first year came round, I had hacked and sawn and chopped a passage of about my height and twice my length into the hedge. It was as impenetrable as ever before me, not allowing a glimpse of what might be on the other side nor a hint that the tangle of branches might be any thinner. Many a time at night I lay hearing my father snore and said to myself that when I was an old man like him, I would cut through the last branch and come out into the forest—having spent my life tunnelling through nothing but a great, round bramble patch, with nothing inside it but itself. I told that end to my story, but did not believe it. I tried to tell other ends. I said, I will find a green lawn inside the hedge . . . A village . . . A friary . . . A hall . . . A stony field . . . I knew nothing else that one might find. But these endings did not hold my mind for long; soon I was thinking again of how I should cut the next thick trunk that stood in my way. My story was the story of cutting a way through an endless thicket of thorny branches, and nothing more. And to tell it would take as long as it took to do it.

On a day near the end of winter, such a day as makes it seem there will never be an end to winter, a chill, damp, dark, dreary, hungry day, I was sawing away with the woodcutters' saw at a gnarled, knotted whitethorn as thick as my thigh and hard as iron. I crouched in the small space I had and sawed away with nothing in my mind but sawing.

The hedge grew unnaturally fast, in season and out; even in midwinter thick, pale shoots would grow across my passageway, and in summer I had to spend some time every day clearing out new growth, thorny green sprays full of stinging sap. My passage or tunnel was now more than five yards long, but only a foot and a half high except at the very end; I had learned to wriggle in, and keep the passage man-high only at the end, where I must have room enough to get a purchase on my ax or saw. I crouched at my work, glad to give up the comfort of standing for a gain in going forward.

The whitethorn trunk split suddenly, in the contrary, evil way the trees of that thicket had. It sent the sawblade almost across my thigh, and as the tree fell against others interlaced with it, a long branch whipped across my face. Thorns raked my eyelids and forehead. Blinded with blood, I thought it had struck my eyes. I knelt, wiping away the blood with hands that trembled from strain and the suddenness of the accident. I got one eye clear at last, and then the other, and, blinking and peering, saw light before me.

The whitethorn in falling had left a gap, and in the maze and crisscross of dark branches beyond it was a small clear space, through which one could see, as through a chink in a wall: and in that small bright space I saw the castle.

I know now what to call it. What I saw then I had no name for. I saw sunlight on a yellow stone wall. Looking closer, I saw a door in the wall. Beside the door stood figures, men perhaps, in shadow, unmoving; after a time I thought they were figures carved in stone, such as I had seen at the doors of the friary church. I could see nothing else: sunlight, bright stone, the door, the shadowy figures. Everywhere else the branches and trunks and dead leaves of the hedge massed before me as they had for two years, impenetrably dark.

I thought, if I was a snake I could crawl through that hole! But being no snake, I set to work to enlarge it. My hands still shook, but I took the ax and struck and struck at the massed and crossing branches. Now I knew which branch to cut, which stem to chop: whichever lay between my eyes and that golden wall, that door. I cared nothing for the height or width of my passage, so long as I could force and tear my way forward, indifferent to the laceration of my arms and face and clothing. I swung my dull ax with such violence that the branches flew before me; and as I pushed forward the branches and stems of the hedge grew thinner, weaker. Light shone through them. From winter-black and hard they became green and soft, as I hacked and forced on forward, until I could put them aside with my hand. I parted the last screen and crawled on hands and knees out onto a lawn of bright grass.

Overhead the sky was the soft blue of early summer. Before me, a little downhill from the hedge, stood the house of yellow stone, the castle, in its moat. Flags hung motionless from its pointed towers. The air was still and warm. Nothing moved.

I crouched there, as motionless as everything else, except for my breath, which came loud and hard for a long time. Beside my sweaty, blood-streaked hand a little bee sat on a clover blossom, not stirring, honey-drunk.

I raised myself to my knees and looked all round me, cautious. I knew that this must be a hall, like the Baron's hall above the village, and therefore dangerous to anyone who did not live there or have work there. It was much larger and finer than the Baron's hall, and infinitely fairer; larger and fairer even than the friary church. With its yellow walls and red roofs it looked, I thought, like a flower. I had not seen much else I could compare it to. The Baron's hall was a squat keep with a scumble of huts and barns about it; the church was grey and grim, the carved figures by its door faceless with age. This house, whatever it was, was delicate and fine and fresh. The sunlight on it made me think of the firelight on my stepmother's breasts.

Halfway down the wide, grassy slope to the moat, a few cows lay in midday torpor, heads up, eyes closed; they were not even chewing the cud. On the farther slope, a flock of sheep lay scattered out, and an apple orchard was just losing its last blossoms.

The air was very warm. In my torn, ragged shirt and coat, I would have been shivering as the sweat cooled on me, on the other side of the hedge, where winter was. Here I shrugged off the coat. The blood from all my scratches, drying, made my skin draw and itch, so that I began to look with longing at the water in the moat. Blue and glassy it lay, very tempting. I was thirsty, too. My waterbottle lay back in the passage, nearly empty. I thought of it, but never turned my head to look back.

No one had moved, on the lawns or in the gardens around the house or on the bridge across the moat, all the time I had been kneeling here in the shadow of the great hedge, gazing my fill. The cows lay like stones, though now and again I saw a brown flank shudder off a fly, or the very tip of a tail twitch lazily. When I looked down I saw the little bee still on the clover blossom. I touched its wing curiously, wondering if it was dead. Its feelers shivered a little, but it did not stir. I looked back at the house, at the windows, and at the door—a side door—which I had first seen through the branches. I saw, without for some while knowing that I saw, that the two carved figures by the door were living men. They stood one on each side of the door as if in readiness for someone entering from the garden or the stables; one held a staff, the other a pike; and they were both leaning right back against the wall, sound asleep.

It did not surprise me. They're asleep, I thought. It seemed natural enough, here. I think I knew even then where I had come.

I do not mean that I knew the story, as you may know it. I did not know why they were asleep, how it had come about that they were asleep. I did not know the beginning of their story, nor the end. I did not know who was in the castle. But I knew already that they were all asleep. It was very strange, and I thought I should be afraid; but I could not feel any fear.

So even then, as I stood up, and went slowly down the sunny sward to the willows by the moat, I walked, not as if I were in a dream, but as if I were a dream. I didn't know who was dreaming me, if not myself, but it didn't matter. I knelt in the shade of the willows and put my sore hands down into the cool water of the moat. Just beyond my reach a golden-speckled carp floated, sleeping. A waterskater poised motionless on four tiny dimples in the skin of the water. Under the bridge, a swallow and her nestlings slept in their mud nest. A window was open, up in the castle wall; I saw a silky dark head pillowed on a pudgy arm on the window ledge.

I stripped, slow and quiet in my dream movements, and slid into the water. Though I could not swim, I had often bathed in shallow streams in the forest. The moat was deep, but I clung to the stone coping; presently I found a willow root that reached out from the stones, where I could sit with only my head out, and watch the golden-speckled carp hang in the clear, shadowed water.

I climbed out at last, refreshed and clean. I rinsed out my sweaty, winter-foul shirt and trousers, scrubbing them with stones, and spread them to dry in the hot sun on the grass above the willows. I had left my coat and my thick, straw-stuffed clogs up under the hedge. When my shirt and trousers were half dry I put them on—deliciously cool and wet-smelling—and combed my hair with my fingers. Then I stood up and walked to the end of the drawbridge.

I crossed it, always going slowly and quietly, without fear or hurry.

The old porter sat by the great door of the castle, his chin right down on his chest. He snored long, soft snores.

I pushed at the tall, iron-studded, oaken door. It opened with a little groan. Two boarhounds sprawled on the flagstone floor just inside, huge dogs, sound asleep. One of them "hunted" in his sleep, scrabbling his big legs, and then lay still again. The air inside the castle was still and shadowy, as the air outside was still and bright. There was no sound, inside or out. No bird sang, or woman; no voice spoke, or foot stirred, or bell struck the hour. The cooks slept over their cauldrons in the kitchen, the maids slept at their dusting and their mending, the king and his grooms slept by the sleeping horses in the stableyard, and the queen at her embroidery frame slept among her women. The cat slept by the mousehole, and the mice between the walls. The moth slept on the woollens, and the music slept in the strings of the minstrel's harp. There were no hours. The sun slept in the blue sky, and the shadows of the willows on the water never moved.

I KNOW, I KNOW IT WAS NOT MY ENCHANTMENT. I HAD BROKEN, hacked, chopped, forced my way into it. I know I am a poacher. I never learned how to be anything else. Even my forest, my domain as I had thought it, was never mine. It was the King's Forest, and the king slept here in his castle in the heart of his forest. But it had been a long time since anyone talked of the king. Petty barons held sway all round the forest; woodcutters stole wood from it, peasant boys snared rabbits in it; stray princes rode through it now and then, perhaps, hunting the red deer, not even knowing they were trespassing.

I knew I trespassed, but I could not see the harm. I did, of course, eat their food. The venison pastry that the chief cook had just taken out of the oven smelled so delicious that hungry flesh could not endure it. I arranged the chief cook in a more comfortable position on the slate floor of the kitchen, with his hat crumpled up for a pillow; and then I attacked the great pie, breaking off a corner with my hands and cramming it in my mouth. It was still warm, savoury, succulent. I ate my fill. Next time I came through the kitchen, the pastry was whole, unbroken. The enchantment held. Was it that as a dream, I could change nothing of this deep reality of sleep? I ate as I pleased, and always the cauldron of soup was full again and the loaves waited in the pantry, their brown crusts unbroken. The red wine brimmed the crystal goblet by the seneschal's hand, however many times I raised it, saluted him in thanks, and drank.

As I explored the castle and its grounds and outbuildings—always unhurriedly, wandering from room to room, pausing often, often lingering over some painted scene or fantastic tapestry or piece of fine workmanship in tool or fitting or furniture, often settling down on a soft, curtained bed or a sunny, grassy garden nook to sleep (for there was no night here, and I slept when I was tired and woke when I was refreshed)—as I wandered through all the rooms and offices and cellars and halls and barns and servants' quarters, I came to know, almost as if they were furniture too, the people who slept here and there, leaning or sitting or lying down, however they had chanced to be when the enchantment stole upon them and their eyes grew heavy, their breathing quiet, their limbs lax and still. A shepherd up on the hill had been pissing into a gopher's hole; he had settled down in a heap and slept contentedly, as no doubt the gopher was doing down in the dirt. The chief cook, as I have said, lay as if struck down unwilling in the heat of his art, and though I tried many times to pillow his head and arrange his limbs more comfortably, he always frowned, as if to say, "Don't bother me now, I'm busy!" Up at the top of the old apple orchard lay a couple of lovers, peasants like me. He, his rough trousers pulled down, lay as he had slid off her, face buried in the blossom-littered grass, drowned in sleep and satisfaction. She, a short, buxom young woman with apple-red cheeks and nipples, lay sprawled right out, skirts hiked to her waist, legs parted and arms wide, smiling in her sleep. It was again more than hungry flesh could endure. I laid myself down softly on her, kissing those red nipples, and came into her honey sweetness. She smiled in her sleep again, whenever I did so, and sometimes made a little groaning grunt of pleasure. Afterwards I would lie beside her, a partner to her friend on the other side, and drowse, and wake to see the unfalling late blossoms on the apple boughs. When I slept, there inside the great hedge, I never dreamed.

What had I to dream of? Surely I had all I could desire. Still, while the time passed that did not pass, used as I was to solitude, I grew lonely; the company of the sleepers grew wearisome to me. Mild and harmless as they were, and dear as many of them became to me as I lived among them, they were no better companions to me than a child's wooden toys, to which he must lend his own voice and soul. I sought work, not only to repay them for their food and beds, but because I was, after all, used to working. I polished the silver, I swept and reswept the floors where the dust lay so still, I groomed all the sleeping horses, I arranged the books on the shelves. And that led me to open a book, in mere idleness, and puzzle at the words in it.

I had not had a book in my hands since that primer of my stepmother's, nor seen any other but the priest's book in the church when we went to Mass at Yuletime. At first I looked only at the pictures, which were marvelous, and entertained me much. But I began to want to know what the words said about the pictures. When I came to study the shapes of the letters, they began to come back to me: *a* like a cat sitting, and the fatbellied *b* and *d,* and *t* the carpenter's square, and so on. And a-t was at, and c-a-t was cat, and so on. And time enough to learn to read, time enough and more than enough, slow as I might be. So I came to read, first the romances and histories in the queen's rooms, where I first had begun to read, and then the king's library of books about wars and kingdoms and travels and famous men, and finally the princess's books of fairy tales. So it is that I know now what a castle is, and a king, and a seneschal, and a story, and so can write my own.

But I was never happy going into the tower room, where the fairy tales were. I went there the first time; after the first time, I went there only for the books in the shelf beside the door. I would take a book, looking only at the shelf, and go away again at once, down the winding stair. I never looked at her but once, the first time, the one time.

She was alone in her room. She sat near the window, in a little straight chair. The thread she had been spinning lay across her lap and trailed to the floor. The thread was white; her dress was white and green. The spindle lay in her open hand. It had pricked her thumb, and the point of it still stuck just above the little thumb-joint. Her hands were small and delicate. She was younger even than I when I came there, hardly more than a child, and had never done any hard work at all. You could see that. She slept more sweetly than any of them, even the maid with the pudgy arm and the silky hair, even the rosy baby in the cradle in the gatekeeper's house, even the grandmother in the little south room, whom I loved best of all. I used to talk to the grandmother, when I was lonely. She sat so quietly as if looking out the window, and it was easy to believe that she was listening to me and only thinking before she answered.

But the princess's sleep was sweeter even than that. It was like a butter-fly's sleep.

I knew, I knew as soon as I entered her room, that first time, that one time, as soon as I saw her I knew that she, she alone in all the castle, might wake at any moment. I knew that she, alone of all of them, all of us, was dreaming. I knew that if I spoke in that tower room she would hear me: maybe not waken, but hear me in her sleep, and her dreams would change. I knew that if I touched her or even came close to her I would trouble her dreams. If I so much as touched that spindle, moved it so that it did not pierce her thumb—and I longed to do that, for it was painful to see—but if I did that, if I moved the spindle, a drop of red blood would well up slowly on the delicate little cushion of flesh above the joint. And her eyes would open. Her eyes would open slowly; she would look at me. And the enchantment would be broken, the dream at an end.

I have lived here within the great hedge till I am older than my father ever was. I am as old as the grandmother in the south room, grey-haired. I have not climbed the winding stair for many years. I do not read the books of fairy tales any longer, nor visit the sweet orchard. I sit in the garden in the sunshine. When the prince comes riding, and strikes his way clear through the hedge of thorns—my two years' toil—with one blow of his privileged, bright sword, when he strides up the winding stair to the tower room, when he stoops to kiss her, and the spindle falls from her hand, and the drop of blood wells like a tiny ruby on the white skin, when she opens her eyes slowly and yawns, she will look up at him. As the castle begins to stir, the petals to fall, the little bee to move and buzz on the clover blossom, she will look up at him through the mists and tag-ends of dream, a hundred years of dreams; and I wonder if, for a moment, she will think, "Is that the face I dreamed of seeing?" But by then I will be out by the midden heap, sleeping sounder than they ever did.

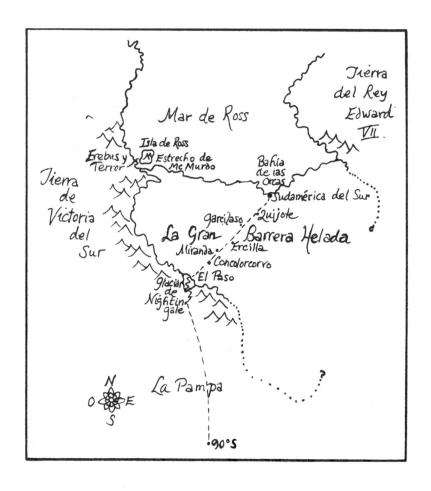

SUR

A SUMMARY REPORT OF THE YELCHO
EXPEDITION TO THE ANTARCTIC,
1909–1910

ALTHOUGH I HAVE NO INTENTION OF PUBLISHING THIS REPORT,
I think it would be nice if a grandchild of mine, or somebody's grandchild, happened to find it some day; so I shall keep it in the leather trunk
in the attic, along with Rosita's christening dress and Juanito's silver rattle
and my wedding shoes and finneskos.

The first requisite for mounting an expedition—money—is normally
the hardest to come by. I grieve that even in a report destined for a trunk
in the attic of a house in a very quiet suburb of Lima I dare not write the
name of the generous benefactor, the great soul without whose unstinting
liberality the *Yelcho* Expedition would never have been more than the
idlest excursion into daydream. That our equipment was the best and
most modern—that our provisions were plentiful and fine—that a ship
of the Chilean Government, with her brave officers and gallant crew,
was twice sent halfway round the world for our convenience: all this is
due to that benefactor whose name, alas! I must not say, but whose happiest
debtor I shall be till death.

When I was little more than a child my imagination was caught by
a newspaper account of the voyage of the *Belgica*, which, sailing south
from Tierra del Fuego, became beset by ice in the Bellingshausen Sea

and drifted a whole year with the floe, the men aboard her suffering
a great deal from want of food and from the terror of the unending
winter darkness. I read and reread that account, and later followed with
excitement the reports of the rescue of Dr. Nordenskjold from the South
Shetland Isles by the dashing Captain Irizar of the *Uruguay*, and the
adventures of the *Scotia* in the Weddell Sea. But all these exploits were
to me but forerunners of the British National Antarctic Expedition of
1902–1904, in the *Discovery*, and the wonderful account of that expedition by Captain Scott. This book, which I ordered from London and
reread a thousand times, filled me with longing to see with my own
eyes that strange continent, last Thule of the South, which lies on our
maps and globes like a white cloud, a void, fringed here and there with
scraps of coastline, dubious capes, supposititious islands, headlands that
may or may not be there: Antarctica. And the desire was as pure as the
polar snows: to go, to see—no more, no less. I deeply respect the scientific accomplishments of Captain Scott's expedition, and have read with
passionate interest the findings of physicists, meteorologists, biologists,
etc.; but having had no training in any science, nor any opportunity for
such training, my ignorance obliged me to forgo any thought of adding to the body of scientific knowledge concerning Antarctica; and the
same is true for all the members of my expedition. It seems a pity; but
there was nothing we could do about it. Our goal was limited to obser-
vation and exploration. We hoped to go a little farther, perhaps, and see
a little more; if not, simply to go and to see. A simple ambition, I think,
and essentially a modest one.

Yet it would have remained less than an ambition, no more than
a longing, but for the support and encouragement of my dear cousin
and friend Juana ————. (I use no surnames, lest this report fall
into strangers' hands at last, and embarrassment or unpleasant notoriety
thus be brought upon unsuspecting husbands, sons, etc.) I had lent
Juana my copy of *The Voyage of the Discovery*, and it was she who, as we

strolled beneath our parasols across the Plaza de Arenas after Mass one Sunday in 1908, said, "Well, if Captain Scott can do it, why can't we?"

It was Juana who proposed that we write Carlota —— in Valparaiso. Through Carlota we met our benefactor, and so obtained our money, our ship, and even the plausible pretext of going on retreat in a Bolivian convent, which some of us were forced to employ (while the rest of us said we were going to Paris for the winter season). And it was my Juana who in the darkest moments remained resolute, unshaken in her determination to achieve our goal.

And there were dark moments, especially in the early months of 1909—times when I did not see how the Expedition would ever become more than a quarter ton of pemmican gone to waste and a lifelong regret. It was so very hard to gather our expeditionary force together! So few of those we asked even knew what we were talking about—so many thought we were mad, or wicked, or both! And of those few who shared our folly, still fewer were able, when it came to the point, to leave their daily duties and commit themselves to a voyage of at least six months, attended with not inconsiderable uncertainty and danger. An ailing parent; an anxious husband beset by business cares; a child at home with only ignorant or incompetent servants to look after it: these are not responsibilities lightly to be set aside. And those who wished to evade such claims were not the companions we wanted in hard work, risk, and privation.

But since success crowned our efforts, why dwell on the setbacks and delays, or the wretched contrivances and downright lies that we all had to employ? I look back with regret only to those friends who wished to come with us but could not, by any contrivance, get free—those we had to leave behind to a life without danger, without uncertainty, without hope.

On the seventeenth of August, 1909, in Punta Arenas, Chile, all the members of the Expedition met for the first time: Juana and I, the two Peruvians; from Argentina, Zoe, Berta, and Teresa; and our Chileans, Carlota and her friends Eva, Pepita, and Dolores. At the last moment I had received word that Maria's husband, in Quito, was ill, and she must stay to nurse him, so we were nine, not ten. Indeed, we had resigned ourselves to being but eight, when, just as night fell, the indomitable Zoe arrived in a tiny pirogue manned by Indians, her yacht having sprung a leak just as it entered the Strait of Magellan.

That night before we sailed we began to get to know one another; and we agreed, as we enjoyed our abominable supper in the abominable seaport inn of Punta Arenas, that if a situation arose of such urgent danger that one voice must be obeyed without present question, the unenviable honor of speaking with that voice should fall first upon myself: if I were incapacitated, upon Carlota: if she, then upon Berta. We three were then toasted as "Supreme Inca," "La Araucana," and "The Third Mate," among a lot of laughter and cheering. As it came out, to my very great pleasure and relief, my qualities as a "leader" were never tested; the nine of us worked things out amongst us from beginning to end without any orders being given by anybody, and only two or three times with recourse to a vote by voice or show of hands. To be sure, we argued a good deal. But then, we had time to argue. And one way or another the arguments always ended up in a decision, upon which action could be taken. Usually at least one person grumbled about the decision, sometimes bitterly. But what is life without grumbling, and the occasional opportunity to say, "I told you so"? How could one bear housework, or looking after babies, let alone the rigors of sledge-hauling in Antarctica, without grumbling? Officers—as we came to understand aboard the *Yelcho*—are forbidden to grumble; but we nine were, and are, by birth and upbringing, unequivocally and irrevocably, all crew.

Though our shortest course to the southern continent, and that originally urged upon us by the captain of our good ship, was to the South Shetlands and the Bellingshausen Sea, or else by the South Orkneys into the Weddell Sea, we planned to sail west to the Ross Sea, which Captain Scott had explored and described, and from which the brave Ernest

Shackleton had returned only the previous autumn. More was known about this region than any other portion of the coast of Antarctica, and though that more was not much, yet it served as some insurance of the safety of the ship, which we felt we had no right to imperil. Captain Pardo had fully agreed with us after studying the charts and our planned itinerary; and so it was westward that we took our course out of the Strait next morning.

Our journey half round the globe was attended by fortune. The little *Yelcho* steamed cheerily along through gale and gleam, climbing up and down those seas of the Southern Ocean that run unbroken round the world. Juana, who had fought bulls and the far more dangerous cows on her family's *estancia*, called the ship *"la vaca valiente,"* because she always returned to the charge. Once we got over being seasick we all enjoyed the sea voyage, though oppressed at times by the kindly but officious protectiveness of the captain and his officers, who felt that we were only "safe" when huddled up in the three tiny cabins which they had chivalrously vacated for our use.

We saw our first iceberg much farther south than we had looked for it, and saluted it with Veuve Clicquot at dinner. The next day we entered the ice pack, the belt of floes and bergs, broken loose from the land ice and winter-frozen seas of Antarctica, which drifts northward in the spring. Fortune still smiled on us: our little steamer, incapable, with her unreinforced metal hull, of forcing a way into the ice, picked her way from lane to lane without hesitation, and on the third day we were through the pack, in which ships have sometimes struggled for weeks and been obliged to turn back at last. Ahead of us now lay the dark grey waters of the Ross Sea, and beyond that, on the horizon, the remote glimmer, the cloud-reflected whiteness of the Great Ice Barrier.

Entering the Ross Sea a little east of Longitude West 160°, we came in sight of the Barrier at the place where Captain Scott's party, finding a bight in the vast wall of ice, had gone ashore and sent up their hydrogen-gas balloon for reconnaissance and photography. The towering face of the Barrier, its sheer cliffs and azure and violet water-worn caves, all were as described, but the location had changed: instead of a narrow bight there was a considerable bay, full of the beautiful and terrific orca whales playing and spouting in the sunshine of that brilliant southern spring.

Evidently masses of ice many acres in extent had broken away from the Barrier (which—at least for most of its vast extent—does not rest on land but floats on water) since the *Discovery*'s passage in 1902. This put our plan to set up camp on the Barrier itself in a new light; and while we were discussing alternatives, we asked Captain Pardo to take the ship west along the Barrier face towards Ross Island and McMurdo Sound. As the sea was clear of ice and quite calm, he was happy to do so, and, when we sighted the smoke plume of Mount Erebus, to share in our celebration—another half case of Veuve Clicquot.

The *Yelcho* anchored in Arrival Bay, and we went ashore in the ship's boat. I cannot describe my emotions when I set foot on the earth, on that earth, the barren, cold gravel at the foot of the long volcanic slope. I felt elation, impatience, gratitude, awe, familiarity. I felt that I was home at last. Eight adélie penguins immediately came to greet us with many exclamations of interest not unmixed with disapproval. "Where on earth have you been? What took you so long? The Hut is around this way. Please come this way. Mind the rocks!" They insisted on our going to visit Hut Point, where the large structure built by Captain Scott's party stood, looking just as in the photographs and drawings that illustrate his book. The area about it, however, was disgusting—a kind of graveyard of seal skins, seal bones, penguin bones, and rubbish, presided over by the mad, screaming skua gulls. Our escorts waddled past the slaughterhouse in all tranquillity, and one showed me personally to the door, though it would not go in.

The interior of the hut was less offensive, but very dreary. Boxes of supplies had been stacked up into a kind of room within the room; it did not look as I had imagined it when the *Discovery* party put on their melodramas and minstrel shows in the long winter night. (Much later, we learned that Sir Ernest had rearranged it a good deal when he was there just a year before us.) It was dirty, and had about it a mean disorder. A pound tin of tea was standing open. Empty meat tins lay about; biscuits were spilled on the floor; a lot of dog turds were underfoot—frozen, of course, but not a great deal improved by that. No doubt the last occupants had had to leave in a hurry, perhaps even in a blizzard. All the same, they could have closed the tea tin. But housekeeping, the art of the infinite, is no game for amateurs.

Teresa proposed that we use the hut as our camp. Zoe counter-proposed that we set fire to it. We finally shut the door and left it as we had found it. The penguins appeared to approve, and cheered us all the way to the boat.

McMurdo Sound was free of ice, and Captain Pardo now proposed to take us off Ross Island and across to Victoria Land, where we might camp at the foot of the Western Mountains, on dry and solid earth. But those mountains, with their storm-darkened peaks and hanging cirques and glaciers, looked as awful as Captain Scott had found them on his western journey, and none of us felt much inclined to seek shelter among them.

Aboard the ship that night we decided to go back and set up our base as we had originally planned, on the Barrier itself. For all available reports indicated that the clear way south was across the level Barrier surface until one could ascend one of the confluent glaciers to the high plateau which appears to form the whole interior of the continent. Captain Pardo argued strongly against this plan, asking what would become of us if the Barrier "calved"—if our particular acre of ice broke away and started to drift northward. "Well," said Zoe, "then you won't have to come so far to meet us." But he was so persuasive on this theme that he persuaded himself into leaving one of the *Yelcho*'s boats with us when we camped, as a means of escape. We found it useful for fishing, later on.

My first steps on Antarctic soil, my only visit to Ross Island, had not been pleasure unalloyed. I thought of the words of the English poet:

Though every prospect pleases,
And only Man is vile.

BUT THEN, THE BACKSIDE OF HEROISM IS OFTEN RATHER SAD; women and servants know that. They know also that the heroism may be no less real for that. But achievement is smaller than men think. What is large is the sky, the earth, the sea, the soul. I looked back as the ship sailed east again that evening. We were well into September now, with ten hours or more of daylight. The spring sunset lingered on the twelve-thousand-foot peak of Erebus and shone rosy gold on her long plume of steam. The steam from our own small funnel faded blue on the twilit water as we crept along under the towering pale wall of ice.

On our return to "Orca Bay"—Sir Ernest, we learned years later, had named it the Bay of Whales—we found a sheltered nook where the Barrier edge was low enough to provide fairly easy access from the ship. The *Yelcho* put out her ice anchor, and the next long, hard days were spent in unloading our supplies and setting up our camp on the ice, a half kilometer in from the edge: a task in which the *Yelcho*'s crew lent us invaluable aid and interminable advice. We took all the aid gratefully, and most of the advice with salt.

The weather so far had been extraordinarily mild for spring in this latitude; the temperature had not yet gone below -20° Fahrenheit, and there was only one blizzard while we were setting up camp. But Captain Scott had spoken feelingly of the bitter south winds on the Barrier, and we had planned accordingly. Exposed as our camp was to every wind, we built no rigid structures above ground. We set up tents to shelter in while we dug out a series of cubicles in the ice itself, lined them with hay insulation and pine boarding, and roofed them with canvas over bamboo poles, covered with snow for weight and insulation. The big central room was instantly named Buenos Aires by our Argentineans, to whom the center, wherever one is, is always Buenos Aires. The heating and cooking stove was in Buenos Aires. The storage tunnels and the privy (called Punta Arenas) got some back heat from the stove. The sleeping cubicles opened off Buenos Aires, and were very small, mere tubes into which one crawled feet first; they were lined deeply with hay and soon warmed by one's body warmth. The sailors called them "coffins" and "wormholes," and looked with horror on our burrows in the ice. But our little warren or prairie-dog village served us well, permitting us as much warmth and privacy as one could reasonably expect under the circumstances. If the *Yelcho* was unable to get through the ice in February, and we had to spend the winter in Antarctica, we certainly could do so, though on very limited rations. For this coming summer, our base—Sudamérica del Sur, South South America, but we generally called it the Base—was intended merely as a place to sleep, to store our provisions, and to give shelter from blizzards.

To Berta and Eva, however, it was more than that. They were its chief architect-designers, its most ingenious builder-excavators, and its most diligent and contented occupants, forever inventing an improvement in ventilation, or learning how to make skylights, or revealing to us a new addition to our suite of rooms, dug in the living ice. It was thanks to them that our stores were stowed so handily, that our stove drew and heated so efficiently, and that Buenos Aires, where nine people cooked, ate, worked, conversed, argued, grumbled, painted, played the guitar and banjo, and kept the Expedition's library of books and maps, was a marvel of comfort and convenience. We lived there in real amity; and if you simply had to be alone for a while, you crawled into your sleeping hole head first.

Berta went a little farther. When she had done all she could to make South South America livable, she dug out one more cell just under the ice surface, leaving a nearly transparent sheet of ice like a greenhouse roof; and there, alone, she worked at sculptures. They were beautiful forms, some like a blending of the reclining human figure with the subtle curves and volumes of the Weddell seal, others like the fantastic shapes of ice cornices and ice caves. Perhaps they are there still, under the snow, in the bubble in the Great Barrier. There where she made them they might last as long as stone. But she could not bring them north. That is the penalty for carving in water.

Captain Pardo was reluctant to leave us, but his orders did not permit him to hang about the Ross Sea indefinitely, and so at last, with many earnest injunctions to us to stay put—make no journeys—take no risks—beware of frostbite—don't use edge tools—look out for cracks in the ice—and a heartfelt promise to return to Orca Bay on the twentieth of February, or as near that date as wind and ice would permit, the good man bade us farewell, and his crew shouted us a great good-bye cheer as they weighed anchor. That evening, in the long orange twilight of October, we saw the topmast of the *Yelcho* go down the north horizon, over the edge of the world, leaving us to ice, and silence, and the Pole.

The ensuing month passed in short practice trips and depot-laying. The life we had led at home, though in its own way strenuous, had not fitted any of us for the kind of strain met with in sledge-hauling at ten or twenty degrees below freezing. We all needed as much working-out as possible before we dared undertake a long haul.

My longest exploratory trip, made with Dolores and Carlota, was southwest towards Mount Markham, and it was a nightmare—blizzards and pressure ice all the way out, crevasses and no view of the mountains when we got there, and white weather and sastrugi all the way back. The trip was useful, however, in that we could begin to estimate our capacities; and also in that we had started out with a very heavy load of provisions, which we depoted at a hundred and a hundred and thirty miles south-southwest of Base. Thereafter other parties pushed on farther, till we had a line of snow cairns and depots right down to Latitude 83° 43', where Juana and Zoe, on an exploring trip, had found a kind of stone gateway opening on a great glacier leading south. We established these depots to avoid, if possible, the hunger that had bedeviled Captain Scott's Southern Party, and the consequent misery and weakness. And we also established to our own satisfaction—intense satisfaction—that we were sledgehaulers at least as good as Captain Scott's husky dogs. Of course we could not have expected to pull as much or as fast as his men. That we did so was because we were favored by much better weather than Captain Scott's party ever met on the Barrier; and also the quantity and quality of our food made a very considerable difference. I am sure that the fifteen percent of dried fruits in our pemmican helped prevent scurvy; and the potatoes, frozen and dried according to an ancient Andean Indian method, were very nourishing yet very light and compact—perfect sledging rations. In any case, it was with considerable confidence in our capacities that we made ready at last for the Southern Journey.

The Southern Party consisted of two sledge teams: Juana, Dolores, and myself; Carlota, Pepita, and Zoe. The support team of Berta, Eva, and Teresa set out before us with a heavy load of supplies, going right up onto the glacier to prospect routes and leave depots of supplies for our return journey. We followed five days behind them, and met them returning between Depot Ercilla and Depot Miranda (see map). That "night"—of course there was no real darkness—we were all nine together in the heart of the level plain of ice. It was the fifteenth of November, Dolores's birthday. We celebrated by putting eight ounces of pisco in the hot chocolate, and became very merry. We sang. It is strange now to remember how thin our voices sounded in that great silence. It was overcast, white weather, without shadows and without visible horizon or any feature to break the level; there was nothing to see at all. We had come to that white place on the map, that void, and there we flew and sang like sparrows.

After sleep and a good breakfast the Base Party continued north, and the Southern Party sledged on. The sky cleared presently. High up, thin clouds passed over very rapidly from southwest to northeast, but down on the Barrier it was calm and just cold enough, five or ten degrees below freezing, to give a firm surface for hauling.

On the level ice we never pulled less than eleven miles (seventeen kilometers) a day, and generally fifteen or sixteen miles (twenty-five kilometers). (Our instruments, being British made, were calibrated in feet, miles, degrees Fahrenheit, etc., but we often converted miles to kilometers because the larger numbers sounded more encouraging.) At the time we left South America, we knew only that Mr. Shackleton had mounted another expedition to the Antarctic in 1908, had tried to attain the Pole but failed, and had returned to England in June of the current year, 1909. No coherent report of his explorations had yet reached South America when we left; we did not know what route he had gone, or how far he had got. But we were not altogether taken by surprise when, far across the featureless white plain, tiny beneath the mountain peaks and the strange silent flight of the rainbow-fringed cloud wisps, we saw a fluttering dot of black. We turned west from our course to visit it: a snow heap nearly buried by the winter's storms—a flag on a bamboo pole, a mere shred of threadbare cloth—an empty oilcan—and a few footprints standing some inches above the ice. In some conditions of weather the snow compressed under one's weight remains when the surrounding soft snow melts or is scoured away by the wind; and so these reversed footprints had been left standing all these months, like rows of cobbler's lasts—a queer sight.

We met no other such traces on our way. In general I believe our course was somewhat east of Mr. Shackleton's. Juana, our surveyor, had trained herself well and was faithful and methodical in her sightings and readings, but our equipment was minimal—a theodolite on tripod legs, a sextant with artificial horizon, two compasses, and chronometers. We had only the wheel meter on the sledge to give distance actually travelled.

In any case, it was the day after passing Mr. Shackleton's waymark that I first saw clearly the great glacier among the mountains to the southwest, which was to give us a pathway from the sea level of the Barrier up to the altiplano, ten thousand feet above. The approach was magnificent: a gateway formed by immense vertical domes and pillars of rock. Zoe and Juana had called the vast ice river that flowed through that gateway the Florence Nightingale Glacier, wishing to honor the British, who had been the inspiration and guide of our Expedition; that very brave and very peculiar lady seemed to represent so much that is best, and strangest, in the island race. On maps, of course, this glacier bears the name Mr. Shackleton gave it, the Beardmore.

The ascent of the Nightingale was not easy. The way was open at first, and well marked by our support party, but after some days we came among terrible crevasses, a maze of hidden cracks, from a foot to thirty feet wide and from thirty to a thousand feet deep. Step by step we went, and step by step, and the way always upward now. We were fifteen days on the glacier. At first the weather was hot, up to 20°F, and the hot nights without darkness were wretchedly uncomfortable in our small tents. And all of us suffered more or less from snowblindness just at the time when we wanted clear eyesight to pick our way among the ridges and crevasses of the tortured ice, and to see the wonders about and before us. For at every day's advance more great, nameless peaks came into view in the west and southwest, summit beyond summit, range beyond range, stark rock and snow in the unending noon.

We gave names to these peaks, not very seriously, since we did not expect our discoveries to come to the attention of geographers. Zoe had a gift for naming, and it is thanks to her that certain sketch maps in various suburban South American attics bear such curious features as "Bolívar's Big Nose," "I Am General Rosas," "The Cloudmaker," "Whose Toe?" and "Throne of Our Lady of the Southern Cross." And when at last we got up onto the altiplano, the great interior plateau, it was Zoe who called it the pampa, and maintained that we walked there among vast herds of invisible cattle, transparent cattle pastured on the spindrift snow, their gauchos the restless, merciless winds. We were by then all a little crazy with exhaustion and the great altitude—twelve thousand feet—and the cold and the wind blowing and the luminous circles and crosses surrounding the suns, for often there were three or four suns in the sky, up there.

That is not a place where people have any business to be. We should have turned back; but since we had worked so hard to get there, it seemed that we should go on, at least for a while.

A blizzard came with very low temperatures, so we had to stay in the tents, in our sleeping bags, for thirty hours, a rest we all needed; though it was warmth we needed most, and there was no warmth on that terrible plain anywhere at all but in our veins. We huddled close together all that time. The ice we lay on is two miles thick.

It cleared suddenly and became, for the plateau, good weather: twelve below zero and the wind not very strong. We three crawled out of our tent and met the others crawling out of theirs. Carlota told us then that her group wished to turn back. Pepita had been feeling very ill; even after the rest during the blizzard, her temperature would not rise above 94°. Carlota was having trouble breathing. Zoe was perfectly fit, but much preferred staying with her friends and lending them a hand in difficulties to pushing on towards the Pole. So we put the four ounces of pisco which we had been keeping for Christmas into the breakfast cocoa, and dug out our tents, and loaded our sledges, and parted there in the white daylight on the bitter plain.

Our sledge was fairly light by now. We pulled on to the south. Juana calculated our position daily. On the twenty-second of December, 1909, we reached the South Pole. The weather was, as always, very cruel. Nothing of any kind marked the dreary whiteness. We discussed leaving some kind of mark or monument, a snow cairn, a tent pole and flag; but there seemed no particular reason to do so. Anything we could do, anything we were, was insignificant, in that awful place. We put up the tent for shelter for an hour and made a cup of tea, and then struck "90° Camp." Dolores, standing patient as ever in her sledging harness, looked at the snow; it was so hard frozen that it showed no trace of our footprints coming, and she said, "Which way?"

"North," said Juana.

It was a joke, because at that particular place there is no other direction. But we did not laugh. Our lips were cracked with frostbite and hurt too much to let us laugh. So we started back, and the wind at our backs pushed us along, and dulled the knife edges of the waves of frozen snow.

All that week the blizzard wind pursued us like a pack of mad dogs. I cannot describe it. I wished we had not gone to the Pole. I think I wish it even now. But I was glad even then that we had left no sign there, for some man longing to be first might come some day, and find it, and know then what a fool he had been, and break his heart.

We talked, when we could talk, of catching up to Carlota's party, since they might be going slower than we. In fact they had used their tent as a sail to catch the following wind and had got far ahead of us. But in many places they had built snow cairns or left some sign for us; once Zoe had written on the lee side of a ten-foot sastrugi, just as children write on the sand of the beach at Miraflores, "This Way Out!" The wind blowing over the frozen ridge had left the words perfectly distinct.

In the very hour that we began to descend the glacier, the weather turned warmer, and the mad dogs were left to howl forever tethered to the Pole. The distance that had taken us fifteen days going up we covered in only eight days going down. But the good weather that had aided us descending the Nightingale became a curse down on the Barrier ice, where we had looked forward to a kind of royal progress from depot to depot, eating our fill and taking our time for the last three hundred-odd

miles. In a tight place on the glacier I lost my goggles—I was swinging from my harness at the time in a crevasse—and then Juana had
broken hers when we had to do some rock climbing coming down to
the Gateway. After two days in bright sunlight with only one pair of
snow goggles to pass amongst us, we were all suffering badly from snowblindness. It became acutely painful to keep lookout for landmarks or
depot flags, to take sightings, even to study the compass, which had
to be laid down on the snow to steady the needle. At Concolorcorvo
Depot, where there was a particularly good supply of food and fuel,
we gave up, crawled into our sleeping bags with bandaged eyes, and
slowly boiled alive like lobsters in the tent exposed to the relentless sun.
The voices of Berta and Zoe were the sweetest sound I ever heard. A
little concerned about us, they had skied south to meet us. They led us
home to Base.

We recovered quite swiftly, but the altiplano left its mark. When she
was very little, Rosita asked if a dog "had bitted Mama's toes." I told her
Yes, a great, white, mad dog named Blizzard! My Rosita and my Juanito
heard many stories when they were little, about that fearful dog and how
it howled, and the transparent cattle of the invisible gauchos, and a river
of ice eight thousand feet high called Nightingale, and how Cousin Juana
drank a cup of tea standing on the bottom of the world under seven suns,
and other fairy tales.

We were in for one severe shock when we reached Base at last. Teresa
was pregnant. I must admit that my first response to the poor girl's big belly
and sheepish look was anger—rage—fury. That one of us should have
concealed anything, and such a thing, from the others! But Teresa had
done nothing of the sort. Only those who had concealed from her what
she most needed to know were to blame. Brought up by servants, with
four years' schooling in a convent, and married at sixteen, the poor girl
was still so ignorant at twenty years of age that she had thought it was
"the cold weather" that made her miss her periods. Even this was not

entirely stupid, for all of us on the Southern Journey had seen our periods change or stop altogether as we experienced increasing cold, hunger, and fatigue. Teresa's appetite had begun to draw general attention; and then she had begun, as she said pathetically, "to get fat." The, others were worried at the thought of all the sledge-hauling she had done, but she flourished, and the only problem was her positively insatiable appetite. As well as could be determined from her shy references to her last night on the hacienda with her husband, the baby was due at just about the same time as the *Yelcho*, the twentieth of February. But we had not been back from the Southern Journey two weeks when, on February 14, she went into labor.

Several of us had borne children and had helped with deliveries, and anyhow most of what needs to be done is fairly self-evident; but a first labor can be long and trying, and we were all anxious, while Teresa was frightened out of her wits. She kept calling for her José till she was as hoarse as a skua. Zoe lost all patience at last and said, "By God, Teresa, if you say 'José!' once more I hope you have a penguin!" But what she had, after twenty long hours, was a pretty little red-faced girl.

Many were the suggestions for that child's name from her eight proud midwife-aunts: Polita, Penguina, McMurdo, Victoria. . . . But Teresa announced, after she had had a good sleep and a large serving of pemmican, "I shall name her Rosa—Rosa del Sur," Rose of the South. That night we drank the last two bottles of Veuve Clicquot (having finished the pisco at 88° 30' South) in toasts to our little Rose.

On the nineteenth of February, a day early, my Juana came down into Buenos Aires in a hurry. "The ship," she said, "the ship has come," and she burst into tears—she who had never wept in all our weeks of pain and weariness on the long haul.

Of the return voyage there is nothing to tell. We came back safe.

In 1912 all the world learned that the brave Norwegian Amundsen had reached the South Pole; and then, much later, came the accounts of how Captain Scott and his men had come there after him, but did not come home again.

Just this year, Juana and I wrote to the captain of the *Yelcho*, for the newspapers have been full of the story of his gallant dash to rescue Sir Ernest Shackleton's men from Elephant Island, and we wished to congratulate him, and once more to thank him. Never one word has he breathed of our secret. He is a man of honor, Luis Pardo.

I ADD THIS LAST NOTE IN 1929. OVER THE YEARS WE HAVE LOST touch with one another. It is very difficult for women to meet, when they live so far apart as we do. Since Juana died, I have seen none of my old sledge-mates, though sometimes we write. Our little Rosa del Sur died of the scarlet fever when she was five years old. Teresa had many other children. Carlota took the veil in Santiago ten years ago. We are old women now, with old husbands, and grown children, and grandchildren who might someday like to read about the Expedition. Even if they are rather ashamed of having such a crazy grandmother, they may enjoy sharing in the secret. But they must not let Mr. Amundsen know! He would be terribly embarrassed and disappointed. There is no need for him or anyone else outside the family to know. We left no footprints, even.

SHE
UNNAMES THEM

MOST OF THEM ACCEPTED NAMELESSNESS WITH THE PERFECT indifference with which they had so long accepted and ignored their names. Whales and dolphins, seals and sea otters consented with particular grace and alacrity, sliding into anonymity as into their element. A faction of yaks, however, protested. They said that "yak" sounded right, and that almost everyone who knew they existed called them that. Unlike the ubiquitous creatures such as rats or fleas who had been called by hundreds or thousands of different names since Babel, the yaks could truly say, they said, that they had *a name*. They discussed the matter all summer. The councils of the elderly females finally agreed that though the name might be useful to others, it was so redundant from the yak point of view that they never spoke it themselves, and hence might as well dispense with it. After they presented the argument in this light to their bulls, a full consensus was delayed only by the onset of severe early blizzards. Soon after the beginning of the thaw their agreement was reached and the designation "yak" was returned to the donor.

Among the domestic animals, few horses had cared what anybody called them since the failure of Dean Swift's attempt to name them from their own vocabulary. Cattle, sheep, swine, asses, mules, and goats, along with chickens, geese, and turkeys, all agreed enthusiastically to give their names back to the people to whom—as they put it—they belonged.

A couple of problems did come up with pets. The cats of course steadfastly denied ever having had any name other than those self-given, unspoken, effanineffably personal names which, as the poet named Eliot said, they spend long hours daily contemplating—though none of the contemplators has ever admitted that what they contemplate is in fact their name, and some onlookers have wondered if the object of that meditative gaze might not in fact be the Perfect, or Platonic, Mouse. In any case it is a moot point now. It was with the dogs, and with some parrots, lovebirds, ravens, and mynahs that the trouble arose. These verbally talented individuals insisted that their names were important to them, and flatly refused to part with them. But as soon as they understood that the issue was precisely one of individual choice, and that anybody who wanted to be called Rover, or Froufrou, or Polly, or even Birdie in the personal sense, was perfectly free to do so, not one of them had the least objection to parting with the lower case (or, as regards German creatures, uppercase) generic appellations poodle, parrot, dog, or bird, and all the Linnaean qualifiers that had trailed along behind them for two hundred years like tin cans tied to a tail.

The insects parted with their names in vast clouds and swarms of ephemeral syllables buzzing and stinging and humming and flitting and crawling and tunneling away.

As for the fish of the sea, their names dispersed from them in silence throughout the oceans like faint, dark blurs of cuttlefish ink, and drifted off on the currents without a trace.

None were left now to unname, and yet how close I felt to them when I saw one of them swim or fly or trot or crawl across my way or over my skin, or stalk me in the night, or go along beside me for a while in the day. They seemed far closer than when their names had stood between myself and them like a clear barrier: so close that my fear of them and their fear of me became one same fear. And the attraction that many of us felt, the desire to smell one another's smells, feel or rub or caress one another's scales or skin or feathers or fur, taste one another's blood or flesh, keep one another warm—that attraction was now all one with the fear, and the hunter could not be told from the hunted, nor the eater from the food.

This was more or less the effect I had been after. It was somewhat more powerful than I had anticipated, but I could not now, in all conscience, make an exception for myself. I resolutely put anxiety away, went to Adam, and said, "You and your father lent me this—gave it to me, actually. It's been really useful, but it doesn't exactly seem to fit very well lately. But thanks very much! It's really been very useful."

It is hard to give back a gift without sounding peevish or ungrateful, and I did not want to leave him with that impression of me. He was not paying much attention, as it happened, and said only, "Put it down over there, OK?" and went on with what he was doing.

One of my reasons for doing what I did was that talk was getting us nowhere; but all the same I felt a little let down. I had been prepared to defend my decision. And I thought that perhaps when he did notice he might be upset and want to talk. I put some things away and fiddled around a little, but he continued to do what he was doing and to take no notice of anything else. At last I said, "Well, good-bye, dear. I hope the garden key turns up."

He was fitting parts together, and said without looking around, "OK, fine, dear. When's dinner?"

"I'm not sure," I said. "I'm going now. With the—" I hesitated, and finally said, "With them, you know," and went on. In fact I had only just then realized how hard it would have been to explain myself. I could not chatter away as I used to do, taking it all for granted. My words now must be as slow, as new, as single, as tentative as the steps I took going down the path away from the house, between the dark-branched, tall dancers motionless against the winter shining.

THE
JAR
OF
WATER

THE RICH MERCHANT MITRAI OF THE CITY BANKALA SUMMONED one of his servants, a man named Kas, and said to him, "You are a loyal man who does his duty faithfully. I am rewarding you for this good service by giving you an important task."

The servant bowed.

"You are to take a gift to the holy man Matua in the city Anun."

The servant bowed. Then, as his master said nothing further, he said, "To go to Anun I must cross the desert of Ses-Hab."

"Yes."

"They say that bandits infest the trade road across the desert and robber tribes haunt the oases. May I take a few men with me, and horses?"

"You are to go alone, and on foot."

Kas said, thoughtfully and respectfully, "It would seem rather a test than a reward."

"It is what you make of it," said Mitrai. "This is the gift you will give to the holy man." He indicated a sealed jar of ordinary brown earthenware with hempen netting around it that stood on the table beside him. "As you see, there is nothing about it to attract the greed of a bandit or a nomad."

"What is in the jar, sir?"

"Water," said Mitrai. "Here is money for your journey. Hide it as best you can, and pray not to meet evil men. Leave tomorrow, and return with what gift or words for me the holy man may send. May your journey be blessed."

Kas bowed once more, took up the jar by its netting, and withdrew.

There were no quarters for menservants in the great house; they lived in a barracks at the back of it. Most of them did rough work, sweeping, carrying water, taking manure from the stables to the gardener's compost. Kas had done such work as a boy, but he had come to his master's notice for his intelligence and diligence. Mitrai used him as a messenger, and he had proved so trustworthy that by now he carried all Mitrai's letters or verbal questions and replies to and from the men of business and officers of government in Bankala; and he was so discreet that Mitrai did not hesitate to send him to deliver a bag of gold coins to a creditor or present a ruby, circumspectly, to a lady.

Because he had to go among rich people, Kas's clothes were finer than his friends' clothes, and he had to keep them much cleaner.

"Taba," he said now as he came into the barracks, "let me wear what you're wearing for a job I have to do, and you can have this shirt."

"You want these?" the young man said, flapping his filthy shirt and the lamentable rag he called a kilt.

"I do."

"And I can keep your shirt?"

"You can."

Taba was naked in an instant, and Kas in the next. Taba took Kas's shirt over to his corner, smoothing it out, stroking it, folding it carefully, and laid it on the shelf over his cot before he pulled on an even more disgusting kilt and pranced back out to work, shouting thanks to Kas. He turned around suddenly and called, "Why?"

"So I don't look worth robbing."

Kas was now wearing Taba's shirt and kilt. Taba looked at him. "You don't!" he shouted, and went off to the stable yard.

Kas went down into Bankala to inns where the leaders of caravans stayed. He often carried messages from his master to these men, and sometimes drank with them; they knew and trusted him. He told them his errand. They said, "Now? Nobody crosses the Ses-Hab now."

"I must leave tomorrow."

They shook their heads.

One of them said, "Old Habgalgat knows what you need to know. He'll be in a pepper seller's booth in the market."

Kas found the old man behind his trays of peppercorns and said, "I must cross the desert to Anun."

"No caravans or traders are going. Not for a month yet, not till the rains."

"But I must go. My master sends a gift to a holy man in Anun."

The old man wrinkled up his face, which looked like the face of a desert tortoise.

"Has he given you a horse? A mule is better."

"I'm to go afoot, alone."

The old man slowly shook his tortoise head.

"Unwise," he said.

Kas turned up the palms of his hands a little, in a patient gesture that said: So it must be.

After a while the old man nodded. "I can tell you the old way. It goes far off the caravan road. Northward. From spring to spring at a walking pace. Fifteen days of walking. Is your memory good?"

Kas nodded.

"Then come into the booth here with me and listen." When they sat together cross-legged, Habgalgat said, "Here is the way you must go." He half closed his dark tortoise eyes, gazing straight ahead as if at a road before him, and began to speak the signs and landmarks, the turns and veerings, of the way across the desert he had walked in the old days before the caravans.

Kas listened and held the words in his mind. In this skill he had had much practice, carrying messages from and to his master word for word as they were spoken. When the old man was done Kas thanked him and asked how he could repay him.

"Who is the holy man you are sent to?"

"Matua."

"Ah. There is no greater saint in all the cities," Habgalgat said. "What is the gift your master sends him?"

"A flask of water."

"It must be the very water of the River of Paradise. Now my throat is dry with speaking so long. I need five coppers for a flask of wine."

Kas gave him ten coppers, and the old man grinned. "Why, you're a rich man under your stinking rags, brother! So, walk at night. Sleep with your head in shade. If the well at Narrow Rocks is dry, as it may be this late in the year, dig in the sand of the streambed under the cliff. May your way be blessed."

"May all your ways be blessed," Kas said.

In the market he bought a new pair of sandals with strong soles and a supply of jerked meat and date-cakes and hard ewe's-milk cheese, then returned home, where he lay down and slept for a couple of hours in the heat of the day. In the late afternoon he went to the women servants' quarters to visit his dear friend Ini, a house servant. They went to a small room behind the storage room. The master did not know this nook existed, but all the servants thought of it as almost a sacred place. Though servants could not marry, they considered couples like Kas and Ini as having the rights of married people, even if those rights were limited to that one small room.

They made long and tender love on the mattress in the small, hot room. He told her of the errand and the journey he was to undertake. "To cross the desert alone?" she cried out. Then she said no more, since her anxiety could only make him anxious. Before he left, she brought two lengths of light, coarse cloth from her box and gave them to him to use as he needed against the desert sun. Then she hurried to the kitchen, took four oranges, and gave them to him. They held each other close and said farewell.

The sun was low in the west as Kas went back to the men's quarters. He filled his pack with the food he had bought and the oranges and cloth Ini had given him, and hung his goatskin water bottle and the gift-flask from the pack. What money he had not given Habgalgat or spent on sandals and food he carried with his knife in the leather pouch at his waist, not trying to conceal it. He said to his friends, "I'll see you in a month or so."

They blessed his way, and he theirs, and he set off eastward across the city and out into the hills. By the light of the rising moon he saw the pale desert stretching before him from the shadowy feet of the hills to where the stars rose out of the earth.

By the first light of day the hills were far behind him and the caravan road a dark streak before him across the desert. The sun rose from the end of that road intolerably bright. The heat of it struck his face along with the light.

In daylight he could see evidence of the traffic of men and animals on the road, hoofprints in what had been the mud of spring now hard as a stone, scraps of canvas, dung, a broken harness strap. There was no other sign of life. The silence was absolute. He had walked some hours in that hot solitude when he came to a track leading away from the caravan road, northward.

Old Habgalgat had spoken of a pile of white stones where the old way met the caravan road. There were some whitish stones scattered about here and there on the sandy earth, but there was no pile of stones. The northward track was clear enough, but there were no signs of travel on it, no footprints or hoofprints.

If it was the old way, it would bring him to the well at Narrow Rocks by evening of this day. On the caravan road there was no water for twice that distance.

He drank one long swallow from his waterskin, which left not very much water in it. He took the road to the north. He walked doggedly in the silent, glaring heat. The sun had begun to descend from noon when he saw a mirage-hill quivering upside down a long way ahead of him. After a while he came among low hills, and saw cliffs to the north. The cliffs grew lower toward the track, and he came to the place old Habgalgat had called the Narrow Rocks.

It was a vast relief to know that he was indeed on the old way, the right way. But the heat in the valley between the cliffs was like an oven. The little stone well that made an oasis of the place was dry, the few palms that had shaded it were half dead. His waterskin held only a couple more mouthfuls.

He followed the narrowing cliffs to a dry watercourse. Where he saw a few scrubby plants and the tracks of small creatures on the gravelly sand of the streambed, he knelt down and began to dig with his hands. The sand felt cool, and as he dug farther, damp. A little water began to seep into the bottom of the hole he'd made. He dug, and waited, dug, and waited. The silent water crept into the hole and shone back the hot brightness of the sky. He waited till he could take up water in the small brass cup he carried in his pack, and drink. Again and again he filled the little cup and drank, slowly and with gratitude, and always the shining water welled slowly back into the hole. He used the cup to refill his waterskin, cupful by cupful. The sun was far down in the west when he went back to the small shade of the palms by the dry well to sleep.

He woke after sunset and went to the streambed to redig the hole, which had already half filled up with sand. He ate one of Ini's oranges while he waited for the slow water. He drank again, and filled his waterskin. The anxiety that had been in his heart all night and day was gone; he was serene. He knew he was on the right road, that Habgalgat had given him good counsel, that all the wells and springs on the west from here were more reliable than the well at Narrow Rocks. All he had to do was walk fourteen days more across the desert under the sun and stars and bring the flask of water to the holy man. And then return as he had come.

For six more nights he walked across the low dunes and levels, the sands and crusted clay of the desert, sleeping through the heat of the day near the tiny well or spring of water to which the old way always brought him. His food was very scanty, but would last him. He saved the last orange as long as he could. He was eating it in the pleasant shade of the big oasis of Gebo, by the pool screened by tall reeds and palms, when he heard the snort of a horse or mule and the voices of men.

He cowered down among the reeds, but they had seen him before he saw them.

There were four of them, nomads, with two small horses and a train of mules. The men came around him and stood looking down at him. They were slight, wiry, wearing trousers, tunics, and white cowls. Their dark eyes burned in dark faces palely shadowed by the cowls. They carried long daggers or light swords and one had a longbow slung across his back. They said nothing.

Kas sat cross-legged among the reeds, naked. After he had drunk at the spring and slept through the worst heat, the big pool of Gebo had offered him the immense luxury of bathing. He had played in the water, rejoicing in its coolness. He had washed his shirt and kilt, even filthier than when Taba gave them to him, and spread them out across the reeds to dry.

He shivered, now, though the evening air was windless and hot. The men were motionless, staring down at him.

He set down the peel of the orange. His pack lay before him. He opened it slowly. Slowly and deliberately he took the pouch off his belt and laid it beside the pack. He looked up at the four men, from one to the next. He turned up the palms of his hands a little in a patient gesture that said: This is what I have.

"Why are you here?" said one of the men, whose sparse, short beard was white.

"I carry a gift from my master in Bankala to a holy man in Anun."

"What gift?"

Kas touched the netted water flask that lay beside his pack.

"What is in it?"

"Water."

One of them smiled. Another looked at Kas with sharp suspicious eyes. They were silent.

The old man squatted down, his thin sinewy arms across his knees, studying Kas and his belongings.

"What is the name of the holy man you seek?"

"Matua."

"Ah," said the old man, with a deep nod.

One by one the other three squatted down on their heels.

One of them pointed a long finger at Kas's pouch.

"My knife," Kas said. "Sixty coppers and a silver coin. Thread and needle."

The man nodded.

Another, a young man, reached out and picked up the empty pack. He shook it, squeezed it, felt carefully along its inner seams, then dropped it. He took up the pouch, examined the contents, and dropped it with a scornful flick of his fingers.

"It is as he said."

"In truth you go to Matua-dei," the old man said, not quite a statement, not quite a question.

"In truth," Kas said.

"Who sends you to him?" the young man asked.

"Mitrai the merchant."

"Does he send out caravans?"

"He sends his goods in trade by the caravans."

The old man asked: "What do you know of Matua-dei?"

"That he is the greatest saint in all the cities."

"Although he was born a nomad," said the old man dryly.

Kas bowed his head a little. "It is as you say."

There was a long silence. The breeze of evening stirred once or twice feebly in the dry fronds of the palms and the long reeds all round them. A mule snorted, its harness clinked.

"Matua the son of my sister's son is kin to you all," the old man said to the nomads. "I wish to see him again before I die. Shall we give this giver of water escort to our kinsman Matua-dei in the city of Anun?"

"They are all liars in Bankala," said the young man. "He is spying."

"Who taught you this road?" asked one of the nomads, a man with a keen, hard face.

"Old Habgalgat."

"Ah," the man said.

"How will the guards at the Desert Gate of Anun welcome us, Uncle-dei?" the fourth man asked, smiling a little.

"The name of Matua will open the gate," the old man said. "We can sell the gray mules at the market there. Come on." He stood up, as lithe as a young man; the others stood. "Saddle the roan," he said to the young man, and to the others, "Fill the skins," and to Kas, "Put your clothes on, water-giver. You will ride to Anun with the nomads."

And before nightfall he was mounted on a tall roan mule, his pack off his shoulders and in the saddlebag, his waterskin and the netted jar in the other saddlebag, riding with the nomads to Anun.

They left the way he knew from Habgalgat almost at once, striking off toward the southeast, on no road or track that he could see in the dusk or when the moon rose.

He had been very frightened when the nomads came on him there at the pool of Gebo. Fear leaves weariness in its tracks. He rode most of the night in a kind of half dream, the mule's reins wrapped around his right wrist, clinging to the saddle horn with his left hand. He marveled at how high above the ground he seemed on the back of the tall, powerful, docile creature, how lordly a thing it was to ride not walk all night, across the moonlit hills.

In daylight they came to the caravan road, unmistakable by its breadth and straightness and the prints of hoofs and piles of stone-dry dung here and there from the last caravans of spring. They spent the middle of the day at an oasis.

The nomads did not give their names to Kas and used only kinship terms among themselves, so he thought of them as the uncle—Uncle-dei, they all called him, giving him the term of respect—the dark cousin, the smiling cousin, and the son. They spoke little to one another, and hardly a word to Kas; but the smiling cousin, seeing him bathing his inner thighs rubbed sore by the saddle, gave him a pair of loose trousers they wore. They shared their food with him. He set what he had out for them to share. The uncle and the cousins politely took tiny morsels of cheese or half a date and signified that they were completely satisfied and could not possibly eat any more. The son would not even look at Kas or his food, yet kept him always in view, as if suspecting him of plans to rob them, murder them, or ride off with the roan mule. He was a boy, constantly proving that he was a man. The men were patient with him.

They mounted again as soon as the sun began to lose its heat and rode on, their shadows growing longer and longer before them. The small tin ornaments on their bridles and saddlebags made a soft, pleasant tinkling, almost like running water.

The nomads' horses were lean, unimpressive animals whose spirit he came gradually to appreciate. The mules were big, handsome, and intelligent. As he listened to the nomads talk during their midday rest-stops, he learned that they had been intending to sell four of the mules, his roan, a bay, and two splendid matched grays at a gathering of their people farther south. Meeting him had made the uncle decide to risk entering

Anun, where they could sell the mules for twice the price, if they could get into the city and out again alive.

Springs of water on the caravan road were much farther apart than on the old way, but like the caravaners, the nomads carried water enough with them to get them and their animals across long dry gaps. They moved much faster than a man walking alone, and their halts were briefer. After his fourth night with them, Kas's eleventh night of journeying, the sun before rising lit a spark of gold far ahead across the dead level of sand desert, the spire of the highest palace tower of Anun.

They thought at first that they might enter the walled city without any trouble, for the guards at the Desert Gate were not on the look-out, not expecting anyone to come out of the Ses-Hab in the hottest month of the year. But as they came through the deep gate on foot, leading their animals, an officious beggar lounging there shouted out, "Nomads!"—and the guard dozing in the gatehouse woke up and ran out also shouting, "Nomads!" Three more guards and a small crowd of onlookers soon stood facing them.

The uncle had dropped back, leaving Kas as the leader of the little procession. The nomads stood holding their mounts' bridles, silent and with bowed heads. The first guard, a broad, burly man, came up, sword drawn, and demanded, "Who are you? What do you want here?"

The uncle had said nothing to Kas about his role at this dangerous moment, but he saw pretty clearly what it must be.

"I am the servant of the merchant Mitrai of Bankala, bearing a gift from him to the holy man Matua," he said. He had long practice in speaking with confidence and without challenge, representing the dignity of his master. "These men have brought me and the gift I bear safe across the desert."

He could see that the name Matua commanded respect; but the guard, after some hestitation, said harshly, "These others are nomads. They have no business in Anun."

"They are kinsmen of Matua. They are horse traders taking their mules to sell at a gathering of their people. They kept me safe from the desert thieves. They come here in peace with me and the gift I bear."

The nomads all stood patient and silent. Even their mules looked humble.

The guard conferred with the other guards; one ran off and came back presently with higher officers, and then officials arrived. Kas repeated his story to all of them. They listened to him. His mission to the holy man clearly gave him status, but they were suspicious. His manner was good, but his company bad. The officials shook their heads and muttered to one another.

One of them, a big man in fine robes with a gold tassel on his cap, was eyeing the gray mules. He turned to Kas and said in the smooth rather toneless voice of a person of power, "Your master Mitrai is a worthy trader, I know, and his errand is to a holy man. Will you vouch for these sand rats?"

"I will. They came here only in kindness to me and hope of seeing their holy kinsman."

"And of selling some mules in our horse market, perhaps," the man with the gold tassle said. Then, with a sudden assumption of authority that the other officials silently acknowledged, he said, "Let them into the city. Two of you guards, stay with them. They must stay with this man from Bankala. They can go to the house of Matua, may-he-be-blessed-who-brings-blessings. They can sell their stock at the market. They can sleep one night in the caravan inn. They must be gone out of the city, by this gate, by this time tomorrow. You can stay on," he added to Kas, and turned and strode off down the street, his gold tassel flicking and winking in the morning light.

"He wants the grays," the smiling cousin murmured to the dark cousin almost soundlessly, and the dark cousin nodded almost invisibly.

So, before the sun was at noon, Kas led his procession of white-cowled men and tin-bedecked animals through the streets of Anun, guided by two guards, followed by many little street boys and lean, light street dogs, much stared at and loudly and rudely commented on from side-walks and doorways and shops and windows and balconies, to the house of Matua.

It was a small house of stone and clay. It had a good-sized courtyard with a well, a wide-spreading fig tree, and a big old orange tree. A man without hands or feet sat dozing in a wicker chair in the shade of the fig tree. Was this Matua? Kas wondered a moment. But then a little one-eyed boy came running out of the open house door to meet them and told them that his master was in meditation. They should return in the early evening.

"May we take water from the well?" Kas asked, for it had been a long way from the last oasis to the city gate, and no one yet had offered water to the travelers or their animals.

"As much as you want," the child said. "The sacred well has water for all!" Proud to be able to be generous, he brought buckets for the animals to drink from. The nomad party watered their animals and filled their nose bags with oats; they drank deep themselves, and washed the dust off their faces and hands, and refilled their waterskins.

Kas would very willingly have spent all that day in the dusty, shady courtyard, waiting to see the holy man. He felt a great and immediate liking for the place, a sense of being at peace, at home. The cripple in the wicker chair did not speak, but watched them with a sleepy smile, as if he was happy they were there. Oranges shone in the shadow among the dark green, glossy leaves of the big tree. Spilt water smelt sweet in the dust. Nobody troubled them.

But the nomads wanted to get to the horse market, and they could not go without Kas, so they all set off again into the hot streets, now half-deserted. On the way they passed food stalls, where they bought bread and fruit and goat meat fried on sticks and broke their long fast with a feast. The nomads would not let Kas pay for his own food. When they got to the horse market and could buy feed for their hungry animals, they did so liberally, paying high for the best grain and oatcake, so that the feed merchants courted them in the hope of supplying their future needs.

The crowd that came round them there was not rude and hostile but intent, businesslike. Nomad horses and mules were highly prized in the cities for both their breeding and their training. The pair of gray mules went to a well-dressed dealer who imperturbably bid up every competing offer and finally paid ten broad pieces of gold and took the mules off to the stables of his master, undoubtedly the official with the gold tassel. They sold the bay and the roan for a good deal less than they'd hoped, Kas judged from what they said to one another, but two or three times what they would have got among their own people. When the roan mule stood waiting to be led off by his new owner, Kas went to him and scratched his forehead under the coarse, stiff up-brush of the mane. The mule grunted companionably.

"A good animal," he said to the mule's new owner. The man grunted less amiably than the mule and tugged at the leading rein.

The roan mule moved off with him, self-possessed, obedient.

As the day began to cool they returned to Matua's house. The man with no hands or feet still sat in his wicker chair under the orange tree, smiling. He had more people to watch now. Ten or more men and women had gathered in the courtyard, waiting to speak to the holy man or to receive his blessing. Some were very poor, two were well-dressed. One man was very lame. A baby in its mother's arms fretted weakly and endlessly. A woman wept, sobbing and moaning, clinging to her younger companion.

Kas and the nomads and the two guards joined these people, sitting or squatting in the dust, which the one-eyed child sprinkled now and then with water so that again it smelled cool and sweet.

Kas sat cross-legged. He was very tired, having not slept the last night and day, but he did not fall asleep. He sat in the deep peacefulness of heart and mind. When Matua came out of the house, Kas watched him with calm delight. He felt as if he were seeing the father he had never known, the mother who had died when he was five, as if he recognized a dear, known face. It was like a dream, but he was not dreaming.

He watched as Matua, a slight, dark man with graying hair, greeted the nomads, embracing them and calling them uncle, cousin, and nephew. They laughed and talked a long time.

Then the holy man came to him, not quite smiling but with a look of kind, alert expectation, and greeted him: "My son."

Kas bowed his head down to Matua's feet, then knelt before him, straight-backed. "Matua-dei, my master, Mitrai, the merchant of Bankala, bade me bring you this gift," he said. He held up in both hands the earthenware jar in its netting of twine.

Matua took the jar and held it up before him. He looked down at Kas and smiled. Then with the jar on the palm of his left hand, he held his right hand over it for a moment.

He took it in both hands again and offered it to Kas. "You have brought me a great gift, my son. I ask you to bear it back to your master with my blessing and thanks."

Kas took the cool weight of the jar into his hands, a little bewildered, but too serenely contented in the presence of this man to have any question. "I will," he said.

Matua looked at him steadily for a time, bent down, and kissed his forehead. "Walk in peace," he said softly. He went on to the woman who could not stop weeping. She and the younger woman held out eager hands to him, whispering his name as he approached.

Kas yearned to spend the night there, sleeping in that courtyard where pain and tears and disfigurement and helplessness were made welcome and given ease, and there was no fear, no cruelty.

But he must stay with the nomads, and the guards were impatient to take them to the caravan inn and be done with them. So they went off through the crowded streets of evening where people stared at them with enmity and contempt. The tired horses were edgy and nervous among the crowds and shouting voices, the narrow walls and flaring torches and sudden shadows. The two pack mules and the two riding mules jogged along steadily on the leading rope. Kas walked close to them. Their resolute calm, their big, warm bodies, and the tinkle of their tin ornaments gave him comfort.

He felt exalted, yet bereft. He felt that he was walking down and down from a high peak to which he had been lifted as if by the wind. All the rest of his life he would walk down from that height.

The caravan inn was a huge place, desolate at this season. They ate together, served by a couple of boys who would have refused to serve the nomads at all if Kas had not taken the tone of a master to them. "Is this the hospitality of Anun?" he said. "The caravaners of Bankala will hear of it from me!" The dinner of cold lentils, boiled wheat, and greens was served with ill grace, but eaten with much pleasure. Kas bought a jug of red wine, and the five of them drank together. For the first time in their week of journeying together the nomads spoke to him openly. The young man, a little drunk on red wine and regretting his distrust of Kas, grew all but sentimental.

Kas could now ask a question that had puzzled him: "Uncle-dei, how is it that Matua, one of your people, lives here in the city?"

The old man told him the story. Over fifty years ago, his nephew had been captured as a little child in a raid of one nomad band on another and sold as a slave in Anun. Freed by his master, this nephew had married a poor woman of Anun. Matua was their child. "His name is spoken among the cities. But he remembers his people," the old man said proudly, with tears in his eyes.

Before they slept, the smiling cousin spoke to Kas: "We go south now. The caravan road is no good to you afoot. Do you know the old way?"

"I know what Habgalgat told me."

"Tell me," said the nomad.

Bringing into his mind the series of places and springs and turns he had learned, Kas began to repeat them, but in reverse order. When he hesitated or drew a blank, the cousin told him what he needed to know. Kas repeated the words until they had gone through all the landmarks and names of the fourteen places of water and turns and forkings of the path to and from the Desert Gate of Anun to the East Gate of Bankala.

"Walk the way lightly," said the smiling cousin.

In the morning when the guards came to escort the nomads out of the city, each one gravely bade farewell to Kas, and the uncle gave him a gift: a white cowl such as they wore. "This is the hottest half month of the year," he said, "and I think it will be very hot this year. Cover your head always. In a sandstorm or duststorm, cover your face like this," and he showed Kas how to tie the cowl to protect his face and eyes.

Then they went on their way with the impatient guards. Kas stood and watched the switching lion-tails of the two pack mules go off down the narrow street.

He went to the market and bought dates, hard cheese, dried meat, bean meal such as the nomads carried, and a few oranges. He added a second small waterskin to his pack. All that took his silver piece, but having still sixty pennies, he went to a jeweler's booth and chose a copper pendant inlaid with a circle of blue enamel for Ini.

There was a longing in him to go again to Matua's house and sit in the dusty courtyard in the shade of the orange tree. He hesitated, from a kind of shyness, and then went there.

The speechless cripple lay in his chair. He smiled at the sight of Kas. The one-eyed child greeted him and went on about his business. Kas sat in the dust in the deep shade and let his heart abide in calm.

As the afternoon wore on people began to come into the courtyard to wait for Matua to appear. Kas went to the well, filled his waterskins, drank deeply, shouldered his pack, and left.

He ate a bowl of boiled wheat and greens at a wayside stall and went on to the city gate. The guard in the booth nodded at him as he went through. He walked out onto the wide road, glaring in the dusty afternoon light.

He had eaten well, was well rested, and had within him now the peacefulness of Matua's courtyard. He knew there was no water until the oasis where the old road, his way, came from the north to join the caravan road: he must walk all night and into the next night to get there. He set off at a steady pace, with the lightened mind of one who knows he is going home.

When he reached the oasis he was very tired and had scarcely a swallow of water left, but there he could drink his fill from a good spring, pour cool water over his head and body, eat an orange and a handful of bean meal, and sleep. The next day he rested, eating a little and drinking often, in the rustling shade of the old, squat palm trees. He studied the faint maze of animal tracks—beetles, sand rats, birds, a fox, and the sharp hoofprints of two tiny antelope he had seen in the dawn light coming to drink at the spring.

In the evening he ate and drank again, filled up his waterskins, and set off on the faint track leading northwest. From then on each night's walk would bring him to water. But though at night the dry air cooled quickly, the rocks and sand held the sun's heat in them like bricks in a kiln. And all the days of his journey were fearfully hot. Every day was hotter, he thought, than the one before.

On the ninth morning he came to Gebo, where the nomads had found him. It had been a long stage from the last small oasis; it was nearly noon when he saw the reeds and palms dancing far ahead on quivering levels of heated air. Low hills to the north stood upside down in the sky. His head was drumming; waves of dizziness frightened him. The weight of the jar of water in its netting, jouncing as he walked, dragged at him as it never had before. He finally came into the shade, threw off his pack and clothes, and plunged into the miraculous soft murky coolness of the pool.

He slept there that afternoon and the next day, not traveling that night. His food was holding out pretty well, he knew the way from here on, and he needed rest. He hoped the terrible heat might break or at least moderate before long. Though this oasis was where he had met up with hostile strangers, he had no fear. The vast solitude in which he walked and slept had come into him and included him, as the peace of Matua's household had come into him and included him. He dozed, lay in the water of the pool, slept again. He watched the creatures of the oasis come to the water: a slender green snake; a dragonfly among the reeds; several sand rats. They too seemed to have no fear. In the afternoon in the shade of the palms he cut and split reeds and wove a tiny basket with them, as he had learned to do as a child. He put Ini's amulet into it, and it was in his pack when he left Gebo in the fiery, breathless evening.

That night as he drank from the waterskin he had bought in Anun it broke open on the seam. He drank all he could of the water, but much was lost. He could not mend the waterskin and buried it in the sand at the Red Hills well. He was sorry to lose that reassuring supply, but after all, he had gone from Bankala to Gebo with only one waterskin; he could go back with only one.

The heat of the days could not grow any greater, but it did not grow any less. There was very little shade even in the oases and no coolness. No wind ever stirred, so that breathing was like breathing heat but not air. Only for a few hours before dawn did the night air grow cool, sometimes enough to make him shiver and wrap himself in Ini's clothes.

The water at the Clay Bank spring was not good, much worse than he remembered it from the journey east. It had a metallic taste that took away his appetite. He forced himself, the day he spent there, to drink it, and to eat. He held each morsel of pressed date in his mouth for a long time before he swallowed it.

He was a little afraid for himself now, but in a detached way. He knew he could not go on walking through the furnace very much longer. But there was not so very much farther to go. The next night would bring him to Narrow Rocks. There was not much shade there, but he would rest in what there was. And from there it was only a night and a day, a long day, to the Dry Hills and the Eastern Gate.

He filled his remaining waterskin with the vile Clay Bank water and set off in the silent heat of the evening. The low sun was so fierce in his face he had to tie the cowl almost shut to keep his eyes from dazzling.

Once in the night he waked from a kind of walking sleep and thought he had lost the track. Everything around him was strange in the starlight. He stilled his panic and told himself that this was the way, he was on it. He trudged on through the strangeness. As the first light came, he began to recognize the hills, but thirst plagued him worse than it ever had, making him feel sick and dizzy. Certain of his way now, he finished the water in his waterskin. The terrible sun came up behind him. In midmorning he came to the streambed and the well at Narrow Rocks.

The well was as dry as ever. He went to where he had dug in the streambed, found the traces of the water hole he had made, and began to dig in the same place.

The sand grew a little cooler as he dug down, but it did not grow damp. He dug far deeper than where the water had begun to seep in before. The sand was dry.

He gave up and tried another place, higher up the streambed, where it might be nearer the buried spring. He came on no sign of water.

He dug once more, at the deepest part of the gully, and then gave up. He went back into the thin shade of the palms and considered the long afternoon ahead, the long night, and the yet longer day that lay between him and Bankala. There was nothing for it. He would rest here, set off in the evening, and walk without water.

He covered his head with the cowl and Ini's cloth and tried to sleep, though thirst made it hard. His head swam even as he lay still, and that troubled him.

He woke suddenly from a heavy sleep. The sun had set and the faintest breeze stirred the fronds of the dying palms by the dead well. An orange haze was dying out of the upper air and a very faint mottling of high clouds, the first clouds he had seen for weeks, caught the last of the afternoon glow. He went back to the streambed, which held the illusion or memory of water, to eat. As he tried to munch on a dried fig, like plaster in his dry mouth, he saw a little movement near the pile of sand where he had dug the last hole. He sat still and watched.

A sand rat came around the pile of sand and nosed at the rim of the hole. They were familiars of all the oases, pretty little animals, tan above and white below, with narrow white feet and large ears so delicate that light shone through them. They were shy, moving quickly and softly, sometimes with a kind of skip.

He watched this one. It went down into the hole he had dug and nosed at the bottom. Then it began to dig. Its little narrow paws were not good at moving the sand. It dug and dug, and the sand slipped back down where it dug.

It was thirsty. It was dying of thirst, he thought. It lived here, this place was its world, and there was no water in it.

He looked up. Only the larger stars were coming out. The cloud layer was thickening. There might be rain in a day or two. The first rain, the crazy rain. This dry streambed might foam with water for an hour before the cloudburst sank away into the sand.

The rat scrabbled weakly at the bottom of the hole. Kas leaned closer to it. It went immobile, a little statue of a rat.

"It's all right," he said. His voice, which had not spoken for fourteen days, was barely a whisper. He unhitched the earthenware jar from his pack and took it out of its netting. He broke the seal of the wooden plug with a twist of his hand and filled his small brass cup with the water. He set the cup in the sand beside the hole, pushing it down to keep it steady. Then he moved some distance away and sat down again.

After a while the rat crawled up out of the hole, moving slowly in fear or in weakness, its long delicate whiskers very busy. It went straight to the brass cup. It put its muzzle in the water and drank, sucking or lapping silently. The water was gone in no time.

Kas involuntarily moved a little. The rat gave a high skip and vanished behind the sand-mounds in the shadows of twilight.

"It's all right," Kas told the shadows.

He put his brass cup in his pack. He replaced the plug in the flask carefully and made sure the flask hung securely from the pack so that it could not leak or spill. The high overcast was slowly hiding even the larger stars. Maybe the crazy rain would come. "Get out of the streambed, little rat," he thought. He set off on the faint track westward.

WHEN KAS CAME TO THE EAST GATE OF BANKALA HE COULD NOT speak. Idlers at the gate had watched the figure shamble along toward them on the road in the late yellow light shaken by distant thunder. When they saw his strained face and blackened mouth they brought him water, and people came crowding around him giving instructions as to how much or how little he should drink at first, saying he was a nomad, saying he was not a nomad, asking him who he was and where he lived and was he mad to walk alone across the desert in the great heat of the year. He heard little of this. Somebody recognized him, and somebody sent to Mitrai's house, and he got home somehow.

His friends in the men's quarters laid him onto his cot and tried to clean him up. Ini came hurrying from the house and did a better job of it. The master sent for him if he was able to appear. He insisted on going. He appeared, shaky but decent, in his master's counting room. He offered Mitrai the earthenware jar in its worn, dirty netting.

"The holy man bade me bring you this. His blessing is on it," he said in his desert-hoarsened voice.

Mitrai took the jar. His face showed no expression.

"His words?"

"Matua said: 'You have brought me a great gift, my son. I ask you to bear it back to your master with my blessing and thanks.'"

Mitrai examined the jar closely and tested the plug.

"The seal is broken," he said.

Kas nodded briefly.

"You drank from it."

Kas glanced up, surprised. His face went still and became stern. He said nothing.

Mitrai watched him.

"You opened it." It was and was not a question.

"I did. At a dry well. I gave water to a rat."

Mitrai studied him a while more, then looked back at the jar. He shook it gently. There was no sound of gurgling. He pulled out the wooden plug and peered inside.

"It's full," he said.

He looked at Kas.

"It is full to the brim," the merchant repeated.

Kas's burnt, cracked lips could scarcely smile. He opened his hands, palm up, in a patient gesture that said: I do not understand, but that is how it is, and it is all right.

Mitrai was silent a while. At last he said, quietly, "Go on, then, Kas. You did well, as always."

Kas bowed and left the counting room. He was not steady on his feet. Ini was waiting for him at the end of the corridor. She wore the copper and enamel pendant on a string round her neck. She put her arm around his shoulders. "Kas," she said, "come outside. It's raining."

RECORD

OF

FIRST PUBLICATION

Part I

⌔

Part II

THE UNREAL AND THE REAL
URSULA K. LE GUIN
READING GROUP GUIDE

In the introduction Le Guin states that she originally considered placing the stories chronologically: "I tried it and didn't like the effect." The obvious question for readers of this book is: "Why?" She goes on to state that the stories in the first half have been described as "mundane." Although her two original categories were *Where on Earth* and *Outer Space, Inner Lands*, this book landed the title, *The Unreal and the Real*. Consequently, if there is any significance to the title, these "mundane" stories (that are anything BUT mundane) are in the "Unreal" half of the book. In the introduction to the second half of this collection, Le Guin says, "I leave it entirely up to you, O Reader, to decide which volume of those two is the Real and which is the Unreal." Are the mundane Earth stories Unreal? Are the outer space stories Real? Or does this single title apply equally to any story in this collection, regardless of its placement? Readers will have fun comparing and contrasting these stories and justifying or arguing about their position in this two-part collection.

Yesterday and Today

The earliest stories in this book ("Semley's Necklace" and "The Rule of Names") were written in 1964. "The Jar of Water" was written in 2014. This is a FIFTY year span of short stories! Many readers speak of the timelessness of Le Guin's writing. It may be of interest to a good number of readers to see a list of current events at the time of publication to contrast against the events of today. This is a time of the Cold War, the Space Race, détente, and more. We had an oil crisis during this span; we had the Kent State tragedy; the Chicago 8 trial; riots in Northern Ireland, Turkey, Singapore, as well as hundreds of Vietnam War protests; Vice President Spiro Agnew resigned; Nixon was impeached because of Watergate and resigned; we launched all kinds of communication satellites and spacecraft; the Beatles came on to the music scene; the Civil Rights Act was passed; and so much more. How do the events at publication render the story unique? How do today's events create the "timeless" feel of Le Guin's short stories? Here is a taste of what was going on in the world at the time of first publication of these stories:

Current Events at the Time of Publication of These Stories

1964   The US severs political relations with Panama

Hindu and Muslim rioting in India

24th Amendment to the Constitution banning poll tax, etc., is ratified

Echo 2, a US communications satellite, is launched

Black & Puerto Rican students boycott NYC public schools

Nuclear testing in Nevada

Nelson Mandela is jailed for life

Gulf of Tonkin Resolution passes, which escalated US Vietnam
    involvement

Race riots in Singapore

1969   USSR lands on Venus successfully

President's salary doubles

Nixon is inaugurated

US and Vietnam peace talks begin in Paris;
    massive US protests in many cities

Rioting in Northern Ireland

Stonewall riots in NYC

Manson Family murders

Mỹ Lai Massacre; Nixon asks "silent majority" to support our war effort

1973   *Roe v. Wade* Supreme Court decision

Peace accord with Vietnam

Watergate scandal

1974   Ford gives Nixon an unconditional pardon

A major US bank is insolvent (Franklin National Bank)

Bombings in Northern Ireland

Major flooding in Australia

Sears Tower is world's tallest building

1975   Vietnam War ends

Margaret Thatcher elected

Suez Canal is reopened after eight years closed

Ford signs $2+ billion loan to keep NYC out of bankruptcy

Jaws hits movie screens

1976   Major earthquake (China), tidal wave (Philippines), and drought (UK)

Isabel Perón is deposed in Argentina

Apple Computer starts

US bicentennial

First Legionnaires Disease affects 4,000 delegates in Pennsylvania

Hurricane Belle

We land on Mars

Jimmy Carter is elected president

1980   Persian Gulf War

John Lennon shot

Iran hostage tragedy

Ronald Reagan is elected

Boycott of Russian Summer Olympics

1981   Poland martial law begins

Reagan is reelected

Antinuclear protesters in Diablo

The *Titanic* is found

Half a million people lose disability benefits

Pope is shot (not killed); Anwar Sadat is assassinated

First test-tube baby is born

1982   Israel invades Lebanon

Israel returns Sinai to Egypt

700,000 people protest nuclear weapons in NYC

Severe US recession begins

Vietnam War Memorial opens

1983   Death toll in Ethiopia reaches four million

China's population reaches one billion

Sally Ride goes into space

US invades Grenada

1985   Volcano kills 25,000 in Columbia

TWA flight is hijacked by Hezbollah

UK coal strike ends but mines remain closed

1986   US bombs Libya

Arms agreement with Russia signed

Iran-Contra Affair (arms deal with Iran by Reagan)

| 1987 | Stock market crash |
| | World population reaches five billion |

1989	Berlin Wall is opened and eventually falls
	George Bush becomes President
	Tiananmen Square massacre
	Old mummy is found in the Giza pyramid

1990	Saddam Hussein invades Kuwait
	Desert Shield begins
	Iran earthquake kills 50,000
	US enters major recession
	Nelson Mandela is released from prison
	East and West Germany are reunited

1991	50 percent of India's population is living in poverty
	Iraq pushed out of Kuwait; signs treaty agreement
	Bangladesh cyclone kills 200,000
	Apartheid in South Africa ends
	Rodney King beating by police captured on video
	Internet unrestricted; computer use on the net is at one million

1992	Somalia civil war
	Ross Perot announces presidential bid
	Great Chicago flood
	Hurricane Andrew
	Bill Clinton is elected President
	US refuses to sign climate accord

| 1994 | Civil war and genocide in Rwanda |
| | Nelson Mandela becomes South African president |

Serbia and Bosnia conflict and genocide

Genetically engineered tomatoes are approved for sale

Netscape Navigator is leading internet web browser

OJ Simpson is chased by police and captured for television

1995   Oklahoma City bombing

Economic sanctions against Iran

Japanese earthquake kills over 6,000

Heatwave kills around 3,000, including around 750 in Chicago

OJ Simpson is found not guilty

Federal workers are sent home in budget deadlock

Windows 95 is released

1996   Taliban captures major cities in Afghanistan

Osama bin Laden is expelled from Sudan

38 million acres of rainforest are destroyed by timber companies

Dozens of black churches burned to the ground in Mississippi

France halts nuclear testing

1998   Southeast Asia financial crisis

Terrorist bombing of US embassy in Nairobi

Monica Lewinski

Stock market drops 500 points

US launches missiles in Afghanistan;

Osama bin Laden declares jihad against the US

2000   Virginia legalizes same-sex couple

Black sludge is released into the Mississippi, creating environmental disaster

Bush v. Gore election ends in the Supreme Court

Bill Gates leaves Microsoft

2002	Euro becomes the official currency of the European Union
	Kmart files for bankruptcy
2014	Ebola epidemic
	Russia/Ukraine fighting
	Israel/Hamas conflict turns deadly
	Republicans take control of US Congress
	Robot lands on a comet in space

Themes, Motifs, and Repeating Characters

As Le Guin states in the introduction about "Half Past Four," she uses the same four characters in eight different vignettes. She is very emphatic that these four different manifestations of these four characters are NOT the same characters, despite sharing the same name. Perhaps they are manifestations of the same character if we first ask, "What if?" An excellent example of this idea is "May's Lion," a story about how our tales twist and turn depending on the person telling it: "'It's still your story, Aunt May; it was your lion. He came to you. He brought his death for you, a gift; but the men with guns won't take gifts, they think they own death already.'" See also "The Silence of the Asonu" for another example (and there are more). The person telling the story has the power, and Le Guin makes us ask, "What if this story were told by . . . ?" And, since this is Ursula Le Guin, she forces us to ask, "What if this story were told earlier or later or by trees or by roads or by penguins or by dolphins or by aliens inspecting human behavior?" Le Guin teaches us how to speak in perspective. ("She Unnames Them," "Direction of the Road" . . .)

Often, such as in "Semley's Necklace," "First Contact with the Gorgonids," "The Shobies Story," or "Diary of the Rose, The Rule of Names," etc., the storytellers come to realize the limitation inherent in speaking for others, or at least the reader does! And out of these limitations comes a conflict, which often has a very direct political connection to events that have happened in real life. This political conflict may ask us to think of environmental issues, government overreach, cultural ignorance (or condescension), and more.

The first four stories have the same Orsinia setting. The first three stories deal with the Fabbre family. The first two were written in 1976, but the the third Fabbre story was written in 1990, fourteen years later. It's almost as if Le Guin reads a story she has written and then deconstructs it: What would happen if . . . ? "Sleepwalkers" and "Ether, Or" tell one story from several different character perspectives; many other stories insert diary quotes or other material to bend the perspective and complicate the tale.

Over and over we see women confronting a patriarchal societal structure that is clearly odious, but the women in these stories do not always make the choices our feminist brains scream that they should, or when they should. In short, they behave as if they are human—humans that may recognize a problem but do not always solve it. For example, take a look at "Gwilan's Harp," "Solitude," "The Wild Girls," "Buffalo Gals" . . . This humanness of the characters is so very evident in all these stories, including the alien characters, ironically, in the "Real" half of this book.

The depiction of men, too, right from the start shows the problems our civilization can impose. Young Martin thinks Stefan is half a man and thinks Kostant is a man and a half. And even though in many of these stories the characters are aware of the problems, they do not make good choices because, as Kostant tells us, "I thought I would fail, so I didn't work." Now take a look at "The Matter of Seggri," a story that sees men as sex toys or babymakers. They are stoned by groups of women if they try to come too close. They are not allowed to live with women, although exceptions can be made for gay men. And while men are often seen as handsome, strong, smart, and other very positive adjectives, they often feel like phonies whose outer looks do not match the inner men, which causes significant problems. This may cause some readers to think of Le Guin's *Where on Earth* and *Outer Space, Inner Lands* sorting device.

Fighting those who control the resources, which often serves as a metaphor for the government, is contained in many of these stories. The first three stories will make you think they were written today. We see a fear of immigrants, walls, greed, corruption, distrust of the government, and more. If we only read one story from this collection, we will not go wrong choosing "The Ones Who Walk Away From Omelas," a chilling dystopian look at a way to ensure social harmony, with Le Guin subtly asking readers whether or not social harmony is possible without subjecting some element of our society to unspeakable brutality. Resistance is a theme throughout this collection.

Although there are many more themes to explore in this thick book, one last one to look for is Le Guin's running debate pitting science against our traditions, especially in how they inform human behavior. Knowledge is clearly necessary—there are very few stories in this collection that do not include scientists, doctors, discussions of science, or scientific reports. Science is often a synonym for truth, but science does not escape this collection without amassing its own collection of bumps and bruises, because there are times when the heart seems better equipped to know the truth than history or measurements. Once again, things are not easy! Readers should have a lot of fun debating the importance of science or the importance of religion and tradition.

Ways to Enjoy This Collection

This thick book has over seven hundred pages. If the book's length is discouraging you from selecting it for your book group or even reading it yourself, here are some suggestions for making it more manageable. These suggestions will help focus your discussion even if you have no trouble getting readers excited about reading. Note: Many of these stories could go in multiple categories, and some of these may fit better in a category other than the one listed. Yes, a few stories may be found in more than one category—feel free to make your own categories.

Political Focus: Current political debates about immigrants, walls, safety, terrorism, racism, etc., can be explored throughout this book. These six stories will allow you full access to these issues: "Brothers and Sisters," "A Week in the Country," "Unlocking the Air," "The Ones Who Walk Away From Omelas," "Betrayals," and "The Silence of the Asonu." The first three stories are the first three in the book, which may tempt readers into finishing the entire book!

Feminist Focus: This focus is one that could include just about every story in the book. These seven stories include a wide range of story styles and should spark some interesting discussions because they are so different: "Gwilan's Harp;" "Hand, Cup, Shell;" "Buffalo Gals Won't You Come Out Tonight;" "Betrayals;" "The Matter of Seggri, Solitude;" "The Wild Girls;" and "The Wife's Story." If you want a smaller focus group, compare "Buffalo Gals" with "The Wild Girls" or compare "Gwilan's Harp" with "The Wife's Story."

Stories Featuring the Role of Stories and Language: This division features stories we have grown up with, including stories that riff off of familiar fairy tales and others that are a product of Le Guin's imagination only, but nevertheless are stories that shape a mythical culture. These stories struggle with ways to accurately describe feelings and attitudes about events and situations that sometimes emanate from traditions that no longer seem to have any rationale for existing. This includes tales in which others appropriate stories and language for their own limited purposes.

Try these: "The Lost Children," "First Contact with the Gorgonids," "The Silence of the Asonu," "May's Lion," "The Rules of Names," "The Poacher," "Solitude," "She Unnames Them," and "The Author of the Acacia Seeds."

Stories with Environmental Themes: This section includes stories in which Le Guin depicts the affect of environmental abuse of some sort. Read these: "Brothers and Sisters," "Semley's Necklace," "Mazes," "Horse Camp," "The Fliers of Gy," "The Ascent of the North Face," and "The Author of the Acacia Seeds."

Stories with a Science, Mythology, Cultural, or Religious Focus: Almost every story in this book includes a science theme, usually compared and contrasted with the cultural/mythological/religious beliefs of the people. Here are several that depict this tension in unexpected ways: "Diary of the Rose," "The Shobies' Story," "Direction of the Road," "The Water is Wide," "Nine Lives," "The Author of the Acacia Seeds," "The Jar of Water," and "Sur." An interesting comparison opportunity in this section is to compare "Diary of the Rose" with "The Water is Wide."

Stories Dealing With Family Relationships: "Brothers and Sisters;" "A Week in the Country;" "Imaginary Country;" "Buffalo Gals Won't You Come Out Tonight;" "The White Donkey;" "Hand, Cup, Shell;" "Small Change;" and "The Wife's Story."

Stories With Multiple Perspectives: "Sleepwalkers;" "Hand, Cup, Shell;" "Ether, Or;" and "Half Past Four."

Your Three Favorite Stories.

General Discussion Questions

1. What is the significance of the title? Does it work?

2. The second introduction in this volume, at the beginning of the "Real" section, states that there are few useful definitions of science fiction and that "Science fiction can be seen as a brilliant modern development of fantasy to use the imagination within the parameters of the rationally possible, or at least plausible." What is your definition of science fiction? Of fantasy?

3. Le Guin also poo-poos genres, calling them commercial product-labels. What value is there in classifying stories by genre?

4. In looking at critical reviews of Le Guin's writing, many speak of her writing as haunting, anything but uplifting. Yet Le Guin only really identifies one story as "dark" ("The Wild Girls") and speaks of the others with obvious love and pride. What evidence in Le Guin's writing suggests hope? Or are these stories truly darker than Le Guin acknowledges?

5. Le Guin says in the introduction that ". . . I was quite certain that reality is often best represented slantwise, backwards, or as if it were an imaginary country, . . ." Many of her stories feature the same event but from very different perspectives. She is also fond of telling history from the point of view of those who were not allowed to write history. With this in mind, what do you suppose would change (if anything) in these stories if Le Guin were writing them today?

6. Many of these stories include music. Some have actual lyrics. If there were a playlist of songs to accompany this book, what would be on it?

7. Throughout this book are titles, phrases, and pairings that seem intended to misdirect our attention or surprise us with unexpected breaches with the rational world. For example, Le Guin has a title, "Ether, Or: For Narrative Americans" (not, Either, Or—and NOT, Native Americans). She has roads and trees that talk and that, if necessary, can kill. What other examples of the unexpected have you found and what purpose does this device serve?

8. Le Guin speaks of her favorite stories and even mentions that one story is in this book because of her editor. Le Guin has written MANY short stories. Are there stories in this volume that you would replace with stories NOT in this book?

9. Are there stories in this book that will be read by students and short story readers fifty years down the road? Fifty years from now, are there stories in this collection that will no longer have an impact?

10. What is your overall evaluation of the book as a whole?